Please return/renew this item by the last date shown on this label, or on your self-service receipt.

To renew this item, visit **www.librarieswest.org.uk** or contact your library

Your borrower number and PIN are required.

Libraries**West**

By Charles Cumming

THE THOMAS KELL SERIES
A Foreign Country
A Colder War
A Divided Spy

THE ALEC MILIUS SERIES
A Spy by Nature
The Spanish Game

OTHER WORKS
The Hidden Man
Typhoon
The Trinity Six
The Man Between

The Man Between

CHARLES CUMMING

HarperCollins*Publishers*

HarperCollins*Publishers*
1 London Bridge Street,
London, SE1 9GF

www.harpercollins.co.uk

This paperback edition 2019

2

First published in Great Britain by HarperCollins*Publishers* 2018

ISBN: 978-0-00-820034-3 (PB)

Set in Meridien by Palimpsest Book Production Limited,
Falkirk, Stirlingshire

Printed and bound in Great Britain by
CPI Group (UK) Ltd, Croydon, CR0 4YY

MIX
Paper from
responsible sources
FSC™ C007454
www.fsc.org

This book is produced from independently certified FSC™ paper
to ensure responsible forest management.

For more information visit: www.harpercollins.co.uk/green

For Luke Janklow and Will Francis

'There is a point of no return, unremarked at the time, in most lives.'

Graham Greene, *The Comedians*

'Would you prefer to talk or to write everything down?'

'Talk,' she said.

Somerville crossed the room and activated the voice recorder. The American had brought it from the Embassy. There was a small microphone attached to a stand, a glass of tap water and a plate of biscuits on the table.

'Ready?' he asked.

'Ready.'

Somerville leaned over the microphone. His voice was clear, his language concise.

'Statement by LASZLO. Chapel Street, SW1. August nineteenth. Officer presiding: L4. Begins now.' He checked his watch. 'Seventeen hundred hours.'

Lara Bartok adjusted the collar of her shirt. She caught Somerville's eye. He nodded at her, indicating that she should start. She brought the microphone slightly closer to her and took a sip of water. The American realised that he was standing in her eyeline. He moved to a chair on the far side of the room. Bartok did not continue until he was still and completely silent.

'In the beginning, there were seven,' she said.

STATEMENT BY LARA BARTOK ('LASZLO')

**CASE OFFICERS: J.W.S./
S.T.H. - CHAPEL STREET**

**REF: RESURRECTION/SIMAKOV/CARRADINE
FILE: RE2768X**

PART 1 of 5

'In the beginning there were seven. *Ivan [Simakov]*, of course, who is still rightly regarded as the intellectual and moral architect of Resurrection; ███████████████ and ███████████████, both American citizens whom Simakov had met in Zuccotti Park at the height of Occupy Wall Street. ██████████ ██████████, formerly of the Service; ██████████ ██████████, the cyber expert who had been active in Anonymous for several years and was instrumental in planning and orchestrating many of Resurrection's most effective operations in the United States. Ivan had a way of contacting such people on the dark web, of gaining their trust over time, of drawing them out into the open. I used to say that he was like a child on a beach, pouring salt onto the sand so that the creatures of the deep would rise to the surface. He enjoyed this image very much. It is no secret that Ivan Simakov liked to think of himself as a man with extraordinary capabilities.

Also present that day were Thomas Frattura, former assistant to Republican Senator Catherine McKendrick, who had been a prominent figure in Disrupt J20; and me, Lara Bartok, originally from Gyula, in eastern Hungary, about whom you know almost everything.

These seven individuals met only once, in a suite at the Redbury Hotel on East 29th Street in Manhattan. Of course, no cellphones, laptops or Wi-Fi enabled devices of any kind were permitted to be brought to the hotel. Each of the guests who entered the suite was searched by Ivan and myself and asked to remove watches and other items of jewellery, all of which we then took – along with personal belongings including bags and shoes – to a room on a separate floor of the hotel for the duration of the meeting. Ivan, who was meeting ██████ and ███████ for the first time, introduced himself as a Russian citizen, born in Moscow and educated in Paris, who was hoping to effect political change in his own country by inspiring 'an international resistance movement directed against the advocates and enablers of autocratic and quasi-fascist regimes around the world'.

Frattura asked him to explain in more detail what he meant by this. I remember that Ivan paused. He always had a good sense of theatre.

He crossed the suite and opened the curtains. It was a wet morning, there had been heavy rain all night. Through the glass it looked as though the thick fog of the New York skyline was going to seep into the room. What he said next was the best of him. In fact his response to Frattura would form the basis of all the early statements released on behalf of Resurrection outlining our movement's basic goals and rationale.

'Those who know that they have done wrong,' he said. 'Those who have lied in order to achieve their political goals. Those who consciously spread fear and hate. Those who knowingly benefit from greed and corruption. Any person who has helped to bring about the current political crisis in the United States by spreading propaganda and misinformation. Those who aid and abet the criminal regime in Moscow. Those who lied and manipulated in order to see England (sic) break from the European Union. Those who support and actively benefit from the collapse of secular Islamic states; who crush dissent and free speech and willingly erode basic human rights. Any person seeking to spread the virus of male white supremacy or deliberately to stoke anti-Semitism or to suppress women's rights in any form. All of these people – we will begin in the United States and countries such as Russia, the Netherlands, Turkey and the United Kingdom – are legitimate targets for acts of retribution. Bankers. Journalists. Businessmen. Bloggers. Lobbyists. Politicians. Broadcasters. They are to be chosen by us – by *you* – on a case-by-case basis and their crimes exposed to the widest possible audience.'

The beauty of Ivan's idea was that it was *individually* targeted. This is what made it different to Antifa, to Black Lives Matter, to Occupy, to all those other groups who were only ever interested in public protest, in rioting, in civil disorder for its own sake. Those groups changed nothing in terms of people's behaviour but instead gave various parties a chance merely to pose, to demonstrate their own virtue. There is a great difference between people of action and people of words, no? One thing you can say about Ivan Simakov, without a shadow of doubt, is that he was a man of action.

At no point did anybody suggest that the targets for Resurrection were too broadly defined. We were all what you would call in English 'fellow travellers'. We were all – with the exception of Mr Frattura – in our twenties or early thirties. We were angry. Very angry. We wanted to *do* something. We wanted to fight back. We had grown up with the illegal wars in Iraq and Syria. We had lived through the financial crisis and seen not one man nor woman imprisoned for their crimes. All of us had been touched by the manifest corruption and greed of the first two decades of the new century. We felt powerless. We felt that the world as we knew it was being taken away from us. We lived and breathed this conviction and yearned to do something about it. Ivan was a brilliant man, possessed of fanatical zeal, as well as what I always recognised as considerable vanity. But nobody could ever accuse him of lacking passion and the yearning for change.

A policy of non-violence was immediately and enthusiastically endorsed by the group. At that stage nobody thought of themselves as the sort of people who would be involved in assassinations, in bombings, in terrorist behaviour of any kind. Everybody knew that deaths – accidental or otherwise – of innocent civilians would quickly strip the movement of popular support and allow the very people who were being targeted for retribution to accuse Resurrection of 'fascism', of murder, of association with nihilistic, left-wing paramilitary groups. This, of course, is exactly what happened.

Ivan spoke about his ideas for evading capture, eluding law enforcement and intelligence services, men such as yourselves. 'This is the only meeting of its kind between us that will ever take place,' he said. There were silent nods of understanding. People already respected him. They had experienced at first-hand the force of his personality.

Once you had met Ivan Simakov, you never forgot him. 'We will never again communicate or speak face-to-face. Nothing may come from what we discuss today. I have a plan for our first attacks, all of which may be prevented from taking place or fail to have the desired effect on international opinion. I cannot tell you about these plans, just as I would not expect you to divulge details of your own operations as you create them. The Resurrection movement could burn out. The Resurrection movement could have a seismic effect on public attitudes to the liars and enablers of the alt-Right. Who knows? Personally, I am not interested in fame. I have no interest in notoriety or my place in the history books. I have no wish to spend the rest of my life under surveillance or in prison, to live as the guest of a foreign embassy in London, or to save my own skin by making a deal with the devils in Moscow. I wish to be invisible, as you should *all* wish to be invisible.'

So much has happened since then. I have been through many lives and many cities because of my relationship with Ivan Simakov. At that moment I was proud to be at his side. He was in the prime of life. I was honoured to be his girlfriend and to be associated with Resurrection. Now, of course, the movement has moved deeper and deeper into violence, further and further away from the goals and ideals expressed on that first day in New York.

They were so different, but when I think of Ivan, I cannot help thinking of Kit. On the boat he told me that I was like Ingrid Bergman in *Casablanca*, the faithless woman at the side of a revolutionary zealot. Kit was romantic like that, always living at the edge of what was real, as if life was a book he had written, a movie he had seen, and all of us were characters in the story. He was kinder than Ivan, in many ways also braver. I confess to you that I miss him in a way that I did not expect to. I wish you would tell me what happened to him. In his company, I felt safe. It had been a very long time since any man had made me feel that way.

MOSCOW

The apartment was on a quiet street in the Tverskoy district of Moscow, about two kilometres from the Kremlin, a five-minute walk from Lubyanka Square. From the third floor, Curtis could hear the ripple of snow tyres on the wet winter streets. He told Simakov that for the first few days in the city he had thought that all the cars had punctures.

'Sounds like they're driving on bubble wrap,' he said. 'I keep wanting to tell them to put air in their tyres.'

'But you don't speak Russian,' Simakov replied.

'No,' said Curtis. 'I guess I don't.'

He was twenty-nine years old, born and raised in San Diego, the only son of a software salesman who had died when Curtis was fourteen. His mother had been working as a nurse at Scripps Mercy for the past fifteen years. He had graduated from Cal Tech, taken a job at Google, quit at twenty-seven with more than four hundred thousand dollars in the bank thanks to a smart investment in a start-up. Simakov had used Curtis in the Euclidis kidnapping. Moscow was to be his second job.

If he was honest, the plan sounded vague. With Euclidis, every detail had been worked out in advance. Where the target was staying, what time his cab was booked to take him over to Berkeley, how to shut off the CCTV outside the hotel, where to switch the cars. The Moscow job was different. Maybe it was because Curtis didn't know the city; maybe it was because he didn't speak Russian. He felt out of the loop. Ivan was always leaving the apartment and going off to meet people; he said there were other Resurrection activists taking care of the details. All Curtis had been told was that Ambassador Jeffers always sat in the same spot at Café Pushkin, at the same time, on the same night of the week. Curtis was to position himself a few tables away, with the woman from St Petersburg role-playing his girlfriend, keep an eye on Jeffers and make an assessment of the security around him. Simakov would be in the van outside, watching the phones, waiting for Curtis to give the signal that Jeffers was leaving. Two other Resurrection volunteers would be working the sidewalk in the event that anybody tried to step in and help. One of them would have the Glock, the other a Ruger.

'What if there's more security than we're expecting?' he asked. 'What if they have plain clothes in the restaurant I don't know about?'

Curtis did not want to seem distrustful or unsure, but he knew Ivan well enough to speak up when he had doubts.

'What are you so worried about?' Simakov replied. He was slim and athletic with shoulder-length black hair tied back in a ponytail. 'Things go wrong, you walk away. All you have to do is eat your borscht, talk to the girl, let me know what time Ambassador Fuck pays his cheque.'

'I know. I just don't like all the uncertainty.'

'What uncertainty?' Simakov took one of the Rugers

off the table and packed it into the bag. Curtis couldn't tell if he was angry or just trying to concentrate on the thousand plans and ideas running through his mind. It was always hard to judge Simakov's mood. He was so controlled, so sharp, lacking in any kind of hesitation or self-doubt. 'I told you, Zack. This is my city. These are my people. Besides, it's my ass on the line if things go wrong. Whatever happens, you two lovebirds can stay inside, drink some vodka, try the stroganoff. The Pushkin is famous for it.'

Curtis knew that there was nothing more to be said about Jeffers. He tried to change the subject by talking about the weather in Moscow, how as a Californian he couldn't get used to going from hot to cold to hot all the time when he was out in the city. He didn't want Ivan thinking he didn't have the stomach for the fight.

'What's that?'

'I said it's weird the way a lot of the old buildings have three sets of doors.' Curtis kept talking as he followed Simakov into the kitchen. 'What's that about? To keep out the cold?'

'Trap the heat,' Simakov replied. He was carrying the Glock.

Curtis couldn't think of anything else to say. He was in awe of Simakov. He didn't know how to challenge him or to tell him how proud he was to be serving alongside him in the front ranks of Resurrection. Ivan gave off an aura of otherworldly calm and expertise that was almost impossible to penetrate. Curtis knew that he had styled himself as a mere foot soldier, one of tens of thousands of people around the world with the desire to confront bigotry and injustice. But to Curtis, Simakov was the

Leader. There was nothing conventional or routine about him. He was extraordinary.

'I just want to say that I'm glad you got me out here,' he said.

'That's OK, Zack. You were the right man for the job.'

Simakov opened one of the cupboards in the kitchen. He was looking for something.

'I need some oil, clean this thing,' he said, indicating the gun.

'I could go out and get you some,' Curtis suggested.

'Don't you worry about it.' He slapped him on the back, tugging him forwards, like a bear hug from a big brother. 'Anyway, haven't you forgotten? You don't speak Russian.'

The bomb detonated six minutes later, at twenty-three minutes past four in the afternoon. The explosion, which also took the life of a young mother and her baby daughter in a corner apartment on the fourth floor of the building, was initially believed to have been caused by a faulty gas cylinder. When it was discovered that Zack Curtis and Ivan Simakov had been killed in the incident, a division of Alpha Group, Russia's counter-terrorism task force, was dispatched to the scene. Russian television reported that Simakov had been killed by an improvised explosive device which detonated accidentally only hours before a planned Resurrection strike against the American ambassador to the Russian Federation, Walter P. Jeffers, former chairman of the Jeffers Company and a prominent donor to the Republican party.

News of Simakov's death spread quickly. Some believed

that the founder of Resurrection had died while in the process of building a home-made bomb; others were convinced that Russian intelligence had been watching Simakov and that he had been assassinated on the orders of the Kremlin. To deter Resurrection opponents and sympathisers alike, Simakov's remains were interred in an unmarked grave in Kuntsevo Cemetery on the outskirts of Moscow. Curtis was buried two weeks later in San Diego. More than three thousand Resurrection supporters lined the route taken by the funeral cortège.

LONDON

EIGHTEEN MONTHS LATER

1

Like a lot of things that later become very complicated, the situation began very simply.

A few days short of his thirty-sixth birthday, Christopher 'Kit' Carradine – known professionally as C.K. Carradine – was walking along Bayswater Road en route to a cinema in Notting Hill, smoking a cigarette and thinking about nothing much in particular, when he was stopped by a tall, bearded man wearing a dark blue suit and carrying a worn leather briefcase.

'Excuse me?' he said. 'Are you C.K. Carradine?'

Carradine had been writing thrillers professionally for almost five years. In that time he had published three novels and been recognised by members of the public precisely twice: the first time while buying a pot of Marmite in a branch of Tesco Metro in Marylebone; the second while queuing for a drink after a gig at the Brixton Academy.

'I am,' he said.

'I'm sorry to stop you,' said the man. He was at least

fifteen years older than Carradine with thinning hair and slightly beady eyes which had the effect of making him seem strung out and flustered. 'I'm a huge fan. I absolutely *love* your books.'

'That's really great to hear.' Carradine had become a writer almost by accident. Being recognised on the street was surely one of the perks of the job, but he was surprised by the compliment and wondered what more he could say.

'Your research, your characters, your descriptions. All first class.'

'Thank you.'

'The tradecraft. The technology. Rings absolutely true.'

'I really appreciate you saying that.'

'I should know. I work in that world.' Carradine was suddenly in a different conversation altogether. His father had worked for British Intelligence in the 1960s. Though he had told Carradine very little about his life as a spy, his career had fired his son's interest in the secret world. 'You must have too, judging by your inside knowledge. You seem to understand espionage extra-ordinarily well.'

The opportunist in Carradine, the writer hungry for contacts and inspiration, took a half-step forward.

'No. I roamed around in my twenties. Met a few spies along the way, but never got the tap on the shoulder.'

The bearded man stared with his beady eyes. 'I see. Well, that surprises me.' He had a polished English accent, un-ashamedly upper-class. 'So you haven't always been a writer?'

'No.'

Given that he was such a fan, Carradine was intrigued

20

that the man hadn't known this. His biography was all over the books: *Born in Bristol, C.K. Carradine was educated at the University of Manchester. After working as a teacher in Istanbul, he joined the BBC as a graduate trainee. His first novel,* Equal and Opposite, *became an international bestseller. C.K. Carradine lives in London.* Perhaps people didn't bother reading the jacket blurbs.

'And do you live around here?'

'I do.' Four years earlier, he had sold the film rights to his first novel to a Hollywood studio. The film had been made, the film had bombed, but the money he had earned had allowed him to buy a small flat in Lancaster Gate. Carradine didn't anticipate being able to pay off the mortgage until sometime around his eighty-fifth birthday, but at least it was home. 'And you?' he said. 'Are you private sector? HMG?'

The bearded man stepped to one side as a pedestrian walked past. A brief moment of eye contact suggested that he was not in a position to answer Carradine's question with any degree of candour. Instead he said: 'I'm working in London at present' and allowed the noise from a passing bus to take the enquiry away down the street.

'Robert,' he said, raising his voice slightly as a second bus applied air brakes on the opposite side of the road. 'You go by "Kit" in the real world, is that correct?'

'That's right,' Carradine replied, shaking his hand.

'Tell you what. Take my card.'

Somewhat unexpectedly, the man lifted up his brief-case, balanced it precariously on a raised knee, rolled his thumb over the three-digit combination locks and opened it. As he reached inside, lowering his head and searching for a card, Carradine caught sight of a pair of swimming goggles. By force of habit he took notes with his eyes: flecks of grey hair in the beard; bitten fingernails; the suit jacket slightly frayed at the neck. It was hard to get a sense of Robert's personality; he was like a foreigner's idea of an eccentric Englishman.

'Here you are,' he said, withdrawing his hand with the flourish of an amateur magician. The card, like the man, was slightly creased and worn, but the authenticity of the die-stamped government logo unmistakable:

FOREIGN AND COMMONWEALTH OFFICE
ROBERT MANTIS
OPERATIONAL CONTROL CENTRE SPECIALIST

A mobile phone number and email address were printed in the bottom left-hand corner. Carradine knew better than to ask how an 'Operational Control Centre Specialist' passed his time; it was obviously a cover job. As, surely, was the surname: 'Mantis' sounded like a pseudonym.

'Thank you,' he said. 'I'd offer you one of my own but I'm afraid writers don't carry business cards.'

'They should,' said Mantis quickly, slamming the brief-case shut. Carradine caught a sudden glimpse of impatience in his character.

'You're right,' he said. He made a private vow to go to Ryman's and have five hundred cards printed up. 'So how did you come across my books?'

The question appeared to catch Mantis off guard.

'Oh, those.' He set the briefcase down on the pavement. 'I can't remember. My wife, possibly? She may have recommended you. Are you married?'

'No.' Carradine had lived with two women in his life – one a little older, one a little younger – but the relationships hadn't worked out. He wondered why Mantis was enquiring about his personal life but added 'I haven't met the right person yet' because it seemed necessary to elaborate on his answer.

'Oh, you will,' said Mantis wistfully. 'You will.'

They had reached a natural break in the conversation. Carradine looked along the street in the direction of Notting Hill Gate, trying to suggest with his body language that he was running late for an important meeting. Mantis, sensing this, picked up the briefcase.

'Well, it was very nice to meet the famous author,' he gushed. 'I really am a huge fan.' Something in the way he said this caused Carradine suddenly to doubt that Mantis was telling the truth. 'Do stay in touch,' he added. 'You have my details.'

Carradine touched the pocket where he had placed the business card. 'Why don't I phone you?' he suggested. 'That way you'll have my number.'

Mantis snuffed out the idea as quickly and as efficiently as he had snapped shut his briefcase.

'Perhaps not,' he said. 'Do you use WhatsApp?'

'I do.'

Of course. End-to-end encryption. No prying eyes at the Service establishing a link between an active intelligence officer and a spy novelist hungry for ideas.

'Then let's do it that way.' A family of jabbering Spanish tourists bustled past pulling a huge number of wheeled suitcases. 'I'd love to carry on our conversation. Perhaps we can have a pint one of these days?'

'I'd like that,' Carradine replied.

Mantis was already several feet away when he turned around.

'You must tell me how you do it,' he called out.

'Do what?'

'Make it all up. Out of thin air. You must tell me the secret.'

Writers have a lot of time on their hands. Time to brood. Time to ponder. Time to waste. In the years since he had given up his job at the BBC, Carradine had become a master of procrastination. Faced with a blank page at nine o'clock in the morning, he could find half a dozen ways of deferring the moment at which he had to start work. A quick game of FIFA on the Xbox; a run in the park; a couple of sets of darts on Sky Sports 3. These were the standard – and, as far as Carradine was concerned, entirely legitimate – tactics he employed in order to avoid his desk. There wasn't an Emmy award-winning box set or classic movie on Netflix that he hadn't watched when he should have been trying to reach his target of a thousand words per day.

'It's a miracle you get any work done,' his father had said when Carradine unwisely confessed to the techniques he had mastered for circumventing deadlines. 'Are you bored or something? Sounds as though you're going out of your tree.'

He wasn't bored, exactly. He had tried to explain to his father that the feeling was more akin to restlessness, to curiosity, a sense that he had unfinished business with the world.

'I'm stalled,' he said. 'I've been very lucky with the

books so far, but it turns out being a writer is a strange business. We're outliers. Solitude is forced on us. If I was a book, I'd be stuck at the halfway stage.'

'It's perfectly normal,' his father had replied. 'You're still young. There are bits of you that have not yet been written. What you need is an adventure, something to get you out of the office.'

He was right. Although Carradine managed to work quickly and effectively when he put his mind to it, he had come to realise that each day of his professional life was almost exactly the same as the last. He was often nostalgic for Istanbul and the slightly chaotic life of his twenties, for the possibility that something surprising could happen at any given moment. He missed his old colleagues at the BBC: the camaraderie, the feuds, the gossip. Although writing had been good to him, he had not expected it to become his full-time career at such a comparatively early stage in his life. In his twenties Carradine had worked in a vast, monolithic corporation with thousands of employees, frequently travelling overseas to make programmes and documentaries. In his thirties, he had lived and worked mostly alone, existing for the most part within a five-hundred-metre radius of his flat in Lancaster Gate. He had yet fully to adjust to the change or to accept that the rest of his professional life would likely be spent in the company of a keyboard, a mouse and a Dell Inspiron 3000. To the outside world, the life of a writer was romantic and liberating; to Carradine it sometimes resembled a gilded cage.

All of which made the encounter with Mantis that much more intriguing. Their conversation had been a welcome distraction from the established rhythms and responsibilities of his day-to-day life. At frequent moments over the next twenty-four hours, Carradine found himself thinking about their chat on Bayswater Road. Had it been pre-arranged? Did the 'Foreign and Commonwealth Office' – surely a euphemism for the Service – know that C.K. Carradine lived and worked in the area? Had Mantis been sent to feel him out about something? Had the plot of one of his books come too close to a real-world operation? Or was he acting in a private capacity, looking for a writer who might tell a sensitive story using the screen of fiction? An aficionado of conspiracy thrillers, Carradine didn't want to believe that their meeting had been merely a chance encounter. He wondered why Mantis had declared himself an avid fan of his books without being able to say where or how he had come across them. And surely he was aware of his father's career in the Service?

He wanted to know the truth about the man from the FCO. To that end he took out Mantis's business card, tapped the number into his phone and sent a message on WhatsApp.

Very good to meet you. Glad you've enjoyed the books.
This is my number. Let's have that pint.

Carradine saw that Mantis had come online. The message he had sent quickly acquired two blue ticks. Mantis was 'typing'.

Likewise, delighted to run into you. Lunch Wednesday?

Carradine replied immediately.

Sounds good. My neck of the woods or yours?

Two blue ticks.

Mine.

2

'Mine' turned out to be a small, one-bedroom flat in Marylebone. Carradine had expected to be invited to lunch at Wheelers or White's; that was how he had written similar scenes in his books. Spook meeting spook at the Traveller's Club, talking *sotto voce* about 'the threat from Russia' over Chablis and fishcakes. Instead Mantis sent him an address on Lisson Grove. He was very precise about the timing and character of the meeting.

Please don't be late. It goes without saying that this is a private matter, not for wider circulation.

Carradine was about halfway through writing his latest book, still four months from deadline, so on the day of the meeting he took the morning off. He went for a dawn run in Hyde Park, had a shower back at his flat and ate breakfast at the Italian Gardens Café. He was excited by the prospect of seeing Mantis for the second time and wondered what the meeting would hold. The possibility of some sort of involvement with the Service? A scoop that he could fictionalise in a book? Perhaps the whole thing would turn out to be a waste of time. By ten o'clock Carradine was walking east along Sussex Gardens, planning to catch a train from Edgware Road to Angel. With a couple of hours to spare before he was due to meet Mantis, he wanted to rummage around in his favourite record store on Essex Road looking for a rare vinyl for a friend's birthday.

He was halfway to the station when it began to rain. Carradine had no umbrella and quickened his pace towards Edgware Road. What happened in the next few minutes was an anomaly, a moment that might, in different circumstances, have been designed by Mantis as a test of Carradine's temperament under pressure. Certainly, in the context of what followed over the next two weeks, it was a chance encounter so extraordinary that Carradine came to wonder whether it had been staged solely for his benefit. Had he written such a scene in one of his novels, it would have been dismissed as a freak coincidence.

He had reached the south-west corner of the busy intersection between Sussex Gardens and Edgware Road. He was waiting to cross at the lights. A teenage girl beside him was nattering away to a friend about boyfriend trouble. *'So I says to him, I'm like, no way is that happening, yeah? I'm like, he needs to get his shit together because I'm like just not going through with that bullshit again.'* A stooped old man standing to Carradine's left was holding an umbrella in his right hand. Water was dripping from the umbrella onto the shoulders of Carradine's jacket; he could feel droplets of rain on the back of his neck. In the next instant he became aware of shouting on the opposite corner of the street, about twenty metres from where he was standing. A well-built man wearing a motorcycle helmet was raining punches through the passenger door of a black BMW. The driver – a blonde woman in her forties – was being dragged from the vehicle by a second man wearing an identical helmet and torn blue jeans. The woman was screaming and swearing. Carradine thought that he recognised her as a public figure but could not put a name to the face. Her assailant, who was at least six feet tall, was dragging her by the hair shouting, 'Move, you fucking bitch', and wielding what looked like a hammer.

Carradine had the sense of a moment suspended in time. There seemed to be at least twenty people standing within a few feet of the car. None of them moved. The rest of the traffic at the intersection had come to a stand-still. A large white Transit van was parked in front of the BMW. The first man opened a side panel in the van and helped his accomplice to drag the woman inside. Carradine was aware of somebody shouting 'Stop them! Somebody fucking stop them!' and of the teenage girl beside him muttering '*Fucking hell, what the fuck is this, this is bad*' as the door of the van slammed shut. The middle-aged man who had been seated on the driver's side of the BMW now stumbled out of the car, his hair matted with blood, his face bruised and bleeding, hands raised in the air, imploring his attackers to release the woman. Instead, the man in the torn jeans walked back towards him and swung a single, merciless punch that knocked him out cold. Somebody screamed as he slumped to the ground.

Carradine stepped off the pavement. He had been taking

boxing lessons for the past eighteen months: he was tall and fit and wanted to help. He was not sure precisely what he intended to do but recognised that he had to act. Then, as he moved forwards, he saw a pedestrian, standing much closer to the van, approach one of the two assailants. Carradine heard him cry: 'Stop! Enough!'

'Hey!' Carradine added his own voice to the confrontation. 'Let her go!'

Things then happened very quickly. Carradine felt a hand on his arm, holding him back. He turned to see the girl looking at him, shaking her head, imploring him not to get involved. Carradine would have ignored her had it not been for what came next. A third man suddenly emerged from the Transit van. He was wearing a black balaclava and carrying what looked like a short metal pole. He was much larger than the others, slower in his movements, but went towards the pedestrian and swung the pole first into his knees and then across his shoulders. The pedestrian screamed out in pain and fell onto the street.

At that moment Carradine's courage deserted him. The man in the balaclava entered the van via the side door and slammed it shut. His two helmeted accomplices also climbed inside and drove quickly away. By the time Carradine could hear a police siren in the distance, the van was already out of sight, accelerating north along Edgware Road.

There was a momentary silence. Several onlookers moved towards the middle-aged man who had been knocked out. He was soon surrounded by the very people who, moments earlier, might have defended him against attack and prevented the abduction of his companion.

Through the mêlée, Carradine could see a woman kneeling on the damp street, raising the victim's head onto a balled-up jacket. For every bystander who was talking on their phone – presumably having called the police – there was another filming the scene, most of them as emotionally detached as a group of tourists photographing a sunset. With the traffic still not moving, Carradine walked across the intersection and tried to reach the BMW. His route was blocked. Car horns were sounding in the distance as a police vehicle appeared at the eastern end of Sussex Gardens. Two uniformed officers jogged towards the fallen men. Carradine realised that he could do nothing other than gawp and stare; it was pointless to hang around, just another passer-by rubbernecking the incident. He was beginning to feel the first quiet thuds of shame that he had failed to act when he heard the word 'Resurrection' muttered in the crowd. A woman standing next to him said: 'Did you see who it was? That journalist from the *Express*, wasn't it? Whatserface?' and Carradine found that he could provide the answer.

'Lisa Redmond.'

'That's right. Poor cow.'

Carradine walked away. It was clear that activists associated with Resurrection had staged the kidnapping. Redmond was a hate figure for the Left, frequently identified as a potential target for the group. So many right-wing journalists and broadcasters had been attacked around the world that it was a miracle she had not been confronted before. Carradine felt wretched that he had not done more. He had witnessed street brawls in the past but never the nerveless brutality displayed by the men who had taken Redmond. He was not due to meet

Mantis for another hour and a half. He thought about cancelling the meeting and going home. Carradine told himself that it would have been rash to try to take on three armed men on his own, but wished that he had acted more decisively; his instinct for survival had been stronger than his desire to help.

He wandered down Edgware Road in a daze, eventually going into a café and checking the BBC for a report on what had happened. Sure enough it was confirmed that the 'right-wing columnist' Lisa Redmond had been kidnapped by activists associated with Resurrection and her husband beaten up in the act of trying to protect her. Carradine opened Twitter. 'Fucking bitch had it coming' was the first of several tweets he saw in defence of the attack, most of which carried the now-familiar hashtags #Resurrection #Alt-RightScum #RememberSimakov #ZackCurtisLives and #FuckOtis. The latter was a reference to the first – and most notorious – Resurrection kidnapping, in San Francisco, of Otis Euclidis, a senior editor at Breitbart News who had been seized from outside his hotel shortly before he had been due to make a speech at Berkeley University. The kidnapping of Redmond was merely the latest in a spate of copycat attacks that had taken place in Atlanta, Sydney, Budapest and beyond. Many of the victims had been held for several weeks and then killed. Some of the recovered bodies had been mutilated. Others, including Euclidis, had never been found.

3

Carradine's apprehensiveness in the build-up to the meeting with Mantis had been completely erased by what had happened on Sussex Gardens. Arriving at the address on Lisson Grove, he felt numb and dazed. Mantis buzzed him inside without speaking on the intercom. Carradine walked up six flights of stairs to the third floor, slightly out of breath and sweating from the climb. The landing carpet was stained. There was a faux Dutch oil painting on the wall.

'Kit. Good to see you. Do come in.' Mantis was standing back from the door, as though wary of being spotted by neighbours. 'Thank you so much for coming.'

Carradine was led into a sparsely furnished sitting room. He laid his jacket on the back of a brand-new cream leather sofa wrapped in clear plastic. Sunlight was streaming through the windows. The sight of the plastic made him feel constricted and hot.

'Are you moving in?' he asked. The flat smelled of old milk and toilet cleaner. There was no indication that Mantis had prepared any food.

'It's not my place,' he replied, closing a connecting door into the hall.

'Ah.'

So what was it? A safe house? If so, why had Mantis arranged to meet on Service territory? Carradine had assumed they were just going to have a friendly lunch. He looked around. Two mobile phones were charging on the floor by the window. There was a vase of plastic flowers on a table in the centre of the room. Two self-assembly stools were positioned in front of a breakfast bar linking the sitting room to a small kitchen. Carradine could see a jar of instant coffee, a box of teabags and a kettle near the sink. The kitchen was otherwise spotlessly clean.

'Did you hear about Lisa Redmond?' Mantis asked.

Carradine hesitated.

'No,' he said, feigning surprise. 'What's happened?'

'Grabbed by Resurrection.' Mantis opened a double-glazed window on to a small parking area at the rear of the building. Cool air poured into the room. 'Thrown in the back of a Transit van and driven off – in broad bloody daylight.'

'Christ,' said Carradine.

He was not a natural liar. In fact, he could not remember the last time he had deliberately concealed the truth in such a way. It occurred to him that it was a bad idea to do so in front of a man who was professionally trained in the darker arts of obfuscation and deceit. Mantis gestured outside in the direction of Edgware Road.

'A mile away,' he said. 'Less! Three men kicked the living shit out of her poor husband, who's apparently some kind of hotshot TV producer. One of them had a pop at a have-a-go-hero who tried to save the day. It's all over the news.'

'What do you think will happen to her?' Carradine asked, though he knew the answer to his own question.

'Curtains,' said Mantis. 'Another Aldo Moro job.'

Moro, the Italian Prime Minister kidnapped by the Red Brigades in 1978, had been murdered in captivity, his body discovered in the back of a Renault two months later. Carradine wondered why Mantis had made such an obscure historical connection but conceded his point with a nod.

'I'm surprised she didn't have any security,' he said. 'People kept saying she was a target. In America, employees in the White House, staff at Fox News, prominent Republican officials, they've all been carrying guns for months.'

'Quite right too,' said Mantis with an impatience that reminded Carradine of the way his temper had flared on Bayswater Road. 'People have a right to defend themselves. You never know who's going to come out of the woodwork and take a pop at you.'

Carradine looked at the sofa. Mantis understood that he wanted to sit down and invited him to do so 'on the plastic cover'. He asked Carradine to switch off his mobile phone. He was not particularly surprised by the request and did as he had been asked.

'Now if you wouldn't mind passing it to me.'

Carradine handed over the phone. He was delighted to see Mantis place it inside a cocktail shaker that he had removed from one of the cupboards in the kitchen. He had used an identical piece of tradecraft in his most recent novel, stealing the idea from an article about Edward Snowden.

'A Faraday cage,' he said, smiling.

'If you say so.' Mantis opened the door of the fridge and put the cocktail shaker inside it. The fridge was completely empty. 'And if you could just sign this.' He crossed the room and passed Carradine a pen and a piece of paper. 'We insist on the Official Secrets Act.'

Carradine's heart skipped. Without pausing to read the document in any detail, he rested the piece of paper on the table and signed his name at the bottom. It occurred to him that his father must have done exactly the same thing some fifty years earlier.

'Thank you. You might want to take a look at this.'

Mantis was holding what appeared to be a driving licence. Carradine took it and turned it over. Mantis's photograph and personal details, as well as a Foreign Office logo and a sample of his signature, were laminated against a pale grey background.

'This wouldn't be enough to get you into Vauxhall Cross,' he said. It was necessary to demonstrate to Mantis that he did not fully trust him. 'Do you have any other forms of ID?'

As though he had been expecting Carradine's question, Mantis dipped into the pocket of his trousers and pulled out a moulded plastic security pass.

'Access all areas,' he said. Carradine had wanted to inspect the pass, if only to experience the buzz of holding a genuine piece of Service kit, but Mantis immediately put it back in his pocket.

'Always worried about losing it on the number nineteen bus,' he said.

'I'm not surprised,' Carradine replied.

He asked for a glass of water. Mantis produced a chipped William and Kate mug and turned on the cold tap in the kitchen. It spluttered and coughed, spraying water onto his hand. He swore quietly under his breath – 'fucking thing' – filled the mug and passed it to Carradine.

'Who owns this place?'

'One of ours,' he replied.

Carradine had met spies before but never in these circumstances and never in such a furtive atmosphere. He leaned back against the thick plastic cover and took a sip from the mug. The water was lukewarm and tasted of battery fluid. He did not want to swallow it but did so. Mantis sat in the only other available seat, a white wooden chair positioned in front of the window.

'Did you tell anybody that you were coming here today?' he asked. 'A girlfriend?'

'I'm single,' Carradine replied. He was surprised that Mantis had already forgotten this.

'Oh, that's right. You said.' He crossed his legs. 'What about your father?'

Carradine wondered how much Mantis knew about William Carradine. A rising star in the Service, forced out by Kim Philby, who had given his name – as well as the identities of dozens of other members of staff – to Moscow. Surely somebody at Vauxhall Cross had told him?

'He doesn't know.'

'And your mother?' Mantis quickly checked himself. 'Oh, I'm so sorry. Of course . . .'

Carradine's mother had died of breast cancer when he was a teenager. His father had never remarried. He had recently suffered a stroke that had left him paralysed on one side of his body. Carradine made a point of visiting him regularly at his flat in Swiss Cottage. He was his only surviving blood family and they were very close.

'I haven't told anybody,' he said.

'Good. So nobody has been made aware of our chat in the street?'

'Nobody.'

Carradine looked more closely at his interlocutor. He was wearing pale blue chinos and a white Ralph Lauren polo shirt. Carradine was reminded of a line judge at Wimbledon. Mantis's hair had been cut and his beard trimmed; as a consequence, he no longer looked quite so tired and dishevelled. Nevertheless, there was something second-rate about him. He could not help but give the impression of being very slightly out of his depth. Carradine suspected that he was not the sort of officer handed 'hot' postings in Amman or Baghdad. No, Robert Mantis was surely lower down the food chain, tied to a desk in London, obliged to take orders from Service upstarts half his age.

'Let me get straight to the point.' The man from the FCO made deliberate and sustained eye contact. 'My colleagues and I have been talking about you. For some time.'

'I had a feeling our meeting the other day wasn't an accident.'

'It wasn't.'

Carradine looked around the room. The flat was exactly the sort of place in which a man might be quietly bumped off. No record of the meeting ever happening. CCTV footage from the lobby conveniently erased. Hair samples hoovered up and fingerprints wiped away by a Service support team. The body then placed inside a thick plastic sheet – perhaps the one covering the sofa – and taken outside to the car park. Should he say this in an effort to break the ice? Probably not. Carradine sensed that Mantis wouldn't find it funny.

'Don't look so worried.'

'What's that?'

'You look concerned.'

'I'm fine.' Carradine was surprised that Mantis had failed to read his mood. 'In fact, it did seem a bit odd to me that a serving intelligence officer would talk so openly about working for the Service.'

'Good.'

'What do you mean "good"?'

'I mean that you obviously have sound instincts.' Carradine felt the plastic rippling beneath him. It was like sitting on a waterbed. 'You obviously have an aptitude for this sort of thing. It's what we wanted to talk to you about.'

'Go on.'

'You have a Facebook page.'

'I do.'

'The other day you were asking for tips about Marrakech. Advertising a talk you're doing at a literary festival in Morocco.'

Despite the fact that C.K. Carradine's Facebook page was publicly available, he experienced the numbing realisation that the Service had most probably strip-mined every conversation, email and text message he had sent in the previous six months. He was grateful that he hadn't run the name 'Robert Mantis' through Google.

'That's right,' he said.

'Get much of a response?'

'Uh, some restaurant tips. A lot of people recommended the Majorelle Gardens. Why?'

'How long are you going for?'

'About three days. I'm doing a panel discussion with another author. We're being put up in a riad.'

'Would you be prepared to spend slightly longer in Morocco if we asked?'

It took Carradine a moment to absorb what Mantis had said. Other writers – Somerset Maugham, Graham Greene, Frederick Forsyth – had worked as support agents for the Service at various points in their careers. Was he being offered the chance to do what his father had done?

'There's no reason why I can't stay there a bit longer,' he said, trying to make his expression appear as relaxed as possible while his heart began to pound like a jungle drum. 'Why?'

Mantis laid it out.

'You may have noticed that we're somewhat stretched at the moment. Cyber attacks. Islamist terror. Resurrection. The list goes on . . .'

'Sure.' Carradine felt his throat go dry. He wanted to take a sip of water but was worried that Mantis would see his hand shaking.

'Increasingly, things fall through the gaps. Agents don't have the support they need. Messages struggle to get through. Information can't travel in the way that we want it to travel.'

Carradine was nodding. He knew that it was better at this stage to listen rather than to ask questions. At the same time he could feel his vanity jumping up and down with excitement; the flattery implicit in Mantis's offer, coupled with the chance to honour his father's career, perhaps even to surpass his achievements, was hitting a sweet spot inside him that he hadn't known existed.

'We had a station in Rabat. It was wound up. Folded in with the Americans. Manpower issues, budgetary restrictions. I'm sure I don't have to tell you that all of this is strictly between you and me.'

'Of course.'

'I have a desk responsibility for the region. I need to be able to put somebody in front of one or two of our agents out there, just to reassure them that they're a priority for London. Even though that may not be entirely the case.'

Mantis flashed Carradine a knowing look. Carradine was obliged to return it in kind, nodding as though he was on intimate terms with the complexities of agent-running.

'I'm afraid it would require you to go to Casablanca as well as Marrakech. Ever been?'

Carradine had heard that modern Casablanca was far removed from the romantic image of the city conjured by Hollywood: a crowded, choking industrial conurbation entirely devoid of charm and interest.

'Never. But I've always wanted to check it out.'

He set the mug of water to one side. In the distance Carradine could hear the sound of sirens, the familiar background soundtrack to life in twenty-first-century London. He wondered if Redmond had already been found and could scarcely believe that within hours of witnessing her kidnapping, he was being offered a chance to work as a support agent for the Service. It was as though Mantis was handing him an opportunity to prove the courage that had so recently been found wanting.

'Can you be more precise about what exactly you need me to do?'

Mantis seemed pleased that Carradine had asked the question.

'Writers on research trips provide perfect cover for clandestine work,' he explained. 'The inquisitive novelist always has a watertight excuse for poking his nose around. Any unusual or suspicious activity can be justified as part of the artistic process. You know the sort of thing. Atmosphere, authenticity, detail.'

'I know the sort of thing.'

'All you have to do is pack a couple of your paperbacks, make sure your website and Wikipedia page are up to date. In the highly unlikely event that you encounter somebody who doubts your bona fides, just point them to the Internet and hand over a signed copy of *Equal and Opposite*. Easy.'

'Sounds like you've got it all worked out.'

'We do!' Mantis beamed with his beady eyes. Carradine must have looked concerned because he added: 'Don't be alarmed. Your responsibilities will be comparatively minimal and require very little exertion on your part.'

'I'm not alarmed.'

'There's no need – indeed no time – for detailed preparation or training. You'll simply be required to make your way to Casablanca on Monday with various items which will be provided to you by the Service.'

'What sort of items?'

'Oh, just some money. Three thousand euros to be paid to a locally based agent. Also a book, most likely a novel or biography of some sort, to be passed on as a cipher.'

'Who to?'

'Yassine. A contact of mine from Rabat. Feeling slightly neglected, needs to have his tummy tickled but I'm too

43

busy to fly down. We usually meet up in a restaurant, Blaine's, which is popular with businessmen and – well – young women of low social responsibility.' Mantis grinned at the euphemism. 'Yassine will recognise you, greet you with the phrase, "I remember you from the wedding in London." You reply: "The wedding was in Scotland." And your meeting can proceed.'

Carradine was surprised that Mantis was moving at such a pace.

'You really *do* have everything worked out,' he said.

'I can assure you this is all very normal and straightforward, as long as you can remember what to do.'

'I can remember . . .'

'As for the money, you are to leave that at the reception desk of a five-star hotel under the name "Abdullah Aziz". A very important contact. He is owed money.'

'Abdullah Aziz,' Carradine was trying to remember his answer to Yassine's question about the wedding. He wondered why Mantis was flooding him with so much information so quickly and wished that he was free to write things down.

'Sounds easy enough,' he said. 'Which five-star hotel?'

'I'll let you know in due course.'

Carradine was seated with his palms face down on the sofa's plastic cover. He became aware that they were soaked in sweat.

'And what about Marrakech? What am I doing there?'

Mantis was suddenly at a loss for words. Having rushed through Carradine's responsibilities in Casablanca, he became hesitant to the point of anxiety. Twice he appeared to be on the brink of replying to Carradine's question only to stop himself, biting the nail on the index finger of his left hand. Eventually he stood up and looked out onto the car park.

'Marrakech,' he revealed at last. 'Well, that's where things will become slightly more . . . *nuanced*.' The man from the FCO turned and looked into the room, slowly rubbing his hands together as he moved towards the sofa. 'It's why we've picked you, Kit. We're going to need you to use your initiative.'

4

Mantis explained that there was a woman.

A 'remarkable young woman, cunning and unpredictable'. She didn't have a name – at least one that was still 'operationally useful or relevant' – and hadn't been seen for 'the best part of two years'. She was on the books at the Service but they hadn't heard 'hide nor hair of her for far too long'. Mantis explained that he was worried. He knew that she was in trouble and that she needed help. The Service was '90 per cent certain' that the woman was living in north-west Africa under an assumed name and '100 per cent certain' that she wanted to come back to the UK. She had been sighted in Marrakech in the winter and again in the Atlas Mountains only three weeks earlier. 'Other officers and support agents' had been looking for her in a variety of locations – Mexico, Cuba, Argentina – but all the evidence pointed to Morocco. All Carradine had to do was keep an eye out for her. The woman knew the country well and it had been easy for her to 'disappear' in a place with such a large number of western tourists.

'That's it?' Carradine asked. The job sounded farcical.

'That's it,' Mantis replied.

'You want me just to wander around Marrakech on the off-chance I run into her?'

'No, no.' An apologetic smile. 'She's a big reader. Fan of books and literature. There's a strong possibility that she might show her face at your festival. We just want you to keep your eyes peeled.'

Carradine struggled to think of something constructive to say.

'If she's in trouble, why doesn't she come in? What's to stop her making contact with you? Why doesn't she go to her nearest embassy?'

'I'm afraid it's a good deal more complicated than that.'

Carradine sensed that he was being lied to. The Service was asking him to look for a woman who was doing everything she could to avoid being found.

'Is she Spanish?' he asked.

'What makes you say that?'

'Mexico. Argentina. Cuba. They're all Spanish-speaking countries. Tangier is a one-hour flight from Madrid, a short hop on the boat from Tarifa.'

Mantis smiled. 'I can see that you're going to be good at this.'

Carradine ignored the compliment.

'What does she look like?' he asked.

'I have a number of photographs that I can show you, but I'm afraid you'll have to commit them to memory. I can give you a small passport-sized photograph to keep in your wallet as an aide-memoire, but you won't be able to keep anything digital on your phone or laptop. We can't risk these images falling into the wrong hands. If your phone was lost or stolen, for example, or you were asked to account for how you knew the woman . . .'

The task was sounding increasingly strange.

'Who would be asking those kinds of questions?'

Mantis indicated with an airy wave of the hand that Carradine should not be concerned.

'If you carry on behaving exactly as you have always behaved whenever you've been on a research trip to a foreign city, it's very unlikely that you would ever be arrested, far less asked anything by anybody about the nature of your work for us. We take every precaution to ensure that our agents – by that I mean you, Kit – have no discernible relationship with British intelligence. Nevertheless, it goes without saying that you must never, under any circumstances, reveal anything under questioning about the arrangement we have made here today.'

'Of course. Without saying.'

'You and I will continue to communicate with one another *en clair* on WhatsApp using the number I provided to you. I will be your only point of contact with the Service. You will never come to Vauxhall, you will rarely meet any of my colleagues. As far as Morocco is concerned, you won't tell anybody about our arrangement or – heaven forbid – start showing off about it on the phone or by email. Did you put my name into a search engine at all?'

Carradine assumed that Mantis already knew the answer to his own question, but replied truthfully.

'No. I assumed it would be flagged up.'

'You were right.' He looked relieved. 'By the same token, you mustn't Google the names of anybody you come into contact with as a result of your work for us, nor carry with you anything that might be at all incriminating. We don't do exploding pens and invisible ink. Does that sound like something you might be able to manage?'

Carradine felt that he had no choice other than to say: 'Sure, no problem.' He was perfectly capable of keeping a secret. He understood the mechanics of deceit. He was keen to do a patriotic job for his country, not least because his own professional life was so low on excitement. The only thing that concerned him was the possibility of being arrested and thrown into a Moroccan jail. But to say that to Mantis, to indicate that he was worried about saving his own skin, might have seemed spineless.

'Mind if I use the loo?' he asked.

'Be my guest.'

Carradine crossed the hall and went into the bathroom. There were no towels on the rail or mats on the floor, no toothbrush or razor in the plastic mug on the basin. A stained shower curtain hung loose over the bath on white plastic hooks, many of which were bent out of shape. He locked the door and ran the tap, staring at his reflection in the mirror. It occurred to him that he was still recovering from the shock of the Redmond kidnapping and had not been thinking clearly about what Mantis was asking him to do. The job certainly promised intrigue and drama. It was a chance to perform a useful service for his country. Carradine would learn from the experience and obtain priceless first-hand research for his books. There was every possibility that he might be asked to work for the Service for a considerable period of time. In short, the situation was profoundly seductive to him.

'Everything OK?' Mantis asked as he came back into the living room.

'Everything's great.'

'Come and have a look at these.'

He was holding an iPad. Carradine sat next to him on the sofa and looked at the screen. Mantis began flicking through a series of photographs, presumably of the woman Carradine would be asked to look for in Marrakech.

It was strange. In the same way that he had recognised Lisa Redmond as she was dragged from the car, without at first being able to put a name to her face, Carradine was sure that he had seen pictures of the woman before. She wasn't a journalist or celebrity. She wasn't a likely target for Resurrection. But she was some kind of public figure. Perhaps an actress he had seen on stage in London or somebody associated with a news story or political scandal. He could not work it out. It might equally have been the case that Carradine had met her at a party or that the woman had some connection to the film or publishing worlds. She was certainly not a stranger to him.

'You look as though you recognise her.'

Carradine decided against telling Mantis that he had seen the woman's face before. His explanation would have sounded confused.

'No. I'm just trying to take a photograph with my eyes. Commit her face to memory.'

'It's a beautiful face.'

Carradine was taken aback by the wistfulness of the remark. 'It is,' he said as they shuttled back through the album. The woman had long, dark hair, light brown eyes and slightly crooked teeth. He assumed that most of the photographs had been culled from social media; they had a casual, snapped quality and appeared to cover a period of several years. In two of the pictures the woman was seated at a table in a restaurant, surrounded by people of her own age; in another, she was wearing a powder-blue bikini on a sunny beach, her arm encircling the waist of a handsome, bearded man holding a surfboard. Carradine assumed that he was a boyfriend, past or present.

'He looks Spanish,' he said, pointing at the man. 'Was this taken in Spain?'

'Portugal. Atlantic coast.' Mantis reached across Carradine and quickly flicked the photo stream to the next image. 'You were right. She has a Spanish mother. Speaks the language fluently.'

'And her father? Where was he from?'

'I'm afraid I can't say.'

There was a fixed, unapologetic look on Mantis's face.

'And you can't tell me her name either?'

'I'm afraid not. It's better that you know nothing about her, Kit. If you were to start asking the wrong questions, if you were tempted to Google her, for example, it's not easy to say what might happen to you.'

'That sounds like a threat.'

'It wasn't meant to.'

Mantis directed Carradine's attention back to the screen. He had a good memory for faces and was confident that he would be able to recognise the woman if he came across her in Morocco.

'How tall is she?' he asked.

'Couple of inches shorter than you.'

'Hairstyle?'

'She might have changed it. Might have dyed it. Might have shaved it all off. Anything is possible.'

'Accent?'

'Think Ingrid Bergman speaking English.'

Carradine smiled. He could hear the voice in his head.

'Any other, uh . . .' He reached for the euphemism. 'Distinguishing characteristics?'

Mantis stood up, taking the iPad with him.

'Of course! I almost forgot.' He extended his left arm so that it was almost touching Carradine's forehead. 'The woman has a tattoo,' he said, tapping the wrist. 'Three tiny black swallows just about here.'

Carradine stared at the frayed cuffs of Mantis's shirt. Veins bulged on his forearm beneath a scattering of black hairs.

'If it's a tattoo,' he said, 'and she's trying not to get recognised, don't you think she might have had it removed?'

Mantis moved his hand onto Carradine's shoulder. Carradine hoped that he wouldn't leave it there for long.

'You don't miss a trick, do you?' he said. 'We've obviously picked the right man, Kit. You're a natural.'

5

Mantis said nothing more about the tattoo. Carradine was told that if he spotted the woman, he was to approach her discreetly, ensure that their conversation was neither overheard nor overseen, and then to explain that he had been sent by British intelligence. He was also to pass her a sealed package. This would be delivered by the Service before he left for Morocco.

'I'm assuming I can't open this package when I receive it?'

'That is correct.'

'Can I ask what will be inside it?'

'A passport, a credit card and a message to the agent. That is all.'

'That's all? Nothing else?'

'Nothing else.'

'So why seal it?'

'I'm not sure I understand your question.'

Carradine was trying to tread the fine line between

protecting himself against risk and not appearing to be apprehensive.

'It's just that if my bags are searched and they find the package, if they ask me to open it, how do I explain why I'm carrying somebody else's passport?'

'Simple,' Mantis replied. 'You say that it's for a friend who left it in London. The same friend whose photo you're carrying in your wallet.'

'So how did she get to Morocco without a passport?'

Mantis took a deep breath, as if to suggest that Carradine was starting to ask too many questions. 'She has two. One Spanish, the other British. OK?'

'What's my friend's name?'

'Excuse me?'

'I need to know her name. If it's on the passport, if I'm carrying her picture around, they'll expect me to know who she is.'

'Ah.' Mantis seemed pleased that Carradine had thought of this. 'The surname on the passport is "Rodriguez". Christian name "Maria". Easy enough to remember.'

'And mundane enough not to draw attention to itself.'

'It does have that added dimension, yes.'

They remained at the Lisson Grove flat for another half-hour, going over further practical details of Carradine's trip, including protocols for contacting Vauxhall Cross in the event of an emergency. Mantis insisted that they meet at the flat when Carradine returned from Marrakech, at which point he would be debriefed and given payment, in cash, for any expenses he had run up in Morocco.

'Feel free to stay somewhere decent in Casablanca,' he said. 'We'll cover your costs, the extra flight as well. Just keep accurate receipts for the bean counters. They're notoriously stingy when it comes to shelling out for taxis and train tickets.'

As Carradine was leaving, Mantis handed him two envelopes, each containing €1,500. There was no limit to the amount of foreign currency he was permitted to bring into Morocco and Mantis did not think that €3,000 would be considered suspicious. He told Carradine that the sealed package containing the passport and credit card would be delivered to his flat in Lancaster Gate the following day, as well as the novel which was to be used as a book cipher. Mantis reiterated the importance of leaving the sealed package intact, unless Carradine was instructed to open it by law enforcement officials in the UK or Morocco. He did not give an explanation for this request and Carradine did not ask for one. Carradine assumed that the package would contain sensitive documents.

'Good luck,' Mantis said, shaking his hand as he left. 'And thanks for helping out.'

'No problem.'

Carradine walked out onto Lisson Grove in a state of confusion. He was bewildered by the speed with which Mantis had acted and strung out by the painstaking assimilation of so much information. It seemed bizarre that he should have been asked to undertake work on behalf of the secret state – particularly after such a cursory meeting – and wondered if the entire episode was part of an elaborate set-up. Clearly the content of his novels, the depictions of tradecraft, his observations about the burdens of secrecy and so forth, had convinced the Service that C.K. Carradine was possessed of the ideal temperament to work as a support agent. But how had they known that he would agree so readily to their offer? While working for the BBC in his twenties, Carradine had spoken to three veteran foreign correspondents – two British, one Canadian – each of whom had been tapped up by their respective intelligence services overseas. They had turned down the opportunity on the basis that it would interfere with the objectivity of their work, undermine the relationships they had built up with local sources and potentially bring them into conflict with their host governments. Carradine wished that he had shown a little more of their steadfastness when presented with the dangled carrot of clandestine work. Instead, perhaps because of what had happened to his father, he had demonstrated a rather old-fashioned desire to serve Queen and country, a facet of his character which suddenly seemed antiquated, even naive. He was committed to doing what Mantis had asked him to do, but felt that he had not given himself adequate protection in the event that things went wrong.

Still in a state of apprehension, Carradine took a detour on the way home, purchased a roll of masking tape and found an Internet café in Paddington. He wanted to be certain that Mantis was a bona fide Service employee, not a Walter Mitty figure taking advantage of him either for his own amusement or for some darker purpose which had not yet been made clear.

The café was half-full. Carradine stood over a vacant computer, tore off a small strip of the masking tape and placed it over the lens at the top of the screen. The computer was already loaded with a VPN. In his most recent novel, Carradine had written a chapter in which the principal character was required to comb the Dark Net in order to create a false identity. He had spoken to a hacker a few weeks before and still remembered most of what she had told him during their cloak-and-dagger meeting at a coffee shop in Balham. The trick – apart from disabling the camera – was to use the VPN both to create a false IP address and to encrypt his Internet usage. That way, his activities would be concealed from any prying eyes in Cheltenham and Carradine could investigate the mysterious Mr Mantis without fear of being identified.

As he expected, none of the 'Robert Mantis' listings on Facebook could plausibly have been the man he had met in Lisson Grove. There was no Twitter account associated with the name, nor anything on Instagram. Carradine ran Mantis through LinkedIn and Whitepages but found only an out-of-work chef in Tampa and a 'lifestyle' photographer in Little Rock. Remembering a tip he had been given by the hacker, he looked on Nominet to see if any variant of 'robertmantis' was listed as a website domain. It was not. Whoever he had met that afternoon was using a pseudonym which had been cleaned up for the obvious purpose of protecting his true identity. Mantis was not listed as a director at Companies House nor as a shared freeholder on any UK properties. A credit check on Experian also drew a blank.

Satisfied that he was a genuine Service employee, Carradine put the computer to sleep, removed the strip of masking tape from the lens and walked home.

6

The following morning, Carradine was woken early by the sound of the doorbell ringing. He stumbled out of bed, pulled on a pair of boxer shorts and struck his foot on the skirting board as he picked up the intercom.

'Delivery for Mr Carradine.'

He knew immediately what it was. He reached down, grabbed his toe and told the delivery man to leave it in his postbox.

'Needs to be signed for.'

The accent was Jamaican. Carradine buzzed the man into the building. He waited by the door, rubbing his foot. A moth flew up towards the ceiling. Carradine clapped it dead between his hands. He could hear the lift outside grinding towards the landing as he wiped the smashed body on his shorts.

The delivery man was a middle-aged, dreadlocked Rasta wearing a high-vis waistcoat. A Post Office satchel was slung over his shoulder. It was possible that he was a convincingly disguised errand boy for the Service, but

58

Carradine assumed that Mantis had simply sent the items by Special Delivery. He signed an illegible version of his name on an electronic pad using a small plastic tool that slipped on the glass, thanked him and took the package inside.

On any other morning, Carradine might have gone back to bed for another hour's sleep. But the contents of the package were too intriguing. He walked into the kitchen, set a percolator of coffee on the stove and sliced the envelope open with a knife.

There was a paperback book inside. Mantis had sent a French translation of one of Carradine's novels, published four years earlier. He opened the book to the title page. It was unsigned. The rest of the text had not been marked up nor were any pages turned down or altered in any way. The book was in pristine condition.

He waited for the coffee to boil, staring out of the window at the treetops of Hyde Park. If the novel was to be used as a book cipher, then Mantis possessed an identical copy which would allow him to send coded messages to Yassine without risking detection. He was using a French, rather than an English version of the book because Yassine was most likely a French-speaking Arab. For Carradine to give him a copy of the novel at their meeting was an ingenious and entirely plausible piece of tradecraft. They would be hiding in plain sight.

He took out the second item, the sealed package for 'Maria'. The envelope was sturdy and bound with tape at both ends. Carradine weighed it in his hands. He could make out the outline of what he assumed was a passport. He bent the package slightly and thought that he could feel a document of some kind moving beneath the seal.

Carradine had an obligation to open the envelope, because it was surely crazy to board an international flight carrying a package about which he knew so little. But he could not do so. It was against the spirit of the deal he had struck with the Service and would constitute a clear breach of trust. It was even possible that the package was a decoy and that the Service had sent it solely as a test of his integrity.

He set it to one side, drank the coffee and switched on the news. Overnight in New Delhi two vehicles had been hijacked by Islamist gunmen affiliated with Lashkar-e-Taiba and driven into crowds at a religious ceremony, killing an estimated seventy-five people. In Germany, an AFD politician had been gunned down on his doorstep by a Resurrection activist. Such headlines had become commonplace, as humdrum and predictable as tropical storms and mass shootings in the United States. Carradine waited for news of the Redmond kidnapping. It was the third item on the BBC. No trace had been found of the van in which Redmond had been driven away, no statement released by Resurrection claiming responsibility for the abduction.

Settling in front of his computer with a bowl of cereal, Carradine watched amateur footage of the crowds screaming in panic as they fled the carnage in New Delhi. He read an email written by the slain AFD politician, leaked to the press only days earlier, in which he had referred to Arabs as a 'culturally alien people' welcomed into Germany by 'elitist pigs'. He learned that one in eight voters had given AFD their support in recent elections and that the group was now the second largest opposition party in the Bundestag. Small wonder Resurrection was so active in Germany. There had been similar assassinations of nationalist politicians in France, Poland and Hungary. It was only a matter of time before the violence crossed the Channel and a senior British politician was targeted.

Carradine took a shower and WhatsApped Mantis, acknowledging delivery of the package with a succinct 'Thanks for the book'. Within thirty seconds Mantis had replied: 'No problem' adding – to Carradine's consternation – two smiling emojis and a thumbs up for good measure. He put the package in a drawer and attempted to do some work. Every ten or fifteen minutes he would open the drawer and check that the package was still there, as if sprites or cat burglars might have carried it off while his back was turned. Later in the afternoon, when his once-a-fortnight cleaner, Mrs Ritter, was in the flat, he removed the package altogether and set it on his desk until she had left the building.

Though he had yet to complete any specific tasks on behalf of the Service, Carradine already felt as though he had been cut off from his old life; that he was inhabiting a parallel existence separate from the world he had known before meeting Mantis and witnessing the abduction of Lisa Redmond. He wanted to talk to his father about what had happened, to tell him about Morocco and to gauge his advice, but he was forbidden by the Secrets Act. He could say nothing to anyone about what Mantis had asked him to do. He tried to work, but it now seemed ridiculous to be writing about fictional spies in fictional settings when he himself had been employed by the Service as a bona fide support agent. Instead he spent the next two days re-reading Frederick Forsyth's memoirs and Somerset

Maugham's *Ashenden*, trawling for insights into the life of a writer spy. He watched *The Bureau* and took a DVD of *The Man Who Knew Too Much* to his father's flat the night before he was due to fly to Casablanca. They ordered curry from Deliveroo and sat in semi-darkness munching chicken dhansak and tarka daal, washed down with a 1989 Château Beychevelle he had been given by an old friend as a birthday present.

'Doris Day,' his father muttered as she sang 'Que Sera Sera' to her soon-to-be-kidnapped son. 'Was she the one Hitchcock threw the birds at?'

'No,' Carradine replied. 'That was Tippi Hedren.'

'Ah.'

He tore off a strip of peshawari naan and passed it to his father saying: 'Did you know she was Melanie Griffith's mother?'

'Who? Doris Day?'

'No. Tippi Hedren.'

After a brief pause, his father said: 'Who's Melanie Griffith?'

It was after midnight by the time the film finished. Carradine did the washing-up and ordered an Uber.

'So you're off to Casablanca?' His father was standing in the hall, leaning on the walking stick which he had carried with him since his stroke. 'Research on the new book?'

'Research, yes,' Carradine replied. He detested the lie.

'Never been myself. They say it's not like the film.'

'Yeah. I heard that.'

His father jutted out his chin and pulled off a passable impression of Humphrey Bogart.

'You played it for her. You play it for me. Play it.'

Carradine hugged him. He tried to imagine what life in the Service must have been like in the 1960s. He pictured smoke-filled rooms, tables piled high with dusty files, men in double-breasted suits plotting in secure speech rooms.

'I love you,' he said.

'I love you, too. Take care of yourself out there. Call me when you land.'

'I will.'

Carradine opened the front door and stepped outside.

'Kit?'

He turned to face his father. 'Yes?'

'I'm proud of you.'

7

Carradine had been on the Gatwick Express for only a few minutes when he saw the photograph. He was seated alone at a table in a near-deserted carriage finishing off a cappuccino and a fruit salad from M&S. A passenger had left a copy of the *Guardian* on a seat across the aisle. Carradine had picked up the paper and begun to read about developments in the Redmond kidnapping. The Transit van, which had been stolen from a North London car park, had been found abandoned and burned out at the edge of a wood not far from Henley-on-Thames. CCTV showed a bearded man wearing a woollen hat filling up the van with diesel in Cricklewood a few hours before Redmond was seized. Resurrection sympathisers had now claimed responsibility for the kidnapping but no images of Redmond in captivity had been released. 'Experts' quoted in the article drew comparisons with the kidnapping of Otis Euclidis, pointing out that Resurrection had waited ten days before publishing footage of an apparently healthy and well-rested Euclidis sitting on a bed in an undisclosed location reading a book. The same experts claimed that the police were at a loss to know where Redmond was being held. At the bottom of the story there was a small box directing readers to a longer piece on the history of the Resurrection movement. Carradine had turned to the back of the paper, intending to read it.

Beneath the headline on the article was a layout of four pictures arranged in a square, each of them about the same size as the passport photograph of 'Maria' that Mantis had given to Carradine in Lisson Grove. The photograph in the top left-hand corner showed Redmond taking part in a reality television show several years earlier. Beside it was a picture of Euclidis in characteristic Instagram pose, wearing a white, gold-encrusted baseball cap, a gold crucifix medallion and outsized designer sunglasses. The photograph in the bottom left-hand corner showed Nihat Demirel, a pro-government talk-show host in Turkey who had been kneecapped by Resurrection outside his summer house in Izmir in May. It was the fourth picture that rocked Carradine.

He had seen the photograph before. It showed Ivan Simakov, the deceased leader of Resurrection, standing beside the woman who was reported to have been his girlfriend when the movement was conceived: Lara Bartok. Carradine stared at her. She had long, dark hair and slightly crooked front teeth. It was 'Maria'.

He reached into his wallet. He placed the photograph of Maria alongside the picture of Bartok. There was no question that they were the same woman. He was about to pull up her Wikipedia page on his iPhone when he remembered that the search would flag. A young woman had taken a seat at the far end of the carriage. Carradine considered asking to borrow her phone to make the search but decided against it, instead reading the article for more detail on Bartok's background. A Hungarian-born lawyer, she had met Simakov in New York and become attached to Occupy Wall Street. Described as 'a latter-day Ulrike Meinhof', Bartok was wanted in the United States on charges of armed assault, kidnapping and incitement to violence. She had reportedly become disillusioned with Resurrection and vanished from the couple's apartment in Brooklyn. Several months later, Simakov was killed in Moscow.

Carradine put the newspaper to one side. The train had come to a halt at a section of track littered with cans and bottles. He stared outside, trying to work out what Mantis was up to. He assumed that the Service had recruited Bartok as an agent, persuading her to inform against Resurrection. But how had they managed to lose track of her? And why was Mantis using an untried and untested support agent to try to find her? In the Lisson Grove flat he had refused even to reveal Bartok's name, telling Carradine that 'several officers and support agents' were searching for her in places as far afield as Mexico, Cuba and Argentina. If that was the case, it was plausible that she was no longer a source for British intelligence, but instead a fugitive from justice. Carradine had learned enough from his father about the workings of the Service to know that they were not a law enforcement agency. There had to be another reason behind Mantis's search. Carradine recalled the wistfulness with which he had spoken about her beauty, his irritation with the photograph of her surfer boyfriend. As the train began to move away, he wondered if Mantis was romantically involved with her. That might explain the furtiveness with which he had spoken about 'Maria'.

Gatwick airport was rammed. Carradine checked the suitcase containing the book and the sealed package into the hold and cleared security without any complications. He was carrying €1,000 of Mantis's money in his wallet and the other €2,000 inside an envelope in his carry-on bag. The departure gate for the flight with Royal Air Maroc was a twenty-minute walk from security along increasingly deserted corridors leading further and further away from the heart of the terminal. A flight attendant wearing a headscarf and heavy mascara clicked a counter for every passenger that came on board. Carradine was one of the last to take his seat. He glanced at the counter as he passed her. There were fewer than fifty passengers on the plane.

As the flight took off, Carradine had the vivid sensation that he was leaving the old part of his life behind and entering a new phase which would in every way be more challenging and satisfying than the life he had known before. His thoughts again turned to Bartok. Was Mantis using him to try to get a personal message to her? If so, how could he guarantee that Carradine would find her at the festival? Was she a fan of his books? Did the Service think that she was going to show herself at his event? Perhaps she wanted to meet Katherine Paget, the novelist with whom he was due to appear on stage.

The sealed package was somewhere beneath Carradine's feet in the chill of the baggage hold; he knew that it would contain the answers to his many questions and felt his professional obligation to Mantis dissipating with every passing mile. He did not consider himself to be particularly cynical or suspicious, but neither would he enjoy the feeling of being duped. He needed to know what was inside the envelope. If that meant breaking his promise to the Service, so be it.

About an hour into the flight, Carradine was handed a small tray with a plastic knife and fork and told that alcohol was not served by the airline. Craving a beer, he ate a tiny, vacuum-packed trout fillet with a bread roll and something the flight attendant claimed was chicken casserole. Leaving most of it unfinished, he decided to go for a stroll. As he passed his fellow passengers bent over their in-flight meals, Carradine could hear a man with a deep, resonant voice speaking in Spanish near the toilets at the rear of the plane. He assumed that the man was talking to a friend, but when he reached the galley he saw that he was alone. His back was turned and he was looking out of the window. He was wearing shorts and a black T-shirt. Religious tattoos completely covered his arms and the backs of his hands. There were tufts of black body hair protruding from the neck of his T-shirt. He was holding a mobile phone perpendicular to his mouth and appeared to be dictating notes. Carradine spoke very little Spanish and could not understand what he was saying. The man sensed that Carradine was behind him and turned around.

'Sorry. You want the bathroom, man?'

The accent was Hispanic, the face about forty-five. He was well-built but not overtly muscular, with long, greasy hair gathered in a topknot. Though not fully bearded, at least three days of dense stubble ran in a continuous black shadow from beneath his eyes to the hollow of his collarbone. He was one of the hairiest people Carradine had ever seen.

'No thanks. I'm just going for a walk.'

The man lowered the phone. He was smiling with forced sincerity, like a technique he had been taught at a seminar on befriending strangers. Carradine had the bizarre and disorienting sensation that the man knew who he was and had been waiting for him.

'Out on the wing?'

'What?'

'You said you were going for a walk.'

Carradine rolled with the joke. 'Oh. That's right. Yes. So if you wouldn't mind stepping aside I'll just open the door and head out.'

An eruption of laughter, a roar so loud it might have been audible in the cockpit. An elderly Arabic woman emerged from one of the bathrooms and flinched.

'Hey! I like you!' said the man. He leaned a hand against the door frame and shook out a crick in his neck. 'Where you from?'

Carradine explained that he was from London. 'And you?'

'Me? I'm from everywhere, man.' He looked like a mid-level drug dealer attached to a Colombian cartel: dishevelled, poorly educated, very possibly violent. 'Born in Andalucía. Raised in Madrid. Now I live in London. Heading out to Morocco for some R & R.'

They shook hands. The Spaniard's grip suggested prodigious physical force.

'Ramón,' he said. 'Great to meet you, man.'

'Kit. You too.'

'So what you doing in Casablanca?'

Carradine went with the story he had agreed with Mantis.

'I'm a novelist. Doing some research on my next book.'

The Spaniard again exploded with enthusiasm. 'A writer! Holy shit, man! You write books?' Carradine thought back to his first encounter with Mantis. There was something similarly inauthentic about Ramón. 'You get any of them published?'

'A few, yeah.'

'Wow! So cool!'

A flight attendant came into the galley, obliging Carradine to step to one side. She was slim and attractive. Ramón stared at her as she bent down to retrieve a bottle of water from one of the catering boxes. He gazed open-mouthed at the outline of her uniform, all of the liveliness and energy in his face momentarily extinguished. He looked up, pursed his lips and shot Carradine a locker-room leer.

'Nice, huh?'

Carradine changed the subject.

'What do you do for R & R in Casablanca?'

It turned out to be the wrong question.

'Oh man! The chicks in Morocco. You don't know?!' The flight attendant stood up, stared at Ramón with undisguised contempt and made her way back down the aisle. 'Last time I was there, I meet this girl in a bar on the Corniche. She takes me to this apartment, we open a bottle of whisky and then – bang! Oh, Kit, man! One of the great nights of my life. This chick, she was . . .'

Ramón's recollection tailed off as a young child, accompanied by his father, was led to the bathroom. Carradine seized his chance to get away.

'Well, it was interesting to meet you,' he said.

'You heading off?'

Ramón sounded distraught, almost as if he had been tasked with befriending Carradine and been judged to have failed.

'Yeah. I've got stuff to read. Work to do. Just wanted to stretch my legs.'

'Oh. OK. Sure. Great to meet you. You're a cool cat, Kit. I like you. Good luck with those books!'

Carradine returned to his seat, oddly unsettled by the encounter. He remained there for the rest of the flight. He thought that he had seen the last of the Spaniard but, having landed and cleared passport control in Casablanca, found himself standing next to him in the baggage hall. As they waited for their respective suitcases, some of the last remaining passengers to be doing so, Ramón continued to grill Carradine on his life and career, to the point at which he began to wonder if he was testing his cover.

'So, what? You're writing a kind of spy story set in Morocco? Like a Jason Bourne thing?'

Carradine had always thought that his novels occupied a literary space equidistant between the kiss-kiss-bang-bang of Ludlum and the slow-burn chess games of le Carré. For reasons of intellectual vanity, he would ordinarily have tried to distance himself from Ramón's description, but he was keen to stop talking about his work. As a consequence, he readily conceded that his 'Moroccan thriller' was going to be 'full of guns and explosions and beautiful women'.

'Like *The Man Who Knew Too Much*?'

Carradine thought of his father the night before munching naan bread and drinking claret. He didn't think the comparison was accurate, but couldn't be bothered to enter into a debate about it.

'Exactly,' he replied.

Ramón had spotted his bag moving along the carousel. He stepped forward, picked it up, slung the bag across his shoulder and turned around.

'You wanna share a cab into town, man?'

Had this been his plan all along? To get alongside Carradine and to accompany him into Casablanca? Or was he merely an over-familiar tourist trying to do a fellow passenger a favour? Out of the corner of his eye Carradine saw his suitcase jerking along the carousel.

'My bag will probably be a while longer,' he said. 'I'm hungry. The food on the flight was terrible. I'm going to grab something to eat in the terminal. You go ahead. Have a great trip.'

Ramón looked at the carousel. Three suitcases remained, two of which had passed them several times. Betraying an apparent suspicion, he shook Carradine's hand, reiterated how 'truly fantastic' it had been to meet him and walked towards the customs area. Relieved to be shot of him, Carradine sent a WhatsApp to Mantis telling him that he had arrived, checked that the novel and the sealed package were still inside his case and walked out into the broiling Moroccan afternoon.

He had expected the chaos and clamour of a typical African airport, but all was relatively quiet as he emerged from the terminal. A hot desert wind was blowing in from the east, bending the tops of the palm trees and sending swirls of leaves and dust across the deserted concourse. Men in jeans and Polo shirts were perched on concrete blocks smoking in the shade of the terminal building.

When they saw Carradine, they popped up and moved forwards, crowding him like paparazzi, repeating the phrase 'Taxi mister, taxi' as he tried to move between them. Carradine could see Ramón less than fifty metres away at the top of the rank standing next to a pranged beige Mercedes. He was negotiating a price with the driver. The Spaniard looked up, waving Carradine forward shouting: 'Get in, man! Join me!' Carradine was already uncomfortably hot. He was irritated by the drivers trying to force him towards their cars and intrigued enough by Ramón to want to know why he had taken such an interest in him. Was he working for the Service? Had Mantis sent him with instructions to keep an eye on the new kid on the block? Carradine raised a hand in acknowledgement as Ramón continued to gesture him forward. Should he stay or should he go? His curiosity began to tip the balance. Where was the harm in sharing a ride into town? He might even learn something. He duly rolled his suitcase towards the Mercedes and greeted Ramón for the third time.

'Chaos back there,' he said. 'Thanks for helping me out.'

'No problem.' The driver popped the boot. 'Where you headed, man? I drop you off.'

Carradine was staying at a Sofitel in the centre of town. It transpired that Ramón was staying in a hotel less than five hundred metres away.

'No way! I'm at the Sheraton! Literally like no distance from where you are.' A part of Carradine died inside. 'We can meet up later, go for a drink. You know any good places?'

'Somebody recommended Blaine's to me.'

73

The words were out of his mouth before Carradine had time to realise what he had said. He was due to meet Yassine at Blaine's the following evening. What if Ramón showed up during their dinner?

'Blaine's? I know it! Full of chicks, man. You're gonna love it.'

He could feel his carefully arranged schedule being quickly and efficiently unpicked by the Spaniard's suffocating camaraderie. He didn't want to be put into a position where he had to work his cover, lying to Ramón about phantom meetings with phantom friends just to avoid seeing him. Why the hell hadn't he taken a separate taxi?

'Sofitel,' Ramón told the driver, speaking in accentless French. '*Près du port. Et après le Sheraton, s'il vous plaît.*'

Somewhere between the aircraft and the Mercedes the Spaniard had developed a case of volcanic body odour. The car was quickly filled with the smell of his stale sweat. It was hot in the back seat, with no air conditioning, and Carradine sat with both windows down, listening to the driver muttering to himself in Arabic as they settled into a queue of traffic. Ramón offered Carradine a cigarette, which he gladly accepted, taking the smoke deep into his lungs as he gazed out onto lines of parked cars and half-finished breezeblock apartments, wondering how long it would take to get into town.

'I never asked,' he said. 'What do you do for a living?'

Ramón appeared to hesitate before turning around to answer. His eyes were cold and pitiless. Carradine was reminded of the sudden change in his expression when the flight attendant had walked into the galley. It was like looking at an actor who had momentarily dropped out of character.

'Me?' he said. 'I'm just a businessman. Came out here to do a friend a favour.'

'I thought you said you were here for the rest and recreation?'

'That too.' Ramón touched his mouth in a way that made Carradine suspect him of lying. 'R & R everywhere I go. That's how I like to roll.'

'What's the favour?' he asked.

The Spaniard cut him a look, turned to face the oncoming traffic and said: 'I don't like to talk too much about work.'

Another five minutes passed before they spoke again. The taxi had finally emerged from the traffic jam and reached what appeared to be the main highway into Casablanca. Ramón had been talking to the driver in rapid, aggressive French, only some of which Carradine was able to understand. He began to think that the two men were already acquainted and wondered again if Ramón had deliberately waited for him to come out of the airport.

'You've met before?' he asked.

'What's that?'

'Your driver? You've used him before?'

The Spaniard flinched, as if to suggest that Carradine was asking too many questions.

'What makes you say that?'

'Oh, nothing. It just sounded like this wasn't the first time you'd met.'

At that moment the driver – who had not yet looked at Carradine nor acknowledged him in any way – turned off the highway onto a dirt track leading into a forest.

'What's going on?' Carradine looked back at the main

road. Paranoia had settled on him like the slowly clinging sweat under his shirt. 'Where are we going?'

'No idea.' Ramón sounded disconcertingly relaxed. 'Probably has to visit his mother or something.'

The Mercedes bumped along the track, heading further and further into the woods.

'Seriously,' said Carradine. 'Where are we going?'

The driver pulled the Mercedes to the side of the track, switched off the engine and stepped out. The heat of the afternoon sun was overwhelming. Carradine opened the door to give himself an option to run if the situation should turn against him. There was a small wooden hut about ten metres from the road, occupied by a woman whose face he could not see. The driver approached the hut, held out a piece of paper and passed it to her. Ramón put a tattooed arm across the seat.

'You look tense, man. Relax.'

'I'm fine,' Carradine told him.

He was anything but fine. He was convinced that he had walked into a trap. He looked in the opposite direction, deeper into the woods. He could see only trees and the forest floor. He used the wing mirror on the driver's side to check if there was anybody on the road behind them, but saw no sign of anyone. The stench of sweat was overwhelming. Through the woods beyond the hut he could make out a small clearing dotted with plastic toys and a children's slide. The driver was coming back to the car.

'*Que faisiez-vous*?' Ramón asked him.

'Parking,' the driver replied. Carradine smiled and shook his head. His lack of experience had got the better of him. He looked back at the hut. The veiled woman was marking the piece of paper with an ink stamp. She slammed it onto a metal spike.

'Crazy!' Ramón produced a delighted grin. 'In Casablanca they pay their parking tickets in the middle of the fucking woods. Never saw this before, man.'

'Me neither,' Carradine replied.

It was another forty-five minutes to the hotel. Carradine sat in the heat of the back seat, smoking another of Ramón's cigarettes. On the edge of the city the Mercedes became jammed in three-lane traffic that inched along wide colonial boulevards packed with cars and motorbikes. Ramón grew increasingly agitated, berating the driver for taking the wrong route in order to extract more money for the journey. The swings in his mood, from back-slapping bonhomie to cold, aggressive impatience, were as unexpected as they were unsettling. Carradine followed the progress of the journey on his iPhone, trying to orientate himself in the new city, the street names – Boulevard de La Mecque, Avenue Tetouan, Rue des Racines – evoking all the antiquity and mystique of French colonial Africa. Mopeds buzzed past his door as the Mercedes edged from block to block. Men hawking drinks and newspapers approached the car and were shooed away by the driver, who switched on the windscreen wipers to deter them. Several times Carradine saw cars and scooters running red lights or deliberately going the wrong way around roundabouts in order to beat the jam. Stalled in the rivers of traffic he thought of home and cursed the heat, calling his father to tell him that he had arrived. He was busy playing backgammon with a friend and had no time to talk, their brief exchange leaving Carradine with a sense of isolation that he found perversely enjoyable. It was exhilarating to be alone in a strange city, a place about which he knew so little, at the start of a mission for which he had received no training and no detailed preparation. He knew that his father had been posted to Egypt by the Service in the early years of his marriage and thought of the life he must have led as a young spy, running agents in Cairo, taking his mother on romantic trips to Sinai, Luxor and Aswan. Ramón offered him yet another cigarette and he took it, observing that the smog outside was likely to do more damage to his lungs. Ramón went to the trouble of translating the joke for the benefit of the driver who turned in his seat and smiled, acknowledging Carradine for the first time.

'*Vrai!*' he said. '*C'est vrai!*'

That was when Ramón showed him his phone.

'Jesus Christ, man. You see this?'

Carradine pitched the cigarette out of the window and leaned forward. The headline on the screen was in Spanish. He could see the words REDMOND and MUERTA.

'What happened?'

'They killed the Redmond bitch,' Ramón replied. 'Resurrection fucking killed her.'

8

They kept her in the van for the first thirty-six hours. She screamed when they took off the gag, so they put it on again and left her to rage. They offered her water and food, but she refused it. She soiled herself. When she had spent all of her energy, Redmond wept.

Towards the end of the second day they took her from the van, still blindfolded, and tied her to a chair in the basement of the farmhouse. They played the recording into the room. A loop of Redmond's words, repeated over and over again. A torture of her own making. The bearded man called it 'The Two Minutes of Hate', after Orwell, but the recording lasted for more than twelve hours.

The immigrants attempting to cross the Mediterranean are the same insects already swarming over Europe. They choke our schools and hospitals. They dirty our towns and cities. They murder our daughters at rock concerts. They mow down our sons on the streets.

It went on and on into the night. Whenever Redmond looked as though she was falling asleep, they turned up the volume. She was prevented from sleeping by the words she had written. 'Sentenced by your own sentences,' said the man who had knocked down her husband.

The only answer is to lock up every young Muslim man or woman whose name appears on a terrorist watchlist. How else to protect British citizens from slaughter? If we cannot take the sensible precaution, outlined by the government of the United States, of preventing potential terrorists from entering the United Kingdom from countries that are known sponsors of Islamist terror, then this is the only option remaining to us.

On the morning of the third day they removed Redmond's gag and again offered her food and water. This time she accepted. The bearded man asked her, on camera, if she wished to defend her words and actions. She said that she stood by everything she had written. She insisted that, given the chance, she would write and broadcast everything again. She had no regrets for exercising her right to free speech and for articulating views held by millions of people in the West who were too cowed by political correctness to speak their minds.

The bearded man was standing behind her as she spoke. He lifted her hair clear of her shoulders, held it in a fist above her head, and sliced her throat with a knife. Redmond's body was dumped at a stretch of waste ground on the outskirts of Coventry. A photograph of her corpse was sent to the editor of the British newspaper who had commissioned her column.

Somerville switched off the recorder.

'What are your feelings about what happened to Lisa Redmond?' he said.

Bartok shrugged.

'I do not know enough about it.' She stood up and stretched her back, twisting one way, then the other. 'I know that Kit was upset. He talked about it a lot. I think it haunted him.'

'What about you?' the American asked. His tone was supercilious. 'Were you upset by it? Were you haunted, Lara?'

Bartok picked up one of the biscuits. She turned it over in her fingers. She liked Somerville. She trusted him. She did not like or trust the American.

'As I have said. I did not know Redmond's writing. I did not have the opportunity to listen to her radio broadcasts wherever I was hiding in the world. She sounded like somebody who we might have gone after.'

The American seized on this, closing the space between them. 'We?'

'Resurrection.' Bartok looked at Somerville as if to suggest that the American was starting to annoy her. 'In the old days. Before the violence and the killing. She was the sort of figure Ivan would have looked at. Redmond, and those like her, men like Otis Euclidis, they gave encouragement to the bigots, to the

82

ignorant. Ivan wanted to teach them a lesson. We all did.' She bit into the biscuit. It was dry. She could only swallow by taking a sip of water to wash it down. 'When I see what has happened to Resurrection, I feel nothing but sadness. It began as something remarkable. It began as a phenomenon. Ivan had a conception of a new kind of revolutionary movement, one which harnessed the power of the Internet and social media, one which was fuelled by international outrage among young and old alike. He wanted to take that revolutionary movement out onto the streets, to fight back against those who had corrupted our societies. He knew that Resurrection would catch fire with people, inspire groups and individuals, oblige the masses to mount operations of their own – however small, however apparently insignificant – so that bit by bit and step by step, democracy and fairness would be restored. But all of the hope and the beauty of those ideas, the purity of the early attacks, has been lost.'

Somerville reached for the recorder. They needed to get the whole story out of Bartok. There was no point letting her talk during the breaks if nobody was keeping a record.

'Would you like to go back to those early months?' he asked.

'Of course, whatever you want,' she said.

'Please. Tell us how it all got started.'

SECRET INTELLIGENCE SERVICE
EYES ONLY / STRAP 1

STATEMENT BY LARA BARTOK ('LASZLO')
CASE OFFICERS: J.W.S./S.T.H – CHAPEL STREET
REF: RESURRECTION/SIMAKOV/CARRADINE
FILE: RE2768X

PART 2 of 5

'Euclidis was our first target. That was the first and most brilliant idea of Ivan's, to capture this snake, this poison in the bloodstream of public life, and to show the world that decent people were prepared to stand up to hate, to put an end to divisive words, to expose Euclidis for the narcissist that he was. For all his expensive clothes and his clever talk, we showed the world that he was just a self-interested clown. He blogged to make money. He spread lies to get rich. To get laid. He was not interested in changing the system, in making the world a better place. He and his friends – the alt-right, the white supremacists, the anti-Semites, the Holocaust deniers – they had no alternative ideology. They had no *ideas*. They just wanted to draw attention to themselves. They wanted to make decent citizens feel uncomfortable and frightened. That was their reason for living. They were bullies, high on hate.

How did Euclidis draw so many admirers? By

making stupid people feel better about their stupidity. By allowing bigots to think they were justified in making anti-Semitic statements, saying that it was OK to hate women, to be aggrieved about people of colour, about immigrants. The sad truth is that there were enough trolls buying his books, reading his articles, attending his talks to make him a rich man. They gave him the fame he craved. Euclidis was a junkie for attention. And if they didn't give it to him in public, they gave it to him on Twitter, on Instagram, on Facebook. We had to take him down.

So Ivan, with my help, and with the assistance of Zack Curtis and ███████, seized him at Berkeley. Grabbed him as he stepped out of his hotel. It was so easy. We were in America so we were able to obtain guns. The hotel had no security, we possessed the element of surprise. We put a hood on him, we put him in cuffs, we threw his phone out of the window. He did not like that, he did not like being separated from his precious phone! We switched vehicles and drove into the mountains. Euclidis of course was a physical coward. He cried like a four-year-old boy. It was pitiful.

We filmed him in secret, as the world now knows. We were able to show on camera that Otis Euclidis was a charlatan, a fraud. He confessed that he had done it all to make money. He had never meant anything he had said or written to be taken seriously. His followers were 'clowns' and 'losers'. When he had said in interviews that black lives 'did not matter', he had been 'joking'. When he had written that feminism was 'the worst invention since gunpowder', he had only been 'fooling around'. He showed himself to be a fraud who believed in nothing but fame. When we screened the film, when we put it out on the Internet for the world to see, and we saw the reaction, well, it was a beautiful moment.

Almost immediately there were copycat attacks. Dozens of politicians and right-wing figures around the world came under threat. My favourite was done by the refugee in Amsterdam. The kitchen porter. A Muslim from Iraq who had been washing dishes in a restaurant so that he could feed his wife and baby daughter. He was no older than twenty-five or twenty-six. Samir. I've forgotten his surname. [JWS: Samir Rabou] He learned that Piet Boutmy, the leader of the Dutch far-right party – again, I don't remember the name of this party [JWS: *Partij voor de Vrijheid*] – was eating in the restaurant. A waiter, a Syrian, I believe, came into the kitchen and told him Boutmy was there. Samir knew about the kidnapping of Euclidis, he told the police who later interviewed him that he had followed Resurrection from its very first statements and that he greatly admired Ivan Simakov. He

86

took off his washing gloves, kept his apron, walked out of the kitchen and went directly into the restaurant. The security guard protecting Boutmy thought he was a waiter. The table was covered in many dishes, including – perfectly! – a soup prepared with beetroots which was still very hot. Also bottles of water, glasses of red wine, cutlery, a vase of flowers. Shouting 'Resurrection!' Samir lifted the whole table on top of this racist animal, soaking him to the bone, also the colleague from the same party who was dining with him. I heard that he faced no charges and soon found another job at a rival restaurant. It was beautiful.

Everything that Ivan and myself had hoped for came to pass. Ivan was worried that the Resurrection movement would burn out. It did not. He wrote that he wanted Resurrection to have 'a seismic effect on public attitudes to the liars and enablers of the alt-right'. This is exactly what happened. The summer homes of criminal bankers were burned to the ground. Cars belonging to producers at Fox News were vandalised and damaged. Those who had attended white supremacist rallies were identified by their peers and targeted for retribution. They paid the price for their hate with the loss of their careers, their friends. All it took was one or two examples for everyone to follow suit.

But, of course, Resurrection changed. What

started as a non-violent movement, symbolic acts targeted against deserving victims, quickly became violent. I was naive to believe that this would not happen, but what distressed me was Ivan's willingness to change his position, not only towards non-violence, but also concerning his own role as a figurehead. He wanted the limelight. He craved adulation. I had not identified these characteristics in him when we first met. His vanity, his stubbornness, his readiness to lose sight of what Resurrection was about and instead to place himself at the heart of what became a hijacked, paramilitary organisation. It became impossible to live with him. I could no longer do useful work. I lost my respect for Ivan Simakov and I left him. That is when they began to hunt me down.

9

Carradine reached his room and switched on the television.

Every major news network was carrying the story. The police believed the murder had been carried out by the same members of Resurrection who had kidnapped Redmond five days earlier. Tributes were being paid by friends and colleagues, inevitable expressions of outrage articulated by politicians, fellow journalists and friends.

Carradine muted the television. He sat on the bed and felt a hollowness inside him close to a feeling of personal responsibility in the death of an innocent woman. Had he done more to help, had he found the courage to cross the street and to confront Redmond's kidnappers, she might still be alive. He thought of the girl who had been standing beside him, chatting away to her friend. *So I says to him, I'm like, no way is that happening, yeah? I'm like he needs to get his shit together because I'm like just not going through with that bullshit again.* Where was she now? How would she react to news of this kind? Would she share

Carradine's remorse or experience nothing but a momentary, fleeting anxiety that Resurrection had again resorted to murder? Would she even be aware that Redmond had been killed?

He went to the window and looked down at the vast city. Low whitewashed buildings stretched in a broad semi-circle to the Atlantic coast. At the sea's edge the vast Hassan II Mosque dominated the skyline; to the northwest, the cranes and wharves of the port were blocks of shadow partly obscured by a high-rise hotel. Carradine had detested Redmond. He had abhorred her character and public style. She had weaved deliberate ignorance into casual prejudice with the sole purpose of inciting outrage, hysteria and fear. She had craved the spotlight of notoriety. In the wake of an Islamist suicide bombing on the streets of London, she had called for 'internment' for male Muslims under the age of forty. Handed a column in a tabloid newspaper with which to disseminate her toxic views, she had advocated the use of naval warships to prevent refugees – many of them fleeing the horrors of Syria and Yemen – from crossing the Mediterranean. When her rhetoric became too vile even for the leather-skinned editors of the Fourth Estate, Redmond merely had to look across the Pond to find any number of right-wing media outlets in the United States eager to beam her prejudices into the homes of the ignorant and the dispossessed. Indeed, Redmond had been only days from moving to the United States to work for Fox News when she had been seized by Resurrection. Carradine knew that if he opened Twitter, or switched to Fox itself, he would be swamped in partisan bile and hate. For every person shocked by Redmond's murder there would be another openly celebrating; for every person applauding Resurrection for taking the fight to the goons and trolls of the alt-right, there would be another – like Carradine himself – who knew that violence only made the situation far worse.

He turned from the window and began to unpack. The sealed envelope was at the top of his suitcase. He took it out and placed it on the bed. To try to clear his head he did fifty press-ups, took a shower and changed into a fresh set of clothes. Whatever was in the package, he knew that he could now be incriminating himself by passing documents to a suspected member of a terrorist organisation. The Redmond murder had changed the game. He had been transformed – without prior agreement – into a foot soldier in the global struggle against Resurrection. To hell with the Service; Carradine needed to do what he had to do. He picked up the package and felt it in his hands. He could make out the edges of the passport, the outline of the document.

He hesitated momentarily – then cut at the Sellotape using the knife on a bottle opener from the minibar. He reached inside the package.

It was a British passport, just as Mantis had said it would be. Carradine opened it to the back. A photograph of Bartok, identical to the one he was carrying in his wallet, looked out at him from the identity page. Bartok was identified as 'Maria Consuela Rodriguez', a British citizen, born 8 June 1983. A Santander credit card fell out of the passport and dropped onto the floor. The name MS M RODRIGUEZ was stamped across the bottom. The back of the card was unsigned.

Carradine reached into the package and pulled out a

smaller rectangular envelope. The envelope was sealed. No name or address had been written on it, only the word 'LASZLO' in block capitals. This time he did not bother using the knife. He tore the envelope open with his hands.

Inside was a single piece of white A4 paper, folded twice. The letter was typed.

IF THIS MESSAGE FINDS YOU IT IS A MIRACLE. TRUST THE PERSON WHO GIVES IT TO YOU.

YOU ARE NOT SAFE. THEY HAVE WORKED OUT WHERE YOU ARE. IT IS ONLY A MATTER OF TIME BEFORE THEY FIND YOU.

I CANNOT HELP YOU EXCEPT BY GIVING YOU THESE GIFTS. USE THEM WISELY. THE NUMBER IS 0812.

I AM THE MAN WHO TOOK YOU TO THE SEA.

10

Carradine read the message several times trying to decipher what was behind Mantis's language. He assumed that 0812 was the Pin number for the credit card though he doubted that Bartok, should he ever find her, would risk using it more than once; to do so would be to pinpoint her location to anyone tracking the account. 'The man who took you to the sea' sounded romantic, but Carradine was wary of leaping to that conclusion without stronger evidence. Yet the tone of the letter was unquestionably personal. Mantis seemed to be distancing himself from the Service in order to send the warning. Who were 'THEY'? The Service? The Agency? The Russians? Almost every law enforcement and intelligence service in the world was hunting Resurrection activists; all of them would have liked to get their hands on Lara Bartok. The only section that seemed unequivocal to him was the opening paragraph, which reinforced the idea that Mantis had employed Carradine in good faith and had been honest about the difficulty of finding 'LASZLO'.

There was a safe in his room. Carradine asked for some Sellotape to be sent up from reception. He sealed the letter, the credit card and the passport back inside the package and put it in the safe. Just as he was finishing he heard his phone ping. Mantis had finally replied.

Glad you've arrived safely. Meeting is at the Four Seasons later this evening. Let me know how it goes.

Carradine understood that he was to go to the Four Seasons and to leave the money for 'Abdullah Aziz' at the reception desk. It was a simple enough task, yet he was apprehensive. He took the €2,000 from his satchel, adding a thousand more from his wallet, and wrote Aziz's name on the envelope.

He looked at the map of Casablanca. The Four Seasons was on the eastern side of the city, close to a cluster of bars and restaurants on the Corniche. It was too far to walk but Carradine set out on foot, intending to catch a taxi en route. He took nothing with him except his wallet, his phone and the envelope containing the money. He was wearing a dark blue linen jacket and walked with both the wallet and the envelope buttoned into the inside pockets. It was still very hot but he did not want to have to take the jacket off and run the risk of it being snatched by an opportunistic thief.

He quickly found himself in a maze of narrow, dilap-idated streets in the old Medina to the west of the port. This was Morocco as he had imagined it: low brick houses painted in blocks of pale greens, blues and yellows with shuttered windows and crumbling plasterwork. He took out his phone and began to take photographs in the fading evening light, the writer in him aware that the details of what he saw – the wooden carts laden with fresh fruits and spices; the old women fanning themselves in shaded doorways; the raggedy children kicking a football in the street – might one day be useful to him. At the same time he was working his cover. On the small chance that he was being followed, C.K. Carradine had carte blanche to snoop around, to be seen taking photographs and scribbling notes, to loiter in the lobbies of five-star hotels or to meet a contact in a fashionable restaurant. If asked to explain why he was carrying €3,000 in cash, he could say that he did not fully trust the safe in his hotel and preferred to carry his personal belongings with him. His legend was foolproof. This was, after all, why Mantis had hired him.

Carradine was lining up a photograph of a rusting truck laden with watermelons when he saw a WhatsApp message from Mantis drop down onto the screen.

Change of plan. Meeting at Sheraton, not 4 Seasons. Sorry for inconvenience.

He wondered if he was the victim of an elaborate practical joke. Ramón was staying at the Sheraton. Was the *Spaniard* Mantis's contact? Carradine hoped that the location was a bizarre coincidence, a consequence of the meagre number of top-class hotels in Casablanca, but could not shake off a sixth sense that Ramón and Mantis were somehow involved with one another. Perhaps Mantis had arranged for them to catch the same flight so that Ramón could keep an eye on him? It was impossible to know.

Carradine looked along the street. He was standing at the edge of a busy market square, a smell of mint and burning charcoal on the air. The narrow switchback streets of the old city had spun him around; he had no idea if he was facing north, south, east or west. He used his phone to pinpoint his position and began to walk in the general direction of the Sheraton, eventually finding an exit from the souk through the old walls of the Medina. Twenty minutes later Carradine was standing on the steps of the hotel. It was just before eight o'clock. A bored, uniformed guard indicated that he should pass through a metal detector. Carradine did so. Despite the fact that an alarm sounded as he walked through, the guard – who was wearing gloves and holding a plastic security wand – waved him on.

The lobby of the hotel was a vast marble atrium dominated by palm trees and wide marble columns. A mezzanine balcony overlooked the ground floor. A cleaning woman was polishing a vase near a window on the street side of the hotel. Carradine was aware that Ramón might be nursing a pre-prandial *mojito* or cup of coffee in one of the nooks and crannies of the lobby. He did not want to be spotted by the Spaniard and engaged in conversation. He did not trust him and was sure that Ramón's ebullient good cheer was a front disguising a volatile, possibly even violent personality. It occurred to him that he was now involved in precisely the sort of scenario he had written about many times in his fiction. The spy – amateur or otherwise – was always at risk of running into a friend or acquaintance in the field. Carradine quickly prepared a cover story, on the off-chance that he was identified, and walked towards the reception desk.

Had he dramatised the scene in one of his novels, he would have made more of the sense of trepidation his protagonist felt as he set about completing his first mission on behalf of the Service. In reality, Carradine found the task almost embarrassingly easy. He approached the youngest – and therefore potentially the least experienced – of three female members of staff, smiled at her warmly, explained that he wanted to leave a package for one of the hotel guests and handed her the envelope. The receptionist recognised 'Abdullah Aziz' as the name of a guest, placed the envelope in a pigeonhole beneath the desk and did not ask Carradine for his name. At no point did he spot Ramón, nor any individual who might conceivably have been the waiting Aziz. It was all very straightforward.

Within ten minutes Carradine was back on the tenth floor of his hotel, basking in the cool of the air-conditioning, sending a message to Mantis informing him that 'the meeting had been a success'. A short time later Mantis responded, telling Carradine that 'everybody was happy with the way things went'. Despite completing the task successfully, Carradine experienced an unexpected stab of disappointment and irritation that he had not been tested more thoroughly. Perhaps it was the nagging sense that all was not quite as it seemed. He did not fully trust Mantis. He was profoundly suspicious of Ramón. Having read the note inside the package, he was concerned that there was a plot to kidnap Lara Bartok, perhaps even to kill her. If that was the case, was he being used as an unwitting pawn?

He took a second shower, went down to the bar, ordered a vodka martini and tried to convince himself that his doubts were just the flights of fancy of a novelist with an overactive imagination. A man sitting two stools away was wearing an aftershave so overpowering that it began to affect the taste of the martini. Carradine ordered a second, carrying it to a table a safe distance from the bar. As he walked across the lounge, a vodka martini in one hand, a packet of cigarettes in the other, he realised that he was casting himself as the central character in a spy story no different to the ones he had written in the pages of his books or seen a hundred times at the movies.

He sat down and tried to work out the link between Mantis, Ramón and Bartok. Carradine acknowledged that he was a need-to-know support agent, not a fully-fledged spy cognisant of all the intelligence about 'LASZLO'. In this respect, Mantis was not obliged to tell him everything he knew. By the same token, the Service was under no obligation to inform Carradine that Ramón had been sent to keep an eye on him. Besides, there was every reason to believe that Ramón was just an overly friendly passenger Carradine just happened to have bumped into on the plane. He had been shown no evidence to suggest that Ramón was 'Abdullah Aziz', nor was it credible that Mantis would have wanted him to pay Ramón for his services. The only thing that Carradine knew for certain was that Bartok was on the run. Mantis wanted to protect her, for reasons that were not yet clear, but had not been in a position to leave London in order to do so. As a result, he had hired Carradine to assist in the search for her.

Carradine stared at the pitted olive at the bottom of the glass. None of it made sense. The vodka had blunted, not sharpened his wits. He had been active as a support agent for less than twenty-four hours and already felt lost in the wilderness of mirrors.

He settled the bill and walked outside. There was a taxi idling in front of the hotel. Carradine climbed in and asked to be taken to the Corniche. He offered a cigarette to the driver who placed it, unlit, in a recess behind the gearstick. Sated by alcohol, Carradine sat in the back seat texting his father, trying to forget about his responsibilities to the Service and to set aside his doubts about Mantis and Ramón. He enjoyed the sepia light of the Moroccan evening and the movement of the taxi as it weaved from street to street. He wanted to convince himself that there was no deeper meaning to the information he had gleaned from the letter, no dark conspiracy playing out on the streets of Casablanca. But it was impossible. He knew, in the way that you know that a friendship is doomed or a love affair coming to an end, that something was not quite right. He was sure that he was being manipulated. He was certain that he had been sent to Morocco for a purpose that had not yet been made clear to him. The chances of finding Bartok were so remote that the words of warning contained in Mantis's letter – 'IT IS ONLY A MATTER OF TIME BEFORE THEY FIND YOU' – seemed to Carradine as vague and yet as terrifying as lines from a work of fiction. So why had he been handed such a task?

The taxi stopped at a set of lights. An elderly beggar came to the window, pressing his face against the glass. The driver swore in Arabic as the beggar knocked on the window, imploring Carradine to give him money. He dug around in his trouser pocket for some loose change and was about to roll down the window and pass the money to the beggar when the taxi accelerated down the street.

Carradine turned to see that the man had fallen over.

'Stop!' he shouted. *'Problème! Arrêtez!'*

The driver ignored him, made a right-hand turn and headed north towards the sea. Through the back window, Carradine could see the beggar being helped to his feet.

'He fell,' he said in French, thinking of Redmond and his failure to act.

'They all fall,' the driver replied. *Ils tombent tous.*

'Pull over!'

Again Carradine's request was ignored. 'I want to go back,' he said, lamenting the fact that his French was not good enough to make himself properly understood. 'Take me back to the old man.'

'Non,' the driver replied. He wanted his fare, he wanted to take the tourist to the Corniche. 'You don't go back, mister,' he said, now speaking in English. 'You can never go back.'

11

By the time Carradine had persuaded the driver to stop, it was too late. They had driven too far from the fallen man. As an expression of his annoyance, Carradine paid him off without a tip and covered the remaining mile on foot.

He found a restaurant on the Corniche where he continued to drink. On top of the two martinis, he bought a bottle of local white wine followed by successive vodka tonics at a bar across the street. Falling in with a group of businessmen from Dijon who knew a place nearby, Carradine found himself at a table in a packed nightclub on the oceanfront drinking Cuba libres until five in the morning. He eventually stumbled back to his hotel at dawn, his mind cleared of worry, his doubts put to rest.

He woke up at midday and ordered room service, necking two ibuprofen with a glass of freshly squeezed orange juice followed by three black coffees courtesy of the Nespresso machine in his room. There was a spa on the third floor of the hotel. Carradine booked a *hammam*, sweating out the night's toxins in a tiled steam room before falling asleep in an armchair to the sound of panpipes and birdsong. By four o'clock he was back in his room swallowing two more ibuprofen and repenting at leisure the oversized tequila shot he had downed at the edge of the dance floor, the entire packet of cigarettes he had somehow managed to smoke in less than seven hours of music and forgotten conversations. He was fairly sure that at a certain point in the small hours of the morning he had consumed an enormous number of grilled prawns.

Mantis texted just as Carradine was preparing to head out to Blaine's. Yassine was running late but would meet him on the first floor of the restaurant as close to nine o'clock as he could manage. Annoyed to have to wait another hour, Carradine tried to grab a quick siesta but found it impossible to sleep. He was too tired to concentrate on the book he was reading so instead ordered a hair-of-the-dog martini at the bar, listening to a local jazz quartet murdering standards from the American songbook as he sat beneath an outsized reproduction poster of Humphrey Bogart and Ingrid Bergman. Just before half-past eight Carradine returned to his room, retrieved the French translation of his novel and took a cab to the restaurant.

It was after dark. Blaine's was not clearly marked. Carradine walked for several minutes up and down Boulevard D'Anfa, eventually locating the entrance at the corner of a poorly lit street lined with shuttered apartments and dusty parked cars. A shaven-headed Moroccan was standing in the doorway wearing a black suit that fitted him like a cube. He looked Carradine up and down, nodding him inside without a word. Carradine climbed the staircase to the first floor. The martini had begun to work through him but he felt no relief from the solemn drudgery of his hangover, only a desire to eat a good dinner and to go back to bed.

He emerged into a well-lit, low-ceilinged lounge uphol-stered in whites and greys. There was an overpowering stench of fruit tobacco. A woman was moving between the tables singing Arabic love songs with the help of a cordless microphone and a pre-programmed synthesiser. The music was very loud. One section of the room was occupied almost exclusively by heavily made-up, well-dressed Moroccan women in their twenties and early thirties. They were seated alone or in groups of two or three at tables towards the back of the lounge. They stared at Carradine as he walked in. He assumed they were prostitutes and ducked the eye contact. Men sitting nearby in grey armchairs were eating dinner and smoking cigars.

A waiter was cutting up a lemon at the bar. Carradine asked in French if he could have a table for two. The waiter appeared not to understand, indicating that he should speak to an older man standing in the centre of the lounge. The man, who was wearing grey trousers and a white shirt badly in need of a washing machine, showed Carradine to a table on the street side of the lounge, close to a large television showing a football match between Real Madrid and a Spanish team Carradine did not recog-nise. The Arabic commentary on the game was inaudible above the noise of the music. A young Arab wearing a thawb was seated opposite, watching the match and smoking a hookah pipe. He did not acknowledge Carradine.

A waiter appeared carrying a long-handled frying pan

lined with aluminium foil and filled with hot coals. He placed several of the coals on the foil cap of the pipe using a set of metal tongs. An attractive woman in a tight blouse and short black leather skirt was sitting at the table adjacent to Carradine's, engrossed in her mobile phone. She looked up and smiled provocatively as he sat down. When he placed the novel on the table she made a point of tilting her head and looking at it, trying to read the title from the spine. In different circumstances Carradine might have spoken to her, but he turned away.

A short time later he received a text from Mantis explaining that Yassine did not expect to reach Blaine's before ten o'clock. This time the delay suited him. He was famished and ordered a lamb tagine. It appeared within five minutes in a burned terracotta pot with a portion of chips piled over the meat. Carradine wondered if this was the traditional way in which tagine was served in Casablanca or if word had got through to the chef that he was British. In any case he ate it all, washed down with a beer, and was restored to something like his usual self. The manager cleared away the tagine and brought Carradine a plate of fruit – 'on the houses' – as well as a second beer. Carradine had line of sight to the top of the staircase and kept an eye out for Yassine while watching the game.

The match had just ended in a two-all draw when a slim, moustachioed man appeared at the top of the stairs, furtively looking around the lounge. Several of the women seated near the bar gestured towards him in the hope of encouraging him to join them. But the man, who was bald and wearing spectacles, did not appear to be interested. Instead he turned and looked in the direction of the television. Carradine was the only white western male in the restaurant. The man picked him out immediately, raising a hand in silent acknowledgement as he approached the table.

'I recognise you from the wedding in London.'

Carradine stood up and shook Yassine's hand. He had to speak loudly against the cacophony of the music.

'The wedding was in Scotland,' he replied.

Mantis's contact smiled nervously and sat down with his back to the room.

'My name is Yassine,' he said. 'I am sorry to be late.'

His voice had a low, rough quality and his cheeks were pinched and sallow. Carradine assumed he was a heavy smoker.

'It's quite all right,' he said. 'Kit.'

Carradine poured Yassine a glass of water. The young Arab who had been smoking sheeshah had long since departed, but the woman wearing the black leather skirt was still at the next table. Carradine was aware that she was looking at Yassine out of the corner of her eye.

'Why did we meet here?' the Moroccan asked, opening a napkin on his lap.

Carradine was confused by the question. Perhaps Yassine was offended by the clamour of the music or the pervasive stench of tobacco.

'I was told it was what you wanted,' he said.

'By who? London?'

'Yes.'

The waiter who had earlier been carrying the pan of hot coals came to the table and spoke to Yassine in Arabic. Years earlier Carradine had been to Tanzania with the BBC and had sat in a safari hutch at sunset as impalas, zebras and giraffes gathered at a watering hole. The wild animals had seemed tense and jumpy, turning constantly to check for predators and bolting at the slightest noise or movement. He was reminded of this as he watched Yassine. He suspected that Mantis's contact wasn't merely a gopher for the Service, but a fully paid-up agent in a state of unremitting anxiety about being caught.

'Have a drink,' he said, in an effort to calm Yassine's nerves. The Moroccan explained that he had already ordered tea from the waiter, but finished his glass of water in one continuous gulp. He then removed his jacket, placing it beside him on a grey armchair. He was wearing a striped green shirt with a heavily starched white collar. Carradine saw that his armpits were soaked in sweat.

'I brought you the book,' he said.

'Good.' Yassine withdrew a packet of cigarettes from his jacket. Carradine had borrowed a lighter from the manager and passed it across the table.

'Here,' he said. They made eye contact as the flame jumped.

'Thank you.'

Yassine blew a column of smoke at the ceiling and inhaled loudly through his nose, flaring the nostrils and releasing the breath as though applying a yoga exercise to control his anxiety. The music in the lounge was playing at a slightly lower volume, instruments Carradine could not identify over a fast electronic beat. Yassine briefly turned around to look back into the lounge. As he did so, the woman at the next table tried to catch Carradine's eye. He looked down and noticed that she had a second mobile phone poking out of the top of her clutch bag.

'How is our mutual friend?' Yassine asked, accepting a glass of mint tea. Carradine assumed that he was referring to Mantis.

'He's fine.'

'And you live here now? In Casablanca? You are writing a book?'

'No, no.' Carradine wondered how much, or how little, Mantis had told him. 'I'm just passing through. On my way to Marrakech.'

'And you have always done this sort of work? You write the books for C.K. Carradine or this is just a cover and somebody else writes them for you?'

Carradine was amazed that anybody could imagine that such a career was possible and laughed as he replied: 'I write them. That's my normal day job. C.K. is just a pseudonym. My real name is Christopher Alfred Carradine. Everybody calls me "Kit".'

'I see.'

Yassine continued to smoke the cigarette and to study Carradine's face with such intensity that he began to feel slightly uncomfortable.

'Why don't I give you the book?' he suggested.

'That would be a good idea.'

Carradine passed the novel across the table. The Moroccan did not open it up or even look at the cover, but instead immediately lifted up his jacket and placed the book on the grey chair.

'Is this all that you brought for me?' he asked.

'I'm afraid so.' Carradine wondered if he had failed to listen carefully enough to Mantis's instructions. Was some of the money he had been given intended for Yassine and not for the mysterious Abdullah Aziz?

'No, this is what I expected,' Yassine replied.

The Moroccan ground out the cigarette and speared a slice of melon from the plate of fruit. Carradine saw the woman at the next table reach down for her second mobile phone, plucking it from the clutch bag.

'What does our friend think about the political situation?' Yassine asked.

'What political situation?'

'The death of this woman in England. The journalist. The one who hated Muslims?'

'Oh. Lisa Redmond.' The name was like an echo chasing Carradine from city to city. 'I only found out about it yesterday. I haven't had a chance to speak to London.'

The ease with which Carradine had begun to use the term 'London' spoke both to his desire to appear professional and to adapt to the language of the clandestine world. He felt self-conscious doing so, almost to the point of absurdity, but it was also oddly exhilarating to be speaking in real life words that his characters had spoken merely in fiction.

'It is the first murder of this kind in London by Resurrection. I am right?'

'That's right. Up to now we've just had beatings, arson attacks, assaults in restaurants and at public meetings. That kind of thing.'

'And what are you doing about it?'

'Excuse me?' Carradine could not prevent himself from laughing. 'What am *I* doing about it? I'm just a writer, Yassine. Writers don't live in the real world.'

'And yet you are here.'

'And yet I am here.'

They were silent. Carradine had begun to believe that he was sitting in front of a much sharper, more reflective man than he had first imagined. He tried to change the subject.

'What do you do for a living?' The woman at the next table was speaking quietly on her phone. Yassine skewered a chunk of banana and waved the fork in front of his face before answering.

'I do not want to talk about that,' he said. 'Let us not leave this conversation. I am interested to know about Resurrection. What you think will happen. Where you think all of this ends.'

Carradine realised that he was being asked to speak on behalf of the Service. Mantis's man wanted to know the party line in London, the thinking in Downing Street and Vauxhall Cross. Carradine was happy to run with the conceit.

'We're all biding our time,' he said. 'We're all living day-to-day not knowing what the future will bring.' Yassine appeared to find this answer vague and insubstantial. Carradine endeavoured to be more specific. 'I'm about to turn thirty-six. My country has been in a permanent state of conflict for almost forty years. From the Falklands to Syria, Great Britain has always been at war. But it's never affected us.'

'What do you mean?'

'I mean that we were able to go about our daily lives without thinking about the battles British soldiers were fighting on our behalf, without being concerned that our own lives might be at risk. We were oblivious to what was going on. In the last few years, all that has changed.'

'In what way, please?'

'The war has come to the streets.'

'This sounds very dramatic. I suppose that I am talking to a writer, so I should expect this.'

Carradine was beginning to like Yassine. Two women, both in figure-hugging dresses and high heels, walked up the stairs, checked their reflections in a mirror beside the bar and made their way to a table on the far side of the lounge. One of them was very beautiful, with long, dark hair, causing Carradine momentarily to think that he had sighted Lara Bartok. But it was just his mind playing tricks. She was too dark, her features too angular.

'It's not meant to sound dramatic,' he said, looking back at Yassine. 'If you walk down the street in London or Manchester, at any moment you know that a bomb could go off, that some maniac in a van could come ploughing through a crowd and mow down fifty innocent civilians.' Carradine had seen huge concrete barriers, close to his hotel, protecting a wide pedestrianised boulevard in Casablanca for just that purpose. 'That was never the case before. We had the IRA, sure. The Spanish lived with ETA. But the existential threat was completely different.'

Yassine removed his glasses and ran a hand across the pointed dome of his head.

'This word, please. I do not understand . . .'

Carradine explained what he had meant by 'existential' and realised that he was talking too fast and in too much detail. He felt a sudden headache flare at a point deep inside his brain and reached for the strip of ibuprofen he had been carrying around in his jacket.

'You are in discomfort?' Yassine asked as Carradine popped two of the pills.

'Nothing to worry about.' It was as though one of the hot *sheeshah* coals had been placed behind his eyes and somebody was blowing on the embers. 'What I was trying to explain is that Resurrection has added to this atmosphere of anxiety, of fear. People know that an incident could occur at any moment. People have been attacked outside bars and nightclubs. At concerts. They've been kidnapped in the street. If you happen to be in the wrong place at the wrong time, you can be caught up in an act of political violence. That was never the way things used to be.'

Yassine was nodding. 'Yes,' he said. 'This must be how Americans have felt for a long time. Living in a society where there are so many guns in the hands of so many people. A mass shooting can occur at any moment.'

'Exactly. And Americans have learned to adjust to this, just as we are slowly learning to adjust to the threat from suicide bombers, from jihadists, from left-wing radicals.'

The hookah waiter passed behind Carradine's chair carrying a pan of glowing coals. He could feel the heat of the coals on the back of his neck; it was like the blast of hot air that had greeted him as he walked off the plane the previous afternoon.

'And now this Lisa Redmond has been killed.' Yassine skewered the last piece of fruit as he spoke. 'Resurrection has changed everything, no?'

'In what way?'

'Murder has become normal for these people. Normal for them, normal for their enemies. Violence is now the currency. People have taken courage from the aggression of others. They have seen how they have acted and they believe that they can behave in the same way.'

'That's certainly what happened in America,' Carradine replied. 'Hate was unleashed. Now it's happening in my own country.'

'Not in mine, thankfully.' Yassine indicated to the waiter that he would like a second glass of tea. Carradine wondered why the Moroccan was sticking around. The book had been handed over. Their business was concluded. Perhaps it was necessary for him to prolong the meeting so that it would seem less suspicious to anyone who might later become aware of it.

'Why do you think that is?' he asked.

'Control,' Yassine replied. 'Leadership.' Carradine looked quickly to the woman at the next table. A man had joined her. His hand was lingering in the small of her back. 'We have undertaken measures to ensure that jihadism is cut off at the roots before it has a chance to flower. Such groups are well infiltrated and – as you will know from your work in London – we share a great deal of sensitive material with our friends in Europe, and beyond.' Carradine began to understand why Yassine had been of interest to Mantis. He seemed to be well connected in political and intelligence circles. 'Our ruling family has strategically placed individuals from the major towns and cities in positions of authority and influence so that each region feels fairly represented. Furthermore, we have ensured that our young men and women are educated in the correct way . . .'

In other circumstances, Carradine would have continued to listen without distraction, but he had heard the sound of laughter emanating from the staircase. As he sat facing Yassine, Carradine looked over the Moroccan's shoulder and saw two young women – one wearing a designer

T-shirt and tight denim jeans, the other a long pink jilaba – climbing the staircase to the first floor. A few steps behind them came a man speaking noisily in a Hispanic accent, his long hair tied in a topknot. The Spaniard's booming laughter was loud enough to be heard above the music playing in the lounge.

It was Ramón.

12

Carradine kept his head down. He knew that Ramón's presence in the restaurant was not a coincidence and cursed himself for recommending Blaine's in the taxi. The Spaniard sounded drunk and fired up, speaking in loud, slurred French as he stood by the bar with the women. Both were attractive and smartly dressed and looked as though they were accompanying him for reasons other than his charming personality. With any luck the manager would show them to a table on the opposite side of the lounge and Carradine would not have to speak to them. He did not want to have to go through the artifice of introducing Yassine.

'Do you recognise somebody?'

'No, no.' Carradine had not realised that his reaction had been so noticeable. 'I thought I saw someone I knew. False alarm.'

'Holy shit! Kit, man! What the fuck are you doing here?'

The timing could not have been worse. Ramón was

shouting across the lounge. Carradine looked apologetically at Yassine, half-stood up out of his seat and faced the bar.

'Great to see you, man!' Ramón was bellowing over the music and waving his hand. Carradine excused himself from the table. Weaving past a waiter ferrying a hookah pipe across the lounge, he reached Ramón and shook his hand. He was immediately clutched in a bear hug so tight that it transferred the sweat on the Spaniard's clothes onto Carradine's shoulders and neck.

'I thought I'd find you here, man! How are you doin'?'

'I'm just having a quiet dinner with a friend.'

'Right!' Ramón put his hands around the waists of the two women. He looked like a Formula One impresario posing for a picture in the paddock. 'You wanna join us?'

Carradine could smell the fumes of several hours of drinking. He was aware of the women staring at him, sizing him up as a potential catch.

'No. No thanks. You're kind to ask.' He played the caricature of a staid, disapproving Englishman. 'We're just doing a business thing. I had a big night last night and . . .'

'A business thing?' Ramón pronounced 'business' like 'beezness'. 'I thought you were a novelist, man?' The Spaniard glanced down at the chunky wristwatch nestled in the forest of hair on his forearms. 'How come you doing business in Casablanca eleven o'clock at night?'

Carradine was not given the opportunity to formulate an answer.

'Hey, girls,' Ramón continued. 'This guy, he's famous writer. In England. Kit Carradine. C.K. right? Not J.K. Rowling. C.K. Carradine. You know him?'

Both women smiled in a polite but obvious demonstration

of their ignorance of the Carradine *oeuvre*. Carradine smiled back. One of them – the girl in the pink jilaba – was extraordinarily beautiful.

'So look,' he said. 'I've got to get back to my friend. Maybe I'll come and join you once he's gone?'

The offer seemed to satisfy all parties.

'OK good, fine.' Ramón slapped Carradine on the back, as if attempting to dislodge any stray chunk of food that might have become lodged in his windpipe. 'We'll be right over here.' He pointed at a table close to the bar. The woman in the pink jilaba jolted Carradine with a bedroom gaze and walked towards her seat. 'Come say hello.'

Carradine turned around and indicated to Yassine that he was going to use the bathroom. As he did so, the woman with long black hair whom he had earlier mistaken for Lara Bartok walked straight past him. She sat in the seat behind Yassine that had previously been occupied by the young Arab smoking sheeshah. Carradine went into the gents, tipped the maid twenty dirhams on the way out and took a stick of Juicy Fruit from a metal plate by the door. When he came back into the lounge, a man in a checked shirt was moving between the tables crooning an Arabic version of 'Careless Whisper'. Carradine could hear the boom of Ramón's laughter above the amplified sound of the music. He walked towards the table and saw that Yassine was checking his mobile phone.

To his consternation, there was a photograph of Bartok on the screen. Carradine was certain that it was one of the pictures Mantis had shown him in London, but Yassine swiped it away before he was able to take a closer look. The sighting troubled Carradine to such an extent that he did not speak for the first few moments after sitting down. Yassine placed the phone on the table.

'I think I will also go to the bathroom,' he said.

As the Moroccan stood up, Carradine noticed him staring at the woman with the long, black hair. His interest in her was so obvious that she returned his gaze. Had Yassine also mistaken her for 'Maria Rodriguez'? The likelihood of such a coincidence seemed remote – unless several Service operatives in the region had all been tasked with finding her? Carradine recalled Mantis's remark at Lisson Grove: there were 'other officers and support agents' looking for Bartok. Yassine could be one of them.

The Moroccan walked towards the bar. He did not take his phone. Had he deliberately left it on the table as a trap? There was no way of knowing.

Carradine realised that he must act quickly. Touching the screen to keep it alive, he leaned forward. In the same movement he picked up the bottle on the table and poured himself a glass of water. He was aware that Yassine was moving in his peripheral vision, passing in front of the bar. He did not want him to see what he was about to do.

As soon as the Moroccan was out of sight, Carradine picked up the phone. He clicked the button at the base of the handset, taking the display to a Home screen populated by icons bearing Arabic script. Carradine's hand was shaking very slightly as he studied the screen. He was frustrated by his inability to control his nerves. He tried to remember the logo for 'Photos', mistakenly opening Facebook Messenger, Instagram and Safari before tapping the technicolour flower that at last took him to the Camera Roll.

He looked up in the direction of the bathroom. No sign of Yassine. He prayed that there was a queue for the gents, that the Moroccan would bump into a friend or be delayed by a woman trying to pick him up. He looked down at the phone.

The screen displayed a patchwork of photos of Lara Bartok, identical to the ones Mantis had shown him in Lisson Grove. Carradine could see the same picture that he was carrying in his wallet, the one used in the Rodriguez passport. He clicked on the photo of Bartok standing next to the bearded man with a surfboard – then closed the Camera Roll, tapped back to the Home screen and locked the phone.

His body was flushed with sweat. He looked up to see Yassine coming back from the bathroom. As the Moroccan passed behind a pillar, Carradine placed the phone back in its earlier position on the table and took a sip of water. His hands were shaking uncontrollably. He decided to sit on them, taking a series of deep breaths, elated that he had successfully managed to access the phone without being caught, but surprised by his inability to conceal his anxiety.

'Your friend is having himself a good time,' said Yassine as he sat down. He had applied cologne in the bathroom. The smell reminded Carradine of the arrivals hall in Casablanca airport. 'Where is he from?'

'Spain,' he replied, rocking forward on his hands. 'Or America. I couldn't really work it out.'

'And the girls?'

'Maybe they're his sisters?'

Carradine had intended the remark as a joke but Yassine took it at face value, indicating with a patronising frown that he thought Carradine was being naive.

'How do you know him, please?'

Carradine explained that he had met Ramón on the

plane and had shared a taxi with him from the airport.

'Do you also know the man who is sitting with him?'

Carradine was caught off guard. He had not noticed that a fourth person had joined their table.

'I didn't see anybody else,' he said. 'Who's there?'

'Somebody I have recognised. Somebody I do not like.'

Carradine peered across the lounge, trying to locate Ramón's table. He could see only the beautiful woman in the pink jilaba and the side of Ramón's head.

'You recognised him?'

Yassine lit a cigarette.

'He is known to me, yes. To the government. He claims to be an American diplomat.'

Carradine understood the euphemism and felt the strange sensation of slipping and losing his balance.

'He's Agency?'

Yassine nodded. All of Carradine's doubts about Ramón crystallised in that moment. He lit a cigarette of his own to hide his disquiet.

'And my Spanish friend? The hairy one. Have you seen him before?'

'Never,' Yassine replied. 'Believe me. I would remember a man like this.'

So who was he? And why was he meeting an Agency officer in Casablanca? Carradine was now certain that he was being followed.

'You look worried.'

He tried to set his concerns aside with a gulp of wine.

'I'm fine,' he said. 'Totally fine.' Needing an excuse for the change in his mood, Carradine plucked a lie out of thin air. 'To be honest, that headache just came back. I should take another pill.'

'I am sorry to hear this.' Yassine immediately gestured for the bill. It was as though he had been waiting for an excuse to end their meeting. 'Why don't we call it a night? Perhaps you should go back to your hotel and rest?'

Carradine heard the bulldog roar of Ramón's laughter burst across the lounge. He thought of all the fictional Agency officers he had written about in his books – the patriots, the traitors, the murderers, the saints – and realised that, for the first time, he was a handshake away from being introduced to the real thing.

The manager brought the bill. Carradine understood that it was the responsibility of the Service to pay for dinner. Yassine did not disagree. He paid in cash, left a generous tip, and kept the receipt for Mantis.

'Before we leave,' said Yassine. 'I have something for you.'

The Moroccan had put on his jacket. He reached into a side pocket and retrieved a small, rectangular object that he passed to Carradine as he shook his hand. Carradine took whatever it was that Yassine was giving him without breaking eye contact, placing it in his back pocket.

'This is for our mutual friend?' he asked. The heat and sweat of his earlier disquiet had suddenly returned like a fever. Mantis had said nothing about Yassine giving him something to bring back to London.

'For our friend, yes.'

Carradine probed the object between his fingers. He was certain that it was a memory stick of some kind. At the same time Yassine picked up the novel. Only then did he look at it more carefully and see the name C.K. Carradine printed on the cover.

'Wait,' he said. 'This is *your* book?'

'One of mine,' Carradine replied.

Yassine walked towards the bar, shaking his head.

'You must forgive me,' he said. 'I did not realise.'

'That's quite all right.'

'Have you signed it?'

Carradine wondered why Yassine was concerned to have a signed copy of a novel intended only as a book cipher. As he returned the lighter to the manager, he asked if he could borrow a pen. Within earshot of the conversation at Ramón's table, Carradine rested the book on the bar, opening it to the title page.

'Who should I make it out to?' he asked.

'Just your signature, please.'

Carradine signed his name and handed the book to Yassine. Anybody within a few metres of the bar would have been able to see the exchange take place.

'Well, it was very good to meet you, Kit,' he said. They shook hands, Yassine making it plain as they did so that he did not want them to leave the restaurant at the same time.

'You too,' Carradine replied.

Yassine suddenly moved a step closer.

'This individual,' he whispered, nodding in the direction of Ramón's table.

'Which one?'

'The one I spoke of,' he said. 'The American.'

'Go on.'

'Be careful with him.' There was a foreboding in his eyes. 'Be very, very careful.'

13

Carradine was acutely aware of his isolation. An over-weight woman seated at a nearby table looked up and curled a smile. He took out a cigarette, turning towards the bar. He felt like a man standing on his own at a party with nobody to talk to. The singer was crooning the end of another love song, drawing out the final notes. All around him middle-aged men were striking deals with women half their age over glasses of cheap champagne and untouched plates of fruit. Sheeshah and cigarettes were being smoked in every corner of the lounge; Carradine watched as one of the waiters picked up the foil crown of a hookah pipe, turned it over and blew a small cloud of ash towards the ground. The private, disci-plined side of his nature was in conflict with his hunger for intrigue. The sensible course of action would have been to slip quietly out of the restaurant and to take a taxi back to his hotel. But he wanted to know the truth about Ramón. Who was he and why was he following him? Carradine also wanted to get eyes on his American contact, to try to discern the nature of the relationship between the two men. He knew that he was potentially putting himself at risk by meeting someone suspected of working for the Agency, yet he was constitutionally incapable of walking away without at least finding out if Yassine's warning had been justified.

He walked towards Ramón's table. The woman in the pink jilaba was speaking rapidly in French. Her friend laughed at something she had said and carefully attended to her mascara. Ramón was subdued, the ebullience and bonhomie sucked out of him. He looked up. Carradine saw the same cold, pitiless look in his eyes that he had witnessed in the cab. There would be no bear hug this time, no slap on the back.

'I just wanted to say goodbye before I head off,' he said.

The American turned. The two women were looking at Carradine with interest. They had their catches for the night, but the solitary English tourist might be worth keeping in reserve for future evenings.

'How are you?' Ramón asked with indifference. He gestured across the table. 'This is my new friend, Sebastian. Sebastian, meet Kit Carradine.'

The American stood up. 'Hey there. Sebastian Hulse. Good to meet you.'

Hulse was a square-jawed forty-five with recently barbered brown hair and blue eyes. Boxing classes had given Carradine a habit of sizing people up in terms of their potential strength and physical fitness. Hulse's bespoke linen suit looked East Coast Ivy League and there was something easeful and well-rested about him. Nevertheless, he looked as though he could handle himself

123

in a fight. Carradine wouldn't have been surprised if he had once been in the military.

'You too,' he said. 'New friend?'

'Yeah.' Was it Carradine's imagination or did Ramón sound uncertain? 'We just met tonight in my hotel. Had a couple of drinks, I told him you'd recommended this place . . .'

'Great bar,' Hulse added.

The meeting sounded plausible enough, but Carradine was wary of what Yassine had said about the American. If Hulse was Agency, could he have engineered the meeting with Ramón in order to find out more about him? Given that they had met at the Sheraton, was it possible that he was 'Abdullah Aziz'?

'Look, I don't want to interrupt,' he said. The remark was an expression both of Carradine's innate politeness but also of his desire not to be drawn into whatever web Hulse might be weaving for him. 'I can leave you in peace.'

Ramón's face suggested that he was hopeful that Carradine would indeed slip away. Hulse had other ideas.

'No, please join us for a drink,' he said. 'You don't have a girl with you?' He glanced in the direction of the over-weight woman who had earlier smiled at Carradine. 'There's one over there. I can't tell if she's built that way or six months pregnant.'

Ramón grunted a half-hearted laugh. The two women seated at the table did not appear to have understood what Hulse had said. He introduced them.

'This is Maryam. This is Salma. Girls, this is Mr Carradine.'

'Kit,' said Carradine, shaking Salma's cool, manicured hand as she adjusted her jilaba. 'And how do you know each other?'

It was a naive question for which he received a suitably blunt look from Hulse. Obviously the women had been plying their trade in the bar at the Sheraton.

'We met earlier this evening,' he replied pointedly.

'Yeah, that's right,' added Ramón.

There was a half-finished bottle of champagne in front of Salma and an empty chair positioned a couple of feet from where Carradine was standing. He did not feel that he could walk away without losing face.

'As long as you don't mind,' he said. 'I'll just have a quick drink.'

In the time it took Carradine to consume half a glass of cheap champagne, he worked out the dynamic between the two men. Slick and self-confident, Sebastian Hulse exuded all of the class and education that Ramón doubtless aspired to but would never conceivably attain. The American was charm personified, asking all the right questions through a mist of aftershave and expensive education. *Have you been published in the United States? Did you enjoy visiting California? Does the current political situation in America look as bad on the outside as it looks from the inside?* At the same time, the two women were vying for his attention. If Ramón was a wallet, Hulse was an ATM. He was solicitous towards them, generous with the flow of champagne, even suggesting to Maryam and Salma that they visit him at his home in New York. Carradine knew that it would be impossible for them to do so: even if they could afford the flights, obtaining visas for the United States would take months. In short, Hulse had ended up cramping Ramón's style. Carradine noticed that he was wearing a wedding ring on his left hand and suspected that the American surfed from bed to bed on a bow wave of charisma and candlelit dinners. An evangelist for the easy, nodding smile, for the steely eye contact that lasted a beat too long, he was at once utterly charming and completely repulsive.

'So how are you finding Casablanca?' he asked.

'He loves it,' Ramón replied on Carradine's behalf, recovering some of his characteristic bombast. 'Our driver take him into the woods. Poor guy thought he was going to get fucked up.'

'That's not exactly true,' said Carradine, wondering if 'our driver' had been a slip of the tongue. 'I wasn't worried.'

'And?' said Hulse.

'And what?' said Carradine.

'What do you think of the place?'

It was the second time Hulse had asked the same question. Either he was possessed of a talent for feigning interest in subjects that were of no importance to him, or he was suspicious of Carradine and testing his cover.

'I like it,' he replied. 'More than I expected to. I'm planning to write a book partly set in Morocco. Thought I'd end up writing about Marrakech, Fez and Tangier. Didn't think I'd be interested in Casablanca.'

'So why d'you come here?'

It may have been his hangover, it may have been a consequence of seeing the photographs of Bartok on Yassine's phone, but Carradine was beginning to feel unsettled. For an almost fatal moment, he could not think of a suitable reply.

'For the waters,' he said, sure that Hulse would recognise Bogart's famous line. 'I was misinformed.'

'What's that? I don't follow.'

There was an awkward silence. Carradine explained himself.

'It's *Casablanca*!' he said. 'I was quoting the movie. I write spy novels, political thrillers. The city is so famous. It has such an ineluctable quality . . .'

'Ineluctable,' Hulse repeated, slowly shaking his head as if to suggest that Carradine was being pretentious. 'What a word. Haven't heard that since they made me read *Ulysses* in college . . .'

Carradine wondered if he had used it in the correct context.

'I'm just here for two nights,' he said. 'Been strolling around, taking photographs, making notes . . .'

'And then I walk in here and find you having dinner with Mohammed Oubakir,' said Hulse, staring at him. 'Of all the gin joints in all the towns in all the world . . . '

'So you *have* seen *Casablanca*!' Carradine replied, feeling his insides dissolve with anxiety.

'Yeah.. I've seen *Casablanca*. Who hasn't?'

Ramón weighed in.

'What does he do, this friend of yours?'

'Who?' Carradine replied, trying to buy time.

'Oubakir,' Hulse answered pointedly.

Carradine scrambled for a cover story.

'Mohammed? He's in the public sector. Friend of a friend. Put me in touch so I could ask him some questions about life in Morocco.'

'Is that right?' Hulse left a pause long enough to suggest that he knew Carradine was lying. 'So what exactly does he *do* in the public sector?'

'What does he *do*?' The American was staring at him. 'I'm not one hundred per cent sure. Something in politics?

127

Something in finance? Those guys speak a different language. I never know the difference between a hedge fund manager, a mutual trust and a leveraged buyout. Do you?' Hulse appeared to be enjoying the sight of Carradine digging himself deeper and deeper into a hole. 'We didn't really get into his job. We mostly talked about books. About Islamist terror. Resurrection.'

Ramón flicked his eyes across the table. It was as if Carradine had used a codeword for which he was primed to respond. 'Resurrection?' he said. 'What about it?'

'Nothing,' Hulse replied. He didn't want Ramón interrupting.

'Nothing,' Carradine repeated, and smiled at Hulse in an effort to take some of the sting out of their exchange.

'So you know people out here? You have contacts?' the American asked.

'A few.' Carradine seized on the opportunity to talk about the literary festival, sketching out what he knew of the event's history and trying to draw Hulse into a conversation about literature. It transpired that he had read a book by Katherine Paget, with whom Carradine was due to share a panel two days later. Carradine offered to arrange some free tickets if Hulse felt like making the trip to Marrakech.

'I might just do that,' he said. 'I might just do that.'

There was a sudden flutter of activity on the other side of the table. Salma was taking a selfie with Maryam. They were adding Snapchat butterflies to their faces and giggling at the results. Carradine hit on an idea. If he could somehow get a picture of Ramón and Hulse, he could send it to Mantis and have London run a check on them. But how to do so without raising suspicion?

'We should join them,' he said, taking out his own phone, activating the camera and looking at Hulse. Seeing that no objection was raised, Carradine reversed the lens, held the phone at arm's length and grinned. 'Say cheese.'

To his surprise, Hulse allowed Carradine to fire off several shots while beaming a matinee idol smile at the camera. Encouraged by this, Carradine turned it on the girls and took several photographs of Ramón sitting between them.

'Do I look nice?' Maryam asked in French.

'You look beautiful,' Carradine replied and received a wink for his troubles. 'Why does nobody want a picture of *me*?'

'*I* want a picture of you,' Salma exclaimed, adjusting the pink jilaba as she raised her phone. A septuagenarian Moroccan businessman at the next table lit up a Cuban cigar the size of a cruise missile. The smell of the tobacco drifted across the room as Salma took a photograph of Carradine and Hulse, their glasses raised, their smiles fixed.

'Man, isn't it great to smell that cigar?' Ramón exclaimed. 'Beautiful! What is it? A Romeo y Julieta? Montecristo? Makes me wanna smoke one. I'd risk getting cancer for that shit.'

Nobody laughed. Carradine was busy watching Salma take the photographs. He placed an arm around Hulse's back. There were years of gym weights in his shoulders.

'Are we done?' the American asked, a sudden edge in his voice. 'That's enough now.'

It was difficult to discern if the source of Hulse's irritation was Salma's flirtatiousness or the fact that Carradine had taken his photograph.

'Don't put those on social media, OK?' he said to the girls in terse, fluent French.

'*Bien sûr*,' Salma replied.

Ramón also seemed concerned by the sudden shift in Hulse's mood. As though wary of upsetting him further, he offered the American a cigarette – which he declined – and ordered another bottle of champagne. Carradine sensed an opportunity to leave. He was strung out and wanted to get back to his hotel. Taking the photographs constituted a good night's work.

'Don't get any for me,' he said. 'I'm going to take off.'

This time there were no objections. As Carradine stood up, Hulse placed a territorial hand on Salma's thigh. Light bounced off his wedding ring. Taking his jacket from the back of the chair, Carradine offered to leave some money for the drinks but was waved away by Ramón.

'Next time, man,' he said. 'Get us next time. And thanks for recommending this place.'

The memory stick was pressing into Carradine's leg as he stepped away from the table. Thanking Ramón for his generosity, he kissed both women on the cheek and shook Hulse's hand.

'You got a card?' the American asked.

It was the same question Mantis had put to him a week earlier. Carradine had been to Ryman's and had five hundred printed up. He passed one to Hulse.

'What about you?' he asked.

'Me?' The man from the Agency smiled at Carradine as though he was being too trusting. 'Don't have one with me tonight. Must have left them back at my hotel.'

There was nothing for it but to leave. Carradine went

downstairs, tipped the doorman fifty dirhams and made his way out onto the street.

Boulevard d'Anfa was deserted. There was a strong smell of urine as he walked along the road. Carradine knew what would now happen. Hulse would have his phone soaked, his emails analysed, every call and message Carradine had made and sent in the past six months cross-checked for evidence of a relationship with the Service. The basic invasion of his personal life was irritating, but whatever privacy he had once enjoyed was now a thing of the past. Carradine had nothing to fear in terms of Hulse learning about his relationship with Mantis; their communications on WhatsApp had been *en clair* and encrypted. Furthermore there was nothing in his online behaviour to suggest an interest in Bartok. What worried him was Oubakir. If 'Yassine' was a source not only for Mantis but also for the Americans, Carradine would inevitably fall under suspicion. He felt for the memory stick, moving it into the side pocket of his jacket, wondering why the hell Mantis hadn't warned him that he was going to have to act as a courier.

Carradine lit a cigarette, trying to gather his thoughts. He stopped beside a branch of Starbuck's about twenty metres from Blaine's. The doorman was staring at him. A cab drove past but it was occupied. Carradine opened Uber and booked a ride in a Mercedes six minutes away on Avenue de Nice. Seconds later a taxi turned into Boulevard d'Anfa with its light on. Carradine swore and let it go past, walking further down the street so that he was out of sight of the doorman. He checked Uber to discover that his own car was still six minutes away, the icon turning in 360-degree circles on Rue Ahfir. He was about to cancel the ride when the car straightened out and began to move. He used the time to check the photos he had taken of Ramón and Sebastian, cropping out Salma and Maryam. He sent three of them to Mantis on WhatsApp with the message: 'Fun tonight at Blaine's. Do you recognise any of these people?' but only a single grey tick appeared beside the message, indicating that it had not yet reached Mantis's phone. Moments later the Mercedes pulled up alongside him and he drove back to his hotel.

Carradine had been lying in the darkness of his room for more than half an hour, wired and unable to sleep, when the screen on his phone lit up, filling the room with a pale blue light. He sat up in bed.

Mantis's message was as straightforward as it was ominous.

You've taken on too much. Thanks for tonight but don't worry about Maria. Other people can handle that side of things. Just enjoy the festival, have a break, come home refreshed and finish your book! Interesting to meet you. All the best for the future, R.

14

Carradine did not know whether he should respond to Mantis's message or even if there would be much point in doing so. It was clear that he had been fired. Sending the photographs had been a grave mistake. Either the Service now wanted to protect him because they knew he was out of his depth or, more likely, were concerned that he was about to jeopardise an operation in which Ramón and Hulse were somehow involved.

Carradine felt an anger and humiliation as intense as any he had known in his working life. The Service had put their faith in him and he had shown himself to be a reckless amateur. He began to compose a reply asking what he should do with the memory stick and the package for Maria but knew that such a message would be pointless. As soon as he returned to London, he would most likely be picked up, taken to Mantis and asked to explain himself. The Service would want the items returned. The fact that he had already opened the package only made the situation worse.

He was exhausted. The long night of drinking, the confusion of finding photographs of Bartok on Oubakir's phone, as well as his subsequent encounter with Hulse and Ramón, had compounded this. Carradine opened his laptop and tried to access the contents of the memory stick, but it was encrypted and would not open. He took a sleeping pill and waited to pass out. There was nothing to be done except to leave for Marrakech, to take part in the festival and to head home. His career as a support agent, a counterpart to Maugham and Greene, and his attempt to live up to the example set by his father, had ended in ignominy.

15

Otis Euclidis was moved three times.

He spent the first two months of captivity in a cabin in the Flathead National Forest, about two hundred miles north of Missoula. He was driven there by Ivan Simakov, Lara Bartok and Zack Curtis and watched by a rotating team of two Resurrection volunteers who were given responsibility for feeding him, making sure that he did not try to escape and filming him for the purposes of propaganda.

When the Montana winter became too severe, Euclidis was driven south to an isolated house outside Round Rock, Texas, where he was kept in a soundproofed attic room for four weeks. Footage of Euclidis denouncing his political views and disparaging his followers as 'clowns' and 'losers' had been widely broadcast. By then, Simakov and Bartok had left him in the hands of Thomas Frattura and two married Resurrection activists who had provided the house. They quickly came to realise that Euclidis had been lying in his filmed statements and still adhered closely to the prejudices which had so enraged Resurrection. Euclidis developed a reputation among his captors for being charming and intelligent. It was obvious that he was quicker on his feet than Frattura and enjoyed puncturing what he described as his 'high-minded left-liberal self-congratulation'. On several occasions, Resurrection volunteers videotaped conversations between Euclidis and Frattura which were later destroyed when Simakov concluded that Frattura had been made to look a fool.

'How can you call yourself a feminist when you defend the right of Muslim men to wrap their wives up in black bedsheets when they walk down the street?' Frattura had been unable to frame a response. 'What's "modern" about that? I'm a gay man with a black boyfriend but your precious gender and racial signifiers are so fucked up you think it's OK to kidnap me on the street with an assault weapon and keep me in captivity for six months just because we disagree on abortion and climate change. Who's the really dangerous person here, Thomas? You or me?'

Frattura eventually left Euclidis in the hands of Raymond Powers, a former British civil servant with links to Momentum who had contacted Simakov on the Dark Net and travelled to the United States as a volunteer. Powers transported Euclidis to his Brazilian girlfriend's rented house in suburban Indianapolis where the basement had been converted into a small, soundproofed prison with minimum ventilation. The room was too low for Euclidis to stand up in and he was chained to a radiator twenty-four hours a day.

Approximately three weeks after Euclidis's arrival at

the house, he developed a kidney infection. Rather than risk taking him to hospital or leaving him out on the street to be cared for by a passer-by, Powers and his girl-friend, Barbara Salgado, took the decision to leave him in the basement with a supply of food and water and some antibiotics. His health deteriorating, they packed their few belongings into a GMC Yukon and drove to Indianapolis International Airport where they caught a flight to London via Newark.

A fortnight later, in the same week that Ivan Simakov was killed in Moscow, Raymond Powers was arrested by British police on charges of premeditated grievous bodily harm. He was sentenced to three years' custody in HMP Pentonville. Salgado, who had been subjected to physical abuse throughout their relationship, recovered from her injuries and moved back to Brazil. She did not tell the British authorities about the whereabouts of Otis Euclidis. The house in Indianapolis remained empty for more than a year.

16

Carradine woke up at nine with a heavy head, went down to the pool, swam thirty laps and sat in the sauna thinking about Lara Bartok. He still had her photograph. He still had the Rodriguez passport and credit card. Mantis did not know that Carradine had identified her as Ivan Simakov's estranged girlfriend. Nor did he know that he had seen photographs of Bartok on Oubakir's phone.

During breakfast he resolved to keep looking for her. Screw Mantis and screw his WhatsApp message. The idea became a fixation. Should Carradine find her and be able to pass her the documents given to him by the Service, Bartok would be saved and his reputation restored. He did not want to return to the mundanity of his working life, the same groundhog routine day after day, without at least putting up the semblance of a fight.

He went back to his room and packed his bags. He took the items out of the safe, wondering why Mantis had not sent any further messages. Surely he knew about the memory stick and was expecting Carradine to deliver it?

Perhaps he was taking on trust the fact that Carradine would fly home from Marrakech and hand it over. After all, what other course of action was available to him?

He took a cab the short distance to Gare des Voyageurs. The first-class carriages were full so Carradine bought a second-class ticket, sitting on his suitcase in the shade of the platform as the passengers for Marrakech began to crowd around him. He was one of only half a dozen foreigners in the station. Two French girls in their twenties were taking giggling selfies a few feet from where he was seated. A Spanish couple, closer to his own age, were waiting on the southern side of the platform, both engrossed in books. At the opposite end, where Carradine expected the first-class carriages to pull in, an elderly man in a Panama hat was engaged in conversation with a member of the station staff. Carradine picked at the idea that he was a British or American official sent to watch him, but knew from his understanding of overseas surveillance operations that locals would have been hired for such a job. On that basis, he had no chance of knowing whether or not he was being tailed. With another fifteen minutes before the train was due to arrive, there were already at least seventy Moroccans on the platform, any one of whom could be keeping an eye on him.

The train was half an hour late. In the scramble to board, Carradine found himself at the front of a crush of passengers, each of them rushing forward to grab a seat. It was fiercely hot in the carriage and no quarter was given as people shoved and barged their way through. Carradine was still dogged by a black mood of annoyance and pushed through forcefully until he had managed to sit by the window at a table occupied by a husband and wife and their two small children. The father nodded at Carradine politely as he stowed his luggage overhead. Those passengers who had been unable to find a seat were packed tightly in the aisles, reaching out to steady themselves as the train pulled away.

The carriage was mostly filled with young Moroccans chatting to one another in Arabic and communing with their mobile phones. Across the aisle, a man with a neat moustache had opened a briefcase and was busy flicking through the pages of a file. Carradine succumbed to the paranoid notion that he was under surveillance, yet he could not tell who was watching him nor exactly how many people had been tasked with the job. An attractive woman of about thirty was standing nearby and kept smiling at him, but he could not know if she was a honeytrap set by Moroccan intelligence or just a pretty girl passing the time by flirting with a foreigner. In a fleeting moment of dread, he thought that he saw the face of Hulse at the back of the carriage, but a second look confirmed that it was just his mind playing tricks. Drifting off to sleep in the clogging afternoon heat, Carradine thought it more likely that the Americans would have organised for a team to be waiting for him at the station in Marrakech. After all, he was hardly going to jump off the train en route. The Agency had him exactly where they wanted him.

A sudden movement of the train woke him more than an hour later. He had been dreaming of Lisa Redmond. Carradine looked across the table and saw that the family of Moroccans had left. In the seat opposite his own was the elderly man who had been standing on the platform at Casablanca wearing a Panama hat. Carradine was surprised to see him; he had assumed that he would have travelled on a first-class ticket. A young, veiled woman had taken the seat beside the window and was listening to music through headphones. The man was reading a paperback book and chewing on the end of a pen. He acknowledged Carradine with a brisk nod. The book was a Lawrence Durrell novel whose title – *Nunquam* – Carradine did not recognise. He was about sixty-five with sparse white hair that in the heat had become matted to his head. There was a bottle of water in front of him, two over-ripe bananas and an unopened packet of Bonne Maman biscuits. There had been no food for sale at Gare des Voyageurs save for a snack bar selling nuts and crisps. Carradine had bought a tube of Pringles and a bottle of water, both of which were in his suitcase. He was hungry after his siesta. He was about to stand up and fetch them when the man lowered his book and touched the packet of biscuits.

'Would you like one?'

He looked, for all the world, like a well-educated, retired Englishman of a certain class and background, but the accent was central European, possibly Czech or Hungarian.

'If you've got one spare, thank you.'

The man smiled in a slightly self-satisfied way and prised open the packet of biscuits. He had large, thick hands with incongruously manicured nails. He was wearing an antique wristwatch with a signet ring on the little finger of his left hand. Carradine assumed that he was comfortably off: his pale blue cotton shirt and beige linen jacket were of high quality and his shoes – at least the one that Carradine had glimpsed beneath the table – expensive Italian loafers.

'Are you going all the way to Marrakech?' the man asked, holding up the packet. It was noticeable that he did not offer a biscuit to the bearded Moroccan nor to the veiled woman sitting beside Carradine. This minor detail was enough to make the already paranoid Carradine think that he had been singled out for attention and that their encounter was not a coincidence.

'I am,' he replied, taking two. 'You?'

'Indeed. We are still two hours away, I think.'

'That far?'

Carradine did not feel like talking yet was pinned beside the window with no chance of escape. It transpired that the price of two biscuits was a conversation of blistering tediousness covering the man's views on everything from Brexit to the difficulty of obtaining a reasonably priced bottle of French wine in Morocco. Carradine suffered in polite silence, occasionally tuning out to look at a cactus crop at the side of the railway or to follow the progress of a donkey and cart bumping along in a small rural settlement. Only as the train was passing through the foothills of the Atlas Mountains, still forty or fifty miles from Marrakech, did the man – whose name was Karel – begin to ask Carradine about his reasons for travelling to Marrakech.

'I'm a novelist,' he said, expecting at least a modicum of enthusiasm on the subject, given that Karel was reading Lawrence Durrell. Instead he replied: 'Really?' in a flat monotone. Carradine might as well have said that he was an Operational Control Centre Specialist at a suburban accountancy firm.

'What sort of things do you write about then?'

Carradine was in an indifferent mood, resentful that the elderly man was taking up so much of his time. He was sick of spies and wanted to forget why Mantis had hired him but knew that he could not lie about his cover.

'Espionage.'

'Ah. No better place for that than Casablanca, I suppose.'

'No better place,' Carradine replied.

The discussion was abruptly interrupted by an announcement, in French and Arabic, on the public address system. The train would be arriving in Marrakech in half an hour. Carradine took the opportunity to get up from the table and to walk to the back of the train where he smoked a cigarette with some students from Tangiers. When he came back, the veiled woman had left and the seat next to his own was empty. Karel was reading a newspaper. As Carradine sat down he saw that it was a copy of *Le Monde*. There was a photograph of Lisa Redmond on the front page and a headline suggesting that Resurrection had 'crossed the line in the United Kingdom'. Karel folded the paper over and looked at Carradine.

'Ah. You're back.'

'Just went for a cigarette.'

'Terrible outcome with this journalist.'

Carradine had the sudden, lurching intuition that their entire conversation up to this point had been manufactured. Karel's sole purpose in sitting with him had been to draw Carradine out about the Redmond kidnapping. He had no evidence for this theory save for his own burgeoning paranoia and the deliberation with which Karel had set about talking to him. But under whose orders was he working? Hulse? Mantis? Or someone else entirely?

'Yes,' he managed to reply. 'Awful.'

'There will be repercussions.'

'What do you mean?'

'They will find whoever did it and they will go after their families.'

Carradine was astounded. He looked around the carriage to ascertain if anybody had picked up the remark.

'Excuse me? You're saying the British government is going to start killing people?'

'I said no such thing.'

'I must have misunderstood.'

'Not the British government. The Russians. It is well understood among people who know such things.'

'Know what things?'

'That Moscow is systematically murdering the families and loved ones of known members of Resurrection.'

It was not the first time that Carradine had heard such an accusation. The Russian government had a reputation for threatening – even for killing – the parents and siblings of slain Islamist terrorists. He had not considered the possibility that the policy extended to Resurrection.

'Why would Moscow care about Redmond?' he asked.

'That's hardly the point.' Karel placed the newspaper on the table. 'I assume you know what happened to Ivan Simakov?'

It was as if a ghost had passed through the carriage. Carradine was conscious of Karel studying his face with great intensity. The mention of Simakov's name was surely intentional; whoever had sent Karel knew that Carradine was searching for Lara Bartok.

'What about him?'

'Blown up by the Russians. The explosion in Moscow was made to look like human error, but they knew exactly what they were doing . . .'

'Agreed,' said Carradine. He had always believed that Simakov had been murdered by Russian intelligence.

'Well, the same applies to his parents.'

'What do you mean?'

A warm breeze was blowing through the carriage. Karel had eaten one of the disintegrating bananas. He used the discarded skin to weigh down the pages of his newspaper.

'I am retired,' he said. 'I speak Hungarian, German, English, French and Russian. I use my time to educate myself. I have met intriguing people in the course of my life – politicians, journalists, civil servants, academics – and these people tell me intriguing things.' The old man had a bland, smug manner that almost short-circuited Carradine's desire to delve deeper. 'They also send articles to me. Books, links to websites, this kind of thing.'

'But what if—'

Carradine began to ask a question but Karel raised his hand, silencing him with an extended index finger. He looked like a cricket umpire giving a batsman out caught behind.

'You merely have to look at the evidence. The parents of Ivan Simakov were killed in a car crash on the outskirts of Moscow. No other vehicles were involved. Mechanical failure was blamed, despite the fact that their Renault was less than two years out of the factory.'

Carradine had known that Simakov's parents had died in a car crash. He did not think that this constituted evidence of a criminal conspiracy.

'You are aware of the name Godfrey Milne?'

Carradine said that he was not.

'I am surprised by this.' Karel employed his customary tone of condescension. 'Milne was a British intelligence officer who lost the faith. Joined Resurrection. Found a new faith in degrading those on the Right with whom he disagreed politically. It is said that he threatened to shoot dead the infant grandson of a senior figure in the NRA. That he waterboarded a member of the Ku Klux Klan. Alleged member, I should probably say. Charming fellow. Some people believe the Americans went after Milne's family as a result.'

The train jolted suddenly to one side at a set of points. Carradine was briefly thrown towards the window. He grabbed the armrest to steady himself.

'The *Americans* are involved in this too?'

Karel shrugged. 'Milne was responsible for orchestrating an attack in Washington DC in which acid was thrown into the face of a lawyer working on behalf of a Republican Congressman accused of taking kickbacks from big pharma. Four weeks later Milne's brother was taken from his apartment – in Salcombe or Padstow, I think, one of those English seaside towns – and murdered.'

Carradine looked out of the window. He did not believe what Karel was telling him. The man was likely a fantasist, a spinner of tall tales and conspiracy theories. The American intelligence community would no more embrace a policy of state-sponsored assassinations against the families of suspected Resurrection activists than they would relocate Langley to the Gobi Desert. It would be political and moral suicide.

'If this is a policy to deter people from joining

146

Resurrection, how come more hasn't been heard about it?' he asked.

The train was passing through the suburbs of Marrakech. In his romantic imagination Carradine had expected mud huts and camels, mosques and souks, but the outskirts of the city were wastelands of concrete housing and roads cluttered with litter. Karel shrugged a second time. He had the self-important man's habit of suggesting that society was beset by depths of ignorance and sloth which caused him great anguish; that his own personal philosophy was the One True Way; and that it was only a matter of time before mankind realised this and came to share Karel's world view.

'There has been plenty said about it,' he replied. 'Plenty written. But perhaps it is not in the British media's best interests to accuse their governments of targeted killings against their own civilians.'

'Hang on,' said Carradine, with a tone that he hoped would convey his contempt for Karel's theory. 'Are you suggesting the British are involved as well?'

'I never said there was British involvement.' Karel fixed him with a sharp gaze. 'But how would I know? Certainly there have been Agency plans to torture or kill the family members of anybody who carries out a Resurrection attack on American soil. It will be very interesting to see what happens to young Otis Euclidis, if he suffered the same fate as . . .' Karel unfolded the newspaper, turning to the photograph on the front page so that he could remind himself of the name. ' . . . the same fate as this poor woman, Lisa Redmond, whose only offence, as far as I can tell, was to write a few immature, reactionary articles about Islam and Brexit and occasionally to be critical of the regime in Moscow. If Euclidis is found dead, you can guarantee they will go after the kidnappers. They probably already know who took him. After all, these people are not amateurs.'

As was always the case when listening to fantasists and provocateurs, Carradine experienced a creeping self-doubt. There was something about Karel's demeanour that convinced him that he should probe more deeply into the accusations he was making.

'Is everything all right?' Karel asked.

'Absolutely,' Carradine replied.

He wished that he had the means to contact Oubakir, to ask him outright what he knew about Sebastian Hulse. Why had the Moroccan warned him as he left Blaine's? What did he know about the American? The other passengers had begun to gather up their belongings and to stand in the aisle. Carradine found himself muttering, 'No, they're not stupid', as Karel stood up, leaving his newspaper and banana skin on the table.

'What did you say?'

'Nothing,' Carradine replied.

Karel looked nonplussed. 'Well, enjoy your visit to Marrakech.'

'I will. You too.' Carradine wondered if they should swap numbers. 'Do you have a card?' he asked. He took one of his own from his wallet and handed it to Karel. He wanted to take the old man's photograph but could not think of a natural way of doing so.

'I do,' Karel replied. He reached into the breast pocket of his jacket and pulled out a die-stamped business card. The name KAREL M. TRAPP was printed on the front. Carradine thought of Mantis and assumed that 'Trapp' was a pseudonym in the same style. He turned the card over. There was a black-and-white photograph of what looked like a lotus leaf on the reverse side.

'Thank you,' he said. 'It would be good to keep in touch.'

'Indeed.'

Karel retrieved his Panama hat from the luggage rack and placed it on his head. He smiled courteously and made his way towards the door on the platform side. Carradine reached up for his bags, lowered them onto the table and sat down. The train moved slowly along the platform, eventually coming to a juddering halt. A woman close to Carradine was knocked off balance. He caught her by the arm. She thanked him in French and smiled gratefully.

Stepping out into the heat of the afternoon, Carradine could not shake off the possibility that Karel was onto something. Simakov. Milne. Redmond. The names were like a roll call of the dead. Bartok could be next on the list. If that was the case, was Carradine being used as a patsy? What if Mantis was not who he had pretended to be? What if the Service had sent C.K. Carradine to Morocco not to save Lara Bartok, but to assist in her assassination?

'I don't like your American friend. I don't trust him. What is his name?'

'Hulse,' said Somerville. 'Sebastian Hulse. He's with the Agency.'

'Tell me something I didn't already know.'

'He was the one trailing Carradine in Morocco.'

'I knew that too.'

They were walking near the safe house. Bartok was wearing sunglasses with a hat pulled down low over her head. Somerville hadn't eaten in over six hours and was cranky for a cigarette.

'What happened to Kit after he left the boat?' Bartok asked.

'I'm afraid I'm not at liberty to say.'

'Why not?'

'Because we don't yet know all the facts.'

Bartok took off the sunglasses. She wanted him to be able to see the despair she was feeling.

'I don't believe you. You know exactly what happened to him. You have all the facts, all the information, but you refuse to tell me.'

'Lara . . .'

'Where is he? What happened to him?'

'Let's go back to the flat.'

She tucked the sunglasses into the pocket of her coat and

turned away. Somerville's willpower broke and he finally succumbed to the desire for a cigarette, only to reach into his jacket and realise that he had left the packet at home.

'Let's finish the interview, get it done,' he said. 'Afterwards I can tell you everything you need to know about Carradine.'

'Everything I want to know, not just need to know,' she said. 'You don't control that.'

He was astonished to see a tear in her eye. Bartok wiped it away and turned in the direction of the safe house.

'Fine,' he replied. 'I'll answer all your questions.'

'All of them,' she said. 'Let's get it done.'

SECRET INTELLIGENCE SERVICE
EYES ONLY / STRAP 1

STATEMENT BY LARA BARTOK ('LASZLO')
CASE OFFICER: J.W.S./S.T.H. – CHAPEL STREET
REF: RESURRECTION/SIMAKOV/CARRADINE
FILE: RE2768X

PART 3 of 5

I left Ivan [Simakov] in New York. One day I was there. The next I was not. I didn't explain myself. I didn't write him a letter or give any reason. I knew that if I told him I was going he would try to prevent me leaving. Surprise was my only chance of escaping and making a new life. Sometimes I regret the choices I have made. I never regretted that choice. His behaviour had become intolerable. He was drinking a lot. He cheated on me with other women. On one occasion, during an argument, he had hit me. I did not feel that I could go to ███████ ████████ or contact ███████████████. I didn't trust anybody – even ████████████████ – to protect me. I had money, I had passports, some of which were known to you, some of which were not. I had enough knowledge of what the Service and the Agency were capable of in terms of trying to find me that initially it was not particularly difficult to vanish and to try to start again.

I went to Mexico, as you know. I always worked on the same set of principles: that it was better to be in cities where a kind of anonymity was guaranteed than to present myself in, say, a smaller community where I could be noticed as I tried to blend in. I found men. Not serious men, but lovers who would want me only for their own short-term pleasure. If a man began to expect more of me, I shut him off. I was ruthless. These men had apartments, houses, places I could go if suddenly I needed to leave wherever it was that I was staying. I lived in hotels, hostels, apartments - at one point in a cabin on a beach in Cancun. I never stayed in the same place for more than a few weeks. At first I relished this freedom. I did not miss Ivan or Resurrection. I felt that I had escaped from a prison of my own creation. I was a free woman - or, at any rate, as free as a person in my situation could ever be.

Then I learned of the deaths of the relatives of Resurrection activists in Russia. I read about Ivan's family. I wanted to contact him, to reach out and to console him. I knew that it was the Russian method and - of course - it is noticeable that while Resurrection actions around the world have continued to increase in the last two years, in Moscow, St Petersburg and elsewhere in the Russian Federation they have come to a stop. Moscow got what Moscow wanted. If you do not care what the other side thinks, if you have no moral compass or sense of shared human responsibility, anything is possible. That is one of the lessons we have learned from the past few years, no? The liars and bullies of the alt-right, the apologists for the NRA, the gluttons of the corporate world, they found a new voice, a new encouragement from the mass population. They became energised. They thought: 'We can do what we want. We can spread lies, we can spread hate, we can spread fear. We do not care about the consequences.' Moscow merely added a sadistic dimension to this: 'We take pleasure in the destruction of our enemies and in the accumulation of power.'

When I heard the news that Ivan himself had been killed, I did not believe it. I screamed. I remember nothing other than falling to my knees and crying for hours. My grief was inconsolable. I knew that Ivan had become paramilitary, that he was planning attacks, bombings and so forth. I didn't think that he would be stupid enough to try to create his own device. He had people to do that. People he knew who could facilitate such things. To be killed while in the act of preparing a home-made bomb, it was tragic and stupid and humiliating. So of course I blamed the Russians. I thought at one point that both the Agency and Moscow was behind it. The Agency or Moscow or even the Service.

Who knew? Anybody in the secret world is capable of anything.

I wept also for Zack Curtis. We had worked together. I knew him well. He was a decent man with only good intentions. He was the best of us. There are things that I did, choices I made, actions I took in those early months of the movement which I regret. I was no angel. One of the newspapers compared me to Ulrike Meinhof, which was ridiculous and lazy journalism. I was never paramilitary. I never fired a gun or planted a bomb. But I was vicious, at times cruel. Zack was better than that. Purer. He had joined Resurrection because he believed in the power of individual action. He believed that one man can change the world by his deeds, however small.

Zack had a favourite analogy. He would say: 'Resurrection will be like the effect of closed-circuit cameras on criminals. If a thief knows that his robbery of a convenience store or the mugging of a defenceless old lady is going to be recorded by CCTV and submitted to the police for prosecution, he stops robbing the convenience store. He does not mug the old lady. Suddenly he is *accountable*. He begins to think about his behaviour and to *reform*.' That was all Zack wanted. Reformed behaviour. A greater accountability. You'll say that I was naive, perhaps even deluded, but I really thought that in time

Resurrection would bring about some kind of return to basic human decency.

We were talking about Kit. This I can tell you with absolute certainty. Before Marrakech, I had never heard of C.K. Carradine. I had never read his books, I had not seen the movie they had made of his novel. He used to joke that the film was 'apocalyptically bad'. His work and career had passed me by. I knew nothing about him personally. That is the truth. I had had no contact with Robert Mantis for more than a year. You suggested that Mantis may have told me about him. How could he? How could this be possible? None of you had any idea where I was.

17

The festival organisers had sent Carradine the address of a riad in the heart of the old city. He was scheduled to stay for two nights. Though his taxi driver claimed to have been born and bred in Marrakech, it quickly became clear that he had no sense of direction and even less idea of the location of the hotel. Criss-crossing the Medina three times, Carradine eventually used his iPhone to pinpoint the riad to a building in the Kasbah. There was no air-conditioning in the car and he was soaked in sweat by the time he arrived at the address. A well-known American author was knocking on a nondescript wooden door half-hidden between a bakery shop and a makeshift stall selling cleaning products. Carradine settled the fare with the driver. He had barely removed his bags from the boot when the taxi screeched off, leaving him standing at the side of a noisy, dusty street in the full glare of the after-noon sun. Carradine crossed the road and followed the American into the building, closing the door behind him.

It was an oasis. Within an instant the clamour and heat

of the Kasbah had subsided. Carradine walked along a narrow passageway towards a reception desk where a young male Moroccan was attending to a guest. Both were speaking in Arabic. On closer inspection Carradine recognised the guest as an Irish novelist, Michael McKenna, who had won a prestigious award for his most recent book. A genial middle-aged Frenchman with a trimmed goatee appeared from a side door and introduced himself as the owner of the hotel.

After five minutes Carradine had been checked in and shown to his room at the edge of a pretty, tiled courtyard with a fountain at its centre. The only sounds were of birdsong and cascading water. He left his bags in the room and explored the rest of the building, passing beneath a series of exquisitely carved Moorish arcades offering glimpses into dark, secluded rooms furnished in leather and mahogany. A woman in a dark green bikini was sipping a glass of mint tea beneath a parasol at the side of a long rectangular swimming pool. The pool was lined on both sides by orange trees in full fruit. Beneath them, dining tables covered in white linen cloths had been set out in neat rows. Carradine felt as though he had been deposited in a travel brochure for the super-rich.

'Enjoying yourself?'

He turned around. The question had been directed at another guest, a celebrity historian with a nest of peroxide blond hair whom Carradine recognised from the television. Behind him, standing in a small group at the edge of a tiled colonnade, were several other writers and academics clutching cameras and bottles of water. Carradine assumed that they had returned from a sightseeing trip. Under normal circumstances he would have approached them and introduced himself, but in the aftermath of all that had happened in Casablanca, he felt strangely alienated from his fellow writers. Writer or spy? He was neither one thing nor the other.

He walked back to his room and began to unpack.

He woke up half an hour later, fully clothed, having fallen asleep on his bed. He looked at his watch. It was almost six o'clock. He searched for a safe in the room in which to keep the memory stick and the package for Bartok but did not trust the small metal box in the wardrobe with only a simple key to secure it. If he was under suspicion, his room would be searched and the envelope discovered in a matter of minutes. Having taken a shower and changed into a fresh set of clothes, Carradine instead took the package and the stick to the reception desk and left them, along with his own passport, in the hotel safe. A member of staff gave him a receipt for the items which he placed in his wallet. He drank an espresso in the dining area before leaving the riad to explore Marrakech. He wanted to search for Bartok, even if his hopes of finding her were infinitesimally small. Mantis was banking on the fact that she might show her face at the festival, but there was also a slim chance that Bartok would go for a walk in the evening, when the intense heat of the Moroccan day had passed, and risk being seen as she searched for a place to eat.

As Carradine walked outside into the chaos of the Kasbah, he recognised the scale of the task facing him. There were hundreds of pedestrians in every direction; it was like looking out over a crowded railway station at rush hour. The pavements were so packed, the streets so jammed with cars and buses and bikes, that surely it would be impossible to make out Bartok's face even if she happened to be in the Medina. Almost all the women Carradine saw – locals and foreigners alike – had their heads covered with shawls or hats. Bartok knew that she was being hunted and had perhaps chosen a Muslim country precisely for this reason; she could conceal her features from the lenses of distant drones and satellites, as well as from the prying eyes of those, like Carradine, who had been sent to look for her.

He walked around the Kasbah for more than an hour. He saw a veiled mother, her children in rags, begging at the side of the road, a sign propped up beside them on which had been scrawled in both French and English: *'Syrian family in need of help'*. He saw an ornate green-and-white painted cart being pulled through the clogged streets by a starving horse, a young couple kissing on the back seat. He spotted hand-painted teapots and wooden chess sets for sale, groups of women sitting on plastic chairs offering henna tattoos to tourists. What he did not see, however, was LASZLO.

Twice Carradine took out Bartok's tiny, crumpled photograph to remind himself of her face; he had begun to doubt that he would recognise her even if she passed him at the festival the following day. At around half-past seven he gave up on his fruitless search and settled in a restaurant at the edge of Place des Ferblantiers, an open square to the south of the Kasbah filled with children playing in the last of the sunlight. He ordered spaghetti bolognese from the Italian page of a pictorial menu and did *The Times* quick crossword on his iPhone.

Just as Carradine's food was arriving, an older couple settled at the next table, placing hats and guidebooks and a Leica camera on the seat closest to him. The woman, who was strikingly beautiful, smiled as she opened the menu. Her husband had gone to the bathroom and she ordered a beer for him. She took out a brochure for the literary festival and began to flick through it.

'Are you going?' Carradine asked, leaning across the gap between their tables.

'Excuse me?'

He put his fork down and raised his voice above the wail of the call to prayer. The woman had an English accent and was wearing a silk headscarf.

'Are you going to the literary festival?'

'We are!' she replied. 'Are you?'

It transpired that the woman, who introduced herself as Eleanor Lang, was a retired lawyer from Canterbury who had been sailing around the western Mediterranean with her husband, Patrick. They kept a yacht in Ramsgate that was currently moored in the marina at Rabat and were coming to the end of a three-week visit to Morocco that had taken them to Chefchaouen, Fez and the Atlas Mountains. Patrick, who shook Carradine's hand vigorously when he returned to the table, was at least ten years Eleanor's senior and had the easy-going charm and worn good looks of a man who had probably made a great deal of money in his life and spent it on at least two wives. In appearance he reminded Carradine strongly of the elderly Cary Grant.

'Kit here is a novelist appearing at the festival tomorrow,' Eleanor told him. Carradine was tangling with his Bolognese.

'Really? What sort of novels do you write?'

They chatted for more than half an hour, gradually pulling their chairs closer together and sharing recommendations on places to visit in the Medina. Carradine explained that he would be appearing on a panel at two o'clock the following afternoon. Eleanor declared that she would download everything he had ever written – 'It's so easy with my Kindle' – and promised that they would come to his event.

'You really don't have to do that,' Carradine told her. 'Thousands of better things to be doing in Marrakech.'

'Nonsense! We find it's so hot during the days, don't we, darling? It'll be nice to be in the air conditioning listening to some intelligent conversation.'

'She doesn't get much of that at home,' said Patrick, reaching for Eleanor's hand.

Carradine was reminded of his parents' marriage. Every now and again he would meet a couple who seemed so content in one another's company that it made him yearn for a relationship of his own.

'Where are you staying?' he asked.

'The Royal Mansour.'

He wasn't surprised. The Leica was state-of-the-art; Eleanor and Patrick were wearing his'n'hers Omega wristwatches; their yacht, an Oyster 575, had been built on spec three years earlier. They could afford five hundred dollars a night at the Mansour.

'I hear it's nice,' he said and listened as Patrick talked about his career in advertising and his 'second incarnation' as a property developer. The conversation felt like the first authentic, relaxed interaction Carradine had experienced since leaving London. Initially it had occurred to him that they might have been Service personnel sent to watch over him and that the meeting in the restaurant had not been a chance encounter. Yet Eleanor and Patrick had seemed so relaxed and happy, and their legend so watertight, that Carradine had quickly set aside any doubts. It was almost eight-thirty by the time he had settled his bill and said goodnight. They swapped numbers and promised to meet after the panel the following afternoon.

'You can sign one of your books for my daughter,' said Patrick.

'Happy to,' Carradine replied.

'She's single,' said Eleanor with a step-mother's knowing wink. 'Doctor, lives in Highbury.'

Carradine went out into the square. Darkness had fallen and swifts were swooping over the rooftops in the moonlight. He walked back in the direction of the riad, quickly becoming lost in the switchback side streets of the souk. Mopeds came at him from both directions, buzzing and weaving along the narrow alleyways. He learned to hug one side of the street and to trust that the drivers would steer around him, just as they steered around the other pedestrians wandering past the jewellery stores and carpet sellers and barber shops lining the souk. Men pushing metal trolleys piled high with boxes would appear suddenly from side alleys, clattering and bouncing along the uneven lanes. There was a constant noise of engines and conversation, smells of exhaust fumes and burning charcoal cut by mint and cumin and manure. Carradine studied the faces of passing women but saw nobody who resembled Bartok. Most of the Moroccan women were accompanied by men or part of larger groups; in an hour he saw only two or three female tourists walking on their own.

Eventually he came into a large open area lined on one side with brightly lit stalls selling orange juice and fresh fruits. Carradine assumed that he had reached Jemaa el-Fna, the great square at the western edge of the souk which he had spotted earlier from the cab. A drumbeat was sounding beneath a black sky lit by the shard of a crescent moon; it was as though the thousands of people crowding the square were being lured to a feast or ancient festival. The central section of the square was crammed with outdoor restaurants serving food to customers at trestle tables under white lights. If Bartok was in Marrakech, this might be a place that she would come to eat, assured of relative anonymity. Each of the trestle tables was crowded with customers, some of them backpackers on a budget, others Moroccan families and groups of friends feasting on fried fish and *merguez* sandwiches. Carradine passed tables piled high with sheep's heads and raw livers, booths selling snails drenched in garlic butter. To a soundtrack of ceaseless drums and wailing flutes he moved through the thick crowds, dizzied by the night-time circus of Jemaa el-Fna, the glow from mobile phones and open fires throwing eerie light onto faces, the atmosphere acting on him like a narcotic dream. Ever since he had met Mantis, Carradine had felt transported into a parallel world, another way of thinking about himself and his surroundings; a world that was as alien to him as a chapter in the Arabian Nights or the Berber poem passed down through the centuries and now repeated by an old, bearded man, seated on a tattered rug in front of him, taking coins from passers-by as he intoned his ancient words.

Carradine sat on a bench beside a wall at the edge of the Medina. He had bought a half-litre bottle of water from a stall in the square and drank it while smoking a cigarette. He looked at his watch. It was already ten o'clock, but the city showed no sign of slowing down. The pavements were still packed with pedestrians flowing in and out of the Medina; the traffic on the road leading north into Gueliz was almost bumper-to-bumper. He stood up from the bench, offering his seat to a frail, elderly man whose face was scarred and as dry as sand. As he walked along Avenue Mohammed V, boys as young as five or six, sitting alone on the pavement with no adults in sight, plaintively offered him cigarettes and plastic packets of Kleenex, begging for coins as he passed. Carradine gave them whatever change he could find in his pockets, their gratitude as wretched to him as their solitude.

An hour later, having walked in a wide circle which had brought him to a shuttered concrete shopping mall in Gueliz, Carradine stubbed out a final cigarette and began to look around for a taxi. He was due to appear at the festival in less than twelve hours' time and had done nothing to prepare for his event. At no point had he seen anyone resembling Bartok, nor felt much confidence that he would do so the following day. This, after all, was a woman who had proved so adept at eluding capture that the Service had been forced to resort to the luck of amateurs such as himself and Mohammed Oubakir to try to find her.

Speak of the devil. Standing directly opposite him on the other side of the road, was Oubakir. The man he had known as 'Yassine' was looking at his phone while speaking to a middle-aged woman wearing a yellow veil

165

and a pale blue *kaftan*. To judge by their body language, she was a close friend or relative; perhaps she was Oubakir's wife. Carradine concealed himself behind an orange tree at the side of the street. A taxi pulled up alongside Oubakir's companion. She opened the passenger door and stepped inside, leaving Oubakir alone. Carradine shouted across the road.

'Yassine!'

Oubakir looked up and squinted, as though he was having trouble bringing Carradine into focus. For a moment it looked as if Mantis's agent was going to ignore him, but he eventually raised his hand in slow, bewildered acknowledgement and watched as Carradine crossed the road.

'Mister Kit,' he said. 'What are you doing here?'

'I was going to ask you the same question. Let's get a drink.'

18

They went to a café on the next corner. It was empty save for two old men playing dominoes at a table on the far side of the terrace. Carradine ordered a Coke, Oubakir a black coffee. He was wearing clothes almost identical to those he had sported in Blaine's: dark cotton trousers and a striped shirt with a plain white collar. The lenses of his glasses were blurred with grease and dust. Oubakir wiped them on a paper napkin. He looked very tired.

'You are here in Marrakech for the festival,' he said.

Carradine took it as a statement rather than a question.

'That's right. And you? London didn't say anything about you coming here.'

Carradine had decided to play the role that Oubakir had assigned to him in Casablanca: that of the experienced writer spy sent by the Service to run 'Yassine'.

'They did not?' The Moroccan looked surprised. 'Perhaps I should have mentioned it.'

'That's all right.'

'You are also looking for the woman?'

Carradine lit a cigarette. He had not expected Oubakir to be so explicit about the search for Bartok. Nevertheless he ran with the conceit, wondering if the Moroccan knew about Bartok's links to Simakov and Resurrection.

'We have people looking for her all over the place,' he said. 'There's a strong chance she may show her face at the literary festival. Have you had any luck?'

Oubakir took a sip of the black coffee, losing his gaze in the cup.

'None.'

'Don't worry about it. Me neither.'

The Moroccan looked up and smiled gratefully, running a hand over the bald dome of his head.

'You know about tomorrow?' he asked.

Carradine played for time. 'What part of it?'

'The envelope. The package for the woman. You are to give it to me at the festival, yes?'

It was confirmation that Carradine had been sacked. He felt a collapsing sense of annoyance and irritation. Why hadn't Mantis told him personally that he wanted the passport and credit card handed over? He checked his phone. Sure enough there was a message waiting for him on WhatsApp.

Yassine is going to come to your talk tomorrow. Can you give him the package I sent to you? Very important that you do so. Hope all going well out there at the festival. Thanks again for all your help.

Carradine lowered the phone. If he did as Mantis asked, and then happened to find Bartok, he would no longer have any way of assisting her. He had to continue to defy

Service orders in order to do what he thought was right.

'You look concerned,' said Oubakir.

Carradine forced a smile. 'I'm just tired,' he said.

'*You* are tired!'

Oubakir's temper suddenly flared. He drained his coffee, setting the cup down angrily.

'I am risking my life for you. My family. My job. I did not expect to do this sort of work when I agreed to help your country.'

Carradine found himself in the unusual position of pretending to be a bona fide British intelligence officer trying to mollify a Service agent on behalf of a man who had just fired him for incompetence.

'Yassine,' he said, wondering if he should have referred to Oubakir as 'Mohammed'. 'Please. We understand the risks you are taking. The Service is very grateful for the sacrifices you are making. Believe me, I know the strain you are under.'

'Yet you are the one who complains of being tired . . .'

Carradine squeezed the Moroccan's forearm in an effort to reassure him.

'I'm sorry. It was ridiculous of me to talk about my own tiredness when you are the one under stress.' He was as bemused by his ability to act out the part of an agent runner as he was bewildered by Oubakir's willingness to lap it up. 'What can we do to help you? Do you want to go back to Rabat?'

The Moroccan's pride prevented him from yielding to Carradine's suggestion. With a stiff shake of the head he folded his arms and looked out at the street.

'I am fine,' he said. 'I am just concerned about the American, that is all.'

'You mean the man in Blaine's?'

'Yes, of course I mean the man in Blaine's. I have seen him in Marrakech.'

Carradine was again obliged to conceal his consternation.

'You saw him today?'

'Yes. Tonight, in the Medina. He was sitting in a café alone. What do you make of this?'

Carradine did not know what to make of it. Sebastian Hulse could have a dozen different reasons for being in the city. Had he come to Marrakech specifically to follow him or did he have other plans? Carradine also wondered what had become of Ramón. Were they working together or had Hulse left him behind in Casablanca? He wished that he knew why Mantis had fired him. It would have been so much easier to confess to Oubakir that he was playing a role for which he was neither trained nor sanctioned, but his pride would not allow it.

'Did he see you?'

Oubakir leaned back in his seat, folded his arms and said: 'Of course not. I was careful. I used my training.'

'Good. I'm sure you did.' Carradine stubbed out the cigarette, wondering what to say next. He came up with: 'Why did you warn me about him?'

'That was in my report,' Oubakir looked affronted. 'Two months ago.'

'I don't see all your reports.' The lie came to him as easily as switching on a light. 'The product you send us is considered to be very sensitive. The circulation on the intelligence is limited to my superiors.'

Carradine had rarely seen a man trying so hard to conceal his delight. Oubakir swayed to one side, fighting to suppress a smile, and turned to order a second cup of coffee.

'Will you have something?' he beamed.

'Not for me, thank you.'

The owner of the café acknowledged the order and went into the kitchen. There was a moment of silence. Carradine could see that he was going to have to prompt him.

'You were going to tell me about Sebastian Hulse.'

'Oh yes.' Oubakir lowered his voice and leaned forward. There was no chance that they could be overheard – the two old men playing dominoes had left the now deserted café – but the Moroccan was plainly keen to sustain an atmosphere of the clandestine. 'Hulse is under suspicion. We think he has made links with the Russian programme.'

Carradine immediately thought of Karel's claim that the Russian government was actively killing the friends and relatives of known Resurrection activists. Did Hulse's presence in Morocco verify Agency collaboration with Moscow's plan?

'I see,' he said. He was trying to think of a way of putting questions to Oubakir that would not reveal his ignorance. 'The Russian programme is something the Service is keeping under wraps. What do your side know about it?'

'Only what the British have told us at a government level. That Moscow is carrying out state-sponsored assassinations. And that Miss Bartok is a target because of her relationship with the late Ivan Simakov.'

So Karel wasn't just a jumped-up fantasist peddling conspiracy theories to strangers on a train. The threat against Bartok was real.

'And you think Ramón and Hulse are involved with them?'

For the first time Oubakir looked at Carradine with a degree of suspicion.

'That is not for me to say,' he replied. Carradine could sense his reluctance to continue with the conversation. Partly out of irritation, partly out of a desire to push Oubakir into further indiscretions, he took a risk.

'It's something that London is worried about.' He lit another cigarette, trying to look nonchalant. 'We've known about the Russian policy for some time. We've been trying to find out what's going on from the American side.'

Oubakir shrugged. He would not be persuaded to talk in more detail about what he knew: perhaps he had concluded that Carradine was too far down the pecking order to be trusted with such sensitive information.

'Well, no doubt we shall see,' he said.

Carradine indicated that the owner was coming back with the second cup of coffee. With the obvious purpose of changing the subject, Oubakir embarked on a discussion about tourism in Marrakech. Less than five minutes later he had finished the coffee and proposed that they go their separate ways.

'Why don't you meet me at my riad tomorrow afternoon?' Carradine suggested. 'Is five o'clock OK? I can give you the package.'

'That would be great.'

They swapped numbers. Carradine gave Oubakir the address of the riad, realising that he would have only a few hours the following day in which to try to find Bartok. That idea now seemed increasingly pointless: he would need to spend the morning preparing for his panel. They hailed separate cabs, Carradine reaching the riad a short time later and banging repeatedly on the wooden door before it was opened by a sleepy night manager in a stained shirt. He was asked to show some identification before being allowed inside.

'I am sorry, sir,' the night manager explained, once it had been established that Carradine was a guest. 'We have many people trying to come into the hotel. It is my job to keep you safe. To preserve your privacy.'

It was only when Carradine was back in his room, swallowing a sleeping pill and setting his alarm to wake him in less than five hours' time, that he began to question whether he should blow the whistle on what he had discovered. A secret Russian plan to kill the innocent friends and family members of known Resurrection activists, a plan with possible American involvement, was a scandal. He had signed the Official Secrets Act – yes – but what was to prevent him contacting one of his old colleagues from the BBC and leaking the story? Something had to be done, not only to protect Bartok but also to expose whoever was behind the alleged plot. Yet Carradine had no evidence to support Karel's theory, nor any way of finding out if Oubakir had been telling him the truth.

What he needed was proof.

19

The chambermaid's name was Fatima. She had been working at the Sheraton for four years, starting in the laundry, graduating to rooms when one of the girls got married and moved to Fez. Fatima was thirty-one. She had two children – a boy of six and a girl of four – with her husband, Nourdin, who was a builder.

Every now and again she would come into conflict with a guest. Usually it was with men, very occasionally with the foreign women who stayed in the hotel. They would shout at her, they would curse, barking orders to change the towels or find softer sheets or make sure they were not overcharged for the minibar. Often Fatima would walk in and find guests asleep or wandering naked around the room. On a few occasions, she had opened the door and heard couples having intercourse in bed. All of this was a normal part of her job. She liked the Americans best because they made sure to leave her money when they left. One man, from San Francisco, told her that tipping was like the time zones on a map: the further east you went – 'chasing sunsets' he called it – the less generous people became.

Only on two occasions had she experienced serious trouble with a guest. Very soon after she first started cleaning the rooms on the upper floors of the hotel, she had encountered a man who was drunk and became very aggressive towards her, closing the door of the room and pushing her up against the wall. Fatima had managed to escape and the guest had subsequently been questioned by the police. She later discovered that he had been mixing prescribed medications with alcohol and that a French diplomat had been summoned from Rabat to represent the guest's interests with the police and with the hotel management.

Never before had any kind of financial offer been made to her. The Spanish man who propositioned her on Tuesday evening was disgusting – his clothes dirty, his skin covered in tattoos and thick black hairs. He offered her two hundred euros to stay in the room with him, waving the money in his hand back and forth with a revolting smile on his face, as though he believed that everything could be bought in Morocco, that he could own any woman. Fatima had never been told that she was beautiful; she did not think of herself as an attractive woman, as the sort of person in whom a guest would be interested for sex. The Spanish guest – she discovered that his name was Ramón Basora – had not seemed drunk or high on drugs. He was instead most probably one of those men who needed a woman all the time, in the same way that some people could not help themselves eating too much or drinking excessive quantities of alcohol. The Spaniard was greedy and vain and arrogant. She had told him no and had left the room immediately.

All the girls knew the story about the French politician and the chambermaid in New York. They had received advice and training from the management in how to deal with sexual aggression from guests of this kind. Even so, Fatima had been so shocked by the offer, so appalled and upset by what the man had proposed, that she had not reported it. She had said nothing to the other girls, nothing to her mother, not a word to Nourdin. She was worried that the Spaniard might be an important man and that she could lose her job. She had felt ashamed and wanted to forget all about what had happened.

She had not seen Mr Basora since he had waved her out of the room on Tuesday saying: 'Fine, no problem, I'll just find somebody prettier.' She had not worked the next day and had hoped that he would have checked out by the time she returned to the Sheraton at dawn on Thursday. This was not the case. She checked the list and saw that he was still registered at the hotel, in the same room on the sixth floor. Passing the room at eight o'clock she saw a 'Do Not Disturb' sign hanging on the handle. It was still there three hours later and had not been moved by midday, when she was due to go off shift. She assumed that he had left the hotel to attend whatever meetings had brought him to Casablanca and knocked gently on the door.

There was no answer. Fatima used her passcard and slowly opened the door, whispering 'Hello, sir, hello' as she walked inside.

The stench of vomit was so overpowering that she gagged and went out into the corridor to take a towel from the trolley with which to cover her face. Fatima then returned to the room.

A man was lying naked on his back, close to the bed, his eyes open, his mouth hanging slack to one side and filled with what seemed to be a dried white paste, like milk which had been left out too long in the sun. She could see a torn condom wrapper on the carpet beside him. Fatima retched, running out of the room into the corridor. She knew that she was not supposed to alarm the guests – she had been trained to be modest in her appearance and behaviour – but she screamed as she ran towards a family at the far end of the corridor. There was a man with them. She grabbed him by the arm, imploring him to find a doctor.

'There is a man,' she said, pointing in the direction of Basora's room. 'A guest. Please help him. He is Spanish. Something has happened to him. Something terrible.'

20

Carradine took breakfast beneath the orange trees, eating scrambled eggs on toast while watching a celebrity chef doing freestyle laps and tumble turns in the swimming pool. The famous American author and the equally celebrated Irish novelist were seated opposite one another at separate tables, the former eating muesli and yoghurt, the latter attempting what appeared to be a Sudoku puzzle on his iPad. Neither man acknowledged Carradine.

He went back to his room to prepare for the festival. He learned what he could about Katherine Paget – speed-reading her Amazon reviews, memorising salient points from her Wikipedia page, watching an interview she had given on *Newsnight* – but felt suspended between two worlds. The first – that of his profession, of his peers – now seemed to him a place of fantasy and escapism which he found faintly preposterous; the second was a real world consisting of tangible threats far removed from the stories C.K. Carradine had woven in the pages of his thrillers. Yet he could no more afford to cancel his appearance at the festival than he could pretend to be a significant actor in the hunt for Lara Bartok. Carradine made his living from writing fiction; men like Sebastian Hulse and Mohammed Oubakir were men of action. He was a writer, not a spy. To think that he could intercede in the Russian plan to assassinate Bartok was foolish, perhaps even delusional.

The festival was taking place at a five-star hotel in Gueliz. The lobby smelled of cedar wood and oil money. Arab teenagers in Yankees baseball caps were slumped on sofas decorating selfies to send on Snapchat. Carradine followed signs to the conference area. A green room had been set up for the guest speakers. Carradine registered with the organisers and introduced himself to a group of sponsors from London, one of whom had read all of his novels and enthusiastically fetched him a plate of biscuits and a cup of coffee before asking him to sign a first edition of *Equal and Opposite*. At around midday Katherine Paget swept into the green room with an entourage consisting of her husband, her publicist, her literary agent and her American editor, all of whom looked exhausted by the heat of Marrakech and the strain of attending to the Great Author's every caprice. It was like witnessing the arrival of a head of state. Her eyes peering over coral-coloured half-moon spectacles, Paget introduced herself to Carradine as 'Kathy' and asked immediately if he had read her latest book.

'Cover to cover,' he told her. 'It's magisterial.'

Paget produced a self-deprecating smile. She did not return the compliment. Instead she said: 'I don't usually appear with thriller writers. Have you written many books?'

'A few,' Carradine replied.

Every ticket for their event had been sold. They were introduced by one of the sponsors from London and invited to the stage by a Moroccan radio broadcaster who had been tasked with chairing the discussion. It quickly became apparent that Paget was interested only in the sound of her own voice, regularly interrupting both Carradine and the chairman in order to promote her latest book and to voice opinions on everything from the BBC licence fee to the Tudor monarchy. In his rattled state, Carradine was happy to take a back seat, managing coherent answers to only a handful of questions, including – inevitably – his views on Islamist terror and government surveillance.

Paget was halfway through an interminable monologue about her daily writing routine when Carradine tuned out and glanced around the room. There were perhaps another five minutes before the chairman was due to take questions from the floor. The vast majority of the audience was comprised of young Moroccan students and elderly European tourists. Carradine spotted Patrick and Eleanor Lang halfway down the aisle on the left-hand side. He gave Eleanor a discreet nod. Patrick caught his eye, looked in Paget's direction and drew a finger across his throat. Carradine suppressed a smile. He looked back at Paget and tried to concentrate on what she was saying.

'Whenever I feel a little bit defeated, a little bit low and flat, I make myself a nice cup of tea and think of my readers.' A bashful smile, a modest tilt of the head. 'I can remember my last publisher but one telling me that the book I dearly wanted to write simply wouldn't sell in today's marketplace. I was dismayed, of course, but I went ahead and wrote it anyway and – thanks to the marvellous people who bought the book all over the world – it became an international bestseller.' Carradine looked at the chairman, wondering how long he would allow her to continue. 'I suppose it's a question of bravery. A writer has to keep up her morale, her desire, her *courage* to tell the stories she wants to tell. For me it's never been about prizes – although I've been lucky enough to have been nominated, sometimes even to win, many more times than I ever expected to – but rather it's about keeping one's spirits up, not getting too dejected, not feeling cross when yet another television adaptation of a period one knows inside-out keeps making basic errors of historical fact, time and again.' Paget appeared briefly to have lost the thread of her argument. Sensing that the chairman was about to interrupt, she quickly picked it up. 'Ultimately it's about the *readers*,' she said. 'It's about *you*. I never forget that.'

Carradine looked out at the audience, half-hoping that Lara Bartok had slipped in at the last minute and was sitting in one of the rows towards the back. But of course she was nowhere to be seen. The chairman was directing a question at him. Carradine turned to listen. As he did so, he was distracted by a face in the crowd. Only three rows from the front, staring at him intently, was Sebastian Hulse.

'Mr Carradine? Kit?'

Carradine was momentarily rendered incapable of speech.

'I'm sorry,' he said. 'Could you repeat that?'

To a gasp from an irritated member of the audience, Paget repeated the question herself and began to answer it, only to be silenced by Carradine.

'Oh yes, the movie business.' He had been asked about the process by which *Equal and Opposite* had been turned into a film. 'Everything you hear about Hollywood is true. It's beguiling, it's ruthless, it's exciting. There's a lot of money flying around, some big egos, some very clever people. What people don't tend to say about Hollywood is how hard they work and how good they are at their jobs. We tend to give the Americans a hard time, depict them as shallow and sentimental. That's not the case – at least, no more than anywhere else. They don't get credit where credit is due.'

Carradine again looked over at Hulse. He had not intended to shape his answer in order to curry favour with the Agency, but the man in the bespoke linen suit looked suitably gratified. He had a smile on his face that might have been interpreted as encouraging and friendly, but which seemed to Carradine slightly forbidding. He recalled the way Hulse had laid on the charm in Blaine's before more or less ignoring him as he was leaving.

'Could I speak briefly about my experiences with the various adaptations of my novels?' Paget asked. It was a rhetorical question. She had soon embarked on a lengthy critique of *Sherlock* and *Doctor Who*, before attacking the 'deleterious effects' of Simon Cowell on popular culture. Carradine scanned the room again. There was no sign of Bartok. The event ended shortly afterwards with a series of questions from the audience, most of which – to Paget's palpable fury – were directed at Carradine. Both authors promised to sign copies of their novels in the pop-up bookstore adjacent to the conference room. More than thirty people queued for Carradine, the last of whom were Patrick and Eleanor Lang, who told him that they were leaving Marrakech the following morning to return to *Atalanta*, their yacht in Rabat.

'It was absurd the way that ghastly woman monopolised the conversation,' said Eleanor as they walked outside into the furnace of the afternoon.

'Unadulterated egomaniac,' Patrick concurred. 'I've known North Korean dictators who were less self-absorbed.'

Carradine thanked them for buying the books and wished them a safe trip to Gibraltar, their next port-of-call. There were perhaps twenty or thirty people milling about outside the hotel in the searing afternoon heat. He wanted only to get back to the riad, to have something to eat and to swim in the pool. A line of taxis had queued on the road, the drivers arguing with one another for prominence in picking up passengers as they emerged from the hotel. A young Moroccan student approached Carradine and thanked him for the event. Carradine signed a French copy of *Equal and Opposite* which the student had thrust into his hands. He was about to hail a taxi when he spotted the Irish novelist, Michael McKenna, standing beneath a palm tree about twenty metres away. Perhaps they could share the ride home. McKenna was talking to a young European woman wearing Audrey Hepburn sunglasses and a cream-coloured headscarf. The scarf completely surrounded her face but not enough to disguise the fact that the woman was very beautiful. Carradine began to watch her. In order to make eye contact with the great Irish novelist, the woman removed her sunglasses and smiled at something McKenna had said.

Carradine froze. McKenna was talking to Lara Bartok.

Her face was unmistakable, right down to the slightly crooked front teeth. This was surely the woman in the powder-blue bikini with her arm around the waist of the bearded surfer. This was surely the woman from the photograph in the *Guardian*, the estranged ex-girlfriend of the late Ivan Simakov. Carradine fought the urge to go immediately towards her, to interrupt her conversation and to introduce himself, not as Kit or C.K. Carradine, but as 'a friend of Robert Mantis'. Another student approached him, asking him to sign a book. Carradine did so, unable to take his eyes from Bartok. As he passed the book back to the student, McKenna gestured at one of the drivers and took a step towards the queue of taxis. Was this his opportunity?

Carradine turned around, looking for Hulse in the crowds. The American was nowhere to be seen. Why had he come to the event only to disappear afterwards? Was his intention simply to unsettle Carradine or was he watching him? In the short time that it took Carradine to scan the crowds, both McKenna and Bartok had made their way to a taxi. McKenna held the back door open as Bartok eased inside.

Without pausing to worry that he might be under Agency surveillance, Carradine whistled for a driver and walked towards the nearest of the taxis on the rank. A young Moroccan man in denim jeans and a Paris St Germain shirt greeted him with a cheery 'Hello there, sir, where you go today?' as Bartok's cab pulled off the rank.

'You see that taxi?' he replied in French.

'Yes, sir.'

'Follow it.'

21

Carradine tracked McKenna's taxi to the riad. Instructing his driver to hold back at a distance of about fifty metres, he watched as McKenna emerged from the front seat and opened the door for LASZLO. Like a celebrity ducking through a channel of fans and paparazzi, she hurried into the riad and quickly disappeared.

Carradine paid the driver and jogged the short distance to the front door. He was embalmed in sweat, assaulted by the chaos and noise of late afternoon Marrakech. He walked past the reception desk and entered the main court-yard leading out towards the pool. It occurred to Carradine that Bartok might have gone to McKenna's room; that they were already acquainted and that McKenna was passing her a message of some kind. Perhaps he was also working for Mantis? Perhaps they were lovers? The latter possibility seemed highly unlikely – McKenna was a bald, psoriatic Catholic homunculus in his early sixties who had been married to the same woman for forty years – but anything was possible when it came to the private lives of novelists.

Carradine stopped in a short passage leading out to a patio in front of the pool. He could hear McKenna's voice. Peering out at the gardens, he saw the Irishman sitting in a low wicker armchair at the edge of the swimming area, already deep in conversation with Bartok. Bartok herself was still wearing the cream-coloured veil and Hepburn sunglasses. A waiter had brought them a bottle of mineral water and two glasses. Hoping to catch Bartok's eye, Carradine walked past their table, eavesdropping on the conversation as he stuck his hand in the shallow end of the pool, ostensibly testing the temperature of the water.

'This is what is so interesting about your books.' Her voice was exactly as Mantis had described: Ingrid Bergman speaking fluent, heavily accented English. 'The ability to sustain a kind of political commitment in literature without losing sight of the essential part of storytelling which is the characters and the relationships and the way we live our lives, yes?'

Bartok must have intuited that Carradine was staring at her because she looked up. He smiled back, trying to appear nonchalant. Bartok gave him a short nod of acknowledgement. He did not want her to be suspicious of him; he knew that she would be on guard against anyone who might have recognised her. Nor did he want to lose what would surely be his only opportunity to talk to her. Walking back past the table he looked down at McKenna and muttered: 'Forgot my goggles', a remark to which neither McKenna nor Bartok responded. On the other side of the tiled colonnade, Carradine then turned sharp left and walked towards the reception desk.

There was a young Moroccan man on duty.

'What can I do for you?' he asked.

Carradine's heart was hammering. 'I gave a package to one of your colleagues yesterday to put in the hotel safe,' he said. 'A large envelope. Can I get it out, please?'

'Of course, sir. Do you have the receipt?'

It was like the feeling of being prevented from boarding a train that was about to leave a station. Carradine explained that the receipt was in his room and that he would have to fetch it. He was desperately worried that in the time it took him to retrieve the piece of paper, Bartok would leave the riad.

'In the meantime,' he urged the receptionist, 'if you could get the envelope. As quickly as possible. It's very important.'

Carradine rushed to his room, scampering through the riad. He unlocked the door, found his wallet and grabbed the receipt. Leaving the room, he looked out towards the pool to check that McKenna and Bartok were still talking. They were. He rushed back to reception.

'Do you have it?' he asked.

'I do, sir,' the receptionist replied.

To Carradine's relief, the package was on the desk. He was asked to sign for it. He did so and took the package back to his room.

What to do next? He heard the sound of movement outside and pulled back the curtains. A maid was sweeping around the fountain on the far side of the courtyard. He picked up the package and wrote 'LASZLO' in large capital letters on the front. He then opened the door and gestured to the maid. She set her broom to one side and came towards him.

'*Oui, monsieur?*'

She was shy, almost wary of him. In his clearest French, Carradine asked if she would take the package to the woman sitting with Monsieur McKenna. She was to tell her that the guest in room five, the man who had forgotten his swimming goggles, had sent it.

'*Oui, monsieur. Quel est votre nom, monsieur?*'

'*Je m'appelle Monsieur Carradine. Je suis l'un des écrivains au festival.*'

He was sure that if the maid did as he asked, Bartok would take the bait. Carradine tipped her fifty dirhams and sent her on her way.

'Remember my name,' he whispered in French as she walked off. 'Carradine. Room Five.'

He had line of sight to the table from a narrow doorway linking the courtyard to the colonnade around the pool. He watched from the shadows as the maid headed for McKenna. After a moment's hesitation, she interrupted their conversation, gestured in the direction of Carradine's room and handed the package to 'LASZLO'.

Bartok immediately turned around. McKenna also looked in Carradine's direction, placing a hand over his eyes to block out a shaft of sunlight. Carradine was sure that he could not be seen. He took a step further back in the shaded doorway as Bartok thanked the maid. She was about to put the package on the table when she saw what had been written on the front. Carradine could sense her shock from fifty feet. Yet he noticed that she controlled her reaction, placing the package face down on the table before continuing the conversation as if nothing had happened.

Carradine waited. The maid came back and asked anxiously if she had given the envelope to the right person.

He said that she had and gave her another fifty dirhams. Other guests came into the courtyard. Carradine wondered if he should go back to the pool and try to signal to Bartok when McKenna wasn't looking. Far from being elated that he had found 'Maria Rodriguez', he was annoyed by the fact that he possessed neither the wherewithal to get her to do what he wanted her to do, nor the training to ensure that their meeting, should it ever take place, would go unobserved.

Another fifteen minutes passed. Carradine hovered around in one of the lounges off the courtyard. He sat in a leather armchair with a view through a partly opened window towards Bartok's table. At no point did she pick up the package nor show any interest in doing so. A third man joined the table. He was African but did not appear to be local: he was too well-dressed and carried himself with the easy confidence and swagger of a European or American. Bartok smiled at him warmly when the man sat down. Carradine hoped that he was not her boyfriend. Then the male receptionist who had fetched his package from the safe came into the lounge. Carradine pretended to be reading a magazine.

'Monsieur?'

Carradine looked up.

'*Oui?*'

'I have been searching everywhere for you, monsieur. There is a gentleman at the entrance who wishes to speak to you. Should I let him in?'

Carradine glanced at an ormolu clock above the fireplace. It was not yet four o'clock. Oubakir was due at five. Why the hell had he come so early?

'Did he give you his name?'

'No, sir.'

Carradine had no choice other than to abandon his surveillance and to find out who was waiting for him. He stood up, walked out of the lounge and followed the man to reception.

There, sitting alone in the narrow passageway, close to the front door, was Sebastian Hulse.

22

'Kit! How are you? Great event.'

The American stood up and shook Carradine's hand, pulling him forwards in a power grab that served only to amplify Carradine's sense of confinement.

'I'm well, thank you,' he said. He was trying to work out what the hell Hulse was doing doorstepping him at the riad.

'Thought I'd pay you a visit.'

'I see that. How did you know where I was staying?'

Hulse ignored the question.

'Enjoyed your talk,' he said.

'Thank you. Slightly took it out of me.'

'What do you mean?'

'I don't know. I don't feel a hundred per cent . . .'

'Oh. I'm sorry to hear that.'

Carradine knew that he had to get rid of him. If Hulse came into the hotel, he would see Bartok. Acting as though he was unwell seemed the most plausible strategy.

'It was a surprise to see you in the audience,' he said.

191

Hulse grinned. 'Gee, I hope I didn't make you feel sick.'

'No, no!' Carradine tried to laugh. 'I think it's a combination of the heat, the food. I'm just exhausted. I was resting actually when you asked for me.'

Carradine glanced in the direction of his room, hoping that Hulse would get the point. He looked down and saw that he was holding a copy of one of his books.

'You bought one!' he exclaimed with more enthusiasm than he had intended.

'That's right.'

'And you came all this way just to ask me to sign it?'

He was certain that Hulse had come for a different purpose. Perhaps Bartok was already under surveillance and had been observed entering the riad. He wondered if Hulse would try to book a room in order to gain access to the building. He had heard that the riad was full for the festival and prayed that this was still the case.

'Would you mind?' The American held up the book, producing a pen from the hip pocket of his trousers.

'Delighted. Who should I make it out to?'

'How about my wife?' Carradine thought of Salma and Maryam, of Hulse's hand on Salma's thigh.

'Sure. I hope she likes it. What's her name?'

'Lara.'

Carradine had already written 'To' at the top of the page. The pen stopped in his hand, a tiny circle of ink forming on the paper as he registered what Hulse had said.

'Lara? That's your wife's name?'

'Last time I checked. You look surprised, Kit.'

'No, no. It's funny. I have a friend called Lara. Dating a pal of mine. In London. I was just thinking about them actually.'

It struck Carradine how easily and seamlessly he was able to conjure the lie. Years of thinking about deception and subterfuge for his fiction had given him a kind of ghastly expertise. He completed the inscription, handing the book back to Hulse. The American looked at him with the same seemingly benign, yet sinister half-smile he had adopted during the festival. It was a look that told Carradine he was not trusted; a look that promised payback should Hulse discover that he was being deceived.

'Well, thank you for coming,' Carradine told him. He tried to appear slightly unsteady on his feet and winced in apparent discomfort. 'I'm sorry not to invite you inside for a cup of tea but I really need to rest.'

'Sure.'

Hulse shook his hand again, moving back towards the door. Carradine was almost in the clear, but at the last moment the American hesitated and turned around.

'You seen Mohammed Oubakir at all?'

He knew it was a test. The Agency probably had Oubakir under surveillance. The two of them had been seen talking in the café the night before. It would be pointless to lie.

'Yeah, as a matter of fact I ran into him last night. We had a coffee up in Gueliz.'

Hulse seemed surprised that Carradine had admitted the truth.

'Really?'

'Yeah. Why?'

'No reason. I thought I saw him at the festival, at your talk. I wasn't entirely sure.' Hulse looked down at the floor, as though lost in thought. He was about to pull open the street door when he said: 'Remind me how you know him again?'

Carradine decided that enough was enough. He had to push back.

'You ask a lot of questions, Sebastian.' A car blasted its horn outside. 'Did you come here to get me to sign a book for your wife or is there something else on your mind?'

'Forget it,' Hulse replied quickly. He stared hard into Carradine's eyes, holding the gaze.

'It's just that you've behaved pretty strangely around me . . .'

'Is that so?'

'Yeah, that's so. I didn't particularly enjoy our meeting in Blaine's.' Hulse looked genuinely offended. The ruse was working. 'Then you show up at my event and kind of stare at me like you're trying to put me off . . .'

'Kit, I can assure you . . .'

Carradine ploughed on.

'Let me finish. I didn't invite you here. I don't know how you found out where I was staying. The thing is, it's awkward for me. I don't feel comfortable around you. You keep asking about Mohammed Oubakir. I don't know why. I don't really know very much about him. There's somebody who helps me with my books in London. An intelligence officer. A spy. She was the one who gave me Mohammed's number. That's why I was meeting him in Casablanca. I'm not really supposed to talk about it but you keep pressing me. I don't know who you are or who you work for.'

To Carradine's delight, Hulse took a step forward and touched him on the shoulder.

'Look,' he said. 'I'm really sorry, man. I didn't mean to make you feel bad. Oubakir is just somebody I know from Rabat. I was trying to work out your connection.'

'It's fine.' A female guest walked between them. Hulse stepped back to allow her to pass. 'But now I really need to go and lie down. I need to rest. I'll see you around, Sebastian. Take good care of yourself.'

23

As soon as Hulse had closed the door, Carradine hurried back to the lounge. Of all people and of all things, he found himself thinking of Simon McCorkindale in *Death on the Nile*, scurrying along the side of a ship having committed murder in the dead of night. He returned to the same armchair in which he had been sitting ten minutes earlier and strained to see what was going on at the swimming pool.

Bartok had gone.

The table where she had been sitting was now empty. There were no guests seated on the patio, nobody swimming in the pool. Panic stretched out inside Carradine. He hurried to the reception desk, looked in the dining room, searched each of the lounges on the ground floor. There was a tradesman's gate at the back of the riad leading to a maintenance area where a van and two cars were parked at the edge of a quiet street. Carradine peered over the gate but could see no sign of LASZLO. He went to the spa and asked if a woman fitting Bartok's description was receiving treatment. The receptionist shook her head. Carradine went out into the gardens, looked up and saw Michael McKenna coming out of his room on the first floor of the riad.

'Mr McKenna!'

McKenna squinted, again raising a hand to block out the sun.

'Hello?'

Carradine walked up a short flight of steps.

'I'm sorry to bother you,' he said. 'I'm Kit Carradine, one of the writers . . .'

'I know who you are.'

'I was just wondering. The young woman you were talking to by the pool. Is she staying here?'

McKenna gave him an appraising smile, making the immediate – and not entirely incorrect assumption – that Carradine was attracted to Bartok and trying to track her down.

'I'm afraid not,' he said. 'I met her at the festival. She wanted to talk about books. I invited her in. Lovely girl. Clever. Hungarian originally.'

'I know,' Carradine replied.

'You were the fella that sent the package. What was that all about?'

'Long story. Did she say where she was going? Did she leave a number, a card?'

McKenna shook his head. He was carrying a swimming towel and a bottle of Factor 50 suntan lotion. His skin was the colour of chalk.

'So you have no idea where she went?'

'Afraid not. You might have to go looking for her . . .'

'Tell me about it,' Kit replied. 'Who was the other man there? The black guy? I thought I recognised him.'

'Oh, just some bigshot editor from New York. Think he was trying his luck as well.' McKenna chuckled to himself. 'Sorry not to be more helpful, young man. To be honest she did look a bit taken aback when she read your *billet-doux*.'

'She opened it?'

Carradine was impressed that Bartok would have taken such a risk in the open.

'Absolutely she did. Caused quite the intake of breath.'

They walked down the steps. McKenna suggested that Carradine join him for a drink at seven o'clock, an invitation he accepted on the basis that he expected never again to set eyes on Lara Bartok and would need several consolation martinis. McKenna headed for the pool, waving the bottle of suntan lotion over his head as he went.

'Good luck!' he cried out. 'May Cupid strike!'

Carradine continued to look in every corner of the riad. He headed to the reception desk with the intention of finding out the name of the editor from New York. It was possible that he was staying in the riad and that Bartok was in his room. He was about to speak to the same member of staff who had earlier removed the package from the safe when he saw Mohammed Oubakir sitting in the same chair that Hulse had occupied less than an hour earlier. In the dismay of losing Bartok, he had completely forgotten about their meeting.

'Mohammed.'

'I apologise, Kit. I am early. I was going to . . .'

'It's OK.'

They shook hands. Carradine was wondering what he was going to say about the package: Mantis would expect it to be handed over intact. If Oubakir was still under Agency surveillance, Hulse would now know that he had visited the riad. Carradine could feel the outside world pressing in on him, the slow, irrevocable squeeze of American power.

'You look well.'

'Thank you,' he replied. 'Listen, I need to talk.'

'Of course.'

He led Oubakir to the table where Bartok had been sitting with McKenna. The Irishman was lying on a sun lounger on the far side of the pool wearing sunglasses and a pair of bright red Speedos. His short, hairless body was entirely caked in sun cream. He looked like a patient in a burns unit.

'What is the problem, please?' Oubakir asked.

'I should have texted you.' Was it his imagination or could Carradine smell a trace of Bartok's perfume on the chair? 'I saw the girl. I've given her the package.'

The Moroccan was stunned.

'Really? This is good news. Have you told London?'

Carradine nodded. It had been an afternoon of lies. One more wouldn't do any harm. 'So you can go back to Rabat,' he suggested. 'No need to stay in Marrakech.'

'I see.'

They ordered mint tea, drinking it in the shade of the colonnade. They talked about politics and Morocco under French rule while the award-winning Irish novelist in red Speedos turned pink by the side of the pool. As the conversation progressed, a distracted Carradine began to feel that he had reached the end of the road. He had defied the Service and found LASZLO. Bartok had been given the package; her future now lay in her own hands.

Doubtless she was already on her way to the airport or to the train station armed with the Rodriguez passport and several thousand dirhams extracted from the nearest ATM. There was, however, a silver lining. Mantis had doubted Carradine's ability to find Bartok and had fired him. Yet he had proven his worth, not least by putting Hulse off the scent. If Bartok survived and made it to London, Carradine could surely expect further work from the Service.

As their conversation drew to a close, he shook Oubakir's hand and wished him well. Oubakir congratulated him a second time on making contact with Rodriguez and headed back out into the Medina. Settling the bill for their tea, Carradine glanced towards the pool. McKenna had long gone. The water looked calm and inviting. He decided to go for a swim and made his way back to his room.

The maid was still sweeping up in the courtyard. When she saw him she smiled, moving quickly into another section of the riad. Carradine took out his key, turned it in the lock and went into the room.

Bartok came at him as soon as he had closed the door.

'Who are you?' she said, pushing her hands into his chest. 'And how the fuck do you know Robert Mantis?'

24

Carradine fell backwards towards the bed.

'Jesus!' he said, regaining his balance and looking quickly around to see if anybody else was in the room. 'How did you get in here?'

'Answer me,' she hissed.

Bartok was taller and physically stronger than he had expected. She had removed her veil to reveal hair dyed peroxide blonde and cut short above the neck. Her eyes were fierce and unforgiving. Plainly she wasn't interested in explaining the whys and wherefores of how she had managed to break into the room. Carradine suspected that she had found it extremely easy.

'Answer you about *what*?' he said.

'Keep your voice down.'

'Answer. You. About. What?' he replied in a comic stage whisper. Bartok looked baffled.

'I want to know why you are here,' she said.

She picked up the remote control and turned on the

television, the news headlines on BBC World smothering the sound of their conversation.

'My name is Kit Carradine,' he replied. 'I'm a writer . . .'

'I know who you are.'

'I met Robert a couple of weeks ago. Less. Or rather he met me. He asked me to work for him. For the Service. To do them a favour while I was out here in Morocco. He asked me to look for you. He wanted me to try to find you.'

Bartok was watching Carradine very carefully, sizing him up, trying to assess if she was being lied to. He heard the sound of laughter in the courtyard and suggested that they move down into the bathroom, which was excavated below ground level and sealed with a heavy wooden door.

'Thick walls,' he explained. 'We won't be heard.'

'Fine,' Bartok replied.

They stepped down into the bathroom. Bartok sat in a narrow rattan chair beside the sink. Carradine perched on the edge of the bath. He looked for the tattoo on her left wrist but could see nothing.

'Mantis gave me a copy of your photograph,' he said. 'The same one that's in the passport. I saw some others in London and Casablanca. That's how I recognised you.'

'What photographs in Casablanca?' she said, plainly concerned. 'Where? How?'

'It's a long story.'

Her watchfulness made him think of the animals at the watering hole, wary of predators, alert to every threat. Yet Bartok seemed at the same time fearless and capable. He had the sense of an intuitive, highly intelligent woman who had made an assessment of his character and intentions within seconds of meeting him.

'I've got all night,' she said.

'I'd better start at the beginning then,' he replied.

He did just that, describing his first encounters with Mantis in London, his subsequent discovery that 'Maria Rodriguez' was the estranged girlfriend of Ivan Simakov. He told Bartok about the €3,000 payment he had left at the Sheraton for a man named 'Abdullah Aziz' who may, or may not, have been Ramón, the Spaniard he had met on the flight to Casablanca. He told her about the photographs he had seen on Oubakir's phone and their subsequent meetings in Marrakech, the most recent of which had wrapped up less than an hour earlier. He described Ramón's appearance in Blaine's in the company of a man identified by Oubakir as an American spy. That same American, Sebastian Hulse, had paid Carradine an unsolicited visit at the riad earlier that afternoon and had asked him to sign a book to 'Lara', a tactic probably designed to unsettle him. Bartok listened intently, interrupting frequently to check a detail and to ensure that she had understood Carradine correctly. She was particularly interested in Mantis's assertion that she had been spotted in north-west Africa and that the Service was '100 per cent certain' she had settled in Morocco.

'Why did he think that I wanted to return to the UK?' she asked.

Carradine told her that he did not know the answer to her question. Rarely had he experienced somebody attending to his words so closely and assiduously. At no point did Bartok give any outward indication that she was frightened, yet her tireless, detailed questions left him in no doubt that she was deeply concerned. The picture he was painting – of a possible Russian–American plot to kill her – was as malign as it was morally indefensible. By the time Carradine had finished, they had moved back into the bedroom. Bartok sat on a leather armchair beside the television, Carradine on the side of the double bed furthest from the door. The television remained switched on to disguise their conversation. The same set of head-lines on BBC World had been broadcast three times, at hourly intervals. A man had been arrested for the murder of Andreas Röhl, the AFD politician assassinated in Germany. Bartok made no comment on the story other than to point out that Röhl had been accused of taking money from sources inside Russia in order to further his political career.

'What more do you know about Robert?' she asked. Carradine could not tell if the question was an attempt to find out how deeply Carradine himself was embedded with the Service or a more personal enquiry into the wellbeing of a man for whom she possibly harboured romantic feelings.

'I think he's in love with you,' he replied.

To Carradine's relief, Bartok looked irritated.

'Still?' she said, as though she expected a man's desire for her eventually to pass a sell-by date.

'I read the note he wrote to you. "I am the man who took you to the sea." It sounded like you were in a rela-tionship of some kind.'

Bartok seemed surprised. 'Really? You concluded this? You must have a very romantic imagination, Mr Carradine.'

'Please, I keep asking you to call me Kit.'

'And you had permission to read this note?'

'I did what I had to do.'

Bartok liked that reply. She smiled for the first time.

Light came into her face and, for a fleeting moment, Carradine saw the woman she must once have been, before Simakov, before Resurrection, before a life on the run had turned her into a fugitive, watchful and suspicious.

'Robert took a great risk by sending me the passport. I suppose I should be grateful to him for that.'

Carradine was not in the mood to give credit to Mantis for anything. He indicated that he had nothing to say in response. Bartok stood up, stretching her back.

'Why did you send the maid with the envelope?' she asked. 'Why not come up to me in person?'

There was a sudden noise from the riad, a door slamming in the distance.

'I thought it was better that we weren't seen together,' he explained. 'In case there was somebody watching me or watching you.'

'So you decided just to stare at me beside the swimming pool?'

She grinned, moving to the opposite side of the bed. He realised that she was beginning to relax.

'I hadn't expected to see you,' Carradine explained, enjoying the shift in her mood. 'I wanted to be certain it was you. You took me by surprise.'

'Evidently.'

She sat on the mattress and began to look at the books stacked on the bedside table. They were both fully dressed, on opposite sides of the double bed, each with one foot secured on the ground. It occurred to Carradine that they must have looked like a married couple in an old Doris Day movie, keeping their distance for the benefit of the censor.

'Did you think it was unlikely I would survive Marrakech?' she asked, flicking through a copy of *Eastern Approaches*. Carradine was reading it for the sixth or seventh time. He found the question interesting. Did she think that Mantis had overestimated the threat against her? Did she think that Carradine himself was being paranoid about Ramón and Hulse?

'I was worried, yes,' he said. 'There were too many moving parts. One minute I was being told the Russians and Americans were bumping people off, the next I was being fired by the Service. I wasn't in a position to know what was really going on. I'm not trained. I write about this stuff. I've never *lived* it.'

'You mean you have no proof that these men mean to kill me?'

'None. No proof at all.'

'But the theory of this man on the train – Karel, was it? – this was confirmed by Mr Oubakir, no? Robert believes that there is a Russian plan to kill me, not simply to arrest me and to bring me in for questioning. That is why he sent this warning.'

'I guess.' Carradine certainly could not think of any other reason why Mantis had acted as he did. 'Isn't that what you think?' He was beginning to feel out of his depth. 'Is there something else going on that I don't know about?'

Bartok placed one of the pillows behind her back and sat up against the headboard. She kicked off her shoes, stretched out her legs and bounced up and down, like a customer testing the mattress in a showroom. Her legs were tanned, her toes slightly bent and calloused. Carradine noticed that the sides of her feet were marked with cuts and patches of dry skin. She saw this and said: 'I have ugly feet.'

'You don't.'

She looked across the bed and flashed him a smile. It was almost as if they had met before and were old friends. Of course, Carradine was aware that this was a misconception: creating an atmosphere of trust and intimacy with a man was doubtless a trick that Bartok could pull off as easily as she had kicked off her shoes. Yet he was convinced that she wanted to remain in the room, not only to extract information from him, but also because she felt safe there. She had stumbled on some sort of sanctuary.

'I was foolish,' she said suddenly.

'What do you mean?'

'I became lazy. I have known that they have been looking for me ever since it was announced that Ivan had been murdered. Before that even. Robert is correct. Your friend on the train and Mr Oubakir last night. They are all correct. The Russians want me dead. Until this moment, I did not know that the Americans had joined their death cult as well.'

'I don't have any proof that the Americans are involved,' said Carradine. 'Only this guy Hulse creeping around and the theories of Karel and Oubakir.' Some kind of machine had been started up in the courtyard outside. 'What do you mean, you got lazy?' he asked.

Bartok gestured into the room. Her gaze was both amused and cynical, betraying the intense strain she had been under for months and months.

'I went to Havana for a long time. Then to Mexico. Eventually down to Buenos Aires. Isn't that what all fugitives do? Run to South America?' Her uneasy smile encouraged Carradine to agree. 'Butch Cassidy. The Sundance Kid. Where did they go?'

'Bolivia.'

'That's right! Bolivia!'

He saw that she had an ability to take pleasure in small, amusing details, even as the world outside continued to press in on her.

'I got scared,' she said. 'In Argentina. Too many repeating faces. Too many strangers coming up to me in bars. I developed a paranoia.'

'So you came here?'

'Not at first, no.' Bartok's answer seemed to conceal a secret that she was not yet prepared to divulge. 'I went to Italy, then to Egypt. Eventually, yes, to Morocco . . .'

'Which is where you got lazy?'

'Eventually a person gets tired of running, you know?'

'I can understand.'

'It becomes almost as if you *want* to get caught, just to bring an end to it. That's how I felt. That's how I *feel*. I don't know how much longer I can go on hiding.'

Carradine was often at his most candid with perfect strangers. He wondered if Bartok had shown more of herself to him in the preceding two hours than she had revealed to any person in a long time.

'Do you have family back in Hungary?' he asked.

She shook her head quickly and decisively, as if to fend off any further questions of that kind. The telephone rang beside the bed and they both flinched. As Carradine reached to pick it up he caught her eye. They looked at one another and he felt his heart kick with desire.

'Hello?'

It was Michael McKenna.

'Michael, I'm so sorry.' He had forgotten about their drink. 'I fell asleep.'

'That's OK. Assumed that was the case. Did you find your beloved?'

Carradine had a sudden, paranoid vision of Sebastian Hulse standing over McKenna in his room, directing the conversation, listening in.

'Sadly not,' he replied. 'Vanished into thin air.'

'Pity,' said the Irishman. 'What a shame.'

'A real shame, yes.'

Bartok looked at him quizzically. Carradine mouthed the words: 'Don't worry.'

'We're all away in the morning,' McKenna continued. 'What flight are you on, Kit?'

Carradine had not looked at his schedule. He had a vague memory that he had been booked on an easyJet flight out of Marrakech that evening.

'I think I'm leaving after lunch,' he said.

'OK. So perhaps we'll see you at the airport.'

They hung up. Carradine explained to Bartok that he had forgotten to meet McKenna for a drink. She did not seem suspicious that McKenna had rung and laughed when Carradine told her about their conversation earlier in the afternoon.

'*Billet-doux*?' she said, a phrase she had never heard before and had difficulty pronouncing. 'I like this expression. He is a brilliant man. We had a wonderful conversation.'

'Didn't you think it was a risk coming to the festival?' Carradine asked. 'That somebody might recognise you?'

She bowed her head. 'That is what I meant about

209

getting lazy. The people who know me, they know that I love literature of all kinds, that I read everything. I devour books. These men who are looking for me, they would also know this. So perhaps they put two and two together and took a chance that I would come to a literary festival, out of curiosity, out of boredom.'

'They were right.'

There was a moment of silence. Carradine was vain enough to wonder if she had read any of his books, but too proud to ask. He picked up two bottles of water from the bedside table and handed one of them to Bartok. In ordinary circumstances, they might have left the room and gone to the bar of the hotel for a cocktail. He would have invited her to dinner, taken her to Le Comptoir or al-Fassia for a tagine and a bottle of red. Simple pleasures that were denied to them. It was becoming increasingly clear that they were going to be stuck in his room. If Bartok showed her face outside the riad she would be scooped up by Hulse and his henchmen within minutes.

'Why didn't you leave straight away?' he asked.

Bartok frowned. 'What do you mean, please?'

'Take the passport. Take the card. Get some money. Why didn't you take a taxi to Fez or Casablanca?'

'I needed to know who you were,' she said. 'Besides, the passport is useless.'

'Why?'

'It has no entry stamp.'

Of course. Any official at a Moroccan passport desk would want to know why there was no record of 'Maria Rodriguez' coming into the country.

'Can't you just say you lost it in the souk and this is a replacement?'

Bartok honoured Carradine with a patient smile.

'Possibly,' she said. 'That was certainly Robert's idea. Or it is a trap and there is a flag on the passport. The Moroccan authorities get suspicious, they make a telephone call, it is all over for me.'

'Why would Mantis be trying to trap you?'

Bartok appeared to have no answer to Carradine's question. He wished that he knew more about the nature of their relationship, but she had closed off his questions whenever he had raised the subject.

'Maybe he is not,' she conceded. 'I don't know. It is even possible the passport is a fake.'

'But it came to me from the Foreign Office!'

Bartok walked around the bed and came to sit next to him. Her perfume was the same scent that had been on the chair by the pool. Their knees briefly touched. She put a hand on Carradine's back, but it was not a new moment of intimacy. Rather it was the sort of gesture that a nurse or social worker might make on the brink of delivering bad news.

'There are things perhaps I should tell you about Robert,' she said.

'Go on.'

'I am afraid you are not going to like them.'

25

Carradine knew what Bartok was going to say before she said it. He let her deliver the *coup de grace*.

'Robert Mantis is not a British spy.'

'I see.'

'Robert Mantis does not work for the Service.'

An awful, hollow feeling of shame opened up inside him. It was the secret doubt that had always nagged at him, but he had never allowed himself to face it head-on. He had wanted Mantis to be genuine. He had wanted to be a latter-day Maugham or Greene, to live as his father had lived and to experience the things he had known. Carradine had taken a business card, a copy of the Official Secrets Act and a photo ID as irrefutable proof that Robert Mantis was a British intelligence officer. He had been comprehensively duped.

'Who does he work for, then? Or is he just a conman? A fantasist?'

Bartok asked if he kept any alcohol in the room. Carradine had bought some Johnny Walker at duty-free in Gatwick; the bottle was in his suitcase. He took it out, handed it to her and fetched two glasses from the bathroom, briefly staring at his own reflection in the mirror as though to remind himself what a fool he had been. She poured him two inches neat and encouraged him to join her in a toast.

'To honest men and women,' she said, clinking his glass.

'To honest men and women.'

Carradine was touched that she was trying to raise his spirits, but he was in shock. He tracked back to the long conversation in Lisson Grove. He wanted to work out why Mantis had made the last-minute switch to the Sheraton. He did not understand why he had set up the meeting with Oubakir in Casablanca. What was it all for? He could not make sense of any of it.

'I can explain.' Bartok sipped the whisky and held it in her mouth, lips pursed, as though reading his mind. She swallowed it, letting out a sigh of pleasure. 'Robert's real name is Stephen Graham. He was born in London, educated at private schools in England. He went to Cambridge, married a French schoolteacher who left him for someone else.'

'He told me he was still married.'

'He told you a lot of things that were not true.' Carradine acknowledged the remark with a defeated shake of the head. 'His father was an academic. From Scotland. You call this a Scotsman?'

'A Scotsman, yes.'

'Gordon Graham. His wife was Russian. This is the key. Yulia. I do not remember the patronymic. She came to England in the 1960s after Stephen's father met her in Moscow on an academic visit behind the Iron Curtain.'

'So she defected?'

Bartok held more of the whisky in her mouth, savouring it, indicating with quick eyes that Carradine was being impatient.

'Wait,' she said. 'Whether she defected or not is not important. I believe they fell in love and she was allowed to emigrate. Stephen Graham has worked for Moscow for his entire professional career.'

Carradine slumped forward, shaking his head. The breath went out of him. 'It's OK,' whispered Bartok and touched his back.

'Mantis tried to recruit me, too. Shortly after I left Ivan and moved from New York. Ivan had become violent, both towards me and in the context of Resurrection . . .'

'Simakov *hit* you?'

She waved away his concern.

'Never mind about that. All anyone needs to know is that I had had enough of him. Mantis wanted me to inform on the people I knew inside the movement. His typical modus operandi, the technique he has used in London and, I suppose, all over the world, with great success, is to pose as the traditional British spy. You said he had a briefcase, that he seemed slightly untidy and disorganised . . .'

'But also sharp, determined, thorough.' Carradine realised that countless others in his position had been comparably gullible. It was scant consolation.

'Of course, of course.' Bartok placed the glass of whisky by the side of the bed, allowing her to gesticulate more freely. 'All of these things. He presents himself as a Service officer, he recruits agents, he runs them, they think they are working on Her Majesty's Secret Service, but all of the information they give to Stephen is channelled back to Moscow.'

'It's very clever.'

'Very simple and very effective. Yes.'

Carradine looked at her. The whisky had brought colour to her cheeks. The nape of her neck was flushed pink.

'So you fell for this as well?' he asked.

Bartok hesitated. 'That is another story, for another time.' It was the second occasion on which Carradine had sensed that she was holding something back from him, something of significance. 'The short answer is that I did work for him, but in the knowledge that he was a liar and a fraud, a false flag. A conman as you describe him.'

Carradine asked the obvious question.

'How did you know he wasn't a British spy?'

Did Bartok possess powers of insight and analysis far beyond his own? Had she rumbled Mantis within minutes of seeing his crumpled FCO business card?

'I just knew,' she replied. 'He slipped up. His story didn't make sense. I allowed Robert to believe that he was running me.'

'Does he still think you're on the books?'

Bartok looked at him as if he had lost his mind.

'Gosh, no!' Someone clipped past in the courtyard. Bartok waited until they had passed before continuing. 'A lot has happened to me since then.'

Question after question formed in Carradine's mind. He still did not know the truth about Bartok's relationship with Mantis, just as he did not understand why Mantis had recruited him under false pretences. Was it simply to use him as an extra pair of hands in the search for LASZLO – or did Moscow have a darker purpose?

215

'Why me?' he asked.

Bartok picked up the bottle of whisky, refilled her own glass and offered more to Carradine. He nodded and she poured him another two inches.

'It sounds as though he is going behind the backs of his employers in Russia. He knows about Moscow's plan to have me killed. He has no means of contacting me, he does not know where I am, he has no way of warning me in person. So he hires anyone he can think of who is coming to Morocco. He uses agents in place in Rabat, such as Mohammed Oubakir, to look for me. From what you have told me, Ramón is almost certainly working for him. Graham knows from Facebook that you are coming here to speak at the festival, so he takes a chance and uses you as another set of eyes.'

'But that's crazy. You were a needle in a haystack.'

'Maybe it is crazy, maybe it isn't. You *found* me, didn't you?' John Simpson was plugging his latest programme on BBC World. The headlines were about to come around again. 'Who is to say there are not five or six other people, all agents of Robert Mantis, walking around Marrakech tonight looking for "Maria Rodriguez"?'

'All armed with passports and credit cards?'

Bartok shrugged. She did not have the answers to all the questions Carradine might ask. She did not pretend to.

'But why send me to the Sheraton?' he said. 'Who was Abdullah Aziz? And why the fuck did Mantis have me deliver a book cipher to "Yassine"?'

She smiled patiently, easing Carradine through his embarrassment.

'Agents need to be looked after,' she explained. 'They

need to be serviced. Mantis asks you to meet "Yassine", to carry out a simple task, he is killing two birds with the one stone. Maybe he needed to get the book to Oubakir for other reasons. You said yourself that this man thinks you are a British spy.' She paused, seeming to weigh up the good sense of teasing Carradine. 'You are no different to Stephen Graham!' she exclaimed. 'You have pretended to be somebody you are not.'

Bartok was apparently delighted by this insight and giggled as she drank the whisky. The sight of her enjoying herself had the effect of making Carradine feel slightly less angry and self-conscious. She was the best sort of company: intelligent and forthright, honest and kind.

'So who was the money for?' he asked.

'I have no idea.'

'Ramón?'

'You meet this Spaniard on your plane. We can say this is a coincidence. There is – what? – one direct flight to Casablanca from London each day? Two, maximum. Therefore it is not unusual that you are on the same journey. He is also probably working for Robert Mantis, looking for me just as you were, just as Mr Oubakir was doing. As for the money, perhaps it was to test you. Perhaps it was for this Ramón. Who knows?'

Carradine stood up. One of his legs had cramped. He walked around the room, shaking it out. Bartok looked as if she found the sight of this endearing.

'Are you all right, Kits?' she asked.

'Yes, thank you.'

He liked the way she mispronounced his name, making it sound like 'Keats'.

'So perhaps now I should leave you in peace.'

Carradine stopped moving. He looked at her. It had not occurred to him that she might leave.

'What do you mean?'

'I mean that I should go. You have done a lot for me. You have an aeroplane back to London in the morning. I have taken up too much of your time.'

'What will you do?'

Bartok hesitated. 'I do not know.'

As strong and resourceful as she was, in that moment she looked vulnerable. Carradine felt a duty of care towards her, a responsibility to protect her from the danger outside.

'Lara, if you walk out of this hotel, you'll be assassinated. The Russians know you're in Marrakech. Now the Agency will suspect I'm involved with you in some way . . .'

'You *are* involved with me in some way!' she said, trying to make light of it.

'You know what I mean.'

The BBC headlines were counting down on the hour. Carradine turned to the television, expecting the same anchorman, the same news, the same guests. He was about to switch channels when he saw that a story was breaking.

'*Gunmen associated with Resurrection have seized control of Poland's parliament building in central Warsaw . . .*'

'Jesus Christ,' he said.

Bartok stepped towards the television in a state of consternation. The anchorman continued:

'*As many as three hundred men, women and children are being held hostage inside the Sejm building. Gunshots have been fired and Polish police are reporting a number of fatalities. We join Peter Hackford, who is live at the scene . . .*'

They watched in silence as the reporter explained that as many as sixteen Resurrection gunmen had managed to shoot their way past security guards and take control of the Parliament building. Carradine was as fascinated by Bartok's response to the unfolding story as he was by the scale of the attack. She knew, as he did, that nothing like this had ever been attempted by Resurrection before. To go after a nationalist government in the heart of Europe, shooting to kill with little chance of personal survival when the siege ended, marked a sea-change in the evolution of Resurrection, perhaps even the death throes of what had metastasised into a violent cult. This was no longer a group of idealistic centre-left activists kidnapping journalists or tipping tables of food and wine into the laps of extremist politicians. This was terrorism, pure and simple.

'The movement is dead,' said Bartok. 'They have stolen it.'

'Who has?' Carradine asked, but saw that she was in no mood to answer. LASZLO was sitting on the edge of the bed, shaking her head in disbelief.

'Why do they continue to come for me when this is happening?' she said. 'Why do they still *care*?'

'I don't know,' Carradine replied.

He had no means of helping her. She was trapped and surrounded, just as the gunmen inside the Sejm were enclosed by those who were determined to bring them to justice. Carradine was merely an ordinary citizen with ordinary powers. When it came to helping Bartok, he knew that he was in over his head.

'I need to leave,' she said, picking up on this moment of self-doubt.

'Leave to go where?'

'Don't worry,' she said. 'I have ways of escape.'

'What sort of ways?'

'A driver. Someone I trust. He can get me to Tangiers. I can catch a boat.'

'How are you going to do that? The Moroccans have eyes everywhere. They'll be watching the ports, the train stations, the airports. The Agency asks them to find you and bring you in, they will find you and bring you in.'

'Why would they involve the Moroccans?' It was as though Bartok thought that Carradine was now exaggerating the threat against her. 'I have been here three months, never had any trouble.'

'It's a risk,' he said.

'This is the nature of my life,' she replied matter-of-factly. 'I could be arrested at any time.'

Carradine thought more carefully about the driver.

'Let's say you get to Tangiers. How will you get out on the ferry? You said the new passport was useless.'

'I have another passport.'

'With you now?'

'No,' she replied. Bartok was carrying a small shoulder bag. 'Not with me now. At my apartment.'

'You have a place here in Marrakech?'

'In Gueliz, yes.'

He was amazed by this. How had she managed to rent an apartment without detection?

'What's the name on the passport?'

'Why?'

Bartok seemed impatient with Carradine for asking so many questions, but a plan had coalesced in his mind. The feeling was not dissimilar to those moments in his life as a writer when an ingenious plot device, born of creative necessity, materialises out of thin air. Carradine suddenly knew how to help her.

'Just tell me.'

'The name in the passport is Lilia Hudak.'

'Is it Hungarian?'

'Yes. Why? What is it, Kits?'

'Kit. No "s",' he said.

'Kit, then!'

All Carradine needed was the driver and a slice of luck.

'I think I can get you out of Morocco another way,' he said. 'A safer way. What's the address of this apartment?'

26

Carradine ordered some food for Bartok on room service and waited for it to be delivered before going out alone into the Kasbah. It was just after nine o'clock. He walked the short distance to the Royal Mansour Hotel, asking for Patrick and Eleanor at the reception desk. They had already finished dinner and sent a message that Carradine should join them in the bar.

The Langs were taken aback by his suggestion at first but it did not take him long to persuade them. The key was his Hungarian girlfriend's love of the sea and the once-in-a-lifetime opportunity to surprise her and sail up the coast of Morocco. He would have been crazy not at least to ask if it would be possible to join them on their yacht for a couple of nights; maybe the extra pairs of hands might also make the journey up to Gibraltar a little bit easier?

Eleanor was the first to warm to the idea, telling Patrick it would be fun to spend a couple of nights at sea with a 'famous novelist' and to get to know his 'lovely young lady' into the bargain. Patrick couldn't remember Carradine mentioning her in the restaurant, but when he saw the passport-sized photograph Carradine kept of 'Lilia' in his wallet, the old man's eyes lit up and he said he couldn't see any reason in the world why the trip wouldn't work. Carradine bought a second round of drinks to celebrate and they spent the rest of the conversation talking about the siege in Warsaw.

'What times we live in,' said Patrick. 'Used to be that you knew who the enemy was. The maniacs who hijacked aeroplanes, drove trucks through crowds, blew themselves up on the Tube. They were identifiable. Nowadays the terrorists look just like you and me – or your nice girl-friend, Kit. Ordinary people bearing a grudge.'

'You mean white people,' said Eleanor archly.

Patrick didn't bother denying it.

'I suppose I do,' he said. 'I can't pretend I haven't worried about Resurrection myself. I've got money offshore. I voted Conservative. I think Brexit, by and large, will be a good thing for Europe in the long term. Apparently that makes me an enemy of the people. I could be kneecapped. Our house in Ramsgate could be burned down. These people are callous.' Patrick took a sip of his Chablis. 'Resurrection isn't about change. It's about hate. Hatred of the rich. Hatred of those in power. They're just thugs. We might get to Rabat and find they've put a hole in *Atalanta* and she's at the bottom of the marina.'

'Let's hope not!' said Carradine, trying to sound cheerful.

'At least we're insured,' Eleanor muttered.

By the time his hosts were ready to call it a night, they

had given Carradine instructions on where and when to meet them and asked only that he and Lilia both buy a pair of suitable shoes for the boat.

'No high heels!' Patrick called out as they parted company in the hotel lobby.

'I'll throw mine away then,' Carradine replied.

He had one more task: to collect the Lilia Hudak passport from Bartok's apartment and to fill a bag with her belongings.

There was a taxi idling on the road at the western perimeter of the Mansour. Young couples on rugs were necking in the long grass, escaping the summer heat of their homes – and doubtless the prying eyes of parents. Carradine arranged a price for the journey into Gueliz, giving the driver the address of a restaurant two blocks south of Bartok's apartment.

The journey took more than half an hour in thick traffic, following a route almost identical to the one Carradine had taken on foot the previous evening from Jemaa el-Fna. Stepping out of the cab at the northern end of Avenue Mohammed V, he realised that he had been dropped off within a stone's throw of the café where he had spoken to Oubakir. Though his circumstances had changed irreversibly since then, Carradine was still fully absorbed in the role of a support agent; he had simply shifted his loyalty to Bartok so that he could continue to ply his trade in the secret world.

At no point had it occurred to him to stop and to think and to wonder if he should stay in the game; he wanted to help Bartok and to outwit Hulse. The particular

characteristics of espionage – the absorption in a clandestine role; the opiate of secrecy; the adrenalised fear
of being caught – were drugs to which Carradine had
very quickly become addicted. At the Mansour, for
example, he had deliberately wedged his mobile phone
beneath the cushions of his armchair, to be collected later
from the bar, so that he would hobble any technical
surveillance the Agency might throw at him. Walking in
loops around Bartok's street, he employed the tradecraft
he had used in his novels to ascertain if he was being
followed. Using reflective surfaces in shop windows, even
the wing mirrors on cars, Carradine ran anti-surveillance
for several blocks, finding the streets too dark, his natural
walking pace too fast and the mirrors too small to enjoy
any degree of success. He remembered a spy in his second
novel stopping on a busy London street and pretending
to answer a mobile phone call so that she could turn
through three hundred and sixty degrees and make a
full assessment of her surroundings. Carradine did not
have his phone, but came to a halt nonetheless and
looked back down the length of Rue Ibn Aicha, peering
this way and that with a frown and a squint, playing the
part of a confused English tourist who had lost his way
in the switchback streets of Gueliz. He saw nothing to
make him suspicious.

After almost twenty minutes of this, he played the
last card in the amateur spy's pack, making a sharp
left-hand turn into a quiet residential street and coming
to an immediate halt. He counted to ten, then turned
around and set off in the direction from which he had
come, hoping to bump into anybody who might
conceivably have been tailing him. The street was

225

deserted. No pedestrians were coming towards him, no vehicles were loitering on the corner or drifting past at a crawl. Carradine was as sure as he was ever going to be that he had reached Bartok's neighbourhood undetected.

Her apartment was on Rue Moulay Ali, a wide residential street with a faux-Spanish restaurant at the northern end. Carradine passed a coffee house that was closing down for the night, a damaged strobe light flickering on the street. Bartok had explained that the entrance was about halfway down the road beside a plane tree sprouting from the pavement, its buckled trunk partly blocking access to the door. Carradine spotted the tree and, having checked up and down the road for surveillance, took out Bartok's keys and unlocked the door.

It was pitch-dark inside the lobby. He gave his eyes time to adjust to the gloom, gradually picking out a row of steel letterboxes on the opposite wall. Moving with zombie slowness, a fumbling hand stretched out in front of his face, Carradine eventually located a timer switch and pressed it with his thumb.

Light flooded the lobby. There were pieces of crumpled newspaper and dust all over the floor. A pot plant had toppled over, spilling earth in dried clumps. Bartok had warned him that the lift was temperamental so Carradine took the stairs. Two-thirds of the way up, the lights timed out and he was again forced to fumble in the darkness, his heart pounding with the effort of climbing the stairs and the fear of being caught. He managed to find a plastic switch in the pitch-black and was able to walk up the remaining flights to Bartok's door, his route illuminated by a series of weak staircase bulbs.

It was a small, stuffy apartment. Carradine was hit by a smell of stale tobacco and unwashed socks. A Berber rug had been tacked to the wall next to a poster of Ziggy Stardust. The kitchen was set to one side of the living room in an open-plan style not dissimilar to the flat in Lisson Grove. A set of French windows led out onto a narrow terrace. Bartok had rolled up a yoga mat and placed it underneath a large wooden coffee table in the centre of the room.

Carradine closed the door behind him and switched on the air conditioning. The room quickly became cooler and the stale smells of sweat and tobacco partially lifted. Every available surface was scattered with books, newspapers and magazines. He spotted some cigarette papers and a small block of hashish on the coffee table. A half-finished bottle of Grey Goose vodka had been left on a shelf in the kitchen. Carradine took a shot for his nerves then went to the cupboard under the sink and reached for the bag of dishwasher salt. It was exactly where Bartok had said it would be, nestled behind a box of soap powder and a plastic bucket full of cleaning products. He untied the knot on the bag and felt inside. He plunged his hand into the salt and felt the hard outline of the passport. He took it out, checked the name – 'Lilia Hudak' – and put it in his back pocket.

Bartok had given him a list of other items to pack. His heart pounding, Carradine went into her bedroom. He was amused by the mess. The bed was unmade and there were books and items of clothing strewn all over the floor. It was as if a tribe of monkeys had been set loose in the room. A small, stained-glass window in the corner fed an eerie technicolour light into the bedroom. Carradine pulled down a soft bag from an overhead cupboard and set it on the bed. He found a drawer full of clean T-shirts and stuffed half a dozen of them into the bag along with two summer dresses from the wardrobe, a pair of denim shorts and some underwear. He was amazed by the number of clothes she owned.

Bartok had told him about the shampoo bottle beside the bed. He found the bottle, removed the lid and tapped out a tin-plate cigar tube. He unscrewed the cap. The tube was filled with hundred dollar bills. Carradine put it back inside the bottle and threw the shampoo into the bag.

Next he looked under the bed and located the pile of Russian novels Bartok had described, each of them translated into Hungarian. He identified *Anna Karenina* thanks to a picture of Keira Knightley on the front cover looking wan and indecisive. He opened it up. The SIM card was taped to the inside back cover. Carradine placed the book in the bag. There was a laptop and an old mobile phone on a shelf beside the window. Bartok had asked him to leave them behind. Unable to remember what shoes she had been wearing, Carradine picked up a pair of trainers and stuffed them into the bag, mindful of Patrick's instructions for the yacht. Finally, he found the one item Bartok had insisted that he remember: an Art Deco silver bookmark given to her by her late mother. He wrapped it up in a pair of black knickers and placed both carefully inside one of the shoes to protect the bookmark from damage. Then he zipped up the bag and went out into the living room.

The man was standing beside the front door. His arms were folded, his legs slightly apart. Carradine was so shocked that he lurched backwards and had to steady himself on the frame of the door. The man was wearing jeans and a black T-shirt. He was slim and looked about thirty-five.

'You must be the writer.' He had a thin voice but with a distinct Russian accent. 'Mister Considines.'

Carradine did not bother correcting him. Instead he said: 'Who the fuck are you?'

Fear boiled inside him. Suddenly he was no longer in an adventure story of his own making, a work of imagination from which he could extricate himself at any time. He was in the centre of Marrakech in the dead of night faced with a man who had been waiting for Lara Bartok. He knew where she lived. He knew that Carradine was associated with her. The game was up.

'Do not concern yourself with who I am. What are you doing here, please?' The man glanced at the bag. 'You make a vacation?'

'That's right.' Carradine's throat was as dry as coal. He looked in the direction of the second bedroom. He assumed that the Russian had been waiting there, though it was possible that he had picked the lock and walked right in. Had he searched Bartok's room? Did that account for the mess? He wondered if there were other men in the apartment or a team waiting on the stairs. He had been so sure that he had not been followed.

'Who is the bag for, please?'

'My girlfriend,' Carradine replied. He knew that he had to play the innocent, to try to find a way of leaving the apartment without exposing Lara or himself to further danger. He could not think of any way of doing that without playing the role of an ordinary man caught up in a conspiracy that he did not understand. 'How did you know my name?' he asked.

The Russian ignored him. He was not a physically imposing person, nor particularly sinister to look at. He might have been the landlord popping in to check up that everything was fine with the apartment. He had no gun – at least not one that Carradine had seen – but his manner was very calm and controlled.

'Where is the girl?' he asked. 'Where is Lara Bartok?'

Carradine played the innocent. 'Lara Bartok?'

'Your girlfriend. This is her place. Where is she please?'

'My girlfriend's name is Sandy.' Carradine plucked the first name that came into his mind. 'She's in hospital. She's not well. She asked me to pack her a bag.'

'Which hospital?'

The question brought an acid surge into Carradine's throat: he was out of his depth, untrained and untested, making things up out of thin air.

'I don't know the name,' he said. 'I just know where it is. Near the Medina. The one all the tourists go to.' He took a further risk, assuming that every city had one: 'The American Hospital.'

The Russian nodded. Perhaps Carradine had miraculously stumbled on a version of the truth.

'I am going to call this in,' he said. 'Please put the bag down. Please remain where you are.'

Those words gave Carradine hope. If the Russian had to make a phone call, that meant that he was alone. There was nobody else in the building. His colleagues were looking for Bartok all over town and had spread themselves thin. If he somehow could get past the Russian, if he could find a way out of the building and back to the riad, he could warn Lara and get her out of Marrakech. He had no other choice. If he did as the Russian asked, if he just stood around watching him call his superiors, he was finished. He had to do something. He had to fight back.

'Listen, mate.' Carradine stepped towards him. He was suddenly possessed of a wild confidence that he could take him out, that one clean punch would drop his man to the ground. 'I don't know who you are or who you're looking for. Sandy is sick. I came to pick up her things. How the fuck did you get in here anyway?'

He was trying to remember everything that his boxing instructor had told him. *Don't swing and hook like they do in the movies. That's just bullshit for the cameras. Drop a low punch into the midriff then drive an uppercut under the jaw. Keep your right elbow close to your body and use the momentum from your pelvis.*

'I can get in anywhere,' the Russian replied, taking out his phone. He started to scroll through the contacts, looking for the number that would seal Bartok's fate.

'It's breaking and entering,' Carradine told him, moving forward. He realised that he was at least four inches taller than the Russian, which only added to his reckless courage. He remembered the day in Gymbox when he had missed the pad and accidentally slammed his fist into his instructor's jaw. The instructor had gone flying, as if a rope had been attached to his back and somebody had yanked on it.

'What are you doing please?' the Russian asked, looking up from his phone.

Carradine wanted it to be the uppercut with which Buster Douglas had floored Tyson in the tenth. He had

231

a vision of George Foreman slumping to the canvas in Kinshasa as Ali loomed over him, his fist primed to strike. He dreamed of recreating the punch with which Sylvester Stallone had floored Drago in *Rocky IV*. Instead Carradine feinted to one side and dropped a hard left hook into his opponent's stomach. The Russian was badly winded, gasping as Carradine brought his right elbow tight to the body and drove upwards from his pelvis with all of his strength, landing a sweet right uppercut on the side of the jaw which drove the Russian back against the door. The contact was not as clean as Carradine had hoped, but there was no need for another punch. He was fit and strong and he had put him down. The man slumped semi-conscious to the ground, eyes glazed over, legs stretched out in front of him like a cartoon drunk propped up outside a bar. Carradine immediately pulled him to one side so that he could unbolt the door. The Russian was extraordinarily heavy; it was like trying to move a sack of wet sand. His phone had fallen to the ground and he picked it up. Grabbing the bag and checking that the passport was still in his back pocket, Carradine hurried out of the apartment, hitting a light switch with his aching right hand before scampering down eight flights of stairs with the speed of a man trying to outrun a rockslide.

On the ground floor he searched for a back entrance but could not find one. He went down to the basement but there were only two doors, both of them leading to apartments. His knuckles were throbbing; it was as if he had slammed his fist repeatedly against a hot brick stove. The Russian might already be coming round; Carradine had no choice other than to go outside onto Rue Moulay Ali and to take his chances.

The street was utterly still. At the northern end he saw a man walking out of the Spanish restaurant smoking a cigarette. He checked the cars parked along both sides of the street but it was too dark to tell if there was anybody sitting inside them. Using the trunk of the buckled tree as partial cover, he headed in the direction of the restaurant, hugging the shadows, the strap of the bag digging into his shoulder.

An engine started up behind him. Carradine did not dare turn around and show his face. Instead he quickened his pace, running past the restaurant and the shuttered coffee house, heading for a busier street up ahead. He dropped the phone into a dustbin. A taxi was coming from the opposite direction with its light switched off. Carradine knew that in Morocco that meant he could share the ride with the other passengers. He waved at the cab. It immediately swerved towards him. There was an old woman in the front. Carradine opened the back door, swung the bag onto the seat and climbed in.

'Where are you going?' he asked the driver in French.

Carradine did not understand the reply but said '*Oui, très bien*' then immediately ducked down, pretending to tie his shoelaces as the taxi passed the northern end of Rue Moulay Ali. For the next several minutes he turned in his seat repeatedly, scouring the vehicles behind him. At one point a young Moroccan on a scooter followed the taxi for four blocks, but eventually turned off, heading in the direction of the Majorelle Gardens. A short time later, the old lady paid her fare and left the cab. Carradine handed the driver a hundred dirhams and asked him to head for the Royal Mansour without stopping to collect any new passengers. The driver did so, leaving him at the western entrance. Carradine walked alone along the private road leading to the hotel. He knew that he looked scruffy and washed out, but he was a white European and the security guard waved him into the building with only a cursory glance.

It was almost one o'clock in the morning. The bar had closed. Carradine found a member of staff wandering in a corridor, explained that he had lost his mobile phone, then searched the armchair where he had been sitting in the bar with Patrick and Eleanor. To his relief, he found it immediately. He tried switching it on but the battery had died. He tipped the member of staff and walked back outside, hailing a cab on Mohammed V that took him the short distance to the riad. Battery or no battery, if the Russians or the Agency were tracking his phone, they would still know that he was back at the hotel. If Carradine was going to be picked up, they would come for him in the next few minutes.

He banged on the front door. Twenty-four hours earlier it had taken several minutes for the sleepy night manager in the stained shirt to come to the door. Tonight he opened it almost immediately, recognising Carradine with a warm smile and inviting him into the hall.

'You are Mister Carradine, yes?' he said.

'That's right.'

'There were men here before. Men looking for you.'

Carradine's heart popped but he tried to remain calm.

'Which men? Did you get their names?'

The night manager shook his head.

'Americans,' he said.

Carradine described Sebastian Hulse: tall, good-looking, slick. He asked if that fitted the description of one of the men.

'Yes, sir. Exactly. It was this man. He says he is your friend.'

'He did, did he? What did he want? Where did he go?'

'He says you invite him for a drink. He not find you so they go to your room. Knock on the door.'

Carradine had established a system with Bartok: three quick knocks followed by three slower knocks to verify that it was safe to let him in; if he tapped out the rhythm of 'Rule Britannia', it was a warning that he had been compromised. He knew that Bartok would not have let Hulse into the room, but that the Agency was more than capable of picking the simple lock on the door.

'Are they still here?'

Carradine's hand was throbbing. He was physically and mentally exhausted. If Hulse and his accomplice were waiting for him in the riad, he doubted that he possessed the wherewithal to lie convincingly about where he had been or what he had planned with Bartok.

'No, sir. They leave. One, maybe one and half hours ago.'

'With a woman?'

'No, sir.'

Carradine thanked him. He tipped the night manager, collected his key and went to his room. He knocked on the door using the system they had arranged and prayed that Bartok was OK.

There was no response.

He knocked again – three times in rapid succession, three times with a pause in between each knock – but she did not answer.

He unlocked the door and went inside.

All of the lights had been switched off. The bed was

empty. Carradine looked to his left, hoping that Bartok would emerge from the bathroom, just as she had done earlier in the afternoon. She did not. He went into the bathroom and looked behind the shower curtain. He searched under the bed. Her shoulder bag was nowhere to be seen and she had not left a note.

She was gone.

27

Carradine ran back to reception. The night manager was sitting behind the desk looking at photographs on Facebook.

'Hello again, sir!'

'Tell me. Did a woman leave in the last few hours?'

Carradine described Bartok: cropped blonde hair, a cream-coloured veil, slightly crooked front teeth. He was desperately worried about her. The night manager shrugged and shook his head.

'Not when I am here at the desk,' he said. 'I do not see this woman.'

Carradine returned to the room. He looked for Bartok a second time, pointlessly, even checking inside the wardrobe, as if he expected a woman of her experience and cunning to be crouched inside it under a blanket, like a child playing hide and seek. He took out the mobile phone and plugged it in to charge. He was worried for her safety, but his concern was mingled with the prospect of personal betrayal. Had she lied to him? Had it always been her intention to leave once she had rinsed him for information?

He looked down at the phone. The screen showed a thin red sliver of power, not enough to start it up. He was starving. The room service tray had not been removed. Bartok had left a bread roll, a scrape of butter and half a bowl of cold chips. Carradine ate all of it, washed down with two cans of Coke from the minibar. Then he picked up the phone and tapped in his six-digit pin.

There were four missed calls, four unread WhatsApp messages and two texts. He looked at the missed calls. Three were from the same unidentified number, the fourth from his father. There were no voicemails. He tapped on the text message icon. The first was from EE, the second from an old friend in Istanbul. He opened WhatsApp.

Two of the messages were from Mantis.

You're full of surprises, Kit! Wonderful news about our friend. Well done. Never doubted you for a moment ;)

Carradine muttered 'Fuck you' to the screen. He bitterly regretted telling Oubakir that he had found Bartok. He read the second message:

Let me know more about it. Also – will still need the stuff Y gave you in Casablanca. Make sure it comes home safely.

Mantis was referring to the memory stick, which was still in the hotel safe. Carradine assumed that it contained information that would be useful to Moscow and therefore damaging to western interests. As soon as he got home,

238

he would hand the stick to a contact in the Service who had helped him, a few years earlier, with a couple of research questions related to his books. Carradine would inform her that a British citizen, Stephen Graham, had been betraying his country to Moscow for more than a decade. With any luck, Mantis would get twenty years.

The second WhatsApp message was from a UK number he did not recognise. There was no name associated with the account and no photograph. Carradine opened it.

Hi Kit. It's Lilia, your downstairs neighbour. Are you in London? I've tried calling you. A package came for you but I couldn't fit it through your letterbox. I've had to go away on business but you'll find it out the back by the tradesman's entrance. It will be waiting for you there.

Carradine was so tired that, at first, he took the message at face value. Just another package to be collected. Just another note from a neighbour.

Then his brain began to work.

Lilia. Tradesman's entrance.

The message was from Bartok.

28

Carradine packed his bag inside three minutes. He knew that he couldn't take his laptop or phone to Rabat and left both under the mattress, having sent a reply to Mantis and scribbled down half a dozen essential telephone numbers on a piece of writing paper. With luck, he could call the riad at some point in the next two days, explain that he had left in a hurry and ask them to courier the laptop and phone, as well as the memory stick in the hotel safe, to his flat in London.

He opened the door and went out into the courtyard. It was blissfully quiet save for the gentle running of the fountain. He shouldered the two bags and walked in the direction of the swimming pool. He glanced at his watch. It was quarter to three. A light was on in one of the bedrooms on the first floor. Perhaps it was McKenna's suite and he was working late or suffering with a bout of insomnia. Carradine turned past the pool, heading towards the spa. He caught his foot on a loose paving stone and almost tripped but managed to retain his balance. He passed the spa and reached the back gate, checking behind him to ensure that he had not been followed.

He peered over the top. The van had gone from the maintenance area. Carradine could see a car parked on the far side of the street. A cat leapt out in the darkness and scurried away from the wall. As Carradine leaned back, he noticed a slight movement in the front seat of the car, a shadow. He was convinced that it was Bartok's driver.

He looked more closely at the gate. There was no way of opening it; it was padlocked from the street side. A line of barbed wire stretched from one end to the next. If he was going to get over it, he would have to sling both bags through the gap between the barbed wire and the top of the gate, then climb over. The maintenance area was overlooked by several residential buildings, all of which were blacked out, save one. Carradine looked up at the lit window. It appeared to be a stairwell or hall of some kind; certainly there was nobody visible in the building. Looking back at the car, trying to signal to the driver, he wondered if he was making life too difficult for himself. Why not just leave through the front door of the hotel and walk around to the car? There was no need for him formally to check out; the festival was covering his costs. The night manager might think it was strange that Mr Carradine was leaving at three o'clock in the morning, but he could tell him that he had an early flight to catch. Yet the risk of outside surveillance was too great. By now the Russian would have come round and alerted his colleagues; they would be en route to the riad. Carradine had to go over the gate to minimise the risk of being caught.

He lifted up the first bag. It was heavier than he had expected and banged against the metal gate as he stretched up and pushed it under the barbed wire. He held it at the top with one hand while stepping up onto a narrow metal bar at the base of the gate. The gate wobbled as it took Carradine's weight. He steadied himself against the brick wall. Pushing his arm through the gap as far as it would go, he lowered the bag on the opposite side, letting it drop to the ground. He had packed the bottle of Johnny Walker and heard a thump against the cement, praying that the bottle hadn't smashed. He then repeated the process with Bartok's bag, letting it drop to the ground.

Having checked his surroundings one last time, Carradine then pulled himself up onto the top of the gate. It was extremely narrow. The barbed wire made it difficult to find a space to plant his feet. The hinge connecting the gate to the wall was also very loose. The gate began to rattle. Carradine crouched down, holding the top with both hands, one leg on either side of the barbed wire but wobbling like a surfer trying to balance on a breaking wave. Feeling exposed, he decided to jump down, almost catching his heel on the wire as he dropped. Pain shot up through his knees as he landed on the concrete. The gate was jangling as though it had been struck by a frying pan. Carradine reached out to smother the din as the cat hissed in the shadows. He half-expected the entire neighbourhood to wake up and to shout at him to keep the noise down.

He heard the man's voice before he saw his face.

'Monsieur Kit?'

Carradine turned to see a young Moroccan man with a neat beard crouched beneath the wall.

'Yes?' he whispered.

'Come,' he said in French, gesturing towards the car. 'I am the driver. I have the lady. Come.'

Somerville went to the window on the street side and peered through the blinds. Seeing nothing in the stairwell he turned and walked back towards Bartok.

'You say this was the first time you had heard of Kit Carradine?'

'That is correct,' she replied.

Hulse stepped across him.

'Come on. You'd never read his books? You didn't know he was coming to Marrakech? You hadn't been told to make contact with him? He just happened to see you walking out of this Irish guy's book event?'

'That is correct.'

'And you expect us to believe that?'

'I have learned not to expect anything from anyone,' Bartok replied. 'People always let you down, Mr Hulse. Don't you find that?'

Hulse hesitated. Somerville dug him out of the hole.

'You hadn't seen Carradine's name in the festival programme? You didn't look in on his talk?'

'I did not.'

'You sure about that?' Hulse asked.

'What reason would I have to lie?'

'To protect him,' he said.

'Protect him from what? From who? People like you?'

'Maybe.'

Somerville had heard enough. Standing behind Bartok, he shot Hulse a look, telling him to back off.

'Let's not get distracted,' he said, filling her glass with water. 'Just tell us what happened next.'

'When?'

'Pick it up wherever you like,' Hulse suggested.

'No.' Somerville was rummaging in his jacket pocket and found an almost empty packet of cigarettes crushed beneath a set of house keys. They had been there all along. 'We know about Mexico. What interests us is the role the Russians played in all this.'

Bartok buried a smile.

'So nothing has changed,' she said. 'Everybody is still playing catch-up with the Kremlin.'

Hulse began to respond but Somerville silenced him again, this time with a raised hand.

'Were you aware of Russian surveillance in Morocco? What did Stephen Graham tell you about their objectives? Did you think Carradine was working for Moscow? Were you immediately suspicious of the Langs?'

'So many questions all at once.'

'Then take your time.' Somerville tucked the cigarettes into the hip pocket of his trousers and sat down. 'You have the stage, Lara. We're all ears.'

STATEMENT BY LARA BARTOK ('LASZLO')
CASE OFFICER: J.W.S./S.T.H. – CHAPEL STREET
REF: RESURRECTION/SIMAKOV/CARRADINE
FILE: RE2768X

PART 4 of 5

Why did the Russians want me dead? Why was it so important for them to find me? Was it just because of my activities with Resurrection – or was there something more? To this day, I cannot answer that question. Why did they come for me when they did? Ivan was dead. I had left the movement. I was no longer a threat to them.

I realise that I was extremely fortunate. If I hadn't risked going to the festival, if I hadn't spoken to Michael McKenna, if Kit hadn't spotted me outside the event. I would now be dead. That's certain. Kit Carradine saved my life. Yes, Mantis knew there was every chance I would show myself in Marrakech. He knew I loved McKenna's writing and had always wanted to meet him. He put Kit in my path for just this reason. Mohammed Oubakir also. But I was still very, very lucky.

I trusted Kit immediately. I felt safe with him. It was obvious that he had been manipulated, that he was embarrassed and ashamed to have fallen for Mantis's trick, but I knew he had done it for noble reasons. Many others would have made the same mistake. Every man wants to be a spy, doesn't he? Every child dreams of being a secret agent. How do you turn down an opportunity like that when it comes about, especially given what happened to his father? Kit had a resourcefulness and a courage, mixed with a kind of romantic naivety – which I suppose is necessary for any writer – which was very endearing and attractive to me.

He was brave to go to my apartment. He wanted to help me and this was the only way he could think of. I don't know how the Russians knew where I was living. If you can find that out I'll be fascinated to know. My suspicion is that one of my neighbours informed on me. He was a creep with a big mouth.

I suppose this would be the best time to talk about Patrick and Eleanor [JWS: Patrick and Eleanor Lang]. Yes, I was very concerned about them. You can choose to believe me about that or you can choose not to believe me. Kit had taken them on trust, just as he had taken Robert Mantis at face value. It was Ivan who taught me a long time ago that when a stranger strikes up conversation in a bar, in a restaurant, on a plane, that stranger may be interested in more than some

light conversation. Kit knew that, too. But
we had to get out of Morocco. At that very
difficult moment, their boat seemed to be the
best way.

29

They ran low through the shadows of the maintenance area. The young driver popped the boot of a Renault Megane and threw the bags inside. Carradine opened the back door to find Bartok asleep. He was amazed that she was capable of relaxing under such intense pressure.

She sat up abruptly as he moved in beside her.

'You made it,' she said.

'We go?' the driver asked in French.

'*Oui*,' Bartok replied groggily. '*Allez*.'

Carradine felt a vertiginous elation, a belief that he had landed in a life that did not belong to him but to which he was ideally suited. He was certain that the car would not be stopped. He was sure that they would make it to Rabat. He was risking his future to help a wanted criminal but knew that the cause was just. He had not fully thought through what he was doing, nor what he was leaving behind. Looking at Bartok as she stared at the road ahead, he felt like a man walking out of church on his wedding day beside a woman he barely knows.

'What happened to your hand?'

Bartok touched Carradine's knuckles. Her fingers were cool and soft. She caressed his wrist and looked into his eyes with such care that the last of his concerns vanished.

'I got into a fight,' he said. He saw that there was a patch of skin on the back of her wrist where the tattoo of the swallows had been removed. 'Does your driver speak English?'

Bartok shook her head. 'Hardly any. Nothing.'

'Somebody was waiting for you in the apartment,' he said. 'A Russian. He knew who I was.'

'How?' She was bewildered. 'This is the man you fought? You *punched* him?'

She was still holding his wrist. He played down his feat, as though he got into fights two or three times a week and always emerged victorious.

'You are brave!' she said and cheerfully kissed him on the cheek. 'Are you OK?'

'I'm fine.' Carradine was watching the pavements on both sides of the road. 'He was knocked out. I hope he's all right.'

'So do I,' she muttered, and just as quickly the thrill of what he had done evaporated. The fact that nobody had come to the riad in the past hour indicated that the Russian was possibly still unconscious. What if Carradine had seriously injured him? He would be no different to Bartok. Another criminal on the run.

'Get down!' Carradine shouted.

The Russian and two other men were walking in the direction of the hotel on the opposite side of the street, no more than thirty metres from the car. He grabbed Bartok, pushing her behind the passenger seat, his head resting on the small of her back as they bent down beneath the windows.

'What's going on?' the driver asked in French.

'That was him. The Russian.'

Bartok swore in what he assumed was her native Hungarian. The driver made a sharp left-hand turn. Carradine held onto the door handle, his weight pushing against her.

'You saw him?' She tried to sit up. Carradine made room for her on the seat. 'The man from my apartment?'

'Right there,' he replied, turning and indicating where he had seen the men. The stretch of road where the Russians had been walking was now obscured by a section of the old city wall.

'So he is fine. And so are you. Did you get everything?'

Carradine looked at the driver. Bartok again reassured him that he would not be able to understand anything they said.

'Yeah. I found the passport. Your place was a mess. Clothes, books, shoes everywhere. I think he'd been looking for it.'

She smiled, rubbing her neck. 'No. This is just me. I am not a tidy person, Kit.'

Carradine laughed. 'Ah, OK.' He wound down the window, looking out on the deserted streets of Gueliz. 'I packed whatever I could. Found the bookmark, the SIM card . . .'

'You were amazing to do this. I do not know how to thank you.'

'You don't need to thank me.'

For a few minutes they were silent, the car moving steadily along wide, empty boulevards towards the outskirts of the city. Carradine was still hungry and hoped that they could stop on the road once they were clear of Marrakech. It would take about four or five hours to reach Rabat on the dual carriageway. Bartok introduced him formally to the driver, whose name was Rafiq. She explained that Rafiq's uncle had found her the apartment in Gueliz. Carradine asked if it was possible that he was the man who had betrayed her to the Russians. She was adamant that this was not the case and thought it more likely that a neighbour had grown suspicious of her and had spoken to the local police; informers were everywhere in Morocco. If the Russians had their ear to the ground, it would only have been a case of putting two and two together. At the same time, she could not be certain that the men who were looking for her might not now question the uncle and connect the dots to Rafiq. For that reason, she had asked him to leave his cellphone at home so that their journey up to Rabat could not be traced.

'Whose car is this?' Carradine asked. He was worried about number plate recognition.

'Don't worry,' she said. 'It's his friend's car. It won't flag.'

They reached a *péage* at the start of the highway. It was still the middle of the night and there was only one lane open. Two large cameras faced the car on either side of a narrow channel. Rafiq moved forward, stopping at a tollbooth. Bartok had climbed over into the passenger seat. Carradine remained in the back, scanning either side of the highway for police patrols. He saw the headlights of a tailing vehicle reflected in the rear-view mirror. There were so few cars on the road that every one of them was a threat. Rafiq opened the window, greeted the guard and paid the toll. The barrier opened and they continued onto the highway. Carradine lit a cigarette to calm his nerves.

'We will be fine,' Bartok reassured him, again giving the impression of reading his mind as she turned in her seat to speak to him. 'Got one of those for me?'

They all smoked as the light gradually strengthened and the suburbs of Marrakech gave way to a flat, feature-less desert stretching out to the horizon. To the east, Carradine could make out the faint outline of the High Atlas Mountains. Bartok spoke in French with Rafiq about his uncle's marriage to a woman who was not permitted to leave the house alone, did not drive a car and had never – to Rafiq's knowledge – drunk alcohol nor smoked a cigarette. This, he insisted, was perfectly normal in Moroccan culture. Carradine enjoyed the way she teased him into confessing that he hoped for a similar marital arrangement of his own.

About an hour into the journey Carradine fell asleep, waking to find that Rafiq had stopped at a Shell garage close to the town of Settat on the A7 highway. He sat up and rubbed his face, adjusting to the bright sunlight flooding into the car. Rafiq was filling up with fuel; Bartok was nowhere to be seen.

The interior of the petrol station was no different to a thousand others just like it, from Inverness to Naples: strip-lit aisles displaying crisps and biscuits, fridges stocked with sports drinks and Red Bull. Carradine tried on a pair of sunglasses and looked around for Bartok. There were tables at the back of the shop in front of a cafeteria staffed by two young women wearing aprons and veils. He queued up and bought several pastries and what he assumed was a cheese bun. One of the girls smiled at him and he realised he was still wearing the sunglasses. He took them off and set them on the counter.

Turning from the till, Carradine saw a woman with long dark hair seated at a table overlooking the highway. It was only when she turned around that he realised the woman was Bartok.

'What did you do to your hair?' he said, absorbing the transformation in her appearance.

She invited him to sit beside her.

'Rafiq brought it to me,' she replied. 'They might work out that we left Marrakech by car. Either we took the road south to Agadir or, more likely, the road to Casablanca. Those were our only options – unless we wanted to get stuck in Essaouira. They might look at CCTV, they might not. But they are searching for a woman with short blonde hair travelling with a man who looks a lot like C.K. Carradine.' She smiled and sipped her coffee. 'You were asleep when I left the car. So I was just another woman in Morocco with long black hair getting out of the passenger seat while her boyfriend filled up with petrol.'

'And now?' Carradine asked, gesturing towards the ceiling where he had earlier spotted two CCTV cameras.

'Now you've ruined it!' she said, as if their escape was all just a game and she had not a care in the world. 'You shouldn't have bought your food and your drinks. You shouldn't have talked to the woman with the long black wig.'

He was stumped for a response, still half asleep but understanding with each passing moment why Mantis had been so bewitched by Lara Bartok. They hurried back to the car. She took the bag Carradine had packed from the boot and placed it at her feet in the front seat.

Carradine shared his food with Rafiq and soon fell asleep again. Seventy miles from Rabat he woke to find that Bartok had removed the SIM card from the copy of Anna Karenina and was busy slotting it into what appeared to be a brand-new handset.

'Where'd you get the phone?' he asked.

'Rafiq too.'

'He bought it just now?'

'No. Before. In Marrakech.'

He took out the list of numbers he had written down from his phone, explaining that it was important that his father should be able to reach him in an emergency. As he said this, he realised that of course it would be impossible to telephone home. Any intelligence service worth its salt would be covering his father's number.

'Will he worry about you?' she asked.

'It's not that.' Carradine did not want to make too much of the situation. He was very close to his father and felt responsible for his happiness and wellbeing. But William Carradine was a tough old bird with a circle of good friends who kept an eye on him. 'It's just for emergencies. I'm his only family in the UK. He doesn't have brothers or sisters. Neither of us do. My mother died a long time ago.'

'I am sorry to hear that.'

'He won't notice I'm gone for a few days. I'll call him when we get to Gibraltar.'

It was then that Carradine saw the cloud of dust ahead of them, about four hundred metres from the car. Rafiq slowed down as other cars in front of him hit the brakes. Bartok asked what was happening and he replied 'Crash' in French as the Renault passed the scene. Two vehicles

255

had come off the highway at speed and careered across the desert floor, one landing on its roof, the other folded almost in half at the base of a pylon. Two other cars had come to a halt at the side of the road.

'We should help,' said Carradine.

'Kit, we can't,' Bartok told him.

He turned and saw two people emerge from the parked cars. She was right. Others would be there to call for an ambulance. If they went back, the police would come and they would run the risk of being identified. Rafiq gradually accelerated away and the crash was soon forgotten. Yet Carradine's nerves had been frayed by the incident – the plumes of dust; the inverted, smashed cars. He tried to wipe what he had seen from his mind. He knew that there had been serious injuries, perhaps even that someone had died, and the knowledge of this acted on him like a portent of things to come.

'Are you OK?' Bartok asked, turning and putting a hand on his leg.

'I'm great,' he said and took back the piece of paper on which he had written down the numbers. 'How much longer to Rabat?'

'Less than an hour now.'

It was past seven o'clock. The other guests at the riad would be awake and eating breakfast by the pool. Had the Russians forced their way in and demanded to see him? Perhaps they had bribed the night manager to let them search Carradine's room. Had they done so, they would now be in possession of his laptop and phone, giving them access to his WhatsApp messages with Mantis.

'You think Stephen Graham was working behind Moscow's back?'

Bartok did not hear the question clearly and asked Carradine to repeat it. He did so.

'I told you already,' she replied. 'I think he knew they were coming for me. He wanted to save me.' Carradine looked out at the dusty road. 'Why do you ask this?' she said.

'My phone is in my room. If the Russians see that Mantis was in touch with me, they'll know he's betrayed them.'

Rafiq was driving past the suburbs of Casablanca, on the edge of the speed limit. Bartok took off her seat belt and climbed over into the back seat in order to continue the conversation.

'There's nothing we can do about that,' she said. Her perfume pushed towards him, a smell he adored. 'He made his choice. He probably saved my life by sending you. But I can't protect him.'

'No.'

'Do you *want* to warn him after what he did to you?'

Carradine found that his bitterness towards Mantis had abated. He was not one to hold a grudge. He understood why 'Stephen Graham' had pretended to be a British spy in order to recruit him. Sending him to Morocco to look for 'Maria' had been an act of love.

'What will happen to Mantis if they find out?'

Bartok bowed her head.

'He will certainly lose his job,' she said. She looked up and met Carradine's eyes. 'Worse, perhaps.'

He took out the list of telephone numbers. As well as the contact details for his father, he had written down numbers for his editor, his literary agent and two of his oldest friends from school days. The last number on the piece of paper had 'RM' scrawled beside it.

'That's him?' Bartok asked.

'That's him.'

Then she did something completely unexpected. Taking the piece of paper, she tore off the bottom section on which Carradine had written Mantis's number, screwed it up into a ball, opened the window and let it fly out of the car.

'There you go,' she said. 'Now you don't have to feel responsible for him any more.'

30

Less than an hour later they had reached the outskirts of Rabat.

'We're going to need somewhere to stay,' said Carradine.

He had blithely assumed that Bartok and Rafiq had already made arrangements. This was not the case.

'Any ideas?' she asked.

'I don't know anybody in Rabat,' he replied. 'Do you want to pop into the British Embassy?'

'Very funny,' she said.

Though he had intended the remark as a joke, the idea took on a certain logic. If Carradine could make contact with the local Service Station Chief and tell them about the threat against Bartok, the Embassy might offer them sanctuary.

'Wait,' he said. He wondered how to pitch it. He did not want to seem rash. 'What if the Service has no idea what the Russians and Americans are up to?'

'Do you think this is likely?'

There was an edge of facetiousness to Bartok's voice

which he had not heard before. The patriot in Carradine, that part of him which had believed in his country sufficiently to want to work for Mantis, could not countenance the idea that his own nation's intelligence officers were involved in the murky business of murder. It may have been because of his father's brief career in the Service, but he had always believed that the British adhered to moral values loftier than those in Washington and Moscow.

'Perhaps,' he said.

She laughed derisively. 'And perhaps they know everything and have chosen to turn a blind eye to targeted killings of innocent civilians. Perhaps they are themselves involved. We cannot know.'

Carradine was again struck by the suspicion that Bartok was holding something back.

'What are you not telling me?' he asked.

She looked at him quickly, as if he had intuited a hidden truth.

'What do you mean?'

'It's like you know something. You know the real reason why we can't go to the Embassy.'

'The *real* reason?' He saw that she was tired and about to lose her temper. 'The real reason is because I was involved in the kidnapping of Otis Euclidis. The real reason is because I assisted in Resurrection operations in the United States and Europe. The real reason is because I was the girlfriend of Ivan Simakov.' Carradine was stunned that she had been involved in the Euclidis disappearance. He could see from her face that she had done things she regretted, things of which she was now ashamed. 'I have no friends. I have only enemies, Kit. If you are with me you must know this. If we are caught, you will be accused of helping a fugitive to escape justice.'

'I'll take that chance.' Carradine had come too far to respond in any other way. 'I don't think the Service would want you dead,' he said. 'I don't think they'd be happy to know that their closest political ally has struck a deal with Moscow.'

Bartok hesitated. Carradine had again glimpsed the secret which she would not divulge. She turned to face him.

'Then go ahead and think that!' Her temper had snapped. All of the anxiety and suffering of her life on the run was suddenly visible to him: a world in which she was never safe, never certain, could trust nobody. 'It does not matter to me what you think. You could be right, you could be wrong. Perhaps the British Secret Service is prepared to sacrifice its good relations with America just to do the decent thing by me. But I doubt it. Let's face it. You write about this world, C.K. Carradine, but you know very little about how it really thinks or how it works.' Carradine's ego took a punch as pure and as effective as the uppercut with which he had floored the Russian. 'I have to trust my own judgement, my own experience. I have to be able to *survive*. You are helping me to do that and – believe me, please – I am profoundly grateful to you. If you want to leave me now, here in Rabat, I would not blame you. Go back to Marrakech. Go back to your phone with its numbers, to your laptop with its words. Take your suitcase and fly home. If I were you and I were able to do these things, believe me, I would do them. I would not stay here. I would not run that risk. I would make the choice to live my life in London.'

'I'm going to get you to Gibraltar,' Carradine replied, taking her hand and squeezing it at the wrist. He was not at all certain that it was the correct decision, taken as it was in the face of Bartok's seeming indifference to his plight, but he did not want to walk away or to let her down. 'We're going to get on the boat and we're going to get you out of Morocco. Then I'll leave. When you're safely in Gibraltar, I'll go back to my life in London.'

31

Then they came to the roadblock.

The first Carradine knew of it was Rafiq swearing under his breath and slowing to a crawl. There was a tailback of about forty cars in two lanes along the main road leading into Rabat. Carradine could see several police cars at the top of the queue, sirens flashing, uniformed officials standing at different points on the road.

'Fuck,' he said.

'Don't worry,' Bartok told him. 'Might not be for us. Arabs love a roadblock.'

They inched forward. It was hot outside. Carradine began to sweat. He closed the window and asked Rafiq to switch on the air conditioner. It was quickly as cold as a fridge inside the car.

'Tell me about Patrick and Eleanor,' she said.

Carradine assumed that Bartok was trying to take his mind off what was happening. Rafiq shunted forward the length of two vehicles and applied the brakes.

'They're a retired couple. Eleanor used to be a lawyer.

I'd say Patrick is about fifteen years older than her, looks a bit like Cary Grant. Very easy-going, very charming. Possible retired ladies' man. Liked the look of your photograph when I showed it to him.'

Bartok smiled. 'Go on.'

Rafiq moved forward another ten feet.

'They live in Kent, eastern part of England . . .'

'I know where Kent is.'

'They have a beautiful yacht. *Atalanta*. Custom made. Showed me some photographs of it at the Mansour. I think you'll be comfortable.'

'How did you meet them?'

Carradine remembered his first evening in Marrakech, trawling the souk for LASZLO. It seemed a lifetime ago.

'I was eating dinner in the Kasbah. Place des Ferblantiers. They were sitting at the next table.'

Bartok turned to face him. A siren squawked in the distance.

'Sitting there when you arrived?'

Carradine realised why she was looking so apprehensive. She thought that he had been tricked.

'No,' he said quickly. 'They came in after me.'

She looked out at the queue of traffic, visibly annoyed. 'Jesus Christ, Kit.'

He leaned towards her. Rafiq briefly turned to look at him.

'I know what you're thinking,' he said, trying to make his case. 'They're Service re-treads, Moscow illegals, Agency personnel keeping an eye on me. That's not the case, I promise you.'

'How can you be sure?'

'Instinct. Common sense.'

'Brilliant!' she exclaimed, with heavy sarcasm. 'So we are OK then. Your instinct as – what? – a *novelist* tells you that Patrick-who-looks-like-Cary-Grant and Eleanor-who-used-to-be-a-lawyer are normal everyday people. Are those the same instincts that told you to trust Robert Mantis?'

Carradine lost his temper.

'Do you want me to get out? Shall I just leave you here? Is that better? Is that what you want?'

Bartok tried to respond but he talked over her. Rafiq asked them to keep their voices down as he shunted the car forward.

'*Pas maintenant,*' Carradine snapped and turned back to Bartok. 'I'm trying to help you. I'm trying to do you a favour. What do you think are the chances of Patrick and Eleanor masquerading as a millionaire couple with an Oyster 575 on the *minuscule*, one-in-six-million probability that a British thriller writer might ask if he can sail up the coast of Morocco with them accompanied by his phantom girlfriend?'

'That's what you told them?' Bartok replied. Her anxiety had vanished as quickly as it had surfaced, to the point where she now seemed almost amused.

'Of course that's what I told them!' he said. 'That's what we agreed.'

'*Phantom* girlfriend?'

Carradine ignored her attempt to lighten the mood. He was still furious.

'Furthermore,' he said, 'how many intelligence services do you know that have a thousand dollars a night to spend on the Royal Mansour? If Patrick's a spook, if Eleanor is Kent's answer to Mata Hari, why don't they stay at the Radisson and save Her Majesty's government a fortune?'

Rafiq was almost at the top of the traffic queue. Carradine realised that Bartok was no longer listening to him. This infuriated him even more. She spoke to Rafiq rapidly in French, so fast that Carradine struggled to understand what she was saying. He asked her to repeat it.

'OK,' she said. 'I repeat.' It was clear that she had already set aside their quarrel and was focused solely on negotiating their passage through the roadblock. 'Here is the situation if they ask any questions.' She nodded in the direction of the guards. 'We are a couple. Not a phantom couple.' To Carradine: a quick, let's-kiss-and-make-up smile. 'We were staying in an Airbnb in Marrakech, OK? Rafiq is driving us to Rabat. We've never met him before. We're flying home to London tomorrow.'

Carradine leaned back in his seat, resigned to letting Bartok take control. He committed her simple lies to memory, rehearsing them in his mind as a policeman in a blue uniform walked up to Rafiq's door. He indicated that Rafiq should wind down the window. Bartok took a good long look at the policeman and smiled the kind of smile that had been working on men since she was about fourteen. Rafiq lowered the window.

'*As-Salaam Alaikum.*'

'*Wa-Alaikum Salaam.*'

The policeman continued to speak to Rafiq in Arabic. He looked into the car and nodded at Bartok. Bartok smiled back. He stepped to his right and looked at Carradine. Carradine tried to smile from the back seat but he was still angry.

'Where are you from, please?' the policeman asked through the window.

'We are from London,' Bartok replied confidently. They were speaking in English.

'Where have you come from today?'

'From Marrakech,' they both said in unison.

The policeman looked at the bag at Bartok's feet. Carradine dreaded the moment at which they would be asked to show their passports. Rafiq posed what sounded like a question, indicating something further along the road. The policeman did not react. Instead, he tapped on Carradine's window and indicated that he should lower it. Carradine did so, his finger shaking as he reached for the switch.

'What is your name please?'

Oh Christ.

'Christopher,' Carradine replied.

'Mr Christopher?'

Should he lie? If asked to show his passport, there was enough ambiguity in the presentation of Carradine's forenames that the cop could not accuse him of deliberately misleading the police.

'That's right. Christopher Alfred.' He did not want to say the surname 'Carradine'.

'Christopher Alfred?'

'Yes.' Bartok was becoming uneasy. Perhaps he shouldn't have evaded the question. Perhaps he should have said 'Christopher Carradine' and taken his chances.

'What is your business in Rabat, please, Mr Christopher Alfred?'

'Tourism,' Carradine replied.

'You arrange tourism?'

'No, no.' Carradine had been momentarily baffled by the question. 'We're tourists. I'm visiting Morocco with my girlfriend.'

'Phantom girlfriend,' Bartok muttered.

The policeman looked up and stared along the line of cars. Carradine's heart was racing so fast he was concerned that it was affecting his appearance. He could feel his chest surging.

'OK, enjoy,' the policeman replied. Without so much as a backwards glance, he moved on to the next car in line. An official in front of Rafiq waved the car forwards with a red baton.

Nobody uttered a sound as Rafiq engaged first gear and drove away from the roadblock. Carradine felt as if he had survived an examination by master interrogators. Bartok looked as calm and unruffled as a model having her picture taken in a photographer's studio. Only when they were at a safe distance, with the windows closed, did she whisper: 'Thank God' and slap Rafiq on the thigh.

'You were brilliant,' she said in French, turning to Carradine. 'Christopher Alfred! Tourism! A fantastic answer.'

'The training kicked in,' Carradine replied, slightly bemused that his response had generated such enthusiasm. 'I'm very experienced in these life-or-death situations.'

'I knew the argument would work,' she said.

Carradine was confused. 'What?' he said.

'Something I was taught.' He realised that she was referring to their squabble in the car. 'We were going into a situation in which we were both tense, yes?'

'Yes.'

'What does a guilty person look like? He looks calm, he tries to seem like he doesn't have a care in the world. But this calmness betrays him.'

'I'm not sure I understand,' Carradine replied. They had turned off the road and were heading into central Rabat.

'Who would get into an argument with his girlfriend while waiting in the queue for a police check?'

'An innocent person,' Carradine replied.

'Exactly. My window was down. Maybe this policeman heard you shouting at me. Maybe he sees that you look distracted and annoyed with your girlfriend in the front. And your girlfriend in the front seat has a scowl on her face? Throws a flirtatious smile at the handsome young man in the nice police uniform . . . ?'

'Who trained you to think like that?' Carradine asked. He had never heard of such a technique, but marvelled at its simplicity.

'I read it in a book,' Bartok replied and asked if she could smoke one of his cigarettes.

32

Shortly after eight o'clock, Rafiq dropped them at Gare de Rabat Ville, the main railway station in the centre of the city. Bartok paid and thanked him for all that he and his family had done for her; Carradine saw that there were tears in her eyes as they embraced inside the car. They took their bags from the boot and banged on the roof as Rafiq pulled away.

'Let's get inside,' he said.

They walked into the station and had only been inside for a few minutes when a young, bearded man in a white jilaba came up to them holding a homemade brochure displaying photocopied colour photographs of a two-bedroom apartment on the seafront.

'Is very clean, very tidy, very cheap,' he said. 'How long you want stay?'

Carradine told him that they would only need the apartment for one night. Bartok tried to establish if he was the landlord but the young man – whose name was Abdul – was evasive on the subject. In the car they had discussed the importance of finding somewhere to stay that did not use a computerised booking system. They would almost certainly have to show Bartok's Hungarian passport to their host, perhaps Carradine's as well. They hoped that whoever registered their details would log them, passing them to the authorities only after *Atalanta* had departed.

Abdul led them out of the station. He said that he had a car parked nearby and that they would drive to the apartment together. Carradine was uneasy but knew that they had little choice: doubtless there would be third parties involved in the transaction at every stage. He and Bartok could be shunted from place to place, from person to person, until they eventually arrived at the apartment. Anything was possible in Morocco. The important thing was not to show their faces for too long on the streets. Bartok was paranoid about satellite surveillance, all the more so now that the Agency also had Carradine in their sights. There was always the possibility that they might be spotted by a passer-by.

Abdul led them across a busy street towards a large open square surrounded by trees and dotted with park benches. A distant trumpeter was busking the melody from 'Michelle'. Songbirds tweeted in the trees as they passed beneath them. Everything to Carradine seemed cleaner, sharper, more functional than Marrakech; he had the impression of a European city that was more affluent than anywhere else he had visited in Morocco. Rabat was the nation's capital, the residence of the king, filled with cops and diplomats, ministers and spies. As a consequence, Carradine felt exposed; it was as though a friend from London might appear around the corner at any moment.

271

'I don't like this city,' Bartok whispered as Abdul led them towards a patisserie on the far side of the square. 'Sooner we get to the apartment, the better.'

'Me neither.'

Abdul had other ideas.

'You wait here, please,' he told them, indicating that his honoured guests should take a seat at one of the tables outside the patisserie. There were customers eating pastries and drinking coffee in the late morning light.

'Why?' Carradine asked.

'I get car.'

They looked at one another. It was inconceivable that Abdul was anything other than the man he appeared to be, but neither of them wanted to hang around in such a public place.

'Be quick,' Carradine told him. 'We'd really like to have some rest.'

'Of course, monsieur.' The Moroccan gave a low bow before hurrying off around the corner.

'Is it always like this?' Carradine asked.

'Not always.'

'We might as well have a coffee,' he suggested.

'Yes,' Bartok replied. 'And text the boat.'

She took out the phone. Carradine passed her the sheet of paper. She typed Patrick and Eleanor's number into the contacts.

'Do you want to text or shall I speak to them?' Carradine asked.

'Text. Always,' she said.

He knew that intelligence services could identify a person using voice recognition, just as he knew that a spy satellite, orbiting Morocco five hundred miles up, boasted cameras powerful enough to read a headline on the newspaper at the next table. Yet Carradine had never had cause to think that these technologies might be brought to bear on himself or on somebody he knew; they were just gimmicks in his books, details in a hundred Hollywood TV shows and movies. There was an awning over their table, providing both shade from the sun and protection from the all-seeing sky. Bartok was still wearing the long black wig, Carradine a pair of sunglasses and a Panama hat he had bought in the souk.

'I'll be back in a minute,' Bartok told him, standing up and going inside.

Carradine assumed that she was off to the bathroom. A waiter stopped at their table. Carradine ordered a café au lait for Bartok and an espresso for himself. He yearned for his phone and laptop and felt an umbilical severing from his old life: what he would have given to check his emails, his WhatsApp messages, just to read that morning's edition of *The Times*. Instead he had only a prehistoric Nokia with which to send Patrick and Eleanor a simple text message painstakingly typed out on an antediluvian keyboard.

Hi. We have made it to Rabat. Having a lovely time and really looking forward to seeing you tomorrow morning. Stupidly lost my phone so using this temporary number. Is 8am still OK? Lilia very excited to see Atalanta – as am I!

Carradine pressed send and put the phone on the table. The waiter returned with the coffees. The espresso was served, as was the custom in Morocco, with a small bottle

273

of water. Carradine opened it and drank the entire contents without bothering to pour it out. The trumpeter was now playing the theme from *The Godfather* as children ran among the carob trees in front of the patisserie. Carradine's table was positioned on a busy corner section of the square. Pedestrians were passing all the time. One of them, a frail, elderly beggar, was moving from table to table, holding out an arthritic hand as he pleaded for money. He was ignored by each of the customers in turn. Carradine leaned down to fetch his wallet, which was zipped into a side pocket of his case. He had some worn ten and twenty dirham notes – the equivalent of a couple of euros – which he could give to the elderly man. He retrieved the money and sat up as the beggar shuffled towards him. Bartok came back to the table just as he was pressing the money into the man's emaciated hand. She said nothing but smiled at the beggar who thanked Carradine effusively before shuffling off.

'Got the phone?' she asked.

Carradine looked at the table. He knew instantly that it had been stolen.

'Fuck.'

'What is it?' Bartok knew it too. He could tell by her reaction.

'The mobile. The cellphone. Did you pick it up?'

She shook her head, very slowly, coming to terms with what had happened.

'I leaned down for ten seconds to get my wallet . . .'

Had the beggar taken it? Surely not. An accomplice? More likely an opportunistic thief had swiped it while moving in the flow of pedestrians passing the table.

'Jesus, Kit . . .'

They searched the ground beneath the table. Carradine frisked himself. He asked a young mother at the next table if she had seen anyone taking the phone. She shook her head in the manner of one who did not wish to become involved in somebody else's misfortune.

'What was on the SIM?'

Bartok did not answer him. She withdrew into silence. Carradine could not tell if she was irritated solely by his lapse in concentration or if the SIM contained vital information on which she had relied for months. Every useful number, every precious message: gone in the blink of an eye.

Abdul soon returned to the patisserie. Carradine told him about the theft. The young Moroccan expressed his sympathy but offered nothing in the way of practical solutions; he was keen only that his guests should accompany him to the apartment which had now been prepared for them.

Shouldering his bag, Carradine walked behind Bartok and Abdul as they made their way towards the car. He was furious with himself. The irritation and embarrassment he had felt when Bartok had told him about Mantis returned in full flood. Perhaps he wasn't cut out for the role in which he had cast himself. For the first time since he had arrived in Morocco, Carradine thought nostalgically of home, of the simple writer's life that had so frustrated him. He was not a man prone to self-pity; nor did he wish that he could click his fingers and somehow remove himself from the complications of Rabat and Lara Bartok. Nevertheless, he was tired of living so much on the edge of his wits. He wondered how Bartok had coped for so long and could only assume that she had enjoyed periods of time in which she had been secure and safely anonymous. He presumed that she had lost contact with old friends from Hungary or New York, but perhaps this was not the case. Did she have boyfriends? Carradine could not imagine how she would be able to build or sustain a relationship with another man, living as she did. He assumed that she took her pick of men, whenever desire took hold of her, then moved on before love had a chance to take hold. But what could he possibly know? All that was clear to him was that his own life, as problematic and dangerous as it had become, was as nothing in comparison to the complexity of her own.

Watching Bartok as she spoke to Abdul, he felt a great sympathy for her, a surge of feeling for which he was rewarded with a smile as she opened the passenger door of the waiting car and climbed in. His sins had apparently been forgotten. The stolen phone was yesterday's news. Carradine was revived and joined her in the car with a strong desire to prove to Bartok, as well as to himself, that he could get them safely to Gibraltar. He had come this far, suffering only a bruised ego and a swollen right hand along the way. If Abdul came through for them and they could lay low in the apartment, there was every chance of leaving Rabat safely in the morning.

33

The bearded man standing on the crowded rush-hour platform at Oxford Circus was carrying a worn leather briefcase and a furled umbrella. It had been raining hard as he entered the station and his thinning hair was pasted to his scalp. Stephen Graham was a man with a lot on his mind. LASZLO had been found, yes, but nobody had seen hide nor hair of her for twenty-four hours. Ramón Basora had got sloppy, fallen in with the Americans – and paid with his life. Kit Carradine had vanished. Graham's hastily assembled house of cards had come crashing down. He had an ominous feeling that he would be next.

Graham had come from a meeting with Petrenko. Not so much a meeting as an interrogation. Moscow wanted to know what 'Robert Mantis' knew about the search for Lara Bartok. Did he realise that she had been sighted in Morocco? Had he had any dealings with one 'C.K. Carradine', a British writer attending a literary conference in Marrakech? Graham had denied all knowledge, fending off Petrenko's questions – *Is Kit Carradine working for the*

Service? Is he romantically involved with Bartok? – as best he could. If Moscow knew that he had been trying to protect LASZLO, they would have him killed. If Petrenko came away from the meeting believing that Graham had deliberately tried to undermine a Kremlin-sanctioned operation to find Lara Bartok, he was finished.

What could he tell them? That he was in love with the estranged girlfriend of Ivan Simakov? That no woman had ever made him feel the way Lara had made him feel? That their brief relationship had been the most sublime and fulfilling of his life? They would think he was a fool who had lost his mind.

The discussion had taken place at the Langham Hotel. Petrenko, the master interrogator, playing the trusted confidant, the old friend, the world-weary spy. Masking his suspicion of Graham in light-hearted asides, posing questions that were not quite questions, levelling accusations that were never far from threats. Graham had felt that he had survived it all until the moment Petrenko mentioned Ramón. That was when he realised that he was cornered. If he was going to escape with his life, he knew that he would have to give something up.

So, yes, he admitted that he had sent Basora to Casablanca. No, that had nothing to do with LASZLO. Yes, he had heard that Basora had been found dead in his hotel room from a suspected drugs overdose. No, he did not have any idea if third parties were involved in the death. Graham explained that he had an agent in Morocco – one Abdullah Aziz – whom he had instructed Ramón to meet at the Sheraton Hotel. Graham himself had not travelled to Casablanca in person because he had been too busy with other projects in London.

It had been hot in the hotel room. Graham had asked if he could open a window. As he did so, Petrenko picked up a black and white surveillance photograph from a table beside the bed. He showed it to Graham.

'Do you know this man?'

The man in the photograph was Sebastian Hulse. Graham could not remember how much, or how little, Moscow knew about the American. He tried to maintain a poker face. Should he feign ignorance? Should he say that he recognised Hulse as the Agency's man in Morocco? In the end, he settled on a version of the truth.

'I do. His name is Hulse. He works for the Americans. He was staying at the Sheraton. He befriended Ramón in the bar, took him to dinner, pretended he was a businessman from New York.'

Petrenko seemed surprised by the candour of this answer. His wistful smile gave Graham hope.

'You mean Hulse suspected that Ramón was working for us?'

'I can't say. I assumed as much. I told him to break off contact. Next thing I knew, Ramón was being taken to a morgue in Casablanca.'

He remembered receiving the text from Carradine, the photographs of Hulse and Ramón in Blaine's. He had wanted to simplify things, to fire Carradine so that he would no longer be in play.

'And you still cannot say who or what may have required him to pay this visit to the mortuary?'

Petrenko's expression betrayed the ghost of a smile. Graham hesitated. It was a toss-up between Hulse and Moscow. He could hardly accuse his own people of murder; better to lay the blame elsewhere.

'My money's on the Agency,' he said. 'But Ramón was always a maverick. Too much of a taste for fast women, for high-living. Didn't they say there were traces of cocaine in his room?'

'They did,' Petrenko replied. 'There were.'

The distant rumble of an approaching train. Stephen Graham moved forward, pushing through the crowds. He hoped to secure a seat. He was worn out after the long conversation and his thighs were aching after an early morning run.

Two men were standing directly behind him. As the train came crashing through the tunnel, one of them placed a hand in the small of his back. The other put a grip on Graham's right arm.

He knew what they intended to do. He had been through the same training course; he had sanctioned the same hits. To give them credit, they had timed their movements to perfection. Turning around, Graham saw that the closest of the two men was wearing a baseball cap and what appeared to be a false beard. He had been given no time to react, no chance to duck or to move to one side.

He was finished.

34

The apartment was a large, two-bedroom conversion on the first floor of a house overlooking the ocean. With a firm throw from the roof, Carradine could have landed a rock in the Atlantic.

They had the place to themselves. The building was owned by a middle-aged woman who lived across the landing with her mother and two teenage daughters. The family greeted Carradine and Bartok like long-lost relatives, showing them around with the passion and enthusiasm of vendors trying to sell carpets in the souk. They were offered hot food and laundry, sightseeing tips, even a lift to the airport in the morning. Carradine explained that they would be leaving at dawn and had already booked a taxi with a friend. When asked by the landlady if they would be sharing the same room, Bartok took Carradine's hand and smiled beatifically in the direction of her elderly mother.

'Thank you, but we are not married,' she said in perfect French. 'Until then, we prefer to sleep in separate beds.'

'Of course, mademoiselle,' the landlady replied, her face a picture of admiration for such old-fashioned sexual mores. The teenage girls looked stunned.

'If we could just have some food this evening, that would be wonderful,' Bartok continued. Carradine's cheeks were flushed with embarrassment. 'Perhaps a couscous? Some salad?'

None of it was too much trouble. The landlady requested only that they enjoy themselves and then closed the door so that the young couple could have some privacy. Minutes later, however, she came back into the apartment, asking if one of them could provide her with a passport.

Carradine fetched his own, as they had agreed, and watched as the landlady painstakingly transcribed his details – in Arabic – onto a registration form. Meanwhile, Bartok settled into what she described as the 'more feminine' of the two bedrooms – a large room upholstered in pink and decorated with floral-patterned cushions – closing the door while she unpacked and took a shower. Carradine accepted the landlady's offer of tea and drank it on a small, enclosed balcony in his room while smoking a cigarette out of the window. Traffic was constant in both directions and the room was noisy, but he was glad to be in a place that both of them considered secure and relatively anonymous. By sheer good fortune, they had ended up in an apartment which was not overlooked by neighbouring buildings. A man was selling pomegranates from a stall beneath Carradine's window. Across the Corniche, on a stretch of waste ground separating the shoreline from the road, a family was living out of a tent surrounded by oil drums and buffeted by the Atlantic wind. They were otherwise out of sight of strangers. Everything was damp to the touch: the sheets on Carradine's bed; the towels in the bathroom; even the sugar in the tiny packets the landlady placed beside the teapot. He thought again of the riad, of the festival organisers wondering what had become of him, but reckoned it would be at least forty-eight hours before anyone raised the alarm. There was no television nor radio in the apartment and therefore no means of keeping tabs on the developing story in Warsaw. Carradine laid a private bet with himself that the siege would already have been brought to an end. It was just a question of the death toll.

After finishing his tea, he took a shower. The ceiling was so low that he had to sit on a plastic stool while dousing himself with lukewarm water. He shaved and changed into some clean clothes, risked a blast of after-shave, then knocked on Bartok's door.

'Come in!' she said.

She was lying on the double bed wearing a pair of denim shorts and a T-shirt. Her hair was damp and tousled from the shower. The room smelled of perfume and the warm sea air.

'You packed my bag well,' she said, kicking a leg in the air. He saw that she was reading a book.

'Lots of practice,' Carradine replied.

He wished they were together, that they could spend the rest of the day and night in bed, passing the long hours until it was time to leave for the boat. In any other situation, with any other woman, he would have tried his luck.

'What's on your mind?' she asked.

'Nothing much.' He walked towards the window, saw

the same view he had been looking at while drinking his tea. 'We have a lot of time to kill.'

'Lots,' she said.

'Good book?'

'I've read it before.'

She flung it across the room. Carradine caught it like a fly-half as it passed behind his waist. It was a French translation of *The Sheltering Sky*.

'Ah, doomed love,' he said, trying to sound sophisticated.

'The wife is called Kit.'

He pretended to be furious. 'Really?' He flicked through the pages, searching for the name.

'Really,' Bartok replied.

'Don't they end up dying in Morocco?' There was a picture on the back of Debra Winger in the arms of John Malkovich. 'She gets sick. Or he gets sick. I can't remember.'

'Don't spoil it.'

'I thought you said you'd read it before?'

'Years ago.'

Carradine threw it back. This time the book bounced off the side of the mattress and landed on the floor. Bartok leaned over the bed to fetch it. Her T-shirt rode up on her back. Carradine stole a glance at her waist, tanned and lithe, blond hairs at the base of her spine. She looked up and caught him staring and for an instant the time stopped between them.

The doorbell rang. They continued to stare at one another. Carradine walked to the door. The landlady walked in carrying a tray covered in plates and cutlery. She apologised for interrupting and said that the food was almost ready. One of the teenage daughters followed her in, holding a bowl of salad and some fruit. Carradine noticed how respectful they were towards Bartok, staring at her as though she were a visiting dignitary. Within a few minutes the family had left them in a traditional, tiled reception room at the back of the apartment, plates of chicken couscous, cheese and pasta salad spread out in front of them.

'Do you want to go down to the marina, see if your friends are there?' Bartok asked.

'Together?' Carradine replied.

'No, no.'

Her answer was quick and dismissive, as if the notion that she could walk around Rabat in plain sight was nonsensical.

'I don't think I should go,' he said. 'Even alone. If somebody picks me up, they'll eventually find you.'

'Only if you crack under questioning.'

Carradine saw her grin as he spooned some couscous into a bowl. 'I'd give you up in a heartbeat,' he said. 'I bet you there's a reward on your head.'

Traffic was growling past on the Corniche. He was still thinking about the lost moment in the bedroom. Yet Bartok's mood seemed to have changed.

'I don't want you to be bored,' she said. 'You can go for a walk. It would be fine.'

'I'm perfectly happy.'

'You strike me as a trapped person, Kit. Like a caged bird.'

'Is that right?' He was by turns flattered by the description and startled that she had intuited his inner restlessness. 'I don't feel like that at the moment.'

'No, perhaps not. Why would someone do what you have done?'

'I don't understand,' he said.

'Become a spy.'

'But I'm not a spy.' He knew that she was referring to his work for Mantis, but did not want to pretend to be something that he was not.

'I realise that,' she replied. 'But many people would not have agreed to work for their country as you did. It was an old-fashioned thing to do. Patriotism. A sense of duty. Of course you were not to know that Stephen Graham was a liar, but this does not really matter. You acted in good faith. You wanted to help. You had the adventure inside you, the restlessness. Does your life satisfy you, Kit?'

Several seconds passed before Carradine answered the question.

'In some ways,' he replied, taken aback by Bartok's directness. 'I'm very lucky. I'm my own boss. I make my own rules. Nobody gets to tell me what time to show up for work, what time I can go home.'

'This is important to you? Not to be told what to do?'

It was like being scrutinised by someone who had not yet made up her mind whether or not to like him.

'I prefer it that way,' he said. 'But it comes at a price. I've started to realise that my life is very solitary. I have no colleagues, no meetings, no team . . .'

'You have to motivate yourself . . .'

'Precisely.'

He ate some of the couscous.

'Are you married?' Bartok asked.

Carradine almost spat out the food. 'No!' he said. 'Why so many questions?'

'I am just getting to know you,' she said, touching her lips.

'But you know that I'm not married . . .'

'Do I?'

He realised that the subject had never come up between them.

'Well I'm not,' he said.

'Do you have a girlfriend?'

Was she making small talk or clearing the romantic ground? Carradine could not tell. He ate a hunk of bread and said that he wasn't seeing anybody in London.

'What about *outside* London?'

'Nowhere.' A sheep, tethered in a nearby yard, let out an anguished cry. 'That's probably our dinner,' he said. 'What about you? Did you have somebody in Marrakech?'

Bartok shook her whole body in a mime of discomfort.

'No. Ivan finished me with men. After him, I was done.'

'You mean you're still in love with him?'

Carradine dreaded the answer. The idea of this beautiful, alluring woman holding an eternal candle for the martyred Simakov was debilitating.

'No!' she exclaimed, with disbelief. 'I was trying to say . . .' She hesitated. 'I was trying to say that I was so disappointed by him that I lost all faith in men.'

'In what way?'

'In the sense that he began as somebody I admired. An idealist, a fighter. He was clever and imaginative, full of energy. But he became vain and angry. He betrayed the principles on which he stood.'

'Which were?'

Quite apart from the pleasure of sitting and talking to Bartok, Carradine was aware of his own good fortune.

To be able to speak to someone who had known Ivan Simakov so intimately was a rare opportunity. It was like listening to a first draft of history.

'Resurrection was intended to be a non-violent organisation targeted against specific people. We always said there would be no leadership structure, no role like that for Ivan. But he quickly became obsessed with the idea that the only way we were ever going to change people was by fighting them. I profoundly disagreed with this. I also saw the way that he cultivated his fame. It became an obsession which has now of course resulted in Ivan being regarded – mistakenly, of course – as some kind of deity. He was nothing of the sort. He was like all of us. He was both good and bad and parts in between. None of us are saints, Kit.'

'Speak for yourself.'

She made a tutting sound and pushed him playfully with her hand. They finished their food. Carradine offered Bartok a cigarette. He lit it for her, opening a window onto the street.

'What did he feel about you?' he asked. He was aware that he was repeatedly, almost fixatedly, looking at her neck.

'I think he loved me,' she said. She was being modest. Simakov had clearly been obsessed with her. 'I think he continued to love me. At least that is what I heard from his friends at around the time he was killed. In some ways I still feel responsible for his death.'

'Why?'

'Because I think losing me made him angry. He wanted to lash out. He became more vicious, more politicised in his general behaviour. He was encouraging Resurrection activists into greater and greater violence with his statements. He was reckless to go to Russia.'

This was all true. Carradine remembered the period leading up to Simakov's death, a phase in which he himself had begun to lose faith in whatever it was that had made so many people in the West sympathetic to Resurrection in the first instance. He spoke of his own attitudes towards the movement and told Bartok that he had witnessed the kidnapping of Lisa Redmond. She questioned him forensically on what he had seen, almost as if she was nostalgic for her own days on the frontline. For the next two hours they sat in the reception room smoking and talking until Bartok said that she needed to sleep. Carradine knew that she wanted to be alone and went to his room where he tried, unsuccessfully, to doze. When he knocked on her door at eight o'clock, she did not answer. He ate some of the leftover food and read his book for an hour, drinking the Johnny Walker and wondering if he should have taken up Bartok's suggestion of going to the marina to look for Patrick and Eleanor. What if there had been a change of plan? What if they had decided to leave Rabat without them? They might have sent a text to the stolen mobile but it was now too late.

Just after ten Carradine heard Bartok moving around in her room. He asked through the closed door if she wanted something to eat but she told him that she was not hungry.

'I'll wait until the morning,' she said. 'I'm just going to rest.'

He wondered if he had said something during their long lunchtime conversation which had upset her. Perhaps she had been thinking of him romantically, but had decided against it. The friction between them, the possibility that they might become lovers, appeared to have dissipated. Carradine wished her a good night and returned to his room. Soon afterwards the landlady knocked on the door of the apartment and handed him a tray on which she had placed a small pot of tea, two glasses and some baklava. He thanked her and took the tray to his room without bothering to disturb Lara a second time. He had concluded that solitude was her default state; she was not used to spending so much time in close proximity to another person. Perhaps she did not want Carradine to think that they were going to become involved; perhaps she was simply taking her time with him. He was not sure.

He took the tray to the window and looked out over the beach. The wind was howling in from the Atlantic, buffeting the shakily erected tent on the stretch of waste ground in front of his room. Thin clouds of yellowed sand and dust were swirling along the Corniche. The landlady had lined the tray with a fresh sheet of newspaper. Carradine put a lump of sugar into a glass, poured the tea and lifted up the plate of baklava. He was on the point of biting into a small, honey-soaked sponge when his eye was drawn to the newspaper. He set the plate to one side and turned the tray through ninety degrees. It was covered in Arabic script. There was a black-and-white photograph of a bearded man hidden within the text. There was no mistaking his face. It was Ramón.

Carradine looked more carefully, wondering if his eyes were again playing tricks on him. He studied the photograph more closely. He could not understand what had been written about Ramón nor why his face was appearing in a Moroccan daily newspaper. Was it a business story – or something more sinister?

Picking up the keys to the flat, Carradine walked outside, crossed the landing and knocked on the landlady's front door. It was some time before she answered. She was adjusting her veil as she opened the door.

'I'm sorry to disturb you so late,' said Carradine.

'It is no problem,' she replied, in faltering English.

He thrust the newspaper towards her.

'This man.' He pointed at the photograph of Ramón. The newspaper was slightly crumpled and sticky. When Carradine tapped Ramón's face with his finger he left a smudge on the bridge of his nose. 'Can you tell me what this story is about? Can you translate it?'

He wondered, for a horrible moment, if the landlady was illiterate and would be unable to do what he had asked. Had he just humiliated her? Would she have to wake up one of the teenage girls to ask them to translate? Yet after a moment's hesitation she took the newspaper and began to read the article.

'It says he was a Spanish tourist.' She was frowning at the text, as though it contained grammatical errors or content that was causing her offence. 'Visiting Casablanca. He has died.'

Carradine had somehow known that she would say this.

'Died? *How*?'

'They say with drugs. An overdose of cocaine. He was staying at the Sheraton Hotel.'

Carradine stood in silence, absorbing what he had been told. He was so shaken that he asked no more questions, merely thanked the landlady and went back to his room.

He poured himself a glass of whisky, wondering if he should wake Bartok. But what would be the point? It would only unsettle her. He could only assume that Ramón had been murdered. Surely there was no possibility that he had accidentally overdosed on cocaine? The coincidence of his death, with Hulse and the Russians at large, was too stark. And yet what proof did he have of foul play? What purpose did it serve to assassinate Ramón? All Carradine knew for certain was that they must get out of Rabat in the morning. If the Russians were going after anybody associated with LASZLO, then he was next on the list.

He drank a glass of water, took a sleeping pill and set his alarm for five. The sun was due to rise at half-past six. He had agreed with Lara to leave the apartment under cover of darkness and to be at the marina at first light. For the next half-hour, he lay on his bed fully clothed, listening to the tick of the air conditioner and to the low roar of the passing traffic. Driving images of the dead Ramón from his mind, he waited for sleep to take him.

35

The police lights woke him.

There were no curtains on the windows in Carradine's room. A bright orange beam was strobing against the walls. At first, he thought that he was in the last stages of a dream. Then he saw the lights and felt his heart jolt as though it had been hit by an electric charge. He got out of bed and walked towards the balcony window, trying to remain out of sight.

He crouched down and peered through the window. Two police cars were parked on the opposite side of the Corniche. Three cops, dressed in the same uniforms as the men at the roadblock, were standing on the pavement beneath a date palm. They were facing in the direction of the ocean. One of them was speaking on a walkie-talkie.

The game was up. They had been found. Police investigating the death of Ramón Basora had established a link to Carradine and run him to ground. The landlady had betrayed them. It was only a matter of time before the police stormed the apartment. Carradine wondered if Bartok had seen the lights. He went out into the passage and knocked on her door. There was no answer. He knocked again, this time more loudly. Still no response. Had she already fled? He turned the handle and walked in.

She was asleep on the bed, naked but for a single white sheet covering her calves and the backs of her thighs. She was breathtakingly beautiful. Carradine felt that he was trespassing on her privacy but he had to wake her. He knelt beside the bed, gently touching her shoulder.

'What is it?' she said sleepily.

She turned over and smiled. It was as though she had been expecting him. She did not seem in any way self-conscious about her nakedness.

'Outside,' he said. 'Police.'

Bartok immediately wrapped the sheet around her and sat up.

'Here?' she replied. She walked towards the window. There was a blanket blocking out the light. She looked out at the Corniche through a narrow gap on one side of the fabric. 'How long have they been there?'

Carradine told her that the lights had woken him up only moments earlier.

'What time is it?' she asked, looking to see if he was wearing a watch.

'Almost five.'

'Wait.'

She had seen something. He stood behind her and looked out through the same narrow gap. His chest was pressed against her back; he could feel the warmth of her body, the shape of her.

'What is it?'

'They're going to the beach.'

Bartok pulled the blanket back a little further. Carradine stepped to one side. One of the cars had driven off so that only one police light remained, sending a clockwise beam, like the beacon from a lighthouse, sweeping across the beach. The headlights of the car were pointing at the ocean. Carradine realised what was happening. The police were clearing the family from the tent. One of them was ushering a woman onto the rocky shoreline while a second policeman, carrying a torch, gathered up their belongings. A child, no older than three or four years old, was being carried in the arms of a man wearing shorts and a dark T-shirt. He put the child down on top of one of the oil drums.

'They're not for us,' he said. 'I'm sorry I woke you.'

'It's fine.' Bartok settled her fingertips briefly on his arm. She released the blanket so that the room was in almost total darkness. 'We have to be up anyway.'

He told her about Ramón. She was surprised, but not shocked. They showered and packed and carried their bags to the door. As Carradine was leaving the keys on a side table in the hall, the landlady's mother peered out from the neighbouring apartment and wished them well.

'*Merci pour tout,*' Bartok whispered.

'*Oui, merci,*' said Carradine, and they crept downstairs to the street.

The second police vehicle had gone. The tent had been cleared from the beach leaving only a scattering of oil drums and the black patch of an extinguished fire. The Corniche was deserted save for the occasional passing car. They stood beneath the balcony of Carradine's room waiting for a taxi for more than ten minutes and had almost given up hope when a dented beige Mercedes rounded the corner and pulled in to collect them. The recalcitrant, elderly driver spoke incomprehensible French. They were obliged to give him directions to the marina using a mixture of English, French and hand signals. They drove to the end of the Corniche and joined a road which passed beneath the walls of the old Medina. Carradine could see the lights of the marina to the north, across the Bouregreg River. He prayed that *Atalanta* was still in dock, that Patrick and Eleanor were fast asleep in their bunks. He was pointing to the bridge which would take them across the narrow river to the marina when it became clear that the driver was refusing to take them.

'*Non*. No go,' he said, spluttering at the wheel. '*Pas permit.*'

'*Pourquoi?*' said Carradine.

'No go! *Pas possible! Là!*'

There was a roundabout at the bottom of the bridge. The driver made a full turn and began to drive back in the direction from which they had come.

'*Attends!*' said Carradine, becoming annoyed. 'Where are we going?'

It was infuriating to be at the mercy of a moody geriatric who refused to take them where they wanted to go. Carradine produced a fifty dirham note and waved it at the driver as a bribe, but still he refused to go back. Bartok explained that there was most probably a local law preventing taxi drivers from leaving the city limits; he would lose his licence if he crossed the bridge. As if to confirm this, the old man stopped at a set of traffic lights, then made a sudden right turn into a car park at the edge of the river.

'*Bateau*,' he spat. It was as if his mouth was full of chewing tobacco. '*Bateau*.'

Only after he had said the word another three times did Carradine understand that they were being told to take a boat across the channel. Realising that he had little choice other than to comply, he paid the driver and removed the luggage from the boot. Two men were sleeping on a low wall running along the length of the car park. One of them sat up and waved at Carradine as the taxi drove off. There was a smell of fish guts and salt water.

'Can you take us across?' Bartok asked.

The man shrugged, as if to suggest that it was too early in the morning to make a crossing. The landing point was less than two hundred metres away on the opposite bank; they could have swum across in a couple of minutes.

'How much?' Carradine asked in French.

The man eventually conceded and they settled on an extortionate price for the short crossing. Carradine carried the bags to a wooden jetty covered in fishing nets and coils of rope. Two skiffs were tied up alongside. There was the same overpowering smell of landed fish. The boatman indicated that they should climb into the furthest of the two skiffs. It was dark and hard to make out the distance between objects: at one point Bartok momentarily lost her balance as her foot landed on a loose wooden plank. Carradine steadied her, helping her down into the skiff, holding her hand as she stepped onto a narrow seat in the stern. He passed the bags, one by one, to the boatman, who was holding one of the oars in his free hand.

'Watch your feet,' Bartok warned as Carradine prepared to step into the boat. 'It's wet.'

He aimed for a point beside her but, inevitably, felt his foot land in a puddle of water. He sat on the seat as the boatman pushed off, resting the foot on a wooden strut. Watching the slow movement of the oars, looking out at the dark channel and the distant lights of the Medina, listening to the sound of the water lapping against the skiff, Carradine knew that this would ordinarily have been a moment for the notebook. But he was so focused on the goal of reaching the marina, and so distracted by his desire for Bartok, that the responsibilities of his profession seemed to belong to a completely different person.

Within three minutes they had crossed the channel. The boatman deposited them at a jetty on the Mellah side of the Bouregreg. The sun was beginning to rise. They shared a cigarette beside a line of outboard motors attached to a wall at the far end of the jetty. They were hungry and wanted to eat breakfast but there were no cafés or restaurants in sight, only empty modern apartment blocks running east in the direction of the marina.

They crossed a narrow strip of waste ground and walked along a deserted road as the call to prayer rose from the distant Medina. There were no cars parked on the street, no early morning pedestrians heading to mosque or taking a dawn stroll. Carradine was reminded of a deserted movie set on a studio backlot and felt that, at any moment, a posse of cops would burst out of an abandoned building and surge forward to arrest them. He tried to distract himself by thinking practically about Patrick and Eleanor. They would need to be convinced that his relationship with 'Lilia' was genuine and that there was no hidden motive behind Carradine's sudden desire to leave Morocco by boat. At the same time, Bartok would have to negotiate customs and immigration using the Hudak passport. If word had got out that she was on the run, or that Carradine had disappeared from the riad, they were finished.

'We're going to have to pretend to be together,' he said.

'I know that.'

'I said that we'd been dating for about six months. They're going to expect us to share a cabin.'

'I know that, too.' She shot Carradine a mischievous smile.

'It's just that I don't think they're going to believe that I'm going out with a born-again Christian . . .'

It was awkward broaching the subject. He wished that he had kept his mouth shut. Bartok put him out of his misery.

'Don't worry,' she said. 'You don't have to be so English about it. Do I look like the kind of woman who would wait until marriage to sleep with you? We can share a cabin and that is fine.'

Carradine spent the next thirty seconds wondering what Bartok had meant by the word 'fine'. He did not want to get into a longer discussion about how they should behave in front of Patrick and Eleanor. He assumed that Bartok would play her part convincingly and that he would not have to change his own behaviour too drastically. It was common in espionage to role-play the part of a couple, though Carradine had never written about an operation of that type in his fiction. As a consequence, he had not had cause to think too deeply about the mechanics of such a deceit. He was sure that body language would play a part, as well as the appearance of a certain easefulness in Bartok's company. But perhaps he was overthinking things and there was no need to be concerned.

Rounding a corner at the end of the street Carradine sighted the tops of masts and a modern, open-air café on a terrace overlooking the marina. He could hear the ping of halyards, the cry of seagulls on the wind. A man was sitting at one of the tables, deep in conversation on a mobile phone. His back was turned to them and he appeared to be in a state of agitation. It was not clear if he was a customer or a member of staff who had arrived early for work. On closer inspection, he turned out to be Patrick Lang.

'I am telling you . . .' Carradine could hear snatches of his conversation. 'They're arriving this morning. At any moment. We had a text message last night . . .'

Bartok took Carradine's hand, pulling him back, sensing the danger. At that moment Patrick turned in his chair and saw that they were walking towards him. Lowering his voice, he quickly ended the call and stood up to greet them.

'There you are! I was just talking about you.'

He looked flustered, as if he had been caught in the act of lying. Carradine wondered who the hell he had been speaking to.

'Hello,' he said. 'Sorry we're early.'

Patrick slipped the phone into his back pocket and ran a hand through his hair as he nodded at Bartok. A pair of sunglasses hung from the collar of his canary yellow polo shirt. He seemed distracted and strung out in a way that was completely out of character.

'Yes,' he replied. 'You didn't answer my text.'

'We lost yet another phone.' Carradine knew that it was now too late to turn back. If Patrick had alerted Hulse or the Russians to their arrival, they were finished. 'This is my girlfriend,' he said. 'The famous Lilia.'

Patrick recovered his equilibrium and made a spectacle of falling for the Bartok charm, kissing the top of her hand as if the ghost of Cary Grant were indeed living inside him.

'Delighted to meet you,' he said, offering to take her bag. 'Kit said you were very beautiful and he didn't misinform. What happened to the phone?'

Carradine explained that the mobile had been stolen and apologised for not confirming their arrival. Patrick waved away his apologies and ordered three cappuccinos from the waitress. His increasingly relaxed manner made Carradine feel that at any moment they were going to be surrounded by Moroccan police.

'So you're Hungarian?'

'Born and bred,' Bartok replied. If she was wary of him, she did not show it. Instead, Carradine was treated to a twenty-minute masterclass in deception as Bartok spoke of her childhood in Budapest, her work as a private tutor in London, her lifelong fascination with boats and the ocean.

'When Kit told me that you had invited us to come with you on your beautiful yacht, it was the happiest moment,' she said, touching Patrick's wrist and speaking with a tenderness that almost convinced Carradine she was telling the truth. 'We have changed our flights to go home from Gibraltar. You are so generous. Both of you so kind.'

They ate breakfast undisturbed. Carradine concluded that Patrick had been speaking to a member of his family on the telephone and that there was nothing to worry about. Having finished their food, Patrick suggested that they walk down to the boat where Eleanor was waiting for them. Carradine settled the bill, shouldered the bags and followed him out of the café. At no point did Bartok shoot Carradine a look of amused complicity or appear to take any pleasure in their shared deceit. She had dropped into the character of Lilia Hudak solely for the purposes of survival and would play the role only for as long as it was required of her.

'We'll get you settled in, then you'll have to go and see immigration,' Patrick announced. They were walking down a gangplank towards a network of pontoons at the entrance to the marina. A young couple with two small children passed them in the opposite direction, nodding at Carradine as he took in the sights of the marina. Patrick pointed ahead at *Atalanta*, sixty feet of teak and fibreglass nestled between two gigantic Qatari-registered gin palaces with crew in pressed white uniforms scrubbing the decks. She was a thing of beauty, gleaming in the early morning sun. A red ensign was flying from the stern, rippling in the slight breeze. Bartok gasped as she stepped on board, walking across a narrow gangplank connecting the yacht to the pontoon.

'Extraordinary,' she said.

Steering wheels were positioned on the port and starboard side of a cockpit protected by a large canvas roof. A hatch at the far end led into the interior of the yacht. Eleanor was sitting on one side of the master cabin at a wooden table spread with the remnants of a classic British breakfast: triangles of half-eaten toast; pots of Marmite and Oxford marmalade; miniature packets of Corn Flakes and All-Bran. It was like a glimpse of home, but for the second time that morning, Carradine had the sudden, giddy sense that they were walking into a trap.

'Look who I found,' Patrick called out with forced cheeriness as he came down the steps. 'They were early.'

Eleanor was dressed in dark blue linen trousers and a Breton sweater. A pair of pyjamas and a dressing-gown with a White Company label were draped over the back of the leather seat beside her. She removed a pair of half-moon spectacles. Just as Patrick had seemed flustered and evasive when they had first spotted him at the café, there was also a palpable change in Eleanor's demeanour. She looked tired, giving off an air of impatient agitation. Carradine wondered if there had been an early morning row.

'Hello,' she said, shaking his hand without moving closer to offer a kiss. 'This must be the mysterious Lilia.'

Carradine was certain that he caught a flash of wariness in Eleanor's first glance at Bartok. Did she know the truth about her? Bartok remained in character, smiling beatifically. *What a beautiful boat. So kind of you to invite us.* Was it Carradine's imagination or was Eleanor looking for a chink in her armour, for some tiny piece of evidence that would convince her that their seemingly innocent voluntary crew were fugitives on the run from the law? Standing in the cabin, watching the two women becoming awkwardly and hesitatingly acquainted, he had to tell himself to remain calm; that whatever circumspection he detected in Eleanor's mood was most likely the aftermath of a row or the natural wariness of a wife who was protective of her husband and all-too-aware that Lilia Hudak was a beautiful young woman.

'Your boat's not at all what I expected,' he said, setting his bag on the ground and taking in the state-of-the-art navigation equipment, the shelves of Everyman books, the wood-lined passages leading stern and aft.

'She does us very well,' Patrick replied as Eleanor stepped past him.

'My husband and I sleep up here,' she said, indicating two separate cabins – one in the bow, another on the portside – both with unmade beds. It was as though she was providing a visual demonstration of the tensions that existed in the marriage.

'It's all so modern,' Bartok observed, plainly trying to think of something to fill the silence.

'Oh yes, Patrick likes all the mod cons,' Eleanor replied coolly.

She showed them a bathroom on the starboard side before turning back towards the main cabin. 'You'll be sleeping here,' she said, leading them through a well-stocked galley towards a master cabin in the stern. There was a large double bed beneath the cockpit and a frosted glass door leading to what appeared to be an en-suite bathroom. This would be the room Carradine was to share with Bartok for the next three days. 'There's a shower, lots of hot water. Hopefully you'll be comfortable.'

'Very,' said Carradine, feeling simultaneously as though he had won the jackpot and yet stumbled on one of the most awkward romantic entanglements of his life.

'This is how the TV works,' Eleanor continued, banging a button on the bedside table with noticeable force. A flat-screen television rose up from a cupboard on the galley side of the cabin. 'State of the art. Apparently.'

Perhaps Eleanor was annoyed that she had been obliged to give up the cabin to her guests. The channel was set to Spanish Eurosport. Cyclists wearing lycra and aerodynamic helmets were bombing around a velodrome.

'So why don't you settle in? We'll see you when we see you.'

The two women exchanged wary smiles as Eleanor turned to leave.

'Lovely,' said Bartok. 'Thank you so much.'

Carradine peered through a porthole. He could see Patrick walking back in the direction of the café, again speaking agitatedly on his mobile phone. Who the hell was he talking to? A mistress? His daughter? Hulse?

'Nice place,' said Bartok, unaware of Carradine's disquiet.

'Very,' he said, closing the door of the cabin. He sat on one side of the double bed. 'Nice digs.'

The commentary on the cycling was loud enough to disguise their conversation.

'Is she OK?' Bartok asked, nodding in the direction of the main cabin.

'I think they had a row,' he whispered.

'Right.' She walked to the far side of the room, looking out of the same porthole. Carradine assumed that Patrick was now too far away to be spotted. 'You are a very clever man, Kit Carradine.'

'Me?' he said. 'Why?'

'Finding us such a beautiful way of escape.'

Bartok turned to look at him. She touched the ceiling of the cabin and the padded wall beside her, as though trying to acclimatise herself to the latest in a long line of strange, impermanent homes. Quite apart from his concerns about Patrick, Carradine was conscious that they still needed to clear immigration. He took out his passport and placed it on the bed.

'Shall we go together or is it easier for you to do it alone?'

At first it looked as though Bartok had not understood what he was asking. Then she nodded and sat on the bed beside him.

'I want to go with you,' she said.

Suddenly she leaned forward, kissing him. The intensity of the kiss, the unexpectedness of it, stripped Carradine of any notion that she might have been acting out of practical necessity. The softness of it was so pleasurable that he grabbed her by the waist and pulled her close against him. No part of him believed that Bartok was engaged in a performance, that she was trying to carry off an illusion of romance. He could sense the desire in her, the excitement, just as he could feel his own.

'What was that for?' he said.

'For everything,' she replied, kissing him again, gently and tenderly, on the cheek. 'Now let's go and do what we have to do.'

36

They walked along a metalled road towards a group of prefabricated buildings overlooking the entrance to the marina. A tram passed overhead, moving towards the bridge connecting Mellah to the old city of Rabat. A television was visible through the window of a deserted restaurant showing a Moroccan news report on the siege in Warsaw. Carradine knocked on the window in the hope of being allowed inside but there was no answer. It was not yet nine o'clock and already very hot. Bartok had put on a hat as protection against the sun.

'It was never supposed to be like this,' she said, gesturing towards the television. The picture had frozen on a bird's-eye view of the Sejm, which appeared to be on fire. 'Large-scale attacks. Innocent people killed as a consequence. These people are no different to terrorists, to the Chechens or ISIS.'

Carradine took her hand.

'If they arrest me or refuse to let me leave Morocco,' she said, 'I want you to go on without me.'

'That's not going to happen.'

'I am serious, Kit.' She stopped and turned to him, touching his face. Carradine wondered if she was acting for the benefit of anybody who happened to be watching: a passing immigration officer; Eleanor on the deck of *Atalanta*. 'They might say my entry stamp is too old. They might want to know why I have been in Morocco for such a long time.'

'When did you arrive?' Carradine asked. He had not thought to look at the dates on the Hudak passport.

'Five months ago.'

It didn't seem too long. Surely she could talk her way around the problem?

'Just say you've been recovering from an illness and I flew out from London to fetch you.'

'They might not believe me. Five months is a long time.'

Carradine was concerned by her sudden lack of confidence. It was the first time that he had seen Bartok display any sign of self-doubt.

'Just tell a version of the truth. Say you rented a flat in Marrakech. I came out to appear at the literary festival. We were offered the chance to leave on a boat owned by a couple who like my books. Simple.'

She squeezed his hand as though she were trying to convince herself that Carradine was right.

'OK,' she said. They began walking again. The customs buildings were less than a hundred metres away. 'If you say so.'

He suddenly remembered their argument in the car the day before.

'Is this one of your tricks?' he asked.

Bartok bristled.

'What do you mean?'

'In the car yesterday, you engineered an argument. Are you genuinely worried about this or just trying to give that impression to anyone who might be watching?'

She let go of his hand. Carradine realised that he had made a mistake. He had questioned the authenticity of her behaviour just at the moment when she had decided to show him a more vulnerable side of her nature.

'I'm worried,' she said. 'I'm worried all the time.'

He had glimpsed the state of permanent apprehension in which she lived. She disguised it with good humour and bonhomie but the months on the run had taken their toll.

'I'm sorry,' he said, annoyed to have misjudged the situation. He held her waist. 'We're going to get through this. They don't know who you are. They won't recognise you. It's too soon for anyone in London to worry that I've not been in touch. They won't be waiting for us.'

'You don't know that. You can't guarantee that.'

The passport office was a nondescript wooden shed not much larger than Carradine's room at the riad. Three uniformed officials were seated at desks covered in ashtrays and paperwork. Cigarette smoke hung in the air; there was an absence of natural light. Carradine knocked on the open door and walked in. Bartok removed her hat as the closest, and youngest, of the immigration officers looked up from his desk.

'*Oui?*'

Carradine explained in French that they were staying

on board *Atalanta*, the Oyster 575 moored in the marina. The captain, Patrick Lang, and his wife, Eleanor, had already passed through immigration. Carradine was their friend, a British citizen travelling with his girlfriend, Lilia Hudak, a Hungarian. They wanted to clear passport control and to set off for Gibraltar.

The immigration officer looked at them carefully. He stared at Bartok. Carradine was certain that she had been recognised. As if to confirm this, the official called out to his colleague at a desk on the far side of the shed.

'Mahmud.'

An older man with a heavy beard, wearing the same light blue uniform, beckoned Carradine and Bartok forward.

'Where are you coming from, please?' he asked in English.

'From Marrakech,' Bartok replied.

The man looked at her with an expression of distaste, as if he had expected Carradine to answer the question.

'And what were you doing in Marrakech?'

'My girlfriend hasn't been very well,' Carradine replied. He was aware that he was lying to a Moroccan official who had the power to arrest and imprison him. 'She picked up a virus in London. She was recuperating in Marrakech.'

A chair scraped back behind him, the grind of metal on the hard wooden floor. The younger official who had spoken to them at the door stood up and walked towards them. He settled in a seat beside Mahmud and stared at Carradine, seemingly with the deliberate intention of unsettling him.

'What does it mean, "picked up virus"?'

Bartok took half a step forward and explained what Carradine had said, this time in French. Mahmud again looked at her as though it was beneath his dignity to have formal dealings with a woman.

'You feel sick now?' he asked.

'I am fine.' Bartok produced a relaxed, summery smile. Carradine was boiled by the heat. There was no air-conditioning in the hut, only a fan in the corner of the room which was making no difference to the quality of the thick, smoky air.

'And you?'

Mahmud had directed the question at Carradine. For a reason that he was afterwards not able to explain, Carradine reached into the back pocket of his trousers and took out his passport. Intending to hand it across the desk, he instead managed to lose his grip on it. The passport sailed over the desk and fell to the ground behind the two officials.

'Shit!' he exclaimed. 'Sorry.'

The third man, seated at his desk in the centre of the hut, looked over and grunted. It was not clear whether he was laughing at what had happened or expressing some measure of disapproval. Mahmud slowly turned around and leaned over in his chair, plucking the passport from the ground.

'That is not what I asked,' he said. 'I asked what you were doing here in Rabat.'

As Carradine answered the question, Mahmud handed the passport to the younger official, who began to study it with forensic attention. A seagull clacked in the marina.

'I am a writer. I was invited to a literary festival in Marrakech. We went together . . .'

The younger official interrupted him.

'But you flew into Casablanca.'

Carradine felt that he was being cross-examined by lawyers with decades of experience. The remark had trapped him in a lie from which there was surely no realistic prospect of escape.

'Yes, well, I came to Casablanca because I'm writing a book that's partly set in Morocco. Lilia came up to join me . . .'

Another lie. Mahmud was writing something down as he listened. Was he keeping a record of the conversation, to be used as evidence against them at a later point?

'Lilia?' he said.

'That's me,' Bartok replied.

Carradine wondered if it was all a sick joke. The officials already knew that Lara Bartok was standing in front of them. They knew only too well that 'Lilia Hudak' was an alias.

'And you are from Hungary?'

'Yes,' she said.

There was a sustained silence. The younger official slowly turned the pages of Carradine's passport. Mahmud was writing something down on a pad. He looked up and addressed a question in Arabic to his colleague at the desk in the centre of the hut. Carradine was amazed to see Bartok spin on her heels and look out of the window, seemingly without a care in the world.

'This is your first visit to Morocco?'

'It is,' Carradine replied.

He wondered what web Mahmud was trying to draw him into. He hated lying. He hated the traps they were setting for him.

'And yet you do not visit this beautiful woman in all that time?'

Of course. It was the simple, gaping hole in their hastily assembled cover story. Carradine did what he could to fill it, improvising as he answered.

'Um, we sort of broke up for a while.' He tried to appear as though the official was prying too deeply into his personal life and was pleased to look across and find Bartok lowering her chin towards her chest, as if trying to forget a painful episode in the history of their other-wise happy relationship. 'That made it difficult to come here.'

'I see,' Mahmud replied.

There was another long silence. Carradine could not tell if his story had been believed.

'So now you go to Gibraltar, on . . .' – Mahmud picked up a sheet of paper on his desk and mispronounced the name of the yacht – ' . . . *Atlantis*?'

'*Atalanta*. That's right.'

'Your passport please, Miss Hudak.'

Bartok smiled and reached into her bag, handing the passport to Mahmud. He stared at the cover as if it was the first document of its type that he had ever seen. He turned it over and looked at the back, his head bobbing back and forth as his mouth dropped into a frown.

'Hungarian?'

'Yes.'

The Moroccan flicked through the pages, looking for the immigration stamp. Carradine felt that his whole future rested on the next ten seconds. He had no idea if Bartok's stamp was real or forged, if there was a record of Lilia Hudak entering Morocco, or if every customs and immigration official in the country had been instructed to search for a woman matching her description.

'You change your hair,' Mahmud observed, indicating that the Hudak photograph showed Bartok with a shoulder-length red bob.

'I did,' she replied. 'Do you prefer that one?'

'I think it looks nice here,' Mahmud replied and pressed a stubby finger onto the photograph. Smiling to himself, he handed the passport to the same official who had earlier copied down Carradine's details.

'And why don't you have British passport?'

Carradine assumed that it was a trick question. A car pulled up outside the hut. He was certain that it was a team of Agency personnel coming to haul them in.

'I don't understand,' Bartok replied.

Mahmud looked at Carradine. His face was blank as he said: 'Why don't you marry this woman?'

Carradine blurted out a laugh.

'I'm thinking about it.' For the first time he began to believe that they might be in the clear. 'Lilia likes being Hungarian. It's a beautiful country.'

'Then maybe *you* should have Hungarian passport.'

'Maybe I should.'

He felt a surge of relief. They were home and dry. All of his worry and agitation had been for nothing.

Then Mahmud opened a drawer in his desk.

He took out a small black machine and passed it to the younger official. Carradine instantly knew what it was. He had seen similar devices in passport booths the world over. The younger official plugged the machine into a computer and switched it on. An eerie blue light glowed from within.

He picked up Carradine's passport. Opening it to the identity page, he scanned it beneath the light, turned to the computer and studied the screen. Various lines of Arabic text appeared inside a small box. Mahmud appeared to be trying to read the text from his position several feet away. The process was taking so long that Carradine began to think that some kind of anomaly had cropped up deep within the Moroccan immigration system. Had a flag been placed on his passport? The younger official said something in Arabic, took Carradine's passport from the machine, hammered an exit stamp onto a clean page, scribbled something on a piece of paper and passed it to him.

'This is fine,' he said.

The younger official then opened the Hudak passport and went through the same routine. He placed the identity page under the blue light, turned to the computer, assessed the information in the small box, placed an exit stamp on the same page as the entry visa granted five months earlier, and handed it back to Bartok.

'Enjoy your trip to Gibraltar.' Mahmud was beaming, as though he knew that he had released Carradine from a personal torment. 'Good weather next three days. Good sailing.'

'So I heard,' he replied.

Bartok put the passport in her handbag, reached for Carradine's hand and squeezed it tightly to congratulate him on a job well done. Then they walked out of the hut into the bright mid-morning sunshine and made their way back to the boat.

37

Patrick was preparing to set sail. When Carradine saw him busying himself in the cockpit, the last of his anxiety about Patrick and Eleanor's true intentions dissipated. If Hulse or the Russians were going to come for them, they would surely have done so by now. The electricity cable had been detached from a panel on the pontoon and the bowline released into the depths of the marina. Carradine had given no thought to the seriousness of going to sea for two nights in the company of an elderly couple who might, at any moment, suffer medical setbacks or become involved in an accident that would require him to take control of a 58-foot, state-of-the-art yacht conservatively valued at a million pounds. He wanted only three things: to leave Morocco as quickly as possible; to reach Gibraltar so that he could contact his father; and to find some way of protecting Bartok from the threats against her.

He was unpacking in their cabin when he heard a noise of distant tapping, growing progressively louder. At first Carradine thought that it was the sound of rain falling on the roof of the saloon. He looked outside but could see only clear blue sky and the glare of the sun beyond the cockpit. Then he heard a dog bark, the rustle of paws on wooden pontoons, and knew what was coming.

Two uniformed police officers, guard dogs drooling and straining on leads, were making their way towards *Atalanta*. Carradine experienced the cold dread he had known only hours earlier when looking out across the Corniche at the police cars.

'Eleanor!'

Patrick was on deck. Carradine climbed up the steps to the cockpit and saw that the Alsatians were already at the stern. One of them began to bark at the sight of Carradine. The man holding the leash had to tug him back forcefully as he spoke to Patrick in English.

'We come aboard,' he said. 'Inspection now.'

Carradine did not know if the search was related to Bartok or was simply a random Customs check on a foreign-registered yacht. The larger of the two dogs continued to bark and was scolded by his master. Patrick indicated that the search party should come on board and explained to Carradine what was happening.

'They're looking for drugs, people smuggling. Best thing is to stay up here. They'll do what they have to.'

'I'll tell Lilia.'

Carradine went down into the saloon and tapped on the door of their cabin. Bartok was folding clothes into a drawer.

'What's going on?' she asked.

'Dogs. They're going to be coming in here. You're not carrying any weed or anything, are you?'

She looked at him in disbelief. 'Are you *kidding*?'

317

Carradine forced a relieved smile but could not escape a nagging sensation that he had done something wrong or had made a slip-up for which they would now pay the price. As he made his way out through the galley he could hear the dogs scampering on the deck above his head, violent, excited blasts of breath. One of them came down into the saloon in the arms of a Customs officer and was released into the boat. The Alsatian wheeled around Carradine's feet, sniffing his shoes and ankles before hurrying towards the bow. Eleanor emerged into the corridor and jumped back as the dog barked at her.

'Get them under control!' she shouted, at first in English, then in bad, schoolgirl French. Carradine spoke to the officer, asking him to put a leash on the Alsatian. He refused, indicating that the animal could only conduct its search if it was allowed to roam free in every area of the boat.

'You are British?' he asked.

'Yes.'

'You are with the girl?'

Carradine thought that he had misheard. Then his mind caught up with the question and he realised that the officer knew about Bartok. Was she under suspicion or had she merely been seen entering the passport hut an hour earlier?

'Which girl?' he said.

'Hungarian.'

'Yes. I'm with her.'

'Where is she, please?'

The Alsatian now tore past Carradine, through the galley and into the master bedroom. Both Carradine and the officer followed.

Bartok was leaning over in the corner of the room, encouraging the dog with a series of delighted cries and whispers.

'That's it! What do you smell? Good boy, good boy!'

Carradine looked at the officer, who seemed more interested in Bartok than in the search.

'Hello!' she said, straightening up to greet him. '*As-Salaam Alaikum.*'

'*Wa-Alaikum Salaam.*'

The Alsatian had found something. It was pawing at a cupboard on the near side of the double bed. Carradine's stomach turned over. The dog began to bark repeatedly.

'I can open, please?'

Carradine indicated that the officer was free to search wherever he liked. He looked quickly at Bartok who indicated with her eyes that she did not know what had caught the dog's attention. The officer opened the cupboard and peered inside. Then the barking stopped.

'What is this, please?'

He had pulled out Bartok's black wig. It looked absurd, dangling from his hand like a prop in a school play. A lie sprang instantly into Carradine's mind. He was on the point of saying: 'We went to a fancy dress party in Marrakech' when Bartok beat him to the deceit.

'I had cancer,' she said in English. '*J'avais un cancer.*'

The officer was visibly embarrassed. He was about thirty-five, good-looking and physically fit; to see a man of such apparent authority looking so awkward was almost touching. Reverently he laid the wig on Carradine's side of the bed, murmuring an apology.

'I am very sorry to hear this.' Bartok touched her cropped blonde hair as though to indicate that it had grown back following radiotherapy. 'I hope you will recover soon.'

'Oh, she's much better,' Carradine interjected, ashamed to be using the illness that had killed his mother for the purposes of deceit.

'We will go now,' said the guard and he led the Alsatian out of the cabin.

Patrick was sitting in the cockpit with Eleanor. The second Customs officer had made his way back to the pontoon. His colleague soon followed. He waved to Bartok as he left.

'Did they find anything?' Patrick asked.

'Only the dead body in my carry-on bag,' Carradine replied.

'And the heroin,' Bartok added. 'I hope that was OK?'

Patrick smiled. Eleanor did not.

Twenty minutes later *Atalanta* had reached the open sea.

'Sounds like you kids got lucky,' said Hulse.

'Kids?' Bartok replied.

'You know what I mean.'

'Do I?'

'Let's not play games.'

'Lucky?' she said, sounding astonished. 'You'd say that what happened to me was fortunate? Losing my freedom. My identity. You call that luck?'

Somerville was tired of the jousting between them. He went outside and finally smoked the one cigarette he allowed himself every day. Walking up Chapel Street, he pretended to make a call on his phone while checking for Russian surveillance. There was movement in one of the windows on the opposite side of the road – a curtain closing two floors up – but no pedestrians, no street cleaners, no vans on a stakeout. He thought about Carradine, grinding out the cigarette underneath his boot, and went back inside.

'Anything?' Hulse asked him.

'Nothing,' Somerville replied.

Bartok was coming back from the bathroom. There was a jar of moisturiser beside the basin and she brought a smell of citrus into the room, rubbing her hands together as she worked the cream into the skin.

'Is everything to your satisfaction, gentlemen?' she said, seemingly in a brighter mood.

Somerville smiled, watching her as she sat down.

'Almost,' Hulse replied.

'Only almost?'

'You were going to tell us about Atalanta,' he said.

'And you were going to tell me about Kit.'

This to Somerville, who shook his head and indicated that Bartok was being taped. He had triggered the voice recorder. The microphone was live.

'Afterwards,' he said. 'The Langs first. Tell us what happened on the boat.'

SECRET INTELLIGENCE SERVICE
EYES ONLY / STRAP 1

STATEMENT BY LARA BARTOK ('LASZLO')
CASE OFFICER: J.W.S./S.T.H. – CHAPEL STREET
REF: RESURRECTION/SIMAKOV/CARRADINE
FILE: RE2768X

PART 5 of 5

The boat trip was the happiest time I had known since New York. I was with a man I trusted, a man I respected. We had great conversations, we became very close. Kit had been worried at times in Rabat, but he began to enjoy what was happening to him. We were both elated to have got away on *Atalanta*. We felt like we had won, you know? Kit had been a little bored with the sameness of his life in London, writing every day, no proper relationship, also caring for his father [JWS: William Carradine] who had not been well. What had happened to him in Morocco was something out of the ordinary. He loved being part of a story larger than his own life. His father had been forced out of his job because of the treachery of Philby. Did you know about that? Philby befriended him, took him under his wing, taught him what he knew, then betrayed Kit's father to the KGB. There were lots of men and women like him, young spies at the start of their careers who were blown once their identities became known in Moscow.

I think Kit saw what was happening as a chance to show what his family was capable of, what Bill Carradine might have been if only he had not been deceived by one of his own. In this sense Kit was making amends. And he loved the world of spying! My shampoo bottle and the passport in the salt and how careful I was about phones and SIM cards. Second nature to me, but not to him. He was like a kid in a spy shop. It was very endearing.

Of course, just as he talked about his own life and his family, I told him about Ivan, about my role in early Resurrection operations, about the way I had lived since leaving New York. He knew that Stephen Graham had been in love with me, that he had taken me away to a beach house he had rented for us in Mexico, that we had spent a weekend together by the ocean. He asked me about my childhood in Hungary and of course, out of habit, I told the stories I have always told, some of which were true, some of which were not true. A lot of the time I felt as though I should protect him from knowing too much about me, because I was aware that I could hurt him at any moment. I wanted to be with him but I knew, deep in my heart, that this could never be possible.

As you know, I had been suspicious of

Patrick and Eleanor. I liked Eleanor particularly and believe that perhaps Patrick was not always true to her. He had a streak of vanity, of arrogance, as if life had always come a little too easily to him. She hinted that he was having an affair, which explained his strange behaviour in the marina when we first arrived. He was always talking on the telephone, presumably to his mistress. I wanted to be able to tell Eleanor more about my life. We had many good conversations. She was a terrible cook! Of course, they had no idea who I was. Kit kept up the pretence very well and it was easy to act as though we were boyfriend and girlfriend because we had become lovers.

My worry was that Kit was too concerned for my safety. He had a streak in his personality, a need to be the knight in shining armour. I've noticed that a lot of English men have this. So I had to be ruthless with him. I had to be cruel to be kind. I was trying to find a way to let him know that, sooner or later, it was all going to have to end.

38

Lara and Carradine had gone ashore for brunch at the marina in Puerto de Barbate. They had been at sea for two days and two nights living off cold cuts and salad and both yearned for a decent cup of coffee, some *jamón ibérico* and the chance to stretch their legs. The decision to delay arrival in Gibraltar by forty-eight hours had been Eleanor's; she wanted to take a hire car into the La Brena National Park so that she could visit the Barbate Marshes. The last-minute change of itinerary had not seemed suspicious to Carradine, who was in no position to argue with Patrick and Eleanor after they had been so generous and hospitable towards him. Besides, it was not as if Gibraltar held any of the answers to Bartok's predicament. When they had been alone in their cabin, Carradine had tried to persuade her to hand herself over to the British authorities. She had refused. She was reconciled to her fugitive status, insisting that Carradine return to London and forget all about her.

He did not want to. On the first night out of Rabat

they had slept together; consequently he was in a state of dazed infatuation and wanted to keep seeing her. He believed that Lara felt the same way and that by trying to persuade him to go home was only demonstrating how much she cared for him. She had explained that she wanted to protect him from the complications of her life on the run.

Their bodies still swaying to the rhythms of the ocean, they walked hand-in-hand through the marina to a small tapas bar where they ordered fried eggs, *patatas bravas* and *jamón*. Patrick briefly joined them before returning to the boat to fix a broken hatch; Eleanor had gone into town to have her hair done.

'Sooner or later they're going to work out what happened to us,' said Carradine, finishing off a second cup of coffee.

'Maybe,' Bartok replied. 'Maybe not.'

It was perhaps the nineteenth version of a conversation they had been having every day since leaving Morocco.

'Where will you go?' he asked. 'What will you do?'

'This does not have to concern you.'

'I want it to concern me.'

She kissed him on the cheek, running her hand along his jaw. They no longer had to pretend to be lovers; a natural intimacy had grown up between them. Carradine toyed with daydreams of smuggling Bartok into the UK so that she could live with him in his flat and make a new life in London. He knew that the crimes of which she was accused in America – armed assault, kidnapping, incitement to violence – would most likely see her extradited to the United States within a matter of weeks. He wanted to believe that he could mount a public defence on her behalf, persuading journalists and broadcasters to campaign for her release, arguing that Bartok had acted under duress from Ivan Simakov and deserved a second chance. He knew that such far-fetched notions were the stuff of fantasy but could not bring himself to face the simple truth: their adventure was over. Looking across the table at the woman who had so bewitched him, Carradine realised that he had only two options: to remain with her, abandoning his life and career in London; or to return home. It was no choice at all. He would have to go back to Lancaster Gate and look back on all that had happened to him in Morocco as a fleeting dream.

'You should telephone your father,' she said.

'Yes.'

An ancient Téléfonica payphone was bolted to a wall on the far side of the tapas bar. Carradine asked the obvious question.

'Won't they have his number covered? If I call, they can trace it.'

'I doubt it,' Bartok replied.

Looking back, Carradine realised that was the first sign of what was to come.

Two hours later he was scrubbing the decks and washing down the windows while Patrick caught up on his sleep. The skipper was tired after sailing single-handedly through the night and had retired to his bunk. It was another fiercely hot day, the marina buzzing with activity. Eleanor had not yet returned from the local town. Lara was below decks reading a book.

Just after midday she popped her head up into the cockpit and told Carradine that she was going ashore to look for a newspaper. He knew her well enough by now to realise that she wanted to go alone. She was carrying the soft bag that he had found in her apartment, into which she had stuffed various dirty clothes as well as their bed sheets and towels. There was a laundromat at the marina. They arranged to meet there and to find somewhere in town to have a late lunch. Carradine had not yet rung his father but planned to do so once they were a safe distance from the marina. Lara had agreed that this was a more sensible course of action.

Just before two o'clock, Eleanor returned from the local town smelling of coffee and hairspray. Patrick was still asleep. She seemed surprised to see Carradine.

'Oh. I thought you were in town. I saw Lily in the taxi.'

She had taken to calling Bartok 'Lily'. The two women had grown close in a short space of time. There was an edge to Eleanor's voice, as though she were admonishing Carradine for a sin he had not committed.

'She went on her own,' he said, wondering why Bartok had taken a cab when she had said she was only looking for a newspaper. 'I'm meeting her in a minute.'

'Ah.' Eleanor frowned. Carradine sensed that something was wrong. 'It did seem odd,' she said. 'She drove right past me. You were nowhere to be seen. I assumed you two lovebirds had had a row.'

'Why did you think that?'

'Because she was crying.'

He knew then that Bartok was gone. Carradine felt unbalanced. He asked in which direction the taxi had been heading when it had passed her.

'Out of town, I suppose,' Eleanor replied. 'Away from here.'

'Are you sure?'

'I think so.' Her expression softened. 'What was the argument about, darling?'

Carradine found himself in the absurd position of confirming Eleanor's belief that there had been a terrible row. What else could he say? That Lily wasn't 'Lilia' but instead a fugitive from justice with a bounty on her head? That she had slipped away into Andalucía without so much as a farewell? That Carradine had taken advantage of their hospitality, potentially putting their safety at risk? It was easier to lie.

'Just boyfriend and girlfriend stuff,' he said, numb at the realisation of Bartok's betrayal. 'Give me a second, will you?'

He went down into the cabin and saw their unmade bed. Only hours earlier they had made love, entwined in one another's bodies, cocooned by the hum of the engine and the hiss of the sea. He opened the cupboard and saw immediately that Lara had taken most of her belongings. Even the absurd wig was gone. Some of her dirty clothes were in a laundry bag leaning against a pile of lifejackets; she had taken one of the *Atalanta* towels to fill out the bag. Carradine opened a drawer on the far side of the cabin. It was no surprise to see that the Lilia Hudak passport had gone. The Art Deco silver bookmark was no longer where Bartok had left it, wedged between the pages of *Anna Karenina*. It was a complete clear-out.

Carradine went out into the galley. Patrick had woken up. He could hear him talking to Eleanor in the cockpit. It was evident that she had told him about the argument because as Carradine came up the ladder he said: 'You OK, son?'

'I'm fine,' he replied, though in truth he was hollowed out.

'Heard from Lily?' Eleanor asked.

'He doesn't have a phone,' Patrick replied.

'No,' Carradine confirmed. 'I haven't heard from her.'

He explained that he was going to go into town to look for her and to apologise for what had happened. Patrick said, 'Don't worry, these things go on all the time,' and Eleanor agreed, adding: 'You two will be fine. You're both lovely people.' Carradine felt wretched for deceiving them. He found that he was intensely angry with Bartok. She had humiliated him, used him up.

He walked to the laundromat. An elderly Spanish woman was removing sheets from a tumble drier and piling them into a plastic basket. She was wearing an apron and a badge. There was nobody else around.

'*Disculpe*,' said Carradine, using what bad schoolboy Spanish he could remember.

'*Hola?*' the woman replied.

Before he had a chance to respond she appeared to recognise him, placing a hand on his elbow.

'*Señor* Kit?'

'*Si.*'

She hurried into a back office. The laundromat was very hot. The vast machines had generated a greenhouse humidity with a smell of soap powder and artificial pine. Carradine broke out in a sweat and opened the door, hoping that the hot summer wind might at least make him feel less claustrophobic.

'Here,' said the woman in Spanish, emerging from the back office holding a large plastic bag and an envelope.

At first Carradine thought it was a bill for the laundry.

Then he looked inside. The shirts and towels had been cleaned and folded. He searched for Bartok's clothes among his own, but of course found nothing.

'For you,' said the woman, this time in English. 'Letter.' Carradine opened the envelope.

My darling Kit

Forgive me for doing this. We hardly know one another but I feel as though I have known you all my life. You have saved that life. I do not know how to repay you except by leaving you in peace. You must not come with me. You must not <u>think</u> of trying to find me. This is the only way. Believe me. It is better.

Carradine's throat was dry. He saw that the letter had been written hurriedly. Certain words had been crossed out, others underlined. The first few sentences slanted across the page. He turned away from the elderly lady because he could sense that she was staring at him.

Go back to London, forget about me. I will go where I have to go and try to do the same. But please know this. As much as it is possible for a person to love another person after knowing him for so short a time, I do love you. I loved what happened between us on Atalanta. I will never forget it. I will never forget you.

Lara

39

Carradine waited for the sheets. It was all that he could do. The elderly woman ironed them and folded them and looked at him sympathetically as he walked outside into the blistering afternoon.

He walked back to *Atalanta* and explained that Lilia had gone to the airport in Gibraltar and booked a flight home to London.

'How did you find out?' Patrick asked.

Carradine had been in such a state of shock that he had not even thought that his version of events would be questioned.

'She wrote me an email,' he said. Lies now came to him as easily as drinking a cup of coffee. 'There's an internet café in town.'

It was agreed that Carradine would also leave the boat. Patrick and Eleanor were sad to see him go, but understood that he wanted to get back to London to try to save the relationship.

'It's all such a shock,' said Eleanor. 'You seemed so happy together.'

'We were,' said Carradine. 'Very happy.'

He went down into the cabin and packed his bags. He put the clean sheets and pillowcases on the bed and washed down the bathroom with an old cloth from the galley. It was as though he was erasing what had happened between them: the shower they had taken together on the first morning at sea; the sight of Bartok's moonlit naked body as she slipped out of bed in the dead of night; her eyes looking back at him as she applied make-up in the bathroom mirror. It had all been a fantasy conjured by Carradine's imagination, an affair so fleeting and unreal that he doubted his own ability to believe it in the months and years to come. He went up on deck to find Eleanor mending a broken china mug with a tube of superglue and some cotton buds. Patrick was eating tortilla and drinking a Mahou in the sun. Carradine asked for their address in England so that he could write to thank them and apologised for the muted way in which the trip had ended.

'I know that Lilia loved meeting you and spending time with you,' he said, angry with himself for making excuses for her.

'Of course,' said Eleanor, hugging him.

'You'll be all right,' said Patrick, shaking his hand. 'Let us know how it all goes.'

Carradine caught a bus to the airport in Seville, checked his emails on a public computer and searched the British and American press for any references to the death of Ramón Basora. He found none. Having expected a tsunami of messages enquiring after his wellbeing, he discovered only an email from his agent asking how the festival had gone ('Hope you didn't get eaten alive by Katherine Paget'), an invitation to a book launch and a message from the manager of the riad revealing that his phone and laptop had been found under the mattress and were being kept in the hotel safe along with the memory stick. Carradine was relieved that Hulse or the Russians had not taken them and sent a reply saying that he would cover the cost of having the items couriered to his flat in London.

He rang his father from the departure lounge. Though he expressed surprise that Carradine had not responded to a text message he had sent two days earlier, he was otherwise oblivious to the fact that his son had vanished.

'Where are you calling from?' he asked.

'Seville,' Carradine replied, relieved at last to be telling the truth about his whereabouts. 'Stopped off near Cadiz on the way home.'

'Cadiz? Really? I went there with your mother.' Carradine was in such a sorry state that he felt tears rising. Father and son, both betrayed and humbled by the secret world. 'Took her to a nudist beach. There's a first time for everything. A last time as well.'

A flight was leaving for Luton at seven o'clock. Carradine bought copies of *The Times* and *Guardian* and sat in a café eating a *bocadillo*. He had looked at both front pages with trepidation, expecting to find his author's photo blown up alongside that of Lara Bartok under a headline about their mysterious disappearance from the Medina. Instead, turning page after page, he found no reference to what had happened in Marrakech, only detailed accounts of the Resurrection siege in Warsaw, which had been brought to an end by the Polish BOA. Parliament buildings around the world were in lockdown. The Pentagon had been evacuated after a bomb scare. In Budapest, a man and a woman had been shot dead after being mistaken for armed Resurrection activists. The movement had metastasised into an international terrorist phenomenon which could erupt at any time, bringing chaos and fear to governments and citizens alike.

Reading the reports, Carradine began to feel that what had happened to him in Morocco had happened to another man. He had not left Marrakech in the dead of night. He had not stayed in the flat in Rabat. He had not slipped onto an English-registered yacht and spent two nights at sea with a beautiful woman who had vanished from his life as quickly as she had appeared. The whole thing had been as unreal and as fanciful as a film noir, with Bartok as the femme fatale. At no point was he tapped on the shoulder by a plain-clothes officer of the *Guardia Civil* nor quietly asked to leave the airport by a representative of Her Majesty's Government in Gibraltar. All that remained was the dismay of losing Lara, the raw disappointment of having glimpsed the promise of love and losing it in the blink of an eye.

The plane was on time. He caught a cab from Luton airport, sitting in late-night roadworks traffic on the M1, eventually reaching home after midnight. Carradine opened the door of his flat expecting to be greeted by a phalanx of officers from Special Branch, but instead there was only the smell of his neighbour's cooking and a note from the Tenants' Association advising him that the date for the Annual General Meeting had been moved to October. He searched each room for any signs of intrusion, but found nobody hiding in the spare bedroom or waiting for him in his office. He opened several windows to stir the warm, uncirculated air of the London summer and smoked a cigarette in the kitchen, wondering what had become of Lara and wishing that he had stayed in Spain to look for her.

It was only as he was falling asleep that he remembered something vital: he had arranged to meet Stephen Graham the following afternoon. Carradine walked into his study and looked at his diary. Exactly thirteen days had passed since his encounter with Mantis at Lisson Grove. Graham was expecting Carradine to debrief him about the trip to Morocco.

He did not know whether to go ahead with the meeting. Graham would want to talk to him about Bartok. He would want to know what had happened in Marrakech. In all probability, he had sent a WhatsApp message to Carradine's phone confirming that the meeting was due to take place. A single grey tick would have displayed against the message as the phone sat in the safe at the riad. What would Graham have made of that?

Carradine went back to bed. He missed the sounds of the ocean, the swell of the waves in the cabin. Instead, traffic was sweeping along Bayswater Road and his married neighbours were arguing in the next apartment. He tried to imagine how it would benefit him to meet Graham and to continue with the facade of working for the Service. He did not have the energy to lie about what had happened. He would have to tell him everything: about Rabat, about the Russians, about *Atalanta*. As a bargaining chip, should Carradine threaten to expose 'Robert Mantis' as a Russian agent? That was surely suicidal: the same men who had come for Bartok in Marrakech would undoubtedly come for him. Perhaps they might do so anyway, grabbing him on the street in the coming days in the hope of finding out what had become of LASZLO. On reflection, this seemed to Carradine the most likely, as well as the most alarming outcome. The Russians knew who he was. They knew that C.K. Carradine had somehow aided and abetted Bartok's escape from Morocco. In this respect, he was going to need Graham's help to get them off his back. If that strategy failed, he would have no choice but to go to the Service and to tell them everything he knew.

40

The courier came at half-past eight, blasting the doorbell and waking Carradine from a deep sleep. He signed for the laptop, the phone and the memory stick, opening the carefully wrapped package from DHL. He wondered if it had been tampered with en route by the Service.

Both batteries were dead. Carradine found chargers and plugged them in. He locked the memory stick in a drawer in his office and walked back to the kitchen. Carradine saw that 'Robert Mantis' had written him two WhatsApp messages, four days earlier, both of which had been sent at the same time. The first confirmed the meeting at Lisson Grove later that day. The second was a reminder to bring the memory stick that Oubakir had given him in Casablanca. There was no further mention of Bartok, nor had Mantis attempted to contact Carradine in the ensuing days. Carradine looked at his diary and worked out that the messages had been sent while he was staying in the apartment in Rabat. He replied, apologising for taking so long to respond and explaining that he had 'accidentally' left his phone behind in Marrakech. He said that he looked forward to their meeting later that afternoon and pressed 'Send'.

The message acquired only a single grey tick.

There were other texts – from his father, from various friends and acquaintances in London. Carradine combed his phone for a covert message or email from Bartok but found nothing. He listened to the voicemails, checked his Twitter feed and scrolled through Facebook looking for clues as to her whereabouts but knew that he was wasting his time. She was gone. He was no different to Stephen Graham and perhaps to countless other men who had fallen under her spell, only to be cast aside when their usefulness had passed.

There were also no messages of any kind from Sebastian Hulse or the Russians. It seemed strange to Carradine that none of them had attempted to make contact, if only to pressure him into giving up information about Bartok's whereabouts. Their absence only added to a burgeoning sense that what had happened to him in Morocco had been part of a dream, a fantasy of escape with no basis in reality.

He spent the rest of the morning replying to emails from his agent and publisher and reading obituaries online of Ivan Simakov, each of them displaying the same photograph of the handsome, martyred revolutionary leader with the implicit visual implication that he was a latter-day Fidel or Che. No fewer than four articles suggested that Simakov had worked for Russian intelligence before setting up Resurrection. Reading the obituaries in his office, Carradine no longer cared who might be looking at his Internet history or reading his private correspondence;

at one point he even typed the name 'Lara Bartok' into Google, finding various articles in which she was referred to as Simakov's 'former girlfriend' with little or no further biographical information provided. He was surprised both by how little had been written about her and by the scarcity of photographs of Bartok online: Carradine found only a cropped version of the picture he had seen in the *Guardian* and a yearbook photo of a teenage 'Lara Bartok' who may or may not have been the same woman. Either Lara had been extremely careful about her digital footprint from a young age or – more likely – somebody had erased her history from the Internet.

Every now and again Carradine would check to see if his message to Mantis had been read. Each time he saw the same thing: a single grey tick beside the text, indicating not only that the message had not been read, but that it had yet to reach Mantis's phone. He began to think that the meeting would not go ahead, but knew that he had no choice other than to appear at Lisson Grove at the allotted time.

As he was leaving the flat, Carradine checked his mailbox on the ground floor. Beneath the piles of junk mail and freebie magazines he found two issues of *The Week*, two copies of the *New Yorker*, a letter from his agent in New York and a handwritten envelope containing what felt like an invitation to a party.

He opened it.

There was a postcard inside. The image on the front showed a four-section collage of photographs from Marrakech: the Koutoubia Tower at sunrise; the Berrima Mosque at dusk; the Royal Palace at sunset; a carpet seller in the souk.

There was a handwritten message on the back.

Kit

Great to meet you in Kech. I'm in London the next few days. Would love to meet up and talk about that girl. You can find me at the St Ermin's Hotel in St James. Staying under Hulse.

I may not be exactly who you think I am.
Sebastian

Carradine could feel his heart racing as he read the message a second time. Two things immediately occurred to him: Hulse knew where he lived but had elected to contact him via the postal service rather than by dragging him into the back of an Agency van. Secondly, he was being explicit about his interest in Bartok. The postcard seemed to suggest that Carradine had outfoxed the Agency. The tone of the message was conciliatory.

Carradine looked at his watch. It had just gone midday. Even if his meeting with Graham lasted two or three hours, that would still leave him more than enough time to go to the hotel and to ask for Hulse. Better still, he could ring up to his room and – if necessary – leave a message. What did he have to lose? Better to make his peace with the Agency, to get Hulse onside, than to leave himself exposed to the threat from Moscow. It might even be the case that Hulse could help bring Bartok in from the cold.

Carradine walked outside. He lit a cigarette. With the first taste of the tobacco, the sharp hit of nicotine, he felt an absolute confusion. *I may not be exactly who you think I am.* What did it *mean*? Was Hulse a freelancer? Another rogue agent like Mantis? Had he even sent the postcard or was it a trap set by the Russians to lure him to the hotel?

It was impossible to know. Carradine was beyond the point at which he could even pretend to know what might happen to him or who could be lurking around the next corner. He hoped that Stephen Graham might be able to provide him with at least some of the answers.

41

Carradine deliberately followed the same route to Lisson Grove that he had taken a fortnight earlier. There was no reason to do so other than a rather melancholy desire to revisit Sussex Gardens and to try to make sense of what had happened to Lisa Redmond.

He reached the intersection certain that he was not being followed. Vehicles were moving normally in all directions. Pedestrians were walking along the pavements and crossing the road at the lights. The cafés and restaurants were full, the shops were open and busy. To the naked eye there was no suggestion that, just two weeks earlier, a woman had been kidnapped and two men brutally assaulted within fifty metres of where Carradine was standing. He tried to recall what he had seen. He remembered the teenage girl jabbering away to her friend. *I'm like he needs to get his shit together because I'm like just not going through with that bullshit again*. Yet Carradine's memory was otherwise warped and confused: he had conflated his own recollections of the kidnapping with other eyewitness accounts. The photographs and videos of the attack later posted online had become a new version of his personal experience.

He stopped at the pedestrian crossing where the girl had held him back. He checked his phone. The WhatsApp message to Mantis still showed a single grey tick. Carradine was convinced that their meeting would not now go ahead, but nevertheless continued to walk east towards Marylebone Road and the apartment block on Lisson Grove.

He rang the bell. There was no answer so he rang it again. He looked at his phone. Still no response from Graham. Carradine pressed the bell a third time and waited another minute. He was sure that something had happened to him; Russian intelligence had worked out that Graham had betrayed them and he had been 'disappeared' as a consequence. Carradine was on the point of walking away when the door suddenly buzzed and a cheerful female voice said 'Sorry!' on the Intercom.

'Hello?' he said, pushing the door ajar.

There was no reply. He climbed the six flights of stairs to the third floor, arriving slightly out of breath and sweating under his shirt.

'There was no need for you to come up.'

A diminutive woman in late middle-age was standing in the door of Graham's flat. She was holding a yellow duster and a bottle of silver polish and spoke in a cut-glass accent.

'I don't understand,' Carradine replied.

The woman looked confused. 'Oh,' she said. 'I thought you were the man from Amazon.'

'Me?' He wondered if he had gone to the correct address

but remembered the *faux* Dutch oil painting on the landing. 'No. I'm not from Amazon. I was supposed to meet somebody here.'

'Here?' Carradine could see various items of brown furniture inside the flat and a rolled-up carpet standing on its end in the hall. The empty room in which he had sat with Graham was in the process of being transformed. He found himself remembering the scene in *Moonraker* when Bond and 'M', expecting to find a control room filled with deadly toxins and lab rats, instead walk into a lavish Venetian drawing room wearing gas masks, only to be greeted by Sir Hugo Drax.

'I may have made a mistake,' he said.

The woman seemed anxious to relieve Carradine of any notion that his presence was an inconvenience.

'Please don't worry, I've only just moved in,' she said. 'Were you looking for Mr Benedictus?'

'Benedictus?'

She picked up an envelope from a stool in the hall. She showed it to Carradine.

'He lived here before me.'

Carradine looked at the envelope. It was a charity circular made out to a 'Mr D. Benedictus' at the same address Graham had given to him two weeks earlier.

'No, not him,' he said. 'Did you know a "Mr Mantis" or a "Stephen Graham"?'

The woman frowned.

'I'm afraid not. You were supposed to meet them here today?'

It occurred to Carradine that she was being unusually helpful. He wondered if she was working for Moscow.

'I was,' he said. 'Never mind.'

He was about to turn around and head back down the stairs when she said: 'Somebody else came yesterday.'

'Somebody who was looking for Mr Benedictus?'

'No,' she said. 'For your Mr Mantis.'

Carradine hesitated. The revelation was not, of itself, particularly alarming. No doubt Graham had used the flat in order to meet all kinds of people.

'Do you remember much about him?' he asked.

The woman wiped a bead of sweat from her forehead. She was wearing three-quarter length tweed trousers and her hair was cut in a messy, knife-and-fork bob.

'Not particularly,' she replied. 'As I was saying, I let you in because I thought you were the man from Amazon. I'm waiting for a microwave oven.'

There seemed no point in continuing the conversation. They would only go around in circles. Carradine took a last look inside the flat – remembering how the plastic wrap on the cream leather sofa had made him sticky and hot – and apologised for wasting the woman's time. It was only as she was shutting the door that he decided to take a chance. He tapped the four-digit pin into his phone and opened up 'Photos'.

'If you could just give me two seconds,' he said.

The woman lingered in the doorway, throwing the Benedictus envelope onto the ground. Carradine searched for the pictures he had taken in Casablanca and found the photographs of Ramón and Hulse.

'These two guys,' he said, showing the woman the shots from Blaine's. As he flicked through them he was conscious that two provocatively dressed Moroccan women were prominent in several frames. 'Was it either of them?'

The woman took the phone and looked through the album. She seemed interested in what Carradine was showing her.

'How do you make it bigger?' she asked.

'Which one?' Carradine replied.

'This one,' she said, pointing at the photograph of Carradine with his arm around Hulse, their glasses raised in a toast.

He moved his fingers apart on the screen so that Hulse's face was enlarged. He realised that his hand was shaking as he held the phone.

'Him?' he asked.

The woman stared at the screen. Hulse's features were slightly blurred but she seemed to recognise him. She took the phone from Carradine. She held it further away from her face. His long-sighted father did the same thing with menus when he had forgotten to bring his glasses to a restaurant.

'Could he have been American?' Carradine asked.

That was the breakthrough. The woman looked at him as if he had solved a particularly taxing clue in a cross-word.

'Yes!' she exclaimed. 'I remember now! Rather good-looking. Isn't he well-dressed? Came yesterday, about the same time. Asked for this Mr Mantis. I only saw him through the camera at the front door, but it was certainly him. Unmistakable accent. American. I could listen to it all day.'

Carradine thanked her and walked down the stairs, trying to work out what Hulse had been doing at Lisson Grove. How did he know about Mantis and why had he sent the postcard to Carradine's flat? He wanted to find a blank piece of paper and – in the style of the great conspiracy thrillers of the 1970s – draw a diagram that would make sense of all the names and places and theories he had encountered since his first fateful meeting with Stephen Graham on Bayswater Road. He sat on the stairs and tried to organise his thoughts but found that it was pointless; only a meeting with Hulse at the St Ermin's Hotel could potentially resolve the myriad puzzles in his mind.

He opened the door onto Lisson Grove. A tall, bespectacled man wearing an ill-fitting lounge suit was staring up at the building. As Carradine came out he smiled at him and raised his hand.

'Mr Carradine?' he said. 'Mr Kit Carradine?'

Carradine was bewildered. He wondered distractedly if the man was a fan of his books.

'Who's asking?' he said.

'The name's Somerville.' It was hard to pick the man's age or to place his accent. 'Julian Somerville.' His voice had an adenoidal quality and the lenses in his round wired glasses were smudged. 'I wondered if we might have a little chat?'

'A little chat about what?'

Somerville had lost much of his hair. Carradine found that he was shaking his hand.

'Oh, about Robert Mantis. About Stephen Graham. About Lara Bartok. About everything, really. Why don't you follow me? I've got a car parked just around the corner.'

42

The car was a Jaguar parked near a fish restaurant off Lisson Grove. Somerville opened the back door and invited Carradine to get in.

'Who are you?' he asked. 'Where are you from?'

'Just hop inside, Kit. There's a good chap.'

Carradine felt that he had no choice. He looked inside the car. There was another man in the back seat. As he climbed in beside him, the man turned. To Carradine's consternation, he saw that it was Sebastian Hulse.

'Kit!' he said, slapping him on the back. 'How you doin'?'

As though in a dream where he wanted to speak but was unable to sound the words, Carradine stared at Hulse. All he could summon was the word: 'You?'

'Me.'

Hulse laughed his seductive laugh, smiled his seductive smile.

'You've given us quite the ride the last few days,' he said.

There was a driver in the front seat, staring ahead with

both hands on the wheel. Somerville climbed in beside him and they pulled away.

'I don't understand,' said Carradine. 'Where's Mantis? Where's Stephen Graham?'

Somerville turned. He had taken off his spectacles and removed his suit jacket. The transformation in his appearance was striking. Carradine had thought that he was completely bald, yet he could now see that Somerville's hair was merely shaved close to the scalp. He had guessed that he was most likely in his late forties but realised that he was closer to thirty-five.

'Stephen Graham is dead,' he said. Hulse wound down a window. 'The man you knew as Robert Mantis has been murdered. Pushed under a train at Oxford Circus.'

Carradine felt as though he had thrown a cigarette out of the window and the butt had blown back into the car to burn him. He stared at Hulse. He was somehow hoping that the American would deny what Somerville had told him.

'What? Who killed him? Why?'

'The Moscow men. Who else?'

The car made a sharp turn in the direction of Marylebone Station. Carradine was pushed back in his seat. He assumed that if Hulse was Agency, Somerville was Service, but anything was possible in the looking-glass world into which Stephen Graham had thrust him.

'He was killed by his own side?'

'Now *that* is a revealing question,' said Somerville, looking immensely pleased that Carradine had asked it. 'How would you know that Mantis wasn't one of us? How did you work that out?'

Carradine's father had always told him that the best

policy in life was to tell the truth, even if you thought it was going to get you into trouble. 'Be honest,' he would say. 'That's what I learned from my time in the Service. People can stand anything except being lied to.' In recent weeks Carradine had grown used to the business of lying. He remembered deliberately misleading Mantis about the Redmond kidnapping. He recalled how wretched he had felt drinking Patrick's Rioja and eating Eleanor's food night after night while blatantly deceiving them about 'Lilia' and their life together in London. It was time to take his father's advice.

'Lara told me,' he said.

'So you *did* find her?'

Hulse looked impressed. Carradine was astonished that the Agency still did not know that he had made contact with LASZLO.

'I did,' he said, with an odd surge of pride.

'And?' said Somerville.

'And what?'

'And what happened next?'

So Carradine told them.

More than two hours later they were in the Members' Room at the Royal Academy drinking tea and eating scones. The driver had dropped them off in Piccadilly. Somerville had confirmed that he was an intelligence officer with the Service, showing Carradine a photo ID and handing him a business card almost identical to the one he had been given by 'Robert Mantis'. Hulse had produced what appeared to be a bona fide security pass for Langley, allowing Carradine to study it closely. It was the first time in his life that he had seen an ID of that kind. A few weeks earlier it would have been a buzz, like handling moon rock or a first edition of *Casino Royale*; now he didn't trust the evidence of his own eyes. Somerville explained that Stephen Graham had been pushed in front of a train by two assailants who had been conveniently disguised to evade CCTV and sufficiently well-trained to vanish from Oxford Circus station without trace. The murder had been blamed on a mugging gone wrong, but the Service had learned through a contact in Moscow that Graham had been killed by his own side. His attempts to warn Bartok of the threat against her constituted an act of treason, a breach of *omerta* for which he had paid with his life. Carradine suspected that Hulse was hearing much of what Somerville was telling him for the first time.

Their conversation had taken place in full view of the RA members, many of whom had visited the Summer Exhibition and were sheltering from an afternoon storm. Carradine was surprised that Somerville had not insisted that they go to a Service safe house or take a room in a hotel; in his novels he had always staged sensitive conversations of this kind in secure environments. He had told them everything he could remember about his initial contacts with 'Robert Mantis', his encounter with Ramón on the plane, the meeting with Oubakir at Blaine's, even his chat with the mysterious 'Karel' on the train to Marrakech. At the mention of Karel's name, both men had looked at one another knowingly and decided, by silent agreement, to tell Carradine that 'Karel M. Trapp' was in fact a Czech émigré and Agency asset in Casablanca whom Hulse had instructed to follow Carradine onto the train and to provoke him into a discussion about Resurrection.

'I needed to know more about you,' he said. 'Didn't make sense you were meeting with Oubakir at Blaine's. Basora was shooting his mouth off, we knew he was one of the Mantis agents. When I called London, Julian here had never heard of you, so I figured either you were researching a book, like you said you were, or maybe you were working for Moscow.'

'So who killed Ramón?' Carradine was back in the wilderness of mirrors, dizzied by names, stunned by the Karel revelation, and all the time wondering what the hell had happened to Lara.

'Who knows?' said Hulse. 'Took a girl up to his hotel room, fucked her, cardiac arrest. Maid found him a day later. Told the cops Basora had offered her money for sex. Kind of a charming guy, wouldn't you say?'

Carradine remembered the girls in Blaine's, the glint of Hulse's wedding ring as his hand caressed Salma's thigh. Had the girls been on the Agency payroll as well?

'So – what? – you looked around town for Lara, you eventually see her at the festival and just follow her back to your riad?' Hulse seemed keen to move the conversation along.

'That's right,' said Carradine.

The American smiled, lowering a dollop of clotted cream onto a scone. By Carradine's reckoning, he had already consumed three scones and four chocolate chip cookies. He dropped a scoop of strawberry jam onto the cream and brought it up to his lips.

'And the Irish guy, the writer . . .' He put at least half the scone into his mouth and attempted to say: 'What was his name?' without dropping any crumbs.

'Michael McKenna,' Somerville replied. 'I read his most recent book. Bloody good.'

'You think he'd met her before?' Hulse asked.

Carradine shook his head. They spoke at length about what had taken place in the riad. He told them about the fight in Bartok's apartment, the meeting with Oubakir on the street, even his doubts and concerns about Hulse when the American had shown up out of the blue.

'Yeah,' he said. 'Sorry about that. I knew you were hiding something. Just didn't know what it was.'

It was a revealing admission of incompetence. Over a third cup of tea Carradine told the men about the drive to Rabat, the flat on the Corniche, the slice of luck with Patrick and Eleanor. He felt bad giving up their names but hoped that any interest the Service or the Agency would take in them would be confined to a quick look at their emails and a light vetting. Somerville had been asking most of the questions.

'So you reached Barbate marina,' he said, 'you went ashore for breakfast, Lara said she was going into town to buy a newspaper, then the lady vanishes?'

'Precisely,' Carradine replied.

'She leave a note?' Hulse asked.

'She did.'

He could remember every word of it, every full stop and comma, even the slant of Lara's handwriting. He kept the letter in his wallet, folded up next to a photograph of his mother. He wasn't going to tell them any of that.

'What did it say?' Somerville asked.

'Just that she was grateful to me for helping her out. That she was sorry to run away, but didn't want to involve me any further in what she was doing.'

'And what *was* she doing, do you think?'

Carradine shrugged. The answer to Hulse's question was surely obvious.

'Running away from guys like you,' he said.

Somerville smiled. Hulse did not.

'Did you sleep with her?' Somerville asked.

'Is that relevant?' Carradine replied.

'Man's got a point,' said Hulse, licking his lips clean of clotted cream. 'Irrelevant.'

'I'm not so sure.' Somerville moved his head to one side in a rather studied, eccentric manner, as though he was still trying to work out if Carradine was saint or sinner. 'What are your feelings towards her? What did you conclude about her work for Resurrection?'

Hulse indicated that he should answer. Carradine wanted to do so without giving the appearance that he was infatuated with Bartok and dismayed to have lost contact with her.

'I thought she was great,' he said. 'Funny, bright, strong.'

'Hot,' said Hulse and received a look from Somerville.

'Yes,' Carradine continued. 'Lara is very beautiful.' His interlocutors glanced at one another, as though Carradine had already provided them with cast-iron evidence of the depths of his love. 'I found her easy to talk to. She was very straight with me, sensitive around what had happened with Stephen Graham . . .'

'Sensitive,' said Hulse. 'You mean finding out you weren't working for the Service, you were actually working for Moscow?'

'Of course that's what I mean.' Carradine wondered why Hulse had seen fit to remind him of his humiliation.

'She said that she'd known Graham, implied that he'd been in love with her, but that he hadn't known that she knew he was a Russian agent.'

'That's about right.' Somerville was absent-mindedly brushing crumbs from the table.

'How would you know that?' Carradine asked.

'Know what?' Somerville replied.

'That Lara knew Mantis was a false flag.'

Somerville reared back in his seat. He looked simultaneously impressed by Carradine's question and extremely cautious about answering it.

'You don't miss much, do you, Kit?'

'Not any more.' Hulse was also staring at him. He smiled automatically when Carradine caught his eye. 'Seriously,' he said. 'Answer the question. How do you know about Lara's dealings with Mantis?'

The two men again looked at one another. It was hard to discern who was in overall command: the Brit or the Yank? Carradine had not yet been able to pin down Somerville's personality or objectives. His mood seemed to depend on what was being discussed and who was discussing it. He could seem distant and formal; he could be jokey and relaxed. These contradictions extended to his appearance: in a certain light Somerville's features were indistinct, even bland; at other times his face came alive with ideas and questions. Even his responses about Bartok had been confusing to Carradine. He knew that Somerville was holding something back.

A mobile phone rang on the far side of the Members' Room. It was a long time before it was answered.

'You've never signed the Official Secrets Act, have you?' Somerville reached into the pocket of his jacket.

'No,' Carradine replied. 'Not a real one, anyway.'

Somerville took out a small piece of paper and placed it on the table. It was identical to the document Carradine had signed in Lisson Grove, down to the texture of the paper. Hulse produced a pen with the flourish of a magician's assistant.

'I suggest that you do so now,' said Somerville. 'Then we can really start to get to know one another.'

43

Fifteen minutes later the driver picked them up on Piccadilly and drove the short distance to a mock French brasserie in Soho. There were reproduction Toulouse-Lautrec prints on the wall, black-and-white photographs of Jeanne Moreau and Yves Montand in the bathroom. The waiters wore black waistcoats and white aprons and spoke with Eastern European accents. Edith Piaf was playing on the sound system. Sitting at a small wooden table close to a zinc-topped bar, Hulse ordered a Diet Coke, Somerville a pint of lager and Carradine a large gin and tonic. He had wanted a vodka martini but thought it would be absurd to ask for one in front of two bona fide spies. No explanation was given for the change of venue. Somerville was very specific about picking the table; Carradine wondered if it was wired. He had now signed the Secrets Act and was effectively under oath. Yet if that was the case, why not take him to a safe house?

'Here's the basic situation.' Somerville was picking at a bowl of peanuts and trying to be heard over *'Non, Je*

Ne Regrette Rien'. 'Ramón was a paid agent of Stephen Graham. Let's call him Mantis for the sake of clarity. One of many on his books. Drug problem, alcohol problem, hooker problem.'

'So he wasn't murdered?'

'Oh, he was murdered all right,' said Hulse. 'Moroccan police tried to make out it was accidental. An overdose. But the Russians got to them. Covered it up.'

Carradine wasn't particularly convinced by that answer. It could just as easily have been the case that the Agency had killed Ramón and paid the Moroccan authorities to keep it quiet. In fact, Carradine hadn't been particularly convinced by anything Hulse had told him. Throughout the debriefing he had developed a sense that neither man knew as much about him as he had expected them to know. He was being assessed and appraised; it was almost as if they were trying to work out whether or not to keep using him in whatever operation they were cooking up.

'Mantis asked Ramón to keep an eye on you and to help in the search for the girl.' Somerville spoke with seeming authority. 'Needed to know that you weren't going to blab your mouth off about LASZLO. The irony being that it was Ramón who was indiscreet. Searched for information about her online. Dropped hints that he was engaged in secret work.'

'He said that to you in the club in Casablanca?' Carradine asked, turning to Hulse.

Hulse nodded. 'Guy was a mess, but I guess Mantis was desperate and using anybody he could find. Bottom line. Moscow wanted to find Bartok and bring her in. Mantis wanted to protect her. Used all kinds of means and methods to achieve that. Moscow found out, pushed him under the train.'

'And you?' Carradine asked. 'Why do you want to find her so badly?'

'I'm afraid at this stage that's above your pay grade, Kit.' Somerville pushed the peanuts away, perhaps remembering that his doctor had warned him not to consume too much salt. 'We just want to talk to her. She knows a lot. She could put some pieces of the puzzle together.'

Carradine could feel his temper beginning to fray.

'Listen,' he said. 'If you want me to help you, I need to know what's going on.'

'What makes you think we need your help?' said Hulse.

Carradine was stuck for an answer. He found himself saying: 'I care about Lara. You're not the only ones who want to keep her alive.'

Somerville sipped his pint. Hulse did the same with his Diet Coke. It was as though they were both thinking the same thing.

'You're in love with her,' said Somerville.

'Is that a statement or a question?'

'Statement,' said Hulse, pulling the peanuts towards him and throwing a handful down his throat.

'I am not in love with her.' Carradine was annoyed to be talking about his personal life with two men he wouldn't have trusted to help an old lady across the road. 'I'm just fond of her. I like her. I'd like to see her again.'

'*Fond* of her?' said Hulse, as if nobody had used the term since the latter half of the nineteenth century. 'What does *that* mean?'

'It means he went native.' Somerville showed a sudden

flash of spite. 'It means Lara persuaded him that Ivan Simakov was Gandhi with a side order of Mandela. It means he thinks she's a paragon of revolutionary virtue, a woman of conviction, a misunderstood heroine fighting for a righteous cause.'

'You have no idea what I think about her, or Ivan Simakov for that matter.' Carradine was shocked by how quickly Somerville's mood had turned. It occurred to him that both men were trying to provoke him, perhaps as a test of his temperament. 'I read somewhere that Simakov was a Russian intelligence officer before he founded Resurrection. Is that true?'

Tellingly, Somerville and Hulse both looked down at their drinks.

'I'll take the Fifth on that,' said Hulse.

'Me too,' said Somerville then, jokingly: 'Come to think of it, we need a Fifth in this country.' He succumbed to the temptation to eat a lone peanut and said: 'You were going to tell us how you feel about Resurrection.'

'Yeah,' said Hulse, glad to be switching subjects. 'How *do* you feel about them, Kit?'

Carradine looked around the deserted brasserie. The floor was a chess board of polished black-and-white tiles. It occurred to him that he was most likely a sacrificial pawn in whatever game Hulse and Somerville were playing.

'First of all, I don't think of Resurrection as "them",' he said. 'It's not a group. Resurrection began as an international movement of individuals, all of whom were seeking the same outcome.'

'What, like Manchester United fans?' said Somerville. Hulse smothered a grin.

'If you like.' Carradine did not want to be deflected from his answer. 'To be honest, when I first became aware of Resurrection a few years ago, the purity of Simakov's intentions, the plain language of the manifesto, I warmed to it. I supported it. The people they were targeting were disgusting. They were liars, narcissists. Many of them were criminals who should have been in jail. I was glad when Otis Euclidis was exposed as a charlatan. I was glad that Piet Boutmy was attacked in Amsterdam. I liked it that the centre Left was finally getting off its arse and fighting back instead of wasting time moaning about the animal fat content in the new five-pound note or protesting about the absence of gender-neutral toilets at the LSE.' Hulse looked confused. 'The world was going to shit and the people who were taking it there were getting a free pass. There had been right-wing coups d'état in my country, in Russia, in Turkey, the United States. Resurrection chimed with me, just as it chimed with many of my friends, my father, with hundreds of thousands of people around the world.'

'You didn't think for a moment it was a bit naive?'

The supercilious tone of Somerville's question suggested that he would tolerate only one kind of answer. Carradine took a long slug of his drink and said: 'In what way?'

'Oh, in the way that a bunch of semi-radicalised, ludicrously idealistic liberal intellectuals trying to make the world a better place is *always* a bit naive. What did they do in those first halcyon months? Throw a pot of paint here. Chuck a shoe there. Kidnap a couple of here-today-gone-tomorrow journalists? "Give me a break", as our friend from across the Pond might say. You didn't think human nature might get in the way?' Carradine opened his mouth to reply but Somerville was up and running. 'Never underestimate the vanity of self-styled revolutionaries. "Man the barricades, guys. Let's revive the spirit of '68. We're the new Black Panthers. This is our Prague Spring." It's all a pose, all nostalgia, like everything nowadays. Revolutionaries? Don't make me laugh. Take away their iPhones for five minutes and they'd have a seizure.' It looked as though he was finished, but Somerville added a coda. 'What was the phrase Simakov used in the manifesto? "Those who know that they have done wrong." Have you ever heard anything so ridiculous? It's a miracle anybody took him seriously.'

'What do you mean?' Carradine was wondering why Somerville had become so agitated. It was as though he had a personal stake in some aspect of Resurrection's activities.

'I mean how are we, as human beings, supposed to identify such people? "Those who know that they have done wrong." They can't even identify *themselves*. What Simakov and his merry band of followers failed to realise is that most people aren't particularly interested in playing nice. They want to *join* the groups that have their hands on the levers of power. They want to gorge themselves at the same troughs that have enriched the so-called "elites". They don't want to smash the state; they want to *assist* it so that they can join in the fun. People are greedy, Kit. Human beings are selfish, competitive. You're a novelist, for Christ's sake. Surely you've realised that by now?'

'The only thing I've realised is that you've been working too long for an organisation that sees only the worst in people.' Carradine was waiting for Hulse to add his two cents, but the American seemed content to listen. 'I have much greater faith in the essential decency of humankind.'

Somerville repeated the phrase with scornful condescension – '*the essential decency of humankind*' – and drained the last of his pint. Hulse looked on with an expression of benign amusement. 'Isn't that touching? You should have known, just as Lara and Simakov should have known, that ideological movements of the Resurrection sort, particularly those that take on a paramilitary quality, are always hijacked by thugs and bigots, by the intolerant, holier-than-thou "no platform" crowd, by the self-righteous and the misguided.'

'Maybe so,' Carradine replied, aware that Somerville had referred to Bartok by her first name twice in the space of five minutes. 'Maybe so. But there was nobility at the outset. The possibility of real change. There was hope.'

'What a load of cock.' Somerville stood up and stretched his back. 'Change? Hope? Save me from the romantic delusions of the artistic classes. Save me from the *writers*. Same again, gentlemen?'

'Just a minute,' said Carradine. It was important to respond to Somerville's accusations. 'I've never been involved in Resurrection actions—'

Somerville interrupted him.

'That's not the point,' he said.

'Of course it's the point.' To his consternation, Hulse was checking a message on his mobile phone. 'I'm here because you wanted to speak to me. I'm here because I'm worried that the people who were hunting Lara in Morocco, the men who killed Ramón and Mantis, may try to do the same to me. I need your help. I want answers.

I don't understand why the fuck I'm listening to you ranting on about Resurrection.'

'Oh, don't worry about the Moscow Men.' Somerville placed a hand on Carradine's back. It was as though he considered the potential threat to his life to be no more serious than the matter of settling the bill in the restaurant. 'They'll never touch you. They think you're one of us.'

'They *what*?!'

Carradine was stunned. Hulse looked up from his phone. 'Think about it,' he said, taking over the narrative from Somerville. 'You turn up in Lara's apartment and beat up on the guy they sent to grab her. You write about espionage with a degree of verisimilitude . . .'

'Ooh, nice word,' said Somerville.

'Thanks, man.' Hulse put his wallet on the table. Carradine could see the outline of a condom pressing out through the leather. 'Then you vanish from Marrakech without a trace, as far as they're concerned with the connivance of the British Secret Service . . .'

'That's what they *think*?' Carradine suddenly understood why he had been left unmolested since he returned to London. 'How do you *know* all this?'

'Pay grade, Kit. Pay grade.' It had become a shorthand for whatever Somerville felt like concealing from him. He ordered more drinks and walked off in the direction of the gents, leaving Carradine alone with Hulse. He had been handed an unexpected opportunity to speak to the American in more detail about what had happened in Morocco.

'What about Oubakir?' he said. 'Can you tell me about him, or is he above my pay grade too?'

'Who?' Hulse was putting the phone back in his pocket.

Either he hadn't heard the name clearly or was pretending not to have recognised it.

'Mohammed Oubakir. How did he know you were Agency? Why did he warn me in Blaine's to be careful around you?'

'He said that?' An Ed Sheeran song came on the sound system. Somebody at a table on the far side of the brasserie shouted out: 'Oh for fuck's sake, not this shit.'

'He said that,' Carradine confirmed.

Hulse took a moment to compose himself.

'Look,' he said. 'I work North Africa. I meet a lot of people. Some of them assume I work for the Agency, some of them don't. Oubakir was on our radar because of his association with Mantis. We knew he was feeding intel back to Moscow thinking it was going to London. We allowed Stephen Graham to continue to operate for precisely this reason. He showed us who the Russians were interested in, where the gaps were in their knowledge, who they were talking to. When I saw you eating dinner with Oubakir, and Ramón told me you were associated with Mantis, I got suspicious. It's what I'm paid to do.'

Not for the first time Carradine wished that he could take some time off, write everything down, try to work out exactly who was telling him the truth and who wasn't. He saw Somerville coming back from the gents.

'So, as I was saying.' It was as if he had been away for no more than a few seconds. The waiter put a pint on the table and returned to the bar to collect the other drinks. 'Here's my theory on the pointlessness of Resurrection.' Somerville sat down, took a draw from the pint and looked as though he expected a rapt audience. 'Life is cyclical, gentlemen. It goes in phases. Seven years of famine. Seven

367

years of plenty. The issues that are aggravating us today have been aggravating our forefathers for centuries. There is nothing new under the sun. A noble, articulate, mixed-race liberal icon takes over the Presidency of the United States. Does he make the world a better place? No, he does not. A narcissistic sociopath with a thin skin and a bad dye job disgraces the Presidency of the United States. Does he make the world a *worse* place? No, he does not.' The waiter put a gin and tonic in front of Hulse, another Diet Coke in front of Carradine. Carradine switched them round. 'We are a planet of individuals. Our happiness is tied to small things: food, water, sex, friendship. Manchester United.' A grin from Hulse. 'The activities of a tin-pot dictator in Washington, Moscow or Istanbul don't amount to a hill of beans in terms of a man's contentment.'

'Try telling that to the people they imprison, the people they humiliate, the people they kill,' said Carradine.

'That's my point!' Somerville exclaimed. 'In any historical cycle there will be people who suffer, people who die, people who are imprisoned because of the actions of their politicians. But to think that you can make those politicians act differently, to think that you can change the outlook or behaviour of a newspaper columnist, a politician, a corrupt banker, a climate change denier – whoever you happen to have a gripe with that week – is the height of fucking stupidity. Nobody ever changes their mind about anything!'

Hulse was about to interrupt when Somerville silenced him.

'Furthermore, it is my personal belief that the more rancid, the more corrupt, the more cynical, the more craven the behaviour of our public officials, the more it brings decent people closer and closer together. To condemn them? Yes. But also to remind ourselves that the vast majority of people are well-intentioned, decent citizens and that the targets of Resurrection are therefore a tiny minority of mavericks and outliers who are best ignored, and certainly tolerated.'

'I wish I could agree with you, Julian,' said Hulse.

'Me too,' said Carradine, trying to square Somerville's optimistic remarks with his earlier tirade against greed and self-interest. Somerville's phone rang. He answered it with a brisk 'Hello' then listened as whoever was calling delivered what appeared to be astounding news. Even Hulse seemed surprised. Somerville's facial expression moved from relaxed good humour to profound shock in the space of a few seconds.

'Say that again,' he said. 'When? *How?*'

There was a lengthy silence. Carradine would have given the world to know what Somerville had been told. Hulse mouthed the words 'What's up?' but Somerville ignored him.

'I see,' he said. 'OK, understood. Yes. We're leaving now. I'll see you as soon as I see you. Bye.'

44

Somerville took £30 out of his wallet, handed the money to Carradine and summoned Hulse to his feet.

'We have to go,' he said. 'Kit, here's a number to reach me at if you're ever worried or get in any trouble.'

Scribbling the number on the back of a menu, Somerville apologised for bringing the meeting to such an abrupt conclusion but explained that something urgent had come up at work.

'What kind of thing?' Carradine asked. He noticed that the first five digits written down were the same as his own and that the number ended with a sequence of twos.

'Pay grade,' said Hulse, adjusting his jacket.

'That should cover the drinks,' said Somerville, nodding at the money. Carradine didn't think that it would.

'So I just go back to my old life?' he said. 'Forget about Lara. Forget about Morocco?'

'Forget about all of us.' Hulse patted him on the back in a way that Carradine found intensely irritating. 'Just keep writing those books, Kit. That's what you're good at.'

That last, patronising remark, delivered as Hulse and Somerville hurried out of the brasserie looking like ushers running late for a wedding, cemented an idea in Carradine's mind. In an instant, his natural curiosity and thirst for risk got the better of him. He pinned the money under his half-finished gin and tonic, tore the number off the menu and followed them out onto the street.

Emerging from the brasserie, he saw Hulse ducking into the back seat of the Jaguar on the opposite side of the road. He assumed that Somerville was already inside. Two black cabs were coming down the one-way street. Carradine raised his hand, missed the first taxi but hailed the second.

'Do you see that Jaguar?' he said, climbing into the back.

'What's that, guv?'

The driver switched on a microphone so that they could hear one another more clearly. He had a central casting Cockney accent, a shaved head and a perfectly horizontal crease of fat at the base of his scalp.

'There's a green Jaguar up ahead on the left.'

'So there is.'

'How do you feel about following it?'

'How do I *feel*?' There was a pause. Carradine remembered tailing Lara to the riad in Marrakech. 'If you're paying, mate, I'll follow whoever you want me to follow. Follow my leader. Follow the money. Follow the yellow brick road. Whatever you want.'

By force of habit Carradine fastened his seat belt, a detail he would have excluded had he been writing the scene in a script or novel. He couldn't imagine Humphrey Bogart or Harrison Ford being concerned about back seat safety.

'Great,' he said. The Jaguar was about fifty metres ahead and already indicating to the right. Somerville and Hulse could be heading to Service headquarters, to the American Embassy, to a safe house or airport. 'Do you take credit cards?' he asked.

'If you've got 'em, I take 'em,' said the driver, making eye contact in the rear-view mirror. 'So who are we following? Jealous husband? Jealous housewife? David Beckham?'

'I really have no idea,' Carradine replied, leaning back in his seat. 'No idea at all.'

45

Hulse and Somerville did not go far. Carradine followed the Jaguar from Soho to Hyde Park Corner then south-west into Mayfair. The driver did such a good job of keeping a discreet distance and concealing himself in traffic that Carradine wondered if he had previous experience.

'Ever been asked to follow someone before?'

'Once or twice, guv. Once or twice.'

The Jaguar pulled up outside a large terraced house on Chapel Street. Carradine recognised the road. He had been to a party in an Italian restaurant on the corner less than a year earlier. The cab loitered about a hundred metres away as Somerville emerged from the Jaguar and looked up at the house.

'Suspect number one,' said the driver. 'Someone should have a word with him about that suit.'

Carradine was trying to work out which address Somerville was heading into. Hulse opened the back door and joined him on the pavement. Somerville tapped on the roof and the Jaguar pulled away.

'Now that geezer's gotta be a Yank. You can tell 'em a mile off.'

'You're not wrong,' Carradine replied, observing the contrast between Hulse's healthy, athletic demeanour and the slightly stooped, anxious-looking Somerville.

'What now?' the driver asked.

'I give you money,' Carradine replied, handing over a twenty-pound note. 'You've been brilliant. Thanks so much.' The change came back but Carradine waved it away. 'Do me a favour and forget this ever happened.'

'Sure thing. Say no more.'

The taxi pulled away leaving Carradine in the middle of the road. He had seen Somerville and Hulse going down a flight of steps towards a basement. They were now out of sight. He jogged towards the house, keeping an eye on a damaged column beyond the gate as a marker for the entrance.

He walked up to the building, staying on the street side of the pavement so that his feet would not be visible to anyone who happened to look up from the basement. He came to a halt and looked down.

Sitting at a table with a piece of paper, a pen and what looked like a voice recorder in front of her, was Lara Bartok. She stood up as Somerville came into the room and shook his hand. There was no question in Carradine's mind that they already knew one another; the body language between them was unmistakable. This was a reunion, not an introduction. As somebody else in the room lowered a set of pale yellow blinds, preventing Carradine from seeing anything else through the window, the beauty and the depth of the operation became clear to him in a moment of overwhelming clarity. He turned away from the house, dumbfounded by what he now understood.

46

Lara Bartok was a spy. Carradine could think of no other plausible explanation for everything that had taken place. Recruited by the Service in her early twenties, she had been played against Ivan Simakov when he had been working for Russian intelligence. She had subsequently fallen in love with him and effectively deserted her post. That was why Somerville had been so agitated by any mention of Resurrection and so dismissive of the movement's ethos. He had recruited Bartok but failed to stop her succumbing to Simakov's charms. He had lost her to a cause greater than his own.

The more Carradine thought about it, the more the theory made sense. When Bartok had decided to leave Simakov, she had not been able to seek the Service's protection. As a common criminal, sought by the American authorities, London had abandoned her to her fate. Carradine thought back to their conversation in the riad. When he had asked her how she knew that Stephen Graham was operating under a false flag, her answer had been vague and evasive. *I just knew.* She knew because there had never been a 'Stephen Graham' on the books at British intelligence.

Carradine lit a cigarette. He was walking along Chapel Street in a heightened state, close to the exhilaration a writer experiences after a creative breakthrough. Yet he was also disturbed by the idea that Lara was so close and yet so out of reach. He wanted to see her, to hear her side of the story. He fought the urge to go to the basement and to ring the doorbell. Quite apart from the humiliation of being followed to the flat, Somerville and Hulse would be horrified to see him. They were hardly likely to welcome him into the fold and make him privy to what they knew about LASZLO. More likely he would be escorted from the building and placed on a watchlist. Carradine's presence might also make things difficult for Bartok. It was better to stay away, to use what he now knew to his own advantage. Whatever Somerville might ask of him in the future, whatever lies Hulse may or may not tell, whatever claims were made, Carradine would know the truth. Information was power.

He returned to his flat on foot. It was a beautiful summer evening. As he walked through Hyde Park, Carradine began to unravel more of the mysteries of Morocco. He remembered Bartok's reluctance to go to the British Embassy in Rabat. She had been afraid of arrest, perhaps even of being handed over to the Americans. If that was the case, why was she now in London? Had she been seized in Spain or had she decided to hand herself in?

It was almost dark by the time he reached his flat. He opened the door and switched on the light in the hall.

He usually placed his house keys in a small bowl on a table facing the door. The bowl was not there. The cleaner, Mrs Ritter, had been to the flat while he was away. Perhaps she had moved it.

Carradine went into the living room. As he put his phone down on a side table, he became aware that the rug in the centre of the room was facing the wrong way. The black horses in the design usually looked out in the direction of Hyde Park, but the rug had been spun through ninety degrees and was now facing towards the kitchen. He wondered if Mrs Ritter had also been that afternoon, though she always texted if she was planning to come on a different day.

He walked into his office. Two vintage movie posters hung above his desk. A Japanese advertisement for *Three Days of the Condor* which Carradine had bought online, and a rare French poster for *The Conversation* showing Gene Hackman with a set of headphones clamped to his ear. Redford and Dunaway were always on the right-hand side of his desk, Hackman on the left.

The posters had been switched.

Carradine began to feel unsettled. He looked at his bookshelves. They were usually arranged by author yet somebody had moved the books around. Updike was mixed in with Ambler, Deighton with Philip Roth. He stared at the shelves, trying to think of any conceivable reason why Mrs Ritter might have put the books back in the wrong order. A complete set of Pauline Kael's collected film reviews were stacked on the ground, as if someone had been dusting the shelves and had forgotten to put them back.

Carradine sat at his desk, aware that his breathing had

become more shallow, his body constricted. He looked in the drawer where he had left the memory stick. It was no longer there. He tapped the keyboard to bring the screen to life and entered his password. The desktop opened as normal. He knew that whoever had been into his office would have tried to access the information on the computer. Then he saw that the backup hard drive usually attached to his Dell was missing from the desk. Whoever had taken the memory stick had also taken the drive.

Carradine felt nauseous. The changes to his flat were a Russian signature; diplomats in Moscow regularly had the pictures and furniture in their homes switched around by local goons. He went into his bedroom and saw right away, like a childish schoolboy prank, that the bottom sheet had been removed. A pile of shoes was stacked up by the door. Carradine went out into the sitting room to find his phone. He would call Somerville using the number he had written on the menu. There was no point involving the police.

As he was taking the torn menu from his jacket pocket, he looked into the kitchen. Light was bouncing off the linoleum floor. Water had spilled from the sink, which had been filled to capacity. Carradine rolled up a sleeve and put his hand into the water, looking for the plug. The water was dirty but still warm. He touched something hard at the bottom of the sink and pulled it out. He knew what it was before it had broken the surface. They had put his laptop in the sink.

Carradine stepped back, water dripping from the computer onto the floor. He prayed that he had a copy of his novel backed up in the Cloud but knew that whoever had broken into his flat would have the where-withal to erase it online as easily as they had switched the posters in his office. He put the laptop on the kitchen table, dried his hands and dialled the number.

Somerville did not pick up.

Carradine tried a second time. There was still no answer. He assumed that the phone was on mute or that there was no signal in the basement. For all the times that he had written about mobile phone technology in his books, he still did not know if a phone rang out if there was no signal or if it had failed to connect.

A WhatsApp message came through from the number.

Everything OK? Sorry to leave you in the lurch.

Carradine tapped out a reply. He did not know how to express what had happened.

Slight problem at my flat. Need advice.

Carradine saw that Somerville was 'typing'. It was like texting Mantis all over again.

Someone will come round within the hour. Stay put.

Carradine didn't bother to give his address. He assumed the Service already knew where he lived. He replied: 'OK' to Somerville's message, lit a cigarette and poured himself three inches of vodka.

Less than forty minutes later a new message came through from Somerville telling Carradine to go to a pub on Bayswater Road. Somebody from the Service would meet him there. Carradine knew the pub – it was his local – and described what he was wearing so that the contact would be able to recognise him.

Don't worry about that. They know exactly who you are.

He grabbed his keys, his wallet and his phone and left the flat. He tugged three separate strands of hair from his head and glued them to the frame of the door with saliva so that he might be able to tell if someone had broken in while he was gone. He applied the last of the strands to the bottom of the door frame and hoped that one of his neighbours wouldn't come out of their flat and ask what on earth he was doing.

He rode the lift to the ground floor. It was dark outside and the street was deserted. The pub was no more than half a mile away. He hadn't eaten for hours and was suddenly famished.

He heard the men coming up behind him before he had time to react. They came quickly, running with light steps. Carradine swung around and saw two of them less than three metres away, closing in. To his consternation, he realised that the man closest to him was the Russian he had knocked out cold in Marrakech.

'Hello, Mr Considine,' he said.

That was the last thing Carradine remembered.

47

Carradine woke up in a comfortable, beautifully furnished bedroom. There was no sound of traffic, only the occasional rush of wind and the regular tweet of birdsong. He felt as though he had slept for twelve hours straight. He was dressed in the same clothes he had been wearing when he had left the flat. His wallet and keys were on a bedside table stacked with antiquarian books. His phone was nowhere to be seen.

Carradine sat up in bed. He was desperately thirsty. There was an en-suite bathroom on the far side of the room. He filled a tooth mug at the basin and drank three glasses of water in quick succession. His muscles were stiff and his head ached but when he looked in the mirror, he saw that his face was unmarked. He needed to shower and shave but was surprised by how calm he felt. He understood that he was probably in a state of shock.

He walked back into the bedroom and pulled back the curtains on the set of windows closest to the door. Carradine was momentarily blinded by bright sunshine but saw that he was standing in a room on the first floor of a dilapidated farmhouse overlooking a muddy yard and, in the distance, a chequerboard of fields. He remembered Somerville telling him that Moscow would leave him alone on the assumption that he was working for the Service. There was a tiny slice of consolation in that thought. Then he remembered that his flat had been turned upside-down and his laptop destroyed. He stepped away from the window and sat back on the bed. He was now afraid.

Carradine tried to shake off a growing dread. He needed to think more clearly. He told himself that he was on a property controlled by Russian intelligence. There was surely no other possibility. It occurred to him that Somerville and Hulse were subjecting him to some kind of training exercise or test, but that theory was too absurd to be taken seriously. Whoever had kidnapped him wanted answers. That was all anybody ever wanted from him. Hulse. Bartok. Somerville. They had all been the same. They had stripped him for information then vanished into the night.

Footfalls on a staircase. Somebody was coming up to the room. Carradine pushed a hand through his hair and stood up, preparing to meet whoever came through the door. He did not know who or what to expect. He assumed that the man from Lara's apartment in Marrakech was the most likely candidate.

It was not him.

The man who came into the room was slim and tanned with shoulder-length black hair tied in a ponytail. He was wearing glasses and sporting a thick, Biblical salt-and-pepper beard. His fast, intelligent eyes grinned at Carradine as he flashed him a benevolent smile.

'Kit,' he said. 'Welcome to our temporary home. Do you like it?'

The voice was deep and rich, the slick international accent hard to place. He was wearing designer jeans and what appeared to be a brand-new pair of Redwing boots. He oozed the easy confidence and poise of the self-made man.

'Who are you?'

The answer to the question revealed itself even as Carradine was asking it. The man standing in front of him, his appearance subtly altered by the addition of glasses and by the fullness of the beard, was the same man whose face Carradine had stared at in dozens of articles and obituaries over the course of the previous fortnight.

He was talking to Ivan Simakov.

48

'You are a hard man to pin down, Kit. Are you just a writer or are you also a British spy? Do you know this world you have fallen into or is all of this a novelty?' Simakov smirked as he gestured outside, loving the sound of his own voice, enjoying the power he was exerting over his stunned and frightened prisoner. 'Are you Lara's new boyfriend, the man who has taken her from me? Or did she play you and manipulate you as she has played and manipulated so many others? Who are you, Kit Carradine? A genius or a fool? Tell me, please. I am fascinated.'

Carradine felt that he was staring at a ghost, a dream of a dead man. Ivan Simakov had been killed in a Moscow apartment and buried in an unmarked grave. The man standing in front of him had somehow managed to fake his own death and to make a new life in the West. How was this possible?

'You are who I think you are?' he said.

'I am!' Simakov replied, revelling in his own myth.

'How?' said Carradine.

Simakov waved a dismissive hand, as if the whys and wherefores of his miraculous rebirth were of no greater consequence than the sound of the wind outside or the persistent tweet of birdsong. He clutched his hands behind his back.

'Where am I?' Carradine asked.

Simakov tipped back his head and smiled.

'Rest assured you are still in your beloved England, that green and pleasant land. Within two hours, driving along the motorway, you could be back at your desk writing another thriller, another little story about spies.'

Carradine was too stunned to be irritated by the slight. He saw that Simakov intended to keep talking. He had the air of a man who was used to supplicants hanging on his every word.

'We are on a farm at the edge of a typical country estate once owned by the English aristocracy, but now lost to those who could afford to keep it in the correct style.' Carradine wondered how and why Simakov had been given access to the property; he assumed that it was under Russian ownership. 'The British ruling class are inexplicably pleased with themselves, don't you think?' He moved towards the window closest to the bathroom and drew back the curtains. 'Your aristocrats can no longer afford to heat their homes. Your banks are owned by Arabs and Chinese. The finest buildings in London belong to Russians. The great English writers and poets have all vanished. Your culture, like so many other cultures today, is an American culture of karaoke, of recycled stories, of political decay and mass stupidity. The great English churches are in the hands of property developers, the schools, so far as I can tell, are controlled not by teachers, but by their pupils. There is no *discipline* in your society. No discipline or intellectual curiosity, only ignorance. Above all, despite this, there seems to be a complete absence of self-doubt in the British character! What is it, exactly, that you are so proud of? You lost an Empire and replaced it with – *what*?'

Carradine saw that he was expected to answer.

'With views like that you sound like you'd fit in very well in Moscow,' he said. 'Everything's a bit binary with you so far, Ivan. Genius or fool? Old Britain good, new Britain bad. I thought you were fighting for freedom of choice, for openness, for decency? I didn't have you down as a reactionary.'

Rather than express any discomfort or annoyance with what Carradine had said, Simakov merely touched his beard and looked out at the farmyard, like an admiral surveying his fleet.

'It's true. All through my life I have been confused by your country. I used to tell Lara this.' Carradine knew the reference to Bartok was intended to unsettle him. Simakov suddenly turned from the window and looked back across the room. 'I thought you would be more upper-class.'

'Excuse me?'

'Kit. It sounds like a character in an Evelyn Waugh novel. Nobody is called "Kit" any more. What *was* William thinking?'

At the mention of his father's name, Carradine felt sick with worry. Simakov pretended to reassure him.

'Please do not worry,' he said, raising a conciliatory hand. 'The old man has not been harmed. Yet.'

The menace of that last word floored Carradine. He wanted to know what had happened, where his father was being held, to demand that Resurrection release him. But he knew that to show his fear would be to play into Simakov's hands.

'Where is he?' he said, trying to remain as calm as possible. 'What is it you want with us?'

Simakov ignored the question.

'Here's the thing.' He offered Carradine a cigarette. Carradine wanted one but refused it. Simakov smiled as he placed the packet in his pocket. 'Mankind has reached its zenith. Homo sapiens has come as far as he can come.' He inhaled deeply. 'We can eat, we can drink, we can fuck, we can communicate, we can travel, we can do whatever we want. About the only thing we are not permitted to do is smoke!' He smiled at his own joke. Carradine knew that he was listening to a man with no moral compass, no values or kindness, only his own self-love. 'There are cures for AIDS and cures for cancer, artificial limbs for the disabled, central heating and hot water and electricity in every home. Every book and film and play and poem and fragment of knowledge ever assembled is available at the click of a mouse or the weight of a finger on the screen of a cellphone. The world has never had it so good. And yet people are still not satisfied! They are so spoiled.' Was this a speech Simakov had prepared in advance or was he making it up off the top of his head? Bartok had spoken about being mesmerised by Simakov's words, but this felt more like an actor giving a performance which had been rehearsed time and time again. 'It turns out that mankind is so competitive, so adversarial, so frightened of change, so geared to cruelty that he will wilfully destroy his own society, his own culture – for what? Independence? *Freedom?* What do Americans mean when they say that they crave "freedom"? Do they not realise that they are already free!'

Carradine could hardly take in what Simakov was saying. He was thinking about his father, wondering if he was a prisoner in the same house. What would Resurrection try to extract from him in return for his father's safety? Did Simakov know that he had once been a British spy? He wished that he had never set eyes on Stephen Graham, that he had never been so reckless or so vain as to agree to work for the Service.

'I will tell you why they destroyed their own societies.' Simakov opened a window. A smell of manure burst into the room. 'They blew it all up for the chance to hate. For a sentimental version of an all-white past that didn't exist and can never exist in the future. People by their millions, here and in America, in Poland, in Hungary, in Turkey, voted for going backwards when they didn't even need to go *forwards*. All they had to do was stand still. Life was never going to get any better. They were never going to be more "free". There were never going to be more steaks in the freezer, more ways in which they could be happy and content. That was the tragedy. Resurrection merely took advantage of that.'

Carradine was confused by that final remark.

'What do you mean?' he said. 'What do you mean you took advantage of it?'

Simakov looked as though he had not intended to speak so candidly. It was the first time Carradine had witnessed a crack in his overweening, theatrical self-confidence.

He had the sensation – so familiar from conversations with Bartok and Somerville – that he was at the edge of a secret which was being deliberately withheld from him.

'So.' Simakov wanted to change the subject. 'You must answer me. Can I expect a visit from the British Secret Service, come to rescue one of their own? Or are you just another penny thriller writer of no great importance who spends his life making up stories rather than engaging with the real world and effecting necessary change?'

Carradine knew that Simakov was not interested in the answer. It was just part of a game designed to unsettle him. All he could do was wait and bide his time and find out what it was that Simakov wanted. Carradine's only concern was to work out where he was and how he was going to save his father.

'Where's my dad?' he said.

Simakov shrugged. 'Safe.'

'My family is not a threat to you. What do you want?'

Simakov walked into the bathroom, ran a tap at the sink, extinguished his cigarette in the stream of water and threw it into the toilet.

'You are well rested!' he exclaimed. 'You feel fit! You feel good! You want to ask me questions and be direct.' He came back into the room and stood in front of Carradine. 'OK, I will be direct with you. You are here because you have been with Lara.'

In that moment Carradine understood that Simakov was still working for Russian intelligence. He had instructed them to find Lara and to bring her to him. That was why Graham had acted as he did; he had known of the operation and had wanted to save LASZLO.

There was no other explanation for Simakov's miraculous survival. Moscow had detonated the bomb in the apartment knowing that their prize agent had long since left the building. Zack Curtis, the Resurrection volunteer who was killed in the blast, had been merely a sacrificial pawn.

'How do you know I've seen her?'

Simakov looked as though he had been insulted.

'Do I look to you like somebody who is short of information? Do I look like a man who has trouble finding things out?'

'Your friends in Moscow told you?'

Simakov did not bother to deny it.

'Yes,' he replied cautiously. 'They heard that you were looking for Lara on behalf of Stephen Graham. Is that correct?'

'Stephen Graham is dead,' Carradine replied. 'But I don't imagine that's news to you. Or to Moscow.'

Simakov removed something from his mouth and said: 'Stephen caused a lot of problems.'

'Really? In the same way Ramón Basora and Zack Curtis caused a lot of problems, or was it something different this time?' Simakov winced. 'Tell me, which one of your flunkies threw Graham under the train?'

It was a brave question. Carradine knew that he was pushing his luck. In his sudden understanding of Simakov's real identity, he had intuited a deeper, terrifying truth.

'You deflect very well, Mr Carradine,' Simakov exclaimed. 'You avoid the questions you do not wish to answer. You ask me the questions which perhaps your masters have told you to ask. Perhaps you have been trained after all!'

'Only media training, Ivan,' he said and regretted it immediately. He knew that Simakov's vanity would be offended by the fact that he did not seem to be afraid. The Russian duly exploded with laughter, the noise carrying outside into the farmyard and beyond to whoever was protecting him, to whoever knew that the supposed icon of non-violent resistance was in fact a murderous thug still in the employ of Russian intelligence.

'You are funny!' he said, and suddenly swept his right arm across Carradine's face. The back of Simakov's hand connected with his jaw, sending him crashing to the ground. Carradine had been hit before, with greater force and skill, but never with such unexpectedness. The side of his face screamed in pain. He could feel a warm, alkaline pooling of blood in his mouth as he tried to stand up. 'You should know when is the correct time to make jokes.'

Carradine's mind was spinning in loops, from fear to determination, from despair to hope. He stood up and faced Simakov. He steadied himself. With the awful clarity of a man waking up to a truth long withheld from him, Carradine realised that, all along, Resurrection had been a Kremlin-approved operation to bring chaos to the West. The movement had been funded and organised with the express purpose of bringing chaos to the streets of New York and Washington and Los Angeles, to the neighbourhoods of Berlin and Madrid and Paris. Bartok had been duped, Somerville and Hulse as well. There had been so few attacks in Russia not because the friends and relatives of Resurrection activists were being assassinated, but because there were no active Resurrection cells in Russia. There was no other explanation for the ease with which

Simakov had been able to fake his own death, to continue to organise Resurrection strikes and to live, like some latter-day bin Laden, on a farm in the middle of the English countryside.

'Who owns this place?' he asked, wanting to swing a punch of his own but knowing that any number of Russian heavies were doubtless on the other side of the door waiting to burst in and defend their boss.

'Why do you ask?' Simakov replied. It pleased Carradine to see that he was rubbing his fist. He hoped that his jaw had smashed a bone in the back of the Russian's hand.

'You're meant to be dead. Anybody sees you, you're finished. Who's protecting you? Who's paying your bills? A man like you should be cowering in a hut in the backwoods of Montana, living under a pseudonym in Ecuador, shuffling from bedsit to bedsit in the north of England, looking for recruits to your shabby cause. But you're not. You're here, living like a superannuated rock star in a Cotswolds farmhouse. Why is that?'

'I am a lucky man,' Simakov replied. 'I have friends in high places.'

'Yeah. I bet you do.' Carradine was gripped by a fatalistic courage, certain that he would never make it out of the house alive, but determined to go out on his own terms. He wanted to express to Simakov the depth of his contempt for what he had done, his conviction that the Russians had picked the wrong strategy, that they would lose in the end, but knew that to do so would be to waste his breath. Instead he continued to puncture Simakov's story.

'I was sorry to hear about your parents.'

'Thank you.' It was the first time Carradine had seen

evidence in his expression of an authentic emotional response.

'It was an accident, wasn't it?'

'Excuse me?'

'The car crash. An accident?'

He wondered if the Great Martyred Leader would bother denying it. He wondered if Simakov would hit him again. Instead, he brought his face so close to Carradine's that he could smell the coffee on his breath as he spoke.

'I hated my parents. I hadn't seen them since I was nineteen years old. Why would I mourn the deaths of two people who had done so little for me?' He paused. 'Yes, to answer your question, the crash was an accident.'

'And what am I?' said Carradine. 'Another Otis Euclidis? You'll keep me here in captivity until everyone assumes I'm dead?'

Simakov looked surprised. 'Oh, you heard about that?' he said.

'Heard about what?'

'Dear little Otis has been found in a basement in Indiana. The Brazilian whore who used to rent the house for us tipped off the police that he'd been left there to die. There wasn't much of him left apparently. I imagine the stench was appalling.'

Carradine shook his head in disgust.

'Speaking of cars,' Simakov continued. 'Do you see that vehicle outside?'

Carradine turned and looked out of the window. A large Transit van was parked in front of the house.

'Yes,' he replied. His throat was bone dry. He could barely voice the word.

'We found the contents of your cellphone very interesting.' Simakov was staring at him, his head tilted to one side. 'You and I are going to be getting into that van, Kit. We're going to set out on a journey.'

49

Carradine was taken downstairs and served food in a large kitchen by a woman who did not speak to him. Simakov came into the room. He was carrying a small bottle of water and a phone. He sat opposite Carradine at a wooden table and told the woman to leave. She took his plate to the sink and went out into the farmyard.

'I want to know what you think about Lara,' he said.

Carradine's jaw was still aching. He had been hungry but had found it difficult to eat.

'Why is that important?' he replied.

'Did you fuck her?'

Carradine had a choice. To lie and to protect himself from further harm, or to make Simakov suffer by telling him the truth. He opted for a sophistry which would achieve both aims.

'What happened between us is private,' he said. 'My feelings for Lara are my own business, just as her feelings for me are hers.'

'Did you fuck her?'

'Grow up, Ivan.'

Simakov pulled out a handgun. For a split second Carradine thought that he was going to fire, but he placed the gun on the table – just out of Carradine's reach – and looked him in the eye.

'What did she say about me?'

Carradine looked at him with pity. 'That you were the best, Ivan.' He laid on the sarcasm, having intuited the extent to which Simakov needed to be praised and reassured. 'She said you were unforgettable. One in a million. She's never got over you. What woman would?'

Simakov exploded with rage.

'WHAT DID SHE SAY ABOUT ME?'

Suddenly Carradine understood why the Russians had wanted so desperately to find Lara. Had they discovered that she had been a Service asset and had proof of Simakov's survival? She had left New York because she no longer loved Simakov and had lost faith in the movement; Moscow mistakenly believed that she knew the truth both about Ivan and Resurrection. That would explain why she needed to be silenced.

'Strangely enough, we didn't spend a lot of time talking about you. We were too busy trying not to get killed.'

Simakov picked up the gun. His face was flushed with anger.

'Your cellphone,' he said. 'You've been to Chapel Street. You know that Hulse is there.'

'Hulse?'

It was obvious that Simakov knew of their connection. There was no point in lying. Carradine heard the sound of movement in a room close by. He wondered if his father was being brought to see him.

'Sebastian Hulse has become a thorn in my side.' Simakov touched the butt of the gun. 'He knows too much. He is going to be eliminated.'

'Eliminated.' The ease with which Simakov spoke of death made Carradine feel nauseous. 'Just like that.'

'Yes. Just like that.'

Carradine looked down at the gun. He knew what Simakov was going to ask him to do. He felt that he was caught in a trap from which there would be no escape. He wondered when he would be shown the photographs of his father in captivity. He could not think of any way to get a message to Somerville or Hulse to tell them what had happened. He prayed that whoever had been sent to the pub to meet him would realise that he had been kidnapped. Would the Service bother to come looking for him – or leave him to his fate?

'Why don't you tell me what it is that you want me to do?' he said.

Simakov stood up. There was an apple in a bowl on the table. He polished it on the side of his trousers and took a bite, staring at Carradine as he chewed.

'I had Mr Hulse followed from his hotel.'

'Your Russian friends again?'

'Excuse me?'

'They followed him? The same friends who stole my hard drive? They're the ones who analysed my phone? That's how you know I read your obituaries, your life story. Moscow does your dirty work.'

Carradine saw that Simakov had no intention of answering him.

'What should we find,' he continued, 'but that Hulse is visiting the same address in Chapel Street that you showed such an interest in.' Simakov took another bite of the apple. 'So I had the basement watched. And who should we see coming out but a certain Mr Julian Somerville. Who is this, please?'

'You know who he is,' Carradine replied. 'He's the man who recruited Lara.'

Simakov threw the apple across the table and landed it perfectly in a wastepaper basket on the opposite side of the kitchen.

'Precisely!'

'What's your point, Ivan?'

In a sudden, swift movement, Simakov stepped forward and pressed the gun against Carradine's forehead. The steel was cold, the contact terrifying.

'My point is that you're going to take me to them. You're going to get me into that basement. Lara is inside. I want to see her. I want to ask her about you and I want to finish what I started. She knows too much. You all do. So let's get on with it.'

50

Carradine sat in the back of the van beside Simakov. A Russian-speaking driver and a woman were in the front. The woman was slight and wiry and looked Eastern European. She stared outside as they drove south along the M40, occasionally eating a boiled sweet and throwing the wrappers out of the window. Only Simakov had spoken to Carradine since they had left the house. There was an atmosphere of practised expertise, as though each of them had conducted raids of this kind many times before. They were not afraid. The clock on the dashboard showed it was late afternoon. Carradine had no idea what day it was or how long it had been since they had taken him.

At no point had he been left alone. He had wanted to try to get a message to Somerville using the number he had memorised from the restaurant but had seen neither a mobile phone nor landline in the house. He had thought about scribbling a note on a piece of paper and trying to drop it out of the van at a set of traffic lights, but there had been no pen in his bedroom or the kitchen nor any opportunity to search for one. When he had gone into the bathroom, the Russian-speaking driver had stood outside, the door wide open, giving Carradine no chance to attempt an escape.

'I want to speak to my father,' he said. They were a few miles south of High Wycombe. Simakov was sipping from a bottle of water.

'Don't worry about your father,' he said. 'Why would we hurt an innocent old man?' He checked himself. 'Perhaps "innocent" is the wrong word in this context. Can a man who once worked against Soviet interests as a British spy ever be described as "innocent"?'

'Where are you keeping him?'

'Somewhere he'll be very comfortable.'

'Just let me talk to him.' Carradine detested the feeling of powerlessness. 'Let me reassure him that he's going to be fine.'

'No,' Simakov replied.

The plan for their attack was straightforward. Carradine was to walk down to the basement in Chapel Street and to knock on the door of the safe house. Simakov knew that Bartok was being held there because she had been allowed out in the morning and had taken a walk around Belgrave Square. A plain-clothes surveillance officer from the Russian Embassy had watched her come out and followed her on foot. A man matching Somerville's description had been with her at all times. There was no security at the flat, not even a CCTV camera showing movement down to the basement. The door had a fish-eye lens. Carradine was to announce himself to whoever answered. Simakov was certain that Hulse and Somerville

401

would let him in. At that point, the Russian driver and the woman would force their way in behind him. They would be armed. Bartok would be escorted outside to the van and driven away. Simakov had told Carradine that he would be allowed to remain at the safe house once Bartok was secured. Carradine knew that it was his intention to kill them all.

'What do you want from her?' he said.

'From Lara?' Simakov screwed the lid back onto the bottle. 'Answers.'

'Answers about what?'

'Why she left me. Why she disappeared with no explanation. Did she suspect the truth about me, about Resurrection? If not, I want to know why she was so cruel. Why she chose to be with a man like you when she could have stayed with Ivan Simakov.'

The sexual jealousy, the bitterness, the self-righteousness: each were as disturbing to Carradine as they were pitiful. He had already seen enough of Simakov to know that he was deranged with power and hate. He remembered everything that Bartok had told him about the breakdown of their relationship and realised that she had been soft-pedalling her reasons for leaving. It wasn't just Simakov's lust for violence that had so appalled her; it was his mania and rage.

'What's going to happen to her?' he asked.

'That is my business.'

Carradine thought again of his father. Was it possible that Simakov was lying? William Carradine was a sociable man. He had a girlfriend – or, at least, a companion with whom he spent a great deal of time. He played back-gammon twice a week in his local pub with a friend who lived nearby. He regularly helped out at a nearby hospice, reading stories to the patients. In short, his absence would be noted. The girlfriend would call round. The back-gammon player would wonder why Bill hadn't turned up at the pub. Before long, the police would be involved, then the Service. They would make the link to Carradine and realise that something was wrong. And where could the Russians hold him? Simakov must have known about his father's ill health. Would he risk kidnapping a recov-ering stroke victim, an elderly man who might, at any point, require hospital attention? It was a horrifying risk, but if Carradine was going to save Bartok, to avert a bloodbath at the safe house, he was going to have to work on the basis that his father was perfectly safe. Simakov was bluffing.

'Can you at least have a photo taken of my dad, a video, just something to reassure me that he's OK?'

The tiny hesitation in Simakov's response convinced Carradine that his hunch was correct. He knew when a man was being forced to summon a lie; he had done it himself many times in the previous weeks.

'Why are you so worried about him?'

'Because he's my *father*, you fuck. He's sick.'

Carradine searched Simakov's face for another tell. There was nothing.

'A photo,' he said again. 'A video. Can you ask for something to be sent?'

'Afterwards,' Simakov replied.

With that, Carradine made up his mind: he would work on the assumption that his father was safe. He had come up with a simple plan. He had one chance to warn Bartok, a single opportunity to alert Hulse and Somerville to the danger. The Service surely knew that he had been kidnapped. With luck there would be a weapon inside the flat: an armed officer from Special Branch, a handgun in a drawer. If Bartok understood what Carradine was trying to tell her, she could prepare them for what was coming. If she was nowhere near the window when he knocked, there was very little chance of success.

They reached the outskirts of London. So many times, Carradine had driven along this stretch of road yet now it felt as though he was seeing the city for the first time. His eyes were not his own, his memories were the memories of a different man. He was numb to the point of confusion, as if he had been cast in a role for which he had not learned his lines nor been directed how to act. He looked at Simakov, who seemed as calm and disinterested as a plumber on his way to a routine job. The Russian driver had his elbow poking out of the window and was smoking a cigarette. The woman was humming along to a song on the radio, sucking on another boiled sweet. The banality of evil.

They turned off the Westway at Paddington, heading south towards Mayfair. A news bulletin reported that a bomb had gone off at the offices of a right-wing newspaper in Paris, killing four people. Simakov appeared silently to celebrate the news, though he said nothing and merely shrugged when Carradine asked if the device had been planted by Resurrection. The van passed a few hundred metres from Sussex Gardens and came within half a mile of Carradine's flat in Lancaster Gate. He felt like a condemned man en route to the gallows being afforded a last glimpse of his home town. He could not think of any way of changing what was about to happen other than to try to overpower Simakov, to grab his gun and to kill him. He had no experience of firing a weapon, nor did he fancy his chances of overcoming a man of Simakov's training and experience in the cramped rear seats of a Transit van. In the time it took him to do so, the driver or the woman could shoot him dead. He had no choice but to do what he was being ordered to do.

They pulled up in almost exactly the same spot that the taxi driver had parked in a few days earlier. Simakov gave his final instructions in Russian. Carradine guessed that he was making arrangements for his execution and that it was merely a question of which one of them was going to pull the trigger.

'Wouldn't it be a good idea for me to know some names? For us to speak to one another in English?'

Simakov took out two black balaclavas and handed them to the Russians.

'Not necessary,' he said. 'Just do what I've told you. We park outside the apartment. You get out. You walk down. Lisa and Otis will follow you.'

'Lisa? Otis?' said Carradine.

'You wanted names.' Simakov was amused by his own joke. 'Now you have names.'

Simakov took out a third balaclava.

'For me?' Carradine asked.

'Of course not for you. They need to see your face.'

Carradine looked at the driver. He was huge and muscular, with dead eyes, almost certainly one of the men who had attacked Redmond. The woman's face was entirely devoid of expression. Carradine cast his mind back to the riad one last time. He could still picture Bartok on the bed, fixing the signals. Three quick knocks followed

405

by three slower knocks to confirm that it was safe to let him in; the rhythm of 'Rule Britannia' tapped out if Carradine was compromised. He wondered if she would even remember the code.

'Everybody ready?' Simakov asked.

Grunts and nods from the Russians. The driver put the van in gear and pulled up a few feet from the entrance to the basement. As he did so, the woman pulled the balaclava over her head and took two handguns from the glove box. She passed one of the guns to the driver as he switched off the engine. Simakov appeared to be signalling to a vehicle or property on the opposite side of the street. Carradine assumed it was to the same Russian intelligence officer who had tailed Bartok and Somerville around Belgrave Square. Some kind of signal came back – perhaps an all-clear, perhaps a confirmation that Bartok was inside – and Simakov gave the go-ahead.

'Now.'

He pulled back a side door on the van. Simakov was going to stay behind while the attack took place. If he saw that something was wrong in the basement, he would join the fight. Otherwise he would remain out of sight.

It was a beautiful summer evening. As Carradine stepped out of the van and heard the door slide shut behind him, he saw a young man making his way towards him carrying a picnic basket and a bunch of flowers. Just a passing pedestrian going about his business, perhaps walking towards Hyde Park to meet his girlfriend or heading to a barbecue somewhere in a garden in Mayfair. Carradine waited for him to pass. The young man did not break his stride, nor look back as Carradine stepped towards the gate and walked down the short flight of steps to the flat. The pale yellow blinds were drawn. There were no CCTV cameras in sight. A smell of stale, mossy damp drifted up from the basement. Carradine felt the temperature drop as he reached the bottom of the steps. He looked up to see the driver and the woman at the gate, both now wearing balaclavas and moving with the silence of cats behind him.

This was his opportunity. By staying in the van, Simakov had given Carradine more of a chance. Reaching out towards the window, he knocked on the glass, loudly tapping out the rhythm of 'Rule Britannia' before coming to a halt at the door. He was aware of the driver and the woman reaching him and crouching down on either side of the door as he waited. He prayed that Bartok had recognised the signal.

He knocked again, loudly, confidently.

Rule Britannia. Britannia Rules the Waves.

At last the driver spoke. 'Use the bell,' he hissed.

'Who is it?' came a reply from inside.

Carradine recognised Somerville's voice. There was a hesitancy in it, but Carradine could not tell if this was the natural caution of a spy or if Bartok was beside him, warning him that Carradine was trying to send them a message.

'It's Kit,' Carradine replied.

'Everything OK?'

'Everything's absolutely great.' Carradine looked down and saw the eyes of the woman staring up at him, impatient, primed to strike. He wished that he had had the presence of mind, the imagination to reply in such a way that Somerville would know for certain that there was a problem, but he could not think of a better response.

Perhaps he did not need to. When Carradine had failed to show up at the pub, Somerville had surely concluded that he had been kidnapped. His sudden appearance at the safe house would therefore have set off alarm bells.

'OK, Kit. Just a second.'

A chain was pulled back on the door. Carradine heard someone reaching for the lock. Instead of stepping to one side and allowing the attack to go ahead, he now did something that he had not intended to do. As the woman leapt up from the ground, Carradine shouted out a warning – 'Two guns! Get back!' – as she burst past him into the narrow hall. A shot went off, the woman firing blindly into the living room. Carradine could not tell who she was shooting at or if the gun had gone off accidentally.

Somerville and Bartok were nowhere to be seen. The driver pushed Carradine violently against the frame of the living-room door as he surged forward. Carradine was so angered by this that he reached out and grabbed at the neck of his jacket, pulling the driver backwards so that he swung around, the gun in his right hand. The balaclava had twisted on his face so that he was blinded. He fired. The shot narrowly missed Carradine, splintering the front door. Sheer rage made him swing a punch at the Russian's face which knocked him against the wall. High on violence, Carradine kicked him in the stomach and he slumped to the ground. He continued to kick the driver repeatedly in the chest and face, his head jack-knifing to one side as Carradine's foot connected with the balaclava. A shot was fired in the sitting room as the gun fell out of the driver's hand. He was unconscious. As Carradine picked up the weapon, he looked ahead and saw the woman lying motionless on the ground. Somerville was standing over her with a pistol. It looked as though he had shot her in the neck.

'Where's Lara?' Carradine shouted.

'Are there others?' Somerville replied.

'In the van, yes. Outside. Simakov is alive.'

Somerville looked at him in consternation.

'*What*?'

Bartok walked into the room. She was carrying a kitchen knife. She saw the dead body of the woman on the ground and looked at Carradine.

'Kit,' she said. She seemed calm, but had heard what he had told Somerville. 'What did you say? Ivan—'

A shadow fell across the room. Somerville looked up towards the steps and shouted: 'Get down!'

Carradine grabbed Lara and pushed her to the floor, covering her body with his own as he turned and looked back towards the door. Simakov came in, his head concealed beneath a balaclava, his right hand clutching the handgun which, only hours earlier, he had pressed into Carradine's skull.

Somerville pointed the pistol at his chest and shouted: 'Put it down! Put the gun down!'

With his left hand, Simakov pulled off the balaclava and let it drop to the ground. He looked at Bartok. She gasped when she saw his face.

'Jesus,' said Somerville.

'Hello, Lara.' Simakov sounded as though he did not have a care in the world. 'You're coming with me.'

'She's not going anywhere,' Carradine replied.

Behind Simakov, in the doorway of the flat, the driver groaned.

'How?' said Bartok, climbing to her feet in a state of bewilderment. 'How is it possible?'

'Lara, get back,' Somerville ordered. He was aiming the pistol at Simakov's chest. Carradine was still holding the weapon he had picked up in the hall. He did not know if he should shoot or if Somerville would want to take Simakov alive. The threat to Lara's life seemed imminent. He had to try to save her.

'There may be others,' he told them. 'Outside. Russian surveillance. They're watching the flat.'

'Telling tales out of school, Kit,' said Simakov. 'I have a van outside.' He was speaking very calmly. 'Here's what's going to happen. Lara walks out with me, nice and steady, no big tears or drama. We take off and finish what we started.'

'That's not going to happen,' Somerville told him.

Carradine could feel sweat on the palm of his hand as he gripped the gun. He was sure that the safety catch was off, that all he needed to do was fire.

'So you were British intelligence all along?' It was as though Simakov was speaking privately to Bartok and believed that they could not be overheard. 'You were so clever. I had no idea.'

'Just as I had no idea about you,' she replied.

'I wonder why Stephen never told you the truth about me. Was it loyalty? Sentiment? Perhaps he enjoyed the feeling of deceiving you. We all did.'

Anger flashed across Bartok's face. 'Put the gun down, Ivan,' she said. 'It's over now. For both of us.'

'Not for you,' he said, indicating Somerville. 'The British will look after you, no?'

Carradine knew then that he had to shoot. Simakov

was prepared to die and to take Lara with him. There was a tiny movement behind the blinds on the window of the basement. Was it Russian back-up? A faint scuffing noise on the concrete steps outside and an almost imperceptible change in the light. Neither Somerville nor Simakov reacted. Lara was staring at Simakov, as though still trying to come to terms with the fact that he was alive.

'We go now,' he said, sweeping the gun towards Somerville, who took a half-step forward but did not fire.

Carradine knew that this was his chance. Shouting 'Lara, get down!' he raised the gun, only to see Simakov's chest explode in front of him in an eruption of blood and tissue. Lara was screaming as Sebastian Hulse came into the room. He had shot Simakov in the back at point-blank range.

'Fucking hell,' said Somerville.

The driver moved in the hall, reaching out and grabbing Hulse's leg. Hulse looked down and shot him in the head.

'Enough!' Bartok screamed.

Hulse stepped forward, crouched and pulled back Simakov's head. His face and beard were clear of blood but Hulse did not recognise the man he had killed.

'Simakov,' Carradine told him, putting his gun beside the digital recorder on the table. 'You just shot Ivan Simakov.'

Hulse let the head fall back. He looked at Somerville for confirmation of what he had been told. Somerville nodded. Carradine was holding Bartok as she stared at the Russian's motionless body.

'We need to move fast.' Somerville picked up a phone. 'All this gets cleared up.'

411

SECRET INTELLIGENCE SERVICE

Extracts from Part 6 of 'Report into Origins and Development of Resurrection'

. . . It is the view of this officer that any information regarding Ivan Simakov's true role in the genesis and development of Resurrection worldwide should remain a matter of the utmost secrecy.

By the same measure, Moscow's hand in encouraging and financing Resurrection attacks in the West must not and should not be disclosed.

Thus:

Ivan Simakov <u>did not</u> survive the bomb attack in Moscow.

Ivan Simakov <u>was not</u> present at the Chapel Street shooting which claimed the lives of two Resurrection activists intent on kidnapping LASZLO. Anatoly Voltsinger and Elena Federova were Belorussian aliens living illegally in the United Kingdom. They were engaged in a burglary of the property at Chapel Street with the intention of stealing jewels valued at over two million pounds sterling. They were overpowered by police and shot dead.

. . . It is also the view of this officer that agent LASZLO, who willingly gave herself up in Spain, should be played back into the field as part of a broader UK-led effort to foment and cultivate opposition to the regime in Moscow under the operational codename 'RETRIBUTION'. The chaos and uncertainty visited upon the towns and cities of the West by the Kremlin will be visited, with interest, upon the towns and cities of the Russian Federation, as well as on Russian government representatives overseas. The time for putting up with foreign interference in the affairs of Five Eyes and other sovereign nations is over. An eye for an eye.

. . . Given the well-established links between the current Administration in Washington DC and Russian organised criminal networks, the Agency should be excluded from knowledge of RETRIBUTION until a changing of the guard takes place at 1600 Pennsylvania Avenue.

J.W.S.

51

Nine days after the shootings at Chapel Street, Carradine was walking through Kensington Gardens smoking a cigarette when he was stopped by a short, jovial woman wearing a bottle-green Barbour and holding an ageing black Labrador on a lead.

'Excuse me?' she said. 'Are you C.K. Carradine?'

Carradine wondered if it was a practical joke. Surely what happened with Mantis wasn't happening all over again?

'I am,' he replied.

'Heard a lot about you,' said the woman. She had rosy cheeks and highlights in her hair. 'Here, take this.'

She reached into the pocket of her Barbour and passed Carradine a mobile phone. He recognised it as an old Nokia 3310. He had owned one himself when he had lived in Istanbul more than a decade earlier.

'I'm to keep this?' he asked.

Only a few weeks before he would have wondered why a total stranger was passing him a burner phone in the middle of a London park. Nowadays he knew better.

'Someone will call you.'

The Labrador rushed forward and jumped up on Carradine's legs. With his free hand he rubbed the dog's head and stroked his jaw before the woman tugged him away shouting: 'Down, Gerald! Down!'

'I'll wait then,' Carradine replied.

'Shouldn't be long,' said the woman with an engaging smile. 'I'll let them know you've got it.'

She nodded at the Nokia before turning away and walking in the direction of Marble Arch. Carradine stubbed out the cigarette on the side of a bin. Less than two minutes later, the phone rang. Carradine took it out of his pocket.

'Hello?'

'Kit! Great to hear your voice.'

Somerville. Despite everything that had happened, Carradine felt that old familiar exhilaration at a renewed connection with the secret world.

'Hello, Julian.'

'How have you been?'

'Well, thanks. Good to be home.'

Two rollerbladers buzzed past him on opposite sides, sweeping south towards Kensington Palace. In the distance, Carradine could hear a siren.

'How's your father?'

His father was safe and well. On the day Ivan Simakov claimed to have kidnapped him, William Carradine had been playing backgammon in his local pub with a friend.

'Took forty quid off me, the bastard,' he had told Carradine over dinner at their favourite curry house on Hereford Road. *'Doubling dice. Who ever thought those were a good idea?'*

415

'He's fine,' said Carradine.

'Glad to hear it. And you? Life going well?'

Lara had left the country. They had spent two days together in a hotel in Brighton before she boarded a ferry for France. Carradine did not know when – if ever – he would see her again. She had told him that she wanted to keep working for the Service, that they had plans for her.

'Life's good,' he said. 'Going to the gym. Working on the book. Fifty press-ups and a thousand words a day. You know how it is for us artistic types, Julian. Same old, same old.'

'Lara is well,' Somerville replied. Carradine felt his heart stretch out. 'She wanted me to tell you that.'

'I appreciate it.'

'We've been getting some interesting results from your famous memory stick.' It had transpired that Hulse's team had intercepted the stick in Marrakech, filled it with chicken feed and played it back to Moscow. 'Our mutual friend, Mr Yassine, is eager to redress the balance. Now that he knows he's genuinely on the side of the angels. Thought you'd like to know.'

'I appreciate that, too.'

Carradine wondered why Somerville was disclosing things that he didn't need to disclose. There was a momentary silence.

'Kit.'

'Yes?'

'There's a lot of admiration in these parts for the way you handled yourself.'

'I'm glad to hear it.'

'Some of us think you might be a useful asset in the future.'

There it was. The narcotic lure of secrecy, still as seductive to Carradine as it had been on that first afternoon with Mantis, only a few hundred metres from where he was standing.

'Only some of you?' he replied.

'All of us.'

Another pause. Then:

'How are you fixed tomorrow? Anything planned?'

They wanted him to continue working for the Service. Maugham. Greene. Forsyth. C.K. Carradine was being presented with a choice. To stay in his office and to stick with his books for the next thirty years, or to work for Queen and country and let the Service decide his fate. It felt like no choice at all.

'I've got nothing planned,' he said.

'Good.' Somerville cleared his throat. 'Why don't you put your pen down for the day and come in for a chat? There's a job we'd like you to think about. Nothing complicated. Nothing dangerous. Right up your street in fact.'

Carradine looked up at the trees. Beside him, two children were giggling on a park bench.

'Right up my street,' he said. 'Sounds intriguing. Then I suppose I'll see you tomorrow.'

Acknowledgements:

My thanks to: Julia Wisdom, Finn Cotton, Jaime Frost, Kate Elton, Roger Cazalet, Liz Dawson, Abbie Salter, Claire Ward, Anna Derkacz, Damon Greeney, Anne O'Brien and the fantastic team at HarperCollins. To Charles Spicer, April Osborn, Sally Richardson, Jennifer Enderlin, Paul Hochman, Martin Quinn, David Rostein and Dori Weintraub at St Martin's Press. To Kirsty Gordon, Rebecca Carter and Rebecca Folland at Janklow & Nesbit in London and to Claire Dippel, Stefanie Lieberman, Aaron Rich and Dmitri Chitov in New York. To Jeff Silver and Faisal Kanaan at Grandview and to Jon Cassir, Matt Martin, Angela Dallas and Lindsey Bender at CAA.

I am also indebted to: Perdita Martell, Max, Stephen Garrett, Sarah Gabriel, Dr Harriette Peel, Natasha Fairweather, Chev Wilkinson, Charlotte Asprey, Natascha McElhone, Roddy and Elif Campbell, Amanda Owens, Nick Green, Jessie Grimond, Stephen Lambert and Jenni Russell, Mischa Glenny and Kirsty Lang, Clare Longrigg, Nicholas Shakespeare, Milly Croft-Baker, Roland Philipps,

Natalie Cohen, Benedict, Finnian, Barnaby and Molly Macintyre, Charles Elton, Rosie Dalling, Rachel Harley, Owen Matthews, Deirdre Nazareth, Kate Stephenson, Anna Bilton, James Rhodes, Nici and Daphne Dahrendorf, Noel, Esther Watson, Lisa Hilton, Dinesh Brahmbhatt, Charlotte Cassis, James S, Rory Paget, Boris Starling, Chris de Bellaigue, Mark Pilkington, Guy Walters, Sophie Hackford, Caroline Pilkington, Ian Cumming, Melissa Hanbury, Stanley and Iris.

C.C. London 2018

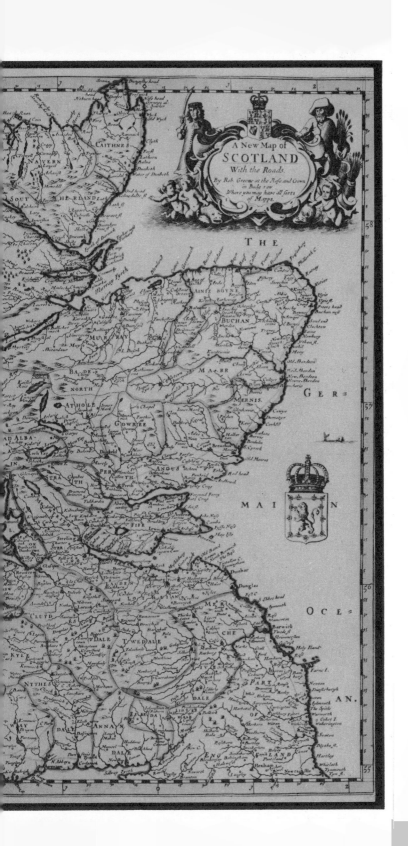

A New Map of
SCOTLAND
With the Roads.
By Rob. Greene at the Rose and Crown
in Budg row
Where you may have all sorts
of Mapps.

THE

GER=

MAI N

OCE=

AN.

Glencoe (Argyll), scene of the infamous massacre of the Macdonalds by the Campbells in 1692, is the most celebrated glen in Scotland, both for magnificent scenery and its historical associations.

Alistair MacLean
Introduces Scotland

Alistair MacLean
introduces
SCOTLAND

Edited by
Alastair M. Dunnett

ANDRE DEUTSCH

First published 1972 by
André Deutsch Limited
105 Great Russell Street London WC1

Printed in Great Britain by
Morrison & Gibb Limited
London and Edinburgh

ISBN 0 233 96349 9

Grateful acknowledgment is made to the British
Tourist Authority and the Scottish Tourist Board
for providing most of the illustrations. The
pictures of Stirling Palace, the Pictish standing
stones and the sheep were taken by Stuart Hood,
to whom our thanks are also due. The map of
Scotland on the endpapers is reproduced by
kind permission of the Trustees of the British
Museum.

Contents

Illustrations

Introducing Scotland

Alistair MacLean

I belong to that larger group of Scots, about twenty million in all, who, according to Alastair Dunnett's calculations, live outside Scotland, in just about any place except where patriotism would have us live. I did not elect to be born in Scotland and can therefore claim no credit for what an Englishman would regard as a somewhat dubious privilege anyway. That I chanced to see the first light in Scotland is pure happenstance and I do not believe that pure happenstance entails a moral obligation to abdicate one's own personality and automatically and blindly identify with the moors, the traditions, the beliefs that hold currency in that particular time and place. So, when I think about Scotland, as I am trying to do now, I try to consider how it measures up to other countries that I know: I try to adopt the attitude of what can he know of England who only England knows: I endeavour to bring to bear the cool and dispassionate eye.

This last prerequisite presupposes a degree of detached impartiality which I know to be impossible of achievement. No man is an island unto himself. Apart from the irreversible and inescapable factor of the transmission of hereditary characteristics via the genes, the weight brought to bear by environmental influence leaves its inevitable mark. The mark so left may be profound or relatively slight: but it is there. Every impinging influence from without cannot but help be a contributory factor in forming the crucible that moulds the individual character. I think of the wonder of sailing on a summer's dusk in the Western Isles bathed in that magical quality of light, diffuse and limpid and wholly indescribable, which I have found nowhere else in the world except in the Aegean in autumn: of driving grouse across the bleak and wind-swept Grampian moors for the benefit of short-sighted American millionaires: of going to three different churches on a Sunday, each in their own way as bleak and wind-swept – inside, not out – as the above-mentioned moors: of

9

cleaning out the byre by the light of a storm lantern in the darkness of a January morning with two feet of snow on the ground: of reading the *Wizard* under the blankets with the aid of a torch in the attic of a venerable Georgian manse deep in a remote Highland glen because not only did the single candle, which was the sole means of illumination, afford little more light than an anaemic glow-worm but the cold in that unheated attic was often so intense that to expose hands, wrists and face was to invite a condition only one degree removed from frost-bite: of the golden harvests of late summer where, because of some unaccountable richness of the soil, the corn was a foot higher than the head of the tallest man: of the illicit removal of salmon from the fishing rights of an absentee Sassenach landlord, who was universally – if the limits of the universe be regarded as the bounds of our glen – and powerfully detested for no reason that I could ever discover other than that he *was* a Sassenach: of what seemed to be half the men in the parish crowding into the manse study to hear the broadcast report of the Scotland-England soccer international at Hampden on my father's radio, the only one in the glen: of fishing for cod with the long lines, or inshore off the island of Gigha – using the wickerwork creels – for lobster and monstrous crabs for whose intransigent belligerence I formed a life-long respect: of sleeping under the stars on a pile of sweetly-smelling new-mown hay, a practice much frowned upon: of the wonders of Hallowe'en, which we took to be All Saints' night blissfully unaware that in Celtic mythology the last night of October was reserved exclusively for the activities of witches of the less desirable kind: of endless reading – I had read all of Scott by the time I was ten: of friends, of schools, ranging from a tiny Highland schoolhouse where the school-mistress was wont to say 'You're no better than your grandfather was' – she'd begun as a pupil-teacher at fifteen and taught for well over sixty years – to a snooty establishment in the west end of Glasgow which had had the misfortune to model itself on an English public school either ignorant of or ignoring the fact that English public schools, like numerous Italian red wines, do not travel very well: of university, where I don't recall that I ever really learnt anything: of twenty years off and on in Glasgow which left me with only one burning ambition and that was to take advantage of the first available opportunity to leave it which I duly did – when and if I return there it will be after I have prudently ascertained, well in advance, that Cliff Hanley is out of town. But I have only to smell a primrose and I am back again on the banks of the River Nairn in Inverness-shire.

How much effect all those environmental pressures may have affected the ability to take a detached view of Scotland is impossible to say: all I can say for sure is that I am indelibly branded as a Scot.

Having admitted that all those myriad and intangible influences may well lead to a distortion of what should ideally be a remote, uninfluenced and detached view-point, I'm still left with no option other than to go ahead and express those views anyway, albeit with a cautious apprehension and an apologetic tentativeness that could easily be interpreted for the trepidation which it probably is.

To me, the most striking feature about Scotland is not Scotland itself but the vast droves of its loyal citizens who regularly depart from their enchanted homeland with a fixed and avowed determination never to return to it again. This cannot be because of any profound and ingrained antipathy towards their fellow citizens who are not headed for Heathrow, Southampton and assisted passages to Australia and divers other faraway places for, with me, the Scots rank with the Austrians, as the warmest, most friendly – when you get to know them, it can take, say, ten years in the more elegant pockets of resistance in Edinburgh – and hospitable people I have encountered. Nor can it be any aesthetic revulsion against the physical features of their homeland, for, the central industrial belt excepted, there is no more beautiful country in Europe. It cannot be that they feel they are being squeezed out by lack of space for, compared to a country like Switzerland, Scotland has a positive embarrassment of space into which to expand. It cannot be grinding poverty that drives them out, for Scotland is not a poor country. Scottish agriculture is in splendid shape and the majority of manufacturing industries are doing well enough. It is true that the shipbuilding industry and, to a lesser extent, the motor industry is in a depressed state and this may account for a certain – but small – percentage of current emigration: but, then, over the generations, the Scots have been heading resolutely for the Antipodes irrespective of the level of unemployment. It cannot be attributed to the uncongenial climate for Finland has an infinitely more extreme climate than Scotland but the Finns, based on their tiny emigration figures, display a most inordinate devotion to the land of their birth. It

11

cannot even be that they are in agreement with the Johnsonian dictum that the fairest prospect in all Scotland is the highway leading to England because, apart from the relatively small number that London finds it essential to import at regular intervals in order to keep the wheels of the City turning, the great majority of emigrants are as eager to shake the English dust off their feet as they had been with its Scottish counterpart.

The true reason for this never-ending exodus lies, I feel sure, in the fact that the Scots are born adventurers, and I use the word in the very best sense of the term. As you can't very well be an adventurer if you spend your life sitting by the hearth it follows, of course, that adventuring is concomitant with roaming and wandering and it would appear to be indisputable that the Scots are the greatest wanderers on the face of the earth. When it comes to making their way to impossibly remote and distant places not even the Jews can hold a candle to the Scots – and the Jews, it has to be remembered, have been on the move throughout the centuries almost solely because they have been subjected to continuous oppression. Apart from the period of the abominable Highland Clearances, the Scots have been subject to no such pressure. The conclusion seems inescapable that they just like wandering.

It would be interesting to speculate on the reasons for this obsessive desire to see what lies round the next corner and over the next hill, but the truth is that we have no information on this. It is easy to explain it away by saying it's in the blood but this is meaningless. Could it be an inherited racial characteristic, a specialized gene which gives rise to itchy feet? It seems hardly likely. More probably it is a mental thing, the carrying on, whether consciously or unconsciously, of an age-old tradition the origins of which are so ancient, so rooted in the long-forgotten past, that they lie beyond any hope of resurrection.

For the tradition is ancient. Scottish history in the first ten centuries of the Christian era is a pretty sketchy affair much given to inspired guesswork, but it is no guesswork but established fact that by mediaeval times Scots had firmly established themselves in many countries on the continent. The Scots are European: the English are not and even today are much given to casting a leery eye towards Carlisle as much as to Calais for it is behind those frontier posts that the unpredictable and dangerous natives lurk. The Scots are cosmopolitan; the English cleave to the parish pump which is their England: even when building up the largest empire in history, which they almost certainly couldn't have done without the aid of the more gifted colonisers from north of the border, they remained invincibly insular and parochial, incapable of either adopting or adapting to the ways of the peoples whom they had colonized. New Delhi never had a chance; it was doomed from the outset to become the London of the sub-continent.

When the English were making their brief forays across the Channel and initiating the French into the more esoteric mysteries of English culture at Crecy and Agincourt, Scottish traders had penetrated into the more remote corners of Europe – although they concentrated chiefly on the Low Countries and the lands that gird the Baltic – and established firm business connections. Many of them achieved positions of eminence as advisers to the heads or governments of foreign states and were particularly active in the military field, being responsible for the building up of navies, the reorganization of armies and, not infrequently, becoming themselves the admirals and generals of those forces, and all this while the English were still virtually engaged full-time in providing the raw and bloody material for Shakespeare's historical tragedies.

None of this, of course, explains *why* the Scots took to wandering in the first place. We just have to accept the fact that they kept on compulsively sticking their noses into other people's business, going either where they had no right to go or where no person in his right senses would have thought of going in the first place. They crop up everywhere. Find a man herding sheep in the furthest reaches of Patagonia and the chances are that he is a Scot. I know of a village in the Italian Dolomites where the most commonly held surnames begin with 'Mac' – the remnants, I assume, of some defeated army although I am not sure. Scottish explorers, almost single-handed, opened up the Dark Continent, while that greatest explorer ever, Captain Cook, was half Scot. (The other half was Yorkshire which is almost as good as being a Scot anyway.) Take the Scots away from Toronto or Melbourne, from the City of London or, indeed, from the whole of New Zealand and the most dreadful confusion and dislocation would immediately overtake those unfortunate places. The list could be extended indefinitely. The word 'ubiquitous' might well have been coined to describe the Scots: to the disgruntlement of large numbers of people, they are to be found virtually everywhere.

13

Equally fascinating is the obverse sign of this wandering coin – the Scot's lachrymal obsession with nostalgia. They are even worse than the Irish and heaven knows that *their* broken-hearted homesickness for the Emerald Isle, especially in song, is appalling enough, although one would have to admit that 'I'll take you home again, Kathleen' could give 'Scotland the brave' a pretty close run for its money. One comparatively recent Scottish song – Andy Stewart's 'The Scottish Soldier' – splendidly epitomizes the mournful depths of nostalgia and self-pity in which the Scot is tearfully prepared to wallow at the drop of a Glengarry. In this particular song, a Scottish soldier is clobbered by the enemy – a jarring note, this, in Caledonian song and story it is invariably the Scot who clobbers the enemy – and is consequently condemned to spend eternity in the green hills of Tyrol, although what he was doing in Tyrol in the first place I have failed to discover. Anyway, that is not the point. Here we have this poor lad, cruelly slain while gallantly defending his beloved homeland – some Scots have rather vague ideas as to the precise delimitations of their national boundaries – condemned to sleep for ever in some foreign field, a horrifying and totally unthinkable idea for everyone knows that there is only one proper place for a Scot to sleep, be he alive or be he dead, and that is Scotland. One would hope, incidentally, that the idea does not take an irreversible hold on the twenty million Scots overseas: to put it at its most delicate, the accommodation factor might pose a problem.

It does not require the facilities offered by a governmental or university research team or, indeed, any particularly acute degree of observation to arrive at the conclusion that there is an extra-ordinarily close affinity between this nostalgia for Scotland, where it exists in its more excessive form, and Scotland's most famous product which the Scots have infelicitously named *uisquebae* or the water of life – whisky.

In conjunction with the above it will equally have been observed that wherever two or three Scots are gathered together, be it in Surrey or be it in Tierra del Fuego, they will immediately set about forming a St Andrew's Society and, inevitably, a Burns Society. The ostensible purpose of the former is to sustain and strengthen the cultural links with Scotia stern and wild by singing a very limited selection of purely Lowland songs – not Highland, for the odds are heavy that none of those present speaks Gaelic – filling a confined space with the hideous banshee wailing of the bagpipes, dancing the Highland Fling in calf-length kilts and, in general making themselves ridiculous. The Burns Societies' dinners, allegedly dedicated to the preservation and honouring of the memory of the immortal bard, should, on the face of it, be even more cultural occasions were it not for the fact that for the majority of people at the majority of such gatherings Burns is synonymous not with poetry but with haggis and an endless river of Scotch: it is compulsory, nay, it is a sacred duty, to drink to the poet's memory and hopeful health in the hereafter: no such ludicrous degree of obligation attaches to the actual reading of his poetry.

The Scot is a hopelessly sentimental creature at the best of times and this is entirely forgiveable: but when he employs his declarations of deathless devotion to the homeland as a supposedly legitimate and natural reason for getting plastered then the amiable nostalgia degenerates into a maudlin hypocrisy singularly lacking in appeal.

This kind of hypocritically expressed longing for one's birthplace is not confined to expatriates: it can be found in as splendidly rich a form within the confines of Scotland itself, and the place where it finds its highest and purest expression – if that's the phrase I'm looking for – is unquestionably the city of Glasgow.

As my father was a redoubtable Gaelic scholar and my mother a Mod gold medallist, as I had to go to school to learn English and was forbidden to speak it at home until the age of fifteen, it will be readily appreciated that I was brought up in an intensely Gaelic atmosphere. As a consequence of this, I was frequently called upon – the permissive age being then not yet to hand refusal was unthinkable – to attend a seemingly interminable series (I was about to use the word 'variety' but they were all exactly the same) of concerts given by the numerous West Highland and Island Associations which were composed of the natives of those remote Utopias who had come to Glasgow to make their fortunes (few failed to do so): more often, I had to attend *ceilidhs*, small informal gatherings in homes, hotels or rented halls, but no matter how large or small or formal or informal those get-togethers were, the proceedings of the evening formed an invariable pattern and no departure from the norm was permitted: speaker or singer, he or she, each mounted the platform in turn and broke their anguished hearts aloud for their little grey home in the west, for that golden beloved isle that had given them birth. It was quite some time before I discovered that it was not only bad form but absolutely forbidden to ask them why the hell didn't they go back and live in their beloved isles if they meant all that much to them for those, it became clear, were thoughtless and crudely distressing questions which could cause a change in the colour of the complexion, make a trembling hand reach out for further sustenance and result in an embarrassingly rapid change in the conversational topic.

This curious ambivalence that is to be found among a people who will venture boldly to the uttermost ends of the earth while loudly proclaiming that they wished they had never left home, is to be found again in their reputation for being a magnificently martial race, a reputation acknowledged and praised the world over but nowhere with quite the fervour that it is in Scotland itself. That the Scots are a warlike race is beyond dispute and nowhere was this more evident than in the internecine warfare that ravaged the country down the centuries when the clans pillaged and burnt the homes and the crops of neighbouring clans, stole cattle and women with splendid indiscrimination and generally, and, in retrospect, for no valid reason, hacked each other to pieces. That those disagreements were, on occasion, economically motivated, which is nicer than saying that they were based on sheer greed, is beyond question: but it seems, basically, to have been a form of national pastime, very likely because there wasn't much else to do in the Highlands in those days. There couldn't have been much else to do in the Lowlands, either, for the border reivers, advanced specialists in cattle rustling before anyone had ever heard of the Wild West, acquired a fearsome reputation to match that of the bloodiest of the Highland clans. Feuds were the great thing then and no clan worth its salt could afford to be without one, although there seemed to be general agreement that a feud that didn't last two or three hundred years wasn't really worth the having. My own clan, the MacLeans, who appear to have made a comfortable enough living from waylaying seafarers so incredibly foolish as to venture within eyeshot of their island fortress of Mull, had a permanent and permanently gory disagreement with the Campbells which both sides cherished down the centuries. It is demonstrative of how long memories can be in Scotland and how hard ancient enmities die that when the chief of the Clan Campbell, the Duke of Argyll, hired – only twenty years ago! – a MacLean as piper for his seat at Inveraray Castle that the consternation, near apoplectic shock and black burning shame of the MacLeans to whom such things were of near paramount importance – and, it would seem, there were considerable numbers of them – would not have been out of place three hundred years ago. In the good old days the claymores would have been out; today, the preference is for Biro pens and some pretty stiff letters to the *Glasgow Herald* and *The Scotsman*. We have fallen upon effete and anaemic days.

In more recent times the battlefields have moved from the glens to the cities. The pitched battles between the pre-war Glasgow gangs, mainly from the Gorbals and Townhead were, I am given to understand, quite something to behold: as Saturday evenings approached, doctors, orderlies and nurses stood resignedly by in the Victoria and Western Infirmaries' casualty reception rooms, with very large quantities of bandages, needle, gut and surgical instruments to hand: the young heroes of those clashes, their martial spirits sadly deflated since the police had relieved them of their knives, razors, bicycle chains, nail-studded clubs and other offensive impedimenta considered essential for the successful pursuit of their street campaigns, rarely kept the doctors waiting for long. Regular confrontations between the supporters of Glasgow's two paramount soccer teams, Rangers and Celtic, also added to the length of the doctors' working day but as those brawls were – it was alleged – essentially religious in nature, I shall return briefly to this topic. The biggest pitched battle I witnessed during the war was in Princes Street, Edinburgh, between our own forces and the American Navy and although I can't swear that the home forces were composed entirely of Scots I can attest to the fact that none of the casualties to whom I spoke later had an English, Irish or Welsh accent.

But although the Scots unquestionably give a good account of themselves when against themselves, it is when they band together against a common enemy that they really come in to their own. Their record in the past seven centuries is unsurpassed. They rank as being among the best, if not actually the best, attacking troops in the world and the English canard that the Scots' history of suicidal charges down the centuries has been motivated solely by the desire to get away from the sound of the bagpipes is no more than a reflection of their admiration for that handful of Scottish regiments – many of them, to be honest, containing not an inconsiderable amount of Englishmen – who have achieved

17

more lustre and fame than any other regiments in the western hemisphere. And, I believe, deservedly so. I recall – mainly because I have in the past written at length about it – the incredible conduct of the Black Watch outside the gates of Tobruk in the last World War. The 1st South African Division were fleeing rapidly to the east with a German motorised division in close pursuit. Who but a Highland regiment would have sent in six hundred and forty of its men, mainly on foot, to stop an armoured division? The battle was brief and terrible and when it was over there was hardly a soldier without a wound and three-quarters of them lay dead. But they had stopped the armoured division and the South Africans made good their escape. It was desperate encounters such as this that helped compile the Scottish regiments' awesome record on the far-scattered battlefields of the world. I defy anyone, even the most dedicated pacifist possessed of the most genuine abhorrence of every conceivable form of warfare, to visit the Shrine in Edinburgh, surely the most beautiful in the world, and come away unmoved.

Possessed, as they clearly are, of this markedly combative nature, the Scots could hardly be expected to exhibit a common front of sweet reasonableness in so important and serious a matter as religion. They don't and they haven't but this is hardly peculiar to the Scots: very few nations ever have.

I am interested in the Scottish attitude to religion. For years it dominated the lives of the people and, as a son of the manse, I was subjected to a very great deal of it in my younger days. I have come to the reluctant opinion that, despite their hardly gained reputation as dedicated church-goers, men of God and even religious fanatics, the Scots are primarily interested in the trappings of religion and not in religion itself. Even from the days of John Knox, who should never have been allowed near an Edinburgh pulpit, and the Calvinists, who carved up everybody in sight for the greater glory of God, down to the latter-day meaningless confrontations of Catholic Celtic supporters and Protestant Rangers supporters, precious few of whom ever darken the doors of chapel or church, the true spirit of Christianity – or what I imagine to be the true spirit – has burnt with a low and guttering flame indeed. The baffling history of the endless schisms that have fractured and ruptured the Protestant church of Scotland, the obsessive concern with form and close to total disregard of content, leads one to sadly suspect that all those generations which memorized the

Sermon on the Mount and the second Corinthians, Chapter 13, were largely wasting their time. I fear that with religion as with nostalgia the element of hypocrisy is never far from the surface. I would like to cite just three little instances from hundreds of my own experience which tend to bear out my contention.

Scotland used to be home of the great divines, those fearsomely patriarchal and immensely learned men of God who knew far more about religion than Jesus, his disciples and all the prophets put together. I had the privilege of listening to one of the last of them – like the dinosaurs, they are now extinct. With his gleaming bald pate, prodigious white beard and cruelly glistening rimless-spectacles he looked a hand-picked choice for the guardian of the gates of Purgatory, although he would have had considerable competition for all the great divines looked the same. Although well past his prime, he was a stayer of note and managed to extend his discourses from eleven o'clock to one, which was about par for the course. He thundered freely and at length about sulphur, brimstone and the indescribable furies of hell which surely awaited the whole lot of us – no milquetoast talk of salvation. But it was not what he said but how he said it that was so memorable. The convolution of argument, the hyperbole, abstruse quotations from and references to long dead divines of the middle ages, lengthy quotations – in the original – from Latin and Greek (he was addressing a primarily Gaelic-speaking congregation), the pulpit-thumping and the voice that ranged from a menacing whisper to a deafening bellow all combined to produce a truly memorable exhibition of histrionic erudition. The only drawback to all of this was that neither the congregation nor the great divine himself understood one word of what he was saying. He was preaching not for the greater glory of God but for the greater glory of the great divine.

Then there was the case of the equally peculiar behaviour of two other quite different break-away sects who practised their beliefs in one of the Western Isles. Both were committed up-holders of the principles of disestablishmentarianism, whatever that means, but otherwise mortal enemies. By some mischance, their two cemetery-encircled churches faced each other across the road. Both church services started at the same time and it became a point of honour for the rival ministers to ensure that the other lot were the first to emerge, partly on the principle that the first man out was a cissy, partly because of a genuinely held belief that

19

inculcated holiness was in direct proportion to the length of time that one wriggled in agony on the iron-hard wooden benches. The respective beadles were posted as sentries to watch the doors of the facing church. As long as the doors of Church A remained steadfastly shut the minister of Church B preached steadfastly on: and, of course, *vice versa*. This state of affairs continued until the services were averaging four hours apiece and the congregations learned the wisdom of not consuming any liquids for a lengthy period before the beginning of the services. The logical extension of this should have been to see the congregations, weakened by hunger and exhausted by sleeplessness, stagger out into the light of day on the Monday afternoon, but the inevitable happened: the ministers found themselves preaching to empty pews. Such was religion in the islands.

And, of course, in any church throughout the country, congregations listen to sermons and sing psalms and hymns praising God and their undying love for their fellow-man. Service over, they cluster in small groups on the pavement or the road outside, and while there is never any mention of God there is plenty about their fellow-man: he is figuratively torn to pieces. I have heard more vindictive gossip and character assassination outside church doors than in any other place I know of.

I do not say that this religious superficiality and hypocrisy is peculiarly characteristic of Scotland – it may very well be a feature of every religion of every country as far as I know: I only say that it undeniably exists. Religion runs nowhere very deep and has long ceased to be the central core of Scottish life. As long as churches are used primarily for christenings, marriages, funeral orations and keeping up with the Jones's, no one, it seems likely, is going to take it very seriously and the impact it makes on people's lives seems certain to lessen even more with the passing of the years. This may be very sad and certainly most cruelly discouraging for the priests of the church, but it probably has one saving grace: in the face of such profound apathy about religion and lack of concern for its true meaning, the appalling strife of religion-ridden Ulster is unlikely to make its way across the Irish Channel.

One can hardly conclude an introduction to Scotland without touching briefly on a subject which is dear to many a Scottish heart – the right to exist as a separate entity and to conduct its own affairs, both internally and with regard to foreign policy.

Because I tend to be an apolitical creature, because I have lived or been in many countries and because I think it is better to be a good European and a good Scot than just a good Scot, I am not a Scottish Nationalist but do sympathize with many of the nationalistic aspirations. It is a most extraordinarily vexed and complicated question. I do think that Scotland should have a much greater degree of autonomy that it at present possesses for Scotland has a much clearer appreciation of the nature of its own problems and how to set about solving them than Westminster will ever have: on the other hand, the setting up of an independent sovereign state is not a matter for airy-fairy contemplation and snap decisions for the excellent Scottish reason that it could well turn out that England has been contributing more to the Scottish purse than *vice versa*.

The extremists who advocate home rule will never be listened to for the simple reason that the great majority of people, in Britain as well as Scotland, are not by nature revolutionary. Any amelioration of what Scotland currently regards as being their unjustifiably subservient condition will come from Nationalists who hold moderate views and they, I fear, have a most difficult task ahead of them. They suffer from the cruel double handicap of their own moderation and the support, if that is the word, of the vociferous and thick-headed who claim to share the same aspirations. I do not doubt that the moderates, of whom this book includes some examples, will eventually win the day: but the battle will be long.

I have touched only, and very generally, upon aspects of the Scottish character which interest me: the true delineation of the country and its inhabitants I leave to the experts who really specialize in their own fields, who don't waffle like me and who know what they are talking about. As I said at the beginning, this is a quite splendid book and I trust, Scot to the end, that the publishers will let me have a free copy of the finished product.

The Scottish Situation

Alastair M. Dunnett

I warned the publishers that they would have to expect some aspects of enthusiasm to pervade the writing of this book. Those contributors I have assembled to have their say on the subject of Scotland had already reached fervent conclusions long before I got to them, and like most of their countrymen they do not tend to be offhand and indifferent on the subject which, scratch them one way or the other, lies nearest to their hearts. To be sure, they can be savagely critical of the local deficiencies they fancy that they see, for like God, with whom they tend to live in neighbourly wariness, they chasten what they love. The intelligent traveller will often find himself becoming involved in these arguments, and who knows to what inward and further congenialities he may not win if he comports himself in such encounters with independent and intellectual modesty. Still, most of the natives he will meet are happy that they live in Scotland and will be prepared to tell him why. The Scot readily induces in himself the belief that a great deal of what is important to the world and its thinking has happened or is happening in his own country.

As a young journalist I worked in Glasgow during the years of the early and middle 1930s when long neglect seemed at last to have prevailed, and men and their works rusted under the sky. One day I went seeking a story in Strathaven, from which I had heard some news that seemed hopeful. When I arrived there I was at once at the centre of a simple incident which fed, in these sparse times, my readiness to believe in the aptness of the Scottish attitude to a hard world. I had to ask the way to a certain factory, for I didn't know where to find it. You know how it is often put forward as a test of a local willingness to help, that the person asked for a direction will turn around and come along to point out the place. I asked a man to show me my direction, and he turned back and came two blocks with me. But he was leading a horse and cart, and he turned them round and took them along also.

My cortege left me at the gate of the factory, and I went in to hear their story. They had been one of the establishments which in that town had built up a prosperous silk weaving industry, manufacturing coloured handkerchiefs. The trade for this had utterly gone out of fashion, and they were left without orders or prospects. It occurred to one of the partners to try making hand-kerchiefs more than double the normal size in the hope that somebody might buy them for scarves, sashes, or anything. The old looms clapped out a sample lot, with their striking designs, and they sent these to an agent in Paris. They hit some market mood, and feverish orders came back. As they told the story to me, what happened then was that some buyers from New York saw this fashion trend in Paris, followed it to the source, and the Strathaven scarf square turned up in Fifth Avenue; where in course of time the London buyers saw them and lined up their orders for the exclusive English trade. In this dogged way the small ancient Clydeside factory on the verge of disaster, had become an arbiter of sophisticated style.

I asked: 'But what about Scotland? Can this stuff be bought here?' 'Oh aye!' they told me. 'But no' just yet. The Scottish buyers will be in London this winter and they'll see what's new, so they'll be stocking. Like enough you'll see these in Sauchiehall Street in the Spring.' The long conditioning to the endorsement of the foreign urbanities had made them perhaps too patient.

As you might expect, I can top all this. There was this long period of inaction at the start of World War II when even journalists got some honest work to do, and by the spring of 1940 I found myself involved in official and Government work in which, as they say, one thing was to lead to another. As the year advanced I was beginning to get engaged in a number of activities which a Clydebank friend of mine described as 'wee jobs for the Foreign Office'. For example, there had come to Britain a group of three Bulgarians sent by their Government as emissaries to report on the long-term prospects our country had in the war which was shortly to break out with the furious assault on France. At that time Bulgaria was under great pressure from Germany, aided by a pro-Nazi faction in their own higher circles, to join Hitler's cause and take part in the destruction of the decadent forces of democracy. The mission was sent to see if we were in fact finished, and if not, what resources had we to last out for any measurable time.

I took them to a rendezvous with an old friend Captain John Eaglesome, harbour-master of the Clyde, and he showed us round one of the great docks crammed with shipping. 'But these ships cannot sail, can they?' they asked. 'Friends,' said Eaglesome, 'they come and go like buses. Over there' – pointing – 'that ship came in this morning from Canada with 11,000 tons of grain. That one – last night from Argentina: 8,000 tons of meat.' He warmed to it, the gestures growing. 'This one here – machinery from America . . . same with these two in the corner. The Americans know a good bet when they see it.' The gestures warmed up. They had been told that nothing was getting to our ports, and the captain, himself a great adventurer, wasn't going to let the wrong impression stay.

As he built up the story, a destroyer towed by a tug started to edge its way round the edge of the dock, crawling for repairs and safety. It had probably hit a mine, for its bows were mostly blown away. 'That ship – ' the Bulgarians started to say. 'Look at that big one in the corner – yes, over there. Loaded up with fruit and meat from New Zealand – that's far enough away, eh. . . .' So went the Captain's hearty narrative, while the stricken ship edged her way to the dock wall where we stood until the ruinous fore hull was almost all we could see. One of the Bulgarians planted himself in front of the harbour-master, demanding – 'What has happened to that warship?' Captain Eaglesome glanced at it, casually, as if seeing it for the first time, and irritated at being interrupted in the real story of the day. 'Ah,' he said, with a little interest. 'I expect she's rammed a German submarine. Our chaps are always doing that. Now if you'll look over to the east side here. . . .'

We sailed then up and down the river alongside the endless building yards, and a whole new fleet was there coming to birth, red steel on the slipways or grey and afloat in the fitting-out berths – cruisers, destroyers, minelayers, boom ships, frigates, craft that were secret and nameless. Their names were unknown, their flags unhoisted, their guns unarmed, their epics still to be told; and yet they looked winners, like the men building them. The Bulgarians had never seen anything like this, and indeed neither had anyone else, and there may never be such a sight again. It was admitted freely by our visitors that their country was deficient in the higher shipbuilding, which was no part of their traditions; but in Bulgaria now there was developing a modern industrial society with factories and available technicians trained under the new dispensation. So

25

we went to the factories that crowded themselves into the central industrial girdle of Scotland, working at it for twenty-four hours of the day, with men and women at their tasks, direct heirs of those who had made the first Industrial Revolution in the shadow of James Watt. They were building vehicles and engines, pieces of secret things, sections of aircraft, ammunition, buttons, uniforms and equipment. They were building everything, fast, accurately, with devotion. We became besotted with lathes and ladles, gouts of steel, shavings of brass, bent overalls above the spindles, the great noise and chatter of making. After enough of this the Bulgarians backed away from the reek of manufacture. Yes, it was true, they said. It had to be admitted that there was nothing on this scale in all Bulgaria. Ah, but the agriculture! That was the pride and achievement of their fertile Balkan garden lands, on the balmy Black Sea, far away from the chill north and its oily guddle among the nuts and bolts. Nowhere was there an agriculture like the Bulgarian agriculture.

So I took them to where, at the very back doors of the factories, spread the best-kept and the most productive farm lands in the world, with more root and grain crops and cattle per acre than any other acres under the sun. In the early quiet summer we saw these fields that had been won over centuries from the bog and the scrub, tended and cherished, passed on from every generation to the new men, who would not let them go. The tractors jostled almost wheel by wheel together, for these farm lands were and remain the most highly mechanized fields anywhere, and they were getting ready for their classic task of feeding us in the siege. We saw the links of the Forth, the carse lands of the Mearns, the Alpine snows of Clyde's fruit banks, while the cattle bloomed thick in the fields, bearing the seed to fertilize foreign herds, the sheep lived fat on the slopes, and the stock-yards were still filled with last year's hay crop and the other harvests.

Late one afternoon we drove through the plain of the River Forth in the direction of Stirling. We were bound for Blair Drummond Castle, to visit its chatelaine, Lady Kay Muir, a Bulgarian. And as we went among the back roads and the farm towns and the small villages, they said: 'Allowance has to be made, of course, for the great technical skills which your farmers have clearly been introducing for long into their operation. It would be true to say that our Bulgarian agriculture, for all its natural advantages, is not yet on this scale. . . . But, ah! In Bulgaria, the vines! Nowhere, not even in France, or Germany, are to be found such vines. . . .'

We were driving at that moment through an unpretentious village, and I spoke opportunely:

'Would you like,' I asked them, 'to see the biggest vine in the world?'

'Where is it?' They were scenting some rude northern jest.

I stopped the car. 'It's here – in this village.' At that moment we were running through Kippen, where below a branching series of glass tunnels flourished the single vine which had for long been a tourist novelty, and which had by then attained rather more than twice the size of the more fashionable monster at Hampton Court. We walked below its steaming yardage, and the pearly black grapes hung in unbelievable clusters, ripe and perfect.

To be sure, you can't always be as lucky as that, even in Scotland, but it was a fair coup in the middle of a diplomatic enterprise. They bought a bunch of the best for Lady Kay Muir, and I steered them, dazed and wary, away from our freak vineyard and on the way to Blair Drummond.

More was to come. Lady Kay Muir was herself a Bulgarian, daughter of the man who in the years after 1918 had been the Bulgarian ambassador in London. Her life for years from girlhood had been composed of the skills of diplomacy. They had made her ambassador after her father's death. On her marriage she came north to be mistress of a laird's castle, and it was there that we found her. They renewed their remote language under that roof as she told them about the heart and soul of the country she had joined. There was a fellow guest at dinner that night, a kinsman of the house. He was General Sir Ian Hamilton, the hero of Gallipoli, who turned out to be the only British soldier for whom the Bulgarians at that time had any kind of respect, and perhaps the only contemporary one of whom they had even heard. The father of one of the Bulgarians had been attached to the Dardanelles forces as an official military observer, and Sir Ian remembered him. Nobody could have invented all this, and that evening in addition the old cavalier had never been more eloquent, more dazzling, more courtly, as he told his unmatched stories.

Their report to their Government recommended that our side was the one to back, and that the delegation believed we had the will and the resources to prevail in the end. But by the time it was delivered to official Bulgaria, the country was committed to the Nazi cause, and Hitler was invading the West. Only two of the delegation went back to Bulgaria. The leader stayed on in Britain and saw out the war with us, and has never gone home.

The Bulgarians are not the only ones to discern that in Scotland we do most things and we have nearly everything. The possession of these manifold endowments could make for a smug situation, but it is sharply corrected by other circumstances which are as easy to notice but more difficult to explain. The best things we are doing in Scotland are the things we are doing by ourselves, because as a rule those who elect to live and work here have the best of inducements for making a job of it, and in any case a unit of five million people is a manageable size. But like the perimeter lands everywhere we are cursed by absentee decision-takers. The imperatives of larger economic destinies and larger comforts call for larger groupings, and with London the enormous bulk it is, you get a lop-sided Britain tilting southwards with more and more headquarters rolling down towards the Thames. The overnight trains from Glasgow or Edinburgh to London are crowded, not so much with holiday-makers, as with business executives. Some of them are going forth to sell, but the most part are off to get instructions or briefings, and to come home to apply these cartel precepts in many cases to businesses that once had distinguished names and wide reputations. A canvass along the corridors of these night expresses would soon produce travellers who had spent 600 to 800 nights of their lives in the sleeper train between London and Scotland.

Of course there are often quite benevolent results from such a situation, and if you mention it as a grievance to a man from London or Oslo or Toronto, you may be told that an equal number of commuters from these capitals is shuttling to and fro for their orders to New York or elsewhere. The essential difference has to be mentioned. The Scottish situation is that we are unique among them all in having at our hand no separate political or economic apparatus by which the situation may be controlled.

This is, in fact, the Scottish dilemma. It is one which is much noticed in these pages, and a great deal of thought, little of it separatist, is going into the matter in all corners of Scotland. The traveller will readily encounter views and arguments as he makes his rounds. There is a great deal of agreement about the ills, and little common ground about the solutions. However, the argument is worth while, and the nimble-witted stranger may enjoy and even add to our regular tours around the predicament. In these debates there will be much reference to the English, our large-scale neighbours who will be mentioned with cautious affection, and sometimes merely with caution. They are, to be sure, a remarkable people, and under some suitable organization would be our most natural and desirable partners. But as things are, they have become practically our greatest problem, in the sense that there are a good many of them, moving about and bearing their own world with them, or staying at home even more securely within that world. By means of radio, television, and the so-called national newspapers of Fleet Street (the description is their own) they send their attitudes and accents into remote corners of our country, expecting them to be greeted as the norm, while expecting our own hard-won views and aspirations to be rated as remote provincial eccentricities. Weight is lent to this trend by the sad fact that important areas of England herself have been kow-towing to London for centuries. In Manchester – that great and wealthy city with much to be proud of – prominent businessmen will tell you that they are 'going to town today'. They mean London, as if there are no other towns. In recent years *The Manchester Guardian*'s circulation in Manchester itself did not start to increase until they took the name of their city of origin out of the title and called the paper simply *The Guardian*. Provincialization had brought the citizens willingly to such a pass that they preferred to read a London-looking paper rather than a Manchester-looking paper. Scottish towns have never been content to accept a status as distant London suburbs, and there are powerful correctives now moving to make this fate less likely. We have a lot of problems in Scotland, but the main one looks like England.

Much is to be hoped from a modernization of the ramshackle political arrangements that make the British administrative package a back number, and the House of Commons the out-of-date grandmother of Parliaments. Almost any type of new executive set-up would be preferable. But you won't get more than a handful of Members of Parliament to admit this in public, and since Cromwell we have on the whole preferred in these islands to bring changes about through a Parliamentary process. In any other modern union this clumsy situation, brimming with ineffectuality and slight, would long ago have been replaced by some structure more likely to release rather than inhibit the genius of the national constituents. Elected MPs go off to Westminster bursting with reforming zeal, and remain to become the captives of a cosy establishment, with more kudos than comfort. As a sovereign nation, with a flair for the wider horizons, Scotland amalgamated her Parliament with the English Parliament in 1707, the two countries agreeing to form a British Parliament and to become British together in all things. The Scots are the only ones who have bent their energies to making the British idea work, while the English, with a natural talent for nationalism, have gone on being English, calling the whole country England, and encouraging kindly foreigners who should know better to do the same. Very few English manufacturers mark their goods 'Made in Britain'. 'England' is good enough for them. Many of the articles you see marked like that have been made in Scotland. Not many Englishmen ever call themselves British. They merely think that in the course of their errant and not ignoble history the bounds of England at some time became extended northwards from their old border at the River Tweed to Shetland. All this they call England, and they have added an almost inextricable confusion to the solving of the problem by forgetting what and where England really is. They have no accurate geographical concept of their own country. When they wave a flag on a purely English occasion they choose the Union Jack, in the belief that it is theirs alone. They even wave the Union Jack, thinking it is the English flag, on the terracing of Wembley or Hampden Park when England is playing Scotland, and the English commentators on such occasions, men who pass elsewhere as informed adults, frequently refer to the English team as the British team, knowing dimly that there is a potential offence to a Scottish audience but failing to grasp what it is.

The terrible truth, to us perhaps more than to them, is that there is no England. Getting the English sorted out and made decently English is, among our other troubles, one of the heavy tasks to which the Scots have pitched themselves. At times we find their blind chauvinism ill to bear, particularly as we imagine, in the light of our performances in partnership and alone, that we are a world people ourselves, and that our small busy plot is a heartland of the British endeavour and a mother country of the Commonwealth. It is this serious belief that keeps us going, and all that belittles it hinders the British fulfilment.

There was a moment in a crowded Dover pub in the early days

of the latest World War when two Scots soldiers in uniform at nine o'clock fell silent with the rest of the drinkers to hear the solemn radio news. A deeper hush fell as the disastrous announcement was given that France had fallen – had given up – and that Hitler's hordes were blitzing a victorious way to the edge of the Channel. In the stricken gathering no voice spoke, until one of the Jocks said to the other: 'Christ, Willie, this is serious! The English will be leaving us next.'

It may well be said that Scotland spends too much time in frustrated preoccupation with the problem of the English overlay, and that we should have been better employed over the last hundred years in achieving some understanding with those of the nations of Western Europe which are most akin to us in size and opportunity. Likely this is true. We could have been learning a great deal from such small and well-run national communities as Norway and Switzerland, not least that when conditions turn against them they tend to solve the problems on the spot in terms of the people who live and work there and will not be uprooted. Unlike us, they have no Canada and New Zealand to run to. The aircraft and trains that we saw earlier, filled with branch employee commuters on the way 'up' to London and back, have had another pay load for as long as they have been running – the Scots who are on their way out of Scotland for good. Their journeys are not concerned with the healthy traffic of commerce but with the one-way pilgrimage of the dispossessed. Emigration, officially and socially blessed as the ready remedy of people prepared to quit too soon, is also our classic control of what would otherwise be an intolerable level of unemployment. It demonstrates, and the rest of us endorse, the sorry blasphemy that we cannot find room for all our own brains.

Along with the late Tom Johnston, at one time a brilliant young Socialist pamphleteer and later our best Secretary of State for Scotland, I worked out once that the world population of Scotland outside of our own bounds was twenty millions. Apart from our home citizens there are twenty million people throughout the rest of the world prepared to call themselves Scots. It is a gratifying total with much goodwill in it, but in manning the frontiers of the new world we have thinned out our own ramparts.

These are Scotland's main problems, and they can be solved only by the Scots in Scotland, and by nobody else. We have, however, a great deal of fun in the bygoing, and it is greatly to be

31

hoped that some of it comes through in these chapters. With the exception of the solitary Englishman among them, who has done more for Scotland than most of us, and one Englishwoman now happily absorbed, the contributors are all home Scots. Being so, we are all looking for an argument, and putting forward conflicting versions of nearly everything, including our own long history. Quite right. A proper editorial purpose is to manage diversity, and not to force a homogeneity which would never in any case be real. You will read here different interpretations, for example, of the Highland Clearances, and notably of the motives and expectations that led to the Union of the Parliaments in 1707. In the latter case there was undoubtedly a merger, and many then expected that something great was bound to happen in the way of change. Even if the Union had been flawlessly successful there would have been some who found it easy to call it a betrayal. Anyway, it didn't work out as most people hoped.

Although we bear many troubles without ever getting used to them nor quietly enduring, there are great areas where the future is bright with endeavour, and all the better for being Scottish-based. In such a field as transport, for instance, where we had many difficulties, there has recently come on the scene the well-run British Caledonian Airways, a world-wide concern with its roots here, the Lion of Scotland on the tails of its planes and tartan uniforms on the stewardesses – a jolly way to come in.

The latest attempt to re-think the political state of affairs is Sir Alec Douglas-Home's proposal for an elected Scottish Parliamentary 'Assembly', accepted as Conservative Party policy. This latest move becomes part of the general adventure of the mind which is always afoot in our country and which is matched by an adventurous expectation arising out of the daily events. Most of the writers here have given their account in this sense. Foremost among the movers for a personal adventure is JAMES S. ADAM who has taken a brisk part in most of the sports he describes. The long-drawn-out canoe expedition we shared has been described in other pages, but I still consider James Adam's solo crossing of The Minch as one of the best lone performances in British waters. A newspaper executive, he was for some years Editor of *The Weekly Scotsman*, and has lately been managing director of newspaper groups in England. TOM COTTRELL is Principal of Stirling University, our eighth and most recent, and the only completely new university to have been founded in Scotland since the sixteenth

32

Crail, a beautiful fishing village with many 17th-century houses, is the most easterly port in Fife.

century. Before he went there in 1965 he had been Professor of Chemistry at the University of Edinburgh, and for some years before that he worked for Imperial Chemical Industries. The man who writes about our separate body of Scots law, NICHOLAS FAIRBAIRN of Fordell, is an advocate at the Scottish bar. Probably the youngest of the book's contributors, he has a growing reputation as a criminal pleader, and is withal a picturesque figure in civil and social life, wearing clothes of 1830 design, and in other ways devoting himself with zest and ability to the brightening of our contemporary life. Among other causes he is Chairman of The Traverse Theatre, and an artist. If he represents in gay aggression something of the traditions of Edinburgh, CLIFF HANLEY, on the other hand, is an implacable Glaswegian, setting forth the virtues of that industrial metropolis in everything that he writes and speaks, and all of these are hearty portions. He was a Glasgow newspaper columnist in his teens, and is now a full-time writer, with handfuls of books (his first was the memorable *Dancing in the Streets*) under his own name and at least one ill-concealed pseudonym. The book-jacket of his latest book carries a picture of Hanley and also one of the author Henry Calvin: the same picture. A hilarious public speaker, he occasionally slips off to the United States to script some film, and hurries back to the superior flesh-pots of Glasgow.

None of us could add to the renown of ERIC LINKLATER. His writings are a library. There is no literate medium in which he has not performed, and it is not likely that there is any better conversationalist in the English tongue. (Has anybody mentioned that Scotland is a great place for conversation?) He belongs to Orkney, and now lives a little farther south, but not too far. Here he writes on the political scene in Scotland, but how much more: a furiously personal and subjective writer, he trails a coat of many colours in all directions. Characteristically, he is up with a solution to the problem of Scotland's political destiny. The intricate task of describing the God of Scotland and our long search for an understanding with Him has been performed by CAMPBELL MACLEAN, a Highlander who is the Church of Scotland parish minister at Cramond, a waterside suburb of Edinburgh which was once a Roman port. He runs a successful television programme, and has moved far from the hard severities of the old Sabbath. RONALD MAVOR, who writes about the arts, was a drama critic who became director of the Arts Council in Scotland, which position he recently

33

Melrose Abbey (Roxburghshire), said to be the burial place of the heart of Bruce, was founded in 1136, though the remains are mainly 15th century.

left to do full-time authorship. He is the son of that Mavor who was the playwright James Bridie, but Ronald is an adequate hand at playwriting on his own account and an articulate focus of people and happenings in an area where much is happening.

Two historians are needed to tell our whole story. The development since the early nineteenth century is recounted by ROSALIND MITCHISON, a professional historian for three generations on each side of her family. She teaches in the Department of Economic History of the University of Edinburgh. Brought up in Oxford, she has lived in Scotland for most of her professional life, and her children regard themselves as Scots. Her husband is an Edinburgh University professor. She writes here an account of attitudes rather than events – the historian's view not only of history but of its teaching and beliefs. The historian who places Scotland in the midst of all its own pageant since the beginning of the record is himself a lairdly romantic in whose chapter there turns up, predictably and early, 'a frenziedly worried ancestor', and who can identify his own personal predecessors for a good many centuries before Bannockburn. Sir IAIN MONCREIFFE of that Ilk has a distinctive scholarship which looks on ancestry as an adjacent accompaniment to all that is happening now, and he is much at ease in the presence of his own forefolk and of ours. He is an attractive and aristocratic card, profoundly read in the available documentation of that long story, and he does a great deal to enliven the Scotland of today, although he claims to know little of what has happened since the nineteenth century came in. MICHAEL POWELL is the only Englishman in the pack, but I do not happen to know of any Scot who knows Scotland better. I have travelled the Highlands and the islands and the borders with him, and of course he has made many a film about the human values within our bounds. Long before *The Red Shoes*, *49th Parallel*, *One of our Aircraft is Missing*, and all that amazing line, he had written and created on the isle of Foula *The Edge of the World*, telling of the evacuation of an island like St Kilda. He turns up in Scotland alone from time to time, in a mobile sleeping wagon with a boat on top and a bag full of his long note-books, and vanishes into the hills. In his chapter here, laid out like what I imagine is a film script, named people suddenly appear and are part of the action, as they do in his films, and as they do to the life in Scotland now.

JOHN RAFFERTY writes about the Scottish tradition in the

steamier and even the seamier sports. He has the right sort of name for it, as well as the chunky build and style. He was the trainer of one world boxing champion, knows football and racing not only in terms of their performance but of their people, and is probably the best sports writer we have in Scotland. On a trip to Wales to cover an international football game, he heard of the Aberfan disaster, immediately went there and in the course of two days produced a series of award-winning articles which are still quoted when great reporting is mentioned. A phrase-maker. He spoke in a dispatch from the Mexico world football games about the nubile girl spectators on whom he clearly doted: 'It's Hell to be middle-aged and faithful!' In the chapter written here he sums up our dilemma: 'Scotland is too big to be wee and too wee to be big'. Lord RITCHIE-CALDER, a journalist who recently became a life peer, is a science reporter with the world for his scene. The University of Edinburgh appointed him a professor, and this status gives rise to an anecdote on the subject of Scots education he tells here, and which is matched by a similar one in the narrative of Tom Cottrell, a more professionally orthodox educator. Ritchie-Calder, a 'lad o' pairts' himself, who made his own way without universities since the day he left school, is much moved by the inheritance of the Scots like him, the original thinkers. Few can know the great and small buildings of Scotland more lovingly than GEORGE SCOTT-MONCRIEFF. His double-barrelled Clan have turned up in all parts of Scotland and Scottish life for many a day and George himself, articulate and versatile like all of them, has written plays, novels, poems, topographical books and much else. He has lived in Highland, Lowland, and Island parts of Scotland, was the first Secretary to the Scottish Council of the National Building Board, and now lives amongst the Peeblesshire hills. DAVID STEPHEN has become one of our best-known naturalists, and he reveals a world accessible to all, but truly unknown. Much of his writing is conditioned by anger at destroyers of animal life and the places where they live. To explore the countryside with him is to see with new eyes. He is an expert on the golden eagle, the hill fox, the roe deer, with many books to his name published in many countries, but he writes also with affection about those other of God's creatures who inhabit naturally the moorland places – the gamekeeper, the forester, the shepherd, the poacher, and others to be readily encountered by the hopeful traveller for whom these words are brought together.

Life in the Cities

Clifford Hanley

It is said of some people and some places that if they hadn't existed, somebody would have had to invent them. This is positively not true of any of the four Scottish cities. Nobody *could* have invented them; they're too improbable. And you can say anything you like about them, in the confidence that it will be true, and untrue, simultaneously.

Glasgow, of course, is more of a myth than an actual place; and if I seem to lean more heavily on Glasgow than on the others, it's partly because it is the biggest of the four, and partly because I was born and dragged up in the place and it has had me half-stunned since the moment I opened my eyes. On the face of it, and certainly at first glance, it isn't the kind of place a man could fall in love with. But to the native, Glasgow is like a raddled but cunning old courtesan, after whom all beautiful and virtuous maidens are pretty pallid stuff; or as the Glaswegian himself would say, peely-wally.

It's old enough, as cities go. Its older university dates back more than five hundred years, to a time when the place was a quiet fishing village living off the River Clyde. It's true that if you dropped a salmon in the Clyde at Glasgow today the poor beast would need a stomach-pump. But this is merely proof that Glasgow is well up with the swinging, polluted twentieth century. At least the air, in recent years, has become fairly breathable. The town acquired a cathedral around the same period, and soon became the scene of spiritual and secular punch-ups, a proud tradition which persists to this day. Scratch a Glaswegian and you'll find a pugnacious theologian, or at least a football fan, and it isn't easy to tell the difference when his fist is coming straight at you.

The physical expansion came with the first Industrial Revolution, and the architectural tradition of the city – in spite of the new epidemic of skyscrapers – is intensely Victorian. This doesn't

36

always mean ugly. John Betjeman, who ought to know, reckons that this is the finest Victorian city in Britain, and the complacent terraces built out in the West End for the nouveau-riche certainly give a whiff of a rich spacious age when money was sprouting out of the pavements and you could buy a servant for twelve pounds a year.

But the basic structural unit, as we call it in the trade, is the working-class tenement, and although the bulldozers and Father Time have removed some of these, and others occasionally fall over in a light breeze, there are still plenty about the place, proclaiming a way of life that is warm, *gemütlich*, vital, brash and even macabre, but completely and intensely Glaswegian. You will find tenements elsewhere in Scotland, but they are definitely a Glasgow invention (or skin growth? because surely nobody could have been daft enough or inspired enough to sit down cold-bloodedly at a drawing board and design such things. They must have been there to begin with, like the river, or Rangers and Celtic).

You have to accept the complacency of the Glaswegian in such matters. He knows that his city is the basic model as well as being the centre of the universe. There's a character in a Glasgow play, a Townhead worthy, who declaims this definitively in the un-answerable question: 'If Abroad is all that hot, how is it everybody lives in Toonheid?'

Anyway, the tenement, briefly, is a menacing stone Thing composed of small houses glued together vertically and horizon-tally to a height of three or four storeys, and the inmates gain access to their narrow cells by the celebrated Glasgow Close, which must be explained in some depth.

To the casual observer, the close is simply a rectangular hole punched through the building from front to back, with a stone staircase leading off the middle to the upper flats. To us aboriginals, it is a shelter from wind and rain, a courting area, a playground, a mode of artistic expression, an echo-chamber, a tribal compound, sometimes a corridor of terror.

Kids play on the landings, housewives wash the thing out and then do strange Celtic designs round the edges in pipe-clay (purely from folk-memory), and on quiet dark evenings, small boys run past closes with their eyes averted from the rectangle of Stygian blackness at the back end, where monsters lurk. And the families who share a close become a community of their own,

37

whether they're on sugar-borrowing terms, or reserved and private.

The close is planted deep in the folklore of the city. There's one venerable tale about a woman whom we shall call Sarah – oh, your genuine Glaswegian, this biddy; built like a reinforced cottage loaf, arms permanently akimbo, mouth clamped like a Mole wrench. To sketch in Sarah's background, she was the kind of woman who widows easy. She had already buried four husbands, one with her bare hands according to rumour, and now that she was nicely fixed for dough, she abandoned all that profligacy nonsense, took a top-floor flat in a respectable tenement, and kept herself to herself. None of that loose habit of living in your neighbour's laps – she had seen the local laps and she didn't fancy any of them.

Yet, the old flame still flickered, and she fell into an intellectual relationship with the milkman. He started making her his regular last call of the afternoon, and they spent a refined hour chatting about the Peruvian situation and atonal music, and hunting the slipper and all that jazz. No question of marriage, you understand. Sarah had her principles and the milkman had a wife and six kids. But it was all very cosy until the day the milkman, on the brink of an aphorism or a half-Nelson, had a stroke and fell dead on her Persian rug.

Here is where the *Gemütlichkeit* of Close society comes in. Utterly at a loss, Sarah finally resorted to neighbourly help, and it came with a bang. Wee Mrs McCafferty rushed in from her house across the landing, sized up the crisis in a glance, and said calmly, 'Don't worry, hen – stick a shammy leather in his hand and chuck him ower the window.'

This togetherness may help to explain the warmth of the citizens – which is real – and the violence of the citizens which is also real. Other animals when packed too closely start lashing out at one another, and the Glaswegian, being human, is an animal. Certainly anybody in Edinburgh would say so. (We'll come to that later.)

The ethnology must have something to do with it too. The people of Glasgow are a mottled amalgam of Lowland Scots, who may or may not be descended from the original Scoti tribe (which came from Ireland, as it happens) and/or those Pictish warriors who annoyed the ancient Romans so much by running about the hills dressed in blue paint and refusing to join the Empire; and the Highlanders driven to the city by poverty and eviction. This adds another confusion, because who the devil is the Highlander descended from? Scotch aborigine. Celt (whatever that is, and nobody knows for sure), a strong flavouring of Norse (from the Vikings) and a wee dash of Spanish (from the Armada). Rattle all this lot about and you have the Glaswegian, but it gets complicated again by the mass immigration of modern Irish in Victorian times. These last arrivals were not only foreign, but Roman Catholic to boot, and booting them became a popular Glasgow pastime. Once they learned the language and could afford a few hobnails, they started booting back.

This confirms our previous findings about the city's love of punch-ups both spiritual and secular. People actually play football in Glasgow, and support teams on the basis of admiration or (in the case of Partick Thistle) resigned fatalism. But the big boys in this game are Glasgow Rangers and Glasgow Celtic, and support for them is strictly a matter of religion. Rangers equal Protestantism and Celtic equal Catholicism, and the truly dedicated fan is throwing his bottle or removing his neighbour's incisors not merely in sport but to the greater glory of God. We don't go in for religious apathy like some people.

The booze plays its part in this merry ding-dong. It plays its part anyway, because the Glaswegian approaches liquor, like everything else, with reckless lust and enthusiasm. There are, naturally, many cultivated citizens with a mellowed taste for fine wines (not always with chips) but your archetypal keelie likes his tipple hard and fast and fairly anaesthetic; either because he is a Celt, or because life has always been hard, or because he just likes it that way. Closing time is 10 p.m., as elsewhere in Scotland, and 10.15 on a Saturday night can have all the raw colour and vitality of a gypsy encampment as Breughel might have painted it if he were stewed to the gills.

The people are *excessive*, that's the point. They refuse to do anything mildly or half-heartedly. If you look at them going about their business, you might take them for pretty stodgy puddings. Greek Gods and Aphrodites are not the norm, though there is a rich sprinkling of beautiful birds. But in most of them there lurks the poet or the tiger, or both. Try a genuine Glasgow wedding for an unforgettable glimpse of man's rich potential. Yes, yes, I agree, there are Glasgow weddings soggy with respectability and hired morning suits; but the genuine article is a riotous sunburst of music and mayhem. They do sing, oh Lord, they sing and no

39

power on earth can stop them. They also suddenly remember old grievances, or just lash out in protest against the machinations of blind Fate. I was talking to a proud newly-wed keelie recently who recalled that during his wedding breakfast, in a room-and-kitchen flat, five guests were singing simultaneously at one point – all different songs, of course. He also recalled, with solemn relish, that he had been compelled to pause in his own rendering of Danny Boy in order to defenestrate his uncle, who had made an offensive remark about the bride. People did notice this at the time, but nobody thought it was too bizarre. One uncle through a window was about par for the course.

In mitigation, if anybody wants some, it must be explained that these hilarities are only the outer limits of a natural energy. In the broad centre it is expressed in a greed for music and talk and hospitality. Glasgow takes strangers in with total abandon, as long as they can stand the pace. And it doesn't take itself too seriously. Its own legend of friendliness and hospitality is the story of an outlandish foreigner who stopped two Glaswegians to ask for directions. They rallied round at once and listened to him pronouncing the address in a dense accent that made no sense at all, and after a few minutes of this non-communication, one of them accepted defeat and said to his mate, 'Ach, we'll just kick the feet fae him and walk away.'

The city's own language ranges from a splendid pure English to an impenetrable *patois*, crackling with glottal stops and elided labials. Specimen of rich native dialect:

'Whaur urry? Erry ur ower err wirra brar.' ('Where are they? There they are over there with the brother.')

But these are the people who for two centuries have been endlessly emigrating to colonies and dominions and foreign lands and mingling effortlessly with their new neighbours, running trade unions and motor companies and becoming mayors. When they do emigrate, disgusted with the grime and the hard times, they turn into hideously sentimental Glaswegians who wear kilts and sing mawkish songs about wee hooses amang the heather, which they never saw in their lives. When they stay at home, they stay because they can't quite abandon the hypnosis of this city, the scruffy cheerfulness and the iron-hard jokes and the surprising beauty.

There *is* beauty. And apart from anything inside the city, Glasgow is the easiest place in the world to get out of. The waters of the Firth of Clyde and the hills of Lanark and the magic of Loch Lomond and the Trossachs are all on the doorstep, and the Glaswegian reckons he owns them too. One keelie, in fact, was walking through the woods somewhere in Dunbartonshire when a pleasant-spoken chap in dogtooth tweeds accosted him and told him he was trespassing. Such arrogance cannot be borne by the egalitarian Glaswegian.

'Get away,' he said. 'This is . . . this is the countryside. How can you own it?'

'Actually, my ancestors fought for it.'

'Okay, Mac, okay – get the jackets off!'

The industrial tradition of Glasgow is heavy engineering, and the character of the city, as of any place, is deeply influenced by its work. Quite apart from the physio-architectural effects – the high density of population around factories and on the riverside – the centuries of tough but highly skilled toil has served to evolve the leathery and laconic flavour of the basic Glaswegian. He may be amused, but he is not impressed. The purest acid of sceptical irony is the tone of a Glaswegian saying, 'Aye, that'll be right.'

None of this prevents Glasgow from having, say, the finest and most numerous parks of any comparable city; or the richest art collection in Britain outside London. But the natives play such honours fairly cool, unless a stranger chances to disparage them.

Cooler than cool, in the view of Glasgow, is the nation's capital city of Edinburgh; and to be fair, the two cities should not be considered in isolation because they interact on each other and entertain themselves by a long-standing, half-joking rivalry. Edinburghers explain that Glasgow's prime asset is the fast train service to Edinburgh. Glaswegians retort that Edinburgh is practically English anyway, and cold-blooded English at that. Edinburgh dismisses the Glasgow native as uncouth, drunken and foul-mouthed. Glasgow's riposte is that a visitor to an Edinburgh home is welcomed at the door with the words, 'Come in, come in, *you'll have had your tea.*'

One of Glasgow's most eminent Elizabethans, Jack House, has summed up the conflicting social attitudes thus: that in Edinburgh, breeding is equated with good form, whereas in Glasgow, breeding is regarded as good fun.

All these things are true and untrue together. There is no doubt that the capital of Scotland is a capital city at first glance. Never

41

mind the fact that the splendid old Edinburgh stores which lined the north side of Princes Street are steadily becoming homogenized into the familiar chain-store pattern; they are still splendid, and Princes Street is the gracious, spacious main drag of what was once called the Athens of the North. It is quite possible to spend a protracted visit to the city without moving a few yards from the Street, in fact. The shops and hotels and restaurants are all on the north side because the south side is virtually all garden, except for sporadic ornaments such as the Scott Monument, the art galleries and the Waverley Station. And above the gardens there towers the Castle Rock, with the absolutely genuine, absolutely historical Edinburgh Castle before your very eyes. Not far away, for that matter, and perfectly visible, the city offers to the lazy viewer its own miniature mountain of Arthur's Seat (on which King Arthur may well have sat). All this without stirring from the centre of the capital. It is certainly the way a show city ought to be designed.

History is the point. History fairly oozes out of the stonework in Edinburgh and you can feel the throb of it through your bootsoles if you have any sensibility at all. That castle is no plastic tourist attraction. Monarchs have reigned from it and plotted in it and stared gloomily down from it at the turbulent mobs they called their loyal subjects. This makes it all the more a tourist gimmick, of course. When they floodlight it during the Edinburgh International Festival, it hangs in mid air like a mirage, and the customers jam into the courtyard every year to see the military tattoo which is the guaranteed box-office smash of this cultural bonanza in which modern show-business cunning mingles with palpable tradition without a trace of unease – because even in the vivid and lethal heyday of the Stewart* dynasty, the city must have looked like an extravagant theatrical set.

Edinburgh's closes are a totally different species from Glasgow's. They are long, devious, steeply climbing alleyways as romantic and dark and durable as the climate. The climate is fine, but it can be unkind to thin clothes or thin blood since it consists largely of the bracing east wind.

The history, by the way, is not at all dry formal stuff, because the star-studded cast is led by Mary, Queen of Scots, and she is

* The spelling of 'Stewart' as 'Stuart' was due to the fact that the French, great allies of the Scots, had no 'w' in their alphabet. The Darnley branch of the Stewarts adopted the French spelling in the fifteenth century.

adored or detested to this day, but never ever overlooked. She is regarded variously as an angel of beauty and a villainous instrument of Papal intrigue, but she was probably no more than an intensely romantic redhead who wanted to be happy but simply attracted trouble, of which she had plenty. She had the distressing experience of having her private rooms invaded one night by Lord Ruthven and a crowd of his drunken friends who leapt on the Queen's Italian secretary Rizzio and stabbed him practically to pieces while she watched. I mention this as an example of the direct and conclusive social mores of sixteenth-century Edinburgh. Some time later her husband, Lord Darnley, was fatally involved in a rather mysterious gunpowder explosion in a suburban house called Kirk o' Field, and criminologists have been probing this incident ever since. It is conceivable that the Earl of Bothwell, Mary's lover, was responsible, and it is conceivable but not probable that the Queen was an accessory before the fact. There is at least no doubt about the final chapter, in which Mary gave herself into the hands of her kinswoman Elizabeth of England for protection, was locked up to moulder for a couple of decades and then subjected to a kangaroo trial and beheaded.

It is worth mentioning all this because the aura is still detectable in Edinburgh, as is also the legacy of John Knox, the fire-eating Presbyterian radical who was a sore trouble to the Queen and helped to infuse Edinburgh (and all Scotland for that matter) with the staunch religious faith that tends to suspect all pleasure as probably sinful and makes us all slightly schizoid because our convictions are inescapable, but our appetites are fierce. Edinburgh in fact is both the scene and the inspiration of that classic work on schizophrenia, Doctor Jekyll and Mr Hyde, and students of abnormal psychology may amuse themselves by relating Robert Louis Stevenson's novel to the conflicting impulses of Scottish puritanism.

There *was* a Jekyll-and-Hyde in real-life Edinburgh, that's the joy of it. His name was Deacon Brodie, and the visitor may still quaff the wine of the country in the pub where once he was accepted for what he was, an elegant man-about-town, a mildly aristocratic pillar of society. By night, he pursued the trade of master criminal – nothing violent or vicious, merely high-class burglary – for which in the end he was soundly hanged after a pursuit to Continental Europe.

The capital city, like any well-regulated family, survives its black sheep, and will even take a wry pride in them after a suitable interval. Edinburgh *is* respectable. It looks respectable and it is. It neither boozes so blatantly nor curses so readily as Glasgow, and it has the feel of a city long established and not given to frivolous changes.

It does change, naturally. New roads are sliced through it here and there, but there is always a vigorous body of citizenry ready to oppose them or divert them to prevent the city from being brutalized. It boasts, to the north, two celebrated pieces of civil engineering both startling and newfangled in their time, the Forth Railway Bridge and the Forth Road Bridge. But it boasts more its Old Town and its New Town (which is new only in the sense of being eighteenth century) and its solid traditions of thrift and the law and old-fashioned decency. You would never think it had also been the home of the prototype body-snatchers Burke and Hare.

To be fair, neither was a native Edinburgher. They were low-class Irish labourers. They were also not body-snatchers as most people understand the trade description. Other men robbed graves to sell the tenants to medical schools. Burke and Hare ran a cheap lodging-house for transients, and produced absolutely prime fresh specimens for the eminent Dr Knox by the judicious use of a pillow held over the guests' faces. Their total output was something over twenty – nobody can be sure of the definitive figure as the company didn't keep precise books.

No, there isn't a trace of that kind of monstrosity in modern Edinburgh. It is a nice town. It's true that Rose Street, running parallel to Princes Street, is one of the densest concentrations of pubs in Britain, all apparently thriving, and reckless young men, native or incomer, sometimes regard a totalist crawl of Rose Street as some kind of initiation. It is not to be recommended except in instalments with a good night's sleep in the intervals. They are pleasant pubs, all the same, and anybody with a taste for tavern atmosphere can soon dispel the legend of the cold, aloof Edinburgher. He may be a little more reserved than his Western neighbours, but he is an amiable and hospitable man once the initial barrier has been breached; and frankly, the city is full of Glaswegians who have gone there to work and have no intention of coming home.

The most probable time for outsiders to visit the capital is during the annual Festival, when the Scottish schizophrenia shows most starkly. Other cities may give themselves heart and soul to some annual junketing, but here it's never quite simple. John Knox is still wrestling for the soul of the pleasure-loving Mary. The city is blissfully proud of its big cultural show, and simultaneously thinks the whole affair is dangerously hedonistic, sinfully ostentatious, tending to corrupt and deprave. The inner conflict shows in curious ways. The city council decides *not* to spend the few trivial pounds required to put up gala lights on Princes Street, or to put a stop to the Festival Club serving dreaded alcohol after the God-ordained hour of 10 p.m. Or local vigilantes rally to repel the irruption of obscenity which always lurks in what decadent outsiders call culture. Shakespeare, I solemnly swear (being a Glaswegian, I solemnly swear quite often) – Shakespeare has been named by the local moralists as one of the upstart purveyors of permissiveness and filth. That is Edinburgh.

The converse is also true. An Edinburgh magistrate has on one occasion delivered a judgment of Solomon which rejected the claim that a naked young woman was *ipso facto* obscene, and confirmed the capital's claim to be a calm, unhysterical and life-loving centre of peace and enthusiasm. And if Edinburgh seems almost to resent its own Festival, how is it that more than half of the audiences at any given entertainment during these three febrile weeks are native Edinburghers? Edinburgh is a great town. You can't pin it down, you can't dismiss it in a flip sentence, you can't even get to know it without pain and surprise. But it is a great town, and as towns or cities go, it is still one of the most habitable places in Europe.

Dundee, now. Ah! Oh! Dundee! Dundee is particular. When I was but a child in the newspaper business, Dundee had acquired the label of being the centre of jute, jam, and journalism. (Journalists tend to cling to labels long after the printing has worn off.) It was, it was. The jute business was a great old affair in its time, and it lingers on although India no longer needs the British Raj to take its raw stuff, turn it into sacks and send it back. Everybody is putting potatoes in plastic bags now anyway. But 'everybody' includes Dundee. Jam, yes. Some of the great names in that alchemical trade were Dundonian and they are still Dundonian. Journalism, yes. The bizarre fact is that Dundee, in an age when the mass media concentrate more and more on London, refuses to yield its own supremacy in the communication business. Generations of impressionable youngsters have been fed their

45

weekly intake of school stories and adventure stories and comic-strip stories from this peculiar outpost five hundred miles from London, and most of those youngsters have been English, and none of them has noticed that they were in the firm hands of an almost foreign power. Outside of Billy Bunter and Tom Merry and a few other English institutions, the folk-heroes of British youth – and of British servant-girls, for that matter – have all been made of whole cloth in this unexpected little city up the East coast of Scotland. The comic-paper industry may not have created Dundee, but it has added its own unexpected flavour to the city, and the legendary publishing family of D. C. Thomson has thriven and expanded by refusing to leave its roots. This is the home, the womb, of Oor Wullie and the Broons, and there is no point in explaining those phenomena here. The visiting Martian has only to ask any Scot – *any* Scot, even in Malaysia or Peru – to discover what they mean in the baffling fabric of Scottish folk-lore.

Dundee is perched on the north bank of the River Tay. It is a tidy, congested place with unexpected discoveries of quiet open spaces, and one thing it doesn't have is a colony of lavish aristocratic town mansions, as you will find in nearly all cities. The millionaire Dundonian has always been careful not to show it. What it has is a slightly other-worldly feeling of ignoring the rest of mankind, at the same time as sucking in huge international investments in modern industries and quietly going its own way as if nothing had happened. It's a pretty hard nut to crack, and if you buy fish-and-chips in Dundee you'll probably get saithe, which no Western Scotsman would even feed to the cat; but it is perfectly eatable. When I was there as a struggling playwright I ate practically nothing else. The city has a theatre, you see, and a thriving theatre although it keeps scrambling about to find new homes from time to time. The life of the spirit surges up in the wee place, and surging with it come rock-carved characters. There is an artist, for instance, who for years when in his cups has had the habit of limning magnificent drawings of horses in the gentlemen's toilets of pubs all over the city. One of these recently reported is eight feet from the floor, and the local theory is that he was high at the time.

This notable man is in the solid tradition of Dundee's legitimate eccentrics, of course, the list being topped by the superb, the immortal William Topaz McGonagall, now universally accepted as the finest bad poet of our language. And since McGonagall can't be mentioned without being quoted, let him give the final word on the city of his adoption, in the deathless ode 'Bonnie Dundee in 1878'.

> Oh, Bonnie Dundee! I will sing in thy praise
> A few but true simple lays,
> Regarding some of your beauties of the present day –
> And virtually speaking, there's none can them gainsay;
> There's no other town I know of with you can compare
> For spinning mills and lasses fair,
> And for stately buildings there's none can excel
> The beautiful Albert Institute or the Queen's Hotel,
> For it is most handsome to be seen,
> Where accommodation can be had for Duke, Lord or Queen.
> Oh, Bonnie Dundee! I must conclude my muse,
> And to write in praise of thee, my pen does not refuse,
> Your beauties that I have alluded to are most worthy to see,
> And in conclusion, I will call thee Bonnie Dundee!

Why did Aberdeen never spawn a McGonagall? It was probably too busy being Aberdeen. It calls itself the Silver City by the Sea, and why not? It's a free country. Aberdeen, to be truthful, is a foreign land to the southern Scot. Anybody who imagines this small country as a homogeneous mass of Harry Lauders has only to travel from Glasgow or Edinburgh those two hundred miles north to realize that it's a very big place indeed. The language is entirely different, the intonation is strange and musical – the pitch rises at the end of a sentence instead of dropping, as if every statement were a question, 'what' becomes 'fit', and if you like far-out linguistic puzzles, try 'a' ae oo'. It is Aberdonian for 'all one wool'. Foreign? Aberdeen is downright exotic.

The city is made of granite and on granite – that is why it remains silver, and it does, it shines in the sunlight; and the people have a granite quality too; but granite is warm as well as hard. Aberdonians are the conventional canny Scots, but they had to invent the Aberdeen joke to cover their embarrassment at not being genuinely stingy. In fact, the first impression of Aberdeen is rich. Rich. The main streets were made to last forever, but they were made broad enough to take a six-abreast chariot race rather than half a sedan chair, and the whole place is startlingly unworn. Frankly, the night life is not vivid. It's there, but it's not vivid.

Nevertheless, the granite city is a wonderful place in which to eat and drink, because the Aberdonian approves of these comforts. It is fair to mention that in this bracing air, a man has to stoke his inner fires fairly steadily. I know a young man, reasonably husky, who migrated from the west to attend Aberdeen University, and lived in trembling misery till he equipped himself with long woollen underwear. It is after all two hundred miles farther north than Glasgow or Edinburgh, and the latitude tells.

There are always compensations. The days are short in winter, but in summer they last almost forever, and there is plenty of sunshine, with or without a stiff east wind to save it from becoming decadent. And one may well glimpse the Northern Lights which figure in the civic anthem. You are far from the other Scottish cities here, both climatically and culturally. To digress slightly, it was only in this century that people in the Norwegian port of Bergen acquired a railway to Oslo, and until then, they could visit Aberdeen faster and more easily than their own capital city. Aberdeen is a notably northern place, and though the native has easy access to the south, he likes his own place and is not much affected by what goes on down there.

The history has been hard, of course. Although the land of Aberdeenshire is lush and fertile, there must have been bitter centuries of digging at it, in the cold blast, to force a living from it; and the sea – because Aberdeen is a great fishing place – has never been soft, or ready to tolerate softness. These elements breed their own kind of child. Here is a conversation, reported in its entirety, between two Aberdonian matrons casually meeting:

'Your man's deid.'

'Aye, I ken.'

There is an even more chilling Aberdeen story, of the poor old woman whose husband died, leaving her very little for the splendid funeral she would have wanted for him. The undertaker was sympathetic and promised something nice and dignified, but she was suddenly taken by one of his current clients, beautifully dressed in striped trousers and clawhammer coat, tastefully reclining in a casket lined in red plush. 'Marvellous,' said the old lady, 'oh, if I could only do that for Alec.'

It wasn't likely – this was the status symbol model at three hundred guineas. But the undertaker promised to do his best.

Glamis Castle (Angus), predominantly 17th century, occupies the site of an 11th-century royal residence. It is the birthplace of Princess Margaret and the childhood home of the Queen Mother.

And when she called in next day, there was Alec, in striped trousers and clawhammer coat, lying in a similar casket, *at a price of thirty pounds.*

'Na na,' she protested. 'I couldna take charity, it'll all be paid, the right price.'

'Ah, shut up,' said the undertaker. 'I just changed the heads.'

I don't actually swear that this is true. Still, it's a hard life, and the Aberdonian is capable of living.

All of this is entirely one-sided and absurd, even if accurate. Aberdeen is a holiday resort. It is one of the best organized and most successful holiday resorts in Britain, and it isn't surprising, because apart from harbours and fishing, the city has some of the most beautiful beaches to be found anywhere. There is a beach smack on the doorstep, thronged during the summer by thousands of tourists from Scotland and England; and a mile or so away is the beginning of a more lavish stretch of silver sand, miles long and sometimes hundreds of yards wide, which can be enjoyed in almost complete solitude.

Aberdeen's visitors tend to be recidivists. Once sampled, the city has them hooked. Clearly, this magic can't be worked simply by providing a beach, or even entertainments. These hard granite Aberdonians enjoy their visitors. They may not serenade them, but they enjoy them. The warmth is all there, below. It is not easily bestowed. But it's there.

There is not a negligible city in Scotland, and there is not a similar city in Scotland. In this absurdly small area, cities stand as citadels apart and they grow and think and laugh and weep in their own ways. They are not bland, and their differences refuse to be smoothed away. It would take a strong and resolute spirit to sample them all thoroughly. But it would be a sad omission to overlook any.

49

Loch Carron, a sea loch in Ross and Cromarty. At its head is Glen Carron, which includes Achnashellach Forest.

Country Places and People

David Stephen

Scotland has much that England has little of, or not at all – a lot of clean water, great mountain ranges, no Law of Trespass, a deer to every twenty-five people, the eagle, the wildcat, the biggest grouse in the world, the finest whisky, and a predilection for being British.

Of course we have plenty of dirty water, so polluted in places that walking on it would hardly qualify as a miracle. We Scots have done our share of dirtying our environment, including its water. We have turned some rivers into sewers, in the best tearaway fashion, but we still have, thank God, oceans of clean water – more clean water per rushing, sparkling mile and gleaming acre than anywhere of comparable size on earth. From the Tay to the Atlantic flank of the Outer Isles the rivers are clear-water arteries with salmon for red corpuscles.

The salmon of the west are Gaelic fish, as those of Aberdeenshire are east coasters, for the salmon homes to its own, to the river of its birth, and not many lose their way even during the great pilgrimage from the sea. Scent memories of icy pools and shingly rapids guide them as upstream they migrate, leaping seal-sleek in the sun, muscling through belching gorges, then out and up and over the falls like Polaris missiles, thirled to the scent of home and owning it with nostrils unclogged by pollution and sophisticated as the red deer's.

Journey's end for the salmon up from the sea is the headwaters of the mountain burns, snow fed, where the pools boil with snaw bree, and if you don't know what snaw bree is you'll have to see it because no one has yet invented the English for it. And on gravelly beds, where the water is so unbelievably pellucid that it might as well not be there at all, the salmon spawn, and that's where life and death begin for the small fish with their yolky belly bags, for of a million born three noughts will be missing before the smolts go down to the sea.

50

There's a river in the Outer Isles, so short that a man could run the length of it almost without drawing breath, where the salmon come up like London rush-hour traffic and where a handful of five pound notes would hardly get you as far as you could hop on one leg. It is one of the greatest salmon rivers in Europe, salmon per yard or £ per ounce.

So the fly fishermen come out as thick as clegs on a sweating horse's belly in summer. The difference between a fly fisherman and a fly fisher is one you'd understand if you were a Scot, although you still wouldn't be able to tell by looking. The fly fisherman fishes fair with fly at all times. The fly fisher has no entomological connections whatever; he is an etymological fly man. A poacher.

Now there are poachers and poachers, and a poached salmon can be a matter of cuisine or origin or both, depending on where you happen to be, and the wavelength you're on, when you ask for it. The more bucolic or less imaginative type of water bailiff or keeper might not appreciate the subtle difference between one poacher and another, but a distinction there is, as most anglers would admit, for anglers are mostly a tolerant and contemplative breed.

The type of poacher who dynamites or poisons a pool, killing a hundred fish for every one he takes out of it, is a despicable character, a crook, and usually violent as well. He is in the same class as the laird or keeper who kills eagles or peregrines – anti-social, blinkered with selfishness.

But there are real poachers, the local men, the natives of the place, who take fish to eat them, or maybe to trade for a bottle or two of the best at some back door, or maybe because they don't accept that salmon evolved for the pleasure of the few. It doesn't really matter. They are simple predators, like anglers, or cannibal trout, or herons, or otters, or dragonfly nymphs, or some keepers themselves. There's a pool somewhere called after a long-dead keeper, not because of his virtues but because of his virtuosity in getting more fish out of it than all the fly fishermen put together.

If you've grown up with the roar and whisper of a salmon water in your ears, who is to say that you can't take a fish out with a gaff, or a net, or whatever? Or even shoot one with a .22 rifle? After all they shoot deer and elephants, and as Horace McCoy once remarked *They Shoot Horses Don't They?* The Wafer, in his day, shot a few salmon as they lay waiting for a big water to take them over the top. He was a poaching artist – lean as a hawk, with

51

fingers like talons – a performer extraordinary. He said it all when he once said:

'I like a salmon!'

Then, enigmatically, he confused the issue by adding: 'So does the polis!'

They said he could wile the birds from the trees, which was a lie – well, except maybe with pheasants. But he could get a salmon out of a pool with the kind of compulsion that must have brought the first prehistoric life ashore from the primordial slime. He was quiet, but not blate as we say. So, fresh from a foray, and with innocent front, he once asked a watchful policeman for directions. It doesn't sound like much until you realize he was using two salmon for legs.

You can talk about the rights and wrongs of poaching until Gaelic becomes a dead language, but there are wildlife fishers with rights beyond dispute, rights more ancient than any legislation about them. The otter is one of them.

Now the otter is a water weasel, a hunter of the tideline and the tide pools as well as rivers and burns. As an opportunist it will raid a rabbit warren, or maybe even a henhouse where some lazybones or incompetent has left a way in for it. But it is, above all, a fisher, with a wide prey range, including frogs, eels, shellfish and other marine life. And, of course, it kills salmon. But it makes as much difference to the number of salmon in the river as I do.

We have plenty of clean water, plenty of salmon, and plenty of otters. The north and the west are otter strongholds, while in England the otter hunters, that not very admirable breed, have had to put away their poles. If ever the angler has to put away his rod it won't be because of otters. Alas! not all river owners see the otter as most anglers do, as something to be preserved, and we still use the gin trap to torture it. So we can't be too superior about otter hunters.

They'll tell you that the otter is a wasteful fisher, that it takes the best fish, that it will take a bite out of a salmon and leave the rest. It does all of these things sometimes, but the general conclusions won't bear looking at. Like any predator the otter usually takes what is easiest to catch, and that means the disabled, the old, the young, the diseased and the dying. It will outswim and tire a pool-bound fish and in so doing tire itself. And a fit otter will hunt sometimes for sport as anglers do all the time. But there wouldn't be a fish more to be caught if all the otters disappeared. And the river would be a poorer place.

They'll tell you the tall tales too, especially the hillmen and the rivermen with their flair for jocular inventiveness: 'This otter' – the man pronounced it *ought-er*, in the delightful way they do in the west – where English is Gaelic thought spoken, with Gaelic imagery, and gentled by the mother idiom – 'this otter caught a salmon and took it to its altar and turned it over and looked at it, but it wassn't made up with it at all, so it threw it back in to the pool, then dived in itself and caught a bigger one, and was pleased with it and ate it up. . . .'

I think of an April morning, with the small-talk of swallows in the air, and the cushats, as we call the wood pigeons, clattering and croodling in the oaks. The flat-topped boulder in midstream that morning was a plinth for a sculpture – the ebony silhouette of an otter, round-rumped, with head high and rudder slack. For long seconds she held that pose, then she padded round in a complete circle and sat tall, like the giant weasel she was. She settled again and trailed her dark, sleek length across the boulder, with her face close to the water on one side and her rudder clamping down on the other. She held this pose for a few moments before curving snake-like into the water, and disappearing as though gliding into a burrow. And that's the most one usually sees of an otter.

Aye, but there's more to clean water than salmon and otters and the tales they tell of them. There are men up there, where each hill burn has its nuances of magic, even if the magic can be measured only in parts per million, who can turn living water into the water of life. *Usquebae*. Whisky. Mind you whisky is a generic name, and each has its own whatever. There are no bad ones, but there are good ones and better ones, and, in the Orwellian phrase, some are more better than others. A good mature malt can go anywhere, but nowhere else can it be made, even in the land of Nippon.

But the finest water, with the true magic, can be subtly and elusively contaminated. There they were, in one of the most famous whisky glens, all set to create a braw new distillery and a new breed that would make Jove give up nectar, and suddenly they find a trace of copper pollutant. Copper in those hills is rarer than butterflies down a coal pit or salmon in the Clyde. Yet there it was; a trace, no more, but a trace just the same.

The experts confirmed the presence of copper, and when they

had all had their say, and been defeated, they called in an old man, a *bodach* who had brewed many a peck of illegal malt, and asked his help. Could he explain it? Of course he could. He took them to a spot upstream, and told them to dig, and behold they unearthed an old copper still, hastily interred there by the ancients when the Excisemen were nosing in on the last whiffs of free enterprise. And that was the end of an era. And may God forgive the Excise for forcing honest men to pollute one of the best and purest streams in all Scotland.

A few years ago, when I was on one of the western islands, looking at eagles and geese and other wildlife, and between times sipping of the scholarly Monsignor's own breed of the malt, I got to know an old keeper who had visited the *Politician* which, you may remember, was the whisky ship that Sir Compton Mackenzie used in his hilarious *Whisky Galore*. Of course the Excisemen, spoil-sports that they were, and are, soon hammered down on the ferry service the islanders were running to get as many of the creatures safely ashore as they could. But many's the one that got to dry land to be drunk, or hidden. And many were reverently interred to be resurrected at a safer time.

The old man sadly produced an empty bottle, and displayed it like some favourite ornament.

'Did that one come from the ship?' I asked.

'Yes,' he said slowly. 'It did. You see there were bottles buried all over the place, and no doubt there will be many of them lying around yet.' He put the bottle down. 'Well, you see, this day my son wass working at hiss peats, building a stack you know, and there wass this little collie pup he had just got, and it would always be digging behind hiss back, and he would always be telling it to come out of there. But always it would be going back, and digging, and digging, and my son, thinking it might be a rat or something, wented and got a spade and dug in the place himself, and found a case of the stuff that had been forgotten about. And he said to me, "Father, look what I haf found, and what shall I do with it?" And I said to him Well we could invite people in and drink it all and that will be that, or we could keep some and sell the rest. Well, we kept two bottles and sold the rest to the skipper of a trawler. And do you know there were men here from all over the island asking my son where did he get his puppy dog.'

If it isn't true it ought to be, and I have no doubt at all that it is, except maybe for the tail piece, which has all the deftness of Gaelic artistry.

Mind you there are plenty of clever collies up and down the country, as anyone who visits Sheepdog Trials quickly discovers. The Border collie is probably the best all round sheepdog in the world, although the Germans might not agree, preferring their own shepherd dog, the Alsatian. The fact is that the collie has gone all over the world as a sheepdog, whereas the Alsatian has gone all over the world as everything else but.

Hill shepherds are sometimes scornful about Trial dogs. Creepers, they call them, yard by yard crawlers, slaves to the whistle, chess players on a standard board, unsuited to the rough and tumble of the hill. This is a libel, betraying the general suspicion of the intellectual's ability in practical affairs. Mountaineers are not all born on Ben Nevis or Annapurna, but the best of them get there eventually. The creeper has made the modern hill collie, and the best hill dogs all have creeper in them.

The best shepherds have the best dogs and the best cared-for dogs. They have the best rapport with their dogs. They carry responsibility as lightly as they carry an orphaned lamb. They have the true dignity of their calling, and a certain family regard for most wildlife on the hill. Good ground, good sheep, good dogs, and the first-rate shepherd, like whisky and freedom, gang thegither.

The good shepherd is easily recognized. If you meet him after breakfast time he'll be coming in, not going out. I was hiding once beside an eagle's eyrie, at half past two in the morning, when I heard the familiar clink of big rocker boots that had to be the shepherd's. The hen eagle flew off and when I looked out of my hiding place I could see white flashes, like badger faces, that were the ruffs of dogs, at heel and alongside the shepherd. Presently the four dogs were sniffing at my hiding place.

'You're up early,' he greeted.

'I've not been down all night,' I told him. 'But you've been up before your eyes were open yourself, surely?'

'Well, we're gathering lambs and I want them down before the sun hots up.' It was typical of the man to pluralize himself when doing a job on his own. 'How are the eagles?'

'They're fine,' I said. 'No lambs in!'

'Aye, just so!' he laughed, and away he went with his dogs.

Such men are a bit thinner on the ground than they used to be; in some places even rare. There are others, of lesser rating, and lesser sensibility. Not unnaturally, the sheepman tends to polarize his frustrations on something he can get to grips with. The fox is one. Governments are remote, almost unreachable; the fox is on the ground, and reachable. It is the most hated of all the hill predators. 'Thou shalt not suffer a fox to live' might well have been the eleventh commandment if Moses had come down out of Cruachan instead of Sinai.

But it was not always thus. It began when the sheep came and drove out the people, and the great Gaelic poet, Duncan Ban Macintyre could write:

> My blessing be upon the foxes,
> Because that they hunt the sheep. . . .
> Deeply do I hate the man who abuses the foxes,
> Setting a dog to hunt them,
> Shooting at them with small shot.
> The cubs, if they had what I wish them,
> Short lives were not their care.
> Good luck to them say I,
> And may they never die but of old age.

People felt like that then. Not now. Duncan Ban would find few sympathizers today for his defence of the Gaelic way of life. Now the hills are for the sheep, and (it is said confidently) the fox is a known predator on lambs. Nobody knows how many lambs foxes kill, and there is little urge to find out. The fox as scavenger, and predator on voles, is not taken into account. It is difficult to rationalize with a dead lamb at your feet, even if the fox didn't kill it. So we hunt foxes as a routine, by habit – almost by instinct.

Nobody in his senses would argue that a big predator, doing significant damage to domestic livestock, should not be controlled. How to do it with the fox has still to be discovered. In the meanwhile we kill a lot of foxes, using guns, poison, gin traps, snares, and dogs. Guns are opportunist weapons, poison illegal, snares an abomination, and gin trapping due to be outlawed, as in England. That leaves the dogs. The dogs used are terriers. And special.

My own view is that the quickest, and in the end the most humane, way to kill foxes is by using terriers, that is the Highland way. The dog is put into a den where a vixen is lying with her cubs. Its job is to force the fox to bolt. When she bolts she is shot by waiting guns. Then the dog kills the cubs. It is a great bloody mess, but it is quick, and sure, and only the quaint get any fun out of it.

Terriers are plentiful enough as breeds, most of them fitter to go to town in motor cars than to ground after the big mountain vixen. The foxing terrier is a special type – varminty, tough, hard-bitten, indomitable, intransigent, long on courage and short on inches – that will fight without noise instead of making noise without fighting, and will trade snash for chop with a big outraged vixen – face on, forewarned, and defending cubs.

Scotland has a few native terriers, but nowadays they are used like most whisky – blended rather than straight. Crosses are mostly the order of the day, and the crosses often skim the cream of courage, bounce, fire and gurry. A favourite one is the Border/ Lakeland. But the one coming to the fore is the Parson Jack Russell – a small, hard dog, sheathed in muscle, all rubber and whipcord, with short legs and a heart you could hardly get into a whisky cask. They'll tell you the Jack Russell isn't a true breed. That it isn't. So it's a faith; and faiths have a habit of outlasting breeds.

The foxhunter may be a keeper or deerstalker or a man specially retained for the work. Whoever he is he usually has a motley collection of terriers, Jack Russells, bits of Border, and others of this and that. But they add up to the quintessence of the meaning of the name terrier.

I knew a terrier called Sionnach who was killing fox cubs when his joints were creaking with rheumatism. He was found once hanging on to a stag's nose in a pool, being swung around and hoisted, and refusing to let go. In the end he came out of a den attached to a bolting vixen, and when she broke away she had all his front teeth in her like banderillas. That left him with a toothless leer while he creaked his way to arthritis and senility. Lots of foxing terriers are called Sionnach, which is Gaelic for fox. How ambivalent is man! to call the beast he likes best after the one he hates most.

Terriers like foxing, but of course they sometimes get hurt. They get their faces painted with blood, their muzzles scarred and holed, their ears cut and squared. And sometimes a lot worse than that, because a big hill vixen knows how to use her weaponry. Then dogs sometimes get buried, in a fall or behind a vixen. There was one down for three weeks, that ate its way out through the fox in the end. Another was down for eleven days, and came

57

back with no nails, no beard, and eyes gummed with blear. Both recovered completely and lived to old age.

But is it right to send small dogs to ground after foxes at all? The difficulty is keeping them from going down. I have yearly trouble with my own and I am no foxhunter. Given that foxes have to be killed I believe that the use of terriers is justified. It is quick death for the cubs, and the terrier that doesn't want the clinch can dodge it, and not be sent down again.

It is different with badgers. The badger is a powerful beast, seldom a problem. He will retreat rather than argue, dig rather than fight. He is a devotee of the peace conference, in love with minding his own business. But he is also thrawn and fearless, strong as a bear cub, with bear claws and jaws like a quarry crusher. A non-starter of trouble he is a terrible executioner at the finishing of it. When his back is to the wall he can do frightful surgery on small, brave dogs, and the man who wilfully sends a boot-high terrier to ground to battle with a badger should resign from the human race.

Not all badgers live in the woods or forests; many live far out on the hill, in fortresses of rock and scree, fearsome places, labyrinths of perils and pitfalls where the badger is impregnable. Mountain foxes live in such places too, and it isn't always possible to tell if there is a badger present where you know there is a fox. So in such wild, unchancy places a foxing terrier will sometimes find itself face to face with a badger.

On Rannoch, some years back, the stalkers were foxing at a cairn where there was a bitch fox with cubs. One terrier was down; the others tied back out of the way. The terrier down for the fox met a badger, was chopped, and came out whimpering. Then the brock burst out into the daylight, fuming at being hustled, and was booted in the seat by Sandy, the head stalker, fuming himself because of his cut-up dog. The sight of the badger in the open almost drove the other terriers off their heads, but none was slipped to follow. The badger shambled on a wide circle, came right back past the dogs, was kicked in the seat again, and dived below via the hole he had come out of. He must have been the only badger in Britain to have his backside kicked twice by a man with a gun, and not a shot fired.

Most Scottish counties have badgers; some have a lot of them. There's much goodwill for them nowadays, and they hardly ever get into trouble. A few find the way to henhouses; but they are few indeed, as few as they who find their way to 10 Downing

Street. In some quarters there is the old hostility; in more there is neutrality, tolerance, or even welcome. If you look along forest deer fences, or rabbit netting, especially Forestry Commission fences, you'll find here and there small, wooden, push-open gates at the bottom. These are to let badgers in and out. If they weren't there the beasts would tear holes in the fence. The badger is a stickler for using his traditional runways, and budging him from them is like trying to get a locomotive on to a branch line without switching the points. He's the same at his set; he puts the *Bydand* sign out and it takes a bulldozer, literally sometimes, to move him.

Cairn and forest are also the haunts of the wildcat, the Scottish tiger, which occupies more of the country today than it did fifty years ago, and is also more numerous. Any big tabby-type cat seen in the Highlands after dark is as likely to be a wildcat as a domestic one. It won't always be; it may not usually be; but it is just as likely to be.

See a big wildcat at sunrise, with the light at his back – ring-tailed, big-fisted, wide-skulled, with out-pointing ears – padding purposefully over rocks or along the face of a crag, and you've seen one of the lords of life. Or hark to the wild pibroch of him in the shadows when the sunset is red, and the pools are plated with gold, and the croaking of the ravens stilled. No alley cat medley could ever match the Wagnerian laughter of this eldritch serenade.

Untameable? Yes, he is, if you try to woo him grown-up, or after his kitten eyes have opened on the light. Bay him on a crag, or in a tree, and he'll simmer and sizzle and maybe explode in your face. But not if there's a way out for him; if there is he'll take it – up, down, right, left, any way at all. He is a man-avoider, not a man-eater. All the pictures you see of the snarling, flat-eared wildcat are of animals at bay. You'll be lucky if you ever see one alive and free, going peaceably about its own affairs. Meet one in the open and you meet an apostle of the direct approach in the opposite direction.

The carnivores are all like that – wildcat, badger, fox, marten, stoat, weasel, polecat, otter – and with reason. The polecat you won't see at all in Scotland, that is if you're a purist. The real polecats are in Wales. Scotland has a lot of feral polecat ferrets, very like the real thing; and there are polecats on the island of Mull, which are the descendants of gone-wild ferrets, introduced long ago to prey on the teeming rabbits there. Many of these look the real thing. For all practical purposes, therefore, Scotland still has polecats. They look like polecats, act like polecats, and breed polecats that look and act like polecats. The argument becomes academic if one raids your henhouse: real or *ersatz*, the result is the same.

The pine marten, that handsome tree weasel with the yellow cravat, is no longer rare. It isn't common, but it isn't rare. Its strongholds are Wester Ross, but it is elusive and secretive, not often seen. For years it had to exist on the open hill, in the wildest places; it is still there, but it is also in the forests, where it belongs. It is an omnivorous creature, eating mice, voles, rabbits, fruit and insects.

Unfortunately, martens get caught in gins set for foxes. That is one of the curses of the gin; it takes anything that happens along, including you or me, your dog or mine. And martens, like other weasels, have no trap sense at all. They'd walk into a trap past a *No Entry* sign. A farmer I know caught two in a week. He didn't like it, and in the end he lifted the fox traps, which says a lot for him. There are others like him. You'll recognize them as soon as they open their mouths to speak.

Now we have the American mink, breeding wild, descended from ranch-bred escapees. You might see one alive occasionally, but mostly you'll see them dead, in traps. The colour of the feral mink is blackish brown, with a rich sheen, which is the standard. The fancy colours, that fetch such high prices on the market, have no survival value in the wild. The mink is trying hard to become a Scot, and likely to succeed. Probably we'll hardly notice it, certainly not in the way we notice the rat, the rabbit or the grey squirrel.

The small mustelids, stoat and weasel, are mousers, preying on voles and mice. The weasel wants 365 of them a year, and kills more; the stoat wants 500 and kills more. Then they have their families to rear, and that requires still more. Of course they take time off now and again to kill something else, like the weasel that killed thirteen canaries in an aviary. It must have been the only weasel in Europe to kill thirteen canaries that year, perhaps even that decade. These two should be protected by law; so should the otter and badger.

Big carnivores, bird or mammal, have a wide prey range and can take the big prey, even red deer calves. Wildcats probably take a few, weaklings or already dead. The fox takes more, including the stillborn. So does the eagle. But hinds don't stand idly by while their calves are taken. They are watchful mothers, who will gang up on fox or wildcat and drive it off, dabbing with their forehooves.

Scottish deer forests, which are still mostly treeless barrens, are usually sanctuaries for eagles; for wildcats too sometimes. Few stalkers molest eagles, unless maybe to the extent of taking a grouse from an eyrie for their own use, which is fair enough. I knew an eagle that killed seven fox cubs, and the stalker tailed them in the eyrie, and said Thank you auld *Chrysaetus*, and collected the bounty on them. A bird that can earn you a five pound note while doing the work of two men and three terriers is worth having around. But that isn't why stalkers leave them alone.

Deerstalkers, in the main, are less bloody-minded than low ground gamekeepers, although there are exceptions both ways, of course. During a discussion on the ecology of the eagle a keeper said to me:

'A' I ken aboot eagles is that they're nae good.' Later on he added: 'I aye shoot a hawk.'

There are still a lot like him; there are many who are not. It is refreshing to meet a stalker who, faced by an irate shepherd who had found two lambs in an eagle's eyrie, said:

'There wass two lambs in the nest; that iss a fact. You say the eagle killed them; that iss an opeenion. We shall see.'

Both lambs had, in fact, been taken dead, and had died of a disease called pulpy kidney. That stalker was an old dog who had learned new tricks of thought and caution. He said to me on another occasion; 'Man, wouldn't it be a hell of a thing now if we reduced the world to people?'

Top line deerstalkers are observant, shrewd men, used to long stints on the hill, in all weathers. Scotland has something like 200,000 red deer, and over 30,000 have to be killed each year to keep the herds at this number. The Scottish method of culling is to stalk the deer with a rifle, and as a system of management it compares more than favourably with any game management system anywhere in the world.

Stalking is, however, more than a system of management; it is a sport, and an expensive one. Deer are now important game animals, and it might cost you a hundred pounds to kill a stag in Scotland today.

If you go out with a stalker after the stag you'll have to work for it. He will stalk for you; but he can't walk for you, climb for you, get wet and dry again for you, lie in puddles for you, or creep and crawl for you. He does them all for himself, stalking ahead; you have to do your own, following on. If you're a foozler he may have to finish off a beast for you; if one goes away wounded he'll track it down for you, and go on until nightfall if he has to.

The stalker has the hardest of it, because the hinds are his work, and you don't shoot hinds in the days of bee-buzz and nodding harebells. Hinds are shot through the winter, often in deep snow, when conditions are more Arctic than Alpine. The deer ponies, the garrons, work hard too, but they are strong beasts able to carry a dead hind, or even two, over many trying, rough and broken miles. They have a long rest at grass after the season, at least until summer when they may be wanted for pony trekking, which is easy work for them.

Like the golfer who will replay you eighteen holes while driving you to town or standing in a bar, the stalker will sometimes recount every move in a memorable stalk, even when it was a failure or a fiasco. There was a stalker who was a skilled boot repairer as well as highly skilled in his own profession, and when he retired he was kept busy mending boots. He was called from retirement to help out during a busy stalking season, and went to the hill with a top-drawer type from the plush south. The man was a poor shot, and missed the same stag three times after three stalks. Like any bad tradesman he blamed everything but himself – the rifle, the wind, a blade of grass moving in front of the sight, the stag moving at the last moment. In the end, and furiously, he turned on the stalker:

'I don't know why the hell they sent me out with you!' he complained. 'You're only a damned shoemaker!'

'Yes, that iss so indeed,' the old man agreed. 'But, look you! I would not be making many shoes if I wass waiting around here for you to supply the leather!'

A much older, and long retired stalker asked me to visit him because he had much he wanted to talk about. We talked deer over a dram while his daughter Morag prepared what we call up here our right tea. And the old man launched on the story of a stag that took as long in the telling as the stalking. . . .

'Well, this stag Mister Stephen . . . he wass a fine ten-pointer, ass fine ass you effer saw . . . but he wass in a bad place, so we crawled a bitty, and waited . . . then hiss head went down, so we were able to crawl into a burn. . . . Now this stag . . .'

'Father!' Morag interrupted him. 'The tea iss on the table, and Mister Stephen will be hungry I'm shure.'

'Yes! Yes!' he said irritably. 'In a minute . . .'

'But father . . .!'

'Ass I wass saying, this stag . . .'

'Father!'

'Well, all right then!' and he rose up. 'Draw in a chair,' he said to me.

'Well, this stag . . .' he began as he sat down. He stopped, bowed his head and muttered 'We thank Thee O . . .' his voice died away. Then his head came up and the voice became strong again, 'Well, ass I wass saying, this stag . . .'

And he went on to finish the story of the stalk in which Grace had been a parenthesis.

Red grouse share the hill with the deer, the cocks staking out their territories on heathery flats and ridges, and holding them against their fellows. Thus the grouse regulates its own population density. The trick of good grouse management is good heather, not predator control. It is a trick many keepers have still to learn. The vermin board, with its fly-blown, eyeless and skeletal remains of harrier, falcon, owl, buzzard, stoat and wildcat, is as out of date and meaningless as the shrew-ash or ordeal by fire.

The frontier between hill and forest is the haunt of the black grouse and here the females, the greyhens, nest. The males, the blackcocks, resplendent in ebony and purple with swollen crimson combs, forgather on spring mornings, on traditional knolls or flats, to perform their ritual display – curduddich and rigadoon to the tune of their own croodles and cat-calls.

The big timber, the coniferous forest, is the territory of the caper-caillie. This fellow is a giant among grouse, the biggest in the world. The cock is a yard long, and can be mistaken for no other grouse.

And in the forest there's the small-antlered deer, the roe. It is small in stature as well as antler; a full grown buck will stand under thirty inches tall at the shoulder. You'll find roe on the open hill, sharing the spartan life of the red deer; but the forest is their true home, and there the master bucks hold their territories, defending them, jealously and sometimes savagely, against all competitors.

July and August are the active months for the roe – the time of the rut. Hark to the barking of the master then! *Bough-bough*! No dog-bark this, or yap of fox, but the chesty bass of a full roebuck with fires stoked for the rut. He is the master of the thickets, with ivory dirks for top tines.

Until a few years ago we did badly by our roe, snaring them, killing at random, driving them to ambushing shotguns. Now we have Close Season for them, and approved weapons. The Forestry Commission in Scotland, once the roe's arch enemy, was ahead of Government with reforms, and now manages its roe as well as they do in Germany.

Roe are found over most of Scotland and are still common in the centre and lowlands, among the pit bings and green connective tissue of the industrial belt. There, where the greyhound is one of the commonest fauna, and every second owner has the best dog ever to come out of Ireland, you are as likely to see a roe as a greyhound at first light or last.

The old mining villages, alive or dead, mark a unique frontier between the green country and the industrial filth, still rich in wildlife, where you'll find more poachers and off-beat skills to the acre than almost anywhere in Scotland.

The Wafer was a deadlier predator on hares and rabbits than any fox. In fact, they said of him that if he ever played tag with a fox the fox would always be het. He could catch rabbits in rough pasture, using only his stalking skill and his bare hands. He is the only man I know who could walk into a field and pick a hare from its seat. He used ferrets and nets, of course, but his liking and flair were for the off-beat, like snatching wild geese when they came to a stackyard to glean corn in the night.

He kept a Bedlington as well as greyhounds.

'See that Bedlin'ton?' he said once. 'She's a great ratter. She wid keep ye shovellin rats tae her, an wear oot you an the shovel!'

When the Bedlington had pups to a greyhound The Wafer kept two of them. One was smokey coloured and he called him Blue Jim. The dog grew to top greyhound size, and The Wafer called him a lurcher. But he was more like a Scotch deerhound, with a shaggy coat. Blue Jim was fast, a sure killer, and had a nose like a foxhound. The Wafer used him for hares.

In the old days the men used to train their greyhounds on a back-of-the-houses track, using an upturned bicycle with a big gear and a drum for winding in the dummy hare. Two men turned hard at the pedals and the dogs chased the lure. One day Blue Jim

Calton Hill, Edinburgh, showing (l to r) the Observatory; 'Edinburgh's Folly', an unfinished monument to Wellington's Peninsular Campaign modelled on the Parthenon; and the Nelson Monument. It affords a marvellous view of Edinburgh.

broke away after them, caught them, and was at the bicycle with yards to spare.

'Jesus!' The Wafer moaned. 'He's just bate some o' the best dugs oot o' Ireland an I canny race him at a track because he's hairier than an ape.'

'Shave him!' I said in jest.

He did. With clippers and razor he cut Blue Jim to greyhound trim and entered him at the flapping tracks. He won race after race, west and east, and broke the track record in one place. Then the bristles began to show and he was warned off.

'Imagine!' The Wafer fumed. 'A' the big men feart o' a bliddy mongrel!'

Blue Jim had other accomplishments. He would go home when sent, even from miles away. That helped The Wafer to talk his way out of one or two situations when caught poaching hares in daylight. With the dog on the way home and the hares hidden he was the injured innocent when accosted. Situations like that appealed to him.

But the day he remembers best is the day he became respectable. He was poaching pheasants in daylight, using a gun, which is something good poachers don't normally do. But that day he had the urge to live dangerously. Pheasants were coming thick over the tall boundary hedge and The Wafer was making every cartridge count, being deadly with rifle or twelvebore. Suddenly a voice hailed him from the other side of the hedge and The Wafer, after a momentary thought of running, decided to brass-neck it as he called it.

A man in tweeds appeared at a gap in the hedge, followed by a well-dressed woman and two Labrador retrievers. Man and woman were carrying what The Wafer called expensive artillery engraved like paper money.

'You seem to be doing all right on that side,' the man said. 'I'm the new shooting tenant here, and we seem to be doing everything wrong way round. All our birds seem to be flying to you. I was wondering . . .'

'Aye!' said The Wafer, monosyllably unhelpful.

'Well, you probably know the ground . . . and I was wondering . . . if you might not care to join us. . . . I'd appreciate it.'

'I ken the grun fine,' The Wafer agreed. 'But I hinny much time . . . For a wee while maybe. . . .' He had all the time till next morning.

65

So he shot with them, and he did well, and they did better because he let them, and for the one and only time in his life he had two quality, no-slip retrievers carrying for him. Then he saw a figure on a bicycle, far along the moor road, and knew it was time to go. The keeper would not appreciate the situation. . . .

'Look!' he said suddenly. 'I'll hae tae go. I've stayed too long already. . . .'

'Oh! Must you? Well, thank you. . . .'

The Wafer was chugging away in his van before the keeper arrived out of breath and almost out of adjectives.

But, as The Wafer often said later:

'There wis'ny much he could hae done onyway. Efter a', I was an invited guest!'

The Look of the Place: Architecture

George Scott-Moncrieff

Amongst my earliest post-natal impressions must have been the sight of the grey ashlar walls of Edinburgh New Town houses. Not the best of the New Town admittedly, for I was born and first took the air in my pram in the Merchiston district, a late, Victorian extension to the City, built when bow windows and plate glass had somewhat marred the primal New Town glories. Nevertheless it was a setting of architectural decency. The stone was fine, the masonry excellent, and the interiors of the houses too maintained the great standard of craftsmanship that persisted in Edinburgh long after tradesmen further south had found that shoddy work need not show up until after a house was safely sold. The panelling of door and wainscot was well designed and made of seasoned wood; plasterwork was good.

Some years later the grandmother in whose house I had been born moved to Randolph Cliff, an earlier and more authentic element of the New Town, part of the Moray Estate development designed by Gillespie Graham which included Ainslie Place and Moray Place. I spent a year or so here, walking with my brother through the stone-built and stone-cobbled streets to school in Coates Gardens. The Dean Gardens, splendidly dominated by Telford's great viaduct, were our playground as they had been for both my mother and my grandmother, while from Randolph Cliff itself there was a superb view of houses tree-embowered along the Water of Leith, seawards to the Firth. The view was best seen from the roof, looking down the dizzy depths of the cliff, and here I often went since it was easily accessible from the parapet in front of the top-floor windows.

But this was some years later. During my earliest months we went to live in Galloway: different houses, a different world. Here hills and sea-coast came close, with some fine woodland, little burns, a sleepy river then still navigable, with rotting hulks along its banks. The houses that went with this landscape were diminutive and rustic. Even when they did congregate together in small townships they were quite different from the city houses. I seem to remember people being rather snooty in my youth about the homespun Galloway townships dating from the late eighteenth century, their architecture hardly changing for the next hundred years, but by now their good proportions, their close-knit rubble masonry, often in Galloway brightly painted, are more justly appreciated. We have learnt better through seeing worse, much worse, in the council-built stark monotony and the vulgarian bungalows that have spread across once-green fields – to say nothing of the high-rise horrors that seem to claim that their inmates can be categorized like index cards.

We lived first in a little low cottage, which we shared with a friendly ghost. Then in another cottage by the sea. And then in a grey granite eighteenth-century house built by the Rattray family, one of whom had founded Rattray's Horse in defence of the British Raj in India. Small, handsome and gentlemanly it survives, a modest mansion set on the outskirts of a modest township. At four years old and after the cottages it seemed huge to me, but every time I see it now I am surprised to find it very small indeed, yet none the less imposing.

When I was three we made a sortie to the home of relatives in Fife, and here I remember a fine old Fifer of a house, its walls harled and gnarled, standing behind a sea-spoilt herbaceous border. I also remember very distinctly a staircase, probably a newel stair but certainly a curving one that went up out of sight, and I felt the fine mystery of a stair that took its passengers swiftly out of one's vision, or brought them abruptly into it.

After Galloway we went to the south of England, to a brick-built area, not a pretty brick, yellow-grey; and brick seemed to me very inferior to stone. But the church tower, adjacent to our rectory, was of mediaeval stonework, and the body of the church, although of brick, was pleasing both within and without. Only long afterwards did I find out that its architect was the Scot, James Gibb, better known in the anglicized form Gibbs since as a Papist he had to leave his native Aberdeen – where however he built his one work in Scotland, the West Kirk of St Nicholas. Gibb trained in Rome. He built St Martin-in-the-Fields and is the real progenitor of the dominant pre-Gothic Revival Anglican church style in both England and America.

But there were many visits to Scotland both to Edinburgh and to Galloway where I used to stay with cousins in a big Victorian mock-baronial house, grand in a pompous way: massive oak balusters and splendid early plumbing, wide-seated loos with gear-lever plugs and huge baths hewn out of solid stone. This house had rather unfortunately replaced a nice little eighteenth-century mansion, and has since had to be scaled down again to meet the needs of today.

It was of course many years later before I began as it were to codify my enjoyment of architecture by learning something of its how and why. I learnt much through that fine architect and close friend, Ian Lindsay. He in his turn, along with many of his generation, had gained the lore to support an early enthusiasm at Cambridge from a fellow Scot, Mansfield Forbes, a man of infectious knowledge whom I was never fortunate enough to meet. Another mentor was an architect of rare taste, Reginald Fairlie, who had trained under Sir Robert Lorimer. A third was James Richardson, HM Inspector of Ancient Monuments in Scotland, a man of vast knowledge if rather too cantankerous and provocative for his own good or to be of as much inspiration as he might have been. All are gone now, but in writings I have done I hope I may have passed on some of their enthusiasm and a little of their knowledge, even though my architectural status is only that of an honorary associate of the Royal Institute of Architects in Scotland. However, as Clough Williams-Ellis has expressed it, flair and passion are the essentials and I hope I possess something of these.

I have lived in different parts of Scotland and in different types of houses, besides visiting many more. At one time I could claim to be tenant both of a but and ben in the Hebrides and of a slum tenement in the Old Town of Edinburgh. There is much I have liked and enjoyed. I see architecture, while supra-national, as always at its best conforming to national tastes, fancies, environments, and, not least, characteristics, and it is these individual glosses put upon the worldwide need for shelter that have created a major source for our delight and culture.

It is sad of course that so much of Scotland's mediaeval ecclesiastical architecture should have suffered destruction, as it did from English raids, a too violent and iconoclastic Reformation, and subsequent neglect, all due to certain historical unhappinesses. However there are some memorable buildings left to us. There is the superb Romanesque nave of Kirkwall Cathedral, a canyon of

69

red rounded pillars and arches, and in Dunfermline some element of the same stony pathway to God survives (the late Sir Frank Mears, that fine architect and wise town-planner, used to say that the composition of palace and abbey at Dunfermline must once have been comparable to anything of its kind in Europe). Glasgow Cathedral is another largely intact and splendid mediaeval work, with a notably fine undercroft. Aberdeen also has preserved its early cathedral, and there are fine churches of the period at Leuchars in Fife, Dalmeny in West Lothian, at Stirling, Paisley, at Haddington (rather defaced), Perth and a few other places.

Scotland began developing its own distinctive curvilinear window tracery, a poorer man's substitute for English Perpendicular, but none the worse – arguably even the better – for that. Yet even before the Reformation we find in the little collegiate churches a move towards a less ornate architecture: as may be seen, for example, at Innerpeffray's long low kirk with its square-headed windows anticipating many of the best of the early Presbyterian kirks.

These little country churches have too often been dismissed as plain. In fact the best of them are thoroughly and righteously plain, justifying themselves by apt proportions and douce decency. They imply too a focal spiritual point, one not dependent merely upon decoration, for the little communities grouped around them in glen and dale, on hillside or burn bank. There has been too much denigration of the shortcomings of that aspect of our lives. Let us take warning from a brilliant essay by the greatest of living novelists, Alexander Solzhenitsyn. Solzhenitsyn tells of the reassuring effect on travels through the Russian countryside of small churches with belfries that 'greet each other from distant, unseen villages', linking community to community by way of something above and beyond the limitations of each. But now when you come to these little churches, he laments, you find them half ruinous, desecrated, with obscenities scrawled over the icons, turned into stores, workshops, or clubs for propaganda meetings: 'We will Achieve High Yields of Milk', as though people could claim no higher destiny than cows.

'People', Solzhenitsyn reflects, 'have always been selfish and often evil. But the angelus used to toll and its echo would float over village, field and wood. It reminded men that he must abandon his trivial earthly cares and give up one hour of his thoughts to life eternal.'

If our Presbyterian village churches are more austere than their Russian counterparts (although in Fife particularly they were often dignified with fine towers), they stood for the same values, and, if they have not suffered so much nor from so great a decline in those values at national level, it is sad to see some of them today degraded to baser uses.

Oddly enough, of greater urban churches built in early post-Reformation days, only one stands out as making an original, promising contribution to an architecture of Presbyterian worship. This is the splendid square-on-plan kirk at Burntisland, its seating centred upon the pulpit set against one central pillar. It unfortunately seems to have inspired no imitators, and the next relatively elaborate phase follows more than a century later with kirks in a cool classical style, often identified by graceful steeples, although these sometimes crowned town halls. The worst fault of the classical churches was that, inspired by an increase of wealth and a flush of building enthusiasm, some of them replaced finer mediaeval churches. Even more misplaced was the replacing or refacing of mediaeval churches with pseudo-mediaeval masonry.

I used to be very dismissive of the Gothic Revival. After all, it was pastiche, an imitation, a work of calculation rather than of inspiration. But if because of that it could never achieve true greatness, the exaltation of art, I have come to gain greater respect and affection for it. Perhaps the increment of years, both by the churches and by me, have modified both masonry and judgment. Anyway I can now enjoy them even though they are inferior to what they too often replaced, perhaps reflecting in their imitativeness man's increased tendency to selfconsciousness. St John's episcopal church in Princes Street, Edinburgh, by the powerful nineteenth-century architect William Burn is a good example. More rustic and more original are such little early nineteenth-century kirks as that of Kilmorich at Cairndow in Argyllshire, in which a certain ignorance of correct forms allowed for a freedom from inhibition.

The Baronial Revival likewise I once regarded with strong intolerance. Again, its products often replaced or spoilt something much better. But now, although some examples must remain forever ludicrous, and only enjoyable in mirth, I find myself impressed by others: particularly perhaps by the fine masonry and something of the assurance that made them possible and leaves its mark upon vainglorious tower and bogus castellation. Mostly, of course, the Revivalists overstressed particular features in ways that cannot have been so apparent at the time; such details as those over-emphatically corbelled turrets that now stick out like sore thumbs. It is interesting that experts on antiques say that a forgery of some piece of furniture can be so perfectly executed as to deceive every-one at the time, but will be quite perceptible as a forgery fifty years later, because at any given period some aspect of the original artefact will be as it were fashionable and therefore subject to unconscious overstressing. This surely applies to architectural pastiche.

Yet the original Scottish baronial can itself be so beautiful that it is difficult not to feel somewhat intolerant of the imitation. Take for example the great Aberdeenshire castle of Craigievar, which Sir Robert Matthew has described as almost more sculpted than built, so sweetly do its austere lower storeys burst into flower with featly corbelled turrets, lead, slate, lum and balustrade. The same sculpted effect is felt within, climbing the winding stairs, or even in the great hall with its pendant plasterwork. Crathes, Midmar and Castle Fraser are other resplendent Aberdeenshire examples. At Midmar the later additions are notable in that they in no way detract from the original splendour but enhance it, only setting it on a wider base. Only lesser in size are the neigh-bouring castles of Barra and Auchanachy, the latter as good an example – on its very modest scale – as Midmar of a building added to at different periods, always harmoniously, achieving a new perfection. At Drum an ancient, bald square tower dating from the days of Robert the Bruce has been most happily added to nearly four centuries later with a wing fully defensible aesthetically if not militarily.

Although the fullest enriching of our baronial architecture is to be seen in Aberdeenshire, many castles equally fine in their own way are scattered far and wide through most of the country. Fife and Ayrshire, one to the east, one to the west, are both particularly rich in examples. At Kellie in Fife three distinct towers are linked by a main block which contains a magnificent hall, and the whole range, looking south seawards has the peculiar sweetness of old masonry delicately detailed. Scotstarvit Tower, of an early type although late in date, is built of hewn honey-coloured stone, a good home with its garret study for the learned Sir John Scot of Scotstarvit (who wrote *The Staggering State of*

Scottish Statesmen, a title that might well be applied to any study of our present lot). Aldie on its hillside is a lovely little tower-house, harled and whitewashed, lovingly restored in recent years. Historic Rossend Castle on its fine site overlooking the sea has been less fortunate, falling into the hands of an undiscriminating local authority. Earlshall was an early and fine restoration by Sir Robert Lorimer.

In Ayrshire old Rowallan Castle with its twin towers flanking the entrance is a very happy example of the small made to loom large by aptness of proportion. Killochan, Kelburne and Cassillis are more massive. Dean is a double castle, two separate towers, in that respect like the smaller Mochrum in neighbouring Galloway. Amisfield in Dumfriesshire is as fine an example as any of a Scottish tower house, its bald, thrawn, defensive lower storeys carried out with a real ecstacy of line to provide more genial accommodation above. Also in Dumfriesshire, Fourmerkland and Isle are two of those baby-size castles, which are perhaps unique to Scotland, endowing cottage accommodation with all the panache of castledom. Another is Craigcaffie in Wigtownshire, and, most perfect of all, far north in Moray, Coxton Tower is the very quintessence on the minutest scale of the Scottish castellated tradition. It was a tradition quite distinct from that of England, and developing in its own way from its French origins.

If the Scottish castle never achieved the same rich magnificence of its French compeer, since Scotland was a relatively poor country, it likewise avoided the decadence of the over-ornate (until of course Baronial Revival days, when indeed French models were often copied). It gave place quite abruptly to the classical-style mansion. Sir William Bruce (1630–1710) was an architect of the first rank. Kinross House which he built for himself on the shore of Loch Leven is his masterpiece, a demonstration of perfection derived out of formality in which the use of academically correct detailing when handled with something of genius can be as surprising in its overall effect as any more apparent originality. Too few of Bruce's houses remain to us. He was responsible for the present form of the Palace of Holyroodhouse, and, near Edinburgh, both Prestonfield and Auchendinny are architectural gems of his devising (both actually incorporating some elements of earlier houses). Two of the men who worked with him achieved distinction themselves. One of them, James Smith, has only recently been accorded the credit he deserves.

James Smith is now considered to have been principally responsible for the Duke of Queensberry's palatial home of Drumlanrig, aptly described by Mr John Dunbar as 'a unique alliance of the Castellated and Renaissance styles in which Scottish Baronial is unexpectedly translated into Baroque'. He was also responsible for adding the courtyard that so delightfully sets off the mediaeval towers of Traquair. Better known amongst Bruce's successors is William Adam, architect of many public and private buildings in different parts of Scotland. The Haddington town hall is his, somewhat changed, and that at Sanquhar. Dundee had a grand one, known as the Pillars, demolished in 1931 after the superb mediaeval heart of Dundee was eliminated and replaced at a time of quite outstanding architectural banality. William Adam (whose actual association with Bruce is putative) continued Bruce's great house of Hopetoun, well enough if not quite to the Bruce standard. He designed grandiose Duff House at Banff, and, along with the laird, Sir John Clerk, Mavisbank in Midlothian which set the fashion for the Scottish version of the Palladian villa.

William Adam's sons succeeded in their father's profession, finally completing Hopetoun, their work more subtle than his. Robert is the most famous of them, working largely in England but responsible for the University, the Register House, and the north side of Charlotte Square in Edinburgh, besides several country mansions. His elegant plasterwork, notably well exemplified at Culzean and Mellerstain, established, as did his furniture, the tradition that is still known by his name. There is no room here to mention the names of some deserving contemporaries and near-contemporaries of the Adam family; suffice to say it was a healthy period architecturally.

The once-renowned beauties of mediaeval Glasgow being practically steamrollered out of existence during that city's impetuous expansion at the close of the eighteenth and the beginning of the nineteenth centuries, it was left to Victorian architects to bring distinction again to the spreading streets. Greek Thomson was the best of the considerable band who gave Glasgow its mid-Victorian heritage. Then, at the very end of the century, came the brief meteoric career of Charles Rennie Mackintosh. His finest memorial, built just after the turn of the century, is the Glasgow School of Art. I have heard a distinguished art historian term it the last great building to be built in Britain. Free and original as it is, I have always been fascinated by its strong links with the old Scots tower house, not this time by way of pastiche but as an inspiration for part of its elevations.

I see I have said too little about our lesser, more rustic, 'vernacular' architecture. Seen where it survives at its best, in the old East Coast burghs, even in humble croft houses, it is delightful. But it is in such fields as these that our own generation shows up particularly badly: due largely in the domestic field to pettifogging bureaucratic regulations, while commerce, with its eye to fashion and the quick kill maintains a dull level of vulgarity in the shop-fronts that compose our streets. We still have good architects, but, particularly in the fields of maximum building, they are generally given too little opportunity.

The Long Story - To Queen Victoria

Sir Iain Moncreiffe of that Ilk, Bart.

Wherever they go abroad, Scotsmen unite. They form Caledonian Societies and Clan Associations. They celebrate St Andrew's Night and Burns 'Nicht'. They back each other up. They have a communal sense and a zest for money, coupled with inventive intelligence and international fluidity, which is rivalled only by the Jews, with whom they have much in common. Like the Jews, too, they are a warlike people, and even their pacifists are militant. Indeed, the Scots pretend that the Stone of Scone, literally their royal family seat, was originally Jacob's Pillow. Many of them are aware that their present Queen is the Chief of Chiefs, head of the whole family of Scots throughout the world, and that Her Majesty's forefathers were already being inaugurated on that Stone in the Dark Ages.

Interested foreigners too have heard perhaps of such architects as Robert Adam and Charles Cameron (who worked mostly in Russia), or artists like Raeburn and Allan Ramsay, of lyric poets like Burns, of writers like Sir Walter Scott and Robert Louis Stevenson and Barrie the creator of Peter Pan, of inventors like 'tinkle' Bell (to coin an irresistibly crashing pun) who devised the telephone, brilliant scientists like Fleming who discovered penicillin, devoted missionaries like St Patrick and Livingstone, great proconsuls like the Dalhousies and Elgins who governed Canada and India, soldiers like Haig who defeated the mightiest war-machine in the then world, philosophers like Hume and John Stuart Mill, Boswell the biographer, Carlyle the historian, Adam Smith the economist, Lister the pioneer of antiseptics, Sir James Simpson the innovator of chloroform for anaesthetics, James Watt the inventor of the modern steam engine, modernizing financiers like William Paterson who founded the Bank of England, and above all, of our world-spanning engineers, and the shipbuilders of the Clyde. Even the Man in the Moon (Armstrong the astronaut) is of Scottish extraction. They will also know of whisky, though not perhaps that it's simply the Gaelic word for 'water', and that the original true name is *usquebae*, meaning the 'water of life': aquavit.

But however much they get together abroad, at home the Scots have always been too independent-minded ever to be united. They were unable to unite even against the English who conquered them by force under Edward I and under Cromwell, by guile in the reign of Queen Anne, and by force again forty years later. Nor are they united today on any subject except perhaps Rabbie Burns. For Scotsmen tend to think for themselves, and if everybody thought alike we might just as well live in an ant-heap run by computers. The snag is that, having thought for themselves, they tend to carry things to their logical conclusion *ad absurdum*: so that they tend to be pretty intolerant of those who disagree with them.

Now, many people seem to think that Scotland was forged out of two conflicting but ancient nations: the Gaels of the Highlands and the Angles of the Lowlands. This is a myth. The rough division between Highlanders and Lowlanders didn't begin before the second half of the 1300s, and even then it was linguistic and cultural, but not at all racial.

The nuclear power around which Scotland snowballed was the High Kingdom of the Picts, centred near Perth. Whether or not the name Pict was originally derived from some name they gave themselves, the *Picti* were Painted Men to the Romans. For they were tattooed in blue with marks that indicated their personal rank.

In pagan times, the Pictish ladies were probably both exogamous and polyandrous. That is, it would be taboo to mate with anyone who belonged to their own clan (in the direct female line), but they could have several paramours or husbands from outside it. In the third century AD the Pictish lady Argentocoxa retorted to the Roman empress Julia: 'We satisfy the necessities of nature in a more commendable manner than you Romans, for whereas you seek secrecy to prostitute yourselves to the vilest of men, we appear in the face of the world enjoying the society of the best'. Pictish men therefore belonged to their mother's and not their father's kin.

Although their aristocracy spoke a Celtic language akin to Gaulish in historical times, they had almost certainly interbred with the Bronze Age population whose language (like that of the Basques) was not Indo-European at all, and both languages seem to have existed side by side, and to some extent to have inter-mingled.

South of the Clyde were Ancient Britons speaking Welsh. Their kings descended from Old King Coel: still remembered as 'a merry old soul'. To the area between Carlisle and Edinburgh belongs the origin of the Arthurian legend; and the original of Shakespeare's Cymbeline reigned here. They warred with invading Angles who conquered Lothian, south of the Forth.

North of the Clyde were the Scots of Argyll, originally Gaelic-speaking settlers from Ireland. Their king came over in person in the fifth century and was forefather of our present Queen: the oldest continuing dynasty in Christendom. A later Scottish king, who was also of Pictish royal blood in the female line, united the Picts and Scots.

By inter-marriage with the Britons' royal family, they also united the area south of Clyde to their realm. But all the western islands belonged to the Northmen of Norway until 1266, when all modern Scotland except Orkney was brought together under one king who was descended from the inter-married royal blood of all its different peoples.

By invitation, a number of Normans and Bretons, Flemings and Franks, also settled in Scotland during the 1100s. They made a considerable impact on our history, as such names as Bruce and Stewart, Douglas and Murray, sufficiently attest.

The progress towards union in the north of Britain should logically have led gradually to union with the south of Britain. The folk of former Pictland, Argyll, the Hebrides, Galloway, Strathclyde, and the Lothians – the Normans and Flemings, Bretons and Franks too – had nothing in common but their King: called for short the King of Scots. Yet the man who welded them all together to form a single nation was the very man who had most to lose by it: Edward I, King of England, 'Hammer of the Scots', who ham-mered them into a sword against himself.

The Celtic idea of high-kingship certainly included a vague hangover from Roman times that the King of England was Emperor of Britain. But high-kings were not supposed to inter-vene in the internal affairs of under-kingdoms. Edward I insisted on doing just this. War followed in 1296. The English conquered Scotland. But the proud Scots smouldered.

The leaders of the country had been defeated. Their children were hostages. The Douglas chief lay dying in an English jail. There was no real reason, since Scotland was so new a country anyway, why they shouldn't have accepted union with England, where many of them had estates already, just as the Hebrides had accepted union with Scotland only thirty years before. But they wouldn't. They encouraged their people to mob up on the English, with whom they themselves dissimulated until they were ready to strike.

The first Rising took place within a year. It was led by a brilliant soldier, young Sir Andrew of Murray, heir to one of the greatest and richest Baronies in the realm, who defeated the English at Stirling Bridge by letting half of them get over the bridge and then cutting it off behind them. But he was mortally wounded. His junior colleague, a laird's son called Sir William Wallace (knighted during the campaign by a Scottish earl who was very possibly the famous Robert Bruce), continued the struggle in such a way as to be immortalized as one of our national heroes.

Although he was a magnificent guerrilla leader, Wallace was defeated when he was lured into a pitched battle. Eventually he was captured and taken to London. There he was hanged stark naked in public, cut down choking but still alive, had his private parts cut off and was disembowelled and saw his own entrails burnt in front of him: next his arms and legs were hacked off, and only then was he finally beheaded.

The greatest and most patriotic Scottish family at the time was that of Cummin, a Norman nickname after the herb that helps to flavour *kümmel*. They had claims to the throne. Their rival was Robert Bruce, whose grandfather had been named provisional heir by his cousin King Alexander II. When the time came, however, the Bruce slew the Red Cummin in the precincts of a church, in an uncharacteristic fit of temper which he regretted all his life; indeed, he got some nervous skin disease which he believed to be leprosy as a result. But this remarkable man could bide his time no more. The resistance movement the Scottish nobles had been quietly organizing (1296–1306) was forced into the open. It was a bit too soon, but they made it in the end. The English were driven out of Scotland. Our present Queen has unveiled on the decisive battlefield of Bannockburn an equestrian statue of her mighty ancestor King Robert Bruce.

Looking back, it's easy to say that it was 'typically Scots' that some Scotsmen had sided with the English, especially when support in some blood-feud was involved. This is a half-truth. The MacDougall chief certainly fought for England against Bruce, for example. But why not? His father had been a Norwegian sea-king, forced to accede to the mainland of Scotland after six hundred years of independence – as long as from 1372 to now. If this union was beneficial, he may reasonably have thought union with the whole mainland of Britain even more beneficial. More-over, he was the Red Cummin's uncle, and Bruce had slain his nephew.

But by 1320, the English had unintentionally created a single nation out of the Scottish mainland, and a nation that was to regard them for several centuries as the Auld Enemy – a nation that was traditionally to ally itself with France to contain England in a military sandwich. It was in 1320 that the nobles of Scotland assembled at Arbroath and sent to the Pope their famous Declaration of Scottish Independence: 'for so long as an hundred remain alive we are minded never a whit to bow beneath the yoke of English dominion. It is not for glory, riches or honours that we fight: it is for liberty alone, the liberty which no good man relinquishes but with his life'.

The Wars of Independence went on intermittently until the 1500s, causing much misery. King David Bruce was captured by the English in 1346 but was wily enough to get liberated by making extravagant promises of what he would do if his Parliament consented, well knowing they would not. He was succeeded by his nephew, the Great Steward of Scotland, first of the kings to be called Stewart.

Between 1437 and 1649 the Stewart kings suffered almost as much as though the old pagan Gaels' fashion of king-slaying still went on. James I was assassinated; James II killed by the accidental bursting of a cannon; James III was murdered trying to put down a rebellion of the Douglases and Homes about an Inland Revenue dispute; James IV was killed fighting the English at the battle of Flodden; Mary Queen of Scots and Charles I were beheaded.

In 1424 James I had returned from years of imprisonment in England, determined to centralize the government on the English model. But the English had been conquered by their king in 1066. The Scots had never been conquered by their king: they regarded him rather as the Chief of Chiefs, head of the whole national

Top: *Sheep from the islands being 'unloaded' from a boat at Oban (Argyll).*
Bottom: *A lobster fisherman at Latheronwheel, Caithness.*

family. That is why he was not normally styled King of Scotland, but King of Scots wherever they were. So James I was slain as a would-be tyrant who had placed his own judgment above the law. It seems odd that the Scots barons are often blamed for forcibly maintaining some of the rights that the English barons are praised for wresting from their King in Magna Carta.

The local magnates and chiefs were regarded as heads of branches of this national family. Their sons and daughters tended to settle and marry within their own districts. So, through constant local inter-marriage they came to be related, however remotely, to most of their following who, being proud of it, were loyal to them but not in the least servile. Being all inter-bred, and classless, there was no syphoning off of innate intelligence into limited groups. Scotsmen of all walks of life were equally well-bred and equally canny: often also, equally cantankerous – but loyal to their ain folk. The Lowlands, contrary to popular belief, were just as clannish in this sense as the Highlands.

Their chiefs (a Norman-French word) were all intensely particularist, in that they regarded their own territories as little semi-independent states whose interests, and thus those of their local folk, it was their duty to advance. Skilled in what is called diplomacy when practised by international politicians, and treachery when practised by earls or chieftains, they were as martial as their people: and well aware that war is an extension of diplomacy.

So the districts or clannish names were often at war with one another. Atholl fought Argyll, Caithness fought Sutherland, Douglas fought Hamilton, Lindsay fought Ogilvy, MacLeod fought Fraser. In a country without moveable and divisible capital, land was the asset needed by each multiplying and expanding group: and as the land itself didn't expand at all, it was often beset by rival claims. But at least they all knew their enemy and why they were fighting; and the casualties were nothing compared with those in the almost meaninglessly remote wars brought about by the existence of the vast agglomerate States of today.

Moreover, as the lairds had no hired men-at-arms, nor could they have afforded them, they relied for protection on a mutual respect between themselves and their own people. It was a two-way relationship. Indeed, it's notable that not only was Scotland perhaps the first country in the world to free its serfs but also that, unlike England and most other European countries, we never had

81

Loch Maree (Ross and Cromarty), surrounded on all sides by mountains, is famous for its sea-trout fishing.

a peasants' revolt. So startling was it for local folk not to get on with their laird, that it's still remembered that 'the bad Lord Soulis' was boiled to death by his own staff, perhaps in the great cauldron found buried on the Nine Stane Rig near his Castle of Hermitage. The monkish Chronicle of Melrose has a terse entry for 1207: 'Randolph de Soulis was slain in his house by his own domestics'. There seems to have been something tasty about such soup, as in about 1420 several people invoked their special sanctuary privileges as kin to the premier Clan Macduff after liquidating an unpopular Sheriff of the Mearns. They had made soup of him and taken a spoonful each.

Before 1400 Scotland had divided fairly sharply into the Highlands of the North and West, and the Lowlands of the South and East – a diagonal line across the country – although there was an intermediary buffer-land known as the Brae Country, and a number of names like Fraser or Stewart held lands on both sides of the Highland Line. In the Highlands and Western Isles, the Norse language died out in favour of Gaelic. In the Lowlands, Welsh and Gaelic died out in favour of a guttural version of north-country English called 'Scots'. The two areas, though racially much intermingled, grew culturally apart. But most of the Highlands long formed an almost separate realm under Macdonald.

The Gaelic-speaking mainland of the southern and eastern Highlands remained feudalized and (when it didn't conflict with local interests) reasonably loyal to the State.

Macdonald, chief of one of the great dynastic houses sprung from the old Kings of the Isles, established a hegemony over the whole Hebrides during the 1300s, and took the style of Lord of the Isles. In the 1400s he doubled his power by inheriting the Earldom of Ross on the mainland, then including much of Inverness-shire as well. For a while it could reasonably have been said that Scotland was divided into two countries: the more especially as Scots Law did not run in Macdonald's island territories. He did not hesitate to make treaties with the King of England against the King of Scots, conducting himself as though a sovereign prince.

In 1475 the Scottish government seized the earldom of Ross, and followed this up in 1494 by the annexation of the whole Lordship of the Isles. The Macdonalds carried on a resistance movement for half a century. It was the unnecessary end of a fine Gaelic civilization.

This bossy action by the gentlemen in Edinburgh who knew best led as so often to untold misery. They had overthrown the administrative machinery that had kept quite as much order in the greater part of Scottish Gaeldom as they themselves had been able to keep among their fellow Lowlanders. But they had no means of filling the power vacuum so created. Anarchy was the result. The government did worse than fail to govern. It kept stirring the chaos quite deliberately by giving charters of the same lands to two different contestants, by giving Letters of Fire & Sword to some chief to invade a recalcitrant neighbour's lands, and by suddenly calling for old charters they knew well to have been lost. It was the old Roman policy of 'divide and rule' with the division but without the rule.

The English close their Middle Ages with the battle of Bosworth in 1485. Ours closed with the battle of Flodden in 1513, when James IV and the 'Flowers of the Forest were a' wede awa' (as the sixteenth-century lute tune laments our loss). It's now adapted as a lament played on the pipes at Scottish funerals.

There was hardly a family in Scotland that had not lost somebody at Flodden. The orphans grew up to become perhaps the wildest generation in all our fiery history. In times of disaster, Scots were reminded that 'there was mair tynt at Flodden': there was more lost at Flodden. Mediaeval chivalry was dead.

The next battle between us and the English was at Solway Moss, shortly before the birth of James IV's granddaughter Mary Queen of Scots and her own father's death. Mary Stewart is perhaps our only Sovereign, apart from her nearest Protestant descendant our present Queen, to be generally known throughout the civilized world today.

The obvious thing would have been to unite federally the Crowns in Britain by marrying the infant Queen to the English boy-king Edward VI. With supreme tact, the English set about a 'Rough Wooing'. The Lord Protector of England invaded Scotland, defeated the Scots at Pinkie and then set about ravaging the countryside: burning towns, towers and abbeys, also raping and slaying wherever his men went. For some reason which the English will never understand, the Scots seem to have resented this.

The Queen herself was packed off to France to be married in due course to the Dauphin, whereupon they were proclaimed Francis and Mary, King and Queen of Scots. An Act of Parliament was passed naturalizing all Frenchmen, and so all French citizens had dual nationality in Scotland until comparatively modern times. Her husband died soon after becoming King Francis II of France: and the widowed Queen returned to Scotland.

Mary Queen of Scots' whole career in Scotland lasted less than seven years. She landed at the age of eighteen, and was only twenty-five when she fled abroad from her terrifying subjects, never to return.

Her difficulties arose from her heredity and upbringing. Her mother was a Guise, of the family seeking to bring France under their control. Her paternal grandmother was a Tudor; sister of King Henry VIII who used Cardinal Wolsey, the 'butcher's dog' who depended entirely on him, to bring down the powerful nobles and centralize the administration of England. This politically-minded girl in her teens set out to try and do the same in Scotland.

But she wanted at the same time to consolidate her claim to succeed to the throne of England. So she married her cousin Henry Stuart, styled Lord Darnley, as they shared the same Tudor grandmother. Before the marriage he was created Duke of Albany and then proclaimed King Consort. Thereafter all public actions were performed in the name of 'Henry and Mary, King and Queen of Scots': even with their two heads on the coins. So it's both ridiculous and misleading, as historians will, to go on referring to King Henry as 'Darnley'. But she refused him the Crown Matrimonial, which would have made him more than king consort and enabled him to go on reigning after her death instead of just becoming a sort of king dowager.

Meanwhile, she set about her schemes for centralization. She had no standing army, and could only call out some nobles to serve her against another. However, she set-to to find herself a Wolsey type, dependent only upon her favour. She found him in an ugly thirty-year-old Italian musician called David Rizzio, certainly no paramour of hers, who became her political *eminence grise*.

Soon he was the most powerful government minister in Scotland, in fact though not in name, and she was thinking of supplementing him by forming a Royal Body Guard of Italian mercenary gentlemen like the Scottish Archers she knew were the 'strong right arm' of the Kings of France. She encouraged Rizzio to swagger haughtily towards the Scots magnates, his equipage and train surpassing that of the King Consort himself. One is reminded of Wolsey's palace at Hampton Court. The King Consort was not pleased at this, nor at being excluded from political decisions.

The other Scots also weren't going to stand any nonsense of that sort. They had no more intention of being conquered by their Sovereign in the English manner now than at any other time in their history. The great clannish territories still felt quite competent to administer their own affairs, and so did those lairds who were now much stronger as a result of land acquired at the recent Reformation.

So, one cold evening in March, the door connecting the Queen's bedroom with her private stair to the King Consort's bedroom below, suddenly burst open. Lord Ruthven stood there in black armour, ghostly pale, as he had risen from a sick-bed. Behind him were other nobles and many armed lairds. They had come to kill Rizzio, who was one of the Queen's supper party in the tiny adjoining room. They dragged him out into the Presence Chamber and stabbed him to death. As a final gesture, they left King Henry's dagger stuck in his corpse.

The Queen was pregnant by her husband, yet by letting the assassins gain access through his private apartments, he had betrayed her in a matter of the highest politics. In those days, there was only one way of getting rid of a secret Leader of the Opposition who was actually sharing one's bed. It isn't surprising that the King Consort Henry was mysteriously strangled while escaping from a mysterious explosion the following year.

Although not much interested in sex herself, the Queen was attractive in an indescribable way not conveyed by her portraits, and inspired great devotion in those who were loyal to her. Fond of gaiety and beauty, she liked to be surrounded by amusing people of talent. But the French poet Chastelard went too far. After she had caught him hiding under her bed twice, he was executed.

Mary Queen of Scots was certainly devoted to King Henry until he betrayed her. If she ever had a lover for a brief moment in her whole life, it was the Earl of Bothwell who abducted her and whom she immediately married. She had certainly had enough Rough Wooing, but so had Scotland.

The other nobles weren't going to have a strong man like

Bothwell to help the Queen overcome them. So they deposed her and, after her romantic escape from the island castle on Lochleven, defeated her general Argyll, who unfortunately had an epileptic fit in the middle of the battle. She fled to her doom in England.

Imprisoned for nineteen years by the English, she lived in pain and misery. For we learn from her son James VI that he inherited from her the hereditary royal malady now identified as porphyria, and from which their descendant George III was to suffer so much pain as to make people think him mad. Nineteen years after Mary Queen of Scots had sought refuge on English soil, she was beheaded at the order of her merciless cousin, Elizabeth I, who had failed to persuade her warder to murder her.

It's an irony of history that in 1952, on the exact anniversary of that execution, it was Mary's descendant, not Elizabeth's, who was proclaimed at the Mercat Cross of Edinburgh to be the present Queen of both countries. For when Elizabeth I died, it was Mary's son James VI who succeeded her on the English throne and became King James I of Great Britain.

The two countries were not yet united in any other way than in having the same king, and it was still necessary for Scotsmen to become naturalized Englishmen and vice versa. Scotland's cave-dwelling family of organized cannibals had only been put to death just a few years before, and the whole clan of MacGregor were still outlawed and being hunted down with blood-hounds on the hill; while the grander English were living in houses like Longleat and Knole and furnishing them with carpets from Turkey. But 1603 at least saw the Union of the Crowns: and James now had such power and cash that he was able to boast that, whereas his ancestors were hard pressed to rule Scotland by the sword, he could rule it from Whitehall Palace by a stroke of the pen. And there was no more need of Rough Wooing between the realms.

At the Reformation in 1560, much of beauty had been lost, such as our church music which was celebrated all over Europe. Lovely buildings were destroyed. The statues of saints were almost everywhere smashed by mobs of loons who enjoyed vandalism then as much as they do now. It's often forgotten that the word 'saint' simply means 'holy'. So it's a good joke that a statue of our greatest Reformation leader, the holy man Knox, now stands outside the hall where the General Assembly of the Church of Scotland meet.

Catholicism lingered on strongly in those districts where the magnates adhered to the Old Faith. But the main conflict came to be between what might be roughly described as the Lutheran system of retaining Bishops, and out-and-out Calvinist Presbyterianism with its emphasis on the authority of the Bible alone: and usually the Old Testament at that.

For the next century Scotland was bedevilled by savage religious persecution. In 1638 Charles I united most of Scotland against him by trying to impose a High Church Anglican-style prayer book on them. Their representatives of all ranks promptly flocked to sign a great protest called the National Covenant, drafted by my frenziedly worried ancestor Johnston of Warriston. The Covenanters mobilized an Army of which the great Montrose was one of the commanders. The king gave way, and the General Assembly abolished bishops.

Glutted with spiritual power, the Kirk now went too far and sought temporal power too. Montrose and the moderates were not standing for this. Civil War resulted on and off until Montrose's execution was followed soon after by the English Conquest of Scotland under the Cromwellians, who ruled us from 1651 to 1660.

The Restoration of Charles II enabled the Episcopalians to persecute the Covenanters in return. We are told that some of the West Country women were tied to stakes to be drowned by the rising tide. If so, it reminds us of a tale that Clanranald once put a thieving woman to death at Castle Tirrim by tying her hair to the seaweed at low tide: and both remind us that the Scots had still much of the blood of the pagan Picts who made human sacrifices in this particular way.

But Charles II's brother, James VII and II, being himself persecuted as a Papist, tried to introduce religious toleration. Such an idea was anathema to the Churches of England and Scotland alike. The high Anglican bishops of England entered into an undoctrinal alliance with our Presbyterians against our Episcopalian bishops. Moreover, having reorganized the English Navy brilliantly while serving as Lord High Admiral, James as king tried to run the two countries as efficiently and to regulate commerce on bureaucratic lines. The freedom-loving English Whig country magnates and capable merchant bankers weren't having this. They threw him out to the tune of 'Lillibulero' in the Glorious Revolution; and the Scots Whigs followed suit. They allowed the Master of Stair to emphasize the mailed fist in their velvet glove three years later (one long dark winter night in 1692) through the Massacre of Glencoe. His coat-of-arms had nine lozenges on it, so the Nine of Diamonds has ever since been called 'the Curse of Scotland'.

Robinson Crusoe was modelled on Alexander Selkirk. This Scottish seaman was marooned for several years on a Pacific island, where I myself observed the characteristic Scottish aumries of that period, niches carved by him as lockers in the sides of his shallow cave. While he was there, a great change happened to his country, all unknown to him. The Parliaments of Scotland and England were united to form that of Great Britain.

The English had deliberately sabotaged the far-seeing attempt of the Scots to form a colony at Darien on the isthmus of Panama: to bestride the Pacific–Atlantic overland trade route. They excluded Scots ships and trade from the English colonies. They maintained a Customs barrier against Scotland. Using these pressures, and refusing the federal solution that had always been the wise one, they forced the Scots most reluctantly in 1707 to accept a Treaty of Union.

A growing myth has it that the Scots leaders were bribed, but it was not so. All that happened was that the British Treasury settled the outgoing Scottish Government's debts. Thus the Duke of Atholl, who had voted against the Union and mobilized 4,000 Athollmen to try and oppose the Union by force, got £1,000 owed to him, while Lord Banff, who had voted for it, only got £11 2s.

We Scots were allowed to keep our own laws, nowadays increasingly whittled by statute to fit the modern English legislative sausage-machine. We still have our own bank-notes, not legal tender in England though the steadily devalued Bank of England notes are legal tender with us.

But the Treaty has never been seriously honoured. The British Parliament assumed the immediate right to amend any part of it by a simple majority instead of by a majority of the Scottish representatives in both Houses. So the negotiated clauses were unprotected and all the Treaty safeguards meaningless. This annoyed as many Scots then as now.

After the Union, its principal opponents were the Jacobites.

They were the supporters of the exiled James 'King over the Water', the Latin form of whose name was JACOBUS REX. Their main following was in the Highlands, although such great clans as Campbell, Sutherland and Mackay were arrayed as Whigs against them under the Protestant and Hanoverian descendants of the Stewart kings.

The Jacobites rose unsuccessfully in 1715, 1719 and 1745. In the meantime, the Government hurriedly built military roads and bridges and forts in the Highlands, and for the first time in history wheeled traffic was possible north of the Tay.

The last of these Risings, 'the '45', was led by the romantic Bonnie Prince Charlie, half Stewart and half Pole. He had with him two of the finest men there will ever have been: Lord George Murray and 'the Gentle Lochiel'. They both knew the enterprise had almost no chance, but gave up everything they had out of loyalty. Lord George was a brilliant Gaelic-speaking Highland general, and defeated the Government troops whenever he was given a free hand. However, the young Prince preferred other and alien advisers, and the result was the complete overthrow of his Cause by his equally young cousin, the Duke of Cumberland, at the woeful battle of Culloden. There the starving, sleet-sodden Highlanders, armed with swords and shields and wearing their clan's lucky plant in their bonnets, were reduced to throwing stones against regular troops armed with cannon and firing volleys of musketry.

The young Prince, hunted through the heather, was never betrayed despite the large reward offered, and escaped to the Continent. Refused all employment for diplomatic reasons, his brave, chivalrous and active spirit consoled itself melancholically with spirits: a very natural and human reaction which meaner men can't resist banging on about today. But the Government crushed his supporters with revolting brutality.

The Lowlands had for some time been Anglicized in their outlook, leading the usual rat-race in the towns and treating rural areas as country estates to be run for economic benefit rather than as the homeland of a community of martial kindred. It was, perhaps rightly, believed that any real increase in wealth would ultimately benefit everybody. Great agricultural improvements were introduced throughout the Lowlands during this century, from Ayrshire to Caithness. As early as the 1730s Argyll had already sent the famous Lord President Forbes of Culloden round his own clan lands to modernize them too.

After the '45 this was attempted increasingly throughout the whole Highlands. The first result was the practical disappearance of the 'tacksman', the gentleman tenant who acted as middleman between the chief and a particular district, with the result that the ordinary Highlandmen were deprived of their local leaders whose modest houses had been centres of culture.

Next came the population explosion. Nobody knew what to do. Reactionary chiefs and lairds tried to keep everybody together on their old homeland, and went bust as a result. Progressive left-wing landlords like the Marquess of Stafford (an Englishman who had married the Countess of Sutherland) were typically radical 'planners' and removed the surplus population in what are still remembered as the notorious Clearances. We must always remember that 'radical' means somebody who wants to 'uproot' and there is nothing a radical likes more than a self-justified clearance of anything old that somebody else is sentimentally attached to. Yet in 1801 the population of Sutherland was 23,117 and in 1831, after the Clearances, it had nevertheless risen to 25,793. Indeed, contrary to popular belief, the population of the Highlands today is greater than it was at the time of the Jacobite Risings.

But the great Caledonian Forest that had covered the Highlands was almost all gone by the 1700s, gradually cut down by men who lived only for the moment and didn't bother to replant. And the basis for any revival of the Highland economy should be a revival of forestry, coupled with tourism and light industry, for the Highlanders in their homeland are not adapted to heavy industry nor used to large cities.

The sad breaks with Highland tradition between the '45 and the Clearances nearly ended it all. The Government banned the tartan, the pipes and the kilt: thus enshrining all three in our hearts for ever. Mr Pitt raised Highland regiments, usually officered and manned from a particular group of clans, and allowed them to go on having pipers and wearing kilts of tartan. Then Sir Walter Scott turned the bitterness of the old feuds into a romantic 'joking relationship', as the social anthropologists would call it, and made episodes from Scots history celebrated throughout the literary world of European culture. His friend George IV set the seal on our revived international grandeur when he took the trouble to wear a kilt on his historic Royal Visit to Edinburgh in 1822, which it's so fashionable nowadays to mock. And Queen Victoria clinched the recovery of our national self-esteem when she made Balmoral her favourite home.

Scotsmen played a dominant part in the establishment of the British Empire, and in the settlement of some of the older Dominions. At home and overseas, they have established Clan Societies to keep together names both Highland and Lowland: Lindsay and Maitland as well as Lamont and Macdonald. I've seldom met a foreigner who didn't long for the right to wear one of our beautiful or hideous tartans: typically divisive and clannish as they are to the last stitch.

And here we come back to the beginning. The Scots are all proud genealogists; no other country in the world has its clannish symbols so meticulously regulated by law enforced by so character-istically grand an officer as the Lord Lyon King of Arms. Scots-men are still intense theologians. But above all, the Scots are all independent-minded, and their historic social combinations were traditionally divided vertically between names and districts, and not horizontally between classes. No true Scot, before the urban maladjustments and makeshifts of the unprepared-for Industrial Revolution, would ever have thought himself of a lower class than any other: a Hamilton or a Murray could be a duke or a dustman, and still can. For, in fact, we are still just one great cantankerous squabblesome family.

Scotland from 1830

Rosalind Mitchison

A recent publication of the Scottish History Society, the *Dundee Textile Industry*, gives us a glimpse of a Scottish town in the 1830s which is as good a starting point as any for a historical survey. Dundee had by then grown to a population of 50,000 and was planning to put new-fangled gas lighting into the parish church. The town had about 80 small schools and a subscription library, but much of the infrastructure required by modern town life had not yet been developed: for instance it still lacked a water supply or a police force. It was in the forefront of industrial advance though as yet there was 'no factory with power looms, no spinning mills that could be called large, very few macadamized streets' and jute was only just appearing in its merchandise. But it was still an isolated social community. Except for the eleven miles of local railway, travel was slow and difficult. It took five days for London news to arrive, and a week for the post, though someone in a hurry, prepared to be uncomfortable, could make the journey in two and a half days.

In spite of the handicap of unmechanized transport, the pull of England was already powerful and Scotland had suffered a loss of national identity. Lord Cockburn in his life of Jeffrey looked back at the later decades of the eighteenth century with admiration and called them 'the last purely Scotch age'. This age had seen striking achievements. In the first half of the eighteenth century Scotland had acquired political stability; in the second she had led Europe into the Enlightenment and had achieved in one generation the pre-industrial economic growth that in England and France had been spread over two centuries. These are probably the most important things that had ever happened to her. They enabled her to come into the Industrial Revolution along with England. In 1830 Scotland was a 'developed nation' by contemporary standards, even if her economic state showed a shortage of both skills and capital, and her development was one-sided. Her industrialists could view the future with a well-founded optimism based on a spectacular achievement in the near past. It was not yet clear whether the businessmen were right to feel confident of the future, or the intellectuals right in their appreciation that they were lesser lights than the great men of a generation before, and that something had gone from Scotland.

Looking back over the last hundred and forty years it seems as if the intellectuals were right and the optimism of the industrialists was misplaced, even in their own sphere of action. The main developments of the nineteenth century were already implicit in the situation in 1830. Scots in the eighteenth century had frequently referred to the process of 'compleating the Union', that is carrying out in political, administrative and social changes the implications of 1707. The fifty years after 1830 can be regarded as completing the Industrial Revolution for the whole of Britain; carrying through the major economic steps of further industrialization and making the adjustments, institutional, social and personal, required by life in a modern society. In concrete terms, there were still to come the railways, the great industrial towns, a new structure of local government, education and welfare services and the disciplining and self-disciplining of the labour force. Society had to become more secular and more tightly organized. Part of the process can be considered either as getting religion out of the system, or at least reducing its share; part of it as getting democracy and bureaucracy in.

This process brought England and Scotland closer together. It was, after all, dictated by a shared economic situation. The legislation that embodied much of it was passed by a Parliament of the two countries, containing men who thought along much the same lines whether the bill before them was ostensibly concerned with Scottish or English affairs. Rail travel soon made the two capitals ten hours apart instead of sixty, and opened up the hinterlands of both cities. Easier travel and economic development in other countries brought Britain more and more into European affairs and movements, a process that was logically completed in the alliance structure of the early years of the twentieth century.

If these were the main trends of the nineteenth century, then in several important aspects Scotland showed herself backward. The basic initial economic backwardness, the fact that her Industrial Revolution had been one-sided, geared only to textiles, was met by the tremendous development of heavy industry after 1828.

93

But social retardation remained. Scotland conspicuously failed to develop, at least in terms of formal institutions, a welfare system capable of dealing with the problems of industrial society; for a time she allowed her educational system to sink into decay; her local government was even more chaotic than that of England. Some of these weaknesses came from a failure to 'get religion out' of parts of the system.

Far, in fact, from reducing the share of religion in the national life, the 1840s saw a resurgence of its power and an intrusion of its claims into the secular world. The quarrel that broke the church in two in 1843 has traditionally been considered as one where her actions were defensive. The church was struggling against the patronage system forced on her by parliament in the early eighteenth century. But the form it took is instructive. The church was claiming that the civil courts should decide property cases in accordance with the views of the General Assembly and in opposition to parliamentary legislation. This was an intrusion into civil affairs equalled, if not surpassed by that of the state into the territory of the church. The state was using the civil courts to prevent ordained ministers holding services in the parishes to which the General Assembly had assigned them. Quarrels between church and state normally involve both intruding into each other's sphere of action. They end, for the most part, officially in a stalemate, in practice with the state getting most of what it had wanted. But in the Disruption crisis, by breaking the church in two, the evangelical side won an outright victory for the time being. Patronage, which it considered the main issue, was killed by the creation of a Free Church, representative of almost half of the country. The Free Church proclaimed that it was prepared to become established on its own terms, but it was more than eighty years before the split was healed, and even longer in some cantankerous congregations. During this time the Free Church showed itself almost as strong in men and means as the established church, and probably stronger in minds. Once its survival became sure, any Church of Scotland congregation involved in a dispute over patronage could be expected to join the Free Church: patronage was therefore dead. But in the end the problems involved in organizing and financing a large religious body in a modern state brought home to the Free Church that the civil courts have to act in accordance with the civil law. The victory of the Free Church also meant that in the end the churches had to admit the rights of the state in its own territory. Both sides can therefore be considered to have won their points. But it is characteristic of received historical opinion in Scotland that only the victory of the church has entered into the popular concept of history.

The economic weaknesses of Scotland in the last two centuries have mainly come from inescapable facts of geology and geography. These, for instance, explain the low-grade end-product of the nineteenth century iron industry, and the need to supplement it with imports. Ship building grew up, in spite of the limitations of the iron industry, because of Scotland's inventiveness in engines, but because Scotland had never had the wealth of diversified techniques in metal work to be found, for instance, in England, the result was a monolithic structure of heavy industry on Clydeside. The fine textile industry there died out, but the coarser and lower-paid survived on the East coast. At the end of the century Scotland had an industrial structure of big industries, relatively narrow in the range of work for skilled men, and in some cases very low-paid. The pay of Dundee jute workers in 1923 was the lowest in Britain. The industries carried a large labour force, and encouraged a tremendous concentration of population in one great industrial area. It was these industries, and therefore this area, that was to be particularly badly hit by the depression between the wars. There were other, more complicated, social results. The gulf in class structure between unskilled workers and the capitalists employing them was not adequately filled by layers of other income groups, *petit bourgeois* or craft workers, for instance, except in the smaller towns. In the countryside the scale and efficiency of Scottish farming created an unbridgeable gap between farmer and labourer. These social chasms may be a reason for weaknesses in the drive for social welfare, already noticeable by the end of the nineteenth century. Some Scottish cities, in particular Glasgow, were among the more adventurous and determined in the early public health movement. This was fortunate, for by all accounts (and there are a lot of them, full of horrors), the problems and evils of nineteenth-century urbanization reached levels unheard of elsewhere. But by the end of that century the impulse for reform was slackening, and the evils were still relatively conspicuous. Scottish cities have a lot to be modest about in their housing records, and accept today norms which would count as overcrowding elsewhere in Britain. They tend to ignore amenity. Parks and other benefits exist by gift of benefactors, great men in terms of land or industry, rather than as a result of civic expenditure. In the mid-nineteenth century there was no shame in this. It was a sign of civic virtue to keep the rates low, a sign of religious virtue not to look for pleasure in the environment. When the workers of Dundee could not get to work in cold weather in the 1850s because they lacked shoes and overcoats, it was natural that they should have to obtain parks, if at all, by benefaction from their employers rather than by local taxation. It is the continuation of a narrow sense of civic responsibility into the relative affluence of the mid-twentieth century that is discreditable.

The dead hand of nineteenth-century industrial structure lies on other parts of modern life. It is one reason for the low economic status of women in Scotland. Scottish industries have either provided reasonably paid jobs for men, and a lot of them, or very badly paid jobs for women: there has been little between. In any case Scotland in the eighteenth and early nineteenth centuries had been a society based uncritically on masculine conceptions. The crucial Veto Act of the General Assembly, the first blow in the quarrel that culminated in the Disruption, giving the right of vetoing presentations to the male heads of households, was a natural manifestation of this. The movement for women's civil rights found relatively little support in Scotland, and did not increase it by injuring property. The more half-hearted efforts for economic equality have met even less.

Perhaps this is to lay too great an emphasis on Scotland's residual backwardness in economic and social achievement in the nineteenth century. It still remains remarkable that she had turned herself from one of the poorest countries in Europe to a modern, industrial state; residual weaknesses are to be expected. And they were accentuated by the political neglect that Scotland suffered for most of the nineteenth century. The system by which Scottish patronage and legislation had been handled in the eighteenth century fell into disuse in the 1830s and was not replaced. The Reform Act of 1832 gave Scotland at last some sort of representative system, but it was not one particularly well worked out. For many years after that Scottish seats became almost a Whig-Liberal monopoly. It was said at one moment in the 1880s that all the conservative MPs for Scotland could travel to London in one first class railway compartment without overcrowding. The explanation for this one-sidedness of Scottish politics still eludes

96

Top: *Details from a Pictish standing stone* (c. 7th century, Aberlemno, Angus), showing typical Pictish symbols and mounted warriors. Bottom: *Detail from the north elevation of the Royal Palace in Stirling Castle. The figure is thought to represent James V, who built the Palace.*

us. H. J. Hanham has advanced the theory that it was gratitude for the Whig party's Reform Act. But this is too naive an explanation of political motives. It also ignores the fact that the parties in the middle and later decades of the nineteenth century were very different from those that had borne the same names in the 1820s. Perhaps we should pay more attention to the efficient organization on the Whig side, to its grasp of the press, of which *The Scotsman* was a conspicuous example, and to the weight of leading families, estates and personalities, in a society very hierarchical. Liberal supremacy, once established, was to some degree self-perpetuating. Scottish conservatives of parliamentary calibre and ambitions had to seek seats in England, and this transportation of ability weakened the quality of and added frustrations to the local party organization.

Liberal dominance did not mean liberal concern. J. R. Vincent, writing on the Liberal party, has described the party's treatment of Scotland, Wales and Ireland, the basis of its parliamentary strength, as like that of 'an inconvenient West African colony'. Scottish legislation was carelessly prepared, usually with deference only to the vested interests of landowners, lawyers and clergy, and postponed to suit English priorities. This was most conspicuously shown in the important issue of creating in Scotland a school system to be run by the State and not by the Church. Bill after bill failed, in spite of the predominance of support from Scottish MPs. Working through the pages of Hansard in the Victorian era for the debates on Scottish issues is instructive. Much of the scanty legislation was not debated at all: the issues had presumably been fought out off stage by the interests concerned. When the House did wake up and speak with vigour, it did so either because of Irish parallels with Scotland and Irish pressure, or because of the intrusion into Scottish affairs of English divisions and issues. Scotland was not well served by the Liberal hegemony. In 1867 the House heard a strong objection to the concentration of political power in the hands of the Lord Advocate and the 'domination of a few Scotch lawyers'. In 1872 Dr Lyon Playfair made a reasoned plea that in this latest attempt at a structure of primary education for Scotland the needs of that country should be considered and not the principles of English politicians. Scotland wanted her state educational structure to give religious instruction, even if it seemed to English liberals an 'illiberal' feature. She got it at last, and with a local government base that did not give a

97

Brechin Cathedral (Angus) with its Celtic round tower (10th–11th century), one of the rare Scottish examples of what is mainly an Irish phenomenon.

built-in position to landowners, an overdue but necessary step to democracy. But this was a rare item in Gladstone's record for Scotland. In 1878 when he held his famous Midlothian campaign, the issues were not local or Scottish ones, though a programme related to Scottish needs could easily have been made up, but the foreign policy of the United Kingdom and the leadership of the Liberal party. It took several more years before Rosebery was able to extract from this party the idea of a Secretaryship for Scotland – the beginnings of coherence for the structure of modern government in Scotland.

Against this much needed reform there was advanced the argument that Scotland did not need government; her douce and orderly people could manage things for themselves. To do the Scots justice, it was English, not Scottish, members of Parliament who talked this nonsense; Scots appear more aware of their problems. Modern nations need a central governing agency, not only to ensure the possibility of coherent legislation, but also to prevent the 'overgovernment' that was inherent in the separation of the various bodies controlling local activities, such as education and poor relief, from elected members of Parliament. In any case the long-standing problem of the Highlands was coming to a crisis at this time, in the issue over the Clearances in Skye.

The special economic problems of the Highlands are obvious to any observer: an unimprovable agriculture, accompanied by too large a population to be supported at tolerable standards even by fertile land, is one aspect. Industry could not reasonably be expected to supply agriculture's deficiencies, because of remoteness. In any case efforts to start up industries had not been made early enough in the Industrial Revolution, or with enough resolution by the landowners or co-operation from the crofters. But this explanation brings into focus the other element in the Highland problem, the lack of contact between landowner and peasant. Improving landowners of the eighteenth century had been men receptive to the new ideas of the virtue of hard work and the value of economic achievement. But they had also taken for granted their own rights of property and had never seriously considered whether the health of the community, local or national, might be incompatible with these. In the Lowlands property in land had not prevented them from endowing their tenants with leases because it had become clear that this was a necessary step to their own economic advantage. But the tenantry of the Highlands were very different from the educated, industrious and profit-making farmers of the Lothians. They had neither the capital nor the skill to put into effect modern farming. There were too many of them anyway, and their cultural inheritance, already weakened by the failure of modern society to absorb and use the positive qualities of the institutions of clanship, was one from which their leaders, the landowners, had cut themselves off. If the landowners thought about Highland culture at all it was in terms of romance or exasperation.

The result of this was that efforts by Highland landowners to develop the economy of their estates had not been formulated in co-operation with the tenantry or with respect for their interests and capacity. We should remember that many of the Clearances that resulted, particularly those in Sutherland, were an attempt to further the economic health of the region, as well as the long-term interests of landowners. The population was moved to coastal villages because otherwise it would starve inland. But in practice this meant removing it from an agriculture which could not support it, to a mixture of agriculture and other occupations which in the long run did no better, and in an economic and social setting which offered almost no welfare and protection beyond the attentions of the landowners, and no alternative except departure. The communities, already shaken and disordered by lack of leadership and this forced resettlement, suffered further shocks from the emigration of those with most initiative and funds to the industries of the central valley or to America.

The worst hardships of the Clearances were probably over by 1850. They had excited a certain amount of attention, but no remedial action. It was, after all, a period when life was hard everywhere for those without property. The shoeless workers of Dundee, the seamstresses of Edinburgh, driven to prostitution by the impossibility of making an honest livelihood on a wage of sixpence a shirt, the callousness of the bothy system for the rural labourers of eastern Scotland, all remind us of the massive weight of deprivation and poverty and their brutalizing effects in mid-nineteenth century Scotland. Compared to that in the towns, the Highlander's destitution was privileged. He had a community to which he belonged, a landowner and a minister to whom he was known and from whom some degree of care could be expected. He was unlikely to be left to starve.

By the 1880s all this had changed in the Lowlands. Wages, housing, welfare and education were all improving. The workers had designed some degree of mutual protection and culture for themselves. This was expressed in protective organizations, trade unions and friendly societies, in the social life of the big blocks of tenements where they lived, in political activity, and, for some, in the temperance movement. The low standards of life in the 'congested' areas of the Highlands now stood out sharply. It was in Skye, long noted for its agitators, that the 'crofters' war' broke out. This was effective because it allied itself to urban and Irish political dissidents. No nineteenth-century government wanted to have a policy about the economic and social development of part of the country, least of all one that reduced the rights of property. But Westminster had been forced to adopt one for Ireland by the threat of civil disorder. The Crofters' Holdings Act of 1886 was not a well-designed measure. It is all too clear that it was the government's reluctantly developed Irish policy reluctantly applied to another area of trouble. It assumed that the rights of landowners and the absence of tenant right in the Highlands were the essence of the Highland problem, and not simply exacerbations of it. But at least it was an attempt at meeting a Scottish need. The half century of parliamentary neglect had been broken by a few determined radicals. It was also a manifestation of an important movement of the late nineteenth century and afterwards, the resurgence of Celtic nationalism with its emphasis on the language, culture and a largely bogus interpretation of the history of the Celtic areas of these islands.

The interpretation of Celtic history has been even more artificial and spurious in Scotland than in other areas. At various times in the last few years it has been stated, often in the correspondence columns of *The Scotsman*, with the sincerity that only total ignorance can produce, that the clan was an institution of real democracy, that all the beneficial elements in Scottish culture are Celtic in origin, that racist opinions are so alien to the Scots that their existence in this country must be the evil result of English influence, that the Clearances were a consistent policy of genocide, and so on. These opinions reflect two important features of nineteenth-century Scotland, the birth of Scottish nationalism and the decline of Scottish intellectual life.

That Scotland lost the remarkable level of eighteenth-century intellectual achievement was inevitable. She had led the world of

100

thought and explored and developed a range of new areas, starting off, for instance, the modern study of economics, economic history, sociology and geology. In the 1820s the great days were over, as her intellectuals recognized, but she was still offering valuable goods, the historical novels of Scott, Hogg and Galt, the review journalism of Jeffrey and Lockhart, the social and medical pioneers of the early public health movement. These found their market not just in Scotland but in Britain as a whole. The financial crisis of 1826 brought down the Scottish publishing houses which had pioneered the expansion of middle-class reading, and evangelical exclusiveness and obscurantism were narrowing the interests of Scotland. The aristocracy had already left Edinburgh and by 1830 the leading Scottish intellectuals were to be found in London. The Scottish universities and middle classes could not retain the doctors trained in the north. London and the interests of the south prevailed.

But Scotland still kept the universities that had been a vital element in the Enlightenment. It was in them that the intellectual leaders had formulated their ideas, and these ideas had provided, in simplified form, the core of university teaching in modern subjects. The level of instruction had been what we today would think of as secondary education, offered in many cases to boys in their early teens. Lockhart, for instance, had completed undergraduate courses in both Glasgow and Oxford before he was nineteen. By the middle of the nineteenth century these new subjects had either developed and gone beyond the illumination of secondary school teaching, or had failed to be incorporated into the mainstream of the curriculum. It might have been possible to create another repertoire of subjects in the Scottish universities, but more and more these institutions were being drawn into the task of equipping the professional men of the future with routine instruction. Parents had paid for the teaching of new subjects in the eighteenth century because they had found them useful and profitable in monetary terms. In the nineteenth century what were useful were formal qualifications in established disciplines. Neither English nor Scottish universities saw any reason to adapt their curricula frequently or radically. By 1914 it was almost impossible for the future aspirant to the civil service to learn anything of value at any British university about recent history, or the structure of government of modern societies. Many of the leading new ideas of the later nineteenth century came from outside the Universities, from independent gentlemen such as Darwin, from politicians, from novelists.

It is not surprising to find the English universities backward in the study of history, for here they merely displayed a strong regard for tradition: the Regius chair of modern history in Oxford had been regarded as a sinecure in the eighteenth century. But Scotland had in the past done better. She had been the pioneer in historiography in the eighteenth century, showing a combination of scholarship and detachment, producing both documentary accounts and the wider historical perspectives of Hume and Robertson. Scott, in the introductions to some of his novels, most notably *Old Mortality*, and in his ability to evaluate the motives of conflicting elements, was the final figure in this period of historiography. Unfortunately the history of Scott that his countrymen latched on to was not that of the novels but of his *Tales of a Grandfather*, which, of all Scott's writings, most clearly reveals the financial pressures of his last years. *Tales of a Grandfather* was written for an eleven-year-old, the novels for adults, and yet it is on the former that the general impressions of Scots about their past has been founded for the last hundred and fifty years, either directly or in embellished form in school text books. Serious historical work went on in the nineteenth century, for instance in the publications of the famous clubs, but these were not for general consumption and made little effect on the writing of secondary accounts. For some peculiar reason the middle classes of Scotland chose to regard their history as enshrined for all time in the worst of Sir Walter's potboilers. They did not want its concepts disturbed, and the concepts were those suitable for childish intellects. There were scholars who attempted to think again on the subject: the early twentieth century saw, in particular, the work of William Law Mathieson and C. S. Terry, but their work was relatively unappreciated by their compatriots and the impulse died out.

History is not just an embellishment on the intellectual life of a people. It is a part of national identity. A modern society needs to have some idea of how it has developed, to give it confidence in its achievements and some understanding of where it is going. If it does not have and use an adult appreciation of the past, it will make do with something lesser. History to Scots has tended to mean antiquarian detail, or Scott in a debased form, or some current of doctrinal opinion, religious or political: all substitutes for the real thing, These substitutes, evasions of the truth, have reduced the vitality of Scottish national life.

Scots have also lost by dropping overboard their national speech as a language of serious communication. This was foreseeable. The process began when the Reformation brought to Scotland the Bible in English. The Scottish educated classes managed to remain bilingual in Scots and English until the late eighteenth century. The disappearance of Scots unfortunately coincided with the end of the great days of the Enlightenment, and at the end of the nineteenth century the new structure of state education was used to divorce both Scottish speech and Gaelic from formal education.

But in the same period we see the arrival of self-assertive modern nationalism to Scotland. At first this took the form of a mild cantankerousness about insults from or mistakes by government. The maximum fuss and the minimum of real heat were generated about the wrong quartering of the royal arms, the attack on the notes of the Scottish banks, the use of English to describe aspects of Britain as a whole, and in 1858 an entirely unhistorical assertion that the word 'Scotch', by which for several centuries Scotsmen had described their nationality, was vulgar, modern and incorrect. 'Scottish' was henceforth to be used by respectable people for respectable objects – 'Scotch' was confined to whisky and vegetables. Behind these minor irritations was a real problem in national identity. Should Scots accept institutions or influences from England, which, even if good in themselves, were in opposition to features of Scottish life and tradition? If they did, would they not find themselves also accepting influences from England which were not even good in themselves? In any case, if Scotland was to be respected by either Scots or Englishmen, she should be giving as well as receiving in cultural exchanges.

In turning from minor bickering to developing a vocal, nationalist movement, Scotland was following a common European fashion, though she was late in joining in. It was a time when satisfaction with the recent achievement of the country could no longer be voiced with total conviction. The aims of society had changed in the 1830s and '40s. Religious seriousness and commitment were the keynotes of respectability for some, social reform for others. Neither section could indefinitely congratulate itself on a period in the recent past when the successes had been intellectual, secular and economic. Yet there was not enough in either political or economic grievance to make a strong movement in the 1850s and onwards. Most of what was wrong in Scotland came from internal maladjustments and not external oppression. Scottish nationalism was therefore in the nineteenth century, as it still is, a minority-held, extremist expression of an uncertainty that is felt by all Scots.

Scottish nationalism, for all that it started as a specific manifestation of a general European feeling, has become insular, even parochial. In the nineteenth century nationalism had, here as elsewhere, a literary and intellectual emphasis, but in the manifestation of the twentieth century Scottish National Party this has disappeared. This may come from the lack of interest in history in Scotland, or it may be, as H. J. Hanham has suggested, caused by the *petit bourgeois* base of the movement. In either case, this has meant that the movement has not been as beneficial to the country as it might have been. At its most influential nationalism has been the means of mitigating the neglect of Scotland by politicians, but it has not understood enough about the realities of Scottish national identity to be taken seriously by most Scots or to make constructive proposals.

In many ways the group nicknamed 'Red Clydeside' in the 1920s, though not consciously nationalist, provided a more essential expression of Scotland's personality than the National Party has ever done. Scottish nationalism has tended to exalt the Celtic element in Scottish culture, which by the late nineteenth century was a minor, and a relatively uncreative, section. But the Left has drawn on a real native radicalism. Scottish radicalism has been vocal and fluent since the early nineteenth century, but as a voting power it was held back until the 1918 extension of the franchise (in Dundee, for instance, the electorate trebled in 1918). It received electoral weight at a time of crisis for Britain's older industries, nowhere more acute than on the Clyde. The international dislocations of the early 1920s put shipbuilding, hitherto supremely successful, into severe depression, and the other heavy industries in Scotland were suffering from loss of initiative or basic faults in structure. The successful economic saga was over. Readjustment would need a real analysis of the problem, help from the government and tremendous organizing energy and ability. It got none of these. Some of this was not material for a specifically Scottish protest. No one in Britain in the early 1920s could give an adequate analysis of the problems of the economy, and consequently there was no adequate remedy under discussion.

But Scotland had her own special element of grievance. London had been drawing Scottish brains to it, for education, government and administration, and still more in the organizations of national scale which now held together the country's economic life.

A country or an area can only flourish if it gives satisfaction, or the hope of satisfaction, to a good proportion of the ability and enterprise it creates. In other words, local health depends on enough people content to look no further than being 'top' locally. Edinburgh or Glasgow, rather than London, must meet their needs. With the coming of the railways the journey to London had fallen to a sixth of the time it had previously taken. Others besides the aristocracy and the writers had taken advantage of this to shift their interest. English schools and universities were used by those whose family could afford them, as a way of entry into English life. Some professional groups, notably the lawyers and some of the doctors, had stayed in Edinburgh, but they had not been enough to keep intellectual life going. The big firm, the amalgamation, the great industrial organization typical of the early twentieth century had a coverage of all Britain and usually put its headquarters in the south. Scotland became the 'knuckle end of England'. There was still a lot of wealth, nominally based on Scotland, but it did not attach itself to the promotion of specifically Scottish ends.

These are some of the items in the inter-war malaise, and explain the left-wing bitterness on the Clyde. The movement there sustained itself into the 1930s, though ultimately it was a failure. Instead of inspiring and invigorating the socialist element in the Labour party, because of personal inadequacy and misjudgment, it broke the old Independent Labour Party element away from the main party to the detriment of both sections. But in its early and optimistic days it offered a varied collection of political thought and expression, and gave a mythology and sense of corporate identity to the Clyde.

Another item in Scottish culture to survive the doldrums of the interwar years was the movement in the visual arts. The impulse here, if it came from anywhere, was certainly not generated in Britain. Starting with Charles Rennie Mackintosh in the 1890s, Glasgow developed a group of modern artists and dispersed some of them to other cities. Gradually they built up a local market for their work and an appreciation of the various styles involved. Painting, for instance, in Scotland has not been in the forefront of modern art, but it has expressed and supported the populace's identity, and as a result has been economically viable. It is an unexpected element in modern culture, for on the whole the Celtic fringe of Britain had had little to offer visually for many decades before.

This may seem a meagre list of cheerful items for the first forty years of twentieth century history, but things have been brighter since. The Second World War emphasized and gave a better setting for the drive to improve Scotland's health statistics, a drive that started in the 1930s with the shamefaced recognition that these were as bad as those of any developed country, and particularly unjustified in one with a long and distinguished history of medical education. With government help, the discovery under Tom Johnston that the Scottish Secretaryship could be something other than a routine step in Cabinet preferment, and the renewed social purpose of the war years, the country began to benefit from the doctors and administrators she had produced. The welfare state legislation after the war maintained the change for the better. The war put back attempts to diversify the industrial structure of the nation but compensated by establishing the concept of a government duty to regulate the economy and keep up employment. It is true that this has been found more difficult in practice than was expected, and the difficulties have been manifest in slow economic growth, particularly in the areas farthest from London. Even so, affluence has spilled over to these areas, creating new patterns of spending and new secondary industries, and at last, in the 'sixties, the problem of regional imbalance has been faced. The decision of the government to invest in higher education has enlarged another set of 'new' subjects in the universities, and this has weakened the grasp of routine and complacency in thinking.

So the status of Scotland within Britain, which declined in the years between 1830 and 1940, has begun to rise again, not only in the eyes of the world outside, but in a place far more important for the country, the eyes of the people of Scotland. Admittedly only some of the reasons for this can be regarded as exclusively Scottish achievements. The capital that has been put into new developments has mostly come from outside. Fertility in the creation and adaptation of ideas has been international in its scope. The new concepts in Calvinist theology, in philosophy, in politics and sociology are not a British, or even an English-speaking monopoly. Since communications are a leading achievement of twentieth-century civilization it would be ridiculous to expect that such a monopoly could exist. What matters for social health is that countries should participate in intellectual life on their own merits and not as poor relations. In the modern world the position of 'poor relations' in the handling of ideas must necessarily be taken by the iron curtain countries, at least until Stalinism has been got out of the system. The smaller countries of the western world can feel like moderately able children in an unstreamed school. They need not fear being bottom of the class, and may hope to do a lot better than this. International organization gives protection and approval to them. Even Scots with little sympathy for expressed nationalism gain from the accepted identity of their nation in the modern world. The fringe element of outspoken separatism has proved a beneficial weapon against the indifference of Whitehall in the 1960s. And the 'overheated' economy of south-east England has added an unexpected element of attractiveness to the more retarded areas. Congestion on the roads, pollution in the air, and impossibly expensive housing are drawing people back from careers that lead to London.

Scotland has thus begun to regain the allegiance of her own ability. She has still some way to go in this process, and she has even further to go in regaining her own money for her own culture. Capital held in Scotland has been relatively insensitive to local claims upon it, for support of theatres, opera houses, universities and learned societies, by the standards of other educated countries. But the return of allegiance and interest to Scotland can be regarded as symbolized in the recent awakening of serious historical thought. It is possible that a turning point has been reached, which might lead to the undoing of the changes of the 1820s. No modern society can hope to do things on its own, but it is possible that Scotland may see how to use and advance the contributions offered by herself, by Britain at large, and by the community of scholars and artists and entrepreneurs of the wider world.

The Political Scene

Eric Linklater

The people of Scotland – I speak of the great majority: the upper classes have had no such benefit – are now better fed, better clad, better paid, and better housed than ever before. It must be admitted that many, especially in Glasgow, are still housed in lamentable squalor and lack what others, more fortunate, regard as the basic elements of comfort; but though their circumstances may be cold, cramped, and insanitary, they are not so cold, cramped, and insanitary as the slums in which their grandparents lived and died. In the last fifty years the furnishings of life – its material conditions – have been vastly improved and generally enriched; it is also true that the spiritual climate has grown no warmer, the intellectual climate is not noticeably brighter, and the emotional climate is inclined to be squally.

It would be foolish and extravagant to say that discontent is rife, but discontent there is – much of it vague but some of it specific – and material advance has done nothing to mute its expression or soften its language. Like other countries, of course, Scotland is suffering from the anxiety and strain of living in a world where too much has happened in too short a time, and the ingenuity of the human mind has created, for all mankind, the novelty of an embracing danger; but on top of that the Scottish malcontent has other reasons for dissatisfaction, anger, and protest. He feels that Scotland has its own importance, its own values and dignity, and he believes that they are insufficiently appreciated because Scotland lacks political independence. Throughout the most turbulent years of its history its only unifying national cause was independence, and the very word has still an emotive quality dear to a romantic mind.

Scottish Nationalists of the thorough, fundamental sort demand partition of the United Kingdom, and assert Scotland's right to govern itself in accordance with its own policies and for its own satisfaction. There are, however, many Nationalists, as committed as the extremists, who profess a more moderate policy. There are Liberals who believe that Scotland could establish its political identity, to the satisfaction of reasonable men, in a federal system. And there are others – very many others –uncommitted to a party line, but deeply aware of their nationality; however close their allegiance to the United Kingdom and its Crown they would declare themselves – and feel themselves to be – Scots first and foremost. In a Scottish context it is impossible to find a precise definition of 'nationalism'; it can, on the one hand, be republican, breakaway, separatist, and on the other it may – with equal reality and perhaps more realism – consist of a pervasive sentiment in which, while there is plenty of room for discontent, there is no conviction that discontent could be erased by radical, political action.

Mrs Winifred Ewing, the Scottish Nationalist whom an enthusiastic Hamilton electorate sent to the House of Commons in November, 1967, once said that her ambition was to see Scotland take its seat at the United Nations between Saudi Arabia and Senegal; and though few of her fellow-Scots would, I think, realize a vicarious satisfaction in such company – for the impotence of the United Nations would seem to be more evident than that of Mrs Ewing's native country – she could summon a host of distant or approximate sympathizers who would like to see Scotland play a more evident and effective part in the world than sometimes it does at Murrayfield or, when Celtic is in a happy mood, upon some foreign field. 'Passion for fame,' said Edmund Burke, 'is the instinct of all great souls', and to desire fame for the country of one's kin and kind is more generous than to seek it for one's self. There is, too, another motive, less generous but at least as common, that prompts the wish for independence if not a place beside Senegal: a motive that is seated in the pocket rather than the heart.

All except those who do not pay them believe that taxes are too high, and for once the majority are right. But in Scotland a minority meet the recurrent demand for income tax with a particular and angry bitterness because they believe that Scotland, as a whole, is taxed too heavily and pays more for the benefit of the United Kingdom than it receives in benefit from Westminster. Ingenious calculations have been made, and published, to prove this; and calculations equally ingenious have been produced to demonstrate that Scotland receives more than its entitlement from a kindly central government. It is true that Covent Garden gets a larger subsidy than the Scottish National Orchestra, and of the money voted for defence more is spent in England than in Scotland. The cost of building extensions to London's underground railways is greater than the cost of building a new road in Wester Ross, and the salaries of the policemen, school inspectors, and dustmen necessary for London's comfort and security exceed the cost of all social services available beyond the Highland Line. But the population of London is very large, and though London may indeed be an extravagance – for bulk has its disabilities, as the great dinosaurs learnt – the people of London pay dearly for the doubtful privilege of living there, and perhaps they also contribute to the maintenance of the infirm and indigent in Scotland. Unemployment in Scotland is higher than in England, so is the birthrate, and more of its people are affected by ill health; it is possible, therefore, that Scotland takes a disproportionately large slice of the social security cake.

It seems likely, however, that the two countries are financially so closely interlocked – that industry and investment cross the Border so often and from both sides – that an exact and true assessment of what each pays and receives cannot be made. To count its wealth Scotland would have to dissolve the Union, and that solution might cost more than it was worth.

Unlike England, where few people remember anything more than a few brightly coloured scraps of their history, Scotland has a memory almost as tenacious as Ireland's and, on the whole, much more accurate despite a natural bias. In any discussion of nationalism – whether political with a capital N or sentimental in the lower case – it is therefore relevant, and perhaps necessary, to say something of the treaty which brought about the Union of the Parliaments in 1707; for everyone in Scotland has a knowledge, as lively as if it happened only a week ago, of the indignation which attended the Union, and Nationalists are still suffused with the emotion that filled the streets of Edinburgh and Glasgow with the noisy wrath of a people who felt they had been betrayed by venal legislators bought by English gold to sell them down the Tweed.

Indignation was fairly general – Jacobites were as angry as the Canongate and Glasgow Green, though the Whig clans of the north may have accepted the Union without much emotion – and to believe that the Canongate and Glasgow Green spoke with a popular voice for Scotland is not unreasonable; but the material

110

reasons which persuaded the Scottish Parliament, whether venal or not, to vote for its final dissolution are less often weighed than the sorrow evoked by 'the end of ane auld sang'.

It has been said, with authority, that the Union was a political necessity for England, an economic necessity for Scotland; and it is undeniable that Protestant England was determined to prevent the return to Scotland and possible restoration, after the death of the heirless Queen Anne, of her Catholic half-brother, James Edward the Old Pretender; while Scotland was so poor – even poorer than usual – that its cherished independence had a famished look, and the prospects of a vastly increased trade, that the Union seemed to offer, were uncommonly enticing. But was Scotland's poverty really desperate – and was it the consequence of its immediately preceding history and two or three years of abominable weather in which crops failed to ripen, or of English machination which had undermined the ambitious and utterly foolish Darien adventure that deprived Scotland of two thousand hale and hearty men and £300,000? Its apparent poverty may have been exaggerated by those who saw in the Union a prospect of profit for themselves; but if indeed its poverty was crippling, it was easier and more acceptable to blame England than God. England, moreover, invited blame by the mean and grasping spirit in which – after insisting on an incorporating rather than a federal union – it allotted to Scotland in the united Parliament only forty-five seats in a House of Commons that already numbered rather more than five hundred, and to a House of Lords where there were nearly two hundred English lordships, Scotland was allowed to send only sixteen peers. That, perhaps, was a representation of which a chartered accountant might have approved – it may have represented Scotland's financial strength – but Scotland was a nation, not a company bought on the Stock Exchange by a much richer company, and England's determination to reduce it to a minor and dependent status was the ugly reiteration of a policy persistent since the angry years of Edward I. Then, in various ways, England restricted the opening channels of overseas trade that Scotland's legislators had confidently expected, and Scotland was harassed by unexpected taxes on salt and malt that turned the Scots into a nation of patriotic smugglers, the English into a race of un-uniformed Customs and Excise officers.

In the terms of the Union, and in their interpretation by the vast English majority of the United Parliament, there were grounds for disappointment and good cause for anger; but in the years that followed the Union what evidence can be found, in Scotland, of a continuing disappointment that provoked a continuous anger? Or, in other words, what evidence is there of an hereditary link between the Nationalism of today and the anger – so noisy in the Canongate and Glasgow Green – of 1707?

The two Jacobite rebellions – or three, if one counts the little Spanish incursion of 1719 – are evidence of a particular kind of anger, of opposition to the Hanoverian monarchy, but it was not the opposition of a nation in arms. It was a factional, dynastic opposition; even in the north and the west the Jacobites could not muster all the clans to their cause, and in the middle and southern parts of the country they found few supporters. To Scotland Bonny Prince Charlie bequeathed a name and a great legend, but added nothing more solid to its history. His fellow-countrymen – who might have become his subjects – were living in a political apathy which lasted for well over a century, during which time Scotland was ruled, in effect, by a succession of managers or party bosses: Dukes of Argyll to begin with, then Henry Dundas and his successors. They found it easy to manipulate, for their own benefit, the two-score Scottish Members who sat in the House of Commons; and the possibility must be admitted that Dundas's autocracy – they called him Henry IX – and a general inertia were a blessing that has never been properly recognized. It was during this period, when politics had been swept under the carpet, that Scotland came to life again.

This was the great age of re-creation when Scotland as we know it – or as we think of it – was brought into being by the genius of David Hume and Adam Smith, of Allan Ramsay and Raeburn, of Robert Fergusson and Robert Burns and Walter Scott and the Ettrick Shepherd, of William Adam and his more gifted sons, of the intellectual grandees of Edinburgh, of the engineers and road-makers and master physicians who created comfort and convenience to fortify the paint and poetry and soaring ideas of their predecessors. It was they, without benefit of politics, who made again the nation that politics seemed to have erased; and its existence may have received public recognition in 1817, when a newspaper, published in Edinburgh, was called *The Scotsman*. But not until the latter years of the nineteenth century did Nationalism, with a capital N, make its modest entry on the stage.

By 1880 a vocal minority – strongest, perhaps, in the old,

112

Elgin Cathedral (Moray), founded in 1224 and considered to have been the most beautiful cathedral in Scotland, was vandalized by order of the Scottish Privy Council in 1567 to raise money for the payment of troops.

Covenanting south-west – was arguing the case for Home Rule; and in 1885 parliamentary reform and extension of the franchise gave Scotland seventy-two Members in the House of Commons and a Secretary – not yet a Secretary of State – whose staff created the Scottish Office. Three years later the Scottish Labour Party was founded by Keir Hardie and Cunninghame Graham, in whose view Home Rule was consonant with a proper policy for Labour. Keir Hardie, born in dire poverty, had gone to work in a coal-mine at the age of ten; Cunninghame Graham, aristocrat, adventurer, and a Liberal Member since 1886, had in 1887 been imprisoned for 'illegal assembly' in Trafalgar Square: a passionate concern for the poor, a romantic faith in Scotland, and a comparable ardour for unpopular causes united them, and the Liberal Party had already expressed approval of Home Rule. For many years, indeed, the Liberal Party continued to advocate Home Rule for both Ireland and Scotland – or, at the least, to speak of it with favour – but brought it no nearer. Then, in the war which began in 1914, Ireland took advantage of England's pre-occupation in France, and Scotland found self-expression in the fame won, at exorbitant cost, by its Lowland and Highland regiments with which – in a small, historically-minded country – the whole population was emotionally involved. But a victorious peace brought few rewards other than unemployment and disillusion, and voices, more numerous than before, began to cry angrily for self-government.

In 1928 the Scottish Nationalist Party was founded under the leadership of Cunninghame Graham, and about the same time economic depression found unexpected company, and what was thought to be the beginning of a literary revival was fondly hailed. Nationalism was fostered by the strange poetry of Hugh McDiarmid, a Communist who dredged from native but forgotten depths a vocabulary that reinforced a suddenly emergent genius. Cunninghame Graham found an ally, almost as romantic as himself, in Compton Mackenzie, and Mackenzie, standing as a Nationalist, was elected Rector of Glasgow University. Neil Gunn wrote of the Highlands with a lyrical intensity that was grounded in his boyhood's knowledge of their life; Lewis Grassic Gibbon devised a prose, in tune with his own emotion and a native habit of speech, to evoke the harsh labour, the intensity of hidden passion, in the Mearns; George Blake promised – but did not quite keep his promise – to give the great drama of the Clyde, its ships and their

113

The Bruce Memorial in Glen Trool (Ayrshire) commemorates Robert Bruce's victory over the English at the Battle of Glen Trool in 1307.

building, enduring and compulsive expression; and James Bridie, who had no sympathy with political Nationalism did much to encourage it by creating for Scotland a theatre, and a corpus of plays, such as it had never known before. But despite this un-covenanted help the Nationalists who fought several by-elections invariably lost their deposits.

One of the reasons for their failure was that they never fashioned and elucidated a policy that would be suitable for Scotland should they succeed in winning a sufficiency of parliamentary seats: their attitude, their belief, was that a mandate for self-government must first be won, and after that it would be relatively easy to construct a policy acceptable to the majority of those who had voted for self-government. But the majority – of the electorates to which they appealed – not unnaturally refused their invitation to what, in the adolescent language of the time, was 'a blind date'. In the General Election of 1935 they put forward eight candidates and polled less than 30,000 votes.

By 1939 the Scottish Office had been transferred to St Andrew's House in Edinburgh, and with it went the Home Department and the Departments of Education, Health, and Agriculture; and in 1939 the war against Germany – at Germany's solicitation – was unhappily renewed. Peace, with a troubled look, returned in 1945, and Dr Robert MacIntyre defeated a Labour candidate at Motherwell to become the first Nationalist MP, but held his seat for only a few months. Three years later the General Assembly of the Church of Scotland gave support to the idea of a separate Scottish parliament; at Westminster the authority of the Scottish Standing Committee was greatly enlarged; and in 1949 the Nationalists issued a Scottish Covenant and within two years two million signatories pledged themselves to work for political independence. By May, 1970, however – despite Mrs Ewing's success at Hamilton and publication of a moderate and reasonable statement of policy – membership of the Scottish National Party was no more than 120,000, and its Secretary admitted that he saw no prospect of any dramatic increase in its numbers. For a year or two the Conservative Party had shown a lively interest in the possibility of some sort of devolution for Scotland, but Mr Wilson's government had become icily cold. In Keir Hardie's time the infant Labour Party had warmly approved of Home Rule for Scotland; but the adult Party ruled by Harold Wilson was implacably hostile to the Nationalists and their cause.

Popular interest in Nationalism, and support for it, have risen and fallen like a troubled sea, and one cannot deny a possibility that from the doldrums there may emerge a new wave of enthusiasm high enough to frighten orthodoxy and break established patterns. It is reasonable, therefore, to consider what sort of legislators would be found in Scotland should Scotland decide it wanted Home Rule; and presumably some who have had experience of municipal legislation would offer themselves as its new parliamentarians. But is that a comforting prospect?

In the first drab years of peace and Clement Atlee's government, Edinburgh startled all Britain and much of Europe by presenting a Festival of Music and the Arts to rapturous applause. Immediately successful – brilliantly successful – the Festival quickly proved its viability, and twenty-five years after its opening performance it appears to have become an institution. It is, however, an institution without material foundation or a material roof, for in twenty-five years Edinburgh's municipal legislators have failed to build an opera house or an adequate theatre. They have done nothing to further or foster the idea – so fondly entertained in Scotland – that Edinburgh is indeed a capital city. They have failed, when opportunities were open, to create that accommodation for music and the arts which they require and deserve, and without which no city, however graced by nature, has the visible character and quality of a capital.

Within the last twenty years, moreover, the north wall of Princes Street has been progressively disfigured by shop-fronts that look as if they had been designed for an oriental bazaar, and the splendid austerity of George Street is much defaced by modern addition. George Square has virtually disappeared, and St Andrew Square appears to be adopting a see-through architecture which must have been inspired by a Chelsea milliner. Thousands of new houses have been built, but nowhere is there any hint of the vigorous imagination which inspired the building of Georgian Edinburgh. Nowhere, indeed, is there evidence of any imagination other than that which can calculate a quick and easy profit.

We look towards the west – and in defence of Glasgow it must be said that Glasgow inherited some appalling problems from the ponderous builders of the nineteenth century, whose massive streets, when they degenerated into slums, for long defied clearance because they looked as if nothing would rock them but an explosion of the sort that destroyed Hiroshima. But heroically Glasgow set

115

to work, and then, with a lack of discretion that sometimes accompanies heroism, it substituted for grim old streets the towering bulk of vast vertical warrens that must dehumanize their occupants, that intimidate the casual observer and his quailing imagination, but may symbolize the ever-mounting size of Glasgow's civic debt. Low rents and a soaring debt: in the city where Adam Smith once taught, the disparity is maintained because politics take precedence over economics.

It is curious that a city so inclined to extravagance should have shown, a few years ago, a pettiness of spirit that prevented the full development of Prestwick as a modern airport. Prestwick is about twenty-five miles from the centre of Glasgow, and has natural advantages superior to those of any other airport in Britain. Had Glasgow decided to make Prestwick its municipal airport, Prestwick could have been developed to match American and European standards – and give Scotland a major, international airport – and a new express rail-service could have reduced those twenty-five miles to twenty-five minutes. But Glasgow – to keep up with Jonestown – had to have an airport of its very own, and acquired one that is much inferior to Prestwick, of little use to the rest of Scotland, and already needs longer runaways. That Glasgow is great-hearted none disputes; but it must be admitted that Glasgow's bosses can be small-minded.

In the north-east there is an admirable town called Aberdeen; but Aberdeen appears to have forgotten that among its traditional distinctions were a respect for learning, and a learning that exacted respect. A single university was not enough: when new ideas began to circulate a second university was endowed to give them houseroom and critical scrutiny. Bishop Elphinstone combined scholarship with statesmanship; in 1638 'the Aberdeen Doctors' refused on philosophic grounds to sign the Covenant; and Clerk Maxwell taught there. There were learned men at the cathedral of St Machar as well as at King's and Marischal, and auxiliary to all three was the old Grammar school where the poet Byron learnt his first Latin verbs. The Grammar School had, until recently, some modest privileges which it had earned by long service to the community, but now, in obedience to a modern whim, the Grammar School has been deprived, not only of privilege, but of its very name. Education, to be useful, needs a maximum freedom. No one can adequately define education, nor state precisely how boys and girls should be encouraged to acquire it. A personal view, however, would certainly be that education will descend to new depths if every school becomes obedient to a deathly uniformity imposed by government edict.

As in Edinburgh there has been a vast amount of new domestic building – Aberdonians, I think, are more generously housed than city-dwellers anywhere else in all Britain – but there has been no town-planning to mass and arrange the new houses in aesthetically agreeable groups and patterns; and Union Street, once a dignified and respectable thoroughfare, has been grossly sullied by recent addition.

But in the matter of new building Aberdeen's unforgivable fault has been to raise a huge, uncomely structure immediately opposite the crenellated white front of Marischal College. The architecture of Marischal is not, admittedly, universally admired; but as decorated granite – an ornate and romantically fashioned granite building – it is unique in Europe, and deserves an open space from which to inspect and marvel at it. The municipal governors of Aberdeen cleared away some small, dismal, dilapidated buildings in front of it, and created that open space. But then they erected a ponderous, clumsily designed, slab-sided arrangement of walls and windows with no better purpose than to obscure the view they had contrived, and house the ministers, agents, and servants of their administration. A truly lamentable decision.

Until a few years ago Dundee – in an academic sense – was part and parcel of the University of St Andrews, and as such served Scotland well. But then Dundee demanded a university of its own; and perhaps one need not say more except that a comparison between Dundee and Glasgow – in respect of their policy vis-à-vis St Andrews and Prestwick – is too obvious to be laboured.

What, then, is the conclusion to which one is led by these examples of recent municipal policy and administration? That if Scotland should vote for self-government, and achieve it, it would do well to avoid recruiting its new ministers and members of parliament from those who have served as governors or managers of its municipalities? It seems a harsh judgment – and how, in a democratic society, could one exclude them?

We must now, I think, return to the theme of discontent – endemic in Scotland, as in all other countries – and the eighteenth century when politics, unless one was a Jacobite, offered no opportunity for protest, but natural dissatisfactions were mitigated by the

117

opportunities offered of strenuous employment overseas. Not everyone, like Walter Scott and Robert Burns, had the talent to write memorable novels and unforgettable poems; not everyone, like Robert Adam and David Hume and Adam Smith, was so gifted as to create new aspects of architecture, philosophy, and economics; but to many, endowed with a sturdy mind and body, rewarding activities were offered in the ever-expanding empire which England designed and Scotland gardened. It has often been observed that Scotsmen do better, for themselves and their neighbours, when they remove themselves from their native landscape and only return to it after they have made a sufficient competence abroad. When that redoubtable man Sir James McGrigor – in effect the creator of the Royal Army Medical Corps – had newly acquired a surgeon's commission in the Army, an agent in London warned him against entering a Scottish regiment. 'Your prudent countrymen,' he said, 'will soon make their way in an English or Irish regiment, but in one of their own corps there are too many of them together: they stand in the way of each other.' So McGrigor was gazetted to the 88th Foot, the Connaught Rangers, and after many adventures achieved high eminence in the Army and his profession. Many of his fellow-countrymen – equally well advised – went farther afield, to India, the distant East, and later to Africa or the West Indies; and those who survived often returned home with more than a competence.

More important than that, they showed in their remote employment a singular aptitude for successfully dealing with situations of extreme difficulty and people, of a sort radically different from themselves, with whom they often discovered an unexpected sympathy, and whose friendship they won by an understanding born of sympathy. When one reads the lives – any forty or fifty of the lives – of the innumerable soldiers, merchants, administrators, and explorers who went out from Scotland in the hundred and fifty years after 1750, one is almost compelled to accept the fact that Scots are incapable of revealing, even to themselves, their true native abilities – their virtue, perhaps their genius – until they find themselves in circumstances which challenge them so strongly that they must respond with equal force if they wish to live. And in their forceful response there was often a remarkable comprehension of their new situation, that unexpected sympathy with their new associates, of which a simple, obvious example is the great camaraderie that used to exist between the Gurkhas of Nepal and Scotland's Highland regiments.

There are, however, more distinguished examples, and out of a multitude of names – from Livingstone in Africa to Macgregor in New Guinea – I choose two of utterly different character and achievement. There was Sir David Ochterlony, of a Forfarshire family, who defeated the Gurkhas and in about 1820 became Resident at Delhi. Not all the stories told of him are true, but it is said, with some authority, that he endeared himself to the inhabitants of Delhi by his ready adoption of Indian pomp and habits: an hour before sunset he used to ride out, 'to eat the air', on a noble elephant behind which strode six other elephants on which, as it were enthroned, were the six ladies who were his current favourites; and as troopers trotted alongside, great crowds loudly applauded the majesty he copied from the country of his adoption.

Totally unlike him, but equally successful, was Major Samuel MacPherson, whose father was the Professor of Greek in Aberdeen. Samuel, a sickly child, grew up into a natural scholar who had to abandon his studies because of failing eyesight; so he became a soldier and went to India in 1827. Within a few years he was appointed to the survey of Hyderabad and became acquainted with the Khonds, and other primitive tribes, whose rites were regarded as pernicious and whose habit was rebellious. Their religion, according to Lieutenant MacPherson, was 'a weak incoherent theism, with a subordinate demonology'; and their ritual included human sacrifice, of which their new British neighbours disapproved. Two campaigns against the Khonds failed to effect their reform, there were insufficient troops to essay a third, and Captain MacPherson, suitably promoted, was given the task of 'humanizing' them. They were a dangerous and barbarous people, who lived in difficult country with a noxious climate, but between 1841 and 1844 he was remarkably successful. Then, after home-leave made necessary by severe illness, he returned to India and as political agent in Gwalior did much to dissuade Scindia, the young maharajah, from throwing his forces into the great Mutiny that soon followed. He was unrewarded for his efforts and died, exhausted, at the age of fifty-four.

A poor advertisement for imperialism? In one way a very poor advertisement; but looked at from another point of view, a justification. There were many others who, like Samuel from the

Greek manse in Old Aberdeen, spent their lives in service to an ideal, and got no reward for it: perhaps a thousand times as many as those who came home with their pockets well lined.

But that ideal, it will be said, is long since out of date: a gross anachronism. We have done for ever with imperialism. . . .

Not, however, with other countries. Now, as it seems – at any moment – we shall find ourselves as closely involved with all those strangely spoken, curiously accented Europeans as ever we were with Gurkhas and Punjabi Mussulmans. On rather different terms, of course, but for Scotland the circumstances may revive old memories. Scots will be able to remove themselves from the inhibiting company of their fellow Scots, they may discover a larger environment such as that which so happily released their dormant energy, their latent virtues, and their suppressed self-confidence when they had an Empire for their habitation and their pleasure. The Common Market will, perhaps, become a market place for talents that have no room to grow in Scotland. It is, at any rate, a challenge, and in the past we have shown a capacity to respond to challenge. *Il faut être toujours botté et prêt à partir*, as Montaigne so appropriately remarks.

The Quality of Life

Michael Powell

Owing to the fact that everything has already been written, particularly by Scots, about the essential Scottishness of the quality of life in Scotland, I am going to trot out a number of impeccable Exhibits, upon which I propose to harness an equal number of personal experiences, and put the whole circus through its paces, for the benefit of the subject of this Chapter, imposed upon me by my friend, the Editor.

First: a Preamble.

Preamble

They are the most personal people in the world. When you cross from Switzerland into France, or into Austria, or from Austria into Germany, or into Italy, it takes some time before you see any difference: when you cross from England into Scotland, the effect is immediate. You are in a foreign country. You have gone abroad. Try it and see.

The Scottish savour is not elusive, but it is exclusive. Engage a Scot, man, woman, or child, in conversation, in London, Kirriemuir, Mandalay, Rhodesia, Townsville, Coppermine, or Cape Cod, and you will appreciate the quality of the race. Naturally, in Scotland it is all-pervasive. You see it in the architecture: in the freshly white-washed but and ben, in the colossal granite walls of Aberdeen, in the majestic sweep into the heart of Dundee of the new road-bridge over the Tay, in the fantasies of Scottish baronial, in the purity of the brothers Adam. You hear it in the speech – direct, literate and colourful – whether broad Lowland, or careful Highland. You enjoy it in the magnificent engineering of the roads, even the smallest; the abundance of public golf-courses; the stupendous high-teas; the generous drams of whisky; the electric blankets in the clean beds; the unpretentious goodness of the small things of life. You appreciate it in the high level of conversation with the people you meet, the fact that it is difficult to find a dour Scotsman, the way that every Scot knows personally every other Scot (or else knows somebody who knows him), the politeness with which your host, or your casually-met acquaintance, draws the facts about you out of you.

Exhibit I: Homely Folk

Beside her I noticed a little pile of books one of which was a Bible. Open on her lap was a paper, the United Free Church Monthly. I noticed these details greedily for I had to make up my mind on the part to play.

'It's a warm day, mistress,' I said, my voice falling into the broad Lowland speech, for I had an instinct she was not of the Highlands.

She laid aside her paper: 'It is that, sir. It is grand weather for the hairst, but here that's no' till the hinner end o' September, and at the best it's a bit scart o' aits.'

'Ay. It's a different thing down Annandale way.'

Her face lit up: 'Are ye from Dumfries, sir?'

'Not just from Dumfries, but I know the Borders, fine.'

'Ye'll no' beat them,' she cried. 'Not that this is no a guid place and I've muckle to be thankfu' for since John Anderson – that was ma man – brocht me here forty-seeven year syne come Martinmas. But the aulder I get the mair I think o' the bit whaur I was born. It was twae miles from Wamphray on the Lockerbie road, but they tell me the place is noo just a rickle o' stanes.'

'I was wondering, mistress, if I could get a cup of tea in the village.'

'Ye'll hae a cup wi' me,' she said. 'It's no often we see ony-body frae the Borders hereaways. The kettle's just on the boil.'

She gave me tea and scones and butter, and blackcurrant jam, and treacle-biscuits that melted in the mouth.

John Buchan, *Mr Standfast**

As we off-loaded rucksacks, sacks, sticks, cameras, our dog and our three be-kilted selves at the door of Alastair's house, two little Glasgow boys lent on the railings:

'Whaur are ye back from? Everest?'

* This extract is reproduced by permission of the Tweedsmuir Estate.

Alastair grunted:

'You see! It's impossible to get a swelled head in Glasgow.'

The three kilts, green, saffron, and MacTavish, were back from the Western Isles, where we had spent three days on Colonsay and Oronsay. So had Sweep, the dog. It was early in March, often a good month for the Highlands and the Isles. The wind had been keen, from the north-west, but the thin sunshine and the high cloud, the clear tops and the green sea, had made up for it.

Colonsay lies out in the Atlantic, about half-way between Iona and Islay, connected with the island of Oronsay by a mile-wide strand, which dries out at low tide. The islands are privately owned by the descendants of Donald Smith who, emigrating to Canada from Forres at the age of sixteen, rose in the service of the Hudson's Bay Company to become Chief Factor and Chairman, one of the builders of the Canadian Pacific Railway, and of Canada. How many steamship-lines, railroads, banks, protectorates and Dominions, have had their origin in a Scottish manse, or a but and ben! The reason is simple: large, vigorous families, in which fools are not suffered gladly and whose individual members all want to be first in their chosen profession. Like many successful Scotsmen, Donald Smith, by then the first Lord Strathcona, returned to Scotland to end his days, and bought the islands from MacNeil of Barra. On the west side is a famous strand of golden sand, the sands of Kiloran (St Oran; the prefix or suffix 'Cille' is Gaelic for Saint, thus Columcille for St Columba), facing Barra and the Outer Hebrides across the herring-black Minch. A more lovely, private, and sacred spot – sacred to Saint Oran and Saint Columba – cannot be imagined, and you can reach it from Glasgow in the day.

We drove in a large, black, sedate, pre-war Humber to the fishing port of Tarbert on the Mull of Kintyre; but the way to go the first time is by the steamer, through the Kyles of Bute, with changing views of the hills and the Isle of Arran. Tarbert is a bright, sheltered, little port, on a neck of land so narrow that chieftains have had their galleys pulled over by hand from West Loch, on the Atlantic side. There the *Lochiel* was lying. She was one of MacBrayne's better boats. We sailed at one o'clock and had lunch on board. The Humber was left on the dock; no cars are admitted to Colonsay.

The sea-loch was calm and so was the open sea under Jura and Islay. We stopped briefly at Gigha, dropping mail and two passengers into an open boat off the north end of the island; next stop was at the pier of Craighouse, on Jura, where we put off a coffin and a band of cheerful mourners; next was at Port Askaig, in the Sound between Islay and Jura, a romantic landing-place, where the tide flows between the islands as fast as a mill-race and as deep as the sea. When we cleared the Sound, the breeze freshened and we felt the Atlantic swell.

By six p.m. we were anchored off Colonsay, scrambling into a large red ferry-boat, along with a horse-box full of cows. Mr Jones, the hotel-manager, was in the boat's crew, a genial Hobbit-like presence. On the quay, beaming and soft-spoken, was David Clark. Beyond him a tall, spare, courteous presence, corduroys stuffed into boots – the third Lord Strathcona. He greeted us and shyly asked us to come and see him at the house, 'any time, any meal, please do come!' The Hobbit, grinning broadly, as Hobbits do, piled us and our traps into a Land Rover – the only one on the island – and whisked us off at supersonic speed up the long, wet road to the hotel, where Mrs Jones, in black satin, received us, supported by a thin maid in an apron, We approved the boiling-hot running water, and Sweep the huge coal-fire, in a small room filled with sofas. After a huge dinner, David looked in, with Duncan Mitchell, the schoolmaster.

When St Columba sailed from Ireland to convert the wild Scots to Christianity he is said to have landed on the islet, now known as Oronsay; but, when he found that he could still see his native land, he set sail again, coasted along Colonsay, and crossed the open water to Iona. Alastair traced a great COLUMBA with the point of his staff on the golden sands where the Saint had trod, and Sweep sat in the capital C. The tide was half out and the sun was trying to push its way through March-coloured clouds. We had brought our lunch. We sought shelter from the wind under a great rock and lit a fire from driftwood. There was a huge log of mahogany, rolling in the surf, that must have drifted direct from Honduras. Black-faced sheep, fat and woolly, came and stared at us.

We arrived at the long, low, pinkish block of Colonsay House at about half past three. Strathcona was working on a new rockery of dwarf trees and rock-plants. The garden is famous, with its sheltering hedges of fuschia, its plantations and one of the best collections of rhododendrons on the West coast. We are three weeks too early, but he shows us the wild garden, with its cascade, and the hanging leaves of the giant plants, like elephant's ears, green above and brown beneath. We had tea in the curving, wood-panelled study. Jimmie, the driver-engineer, ran us back to hot baths and an early supper before the Show.

We were showing *I Know Where I'm Going* to the people of Colonsay, which was the 'Kiloran' in the film. Few of them had seen it; I hadn't seen it myself for ten years, and suddenly I got stage-fright. Suppose they didn't like it! However, all went well. The projection was good and the show was in the same long, low room, where we had the *ceilidh*, which inspired the one in the film. I said in my speech that this was where it started. The remark was received in respectful silence. Strathcona said some homely words: he was moved by the film. David murmured some soft nothings in the Gaelic. Niall Oronsay made a speech, which nobody understood, but gave general satisfaction.

Dancing, singing, and reciting followed until midnight. A small but select party, consisting of Mr and Mrs Jones, Mr and Mrs Donald McNeill of Garvard, Mr and Mrs Andrew McNeil of Oronsay, plus one or two others, plus the visiting shentlemen, came back to the hotel and whooped it up until three in the morning.

The next day we went to Oronsay. Before breakfast Bill and I went down to the pier where half the male population of the island were loading stirks into the ferry-boat; this was not accomplished without argument on both sides. Time and again a bullock broke away and came panting up from the jetty, surrounded by dancing and shouting sheep dogs. Once, a heifer plunged into the sea; and, once, Bill nearly followed it. At last the ferry sailed, lop-sided, out to the waiting steamer.

The tide was just uncovering the strand when we got to the hut. If you know the ford you can cross over to the island half an hour earlier and cross back again on the same tide before it starts to flow. Donald came down driving a red tractor with a small iron trailer to drive us to Garvard Farm and, for fun, headed out over the strand, showering us with sand and water, paying no heed to our yells. Sweep sat in my arms, shivering with disdain. At the farm Nora gave us tea and scones. We got into a solid old bone-shaker of a market-cart, with a solid, old, bony, black horse between the shafts and splashed out across the mile of sand, intersected by channels of water.

We sat in a row, freezing in the cold sunshine. Occasionally a thin flurry of snow blew clear through us and out the other side. The horse splashed steadily on. The ford curves around seaweedy rocks and through acres of foot-deep sea-water flurried by the wind. We scraped between walls of rock, blasted and cut out of the low cliff, climbed the hill and crossed Oronsay, opening up the view of the Paps of Jura, across the machair, and the hill, Carn Cul Evrinn, from which Columba saw, for the last time, the hills of Donegal.

We drove into the yard and fell out like frozen mutton. The horse and cart returned across the ford. I dragged the others to see the great Cross and the rows of stones, carved with swords, effigies, and ribbon-animals, which lie sleeping, like their owners, in the shadow of the priory walls. We had a cup of tea with Andrew and sat by a roaring fire in a tiny, panelled study. Andrew got out the tractor and a big trailer, which we filled with armfuls of hay, into which Sweep burrowed thankfully, and trundled us rapidly back over the island and across the ford. It was a four-mile, frozen, march home; the March wind would have taken the skin off an onion.

Strathcona speeded us with presents of whisky; my bottle was Laphroaig, a straight malt, heavy and smoky, distilled on Islay, in white-washed buildings with their feet in the sea.

When we reached the car again at West Loch Tarbert, I tele-phoned Crinan Hotel: Iain Mackenzie was at the cattle-sales at Lochgilphead. The town was dressed with flags. A sixth sense led me round the back, where we drew up beside Iain, in the same battered bonnet and darned kilt, leaning on his shooting brake, talking to a black-bearded man and a sturdy girl, who turned out to be George Orwell's sister, from Jura. Iain said: 'If you don't make that film of the Lord of the Isles soon, Gordon and I will be too old to kill Campbells.'

We drove back by Crianlarich and the road down the length of Loch Lomond. We had been away three days. It seemed like three weeks.

Everest my foot!

Exhibit II: Legend

When the last laird of Ravenswood to Ravenswood
shall ride,

And woo a dead maiden to be his bride,

He shall stable his steed in the Kelpie's flow,
And his name shall be lost for evermore.

Sir Walter Scott

There is talk in Ullapool of a Sabbath day when the Devil played the pipes on the top of Ben More Coigach; and this is the truth of it.

Bill, Alastair and I had met in Assynt, in Sutherlandshire, at the little inn at Kylesku Ferry about thirty miles south of Cape Wrath. We had climbed Suilven, that amazing sugar-loaf mountain, which starts bolt upright out of the rocks above Lochinver. All that deer forest belongs to Vestey, the meat king, and his stalkers accompanied us to the top just to stretch their legs and watch where the deer were moving. It had been a clear day and we had a great view over Assynt's thousand lochs and hills. A great lump of a hill, beyond Stac Polly and above the Summer Isles, attracted my attention and Seton, who had come over the sea from Skye to join us, said it was Ben More, one of the many Ben Mores in the highlands – Ben Mhor means Big Mountain in Gaelic. We planned to move on down the coast to Achiltibuie and stay at the little hotel, which looks out to Tanera More and Tanera Beg; from that comfortable base we would climb Ben More.

Seton Gordon, of course, had brought his pipes and had been playing pibroch after pibroch in the long summer evenings, marching with short and stately step along the edge of the awesome loch, listened to by an appreciative audience of seals, moaning in sympathy with the drone of the pipes, as Seton played the Lament for MacSweyn of Roag. How the suggestion arose, I don't remember, but by the time we were all installed at Achiltibuie it was settled that he would play the pipes on the top of Ben More, which rose up 2,500 feet above sea-level – our level. The snag was, the next day was Sunday, and quite apart from what the local people would think of such goings-on on the Sabbath, there were Seton's neighbours on Skye to consider: if it should ever be known in Uig that Maister Seton Gordon, CBE, laird of Upper Duntulm, world-famous zoologist, naturalist, and judge of piping, author and nature-photographer, had put his lips to a chanter on the Sabbath, there would be hell to pay. He would have to leave the island.

A circuitous approach was indicated; postponement was not to be thought of: we all had to be back at work, and were going on

127

to Ullapool after conquering the mountain, to catch the bus next day to the little railway station at Garve, thirty miles to the south. Alastair was to carry the pipes in his rucksack; Bill and I would cram everything else, including food, on our backs; and we three would assault the mountain from the seaward side. Seton and Dara, his black and white Border sheep-dog, would drive around the mountain and, coming up the eastern slopes, would meet us on the top; that is, if the day were pretty. It dawned fine and clear, and after a huge breakfast of porridge and sea-trout, the assault-party trudged off along the road, speeded gently on its way by Seton, who knows every path of every hill in the Highlands and had several hours in hand.

Seton is tall and romantic, spare and active, gentle of voice and hard of hearing, so that his eyes, which miss nothing that moves on the hill, are always full of humour and enquiry, when he takes part in the conversation, his slender hand curved around his ear, turned to the last speaker. His stride is long and his pace seems slow on the hill, for he stops often to pull out his glass and, steadying the heavy end with his hand against his long staff, follow the movements of deer, or eagle. But his pace is not as slow as it seems, he never pauses for breath, keeps his height and is seldom more than five minutes behind the thrusters. He wears Highland dress, his feet shod with stout brogues, a bonnet or a shooting-hat on his head, the glass slung on his back, a long staff in his hand. He loves bright colours and today wears a red flannel shirt and a knitted tie, under his short-cut Highland jacket, patched with leather.

'Keep a good, slow pace. It's going to be hot. Dara and I will see you on the top about noon.'

Bill only knows one way up a hill: straight up. He is built like a tank and takes obstacles in the way that tanks do – with contempt. We were happy that he should lead. We had about four miles along the road by Loch Broom before we flung ourselves at the great hill. The south-west side of the Ben falls down steeply to the Loch, but on the West it rises in giant steps. It was April, but the sun was hot. As we climbed the great country to the north of us opened up. What a country that is! The ribbed hills were blue and stark, we could see half Sutherlandshire: nearest to us the bare mass of Stac Polly, beyond the double hump of Suilven, over to the right Ben More Assynt, and everywhere the gleam of water. This is the country of giant lake-trout and of the beautiful black-

128

throated diver. There are thousands of red deer. There is a waterfall near Kylesku, where the stream plunges over the lip of rock to fall into a cup three hundred feet below, only to bounce out and fall another three hundred feet or so into the glen. It must be one of the highest falls in the British Isles and hardly anybody knows it is there: the country is so big. It is called Eas-Coul-aulin: the tresses of a maiden's hair.

There was nobody to greet us on the flat top when we arrived. Bill took off his kilt and rung it out. I took a picture of him with his shirt-tails flying. Alastair got out the pipes and played a tune on the chanter. A few minutes later Dara appeared over the edge of the rocks followed by the slow, deliberate figure of Seton, leaning on his staff.

The first thing he did was to get out his glass and spend a quarter of an hour examining the country at his feet. Nothing that moved escaped him. The air was clear as it is only in early Spring. Then, urged on by us, he took the pipes and started his slow march to and fro, on the flat top, in the bright sunshine, with the greatest background a piper ever had for his performance. He played a pibroch. I remember it had a long and complicated name, even for a pibroch and even in the Gaelic, something about the Battle of the Pass of the Shoes: either they lost their shoes and lost the battle or threw them off and won the battle. I don't remember, although I am sure Seton does. For although there wasn't a house, nor a man, within ten miles of us, and we could only be over-looked by eagles, they knew in Ullapool before we arrived there, that the pipes had been heard on Ben More and, since it was the Sabbath, it could only be the Devil himself. We had tramped eight miles and wanted our tea, so we agreed with them; and that is how the legend started.

Exhibit III: Romance

Kingsburgh was completely the figure of the gallant High-lander – exhibiting the graceful mien and manly looks which our popular Scotch song has justly attributed to that character. He had his tartan plaid thrown about him, a large blue bonnet with a knot of black riband like a cockade, a brown, short coat of a kind of duffel, a tartan waistcoat with gold buttons and gold buttonholes, a blueish philibeg, and tartan hose. He had jet

129

A Pictish settlement at Jarlshof (Shetland mainland), where there is evidence of a sequence of occupations dating from the second millennium B.C.

black hair tied behind, and was a large, stately man, with a steady, sensible countenance.

There was a comfortable parlour with a good fire and a dram went round. By and by supper was served at which there appeared the lady of the house, the celebrated Miss Flora Macdonald. She is a little woman of a genteel appearance, and uncommonly mild and well-bred. To see Dr Samuel Johnson, the great champion of the English Tories salute Miss Flora Macdonald in the Isle of Skye, was a striking sight; for though somewhat congenial in their notions, it was very improbable they should meet here.

The room where we lay that night was a celebrated one. Dr Johnson's bed was the very bed in which the grandson of the unfortunate King James the Second lay, on one of the nights after the failure of his rash attempt in 1745, while he was eluding the emissaries of government, which had offered thirty thousand pounds as a reward for apprehending him. The Doctor smiled and said, 'I have had no ambitious thoughts in it'.

From Boswell's *Journal of a Tour to the Hebrides*

Historians and schoolmasters rap us over the knuckles and tell us that the Act of Union is more important than the '45 Rebellion, that the Clearances were more fatal to the Highlands than the Massacre of Glencoe, that Mary Queen of Scots had no political sense: they point out that the '45 Rebellion was a Jacobite rebellion, not a rebellion by Scotland against England, that the Highland chiefs themselves were divided in their loyalty, that the mass of the Scottish people had no interest in the cause of the Young Pretender, until he looked like winning; that the Glencoe incident was a Balkan scuffle between rival clans; that Darnley was an adventurer, Bothwell a Border cattle-thief, and that the only question of interest in Queen Mary's brief reign is the authenticity of the Casket letters; and yet – and yet – in modern Scotland, with her hydro-electric schemes, atomic power-stations, new bridges, roads, and tunnels, her deep-sea fishing fleets; in the bustle of Glasgow, the dignity of Edinburgh, the excitement of Aberdeen, the deliberation of Inverness, you are never far from the world of romance, where lost causes, bright heroes, and tragic ladies, make the eye moist, and the heart beat faster, where the sacredness of hospitality is part of life, where a Cameron will not sit on a Board with a Campbell, and where there is no mistaking when you pass from MacDonald country into that of MacLean.

Exhibit IV: Sensuality

> O wha's been here afore me, lass?
> And hoo did he get in?
> – A man that deed or I was born
> This evil thing has din.
>
> And left, as it were on a corpse,
> Your maidenheid to me?
> – Nae lass, gudeman, sin' Time began
> 'S hed ony mair to gi'e.
>
> But I can gi'e ye kindness lad,
> And a pair o' willin' hands
> And you sall ha'e my breists like stars,
> My limbs like willow wands.
>
> And on my lips ye'll heed nae mair,
> And in my hair forget,
> The seed o' a' the men that in
> My virgin womb ha'e met.

Hugh MacDiarmid *A Drunk Man Looks at the Thistle*

It will come as no surprise to the countrymen of Burns that I regard sensuality as an essential and attractive quality in Scottish life, as it is in France. No doubt this was the solid basis of the Auld Alliance. A country and people that respects brains, and reveres education, is not usually lacking in the other appetites: they go together. Frank and bawdy in sex, passionate in love, steadfast in marriage, possessive of their children, the Scots demand good food and strong drink, solid comfort and good quality clothes. Maybe the French find their old ally's tastes a wee bit sober, but they, too like value for money, and they would have to admit that the Scots have the better of it: Scottish houses, Scottish tweeds, Scottish roads, are built to last; Scottish matrons, for comfort, rather than speed; Scottish whisky is a nonpareil.

You may have noticed that the word, pride, did not appear in the preceding paragraph, as it certainly would if I had been writing about France. It seems to me that the pride of the Scots in their history and their achievements is buried so deep in their nature that it seldom appears in public. When it does it is magnificent, as when Colin Campbell, at Balaclava, seeing the thin red line of Highlanders start to move forward against the squadrons of Russian cavalry, shouted:

> '– Ninety-third! Ninety-third! Damn all
> that eagerness.'

No, the Scots are not proud of their possessions, they are too generous to be proud. This is the basis of their famous hospitality: the good things in life are to be shared: families are large and have many ramifications: the branches spread all over the world: every Scottish matriarch spends at least a quarter of her day writing letters and doing up parcels: every busy Scot must know, I sometimes think, a million other Scots, by name and occupation, in Scotland alone; and when it comes to the Commonwealth, well – it's a Scottish preserve; and everywhere the Scot takes his standards with him; and his whisky.

> Inspiring bold John Barleycorn!
> What dangers thou canst make us scorn!
> Wi' tippeny we fear nae evil;
> Wi' *usquebae* we'll face the devil!

How true! How very true! Whisky is the life of man, and frequently the death of him. It is not my intention to launch into a dithyramb to whisky. I will only say that in my opinion the sweetest words I remember were uttered by a monosyllabic stalker of my acquaintance, after my first stag, when, stopping by a peaty-brown spring that rushed from the hill, he filled two horn cups with Islay Mist, topped up with cold spring water and said: 'Will ye have a dram?'

We had been out twelve hours and covered about twenty-five miles on the hill before I got my stag, and we had dragged him by the horns and hoofs nearly a mile to the track, where the fat, white pony with the sledge could come bumping up the glen to bring him back to the castle. What a dram that was!

And the bakeries! The bread, the morning rolls, the oatcakes! The butteries, the baps, the bannocks! Soda scones, made with buttermilk! Girdle scones, large and small! Potato scones, without which no Glasgow Sunday breakfast is complete! The pancakes, the crumpets, the biscuits! The shortbread that melts in the mouth! Buns of every size, shape and stickiness! There is even a Black Bun. The gingerbread, the ginger-cake, the currant loaf, the hold your breath, now! – the Dundee Cake! Ah! I thought that would stop you! And next – with tears choking my throat – the pies! The meat pies, the mince pies, the Forfar Bridies – but I can't go on, or I'll leave no space for the butchers.

If all the beef advertised as Scottish in London Steakhouses comes from over the Border there must be twenty million head of beef cattle between Carlisle and Thurso; because the Scottish housewife likes to buy her meat fresh, and sees that she gets it. She likes the meat off the bone and rolled, as in France, and the Scottish butcher is an artist at his trade. Most of the cuts are different from England and have different names. Sirloin, you would understand, but what is Nine Holes? Steak is steak in any language, but what is Pope's eye, or heukbone steak? My dog, Johnnie, knows shin when he hears it, but what is his reaction to hough? A spalebone stew sounds almost as kailyard as Barrie. Nae worry! Never heed! The Scottish housewife is an artist in her kitchen.

And then the puddings! The black puddings, the white puddings, the mealy puddings! And King of Puddings, the Haggis! What's in a Haggis? I know. But I know no reason why you should. All you need to know is that it should be served with mashed potatoes and bashed neeps, and you must drink whisky with it. You will discover that the oatmeal in the haggis absorbs the whisky, and so you can drink more of it. What else do you need to know?

And then the lasses! O, the lasses!

> Auld Nature swears the lovely dears
> Her noblest work she classes, O:
> Her prentice han' she tried on man,
> And then she made the lasses, O.
> Green grow the rashes, O,
> Green grow the rashes, O,
> The sweetest hours that e'er I spent,
> Were spent among the lasses, O.

I had once a Scottish secretary. What a mundane phrase! She was as golden as a daffodil in the wind, as tall and straight as a birch-tree, as fresh as an unpicked peach. I first saw her at Tobermory being chased indefatigably by young naval officers. I knelt and offered her a job. She refused me. A year later I stepped off a tram in Glasgow into her arms. I know nothing else good about Glasgow trams but, for Elspeth's sake, I love them. I knelt again, she wanted a change from Glasgow, and this time consented. She was as perfect a secretary, as she was in every other way. All my friends and associates were in love with her, but since everyone was in love with her it didn't matter. After two years I dreamt she might stay forever. But the Glasgow doctor whom she was running away from, bided his time, got his degree, swooped down like Lochinvar, and bore her away to be a brain-specialist's wife. Nothing wrong with *his* brain at any rate! What a girl that was!

Exhibit V: Guts

> Upon the bridge his strength he threw,
> And struck the iron chain in two,
>   By which its planks arose;
> The warder next his axe's edge
> Struck down upon the threshold ledge
> 'Twixt door and post a ghastly wedge
>   The gate they may not close.
> Loud came the cry, 'The Bruce! The Bruce!'
> No hope, or in defence, or truce –
>   Fresh combatants pour in;
> Mad with success and drunk with gore,
> They drive the struggling foe before,
>   And ward on ward they win
> Unsparing was the vengeful sword,
> And limbs were lopped and life-blood pour'd
> The cry of death and conflict roar'd
>   And fearful was the din.
>   Sir Walter Scott *The Lord of the Isles*

We are told that Walter Scott composed the Lord of the Isles 'in the cottage at Abbotsford, surrounded by his family and casual visitors, neither conversation nor music seeming to disturb him'. We can well believe it. Only a determination to finish Canto Fifth before going to bed could produce such ruthless rum-ti-tum. But who cares? What a story-teller! What guts! What ferocity! And how true to Scottish nature! There may be many other nations, who are bonny fighters, but I am concerned here with the Scots. Not for nothing was the Bible often the only book in a Scottish household: 'Whatsoever thy hand findeth to do, do it with thy might; for there is no work, nor device, nor knowledge, nor wisdom, in the grave, whither thou goest'. Upon this text the Scots have converted heathen, brought medicine to the savage, explored rivers, discovered riches, founded dynasties, won battles, and caught the 9.15.

MacBrayne's boats to the Western Isles have remarkable Captains; Squeaky Robertson was perhaps the most remarkable in his day. The Minch can be one of the nastiest pieces of water in the world, but it is rare that a sailing is cancelled. One crossing to Lochboisdale, which ended by nearly ramming the pier, will never be forgotten by a friend of mine. He went up to the bridge and found Captain Robertson holding a cup of tea in his hands.

'Thanks to the Almighty and to you, Captain Robertson, we weren't drowned.'

The Captain looked over his teacup and, in his husky Highland voice (of which he was fully conscious) squeaked:

'Two goot men.'

Exhibit VI: Highland Landscape

It was near noon before we set out; a dark day with clouds, and the sun shining upon little patches. The sea was here very deep and still, and had scarce a wave upon it, so that I must put the water to my lips before I could believe it to be truly salt. The mountains on either side were high, rough and barren, very black and gloomy in the shadow of the clouds, but all silver-laced with little watercourses where the sun shone upon them. It seemed a hard country, this of Appin, for people to care as much about as Alan did.

There was but one thing to mention. A little after we had started, the sun shone upon a little moving clump of scarlet close in along the waterside to the north. It was much of the same red as soldiers' coats; every now and then, too, there came little sparks and lightnings, as though the sun had struck upon bright steel.

Robert Louis Stevenson *Kidnapped*

135

Looking back to Scotland from 'Skerryvore', in Bournemouth, setting the Highland scene for the murder of the Red Fox, R.L.S. saw the country of Appin as if he were there. That is one of the magic qualities of the Highlands: the great hills, the silver of lochs, or burns, the movement of living creatures, like the patch of red of the soldiers' coats, establishing the scale, making you realize how many miles lie before you, all this comes back to you in a wink as you sit dreaming in your chair; and then there is nothing for it, but to reach for a time-table, and book a sleeper, and step out into the heather in the early morning at one of the stations between Perth and Aviemore; unless you are a story-teller like Stevenson and Buchan who, with a few words, can put the dusty road under your feet and the taste of the peaty hill-burn to your lips.

It was in the second week of November, when Bill and I walked across Ardnamurchan. We had crossed to Kilchoan the night before, on a lobster-boat from Tobermory in Mull. We had telephoned from Oban that we wanted to cross that night. Mr Courie of the MacDonald Arms said it would depend on the tide: the boat was on the mud. When we got there, by the steamer *Loch Nevis*, we saw that the boat was nearly floating and three boys were working on it. Mr Courie was waiting at the door for us, the bar was open at half past four, and we all pressed in. A fat man, with a fine face and a mass of grey hair, had a fiddle thrust at him and played some tunes rather well. The boat was floating! They had gone to find some fuel. We had another glass of Old Mull. The boat was ready. We shook hands all round, picked up our huge rucksacks and staggered to the pier. It was a thirty-foot lobster-boat. Courie Junior, our skipper, was twenty-three; they have another boat, fifty-three feet long. The sun had set as we cross the Sound, but there was so much afterglow in the clear sky we could see for miles. Mull looked as if cut out of black paper, and a crescent moon hung above the cliffs. The skipper told me they got 800 pounds of lobsters on their last trip around the Treshnish Isles. They used 250 pots, all home-made. They haul in by winch. Lobster fetches about 50p a pound in Oban. A flashing light from a torch held by the driver of the car from the hotel guided us in to Kilchoan.

Now we were following the old track over the peninsula to Acharacle in Glen Shiel. The morning was gloriously clear and cold. The track was rough and wet, but had once been very good, and the keen frost made it possible to pass over the boggy patches, occasionally breaking through the frozen surface, as thin sheets of ice crackled under our feet. The burns were roaring down, but the stone bridges stood. When we stopped for lunch at Kentra Bay, two boys on ponies passed us, the bigger one on a tiny Shetland, the smaller on a brown garron. The tide was out, so we cut across the bay and came to Loch Shiel Hotel. Next morning we took the red-painted motor-boat up the loch to Glenfinnan, the road the Prince took that morning in '45. We caught the train to Mallaig and the steamer up the Sound of Sleat. As we passed Gavin Maxwell's cottage at Sandaig I looked for signs of life, but even with glasses I could see nobody.

We reached bright and busy Kyle of Lochalsh at about two o'clock. So far we had changed from lobster-boat to motor car, to flat feet to motor-boat, to Highland railway to MacBrayne steamer as if the whole journey across Ardnamurchan and Moidart had been planned by Thomas Cook. Quick now! Where was the small motor-boat at Kyle, which is rumoured to go back down the Sound again to Glenelg?

'Ye'll find a wee boot the other side o' the pier.'

We went and peered over – into a fibre-glass swimming pool. Underneath it we finally made out a dingy motor-boat at the end of a rickety iron ladder.

'Are ye for Glenelg?'

He was a tall, shock-haired young man, in startlingly dirty dungarees. We said we might be, but was there any room under the swimming-pond?

'Ach! plenty. It's for Major Maxwell and his otters. We are taking it down to him tonight. You can get on at the ferry-pier, when we come for mail.'

'We'll get a cup of tea. Mind now! wait for us!'

Bill is a great believer in tea while it is going. When we saw the swimming-pond at close quarters it looked even larger. It was being transported with the fore-part propped up on the wheel-house, with the skipper, crew and passengers under it. It weighed about three and a half hundredweight, they said. We slipped down with the tide to the village of Glenelg, where we landed somebody's greenhouse, and the crew went to have tea, while the sun inconsiderately set in glory over the Coolin hills of Skye. By the time they came back, wiping their mouths, it was nearly dusk. Sandaig Light is four miles south of Glenelg and by the time we had rounded the islands and started to nose our way in we couldn't see a thing. Fortunately it's a shallow, sandy beach by the cottage. Two torches started to flash on shore and we launched the swimming-pond with a splash like one of the Queens entering the Clyde. Tosh, the skipper, jumped inside and started to drift rapidly away to the island of Eigg, but Bill hurled an oar at him, and they pulled and poled their way back struggling with the eight-knot tide. I went ashore in the dinghy and met a tall beautiful youth in the light of the torch (Jimmy). I went with him up to the cottage, carrying two cans of kerosene, escorted by a stream of curses in the Gaelic from an old fellow in a cap, who had fallen over an outboard motor and a length of copper-tubing. Evidently Gavin was on a spending-spree.

He was cleaning mussels in the sink, when we entered and greeted me genially:

'Damn you, Micky. There's a bed for you with someone else's sheets and moules marinière for supper. Did you bring any whisky?'

'Certainly.'

'Then you're welcome.'

Meanwhile Bill, who is a Shetlander, and looks on the Western Islanders as effete Neapolitans, was in his element, laying about him in the dark and practically bringing the swimming-pond up to the cottage single-handed.

We played Gaelic folk-songs on the gramophone after dinner while Edal's flat feet tramped up and down on the ceiling, occasionally stopping to roll her marbles and other playthings, while the big dog-otter, Teko the Slob, whistled in his house outside. Gavin drank my whisky and we drank his brandy.

In the morning we walked up the track to the cottage on the road:

'Good morning, gentlemen! I hope you slept well and that the Major looked after you. They already know at the Estate office about your irregular arrival. Thank goodness, I have the Gaelic and can say what I like in the presence of the English, me cursing them in most beautiful phrases and they not understanding a word I am saying. It is a great safety-valve. But I am boring you with my talk. I see the yawning jaws of aching weariness, as Nietschze put it.'

We were staying the next night with Angus Campbell, the foreman of the Estate, but before we met him we saw a lady hanging perilously over the bridge of the burn.

'See any big ones?'

'Ay. There's a whole lot of them together, and there's one a pound and a half at least. Do you mind his tail?'

We did. It was a sea-trout.

'They're late coming up,' said Angus, a very handsome man, speaking the Gaelic of South Uist, although he was born in Mallaig. After high tea Mrs Campbell and one of her sons, a red-headed young man in the Merchant Navy, went to the whist-drive. The Campbells have six children, all away from home.

The next day we went back by Inverness to London.

Exhibit VII: Lowland Landscape

Having abandoned my fishing-rod as an unprofitable implement, I crossed over the open downs which divided me from the margin of the Solway. When I reached the banks of the great estuary, which are here very bare and exposed, the waters had receded from the large and level space of sand, through which a stream, now feeble and fordable, found its way to the ocean. The whole was illuminated by the beams of the low and setting sun, who showed his ruddy front, like a warrior prepared for defence, over a huge battlemented and turreted wall of crimson and black clouds, which appeared like an immense Gothic fortress into which the lord of day was descending. His setting rays glimmered bright upon the wet surface of the sands, and the numberless pools of water by which it was covered where the inequality of the ground had occasioned their being left by the tide. The scene was animated by the exertions of a number of horsemen, who were actually employed in hunting salmon, chasing the fish at full gallop and striking them with their barbed spears, as you see hunters spearing boars in the old tapestry.

Sir Walter Scott *Redgauntlet*

Between Solway and Clyde, between the Mull of Galloway and the Grey Mare's Tail, I have seen nearly everything, and what I haven't seen I've heard of – especially during the war-years! – but I have never seen horsemen salmon-sticking in the tidal rivers of Solway, and I would like fine to know whether good Sir Walter saw the sport with his own eyes, or whether he was kidded along by some Border chiel. But one thing I do know (because I had a house on the edge of Galloway for many years, in a glen in those green bare hills, where the lonely graves of the martyrs are lying), and that is the low, rocky coast, the hirpling tides, and the salmon-rivers of the Border Ballads, of S. R. Crockett, of John Paul Jones; the hills, fold upon fold, inhabited only by shepherds and forestry workers, with the small friendly inns in their glens, early tramping-ground of young John Buchan; the clean, sturdy villages and towns, with names from Ballads – Moniaive, Castle Douglas, Gatehouse of Fleet, Wigtown, Glenluce; Dumfries herself, the biggest small town in the world, Queen of the River Nith, where they say that in the great floods a few years ago, a twenty-six pound salmon was found in the police station after the floods receded – it was the only place it would be safe was the Superintendent's explanation; as I was saying, at the beginning of this splendid sentence which has attempted to contain Annandale as well as Galloway in its clauses, there is no place in Scotland like Galloway, and we lovers of Galloway gape to see the cars rushing by to the Highlands in order to crawl head and tail up the shore of Loch Lomond, and down the Great Glen when they could be bowling along the winding but empty roads of Galloway; but we are very glad that they do.

Highlanders are affronted, when they realize the beauty and wildness and bigness of Galloway for the first time. I know Alastair was, when we drove from Edinburgh, in March, to the Isle of Whithorn which, as you will remember, is not an island, but a promontory, jutting out into the Irish Channel, parallel to and not far from the great Mull of Galloway itself. It is the most southerly village in Scotland. We took the road by Clatteringshaws Loch, through the hills, nodding to giant Cairnsmore of Fleet, and by the time we crossed the golden and red moor and I had introduced Alastair to the grey House of Mochrum, among its lochs, he was as near speechless as he has ever been. The object of our journey – for all journeys should have an objective – was to visit Saint Ninian's Chapel. Alastair and I are powerfully protected, so far as Celtic Saints are concerned, for his two sons are Ninian and Mungo, and mine are Kevin and Columba. Between us we move under a saintly umbrella which stretches from the monasteries of Donegal to the brochs of Shetland. It was sunset by the time we got to Whithorn, so we stayed the night, at the Steam Packet Inn, on the end of the jetty, kept by Mrs Kinnear-Browne and her two poodles. There was a remarkable bar, carved from a great block of granite, and we kept it busy. There

140

was company: a mad accountant with his family and an eccentric Edinburgh lawyer. Inside the fire roared and there were electric blankets; outside it was calm and very, very cold.

The sun rising over Cumberland got me up and out to take photographs. I had to put my hands in hot water before I could handle a knife and fork.

Whithorn, the White House, Candida Casa, Leuk'oikidia, is mentioned under its name by Ptolemy, the geographer of Alexandria, in AD 135, so it is reasonable to assume it was of some antiquity, even before Bishop Ninian built his cathedral there, in 397. It became a great place of pilgrimage in the Middle Ages, particularly for the reigning monarch: it gave him an excellent excuse to proceed in leisure and comfort across his kingdom to the shores of Solway, perform penances for his sins, and see what the English were up to. We admired the Scottish coat of arms over one of the archways: supporters, two white unicorns.

We returned through Wigtown where friendly people run the County Hotel. He keeps his Springer spaniels in the hotel office and they pass the time by chewing up the account-books and eating all the bills.

The wonder of the Solway is the geese. They come in thousands in November and stay until March when they fly north to breed in the lands of ice and fire: to see and hear them feeding on the mud, moving before the moving tide, rising in a roar of wings, settling again, then, as the flow covers the sands, taking off, getting into formation, streaming across the dawn sky by hundreds, calling and re-forming, following their leaders into the plough-lands, is as exciting as watching a charge of cavalry; and like cavalry before snipers, the geese fall before the concealed hunters, far out on the merse with their dogs. For hours they have crouched in a mud-hole, reached in darkness by wading down some drain: for hours they have shivered with their dogs, while the sky lightened and revealed the vast landscape around them: now their moment has come: those black blotches on the mud are revealed as men and dogs, a skein of calling geese heads within range, they stand and fire: the leaders cry 'Ware guns! the line swerves, breaks, alters course, re-forms, geese leave the line, mortally wounded; some fall dead and hit the mud with a thud; but still they call to one another, urging each other on against the deadly fire, like Greeks, assailed by Trojan javelins, calling and answering, with that thrilling sound that needs a word invented to describe it, and that no composer but Sibelius has yet heard in his music. To hear it in the wide Solway sky, flailed by the wings of a thousand geese, one moment invisible, the next overhead, is an experience worth travelling round the world to see and hear. The Scots are born with it in their ears.

Postscript

So you have been abroad with me. In a foreign country. If the extremes of climate daunt you, if the mild air and blowing rain of the West Coast, which covers the machair in flowers and enriches the fuschia-hedges, irritates you, if the great sea-cliffs and roof-lifting storms of the Orkneys and Shetlands give you pause, if it means nothing to you to fight a twenty-pound salmon to a finish, to watch male black-cocks rookooing at the lek, to shoot a red-grouse out of the sky at forty miles an hour, to creep close enough to a Black-throated Diver on its nest to count the delicate black and white bars on its neck and chest; if mountains mean to you no more than they did to Doctor Johnson, a considerable pro-tuberance; if you are no nympholept; if islands, lakes and rivers, mountain tarns and waterfalls leave you cold; if blunt speech and high temper displease you, if independent minds and hearts affront you, if you don't wish to carry another country beside your own, in your mind and heart and memory for ever, then don't go to Scotland.

Education
in Scotland
T. L. Cottrell

If anything going on in Scotland now is essentially, characteristically Scottish, it ought to be found in education, in the law, or in the church, because these three social activities were left formally unchanged by the Act of Union. I don't know much – or at least any more than the average modestly informed Scottish layman – about the last two of these three, but I should know something about the first. As a native of Edinburgh, I had my schooling in a Merchant Company School there. Living at home, as most Scots students do, I studied at Edinburgh University. Sixteen years later I went back to Edinburgh as a professor, and I am now the Principal of a new Scottish university. What, then, can I describe as particularly Scottish in my own educational experiences?

In my first month as a professor at Edinburgh University, working in my office one Saturday afternoon, I heard a curious banging noise in the corridor outside my door. I looked out, to see the secretary of one of my colleagues trying to push a filing cabinet from one office to another. She was a lightly built woman, and it was a standard filing cabinet, so she was having little success.

I offered to help, and started to push as well. 'Oh no, Professor,' was her response, 'I couldn't allow you to help me.' My initial indignation passed off when it became clear that she didn't object to me personally, but that she felt that such a task was beneath the dignity of the holder of the office of Professor. I argued that it would be even worse for the dignity of a Professor to have a secretary trapped by a filing cabinet immediately outside his door. She saw the point, and said that the obvious thing to do was to leave the cabinet where it was until Monday, when a servitor could be summoned to move it. Thus the respect due to the holder of a Chair could remain intact.

Academically, I suppose, the office might very well command respect. Although the University of Edinburgh was at that time the youngest of the Scottish universities, the Chair of Chemistry, which I occupied, had been founded about two hundred and fifty years previously, to make it one of the earliest Chairs of the subject in Great Britain.

What seems to me to be significant about this incident is not so much the respect, but that it was shown by a member of the non-academic staff. This argues that it may represent an attitude which is fairly widely spread throughout the community, and one could provide plenty more anecdotal evidence for this. It might be argued, too, that respect for the persons engaged in education would be characteristic of a respect for 'authority', and hence of a somewhat authoritarian attitude to education. Indeed, a rapid opinion poll of some Scots I happened to find in a Dorset hotel in which I started thinking about this article produced 'authoritarian' as the most appropriate epithet for Scottish education.

Thus if one looks for a single, and therefore probably misleading, phrase to epitomize education in Scotland, one might be tempted – to say 'authoritarian and widely diffused'. With more caution, one might rather say 'authoritarian and widely diffused – *but . . .*', and it's this latter thesis I'd like to defend.

So many twentieth-century attitudes are foreshadowed in a rawer form in the nineteenth century that it's worth looking at that most searing of guides to late nineteenth-century Scotland – *The House with the Green Shutters* – to see how the generalization stood up at that time. The respect for education – at least as a social convention – appears as a generalized respect for a learned profession – at least as a career:

> 'What does Wilson mean to make of his son?' he enquired – a civil enough question surely.
>
> 'Oh, a minister. That'll mean six or seven years at the University.'
>
> 'Indeed!' said the Provost, 'That'll cost an enormous siller!'
>
> 'Oh,' yelled Brodie, 'but Wilson can afford it!'

On hearing this John Gourlay, the self-made owner of the house with the green shutters, determines that his son shall go too. His respect for the ministry is slight, but he tells his son:

> '. . . I mean to make you a minister; they have plenty of money and little to do – a grand, easy life o't. MacCandish tells me you're a stupid ass, but have some little gift of words. You have every qualification!'

144

A beach near Tolsta on the Island of Lewis (Outer Hebrides). On a clear day the mainland can be seen 40 miles away across the sea.

Mrs Gourlay was more enthusiastic.

> 'Mrs Gourlay, for her part, though sorry to lose her son, was so pleased at the thought of sending him to college, and making him a minister, that she ran on in foolish maternal gabble to the wife of Drucken Wabster.'

Gourlay saw education as authoritarian enough too. He finds his son playing truant, and brings him back to the High School, where the master asks what he can do about it. Says Gourlay then:

> 'Do – do? Damn it, sir, am *I* to be *your* dominie? Am *I* to teach *you* your duty? Do! Flog him, flog him, flog him! If you don't send him hame wi' the welts as thick as that forefinger, I'll have a word to say to you – ou, Misterr MacCandish!'

Respect paid to well-paid learning, and flogging to enforce it: is that Scottish? It might refer to nineteenth-century England too. But I imagine it went deeper, socially, and the opportunity for education was more widely spread. But . . .

But . . . in the first place it wasn't all that authoritarian. The tendency in secondary education, to concentrate on knowing the facts is reputedly Scottish – but is it *authoritarian*? The facts are important: one cannot intellectualize usefully without them. There is perhaps a sense in which insistence on the facts is authoritarian, and it's partly this insistence that has given Scottish education its reputation. But facts are their own authority, and this sort of authoritarianism is simply a useful inoculation against disappointment when beautiful theories are broken by ugly facts: the point is that it's not arbitrary, and the typical modern use of the word authoritarian implies an arbitrary authority.

And again, although the authoritarianism of the dominie has been a characteristic of Scottish education, there have been substantial counter-movements. Professors have not been without criticism. The fifth university in Scotland (in order of foundation) was started at the end of the eighteenth century partly as a criticism of the way in which the existing universities had neglected what the founder regarded as their social duty.

John Anderson, who was Professor of Natural Philosophy in the University of Glasgow from 1757 to his death in 1796, left his property 'to the Public for the good of mankind as an Institution to be denominated "Anderson's University".' It was to be under

145

Once the largest church in Scotland, the Cathedral of St Andrews (Fife) was founded in 1161 and destroyed by the Reformers in 1559, aided by local citizens who used its stones to build houses.

the control of the community, not of the teachers. Its trustees, who were to elect nine ordinary managers, were to be representative of tradesmen, manufacturers, merchants, and the professions. There were to be visitors, including the Lord Provost of Glasgow, to inspect the activities of the trustees. But, above all: 'The Professors in the University shall have no incorporate power like the Professors of the Faculty of Glasgow College.'

Professors may have been respected by the laity, but Anderson, a Professor himself, felt that an institution governed by its own teachers was insufficiently sensitive to public demand, and could become corrupt. 'The Professors in this University,' wrote Anderson, 'shall not be permitted, as in some other Colleges, to be Drones or Triflers, Drunkards or negligent of their duties in any manner of way . . .' Thus was academic syndicalism rejected.

In the event Anderson left very little property, but his ideas bore fruit, and in 1796, the very year of his death, 972 students attended lectures in Physics in what was originally known as 'Anderson's Institution' and became Strathclyde University in 1964.

Authoritarian but. . . . Although, apart from Anderson's Institution, and University College, Dundee, in 1883, the professoriat were accorded not only a proper respect but the power to run their university (apart from various skirmishes between the Town Council and the University of Edinburgh), the view that on the whole prevailed was that they were there to earn their keep in the teaching of their subjects. Professors could and should be authoritarian within their field, but when it came to deciding what they were there to do, society – or at least its representatives – knew best.

The main consequence of this attitude is that the research record in Scotland is pretty unimpressive for a nation that prides itself on its education: or rather it's unimpressive if you believe that pre-eminence in research is a good criterion of success in education. The University of Edinburgh has the distinction of having turned down for its Chair of Natural Philosophy (as Physics is called in Scotland) the greatest theoretical physicist of the nineteenth century. When it next became vacant the greatest experimental physicist of the twentieth century considered applying, but did not, because of the University's reputation for parochialism. Public speculation at the time did indicate why Clerk Maxwell's application for the Edinburgh chair in 1859 was unsuccessful. In these days general public interest in who might get chairs in Scotland reached an intensity only experienced today in connection with the Oxford Chair of Poetry. Of the rejection of Maxwell, the *Edinburgh Courant* wrote: 'Professor Maxwell is already acknowledged to be one of the most remarkable men known to the scientific world . . . there is another quality which is desirable in a Professor in a University like ours, and that is the power of oral exposition proceeding on the supposition of imperfect knowledge or even total ignorance on the part of his pupils. We have little doubt that it was a deficiency of this power in Professor Maxwell that made the curators prefer the claims of Mr Tait.'

The curators were competent enough. They got a first-rate expositor in Tait. Maxwell did not suffer – he held chairs in Aberdeen, King's College, London, and Cambridge, and it may well be that he, like Rutherford, contributed more to physics in Cambridge than he might have done in Edinburgh.

So although the educators might have been authoritarian enough in their field, they were not in a position to be authoritarian to their employers. If this is true for professors, how much more so must it have been true for schoolmasters.

And yet again, authoritarian – but . . . It must be repeated in a different context that although respect for learning in a defined field was there in abundance, the notion of defined fields was – and is – fairly narrow. I'd like to take two examples, one from universities, the other from schools.

Until the Latey Committee took the ground from under their feet, it used to be thought by many British universities that they acted *in loco parentis* to their pupils. Not only did they, quite properly, know more Latin, or more Physics, or more about any given aspect of systematic learning than their pupils, they knew more about what was good for them in other respects as well. They knew where they ought to live and when they ought to be in at night. The original Scottish university foundations knew this too, but with expansion this idea was abandoned. It's easy to see from young Gourlay's experiences in Edinburgh that the university formally cared nothing about the behaviour of the son of the house with the green shutters: what he was expelled for was not his drunkenness but his insolence to a lecturer during a lecture – that is, for lack of respect for authority.

For the most part, students at Scottish universities live at home, or in lodgings. And, although universities are prepared to help students find lodgings, they do not, again for the most part, enquire too closely into where they stay. Thirty years ago, attempts by the authorities in Scottish universities to introduce halls of residence were regarded as dangerous inroads into student freedom, and as attacks on a valuable feature of the system. In *Scottish University*, written in 1944, by two Edinburgh students, J. H. Burns and D. Sutherland-Graeme, it is said:

> 'Edinburgh University without the landladies of Marchmont and kindred districts is not to be thought of; and if the system of halls of residence triumphs at last so that the landlady disappears, something quite irreplaceable will have been needlessly taken away. There is something in the "digs" system which chimes in with that tone of independence which is so characteristic of academic life in Scotland. It binds the student searching wearily for a room to his predecessors who came in from their farms with sacks of meal on their shoulders to see them through the winter. The student *vis-à-vis* his landlady stands on his own feet, and must fight his own battles; for battles, of course, at one time or another there must be.'

It is easy for me to be accused of looking back sentimentally to my own student days particularly when I contrast them with the sad decline of the present. Happily, Burns and Sutherland-Graeme and I were contemporaries, and they wrote down what we felt at the time. So I can turn to their pages and see what was written then and I can say without laying myself open to an easy charge of sentimentality that things have indeed changed. 'That tone of independence' referred to by Burns and Sutherland-Graeme still exists, but at present, and in Stirling University at least, it is chiefly employed in criticizing the university authorities for not providing more halls of residence!

But 'digs' rather than halls, though chosen for praise by Burns and Sutherland-Graeme, form only one aspect of an even more significant difference between a Scottish tradition of living and a current English belief. Probably between a quarter and a third of Scottish students live at home: a state of affairs as rare, from a world point of view, as it is obviously advantageous. Who better to look after the young than their parents? This view seems to me to have a good deal more plausibility than the current fashionable view that the best thing for half a dozen eighteen-year-olds is to set up in a flat together – or indeed to occupy adjacent study bedrooms in a hall of residence. Moreover, some of us tend to blame the young for their rejection of the aged, or even the middle-aged. But is this surprising, if the wisdom of the parents has been that the young should be sent away from home to boarding school or to college as soon as possible? I believe, and it doesn't seem to me that there's anything revolutionary about the belief, that eighteen to twenty-two-year-olds are no more nearly unique than zero to four-year-olds, or even twenty-eight-year olds to thirty-two-year-olds, and that there's no good reason to lock them away from the rest of society for half the year. Moreover, I believe that if you do this, you've no good reason to be astonished if they reject your culture as well. I think that Scottish education, which relates students in their own homes directly to their fathers and mothers, and their younger brothers and sisters, and with luck their grandparents, and through them all, with luck, to some sense of social and economic reality, shows a degree of sense which has never appeared more sensible than now, when the generation conflict is becoming institutionalized.

Another way, exemplified in the schools, in which the pretensions of the learned to know about everything are mercifully less in Scotland than elsewhere is the way in which, for the most part, they refrain from dictating to their pupils how to enjoy themselves. Compulsory games, which to me sound as much a ghastly contradiction as compulsory fun would be, are less prevalent in the Scottish system, although they exist in parts of it. I was at a school that was well-known for its enthusiasm for rugby football – but it provided its pupils with the *opportunity* to play rugby, without any *obligation* to do so. It's still true of that school. The fact that the professional educators knew more Latin and Mathematics than I or my parents, did not seem to them to justify the attempt to organize my leisure.

Authoritarian ... but. What British university first had statutory recognition of student representation? Sussex? – Wrong, in spite of its first Vice-Chancellor having been educated in Scotland. The Students Representative Council was initially an Edinburgh institution, conceived by Robert Fitzroy Bell, welcomed by the university authorities, and established in 1884. The first Council worked hard to establish the University Union, which opened in 1889 without having had funds provided by the state.

So the general academic position appears to be that there are areas in which the charge of authoritarianism doesn't seem to stick. The main authoritarian area not yet explored must be limited to the subject content of the education. There at least it would be agreed by many products of the system that authority still holds sway: the facts are taught, and must be known. Academic syndicalists may be kept in order by the students and the civil power, but their great strength still remains in the living tradition of sound learning – or so we might be tempted to say. But – what does my own experience say?

I graduated with a first class honours degree in Chemistry from Edinburgh University. Just three years later, I found myself going to do chemical research in a laboratory of the University of Oxford. What different characteristics did I expect to find in my Oxford-taught fellow research workers? Easy. Chemistry was chemistry the world over, and I had a good honours degree in it. Therefore Oxford chemists would not be too different from me as chemists, at least. But what was the main characteristic of Oxford? The existence of colleges, so that students there would not become narrow specialists, because they lived and learned with students studying other subjects. Their general knowledge, their general intellectual sophistication, would therefore outshine mine. I was totally wrong in the event. The only thing that was obvious was that they knew much more chemistry – not only knew more, but they understood it better.

I hadn't read the history of the Scottish universities carefully enough. Specialist excellence was far from being the traditional goal of Scottish education. How far the Scottish universities fell short of achieving this was revealed in the mid-nineteenth century when the Indian Civil Service was thrown open to entry by competitive examination. The *Edinburgh Review*, in 1858, calling for changes in Scottish education, pointed out that 'at the very first trial, those candidates who had been educated in Scotland failed egregiously'. Principal Sir David Brewster of Edinburgh, whose statue still stands at the entrance to the Chemistry Department there, said in 1859 that 'the result of the competition has been both painful and instructive'. At about the same time, Professor J. S. Blackie explained the situation as follows: 'Students from the English universities must possess an immense advantage in all public examinations, owing partly to the fact of their more thorough, long-continued training in certain departments of science and learning. . . .'

So, on the assumption that nothing had changed, I shouldn't have been surprised. That assumption would have been unjustified. The single subject honours degree had been introduced in Scotland, largely as a result of that sort of criticism. Nevertheless, habits of thought have their own momentum. In my honours degree in chemistry, begun in the late nineteen thirties, or eighty years after these criticisms, I was formally required to spend only 57 per cent of my time over four years in the study of chemistry itself, and the same regulations still hold. The Oxford chemistry graduate had also spent four years in getting his degree, but he had no other required subject of study over this period.

In the struggle between general and specialist education, the Scottish university system has moved some way towards the latter from its early nineteenth-century position, but it's still clear – at least in relation to the English system – where it effectively stands. And it's no use imagining one can get the best of both worlds: in a fixed number of years, compulsory breadth is likely to be accompanied by some concomitant shallowness. But, when I decided that I really wanted to be a chemist, I could then go on to read and understand the books that my Oxford contemporaries had read at an earlier stage of their education. In this impressionist survey, I've been switching from what was said and done over a hundred years ago, to what was said and done when I was a boy, to what is now said and done now in a university which didn't exist until five years ago. This is more natural than logical. One cannot be brought up in Edinburgh without some sense, however imperfect, of the weight of the past on the present, and most Scots graduates must be conscious of this. What I have to do, and what I shall try to do before I have finished, is to sort out the quasi-historical myth from the facts, and to sort out the present from the past. So I'll digress about the history of Scottish universities at this point.

The four ancient Scottish universities were founded before the Union of the Crowns, that is, before 1603, and the remaining four in the seventeenth reign since then, that is, between 1964 and 1967. Thus we can, perhaps deceptively simply, divide the Scottish universities into the ancient – St Andrews (founded 1410), Glasgow (1451), Aberdeen (1494) and Edinburgh (1583) – and the more recent, Strathclyde (1964, as such, but parent institution dates back to 1796), Heriot-Watt (1966, but parent institution

1821), Dundee (1967, parent institution, 1881), and Stirling (1967). There are other ways of division. One can talk of the three pre-reformation foundations, or of the two technological, or of six urban and two rural. But, most importantly, one can talk of seven with roots firmly embedded in the nineteenth century or earlier, and only one a purely modern creation. So a sense of history is not misplaced in these institutions.

For example, in considering student representation we – though not always the students – remember that Student Representative Councils began in Edinburgh. And in considering 'student power' we might usefully remember what happened in Anderson's Institution in Glasgow in 1823. In that year, the mechanics' class, 1,000 strong, dissatisfied with the education and treatment they were getting, seceded from the Institution to set up a new body of its own. The break-away was successful. By 1825 the new body, with Birkbeck as its honorary president, had 1,300 students. The committee of management consisted of students elected by and from the Physics and Chemistry classes. Appointment of lecturers was originally by popular vote of the classes they taught – an innovation which proved so unsatisfactory that it was discontinued. The Glasgow Mechanics Institution gradually lost its direct democracy, and by 1886, full of respectability, it re-united with the parent body.

How widely diffused among the student body this sense of history is I don't know. A wretched consequence of the success of the mass communications media is that the widening of geographical horizons appears to have been accompanied by a narrowing of historical ones. But I do know that this sense was firmly there as recently as thirty years ago, and that the appreciation of the past extended beyond the history of the Scottish universities themselves to that of universities in general. My authority is again *Scottish University*. To begin a chapter, as they do, with the arresting sentence: 'It all started in Bologna in 1155', is easy enough, and it may or may not reflect a sense of history. But the following quotation from Burns and Sutherland-Graeme, written, be it remembered, not in a late afterglow of sentimentality, but when they were students themselves, gives something of what I have in mind:

'As well as this mental background there is another physical background to be borne in mind when reading of Edinburgh

University: it is the background of Edinburgh itself. Lying on its hills and the Forth coastal plain, with less than half a million inhabitants, Edinburgh is of a size and situation to be one of the loveliest of cities; and this cannot but have its effect. That the physical environment must affect the climate of mental endeavour is obvious: and there is enough in Edinburgh, away from its modern suburbs, to be a beneficent influence indeed. A City's character is determined by the age in which it has seen the most vivid life. It was late when Edinburgh became the Scottish capital – and it is essentially a city of the Renaissance and later. The religious disturbances of the sixteenth century mark the stormy dawn of its splendour; but its noonday, despite the Nationalists, came after the Union of 1707, in the height of the eighteenth century. Two periods of widely differing character have had most influence on Edinburgh's personality: on the one hand is the city of Mary Queen of Scots and John Knox; and on the other the city of David Hume, William Robertson and James Boswell. All this, then, is the Edinburgh student's home. He lives with the dignity of the Old College, built by Adam; with the mellow beauty of Charlotte Square bathed in the setting sun; with the stateliness of Royal Terrace; with the dingy history of the Royal Mile; with the cool memory-laden air of Holyrood. . . .

'We may despise and distrust romanticism – but we live in a romantic town and cannot escape from its spirit, the city of Robert Louis Stevenson and *Rab and his Friends*, the cold windy city which once harboured the fiercest mob in Europe, the mob of *Cleanse the Causeway* and the Porteous Riots – our daily lives are spent in an atmosphere steeped in peace and riot, an atmosphere of prosperity and poetry, of cruelty and caution. . . .'

It's no longer the fashion for student authors to write like this – indeed, I wouldn't say it was all that the fashion to do so thirty years ago – but I find it difficult to believe that Edinburgh students are no longer conscious of Scotland's past. The Scots, like the Irish, but happily under conditions of greater political stability, cherish the past to preserve a sense of national identity which the electronic village of the present seems hourly to threaten.

My thesis had a second term. Scottish education, I argued was 'authoritarian and was widely diffused – but . . .'

153

What about wide diffusion? Anyone in Scotland, it is often said, can be well educated if he chooses.

How widely one imagines education is diffused depends partly on one's view of who is educated. The criterion nowadays seems to be: who gets a degree? The traditional Scottish view – now almost totally disappeared – is that the degree itself is relatively trivial, and the 'class ticket' is the thing. The 'class ticket', in the ancient Scottish universities, was the bit of paper that said one had duly performed the work of a given class. One had to have this to sit the examination that would allow one to qualify for the degree. At the turn of the century it was said: 'A comparatively small percentage of these students obtain a degree. . . . They seek a certain amount of solid, valuable information on certain subjects . . . and when they have obtained this, they drop themselves quietly out.'

So 'drop out' had a different meaning. The sensible man got some education that suited him, and went away – but he went away to a society that was prepared to accept him. Apart from the right of entry to specific professions, being a drop-out wasn't a problem. This is indeed a characteristic of a society, now in this respect past, that could live with its education, that could take it or leave it alone.

Thus a 'completed' education may not have been all that widely diffused, but the notion of post-school education being something that one might reasonably be expected to have a go at was. And this notion implies that schooling to reach this point was widely available and widely accepted in Scotland.

Before saying 'but . . .' to this encouraging belief, I should give some clearer definition of the Scottish educational system. The characteristics that I think are most important stand out sharply when we consider the interface between the secondary school and the university. So what's peculiarly Scottish about that?

To say even this requires a knowledge of what I'm supposing to be in the system. With the Scottish universities – which I have already listed – I've no difficulty in equating 'universities in Scotland' with 'Scottish universities'. The individual universities differ of course. It could be argued that the second foundation in point of date, the University of Glasgow, is in a sense the most characteristic. In its predominantly Scottish, home or 'dig-dwelling', student community, in its proud conservatism and loyalty to its past, and in the breadth of its impact throughout Scotland,

Glasgow must be the archetypal Scottish university. But all the Scottish universities, despite their differences, are within the system. As far as the interface is concerned, they all have a common pattern of entrance requirements, and these requirements are thought of primarily in terms of the examinations for the Scottish Certificate of Education. These examinations are normally taken in the fifth year of secondary school, so that the formal requirements for entry to the Scottish universities relate to attainment at that standard.

Definition of a Scottish school is less easy. As in the rest of Britain, there are at present three main categories of school: those run by the public authorities; those run by a private trust or similar body, but with state support ('direct grant' schools); and those run wholly independently of the system ('independent' schools, of which the so-called 'public' schools form an important part). All these are schools in Scotland. But some of them are essentially organized to prepare pupils for the Scottish Certificate of Education, and implicitly therefore for entry to the Scottish universities, whereas others are primarily organized to prepare pupils for the British General Certificate of Education, the advanced or 'A' level of which is normally taken in the sixth year at secondary school, and which is the qualification in terms of which the entrance requirements of most English (and Welsh and Northern Irish) universities are framed. This means that these schools in Scotland that are organized primarily for GCE 'A' levels as the main leaving qualification to be sought by the pupils are choosing to separate themselves from the distinctively Scottish educational system as a whole, and, although they may be Scottish in geographical location, and perhaps in respect of an enthusiasm for wearing the kilt, are essentially not Scottish as far as the type of education they offer is concerned. All of the secondary schools run by the public authorities are primarily organized to fit the Scottish Certificate of Education (SCE) though many of them will do their best to prepare pupils for GCE 'A' levels should they for any reason wish it. Most of the 'direct grant' schools are organized for the SCE, although there is some interest in GCE examinations as well. Almost all of the independent schools are organized primarily to prepare pupils for the GCE examinations.

There is therefore a sense in which Scottish independent schools are epiphenomenal as far as the Scottish educational system is concerned. They avoid both the virtues and some of the defects of the system.

This distinction makes it possible to define the intentions of the system with greater clarity. Essentially the Scottish secondary and higher educational system, taken together as a unity, is concerned to attain two things: a general education rather than a specialist one, and a situation in which the career choice of the individual can be postponed till the end of his or her school career. To this end, the 'Highers', the most advanced examination in the Scottish Certificate of Education, are not very advanced in a specialist sense, so that it is possible to take as many as six subjects simultaneously to the Higher grade with a reasonable prospect of success. Thus the pupil will have not only a general university entrance requirement, but the specific course requirements for a wide range of university courses. For example, I passed 'Highers' in English, Latin, French, Mathematics, Science (Physics and Chemistry) and Dynamics (this last being rather the odd one out), and this group was sufficient to let me study almost anything in the university except Greek. That was thirty years ago, and things change. But this year, at the same school, my son sat six 'Highers': English, French, Mathematics, Physics, Chemistry and Art which again, if he passes, should allow him to enter any of a wide range of university courses.

The very fact of taking a wide range of subjects at school acts in both the desired directions: general education rather than specialist education is fostered, and career choice is widened. Now, if, as I suggest, these are major objects of the Scottish educational system, and I believe they are major virtues as well, then schools in Scotland, no matter how Scottish they may be in location, do not fall within the system if they do not seek to serve these ends. And I'm completely clear that paying primary attention to the British General Certificate of Education does not serve these ends, and that English educationists do not think that it does either.

With this clarification of the nature and purpose of the system, we can return to the question of its widespread diffusion and acceptance.

There is of course no doubt about its widespread diffusion, numerically. The vast majority of the population, either from lack of money or lack of initiative, simply accept what is offered by the state, and in Scotland, the state offers the Scottish system. The exercise of choice implicit in the direct grant school principle tends to show itself as a vote of confidence in the system – most of their pupils take the SCE examinations, and most of those who go to university go to Scottish universities. But the further exercise of choice – coupled in this case with massive financial expenditure – implicit in choice of independent schools tend to go with a massive vote of no confidence in the system. Scottish universities appear to be a second best for the patrons of independent education. If these patrons tend to come, as of course they do come, from certain classes in society – after all, they could hardly come from the poor – any notion of the essential unity of Scottish society, associated with a general acceptance of an educational system open to the talents, must be contrary to the facts. This raises the question of where the leaders of Scottish society were educated.

Let us look firstly at our political masters, those we ourselves elected to serve us. Where were they educated? The present Secretary of State for Scotland (I write in July 1970) was educated at an independent school in England. The Minister of State was privately educated in England, Germany and France. Of the three Parliamentary Under-Secretaries to the Secretary of State for Scotland, one was at school in England, one was at a school in Scotland but not within the Scottish system, and one was at a school within the system. Two of these three were at Scottish universities. Thus *one of the five* ministers was at school within the Scottish system, and *two of the five* were at Scottish universities.

Our previous masters were different. Of the five Scottish ministers in the government that went out of office in June 1970, all were educated in schools within the Scottish system, and all of those – three in number – who went to university went to the archetypal Scottish university: Glasgow.

If the parents of our present politicians opted out of the system for them, this isn't true of our senior civil servants. The permanent under-secretary of state was at a Scottish school and Edinburgh University as well as Cambridge. Of the six next most senior civil servants in the Scottish office, five were educated within the Scottish system, and the one who wasn't doesn't come from Scotland anyway. Five of them were at Scottish universities (Edinburgh or Glasgow), and of these five, two went to other universities as well.

These are interesting facts. The administration of Scotland through the Scottish Office is often criticized as unrepresentative, because it tends to be run by the civil servants. But as far as

157

education goes, the civil servants seem to be more representative than the politicians from at least one of the parties.

So much for the government and the administration: what about the representatives of the Queen? Of the Lords Lieutenant of the counties of Scotland, only three or four out of over thirty were at schools within the Scottish system (over a third of them were at Eton!), and only one or two appear to have been at a Scottish university, although nearly half have been at Oxford or Cambridge.

The notion of the Scottish educational system promoting social homogeneity because of its widespread acceptance seems a little thin, in view of these facts. We should look a little further.

What about the leaders of opinion? The Controller of the BBC in Scotland was educated at an English independent school and at Oxford. Of the editors of the two major quality Scottish daily newspapers, one was educated within the Scottish system, the other was educated at school partly within the system, and at Glasgow University. One could carry this sort of research much further, with results which would be fairly well in line with those given above.

What does it amount to? It would be wildly unreasonable to expect those who come into Scottish life from England or overseas to have had a Scottish education. It would be at least equally unreasonable to believe that Scotland had nothing to gain from the introduction of people from elsewhere, bringing us new ideas and new values. It follows that it would be absurd to expect all, or even nearly all, the people playing an important part in Scottish life to have been educated within the Scottish system. And yet it should be clear from the general tone of what I've written that I'm not wholly happy about what the statistics I've presented reveal, or what I'm pretty sure further investigations along the same lines would reveal.

I believe that the objects of the Scottish educational system are worthwhile. I believe I have gained by being brought up in it, and I'm doing my best in a new university to see that these values—a sense of the past, an aversion to specialization, and flexibility of outcome, play a proper part in the shaping of the first completely new twentieth-century university in Scotland.

But there are difficulties. I have already mentioned the decline in the sense of the past that I detect in the young of today, and said that I blame it chiefly on the technical success of the mass media. But another major difficulty is the heavy legacy of the vast and obvious, though I believe essentially limited, success of academic specialization. This success means that most academics have a vested interest in their specialisms, and are reluctant to accept any apparent diminution in their rated importance. Thus in a twentieth-century university it's very difficult indeed to persuade one's colleagues of the disadvantages of specialist education. And as other specialists have gone out and taught in schools, it's difficult, perhaps even more difficult, to persuade students of the disadvantages of specialization. The advantage of specialization only exists when there is a clear need to go on doing what one has specialized in, and in a rapidly changing world that's not always obvious. As for flexibility, that of course is fine as long as it doesn't interfere with specialization – which of course it's bound to do!

It would be nice to be able to reinforce the very strong pragmatic arguments that allow me to conclude that the virtues of the Scottish educational system are peculiarly appropriate to the present historical situation by some appeal to a feeling for the continuity of a tradition. But if the sense of the past is being knocked on the head, that's not much help. It would be even nicer to reinforce the arguments and the appeal to tradition by pointing to the evidence of social pressures working in the direction of reinforcing the tradition.

And what way are the social pressures working? We've already seen that a substantial proportion of the influential people in Scotland, even of those born in Scotland, had parents who chose to send them outside the system. Thus there are in fact social pressures acting against the system. Why?

I believe the answer is related to the fact that Scotland is not an independent centre of political or industrial power. People who feel they have a talent for organizing or leading their fellows naturally wish to exercise this talent on as large a scale as possible, and therefore on a United Kingdom scale rather than on a Scottish scale. Education, with this prospect in mind, is only partly a matter of acquiring useful knowledge, useful skills, and useful attitudes: it is also a matter of meeting useful people. And for someone who sees himself as a leader, it is a matter of meeting the most able or the most influential people in the whole society in which he proposes to exercise his leadership. England is the most populous, the richest, and therefore the most influential of the countries that make up the United Kingdom. Therefore the

159

aspiring leaders go to England for their education, because, if they go to the right place there, they will meet the influential and probably the most able people in the society they hope to lead. This answer depends on the view that the explicit content, and the structure, of education are less important than the contacts one makes in the course of acquiring it, and it would be absurd to deny that there is considerable truth in this point of view.

Under these circumstances one might well ask what vital future there can possibly be in Scottish education, at least within the framework of the continuation of the United Kingdom. I think there *is* a vital future for it, provided we who are involved in it believe that its characteristic virtues are important.

If my analysis of the social pressures acting against the Scottish system is correct, the last thing we should do is surrender our own judgment at this time, and try to assimilate the Scottish system more closely to the English one. The reason why there is a social pressure in Scotland, among those who have the money to react to it and the wit to see it, in favour of the English system is not any intrinsic superiority in the latter but simply that people believe that more fruitful interpersonal interactions can take place in it, because it serves a larger and richer community. Thus even if the Scottish system were to disappear totally, and to be replaced wholly by the English one, there would still be a drive in Scotland to seek education beyond Scotland. To ensure a future for Scottish education, the thing to do is not to abandon it but to build on its strengths.

The greatest strength of the Scottish system is that in its insistence on flexibility and generality it emphasizes features which are only now being recognized to be firstly, important, and secondly, relatively lacking in other systems. Like many other people whose successes and failures should sober us if we were to become intoxicated by the thought, history is with us.

So what we have to do in Scotland to ensure an exacting future is not to say 'we are Scottish', but to say – and act as if we believed in it – 'we believe in general education'. And as other people who are already saying that this is important see that it is characteristic of Scotland, then they'll begin to come to Scotland to be educated.

One thing that we have to remember is that already (in 1961/62, Robbins figures) some 4 per cent of the students from England and Wales who enter universities go to Scottish universities. We don't know the motives of that 4 per cent. Some of them no doubt are the

160

children of Scottish parents, perhaps of Scottish graduates, whose ambition for their children is that they should study in Scotland. Some of them are probably under the impression that because the Scottish 'Highers' are taken in the fifth year at school it should be easier for them, with GCE 'A' levels, to get in to Scottish universities. Some of them perhaps feel that the social cachet of St Andrews (failing that of Oxbridge, Bristol and Sussex) is superior to that of some (academically eminent) English civic universities. Some of them want to ski. But if the growing belief that academically respectable generalists are more useful employees than esoteric specialists were to strike deep into recruitment patterns – and why not, if these beliefs are correct – then the motivation could gradually become that one got (in practical terms) a more valuable education in Scotland.

This could alter the social pressure forcing the Scottish young to go south. If employers were to believe what they say about the superiority of generalist to specialist education, they would look to the graduates of Scottish universities for their most promising recruits. Even if this fact were realized, the system in the rest of the United Kingdom could hardly change very rapidly, such is the inertia of all educational systems. Potential leaders in the rest of the United Kingdom – such is the sensitivity of potential leaders – would seize the point rapidly, and seek entry to Scottish universities. The Scots, reluctant as ever to believe that any good could come out of the efforts of their own contemporary countrymen, would see the point shortly after the rest of the United Kingdom saw it. The epiphenomenal Scottish schools would – or some of them would – then see the point as well. And the weight of the evidence would finally convince the wealthy parents of potential Scottish leaders.

In a few words, my prescription for a revitalization of Scotland would be to convince the English (the influential Scots being beyond conviction) that the basic values of Scottish education are the basic values appropriate to the future. The resulting increased competition for places in Scottish universities would convince the Scots that they had something worthwhile.

But . . . how much of this is mere sentimentality? Not all that much. Some things are true beyond doubt. Firstly, many government reports on education have stressed the value of generalist rather than specialist education. Secondly, both the critics of and the apologists for Scottish education have stressed that it is

Inveraray Castle (Argyll), the seat of the Campbells of Argyll, was completed in 1770 and is among the earliest examples of the Gothic revival and the neo-Scottish baronial style.

generalist rather than specialist in intention. Thirdly, and perhaps more controversially, the Scots tend not to appreciate their own assets till the hard-headed English seek to steal them.

I seem to have gone beyond my remit. I was asked to describe the Scottish educational system, rather than tell it what to do. But in trying to see what its possibilities are, I hope I have been able to illuminate its present situation.

The Thinking Scot

Lord Ritchie-Calder

During the Great Depression an indulgent uncle from foreign parts treated me to a round of golf at Gleneagles and the extravagant luxury of a caddie. My score disgraced my own modest proficiency and affronted my uncle whose golf was tournament standard. It was the caddie's fault; he talked too much and I encouraged him.

He was an unemployed miner, 'ower frae Fife and living like a tinker'. He was a wee shilpit creature, with bandy legs from going into the pit with ricketty bones when he was thirteen. His well-scrubbed and shaven face was tattooed with indelible carbon from the shot-firing. He was not so old but he was toothless. He was an unprepossessing gnome – until he started to talk.

Among the whins, looking for the ball, I asked him how long he had been out of work and he said six years. What did he do with all the unwanted spare time? He said he studied philosophy. And from there on he talked about Karl Marx, Hegel, Spinoza, Hume, Locke and even Bishop Berkeley. It was a bit above my head but the intellectual name-dropping was not for effect; he was earnest and erudite. I asked him who was his teacher. His gums grinned: 'A bluidy capitalist – Andra Carnegie!'

The Pittsburgh multimillionaire had endowed his native Scotland with public libraries and my wee Fifer was self-taught.

Scotland's libraries have a lot to answer for. In my native Forfar, a town of weavers, who could rarely afford to buy books, we had a good library and we youngsters had the run of it – except for The Forbidden Shelves. In the Non-Permissive Society of those days books by Richardson, Fielding and Smollett and the Restoration Dramatists were unfit for juvenile consumption. That proscription had an unintended effect on my own life.

At the age of twelve, for no reason other than that the local paper, of which my English teacher was the literary editor, had printed one of my essays, I had decided to be a writer. There was a general election coming on and one of the candidates was an author. I had never seen a real live author and in anticipation I went to the library to get a copy of his book, *The War of Steel and Gold*. I did not know it was a 'subversive' book but the librarian was appalled. He refused to give it to me saying 'It isna a fit book for a laddie to read'. So, of course, I used the method by which I had got hold of the other forbidden books, *Tom Jones*, *Peregrine Pickle* – the lot. I asked my obliging father, who was not much of a reader himself, if he would fetch it on his own ticket on his way home from work. I was dismayed when I got it. If the librarian had handed it to me normally, I should have handed it back hastily but, now, I read it from cover to cover, trying to find the juicy bits. I did not, but in juvenile non-conformity I learned a lot. I smuggled myself into the hustings. My author, H. N. Brailsford, did not win but years later I joined him on the editorial board of *The New Statesman*.

Occasionally my fellow Forfarians did buy books. Once I was in the bookseller's and noticed a collection of 'Teach Yourself' books including *Teach Yourself Greek* and *Teach Yourself Hebrew*. I said to the bookseller 'Now, who would come in off the street to buy these?' He said, 'You'd be surprised. You remember So-and-so?' I did; he was a factory worker. 'His son has gone to college and he is studying Hebrew. The father's teaching himself, so's he'll not be behindhand.'

An auld wifie was asked what she did when she was alone. She replied, 'Sometimes I sit and think. And sometimes I just sit.' Maybe there are lots of Scots who 'just sit' or who let the 'telly' do their thinking for them but positive thinking is a Scottish characteristic bred through generations of enquiring and protesting minds, in a spirit of non-conformity and a democracy of learning.

There are those who, with some justification, will question the 'nonconformity' and the 'democracy'. They will say that the Scots tend to be educationally conventional (I would say 'canny') and that the equality of opportunity for learning has not always been, and maybe is not now, what we crack it up to be. Like others I had the 'conventions' and the 'learning' impressed upon me with the leather taws. The beatings were not always for misbehaviour; sometimes they were for bad marks (i.e. the results of bad teaching) and sometimes I felt that the master just thought that I would be 'nane the waur for a leatherin'. I resented it then and I resent it for others now. But it acts contrariwise; within, and against, the constraints of convention we have produced rebels, not just constitutional but intellectual.

It has been said that John Knox founded Scottish education on religion and it became a religion. What happened was that with the onset of Protestantism, Knox wanted to break the priestly monopoly of the Bible by giving ordinary people access to it. In the *Book of Discipline* of 1560, there was to be a Bible in every church for the whole parish to use. The minister was to read it systematically through to his congregation and the head of every household was to instruct everyone, at family service, to understand enough to be interrogated by the kirk session. But the *Book of Discipline* also proposed that each parish should have a school and a schoolmaster, each town a college and the universities should be enlarged to train the children of rich and poor alike. This was to be financed from the revenues from former church properties but the nobility, who had already helped themselves in the confiscation, baulked. The idea, however, was there and persisted, through charity. In 1633, the Kirk was strong enough to carry through the Scottish Parliament an act permitting a school-rate to be levied. In 1696, the 'Act for Settling of Schools' ordained that every parish was to have a schoolhouse and a schoolmaster with a salary paid by the landowners. In principle, though dilatory in practice, the system of education in Scotland entered the eighteenth century offering the possibility for any boy of ability to start at school in his parish and go on to the university. In the middle of each term (still hallowed as 'Meal Monday') he would go home to refill his mealpoke for his porridge and replenish his portable larder with whatever comestibles were then durable.

In one sense education became a religion. The respect for knowledge became a reverence for learning and with it a deference to its exponents. (It still persists. Long after becoming a peer, shopkeepers in Edinburgh with a proper sense of values still greet me 'Good morning, professor. How is her ladyship?') To send a son to the university became the ambition of even the humblest family – an ambition too few of them could achieve. Too often they could not even keep the children through the years at the parish school, when there were fields to be minded or the family keep to be earned. But most children got some – at least the Three R's. Robert Burns could break through the limitations of home and school and hold his own in discourse in the Edinburgh drawing-rooms. And it was not always the child of most ability in a family who got to the university. He had, of course, to have the qualifications to enter but elder brothers or sisters, whatever their ability, would have had to stifle their own ambitions and have gone out to work so that the Benjamin could wear the gown.

The university (or 'college' as it was usually called) had a special meaning among my contemporaries. If you asked a bunch of my cronies at Forfar Academy what they were going to do when they left school, there would be those who would say 'a butcher' or 'a farmer' or 'a baker' or 'I'm gaun into the factory' and they would add 'like ma fayther'. Or one of them might say 'I'm going to be a doctor' and add 'like ma fayther' because there was the succession in the family practice to be considered. But there would be those who would say 'I'm gaun tae college'. They did not say to be a minister, a doctor or a scientist. The university was a plateau which you reached and from which you surveyed the professional peaks you might choose to ascend. The university was where you went to become a rounded person – the purpose of the traditional Scottish MA. The vocational training was something else to be added unto you.

In this religion of education, there was a presbytery of knowledge. Just as the kirk elders could catechize the minister and dispute his theology, be he a doctor of divinity, so the cottar or the weaver or the mechanic from the parish school, or the burgh school, reinforced by the Three R's and the dominie's college acquired Seven Disciplines, was prepared to argue with his academic betters. To the Ancient Greeks *nous* was the Reason which brought Cosmos out of Chaos. To the Scot *nowse* was (and is) inborn common-sense, fostered by a schooling which, given the information, would produce the confidence to deal with any situation. The educated Scot of the nineteenth century, whatever his origins, could stand foursquare against Thomas Arnold's elite, from the gymnasia of privilege, the English public schools. Those homespun Scots became the proconsuls of empire and the leaders of finance and commerce even if they had been born in a but and ben or a bothy. Before the Second World War, three-quarters of the medical officers of health in England and most of the colonial medical service were Scots. The reason was simple: the 'lad o' pairts' could go from the burgh school to medical school by his bursaries and qualify alongside the scions of the medical dynasty but could not afford to buy a practice, so he went into the salaried medical service. I knew a general in the

RAMC who had held his own in the officers' mess by maintaining he had been to a public school. He had: in the East End of Glasgow.

From these eighteenth-century Folk Schools came remarkable and original talents, some of them changing the direction of human thought and human enterprise and none of them burdened by the Schoolmen tradition. There was James Hutton, of Edinburgh, who was the 'father of geology' confronting and affronting the kirk-ridden theologians. He was not disputing theology; he was denying the very story of the Creation by letting the rocks speak for themselves. There was Adam Smith, the orphan son of a Kirkcaldy excise man, who won through to Glasgow University at the age of fourteen and to Balliol, the Scots-founded college at Oxford, three years later, to become the author of *The Wealth of Nations* which was the first great survey of economic life and the framework for the development of political economy as a separate discipline.

There was James Watt, from the burgh school of Greenock. He became the 'philosophical instrument maker' (laboratory technician) to the University of Glasgow. Two of his clients among the professors were Joseph Black and John Anderson. It was Anderson who sent him a small model of the Newcomen engine to be repaired, 'the cylinder', according to Watt, 'being not more than $1\frac{1}{2}$ inches in diameter and the boiler no bigger in size than a tea-kettle'. (So much for his mother's tea-kettle of the legend.) Watt realized how inefficient it was but he himself had found that a small quantity of water in the form of steam could heat a large quantity of water – six times its own weight – to its own temperature. The burgh schoolboy took the problem to Joseph Black, the Professor of Chemistry, the discoverer of carbon dioxide, who then explained to Watt something that he had only so far discussed with his students, the theory of latent heat for which he is famous. Its practical significance dawned on Watt as he walked over Glasgow Green: 'I had not walked further than the golf-house,' Watt wrote later, 'when the whole thing was arranged in my mind'. The waste of heat could be avoided by keeping the cylinder at steam heat and condensing the steam in a separate boiler. He made a model embodying his wife's thimble. The result was the condensing steam engine and its decisive part in the Industrial Revolution. It would not have got anywhere, however, if he hadn't been introduced to the Birmingham industrialist, Matthew Boulton, by

William Small. Small was a Scottish medical graduate who had emigrated to America and who had become Professor of Natural Philosophy at William and Mary College at Williamsburg, where one of his students was Thomas Jefferson. Jefferson wrote in his autobiography that 'Small probably fixed the destinies of my life'. He may have done more than that when one considers the peculiar marks of scientific influence which are plain in the American Constitution. As Woodrow Wilson pointed out, the Constitution was based on the theory of political dynamics 'a copy of the Newtonian theory of the Universe', a system of government in which the action and re-action are equal and opposite and all bodies are nicely poised by the balance of forces acting on them – the Executive, the Legislature and the Supreme Court. Small had taught Jefferson Newtonian physics. Small left Williamsburg with a letter of introduction from Benjamin Franklin to Boulton who helped to set him up as a physician in Birmingham, England. When Boulton was looking for a pump for his factory, Small remembered Watt.

In passing we should remember John Anderson, Watt's patron. Anderson, the orphan son of a minister and a product of the burgh-school of Stirling, became at the age of twenty-eight Professor of Oriental languages but three years later transferred to the Chair of Natural Philosophy. As a man of science he 'delighted in visiting the workshops of the artisans and mechanics and giving them such information as was likely to benefit them in their respective arts receiving in return knowledge which he would not otherwise have obtained'. He started in the University what he called his 'anti-toga' class attended by hundreds of mechanics who had to come in their 'working-clae's'. When he died at the age of seventy he left all his effects to be devoted to the establishment of 'Anderson's University' for the 'unacademical classes'. The intention was bigger than the resources but he can be regarded as one of the founders of the adult education movement and the technical training part of the enterprise became, in time, the Royal Technical College and, eventually, the University of Strathclyde.

David Hume, an intellectual giant on the world scene, was the son of an impoverished Border laird, a poor relation of the aristocratic Earls of Home. As a boy he lodged with his mother's relative in Edinburgh and attended the High School. He went to Edinburgh University at the age of thirteen and left at the age of fifteen! From thereon he was, intellectually, fending for himself.

The well-spring of genius was there, within, but it was artesian. At twenty-six, he produced *A Treatise on Human Nature* and at thirty, *Essays, Moral and Political*. On the strength of that he hoped to become Professor of Moral Philosophy at the University of Edinburgh. He was rejected, the objectors alleging heresy and atheism. Later, he was rejected by Glasgow University when he applied to succeed his friend, Adam Smith, in the Chair of Logic. It is true that his books qualified for the Papal *Index Expurgatorius* but that should scarcely have weighed with Scottish universities, then becoming venturesome in secular science. One suspects that the professors resented the presumptuousness of a fifteen-year-old university drop-out. At the age of forty-one, he became the keeper of the Advocates' Library in Edinburgh and 'master of 30,000 volumes' with opportunity to indulge in his desire to write history. His reputation as a historian is diminished by his stature as a philosopher, but it was as a historian he first acquired his international reputation. In the fullness of time, the David Hume Tower became the centre-piece of the University of Edinburgh, which had refused him a Chair.

The discrimination against Hume is interesting because, whether the academic 'squares' knew it or not, the Scottish universities were leading the world into a bigger revolution – in ultimate effect – than the contemporary political upheavals, than even the French Revolution which sorted out the Jacobins from the Jacobites in the Scottish disputations. They were spearheading the Industrial Revolution. Not just Professors Black and Anderson consorting with James Watt but, insidiously, the medical faculty of Edinburgh. This is long before the great 'medical' days of Tait, Lister, Knox (the Burke and Hare anatomist), of Simpson. The eighteenth-century medical school produced Roebuck, who gave heavy industry its mass-produced sulphuric acid and founded the Carron Iron Works, and Keir gave the revolution its synthetic alkalis, without which the textile industry could not have coped with its mass-produced fabrics. Why 'medical'? Why Scots-trained medicals? Because medicine is both an art and a science and the nonconformist Scots were adventuring into the science, into physics and chemistry which seemed to have little to do with pills, or drenches or leaches. Scots medical graduates were ambivalent, like physician William Small unwittingly inspiring the American Constitution through professing Newtonian physics, or physician Hutton deciphering the rocks, or Roebuck or Keir going into Big Business, the very Big Business of the Industrial Revolution.

Perhaps 'Scottish Enlightenment', as it was called in the intellectually insurgent days of the late eighteenth century, can be explained as the paradox of Calvinism. Its austere theocracy had within it the right of disputation, encouraged, or monopolized, by the long rhetorical sermons. There is the story of the minister preaching a sermon on Jonah and the Whale:

'And Jonah was swallowd by a muckle fush. Noo, ma freen's, was it a salmon? No, it wasna' a salmon. Was it a troot? No, it wasna' a troot. Was it a shark? No, it wasna' a shark. Was it a ...'

An impatient voice interrupted: 'Wheesht, minister, it was a whale.'

The minister thumped the pulpit and thundered: 'Wumman! Would ye tak' the verra word o' God oot o' ma moo?'

Or (my favourite) about the minister who was interrupted during his sermon on the miracle of the loaves and fishes by a voice saying, 'But, minister, I could do that'. He ignored the interruption but, back at the manse, he said to his wife, 'Did you hear that carlan, Willie McGillivray say he could do the miracle of the loaves and fishes?' 'That I did,' said his wife, 'but you got your figures wrong: you said "two thousand loaves and five thousand small fishes".' So the minister, being a scrupulous man, returned to the theme in his next sermon and got the figures right. He leaned over the pulpit to say 'Noo, Willie McGillivray, could you do that?'

'Fine, minister, I could do that.'

'Ye blasphemer. How could you feed the multitude with two small loaves and five small fishes?'

'Wi' whit was left ower frae last Sabbath, minister.'

If you can debate and question, albeit within the paradigm of scriptural tenets, you get the habit of questioning nature itself – like Hutton questioning the rocks and finding that six days was a bit short if you have to account for fossils. So the Scots are predisposed to the dialectic and to experiment.

One finds a lot of insight into the Thinking Scot in the now-neglected 'Thrums' books of J. M. Barrie (Sir James Matthew Barrie, Bart, OM). Gavin Dishart, the Little Minister, hostage of his kirk-elders for all his colleging. John Shand, the railway porter, nonchalantly breaking and entering the Wyllie home to study from their neglected books, in *What Every Woman Knows*. Cameron, the student-gillie in *Mary Rose*. And, of course, the story of his own family. His father was a handloom weaver when the family was young in the town of Kirriemuir. Yet he, or they, because the sisters had to help, sent one son to Aberdeen University to get his MA and the student undernourishment which killed him prematurely but not before he helped to send his brother, Jamie, on his way to Edinburgh University and his MA.

Barrie to me was one of The Immortals. (He is not now so imperishable as he was.) He was born five miles from Forfar, my birthplace. When I was a boy he was already dazzlingly famous as a writer and playwright. He had, for a time, been a pupil at my school, Forfar Academy, and in one of the classes there was a desk at which I contrived to sit regularly. It had carved on it 'J.M.B.' I persuaded myself that they were his and carved my own to keep them company, with a ritual sense (borrowed maybe from my long-dead gypsy grandmother) that we might be brought together. (We were, but that's another story.) He, too, had decided to be a writer and his MA was to get him a leader-writer's job.

To me the classic story of the Thinking Scot is that of John Boyd Orr. He was born in Kilmaurs in Ayrshire, not far from that other 'lad o' parts', Alexander Fleming, who was to be awarded the Nobel Prize for the discovery of penicillin. John Boyd Orr's father was a man of many trades and not over successful in any. He was a Fundamentalist. He wanted John to be a clergyman. (Two other sons wagged their pows i' the poopit.) John, after being a pupil-teacher, teaching boys not much younger than himself, got himself a teacher's grant to go to Glasgow University and get his MA. He was still being pressed to be a minister but, as he told me once, he happened one day to be passing the Zoological Department of the University and just happened in to hear a discourse on Darwinism, then a hot subject. That decided him he could not be a Wee Free Minister and the net result of any theological insights was his book *The Schism in the Scotch Kirk*. With his MA he worked himself back to the University to study for a medical degree. He took his MD and the Bellahouston Medal, the highest prize in medicine at Glasgow. But, except for a short time as a locum, and his front-line RAMC experience (MC twice over) he did not practise. He realized that there were diseases for which medicaments offered no cure – diseases of poverty and malnutrition. So he went on to his DSc in physiology and biochemistry, which brought him £350 a year as director of research in animal nutrition at Aberdeen. There, on

171

his return from an adventurous war (in both the army and the navy) he built up the world-famous Rowett Research Institute. But nutrition of animals only reminded him of malnutrition in people and in the desperate days of the Depression he began the survey which was to become *Food, Health and Income*, to produce the 'marriage of health and agriculture', the Mixed Commission of the League of Nations and led to the post-Second World War UN Food and Agriculture Organization, of which he became the first Director-General. But not before he had become MP for the Scottish Universities, and, first, students' Lord Rector (1945) and then Chancellor (1946) of his own University. Add on the Nobel Peace Prize, a peerage and the Companionship of Honour and you have the potted biography of a Scottish 'lad o' pairts'.

I once wrote a book on the great advances of science, *The Profile of Science*, and I used the device of giving a profile of the persons whom I personally knew and who were identified with the great advances. I had to apologize in the preface. I had used Lord Rutherford, New Zealand-born son of a Perthshire saw-miller as the 'father' of nuclear-research; Sir Alexander Fleming of Darvel for antibiotics; Sir Robert Watson-Watt of Brechin for radar, i.e. electronics; and Lord Boyd Orr of Brechin-Mearns for nutrition. And where is Brechin? Twelve miles from my hometown. Scientific chauvinism is bad enough but this was downright parochialism!

There is no niche for me in the Pantheon of the Thinking Scot, but my record would rate as that of a 'lad o' pairts'. At least my upbringing and my education encouraged that 'nowse' and that habit of questioning which cannot be cowed by social or academic pretentiousness. I left school at fifteen to become a police-court reporter in Dundee and that was the end of my formal education. Forfar Academy had given me a little Latin and less science. But from crime reporting I could turn to science writing. It was on-the-job training with, as my teachers, the famous scientists to whom my press-card gave me access. Came the day when my American publisher described me as 'a common-law scientist. He has cohabited with scientists for so long he is married to them by habit and repute'. I could hold my own in the Foreign Office as Director of Plans of Political Warfare without anyone quizzing my Old School Tie. And I became Professor of International Relations at Edinburgh University. In order that I should not appear academically naked before my students the University made me an MA 'as by examination'. When Sir Edward Appleton, as Vice-Chancellor, capped and gowned me he said, 'And now, Professor, you can tell everyone that you are a genuine MA and not an honorary MA'. My reply was 'Thank you very much. I now know the title of my autobiography – *Forty Years an Undergraduate.*'

Which is another way of saying that the Scot never stops learning.

The Law of Scotland

Nicholas Fairbairn of Fordell

The kingdoms of Scotland and England were united in 1603. A century later on October 3, 1706, the people of Edinburgh watched for the last time with tense regret, the Riding of the Parliament. On April 22, 1707, the Scottish Parliament adjourned for ever; since when Scotland has survived as a nation largely through her separate laws and legal system which were safeguarded in the Act of Union. The personality of Scotland passed from the King on his departure to the Three Estates; and Parliament House became the focus of national life. On the departure of our Parliament the members of the College of Justice alone remained the inhabitants of Parliament House and they became, for two centuries at least, the public expression and embodiment of the Scottish character. Now perhaps St Andrews House with its unseen occupants behind its blank facade may claim, through its dull politicians, to mirror the national face.

The Act of Union separated a period of comparative barbarity from two centuries of great civilization. One final act of frightfulness ushered in the United Kingdom. The English had obtained the consent of the Scottish Commissars at the cost of £20,540 17s 7d in bribes. Of that sum the Duke of Queensberry as Lord High Commissioner received £12,235 whereas Lord Banff was converted for the minor sum of £11 2s. The Duke's vanity was no less than his greed and he took his entire household to witness the final act of his disgraceful triumph in Parliament House. In Queensberry House, near the Palace of Holyroodhouse, he left a small boy roasting a fatted ox in the kitchen and his squint son Lord Drumlanrig locked in a darkened room. The unusual silence overwhelmed the reason of the glaikit youth and mewing his gangling strength he broke free from his forbidding confinement and having torn in pieces and devoured the half-cooked ox he replaced the sacrifice with the awestruck boy thus reversing the story of Isaac. The Duke returned to celebrate the success of his treacherous contract with the 'Auld Enemy' to be greeted by the sight of his cannibal son devouring the remains of his minor servant. An unromantic dullard has blocked up the site of this gruesome tale in the great house which is now a home for the invalid aged. And this horror which has all the elements of frightfulness of classical mythology heralded a glorious period of classical taste and classical civilization in which the law and lawyers played a leading part.

Scots law is very similar to other European systems which have developed from Roman and feudal sources. The origins of the law of Scotland are feudal. Feudalism was European and came to Scotland by way of England from France and was much developed by David I. Previously the law was Celtic but very few remnants of Celtic law remain. The Lord Lyon King of Arms is the only officer of the law who can trace his origins to the tribal and patriarchal society of Celtic Scotland. The office of Lord Lyon was created in its modern form in 1318 to denounce war and proclaim peace, a function now usurped by less colourful figures. He has jurisdiction in all armorial and genealogical affairs and may prosecute in his Court those who usurp heraldic devices and clan badges. Beware, the tartan tourist! He is the Chief Herald and appears in his splendid tabard with the Scottish Royal Arms with his Court on state occasions. The office was greatly enhanced by the rambling brilliance and eccentricity of the late Sir Thomas Innes of Learney. His wispy hair, shrill, trembling voice and gangling gait made him a beloved national figure.

In 1532 the foundation of the College of Justice and the Court of Session marked the end of the ascendancy of the feudal law and the beginning of the professional tradition of the law in Scotland. At that time the admiration of classical civilization and the ceaseless martial hostility of England combined to create a zeal for reform of the law on the principles of Roman justice. For two centuries and more Scottish scholars, numbered in thousands, studied in the universities first of France – the 'Auld Ally' – and then in the Low Countries. In the sixteenth century all the Scottish lawyers of eminence, Mackenzie, Craig, Fountainhall, studied at Orleans, Poitiers, Bourges and Paris and in the seventeenth and eighteenth centuries at the universities of Leyden and Utrecht. At Leyden alone some three thousand Scots studied during this period and Scotland produced some of the most eminent European lawyers. In 1681 James Dalrymple, First Viscount Stair who had been appointed Lord President of the Court of Session ten years earlier published his *Institutions*, described by Lord Cooper in his selected papers as 'an original amalgam of Roman law, feudal law and native customary law systematized by resort to the law of nature and the Bible and illuminated by many flashes of ideal metaphysics'. This marked the creation of modern Scots law and laid down its basic principles. In the same year as he published his classic tome, he was ejected from the Presidency for refusing to take the Test and he set out forthwith for Leyden where he studied for six years, returning in 1688 with King William III who restored him to the Presidency in the following year. Such a period of enforced sabbatical retreat to study the principles of law would be of immeasurable benefit to the Law today and could be undertaken without loss of face by claiming that it was based on the example of the father of the law in Scotland.

The Napoleonic Wars brought to an end this splendid European tradition which had produced the Roman structure of the law in Scotland, enshrined the concept of principle rather than precedent and avoided the traditional insularity of the English approach.

The historical origins of the law of Scotland are thus quite different from the law of England but its peculiar identity and principles have come under increasing English influence since the Union of the legislatures, and in the present century this eroding process has greatly accelerated owing to the ever growing proportion of the law which is embodied in statutes passed by an English-orientated assembly, and to the habit of applying the solutions of the law of England where the law is common to both countries. If the principles of the law of Scotland are to survive, a separate Scottish legislature is essential since the present system effectively prevents Scots lawyers from taking part in legislation. The true importance of Sir Alec Douglas-Home's proposals for a Scottish Convention are as yet unappreciated by many Scotsmen, who may not realize that Scotland is the only nation with a separate system of law but without a legislature.

There are five sources of law. The first is legislation passed either before the Act of Union by the Scottish Parliament, or since, by the British Parliament. Today there are some 3,000 Acts of Parliament and 25,000 Statutory Instruments all tending to restrict the activities of the citizen allegedly in the interests of the majority but frequently for the joy of those who like making rules. The simple principle that the law is for the adjustment of competing

The Forth Road Bridge, completed in 1964, is the longest suspension bridge in Europe, spanning 1.25 miles including the approach viaducts.

freedoms and the guarantee of liberty is being replaced by the bureaucrats' chief cannon 'What is not compulsory is forbidden'. The courts alas, are bound to apply legislation strictly – much of it makes no sense – most of it makes bad law.

The second source of law comes from the authoritative writings of the great lawyers of the past, called the institutional writers. In civil matters Craig, Mackenzie, Stair, Bankton, Erskine and Bell are the chief writers, while Mackenzie and Baron Hume are authorities in the criminal law. Sir Thomas Craig of Riccarton (1540–1601) wrote his *Jus Feudale*, the first Scottish institutional text, because he was sorry for the students of the law who had no books they could consult. Sir George Mackenzie of Rosehaugh (1636–1691), who founded the Advocates' Library and became known as 'Bloody Mackenzie' for his prosecution of the Covenanters, wrote innumerable books on the law, religion, poetry and other subjects. Andrew McDowall, Lord Bankton, wrote his *Institutes* in 1751. John Erskine of Carnock was Professor of Scots Law in Edinburgh till 1765 and wrote both a text book for his students and an authoritative text which was published after his death. George Joseph Bell, Professor of Scots Law at Edinburgh from 1822 until his death in 1843, was the son of an Episcopal clergyman and brother of an eminent surgeon and artist. He was appointed on the motion of John Clerk of Eldon seconded by Sir Walter Scott. He contributed immensely to the creation of Scots mercantile law and his commentaries were claimed by Lord Cockburn to have done more for the fame of the law of Scotland in foreign countries than had been done by all our other law books put together. In later life he was appointed principal Clerk of Session in succession to Sir Walter Scott. Lord Jeffrey observed that it was sufficient recompense for accepting the office of Lord Advocate to be able to reward so honest and ill-used a man as George Joseph Bell. He followed David Hume, the nephew of the great philosopher of the same name whose commentaries on the law of Scotland relating to crime, published in 1797, remain the foundation of Scots criminal law.

Sir Archibald Alison who was Sheriff Principal of Lanarkshire also wrote an authoritative text on the criminal law. He was a great historian and was so popular that one hundred thousand people attended his funeral in Glasgow. Bell's successor, John Schank More, published the modern annotated edition of Stair and Erskine though it was said of him that he could never deter-

Braemar Castle (Aberdeenshire) was built by an Earl of Mar in 1628. The rectangular rampart, or curtain-wall, is a later addition as are the crenellated top stories of each turret.

mine in his own mind what the law actually was. He was scarcely unique in that! From the Bench, Lord President Inglis set out many of the developing principles of law and Lord Fraser wrote authoritatively on the law of husband and wife, master and servant, parent and child. In the present century Lord Dunedin and Lord Cooper continued the great tradition.

The writings of lawyers attract notice or authority in Scotland according to the merit of the author. Death is properly regarded as promotion. No lawyer, however eminent, is accorded much authority until he is dead – and some not even then. No doubt the maxim *Nil nisi bonum de mortuis* extends its pity to their works. And Scotland awaits with ill-concealed anticipation the deaths of Professor Walker, Professor T. B. Smith and Professor Gordon who have made particularly extensive and valuable contributions to the law in the recent past.

The third source of law is judicial precedent, though the idea that it has to be treated as binding in preference to principle is an English introduction. The higher the Court the more binding the precedent and since the House of Lords is the Supreme Court of Appeal in civil matters, considerable quantities of English legal doctrine have forced their way into our law through this noble door. In criminal cases no appeal lies to the House of Lords but the traditional reluctance of the High Court of Justiciary to develop the law of Scotland on the principles laid down by Hume has led to the law of England providing precedents for the law of Scotland in matters such as Road Traffic law under the excuse that the law should be the same in both countries regardless apparently, of whether it is good or right. There is however, a splendid machinery in Scotland for the resolution of bad precedents whereby a fuller court of five or seven judges can reconsider an old and binding decision; this is an excellent source of law reform and it is sad that it is used only very occasionally.

The fourth source of law is custom, whereby certain conduct gains general acceptance or rejection in the community and is given the force of law. This is in effect the Common Law, our ancient and immemorial custom which forms the broad base of all the law.

The fifth source of law is equity. Scotland has never had a separate Court of Equity. In 1760 Henry Home, Lord Kames, published his *Principles of Equity* among many books which he wrote on all manner of subjects from religion and morality to farming. The law of Scotland still stands in his debt. Apart from its ordinary equitable jurisdiction the Supreme Court has an ultimate equitable power called the *Nobile Officium* to ensure that no lapse or omission of the law shall frustrate the rights of the aggrieved subject or the interests of justice.

These are the sources of law which the judges apply. There are eighteen judges of the Supreme Court who are called Senators of the College of Justice. The same eighteen act as civil judges in the Court of Session and criminal judges in the High Court of Justiciary. They dress in different robes for their different roles – like Deacon Brodie, the notorious Edinburgh merchant who was respectable by day and crooked by night – blue robes with plum facings and crimson crosses in the civil courts and scarlet robes with silk facings and crimson crosses for the criminal court.

Under some pressure King James VI bestowed upon the judges the right to the honorary title of Lord (but with no right to sit in the House of Lords), but with the right to assume a judicial title. The King, true to his reputation as the wisest fool in Christendom, refused to extend the pretence of grandeur to their wives. This resulted in the husband and wife bearing different styles and sometimes different names. The custom was changed by a bourgeois and unromantic government, at the request of a priggish sovereign, Queen Victoria, after one of the Senators was ejected from a Paris hotel for signing-in himself and his wife in the register, as Lord Ardwell and Mrs Jameson!

The highest civil court is the Court of Session which always sits in Edinburgh and thus compels all its litigants and witnesses to come to the capital. This has resulted in the benefit of a resident legal community and the disadvantage of a parochial approach. Originally the Court travelled to the place appointed by the King. The judges of the Court sat by rotation, changing when they had sat for forty days, but they became so idle and negligent that the Court became a daily council sitting in Edinburgh, where the King could see that they sat. Like so many traditions of importance no one has bothered to question the wisdom of their continuing to do so but a howl of sedentary protest would arise from those who are in a position to veto a change if one were suggested.

The Court of Session was founded in 1532 and for three centuries the 'Haill fifteen' sat to determine any cause of consequence. It is still theoretically a collegiate court but today the ten judges of the Outer House called Lords Ordinary sit alone as a civil court of first instance and hear claims for damages or defamation and all cases of divorce since all matters affecting status are reserved for the Supreme Court. The rest of the Senators form two civil appeal courts called the First and Second Division of the Inner House to hear appeals from the Lords Ordinary and judges of the lower courts and certain matters at first instance. Until 1933 the pursuer could choose his judge and his appeal Court. This resulted, as it would even more today, in some judges having little to do, which illustrates the fallibility of human beings. Some advocates cannot achieve that withdrawn and conscientious impartiality and devotion to the principles of law and justice which is the hallmark of a great judge, and litigants and their solicitors in so small a community are quick to learn to read the Bench and act accordingly.

Civil cases are heard before a judge, or a judge sitting with a jury of twelve. Contested cases in the Court of Session are usually conducted by Senior and Junior Counsel on each side. Before a jury, the Junior Counsel outlines the case for each side before it begins and Senior Counsel sums it up at the end. Senior Counsel asks the questions and Junior Counsel notes the answers. The solicitor sits behind, impotent and anxious. The judge outlines the law. The whole process begins with a written summons setting out the case for the pursuer and written defences in reply. These are adjusted and printed as a closed record so the case for each side is committed to paper and restricted to that. There may be preliminary hearings on matters of law by the judge before the final hearing by judge or jury. Most pursuers in the Court of Session seek damages for injury or seek divorce – employee and employer, or husband and wife. In both categories the less powerful party has been gaining rights increasingly over the years.

Marriage may be celebrated by a minister of religion or a registrar. Formerly there were many forms of irregular marriage but the Marriage (Scotland) Act 1939 abolished most of them. Declaration of consent to marry before witnesses was described by Lord Neaves, a Judge of note in the last century, in verse, in his Tourists' Matrimonial Guide throughout Scotland:

> This maxim itself might content ye,
> The marriage is made by consent,
> Provided it's done *de praesenti*,
> And marriage is really what's meant.

Suppose that young Jockie or Jenny,
Say 'We two are husband and wife'
The witnesses needn't be many,
They're instantly buckled for life.

From the Canon Law there came the form of promise *cum subsequente copula*. If on a promise of marriage the woman allowed the man to go to bed with her the marriage was obtained from the moment of union. The 'permissive society' requires stricter rules and administrative neatness has swept away forms of marriage which were real and useful. Until the Age of Marriage Act 1929 the age of consent at common law was 14 for boys and 12 for girls. By that act it was raised to 16 but parental consent has never been required for marriage; hence the popularity of Gretna Green. Scotland has always taken a more genuine view of the responsibility of its fledglings and treated the lieges as one species. The modern hackneyed trope of speech about the young and the generation gap is alien to the Scottish tradition, which has treated young people with neither awe nor disdain. The condescension which isolation of the young and discussion of them as a different species implies, is English or American in concept and brings with it social problems which the Scottish approach has always escaped.

Marriage may be nullified on various grounds but the contract more usually is brought to an end by divorce on the ground of adultery, cruelty, desertion for three years, incurable insanity, sodomy, bestiality or presumed death. Most divorces are undefended which suggests that the grounds of divorce are merely symptoms of the regrettable fact that the parties can't get on with each other and the proposed change to the ground of irretrievable breakdown may be more logical but is likely to be more complex. Adultery, like crime, must be proved beyond reasonable doubt while all other civil matters need only be established on a balance of probability. The concubine attracts the name of paramour.

The First Division is presided over by the Lord President, the administrative chief of the law, presently Lord Clyde, son of a distinguished father and father of an erudite son; electric and wiry, he is a man upon whom flies settle at their peril. Originally judges received no salary and kept the fines they imposed and some of the damages they awarded. How few would go to prison, how high the awards would be! By 1753 however, the Lord President received £3,000 per annum. The Second Division is presided over by the Lord Justice Clerk, Lord Grant, a tall man, bluff and gruff, fond of high living and low jokes and champion of Scottish opera. The decisions of these two Appeal Courts are subject to a restricted right of appeal to the House of Lords whose justiciary includes two Scottish judges. Through the years this 'barbarian minority' sitting among the Sassenachs in London, has exercised a wholesome and brilliant influence upon the law of both nations.

All the judges in their scarlet robes act as Lords Commissioner of Justiciary. They sit alone with a jury of fifteen to hear criminal trials in the High Court of Justiciary which was founded in 1672. This court sits in the jurisdiction of the crime and therefore travels on circuit from time to time to wherever it is required. Formerly this was a great occasion, the officers of Court parading with great ceremony through the streets but now almost all the panoply is gone. In Aberdeen a Guard of Honour still parades for his Lordship to inspect and a banquet of shrinking grandeur is provided at the mid-day adjournment of the Court. Elsewhere the sole sign of panoply, the two state trumpeters who heralded the entrance of the judge and paraded in uniforms provided by the mean but spendthrift Treasury, covered in the insignia of the sovereign who died in 1910 was abolished by order of the Lord President in 1971. The mace is borne by a Macer but all the criminal maces in Scotland are cheap and vulgar, being made of iron and chrome and gold paint. The High Court on circuit sits longer hours than the Court of Session because the judges don't like staying outside Edinburgh a minute longer than they have to, and the former habit of making a circuit an event for those who took part in it has gone. Had the tradition of good fare and old port obtained in Scotland as it does in England, their lordships might never come home.

All criminal prosecutions are taken at the instance of the Lord Advocate on a written indictment. When a crime is committed in Scotland the police take preliminary statements and report their findings to the Procurator Fiscal. He interviews the witnesses and takes precognitions from them and he decides if a prosecution should be taken in summary matters. If the crime is serious he reports to the Lord Advocate who decides whether to prosecute, whom to prosecute, what to charge and where to charge him. There is no preliminary hearing as in England, where the prospective members of the jury are free to read the evidence and form their view of the case from reports, accurate, full, or false, of the Magistrates' hearing. Prosecution by an impartial law officer and his advisers in contrast to the English system of prosecution by the police and the Director of Public Prosecutions, and the absence of the preliminary hearing, so that the jury comes fresh and free to the case at the trial, are two of the cardinal guarantees of justice in Scotland – an impartial prosecutor and an impartial jury.

The case is conducted by one of the Advocate Deputes who are salaried advocates entitled to engage in private practice as well. There are no opening speeches, so the jury hear the evidence and not, as in England, what it is supposed to be going to be. Gradually as the case proceeds they twig what it is all about. Each witness is examined, cross-examined and re-examined by Counsel for the Crown and Counsel for the Defence. Both Counsel then address the jury. The judge gives them the law in his charge. He usually tells the jury as he is bound to do, that all the matters of fact are for them to decide, though he sometimes proceeds to decide them himself. In the last century the Court sat without cease until the case finished, however long it lasted, and the unfortunate jury had to stand throughout the judge's charge. Though this exhausting practice has been abolished, the remnant persists in the rule that juries may not eat or drink once they retire. It is usual for accused persons, sometimes quaintly called the panel, to be defended by an Advocate or Queen's Counsel and a Junior Counsel. There are occasional exceptions, the most noteworthy of which was Peter Thomas Anthony Manuel who sacked his eminent Counsel in the course of his trial in Glasgow in 1957. He conducted his impossible defence with a skill which displayed great talent but which was insufficient to obtain his acquittal on the six charges of murder which he faced, and Lord Cameron pronounced upon him the awful words of the Scottish death sentence 'which is pronounced for doom'. On the Bench a man of set ambition, power and prodigious ability turned to right – in the dock, the same turned to evil. Each received his likely rewards, though doom is now happily a past concept.

From the High Court appeal lies since 1926 only to the High Court of Justiciary. Appeals are granted by these courts with increasing reluctance. In 1674 the Lords of Session to strengthen their own power refused to admit any appeals. The Faculty of Advocates taking this to be an encroachment on the liberty of the subject 'laid by their gowns and gave over pleading' and the Lords of Session banished them twelve miles from Edinburgh. In a noble speech in November 1674 Sir George Mackenzie resolved the dispute. Three hundred years later in 1969 a similar dispute arose over the hearing of criminal appeals but on this occasion no advocate was banished.

The Scottish Bench has always attracted a proportion of men of great scholarship in the civil law and barbaric brutality towards wretched criminals. This was especially so in the eighteenth and nineteenth centuries and caused Charles James Fox, the English Whig, to say of the Scots 'God help the people who have their judges'. Braxfield was the Judge Jeffries of Scotland and was able to condemn to death a friend with whom he often played chess with the words 'That's checkmate noo, Willie'. He was succeeded by David Rae, Lord Eskgrove, who took even more delight in the infliction of suffering and earned from Cockburn the great taunt that the value of all his words and actions consisted in their absurdity. The ghost of Braxfield is not laid yet.

No person in Scotland can be detained without a charge being made against him and if within 110 days of his committal his trial has not been brought to a conclusion he is entitled to be released and declared free from all liability in respect of the crime with which he is charged. In 1967 a prisoner was released without trial from the dock under this procedure on a charge of attempted murder, by Lord Milligan, a Senator renowned for athletic prowess, great humanity, drinking Guinness and cracking jokes. He may also be remembered as the first judge forced to retire at seventy-five. Formerly the Senators were appointed *ad vitam aut culpam* and many great men came near to shaking the concept of human mortality. But now Parliament in its self-taken omnipotence has declared that life is over at seventy-five.

Below the two great branches of the Supreme Court is the Sheriff Court which exercises civil and criminal jurisdiction in the territorial district to which it is assigned. The office of Sheriff is very old. Originally they were potentates rather than lawyers but these were replaced after 1748 by Sheriff Deputes who appointed Substitutes to sit in their absence. In 1838 Sheriff Substitutes became full-time judges resident in their sheriffdoms, which is what they are today. The Sheriff Deputes are now called Sheriff Principals and they are salaried part-time members of the Senior Bar. They exercise an equal criminal jurisdiction as their Substitutes but in civil matters act as a Judge of Appeal. The powers of penalty are limited to two years imprisonment and prosecutions are conducted in these courts by the Procurator Fiscal on behalf of the Lord Advocate. The Sheriffs wear black robes and white falls which reflects the taste of a Calvinist country. Some of the Sheriff courthouses are noble but most are dreary and have the appearance of a schoolroom rather than a court. In Glasgow the Corn Exchange has been used as the Sheriff Court since the last century. The building is tawdry, ill-equipped and badly designed and lowers the whole scale and face of justice. Its continued use must be one of the strangest denials of national pride. Lucky that justice is blind!

By contrast the Court of Session has a magnificent home in the Parliament House. In the year 1632 Edinburgh was greatly straitened for want of proper places for holding the courts of Parliament and Session which the citizens were afraid might occasion removing the courts elsewhere. The Town Council resolved to propose to the citizens the erection of a proper place and called them to subscribe such sums as were needed. The subscriptions were so considerable (£56,000) that the Town Council embarked on the building and such money as was needed further was raised by tax, the whole cost being 209,340 merkes in Scottish money. In his history of Edinburgh, published in 1753 William Maitland claims that this is an affair not to be paralleled, that a national building for the service of the kingdom should be erected at the expense of the Edinburghers without the least assistance of Parliament. The empty site of the opera house confirms that it has never been done since. The maiden, the machine for beheading criminals was kept with the city's hundred lamps in the laigh, or lower, hall and it was there that Argyle heard that it was to be used to behead him. The Parliament Hall contains many good portraits and statues, the best of which is of Lord President Forbes of Culloden, by Roubillac. The great window, the work of two German artists, was erected in 1868 representing the inauguration of the College of Justice by James V in 1532 and under its mighty hammer beam roof all the great debates of Scotland's history have occurred. Now it is used for lawyers to ponder over lesser matters.

The members of the legal profession in practice are either solicitors or advocates. The advocates are all members of the Faculty of Advocates and form the Scottish Bar. They wear morning dress and wigs and gowns in court. They have an exclusive right of audience in the Supreme Court and they may appear before any other court or tribunal. They number about one hundred and from their number are appointed the Senators of the College of Justice, the Sheriff Principals and most of the Sheriff Substitutes. The advocate is a specialist like a surgeon and no client may consult him direct; he must be instructed by a solicitor. The advocates provide specialist opinions on questions of law submitted to them. It had always been assumed that the advocate could not be sued for negligence so that a solicitor could safeguard himself by obtaining Counsel's opinion, but a recent English decision has called in question the validity of the rule though it has yet to be decided in Scotland. The equivalent disadvantage is that an advocate cannot sue for his fees. The Bar is so small that advocates have never been able to specialize to any extent in a particular branch of the law without great risk. This has greatly reduced the calibre of their contribution and superior specialists in Company Law, Taxation and Conveyancing are frequently to be found among the solicitors and academics.

The dignity of Queen's Counsel has been conferred on Senior members of the Bar since 1897, when a dispute arose as to precedence of senior members of the Scottish Bar and English QCs in the House of Lords. The taking of silk bars an advocate from appearing alone in any Court unless he is a prosecutor. It is an English tradition entirely inappropriate to a Bar so small as Scotland's which reduces the choice to the solicitor, increases the cost for the client and restricts the work of both halves of the Bar. It was demanded by the inherent Scottish sense of inferiority and should be abolished forthwith.

Advocates have existed in Scotland since the reign of James I. In 1424 by Act of Parliament judges were required to ensure any poor and ignorant litigant should be assisted by a 'lele and wys advocate to follow sic pur creaturis caus'. In 1587 advocates were first allowed to appear for criminals. In the reign of Charles II, Sir George Mackenzie of Rosehaugh founded the Advocates' Library. It was the custom of those who studied abroad to return with a large collection of treatises on the law which formed the basis of their private libraries. These found their way to the Advocates' Library. As a result, a collection of special distinction and vast size was accumulated and this magnificent asset was presented to the nation in an act of singular self-sacrifice in 1926.

It is now the basis of the Scottish National Library to which all scholars have resort.

The king of the Bar is the Dean of Faculty of Advocates who is elected by his fellow advocates and reigns over their necessary affairs. If ever it is essential, he enters the Court to guarantee the right of any advocate to be given a fair hearing and he resolves disputes between Bench and Bar. The Dean of Faculty is usually appointed to the Bench and five former Deans are presently judges in Scotland. The most senior, Lord Cameron, revived and restored the Cockburn Society, named after the great judge, which was founded to preserve all that is best in Edinburgh. He has given impetus and respect to the great task of preserving one of the most notable expressions of the second Scottish Renaissance by the support of his gigantic image and energy. He is frequently to be found dining in the Arts Club with another Senator who was Vice-Dean of Faculty, Lord Walker, the oldest of our judges, whose chief joy is making subtle distinctions and twisting the tails of serious Counsel with his endless sense of fun. In a recent case in which a man was assaulted and had his teeth knocked out, the tender judge enquired whether they were his own teeth or false teeth. The advocate depute explained that the distinction was immaterial. 'Not at all,' replied the judge, 'one is an assault on the person; the other is an offence against his property.' Lord Kilbrandon succeeded Lord Guest as Dean and has now succeeded him in the House of Lords. He formerly presided over the Scottish Law Commission and investigated fields of reform. Lord Fraser his successor as Dean is distinguished by his nimble lawyer's brain, his shy retiring nature and his constant assistance of the Arts. Lord Thomson is unceasingly congenial, and has an endless repository of good nature and good sense. The last Dean, Lord Emslie is distinguished by his impeccable capability and kindness alike.

But by far and away the most important member of the Bar is the Lord Advocate. He is a member of the Government and falls when the party of government changes. He is in unfettered charge of the conduct of criminal prosecution. His greatest power is patronage. All judicial appointments to the Supreme Court and the Sheriff Court are made on his recommendation; moreover the appointment of the Prosecutors in the Supreme Court and the Procurators Fiscal in the Sheriff Court are subject to his choice or whim, as are the Standing Counsel to all government ministries and many other subsidiary appointments to the Civil Service. There are indeed only four judges who have not held political office or become Dean of Faculty; Lord Migdale, Lord Robertson, Lord Kissen and Lord Hunter. Two more, Lord Keith and Lord Dunpark, have just been appointed.

After the Union of the Parliaments in 1707, the Lord Advocate was undoubtedly the most powerful man in Scotland and the great Dundas of Arniston was called 'King'. Many of our greatest judges and greatest men have been Lords Advocate. They towered over the nation and the continent in the eighteenth and nineteenth centuries. Their patronage, though mightily beneficial, did not guarantee the salaries that the Lord Advocate can hand out today. As the stature of the occupant of this great office declines his power becomes increasingly beneficent. This cauldron of power has attracted many advocates, some by aptitude, some by ambition, to stand for Parliament. Great are the risks of such a course. Some win, some lose, some rise, some fall; but it is important that advocates should continue to enter Parliament in much larger numbers than they have of recent times. Apart from the Lord President and the Lord Justice Clerk, there are three Senators who have held the office of Lord Advocate – Lord Wheatley, made a Life Peer in recognition of his public service, and, in the Outer House, Lord Avonside and Lord Stott. The second law officer is the Solicitor General who is also a member of the Government and provides the Lord Advocate with another pair of hands and a second, or sometimes a first, brain. Two of the Senators were once Solicitor-General, Lord Johnston, who is a gentle man, and Lord Leechman, who must be the most meek and merciful person ever to wield the sword of justice.

The contribution of the Faculty of Advocates to the national life is far beyond the law. The tradition of scholarship and culture is as old as the profession itself. Sir George Mackenzie, apart from founding the great library, was a poet and philosopher, Sir Walter Scott was a Clerk of Session, James Boswell and Robert Louis Stevenson were advocates, Lord Kames who always referred to his brothers on the Bench as 'auld buggers' and Lord Monboddo who never sat with his fellow judges because they once decided a case against him, were men of deep learning who made great contributions to letters. The brilliant revival and renaissance of the eighteenth and nineteenth centuries in Scotland, was due in large measure to the initiative and prestige of the advocates and solicitors. This great liberal and cultural tradition has greatly benefited Scotland. Sadly it is in decline and golf has replaced art and letters as the common culture of the Bar.

Hand in hand with their good minds was the tradition of good living. Before 1800 judges had wine and biscuits on the bench in the Court of Session, a practice which lingered on more discreetly when some judges put port in their inkwell and sucked their pens. On circuit the court adjourned from time to time and all proceeded to the inn before returning to deal with the business of death and transportation. Lord Hermand made his drinking into not merely a pleasure but a virtue and in the Oban circuit of 1840 Lord Cullen, Lord Hermand and Lord Cockburn presided. The night before the circuit began the three judges and two advocates consumed 16 bottles of claret. Lord Cullen was in bed all next day and as the evening jollifications continued for fourteen nights, he never saw his circuit court. The immortal head of Hermand was clear and cool each day and he and Lord Cockburn discharged the calls of justice together and alone. In this century the great Lord Justice Clerk Aitchison who did so much to humanize the criminal law was only at his brilliant best when he had indulged in a suitable libation, and his successor the present Lord Justice Clerk is not ashamed to sample the national drink of which he bears the name of one brand.

Alas the consumption of the bacchanalian dew of grape and grain has begun to attract a puritan frown and the law of motoring has helped to create the view that alcohol is a drug consumed only by the ill and the irresponsible. The age of the technocrat is indeed at hand. All these traditions of broad minds, big men and high living have done much to mould the character of the Scots nation and to confound the narrow national ecclesiastical doctrine that fun is sin and the only joy to be had is hereafter.

The licensing laws in Scotland make a mockery of all principle. Before 1955 only *bona fide* travellers could drink on Sunday and many a Scotsman made a short round trip from home to hotel and back again. Now hours are restricted everywhere to standard times and Scotsmen abandon self-control and abdicate the decision when to stop since they know that at 10 p.m. the publican will take it for them. Not so in the Islands where the law is less harshly applied. On being asked why he drank beer and whisky together, the Scottish habit of a 'nip' and a 'chaser', an old high-lander explained, 'If ye just drink whisky ye get tight before ye're fu' and if ye just drink beer ye get fu' before ye're tight but if ye drink them together ye get fu' and tight at the same time and ye know when to stop.' For those who like to drink unrestricted all day the law makes due asinine and unintended allowance. If you are resident in a hotel you can drink all day and invite the whole world to drink with you and if you don't like hotels you can do it on a train once it starts moving. Both pastimes are expensive. The law is mad. Foreigners are dismayed to discover that they can drink at 11 o'clock in the morning but not at 11 o'clock at night. The licenses for public houses and hotels are granted by local councils sitting as the licensing court. Here justice is rough, strange and unpredictable – except for some. All the things the law should not be. In 1702 the Rev. Areskine prayed in the Tron Kirk in Edinburgh's High Street, 'O Lord have mercy on all Fools and Idiots and especially the Magistrates of Edinburgh'. If there had been a licensing court in those days he might well have prayed for their victim. It is surely time that a bad practice was brought to an end.

The great majority of the legal profession are solicitors. The senior society of solicitors in Scotland is the Society of Writers to the Signet, who attract the brocade that they never waste an estate on the beneficiaries. This august body has produced a superabundance of excellent men whose portraits and busts line the noble library and hall which they bought from the Faculty of Advocates. The Society had a most valuable library but being poor they sold many of their best books to restore their splendid halls. What the advocates gained in prestige from giving their library to Scotland, the Writers to the Signet gained in capital from selling theirs to foreign bidders who would read them. Utilitarians may decide for themselves which is the fool satisfied and which Socrates dissatisfied. In all the major towns in Scotland solicitors' societies with strong traditions exist. In Glasgow the Royal Faculty of Procurators has a splendid library, recently restored, and in Aberdeen to emphasize their traditional preference for independence the solicitors call their club The Society of Advocates.

The solicitors provide the personal services to their clients. They buy and sell their houses, and record the title deeds. One of the most excellent features of the law of Scotland is that from early times titles to all land and heritable property have been recorded in the Register of Sassines kept in Robert Adam's beautiful Register House. The law of land tenure in Scotland has hitherto been feudal in form; this land may be held direct of the Crown but it is usually feued from a Superior. The Superior in granting this everlasting lease could impose conditions on building and development and this proved to be a most enlightened form of town and country planning to which the creation of Charlotte Square bears witness. Now we are left to the mercy of local authorities whose taste and planning could hardly leave more to be desired.

The solicitor also makes wills and contracts and sets up companies and trusts and provides all the manifold requirements of the citizen for the law. They advise the client whether to litigate or get Counsel's advice and they prepare the cases and interview the witnesses thereafter. In the Sheriff Courts the bulk of litigation and defence is undertaken by the solicitors and they are often experts in the fields in which they play the most part such as the law of inheritance.

The law of Scotland has always ensured that a family should not be entirely excluded from its inheritance. This tradition can be traced back to the early burgh law of the twelfth century whereby testing on heritage was not allowed. The house went to the eldest son who had to accommodate the widow if she was his mother. Children were entitled to one-third of the movable property, legitim fund, or bairn's part, and the widow to a third, the *jus relictae* and the remaining third could be tested subject to the takings of the Church. Now the Government takes its self-declared whack before the family and thus their inheritance, upbringing and way of life may be peremptorily destroyed by the mere accident of death. The Roman law made similar distinctions between heritable and movable property and similar provisions for the widow and children and this safeguarding of the family of the deceased has always been the principle of the Scottish law of inheritance.

The over-riding social humanity which is to be found in all branches of the law of Scotland is one of its most substantial traditions. There has, for instance been a system of free legal aid since 1424. Half a millenium later Parliament passed the Legal Aid (Scotland) Act 1949 giving financial legal assistance from Government funds to litigants of moderate means. In 1964 it was extended to criminal cases, though free defence had always been provided for those of small means since the foundation of the

Justiciary Court in 1672. The criminal law has always been liberal towards social crimes in contrast to our Calvinist image. Recent legislation in England on such matters as homosexuality, abortion, majority verdicts and the defence having the last word, has been heralded as triumphantly broad-minded and progressive. But in Scotland in 1685 Sir George Mackenzie introduced the accused's right to challenge juries without reason and the right of his counsel to speak last to the jury in 'full harangue'. The common law of Scotland has always been more liberal and compassionate in all these matters than the law of England has even now become.

The tradition of intelligent compassion has nowhere been more enshrined than in the famous idiosyncratic verdict of 'not proven' in criminal cases which foreign lawyers find difficult to understand far less to justify. Madeleine Smith who was defended in the High Court at Edinburgh for murder by the great Lord President Inglis, then Dean of Faculty, was acquitted by a verdict of 'not proven'. Inglis' speech to the jury is one of the classic forensic orations of all time and opened with the mighty words 'The charge is murder and the penalty is death'. In the recent case of McNicol against Her Majesty's Advocate in 1964 the Lord Justice General Lord Clyde, rehearsed the virtues of the 'not proven' verdict in a classic judgement. 'It is of course quite true that under the English system there are only the two verdicts and periodically the cry is raised from across the border that we in Scotland should tamely accept the rule established in the law and practice of England. But for upwards of two centuries a "not proven" verdict has been available as a third verdict in the law of Scotland and no convincing argument has been advanced to justify its elimination from our law. It is unnecessary to consider all the reasons in its favour but perhaps I might just mention two. Its inclusion in the list of possible verdicts is much more humane and much more advantageous to the accused than if it were not so included. It gives a jury who have some lingering doubts as to the guilt of an accused, and are certainly on the evidence not prepared to say that he is innocent, the chance to find the charge against him not proven. If that third choice were eliminated and if the jury had only two alternatives left it is almost inevitable that in the situation that I have just envisaged they would hold that their doubts of guilt were not enough to amount to a reasonable doubt and he would be convicted. In the experience

of all of us here there are many cases where a verdict of "not proven" has been reached and where had that verdict not been available the jury would have found the accused guilty, and there are many men and women today in Scotland who have been acquitted on a "not proven" verdict and who had it not been available to them would have been in prison. But apart from this aspect of the matter the three verdicts are more logical and in accordance with principle than merely to give a jury two. Juries are not all-seeing and all-knowing. They are merely human beings and they can never know with certainty that a man is guilty. The furthest they can go against him is that on the evidence led before them it is proved beyond reasonable doubt that the accused did commit the crime. That after all is all that a verdict of guilty means. The true alternative to that verdict is that the Crown has not proved its case beyond reasonable doubt and the truly logical alternative therefore is a verdict of "not proven". But there are cases where the jury can go further in the accused's favour. The crucial witnesses may be disbelieved or may be proved discreditable and the defence may be shown to be a true defence which they accept. In that case a jury may well be prepared to hold it positively established by the evidence that the accused did not commit the crime and the appropriate verdict would then be a verdict of not guilty.'

Let us close with these words. It is prudent to let the Lord Justice General have the last word. He usually does.

Pony trekkers at Ruthven Barracks (Inverness), which were destroyed by supporters of Bonnie Prince Charlie in 1746.

Who Is Their God?

Campbell Maclean

The eminent Highland divine who allegedly opened his prayer with the words 'Paradoxical as it may seem unto thee, O Lord', offered a major clue to the distinctively Scottish notion of God. On the one hand the Lord is credited with intelligence of a high order of subtlety and complexity; on the other, there is a genuine appreciation, amounting almost to fellow-feeling, of how this makes for a correspondingly burdensome existence. For a full expression of Scottish piety it is essential that the twin notes of reverence and commiseration be simultaneously struck. Doubtlessly liturgical practices elsewhere fittingly express the splendour of God, although none have made him grander. And perhaps the Scots have not been alone in contriving sufficiently magniloquent language to do justice to his absolute otherness. But Scottish worshippers may also wish to suggest that they understand what it looks like from that other side, and for this the only apparatus available to them is the uniquely metaphysical usages of Scottish devotion. This attitude of awesome familiarity, which is neither presumptuous nor disrespectful, is the classic distillation of their native spirituality. In all fairness, the Devil is treated in the same way. A proper apprehensiveness is, of course, called for. But as in Robert Burns's rollicking poem, Auld Nick is both less formidable and more credible when approached in a mood of teasing and affectionate jocularity. Even the Devil stands in need of a little understanding.

Understanding is the key category of Scottish Presbyterianism. Other modes of apprehension are all very well but they do not match hard rationality and they may be dangerous obstructors of true religious communication. In Scotland you will hear the time honoured and universally practised rituals of Christendom dismissed as mumbo jumbo; and often in the kirk itself, the items of public worship which precede the sermon, through hymn and prayer and anthem, are slightingly referred to as 'the preliminaries'.

194

The sermon is the main feature. It is the reason for going to church. Indeed for centuries Divine Service was known as 'the sermon'. In many parts of the country singing was suspended entirely to allow more time for talking, and Communion came to be celebrated infrequently, usually twice a year. The most electrifying moment I have ever spent in a church followed the announcement by the minister that, as a result of a pastoral emergency which cut into his preparation time, he did not propose to preach a sermon that day. In almost any other country in the world this unhoped-for news would have been greeted with the jubilation it merited. But in the Scottish kirk it fell like a thunderclap upon incredulous and resentful ears. In so threatening an atmosphere it looked as if reimbursement of payments already made would be the least of the public demands. For all of them it was a wasted Sunday, called out, as they had been, on false pretences.

Religion may be more than the attempt to confer ultimate significance upon immediate social values, but people inevitably create a god to suit themselves. And though ideally any advanced deity should be immune from human influence he can hardly be conceived in terms other than those which have been strongly tinged by the aspirations and prejudices of his subjects. In Scotland, where rationality reigns, God is an intellectual. He may not excite mystical adoration. He does encourage argument. Of all the national gods Scotland's is the most sensible. In a rural parish, where it was customary to pray for rain during a spell of drought, one minister excused himself from these exercises on the grounds that on that particular Sunday morning, as he put it, 'the gless was ower high'. (The barometer was on the high side.) His congregation both understood and approved. You do not fly in the face of proven unfavourable indicators. In a sensible world, miracles are more likely on a falling barometer.

Faith by cerebration was Scotland's answer to the enfeebling mystification of pre-Reformation Catholicism. Elsewhere faith might be expressed with that degree of vagueness which might seem natural to it, but in Scotland no descriptive leeway was permitted. Faith had to make sense, and it had to make sense to everybody. This helps to explain the Reformers' preoccupation with the vision of a system of universal education, a vision never wholly realized, but for its time and in such a poor country, marvellously ambitious. It may also help to explain to visitors that streak of dogged academicism which many of them have singled out as the drollest of the national obsessions. They point to it daily in the public notices of the newspapers where it seems almost indecent to announce, for example, an engagement, without both parties having acquired some kind of reputable academic append-age. They do not know it at its best, seen through the eyes of generations of education-hungry peasants, themselves devoid of schooling, whose long, hard years of thrift and penury were hand-somely rewarded because it enabled them to send their clever son to university. But it is important to know that the inspiration behind this national drive was primarily religious. Education was a safeguard against obscurantism and clericalism. In Scotland it gave rise to an impressive compendium of religious instruction which centuries of children learned by heart. It produced the most knowledgeable and articulate lay theologians in the history of the Christian church. There are stories galore of the momentarily careless preacher beseiged after church by infuriated elders and deacons come to tell him, with a wealth of sophistry and learning, that the hairsbreadth by which he had dared to deviate from the norm of confessional orthodoxy had not escaped their attention. This is hardly true nowadays, but it has left behind a legacy of steely intellectuality, perhaps too inflexible for some, which still stands guard against alien intrusions into Presbyterian territory and is as suspicious as ever of non-rational elements in religious experience. Visitors who find the Presbyterian style unattractively top heavy should know that it springs from a desire to give sound understanding of the faith pride of place within a historical tradition in which the irruption of mystical and intuitive stimuli, so refreshing elsewhere, tended to get out of control. It is not easy to determine whether it was Presbyterianism which made the Scot a notably rational being or whether it was the intrinsically rational Scot who fashioned for himself a religion after his own heart and called it Presbyterianism. This is an instance where cause and effect are inextricably confused. What is not in doubt is that the series of explosive events which began in 1560 and continued off and on for the next hundred years contributed decisively to the shaping of this dilemma.

The twists and turns of these events take some unravelling. They have often been recorded. In the process much passion has been spent, many axes ground. It is too late in the day to hope for objectivity in the depiction of moments in which the heart and soul of Scotland was won and lost. What might be attempted is a description of two of the most obstinately-held attitudes towards the Reformation which have now acquired the status of folk myths and which visitors must learn to distinguish.

The first might be said to take its cue from T. S. Eliot's dictum 'Scotland is a country ruined by religion', and by religion he meant the Calvinist Reformed Faith which took root in the sixteenth century. Before that time (so the story goes) religion had been, on the whole, something of an asset. It had begun well. The first missionaries who came from Ireland in the sixth century, led by St Columba, had brought with them a romantic and mystical version of Christianity which finally centred itself on the idyllic Hebridean island of Iona. This form of the Faith was later Romanized and refined chiefly through the influence of the saintly Queen Margaret, English wife of King Malcolm Canmore, who, although not everyone's idea of Christian sweetness and light, went about doing an endless amount of good. From that time onwards we are to think of Scotland as a land of fun-loving rustics, poor but happy children of nature, whose chief pastimes were singing, dancing, drinking and innocent fornication. We are to see in the works of the Rabelaisan-type poets and balladists of the day a reflection of their brave and often hilarious encounters with the supernatural and their delightfully ribald view of the natural. All this was exercised within the dispensation of a benign and lethargic church which contented itself with presiding over the rituals of birth and death and regularizing the miscalculations of love.

It was then that the blow fell. The fanatical John Knox, with all the choking fury of the exiled revolutionary and bearing a monstrous grudge against all authority, particularly that exercised by women, landed in Scotland carrying with him a blueprint for salvation based on his besotted admiration for Calvin's Geneva, which he was determined to impose upon his fellow countrymen. Soon his rabble-rousing sermons won him popular support among the nobility and the crowd, and before long his howling hooligans made their first characteristic move. They tore down, stone by stone, every ancient building connected with the old order – which will explain the desecration of Scotland's loveliest religious foundations to puzzled visitors. Then began the long, dark night of Puritanism, from which Scotland has yet to emerge. Festivals, merrymaking, songs and dances, carousals late and early, were all banned. Fiddles and pipes were burned, and laughter vanished

197

from the streets. In its place came the dolorous discipline of Sabbath-keeping and soul searching, compulsory church attendances, and the receiving end of interminable pulpit harangues. Theological discourse ousted poetry: the catechist took over from the troubador: and witch-burning displaced cock-fighting as a public spectacle. Artistic inspiration disintegrated before the brutalizing vehemence of the new evangel. And God himself, heartless, arbitrary and terrifying, trapped in Calvin's inexorable logic, became its final victim.

This version of ecclesiastical history is held by the majority of Scotland's Roman Catholics. Indeed, it is the stuff of their text books. It is the stock-in-trade of leading members of the intelligentsia, especially when they feel they need to make excuses for Scotland's cultural backwardness. European visitors go away convinced that only some such bizarre historical experience could account for the Scottish idea of what constitutes entertainment on Sunday or civilized drinking time on weekdays. It is fanned into almost daily life by the diligence of English journalists. These busy fellows, themselves ignorant of the many-sidedness of Presbyterianism, and unable to detect when they are within the orbit of some tiny extremist sect whose affairs are the subject of many a Scottish joke, solemnly report its latest lunatic antics as if they were within the mainstream of Scottish life, and thus confirm the suspicions of their readers in Tunbridge Wells and elsewhere that the Scots are still in the grip of a raging Puritanical fanaticism.

The second version, which has just as many devotees, might be said to locate its finest moment in that scene of honest toil and homely piety described in Burns's *The Cottar's Saturday Night*. This typical expression of eighteenth-century rural life is the norm by which the Calvinist Reformation wishes to be judged. Before 1560, we are asked to believe, the picture is one of a tired and cynical church abandoning the sick soul of Scotland to the Devil. Only its rotted framework remained. Corrupt bishops had exhausted its revenues: an indolent and licentious priesthood absented themselves from its ordinances. Yet somehow its tottering structure remained intact, propped up by a French army, defying reform.

Then came the year of grace, 1560. The hand of the Lord had long been ready to smite, and when John Knox returned home, bringing with him an unrivalled knowledge of the target area, it smote to some effect. Out went Popery, prelacy, and priestcraft. Down came the idols, the Mass and the Confessional. Out went the saints, holy days and penances and the whole pestilential rigmarole of Popery. The Lord's church, at last, was cleansed of the suppurating foulness of Romanism. Almost overnight the cesspool of superstition was transformed into the clear water of Biblical truth. The true Kirk, shed of its past shame, was restored in its original purity and power. It could not have happened without John Knox. It was he who held to the vision of reform while others faltered. It was his faith and determination that carried the day. It was his words, God-given, loud and clear, that raised the nation to action. And all this we know for a fact, for is it not all recorded in Knox's own *History of the Reformation in Scotland*?

But the struggle to consolidate the triumph of the Reformed Church was to go on for many years. Two of its most hard-won excellences, its democratic government and its simple services, were constantly under threat from London-based Stewart kings, English Parliaments and upstart bishops, all wanting more power over the kirk and a return to High Church practices. The harassed people of God banded themselves together in a new declaration of purpose, called themselves the Covenanters, and prepared to do battle to the death. We are to imagine this episode, the Killing Times, as one in which peace-loving, pilgrim souls, with no other desire than the right to worship God in their own way were pressed unwillingly into a struggle against the forces of a new ecclesiastical tyranny. Ousted at bayonet point from their beloved kirks, they continued to worship God together at hillside conventicles, setting guards to warn them of the approach of the King's troopers. Though cut down savagely in their thousands, they persisted. The blood they shed was shed freely, knowing that Scotland's religious future, independent and democratic, lay in their hands. In the end they won, as they always knew they would. God, after all, was a Presbyterian, plain like themselves, and a faithful supporter of all righteous causes.

Scottish children have been reading their history that way for centuries, and Scottish exiles, generations removed, continue to rear their offspring on it. It has cut deeply into the emotional life of the nation. It is the substance of every peroration worthy of the name on festive Presbyterian occasions. Its morale-raising properties hardly ever fail. It may also be used for devious ends.

There are instances in recent times where two neighbouring congregations of the Kirk, having firmly decided to unite for sensible economic reasons, have been dissuaded from doing so at the last minute by some disaffected local orator, who, citing vaguely but passionately from the Killing Times and jogging the folk memory with a sigh or two, has accused them of betraying their glorious Covenanting heritage of independence. Visitors are warned about its use in Scottish pulpits. When they hear a preacher on the theme of the Blood of the Martyrs, he is not referring, as they mistakenly suppose, to the sufferings of the early Christians in the Roman arena. He is talking about some desperate encounters on the Lanarkshire moors three centuries ago.

There are more important confusions of which the visitor must be aware. One of them springs from the understandable tendency to judge Scottish issues by English standards. The English, as every Scot knows, are not a serious people. About cricket and beer, perhaps. But on every other subject of real importance, like religion, they are maddeningly facetious. For example, to the Scot, argument is a kind of sacred dialogue, dedicated to the enhancement of truth. It is a rough and unmannerly affair, full of vicious personal innuendo, unlit by smiles or concessions, and pursued in a spirit of unflagging immoderation. To the Englishman, especially the donnish Englishman, argument is a kind of parlour game in which the idea is to create a mood of effervescence where everything, however pungent and surprising, evaporates quickly. To embark on an argument with an Englishman is a frustrating business. He will, of course, be splendidly original and exploratory. He will catch you flat-footed in many a humiliating contradiction, and fend off your crude lunges with the adroitest of side-steps. But get him to within sighting distance of the heart of the matter and watch him sign off, panic-stricken, with some desperately jolly witticism. The English are embarrassed by strong convictions. It is typical of them that their religion should be the offshoot of a royal divorce, and that, in the absence of any remotely suitable term from the entire history of theology, it had to be described as Anglicanism.

But if the English toy with religion, the Scots are obsessed by it. Even those who are against religion are seriously against it. The finest refutation of the case for religion is by a Scot, David Hume. When a modern poet like Hugh MacDiarmid wishes to dispose of Christianity quickly he does so with venomous irreverence.

> Wull ever a wumman be big again
> Wi's muckle's a Christ? Yech, there's nae saying
> Gin that's the best that you ha'e comin'
> Fegs but I'm sorry for you, wumman.

It is this quality of seriousness, for good or ill, that stands behind the great Reformation enterprise. Only a people who took themselves seriously could have embarked upon so ambitious a programme. For it was nothing less than an attempt to dedicate the total life of the nation to a single end. In theological terms, it was the attempt to realize the Kingdom of Heaven on earth. Most nations, however Christian, have retreated from this dangerously Utopian hope and have been content with more realistic and attainable ends. Where it has been tried, the communities have either been territorially smaller, as in Calvin's Geneva, or have opted out of the general life of society, like Catholic monastics or like some of the Puritan primitives in the United States. But this is the single instance of a whole nation, over a period of centuries, being absorbed by the vision of a communal attainment of such ambitious proportions. Only the great Communist states of the twentieth century have shared a like vision. It began with a necessary assumption – not everybody wants the Kingdom of Heaven on earth. Many indeed prefer the Kingdom of Heaven to remain in heaven. Then they must be made to want it and like it. This meant the imposition of a structure of discipline which could be made effective nationally. It also called for the systematic indoctrination of the people in the content and hopes of their new society. And these twin factors of discipline and education became the cornerstones of the Reformers' scheme. The fact that it failed and was finally abandoned by the start of the nineteenth century should not detract from its considerable achievement. It failed because the executors of the mechanisms of godly discipline, the Kirk Session, became the wielders of a power that eventually became too far-reaching for them to control. Of all the absolute powers, spiritual power corrupts most absolutely. But the great experiment left a permanent imprint. It made the Scots the best-educated nation in Europe for three hundred years. It made the millions of Scottish pioneers in the New World and the Antipodes unusually impervious to adversity – those who have inherited convictions concerning the predestinated children of God are not broken by his occasional chastisements. Above all it confirmed the Scot in a love for democracy and for free institutions, and in the conviction that the final test of any nation's grandeur is a moral one. The Reformation experiment was undertaken by earnest people in a perfectionist mood: it demanded too much from human nature, but it was a magnificently ventured expression of their seriousness of purpose. They rejoiced in a God who set them such high standards. Alas, they could not keep up with Him.

The Kirk maintained its structural unity for nearly two hundred years. After that it broke up. You might say that a church which so emphatically encouraged independence of mind precipitated its own dissolution. It is true that many of the departures from the established church were undertaken more in a spirit of sorrow than anger and always with a high-minded disregard for the subsequent loss of privilege and property to the dissenters. But inevitably, once the flood began, it gave rise to a spate of perverse and self-indulgent sectarianism so farcically delicate of conscience that it could only be satisfied by every Presbyterian having a kirk to himself.

The proof of this is the way in which the splinters themselves splintered. Some of the smallest groups of seceders reached a stage where they enjoyed up to a dozen officially recognized incompatible sub-divisions, so allowing every one of the sub-seceders to choose the permutation most agreeable to him, and practically assuring him of a doctrinal position shared by no one else. There is no divisiveness like Presbyterian divisiveness. Now that, in the twentieth century, the splinters have been happily re-assembled in the present Church of Scotland all this may be viewed from a cooler perspective, although disentangling their ecclesiastical pedigree is still a favourite diversion among Presbyterians. Every visitor is advised to get to know that special look of smirking pride which lights up the Presbyterian visage whenever the account of a pedigree of tediously labyrinthine complexity is about to be embarked upon, and have a means of escape prepared. Otherwise he will be taken through an endless jumble of mysteriously named or initialled sects, all of them apparently of crucial importance to man's understanding of God. On the other hand, should he be in an ingratiating mood, an indication of how spiritually impoverished he now knows himself to be by not belonging to such an incomparably diverse heritage will endear him to his host forever more.

But the major rift in the Kirk, the Disruption of 1843, reflects a permanent clash of temperament in Scottish church life. At that time the Evangelicals, the radical and activist party, found themselves irreconcilably at loggerheads with the Moderates, who represented the aristocratic and gradualist tradition. They quit the Auld Kirk, and created a formidable alternative to it, the Free Church. For almost a century the two remained apart, licking their wounds, feeding their children on scorn and brag, competing for the allegiance of Scotland. The Auld Kirk, as all Free Kirkers knew, was lax and soulless, tainted with government money, socially pretentious. Their ministers were dressy and worldly, they dined and wined with the laird, played cards, and read their sermons. (Visitors should note that in Scotland reading a sermon is regarded as the clearest possible admission of spiritual bankruptcy.) The Free Kirk, on the other hand, as their depreciators well knew, was a church of upstart and quarrelsome busybodies, devoid of tolerance and good taste, aggressively self-righteous. Their ministers were uncultured pulpiteers, purveyors of fear-ridden religious emotionalism. School children jeered their jingles at each other:

> The Free Kirk, the wee Kirk
> The Kirk without the steeple
> The Auld Kirk, the cauld Kirk
> The Kirk without the people.

School children today know nothing of this historic vendetta. They are unaware of the wrangles that upset and inspired their grandparents. Yet these same grandparents, ecumenical age or not, will frequently be heard regretting the loss of the old competitive spirit in parochial church life. Since their attachments are no longer polarized and their enemies named, the fun has gone out of religion. But this tension from the past, however softened, remains an important and not uncreative ingredient of the re-united Church of Scotland today. If a little left of centre is the happiest pivotal point in a political party then a little right of centre may be said to be the Kirk's most characteristic resting place. From that stance it has been able to focus the concerns of the whole nation; it has kept a foot in high places without belonging there. Whenever the balance tips, the Kirk is in danger of becoming either mistress to the establishment or champion of the passing enthusiasm. The church is now wide enough to encompass both the Moderate and the Evangelical, although these in their purest forms have all but died out. But their echoes still reverbate powerfully. A young minister may save himself years of needless friction with his elders by taking the trouble to find out which of them were Auld Kirk and which U.F. or U.P. (two variants of the opposition) and by handling them accordingly. The lazy assumption on his part that they are all really the same will not be well received. This young man has clearly forgotten that not so long ago, whoever God was, he could not be the God of the Auld Kirk and the Free Kirk at the same time.

The re-unions of Presbyterianism have been as untidy as the separations. Every re-union left behind its trickle of stragglers, obstinate defiers of the majority cast of mind. Not all of them have yet been absorbed into the great Presbyterian consortium, although some of them must do so or perish. The visitor is likely to encounter the most influential of them if he travels in the North-West Highlands and Islands. They are a remnant of the Disruption, still rejoicing in the great name, but now known popularly as the 'Wee Frees', sometimes in ridicule, sometimes affectionately. He will know at once when he is in their territory. Should he arrive on a Sunday it will be all the more unmistakably evident. Not a movement anywhere, no petrol, no food, no newspapers, no room at the inn. Indeed 'Bed and Breakfast' signs would have been dutifully covered up in their Sunday night sacking to discourage such a request. This is the holiest part of Scotland, where God's known dislike of Sunday travel is scrupulously respected. Since God is known to dislike every other form of mischievous pleasure from Highland Games to Christmas dinners, indeed the very sound of laughter itself, a great deal of respect is called for. If there are transgressions, as well there might be, what with the notorious example of members of the Royal Family, they are in defiance of the prescriptions laid down by the godly minority, the Lord's chosen taskmasters. The visitor may wonder how so austere a regime became the provenance of a people who, as he will quickly discover, are notably hospitable, courteous, intelligent, and charmingly good-humoured. He may conclude that they have been saddled with the wrong religion. However much he envies them their stable and unquestioned standards he may wonder whether the burden of so uncongenial a God was not too high a price to pay.

Some parts of Scotland, miraculously, were untouched by the

Reformation. In the Lovat country, in Arisaig and Glenfinnan, on Barra and South Uist, not having met the New Faith, they kept to the Old. Miraculously again, in a country which has a record of savage and wasteful Protestant–Catholic hostility second only to Ulster, they have never fallen out with their Presbyterian neighbours. The Hebridean way of interpreting this exceptional cordiality would be to conclude that when the rival Gods are native and preferably Gaelic-speaking there is never any trouble. But for most Scots Roman Catholicism is a foreign religion. In its most harmless form it was smuggled in by prospective restaurateurs from Italy whose delectable fish and chips soon replaced both porridge and haggis as the staple diet of the nation. But its most infamous importers were the necessitous Irish labourers of last century come to find a living of any kind within the roaring jungle of industrial Clydeside. Their desperation drove them to the most unpleasant jobs and the lowest wages, and into fatal conflict with the native proletariat. As their numbers grew, the struggle intensified. They made their alien God a symbol of their will to survive and industrial Scotland became the battleground of a holy war. Although today the fires burn low, this war of two generations has had lasting consequences for the religious community in Scotland. Ghettoed Catholicism was forced into a conservative and autocratic stance: and Protestantism came to regard it as a wholly sinister and opportunistic movement. Visitors from Europe who have enjoyed a tolerant tradition of Catholic–Protestant relations at home will be surprised at the degree of primitive animosity shown on this subject by their otherwise sophisticated Scottish friends. Catholics feel there are hidden criteria employed against them. Although they have now naturalized their God and begun to play a more significant role in public life their faith is still a barrier to the highest offices. Even when they make light of their origin an Irish surname is assumed to conceal a Catholic adherence. (Promotion-seeking Protestants with Irish surnames have an even stronger case for disgruntlement.) More unforgiveably, this sustained mistrust at the heart of Scottish life confuses natural relationships. A young lad from a staunch Presbyterian home realizes what is in store for him when he announces there that the charming girl to whom they know he has become seriously attached is called Teresa or Bernadette. There is one further instance of the singularity of the Scottish scene that a visitor should bear in mind. His booklet of handy English phrases is likely to define a chapel as the meeting place of implacably nonconformist Protestants. He should know that in Scotland it means just the opposite.

In terms of numbers it is only the Roman Catholic community which threatens the Presbyterian monopoly. Indeed it is not too fanciful to suppose that if both stay the course for another hundred years they will have reached a position of parity, especially since the Catholic disinclination to interfere with nature gives them a clear advantage. But all the other Gods are on the wane. The Episcopalians, 'the Piskies', who once challenged the Presbyterians for control of the Kirk and have given rise to its gentlest spirits are now so reliant upon southern immigrants that they are everywhere known, much to their annoyance, as 'the English church'. The social distinction of their God continues to appeal to the aspiring, and no lordly wedding or double-barrelled christening may be said to be adequately celebrated outside his jurisdiction. But their future rests in some kind of accommodation with the kirk, which is now being painfully negotiated. In the common mind they are insuperably handicapped. Firstly, they kneel. Genuflexion is an exercise darkly connected with the most grievious of Scotland's past misfortunes and kirk pews have been so designed as to make its reintroduction impossible. It is doubtful if there is any sneer so heartfelt as this popular rhyming dismissal of Episcopalian piety:

> Piskie, piskie, palian
> Doon on your hunkers and up again.

Church-going visitors are recommended to suspend life-long habits of devotion while in Scotland for fear of arousing suspicions that they may never be able to remove. Secondly, and worse, they have bishops. Mention of this office, so revered in the universal church, and graced by the most eminent of the saints including Augustine and presumably Peter, puts every Presbyterian on the alert. Resistance to it is the holiest of causes. It is the only subject in the public life known to rejuvenate the faith of backsliders, unite sworn enemies, and transform the assemblies of wise and charitable men into ungovernable rabbles. Circulation managers of certain newspapers have also discovered that if periodically re-injected into the bloodstream of Scottish life it is an ideal way of serving both God and Mammon.

The encounter with other churches has helped to expose the Kirk to herself. For example, though she may rejoice in the democratic instinct which warns her against bishops she now finds herself alarmed at the unfettered democracy of the Congregationalists with whom she is supposed to be on the way to uniting. Other friendly Protestants who come to settle in Scotland frequently express their disappointment at the lack of a genuine lay participation within the Kirk. They experience it most clearly at Sunday services. At home they are used to a friendly, intimate and cheerful atmosphere where spontaneity of response is readily achieved. In Scotland they are unsettled by the awkward, styleless formalism of the occasion, the limp singing, the unwillingly grunted Lord's Prayer, the resentful postures of devotion, and the bold, expressionless staring towards the pulpit. It might be as well to explain what is happening here since it will spare the best-disposed of visitors some moments of consternation. The fact is that in Scotland public expression of the deepest religious feelings is suspect: spontaneity, especially joyful spontaneity, is a sure sign of insincerity. If, for instance, a minister should happen to overhear one of his congregation refer to his sermon afterwards in some such phrase as 'I've heard worse' he is entitled to feel that his time has not been wasted. Another example may help to underline the liturgical limitations of the Presbyterian service. An English summer visitor who happened to belong to one of the more ecstatic versions of the Faith found himself in a country kirk at morning service. He called attention to himself immediately by his hearty bonhomie and by the energetic way he took part in the singing. Later he began to punctuate the sombre-toned sermon with cries of 'Hallelujah! Praise the Lord!' At last, an aged worthy, unable to abide these intrusions any longer rose from his seat and addressed him in a cold, emphatic voice: 'We dinna praise the Lord here!'

It might be argued that Scotland's God is no longer a church-goer; or that if religion means that to which a man attaches total and unconditional significance, he never was. He is just old-fashioned Success, or Money, or more likely, Self. If he has to be a native he could be Golf, but undoubtedly, among the lower orders, he is Association Football. Visitors should know that Scotland is the only country in the world where the historic dispute of institutional religion is regularly re-enacted on the football field. Yet most Scots act as if their God were in the church and, however indifferent they have become, like him to be present at their marriages and christenings. Cynics and sceptics are uncommonly well-informed on ecclesiastical trivia. Many of them still feel guilty about buying newspapers on Sunday, or leaving their washing on the line, and regard bishops with much the same hostility as the most irrational of Presbyterians.

The Scottish religious tradition is subject today to the same unavoidably explosive pressures as every other deposit of belief. Much of what is definable within it is already dissolving and may not be reconstituted in a recognizable form. Meanwhile, until the dust settles, the Church of Scotland has already shown that it is prepared to respond instinctively. Visitors should be careful not to allow the flickering, and occasionally irritating, survivals of a Puritanism which the Scot has learnt to accommodate, to predetermine their view of the Scottish religious achievement. They should know, for example, that the Kirk has been in the forefront of experiments in industry and social service, that it is the first church to appoint a full-time technologist to its staff, and it has been consistently prepared to break with tradition in the sphere of sexual morality. These are not the signs of a church living off its past, but rather evidence of a determination to remain relevant to the interests of the nation.

Top: *Throwing the Hammer at the Royal Braemar Gathering.*
Bottom: *Snow scene at Glen More (Inverness), with the Cairngorms in the background. Scotland is becoming increasingly popular with skiers.*

The People at Sport

John Rafferty

A quick count reveals that there are Scottish champions at forty-four sports. The point is made to show that although in Scotland there is a persistent compulsion to play football and watch it and argue about it and make it a way of life there is a parallel and calmer-running sports stream which is often not noticed. The figure shows that there is a wide scope and growing enthusiasm for participation in the formal sports.

This healthy stream has developed along with the social changes that took young people out of the slums and their parents out of the bad times. Once the only sports equipment that young fellows in the towns could afford was a ball. A good one for playing with in the streets cost sixpence and a crowd of boys could usually raise sixpence but if money was short then a ball could be made from rags and string and there was a considerable knack in rolling and tying such a ball to make it spheroid and have it remain so.

In the twenties, in towns such as Glasgow, football was played interminably in the poorer streets and there were still enough green fields on the outskirts to provide ample pitches for those who had a real football. Ever increasing traffic cleared football from the streets and houses crushed into the green spaces, and now the game is played more formally. Despite difficulties and counter attractions, nearly all our young boys still play football as is shown by the records of the Scottish Football Association.

Urchins and crowds gathered around street corners used to seek their own opposition but now competitions are widely organized by the schools and the youth organizations and any boy who wants to play can soon find a place in a team.

There is however a difference in that urban youths now have a choice of sports. They are not hampered in that choice by a lack of equipment for there is public money available for it through the Department of Education and the Sports Council, and if a

Top: *Statue of Robert Burns by Greyfriars Church in Dumfries.*
Bottom: *Abbotsford (Roxburghshire), last home of Sir Walter Scott, is now lived in by his great-great-great granddaughter.*

school wants a boat at £350 and oars at £25 a pair then they can have them.

This alone would not have caused such a sudden and spectacular move towards the present diversity of participation. That was spurred by the Scottish Council for Physical Recreation, when they opened the Inverclyde National Recreation Centre at Largs. They started there a sports tasting scheme for town children.

Classes of school children from Glasgow and elsewhere in the Industrial Belt of Scotland were taken on residential courses to Inverclyde. Most had known no sport but football and some had never seen the sea. At Largs they were introduced to badminton and archery, to tennis and basketball. They climbed the hills and sailed on the Firth of Clyde and rode on the ponies.

With some astonishment they discovered that there were things to do with a ball other than kick it. They discovered new interests. Those with a D'Artagnan turn of mind liked fencing and were steered to a club and as class followed class more and more had their sporting horizon widened and the stimulus was given to participation and a blow struck at spectating.

There was an explosion in Glasgow in such an unlikely sport as rowing and the Clyde at Glasgow Green became an astonishing place for those who remembered the old narrow sports ways. The water was booked for every minute of a Saturday morning from nine o'clock by school crews and then the seniors took over.

The Scottish Council for Physical Recreation worked at encouraging the building of sports halls and so there was more badminton and basketball and the weight lifters and the wrestlers had facilities for practice, and the judo men multiplied.

Scotland employed a *Maitre d'Armes* and he brought fencing to the schools and to the universities. More indoor ice became available and with it more skaters and curlers and when championship swimming pools began to be opened throughout Scotland, swimming flourished.

There was one unfortunate side effect. Scotland has a population of only five millions and so few spread among so many sports gave so small a base to the pyramid of participants that there was very little chance of the peak being high enough to produce champions of British or world stature. Some are not interested in producing champions but champions are the inspiration for the young to take up a sport.

And so Scotland settled into an era of wide participation which was only exciting in that it was healthy. There were too many sports chasing too small a population for any to be of exceptional standard and it was all happening in the shadow of the monster football which was demanding attention and attracting the most athletic and aggressive participants.

With so many outlets available for healthy competition young people began to turn away from the more demanding amateur sports. Standards in athletics elsewhere soared above what could be achieved by normal training and living and some who had fancied running turned to sailing or ski-ing or golf where only reasonable fitness is necessary. Athletics became a minority sport, participation-wise.

It was unfortunate that the interest in running should have dwindled when it did. When athletics was healthy there was a recurring complaint that the standards would not improve spectacularly until proper tracks and training facilities were made available. Then when good tracks were built by the universities and the cities there were too few making use of them to push up the general standard enough to overtake the improvements elsewhere.

The sport had not been well administered. Attention was focused on rule books, stop watches and arena plans and not enough on people and a split was allowed to develop which sent a body of runners into professionalism and kept them out of championship competition.

The big professional foot race is the Powderhall Sprint which is staged as a New Year's Day festival in Edinburgh but the Games Meetings, as the professionals call them, involve so little prize money that enlightened negotiations would surely have brought the two sides together and produced a united athletics front to the good of all runners.

Boxing which like football was the traditional sport of the urban districts fell into decline when modern youth found more civilized ways of passing an evening. They still had the urge to be combative but found a way of satisfying the urge without taking a punch on the nose. Judo and karate gave them the chance to destroy an opponent but it was all done in mime and nobody got a sore face.

Boxing clubs used to be sweaty, dirty, tumbledown establishments and modern youth with its sophistication would not have tolerated them, but the judo and karate clubs are more to their liking. They are mostly pleasant well-appointed establishments to which a young man can bring his girl friend and leave her at the soft drinks bar until he has had a work-out and maybe a sauna bath.

Then he appears before her glowing from the conflict and the sauna and looking like James Bond and that in his view is not a bad state of affairs and certainly to be preferred to the old days when a young fellow came out of a boxing club with his face marked, his body aching and his lips cut or puffed. He was in no state to do himself justice with his girl.

This is a new sports stream, sweeping through Scotland, laughing as it goes but it is only a parallel stream to the flooding river that is football. That sombre flow more often bubbles with indignation and anger than with fun but it is as enduring as the Clyde itself and like it replenishes itself from the hills and valleys and the towns.

From the first moment a Scottish baby boy is set by doting parents on shaky bow legs he knows that his feet are for kicking. His first ball is no problem to him for kicking a ball comes as naturally as soiling nappies.

In the parks on a sunny day as young mothers gossip beside parked prams toddlers can be seen in an eager stumbling run, with elbows high, chasing and kicking a ball and at times tumbling grotesquely over it.

Before they have gone to infant school they have identified with the professional heroes and even in schools where rugby rather than football is the compulsory team game a round ball is kicked in the crowded playground.

Inevitably with football so firmly involving young minds there is an obsession with it in later years. It could never be said of football in Scotland that it is only a game.

Some may regret that football so fills the minds of the great mass of the population but there is a need in a human being to argue and to take sides, to have a cause. In some places this is served by religion or politics. In Scotland from the middle to the lower end of the social scale football serves the need. There are some to argue that it is as well it were so. They contend that had it not been so then in the bad times, in the 'hungry twenties', there could have been revolution.

Then there were strong feelings on 'Red Clydeside' about unemployment and social conditions and there were critical days with strikes and hunger marches but there was football to argue over and thus many minds were channelled towards less dangerous issues. Even poverty and unemployment were less obsessive than football.

The Scottish obsession with football goes back a long time. In the Year of Our Lord 1424 James I, King of Scotland, decreed: 'It is statut and the King forbiddes that na man play at the futball under payne of IVd. to be paid to the lord of the land as often as he is taynted'.

Every Scottish King of the fifteenth century passed such an act. They were alarmed that so many Scots preferred to kick a ball rather than practise archery. The Kings maybe had a flash of intuition that a war with bows and arrows would be less violent than a conflict with a ball.

In the middle of the next century the councils of the towns of Peebles and Perth were to show concern over the playing of football in the streets and with good cause. The game then was played with enthusiasm uninhibited by referees or rules and there was bruising and blood-letting and property was damaged as high spirits were fanned to rioting.

The fine by then had gone up to eight shillings which seems to show that inflation is not a modern phenomenon. The game was not organized on more civilized lines until three hundred years later.

Then on the night of July 9, 1867, 'a number of men met at No. 3 Eglinton Terrace, Glasgow, for the purpose of forming a football club'. The Queens Park Football Club was formed and for many years the history of football in Scotland was the history of that club.

Queens Park still exists as a senior club but as an anachronism in the modern commercial game. They elected to stay amateur and as professionalism spread their stature diminished but they have retained one reminder of their former greatness. They own Hampden Park in Glasgow, the biggest football stadium in Great Britain with a capacity of 150,000. It is the setting for all the Scottish show games, but it is an embarrassment to Queens Park for they cannot afford to maintain it adequately.

Queens Park played their first challenge game in 1868, against Thistle Football Club, and they still preserve the letter of acceptance from Thistle. This demonstrates the fluid state of the rules then.

The letter agreed to twenty players on each side then went on, 'We consider that two hours is long enough to play in weather such as at present. . . . We would also suggest that if no goals be got by either side within the first hour that goals be then exchanged, the ball of course to be kicked off from the centre of the field by the side who had the original kick so that both parties may have the same chance of wind and ground.'

There was a neat plea to conclude. 'Would you also be good enough to bring your own ball with you in case of any breakdown and thus prevent interruption.' They were just feeling their way in those days.

Football as it is now known in Scotland could be said to have started on June 2, 1869, when a Glasgow newspaper carried a report on Queens Park v. Hamilton Grammarians. It was the first newspaper report of a football match in Scotland and a forerunner to the struggle by newspapers to satisfy the need of the masses to read about the game.

In 1872 the followers of football in Scotland were given a cause when the first international against England was played. It is a peculiarity of the football supporter that not only must he have a team to cheer but he must also have one to hate.

In the international field England was the natural opponent to hate and since that first match was played in Hamilton Crescent, in Glasgow, Scottish supporters have worked hard against the English.

The first match was a calm, civilized affair. A mere 2,500 crowded round the ropes. They had bought their tickets at a shilling each from McMillar's hatters shop and Mr Keay's hosiery shop. They walked to the match or travelled by pony and trap.

There was a game at Kennington Oval but nobody travelled from Scotland and all the Scottish players were resident in England. It was reported: 'Scotland was severely crippled at the eleventh hour by the enforced absence of their best back W. H. Gladstone MP owing to the exigencies of his political duties.' It was not long until the priorities were set right and nothing was allowed to interfere with football.

Support for Scotland and consequent antagonism to England was hardened when Wembley Stadium was opened in 1924 and then was instituted a continuing biennial pilgrimage which has only altered in the mode of transport.

With all the discomfort, inconvenience and dedication of

pilgrims, 30,000 supporters travel every second year to see Scotland play at Wembley. Before the popularity of aeroplanes they mostly travelled 450 miles by special trains and immediately on returning started to save up for the next game two years hence.

They travelled by outdated uncomfortable stock well-laden with liquid sustenance for the long night. They would leave their bottle-littered compartments in the grey hours of Saturday morning, half-slept, unshaven, damp after washing in flooded toilets and trying to dry on paper towels.

They dressed quaintly in tartan and it is strange that for no other event would they have accepted such discomfort nor dressed as grotesquely except at Hallowe'en. The ritual of Wembley became firmly established but now the travelling is more sophisticated.

Now travel is not so hard as it was on the 10.30 out of Glasgow Central in 1949. Two men fell from that train and were killed. One man was found astride a buffer and another sitting on a running board. These were strange goings on.

There were recompenses in being in Wembley Stadium for Scotland sometimes won. There was the long-remembered year of 1928 when a little fancied Scotland team won by five goals to one and were immediately the Wembley Wizards. So 1928 took on the importance of 1314, the year of the Battle of Bannockburn. There had been other Scottish victories over the English in between but the big ones were all that mattered.

The mob in later years flocked south to lament over the Wembley Follies, the Wembley Strugglers, the Wembley Unfortunates. Luckily the practice of naming a team flamboyantly as in 1928 died out.

In the years between Wembleys, England meet Scotland at Hampden Park in a match for which the 134,000 tickets are allocated rather than sold. Men have been known to become directors of Scottish football clubs mainly to qualify for an allocation of international tickets.

In 1933 there were 134,700 spectators at Hampden for the England game. They paid £7,660. Now the attendance is restricted to around the same figure but the receipts approach £100,000.

In 1937, 150,000 tickets were sold and 149,407 spectators turned up. This was the biggest crowd ever at any football match in Great Britain and on that day was born the Hampden Roar, an awesome maintained crescendo of cheering which has been inadequately described as like the finish of the Derby or a six at Lords. Scotland teams afterwards asked for it and England dreaded it. This was stirring audience participation from a willing audience.

And in club football, too, the masses needed a team to identify with and another to hate. Their problem was easily resolved in those towns which had two clubs.

In Dundee the United supporters would not want to cross the street to watch Dundee, the other team. It is strange that in that town the grounds of the two senior clubs are in the same street. The supporters have no such common link.

In Edinburgh there is a long-standing rivalry between Hearts and Hibs. One Hearts supporter I knew was a bit more biased than need be. I have known him lament about the sun shining on a Saturday afternoon when Hibs were playing at home. He grudged them the good crowd that would come out in the sunshine.

That was partisanship gone berserk but there is no sweet reasonableness in the Scottish football supporter and nowhere is that more depressingly shown than in Glasgow.

The differences that split Celtic and Rangers supporters are the most explosive in sport because they are based on a pseudo allegiance to religion. Their rivalry is the most publicized in the world because of this and I have had the differences between the supporters explained to me by a Georgian in Tbilisi a thousand miles south of Moscow.

Much violence has been provoked over the years by the temper which religious differences among the untamed can arouse. Celtic and Rangers played traditionally on New Year's Day but in recent years the magistrates of Glasgow have changed the date to January 2, because they consider the drink situation less acute on that day.

The match between the clubs has been described as the greatest club game in the world but often it was no more than the most disgraceful. In recent years the Glasgow police have curbed the violence but the unpleasant chanting of religious slogans and the singing of party songs still persists. The origin of the differences has never been fully explained.

Celtic were instituted by Irish Catholic immigrants in 1888 for charitable purposes and although since then they have ceased to be sectarian and have a Protestant manager and many Protestant players they still are acclaimed as a Catholic Club.

216

From the start they were unpopular with many for at the end of the last century Irish Catholics were looked on by the general public much as Pakistani and West Indian immigrants are looked on today. They were ill-educated hewers of wood and drawers of water, who lived in conditions beneath the local standard. Into the bargain the Irish Catholics were considered cheap labour and a threat to the natives' jobs.

The Celtic Football Club in its infancy aroused the opposition that a Pakistani club would arouse now and if such a Pakistani club were later to play Scottish players it still would be considered Pakistani.

The Rangers Football Club was instituted by Scots and originally had no sectarian interests and the opposition of their supporters to Celtic was no more than the general opposition to an Irish Catholic institution at the time.

The best evidence is that a change took place during the First World War when a Belfast shipyard opened a branch in Glasgow and sent workers from that sectarian ridden city to staff it. They immediately attached themselves to Rangers and brought Orangeism to their support.

Rangers have since claimed that they have always been a Protestant club but this is not so. Catholics did play for them and there is irrefutable evidence that the Rangers' manager in the late twenties was prepared to sign a Catholic player but was dissuaded from doing so by the other players who wanted to have everybody in the club of the same religion.

The strife has been good for business and Celtic and Rangers have become the monsters of Scottish football growing ever fatter as the others struggle through lean times. In a season each plays to well over a million spectators. No other club plays to 300,000.

The development of the internal combustion engine added to the popularity of Celtic and Rangers and allowed supporters from the outlying districts to travel to see them. There is a terrible compulsion among Scottish football supporters to be identified with success.

In the twenties most little townships in Central Scotland had their own football club. Towns like Armadale, Bathgate and Bo'ness could maintain a senior team because the workers were trapped on a Saturday and had little to do except support the local team.

217

By the time they had arrived home from work on Saturday at lunch time and eaten and changed, it was time for the football match. Later when the five-day week made Saturday a free day and motor cars made travel easy they could travel to Glasgow to Celtic and Rangers comfortably. The little clubs were neglected and closed and the bigger ones saw their gates diminish perilously.

Now on a Saturday buses laden with Celtic and Rangers supporters leave towns like Kilmarnock and Motherwell where the local clubs struggle to survive. They pass the grounds of their local clubs which expect and need their allegiance and, adorned with the green of Celtic and the blue of Rangers, make for Glasgow. They wear their club colours interminably and one frustrated manager of a small club said memorably, 'You can tell Celtic and Rangers supporters easily. They are the only people who wear scarves in the summer time'.

Much of football in Scotland is about supporting and there is a danger of the game becoming a talking point rather than a sport. European competitions have brought a new dimension to supporting as the clubs have moved into Europe.

Many thousands have bundled into Europe's football centres to support Celtic and Rangers. Celtic had 15,000 followers swarming rapturously in Lisbon and 20,000 suffering misery in Milan. Some have hitch-hiked across Europe, others gone on credit and many have looked as if they could put the money to better use.

The unemployed somehow have travelled and the startled citizens of European cities have seen them arrive in trousers and shirt and maybe a jersey as if they were going to crush on to the terracings at Celtic Park or Ibrox. Those strange-talking foreigners have perplexed them by not accepting good Scottish money. Old habits die slowly in the transition from bus to plane and they still put the hat round for the driver.

One at least came back in a supporters' plane in which they were all pals together in drink, then, when he landed in Glasgow the cold air hit him and he lamented, 'What am I doing here? I went by car'. His car was a long time in Lisbon.

Even Celtic and Rangers supporters have been brought together temporarily on these trips. One Rangers supporter travelled to Portugal with three friends who were Celtic supporters. They went to a club for dinner and on the way met two Scottish priests and invited them to join in.

218

During the floor show the Rangers supporter, relaxed by the wine, sent a note to a dancer inviting her to join them for a drink. His Celtic pals with righteousness inspired by the presence of the clergy, even if they were in plain clothes, remonstrated, 'You're out of order. You've a wife at home'.

He answered steadily, 'I've a wife at home and she's a good Orange woman from Belfast. If I had a drink with that girl and took her to a brothel and my wife found out she would be very angry but she'd forgive me. But if she found out I was having dinner with two priests she'd cut my throat!'

Before there can be spectators, however, there have to be players and Scotland is rich in them. English managers habitually raid the Scottish cradle and Bill Shankly, the Liverpool manager, has explained why: 'You're liable to find an internationalist on any street corner.' The leading teams in England are well bolstered with Scottish players who are noted for their flair for the game and for their courage and aggressiveness.

These players are either taken as schoolboy apprentices to England or go for heavy transfer fees. The Scottish football economy depends on these fees and only Celtic and Rangers can survive comfortably without selling players.

The reason for this is that Scotland is short of another five million inhabitants. The present five million cannot support Scottish football on a big enough scale to satisfy the Scottish ego over the game. It is impossible to convince the Scottish football enthusiast that the game in his country is not as big and as good as in other countries with multi-million populations.

In Glasgow there are three grounds, Hampden Park, Ibrox Stadium and Celtic Park, each capable of holding 100,000 spectators and that a city of a million inhabitants should be so endowed with spectating space is indicative of the exaggerated accent on the game. Firhill Park and Shawfield are also senior grounds.

National pride has often been dented, especially in the World Cup, but the Scot is brilliant in manufacturing excuses and is sustained by the many great individuals produced in the country and recently by the success of Celtic in the European Cup. Scotland's frustration is that in football she is too big to be wee and too wee to be big.

And so in recent seasons Scottish clubs have been taking from half a million to three-quarters of a million pounds out of England in transfer fees. Scottish clubs have thus been strengthened financially but weakened on the playing side.

Celtic and Rangers have remained strong and so on them the main following has centralized and they approach the point at which they would be impregnable. Had it not been for the broadening of interest into Europe, Scottish football ere now would have developed a fatal monotony.

But football in Scotland is not all big crowds and spectacular professionalism. At the fun level of the game there is wide participation. There are few schools without their football teams. Youth clubs and church organizations have their leagues and if there is a clear stretch of ground around 100 yards long then football will be played on it.

This is recreative football, the big face of football too often not noticed because the big nose of professionalism catches the attention. To this branch will drift most of the toddlers who stumble over a ball in the parks while their mothers watch and their fathers hope.

Those who fear that football in Scotland could deteriorate outside Celtic and Rangers until it is no more than a talking point have the example of professional boxing before them.

Going into the sixties there were around 200 professional boxers registered with the Scottish Area Council of the British Boxing Board of Control. Going into the seventies there were no more than thirty and half of these were inactive. They maintained a licence out of innocent conceit.

It may seem strange that young men ever did want to take a punch on the nose but pre-war there were enough of them to man a professional boxing show every night of the week and three on a Saturday. In these days the tales of hungry fighters were born. At least then young men were taught to trim their aggressiveness to the rules of the British Boxing Board of Control.

There was the stimulant of the great champions, coming out of the slums and becoming famous and apparently rich. The more tragic and sordid aspects of boxing were overlooked. Elky Clarke came out of a Glasgow tenement to reach world stature, then lost an eye. Johnny Hill soared to the top and died of pneumonia caught in training. Benny Lynch was the gallant and dashing champion of the world then died prematurely, a drunkard and a pauper. Jackie Paterson earned a fortune but died, broke, in a drunken brawl.

There were plenty of more pleasant stories to fan ambition in young fighting breasts and boxing was one of the few chances for quick riches for the slum kid. But now in Scotland professional boxing is no more. The young now have other less strenuous occupations to amuse them.

Amateur boxing persists in a diminishing degree and is sustained by television fees. Boxing makes exciting viewing and stimulating argument and if only the participation were so pleasant then it would flourish.

Amateur boxing was set on respectable lines in the twenties when Sir Iain Colquhoun, the Laird of Luss, was a participant and the Marquess of Clydesdale, later the Duke of Hamilton, won a Scottish amateur championship. But now amateur boxing shows the same symptoms that killed the professional game. There are too few participants.

It has regular stimulation from the Olympic Games and the Commonwealth Games but quickly sags when only club tournaments offer boxing practice and even the Scottish Championships raise little interest. Television has kept amateur boxing a long time a-dying.

A visitor to Scotland must notice the betting shops. They are in the towns and the villages and some are decrepit and dingy but others are marble-fronted and comfortable. All denote an obsession with horse racing second only to that with football and the variety marks the breadth of society who bet. Many who bet have never seen a horse race although to hear them talking about trainers and their methods and jockeys and their strengths and weaknesses one would think most of the population had been brought up in a racing stable. The huge coverage of horse-racing in newspapers has educated the punters.

There are five racecourses in Scotland at Ayr, Hamilton, Edinburgh and Lanark and National Hunt Courses at Perth and Kelso. The course at Ayr is a particularly fine one, ranking in Great Britain in the grade just below Ascot and Goodwood.

There is no record of when racing first started at Ayr but there is a report of a race there in 1576 and this was noted not because it was the first but because of a quarrel over the starting of the horses. One John Kennedy was shot through the leg and James Crawford was shot in the thigh so that he was lame all his days.

There was a two-day meeting at Ayr in 1771 and in 1804 the Gold Cup was first run for, and since then has been the prize for the principal race at the Western September Meeting, the high-light of the Scottish racing season. The September meeting is one of the best in Britain.

The present course was opened in 1907 on 150 acres of good sandy soil close to 'Ye Banks and Braes O' Bonnie Doon' immortalized by Robert Burns. The surroundings make a fine pastoral picture but to the racegoer a more beautiful prospect is the horse he has backed two lengths in front in the final furlong and going away.

Modernization is making the Scottish courses increasingly comfortable but the Perth meeting on very old turf in the Palace of Scone, and Kelso in the Borders retain a pleasant 'country' atmosphere.

There are many Scottish racing stables turning out horses to supply these meetings and to raid the meetings in the North of England. The most northerly training stable in Great Britain is that of John Sorrie in Inverurie.

John Sorrie, who raises turkeys as well as horses, used to laugh about his horses behaving like country cousins when he took them among the sophisticated thoroughbreds of the south.

He once sent a two-year-old filly, Firegirl, to Ayr. Because of frost he had not been able to train her over more than three furlongs. Going to the start a jockey shouted to Joe Sime who rode her, 'I don't think that one has seen a course before'. Sime called back, 'I don't think she has seen people'. The shaggy Firegirl won to the astonishment of one and all.

Mainly, however, horse racing is about betting which fits in with the natural characteristic of tilting at the big fellow. The punter sees nothing incongruous in eternally challenging the book-makers who live off him or in backing his second-hand knowledge against that of the professionals. At least if the punter is at the racecourse he has the recompense of pleasant surroundings and an exciting, colourful spectacle and although John Sorrie may joke about his horses there is in Scotland much sophisticated racing scrupulously administered.

Soon in Scotland there must be an increasing interest in swimming. In the past there have been sporadic bursts of greatness but these were the result of inspired coaching by dedicated bath masters.

Motherwell had David Crabb who produced great international swimmers in the Wardrop twins, and Nancy Riach and Cathie

Gibson. Andy Robb, at Aberdeen, produced Ian Black; and David McGregor, at Falkirk, his son Bobby. There were others from Dunfermline and Kilmarnock but now there is a new interest.

Swimming pools of international standard have been built with the Commonwealth Games Pool in Edinburgh of Olympic standard and these magnificent facilities, now fully used, must inevitably produce their quota of competitive swimmers.

The provision of new facilities for participation in so many sports keeps chipping away at the obsession for football and for spectating and soon there is to be another diversion in the provision of a National Park in Central Scotland to offer opportunity for healthy recreation in the age of increasing leisure time.

Strathclyde Park is being developed in 1,750 acres of the Clyde Valley near Hamilton and Motherwell. It will have a loch 1½ miles long suitable for a 2,000 metres Olympic standard rowing course. There will be athletics grounds and ski-ing on land and water and a diversity of sporting opportunities.

Four-fifths of the population of Scotland live within 50 miles of this valley park and inevitably many will be drawn to it, and the depth and breadth of sporting participation will increase further.

But alongside the Strathclyde Park flows inexorably the River Clyde and as it replenishes itself and ignores the more sedate waters of the park it symbolizes the strong persistent flow of football which will carry on despite distractions of sporting intellectualism. Football is basic in Scotland.

The Land of Adventure

James S. Adam

'There are far more scientific ways of travelling than that.'

The speaker was an engineer on one of MacBrayne's ships. The time was October 1935. We were in Tarbert, Harris, and I had brought my canoe aboard to go back to Glasgow. There it lay on the deck, 14 feet of canvas and wood, a beautiful little craft whose lines were a delight, but not to this sea-going engineer. I forbore to make the comments about the other ways of travelling the Hebrides that sprang to mind and, beyond saying that it was a good craft in a sea, I let his comment drop. Indeed, the canoe, a kayak made by John Marshall of North Queensferry, had served me well.

In it I had completed the second bit of the sea canoeing that Alastair Dunnett and I set out to do in 1934 when we travelled from the Clyde to Skye, a journey which Alastair Dunnett subsequently recounted with verve and style in *Quest by Canoe*. This time I had started off from Kyle of Lochalsh up the coast of Skye, over the Minch to Scalpay, Harris, up Loch Seaforth, down Loch Erisort and up to Stornoway. It was the first solo canoe crossing of the Minch.

Some of the weather was good but for the most part it was tough battling in rough conditions. Three stretches in particular tested both my kayak and me; I was setting out from Portree for Staffin when one of the teachers from the Portree High School whispered in my ear: 'There's a wind outside. It's the general opinion you'll never see Staffin tonight.' The context was more than a little sinister for there was nothing soft about the Portree schoolmasters, or the Portree boys. One of the teachers, indeed, was going around with a broken collar bone, his arm in a sling. He had, he explained, been playing shinty with the boys. When I got out of Portree bay and turned north, I knew what the valediction meant. There was more than a wind. It was a northerly gale, right into my teeth, and on an exposed coast with no shelter for eighteen long miles. The gale and the short steep sea stopped all forward motion between strokes and for eight fierce and wearing hours the kayak had to be lifted into motion again with each stroke of the paddle. If that remark had not been made to me in Portree, I might have turned back but I was too young then to admit public defeat and I finally made it to Staffin as dusk was falling; at the head of Loch Seaforth in the narrows where the tide drove through a wicked rocky channel one of the heaviest rainstorms I have ever experienced blotted out the landmarks, the pattern of the tidal flow, and the sea itself. Such was the force of the rain stotting off the loch, that I went through the narrows engulfed in sea and rain water; the third testing stretch was just a day or two before I boarded MacBrayne's ship. I came down Loch Seaforth to the narrows of Scalpay to as wild a stretch of sea as I have seen. Caolas Scalpay was white from shore to shore, a turbulent malevolent maelstrom whipped into a fury by contending winds and tides. It was a bonnie sight to be viewed from the shore. In the middle of it and from the tiny cockpit of a canoe it looked somewhat less than bonnie and, although I was then at my fittest and most expert, I was not at all sure that I was going to make the passage to Scalpay.

The next day on the island an old man said to me, 'I was watching you yesterday in Caolas Scalpay. You know, not one of the men of Scalpay would have taken a boat out in that sea.'

It was on the day after the old man's comment that the MacBrayne engineer read me his lecture on scientific travelling.

Not every disparaging comment meant what was said. The year before, we had people on the coast saying to us, 'Ye should be put in jail for going to sea in boats like that', and, 'You're hardy, boys'. Both comments were acknowledgments to us that we had succeeded in part in what we had set out to do – to demonstrate as dramatically as was in our power that adventure was there for the taking.

Away back in the depression years of the twenties and thirties when Alastair Dunnett and I were working with young boys in Glasgow, many of them underprivileged, we set out to introduce them to the adventure that their own country offered. It was a brave concept, gallant indeed, for few of the boys in one group had fathers in jobs. Life in the depressed city seemed to hold only the promise of a bleak grey future and a deprived and hungry present. Yet the progression from weekends at the Glasgow

225

Scouts camp site at Auchengillan was natural and smooth. That incomparable camping ground looking out to Loch Lomond, the Argyll hills, Menteith and the Trossachs provided the stimulus. The prospect of pioneering into the Highlands stirred most of those boys and to their instinctive response to the physical challenge, we tried to add an awareness that, concurrently with their awakening to the adventure of living in their own lovely land, there were also the more exciting challenges to be explored in the mind. As they began to enjoy the freedom and the healthy life that the depression denied to many, we talked about the future and what had to be done to use our country's assets to make a fuller life for those who would follow.

Not for us the empty vociferous protests. Then as now, we left that to others. We were too busy making our direct contributions to social service, together with like-minded contemporaries, helping to give some boys a zest for living. I doubt if any of these boys thought of himself as underprivileged. They were a cheery and lively lot who took to the country and to the hills and gradually came to realize just how wonderful their heritage could be. With the realization came the dreams, and the visions, and the passionate questions; questions that ranged over the great problems of the why and how of democracy, economic policies, industrial requirements, and the vital need for a parliament in Edinburgh to bring an urgency to the tasks we saw so clearly. But let me confine myself to one aspect of the aspirations and questioning.

Why, we asked, looking around our empty glens and bare bens, why are they not put to better use for forestry, for food, for sport? There was no need, we said, for anyone to seek adventure half a world away. It was here in plenty, right at our back door. In any case, we argued, people of our race and clan had made a fair contribution to pioneering and building other countries. Now it was time to examine what had been neglected at home in the bygoing and to set the balance right. That, we decided away back in the early thirties, would be the Great Adventure and the most satisfactory of all – if only it could be made possible.

Well, it was made possible and many of these dreams have been brought to realization by devoted men and women who have followed the gleam. In outdoor sporting activities, it is the Land of Adventure indeed.

There has been a post-war explosion in mountaineering. Not

so very long ago mountaineering was regarded as a sport for the affluent. That has long since changed and there are now all kinds of people climbing, standards are rising steadily and hitherto 'unclimbable' faces today tend to be regarded as easy.

One of the newer clubs was the Creag Dhu. They were from Glasgow and they were tough and lively, sometimes on the rough side too, be it said. In Fort William for a weekend, I tracked the sound of singing in a pub. The songs were Gaelic and the accent was Glasgow but there in the Highlands where the native tongue is dying, the disinherited from the city had returned to reclaim their heritage of freedom in the hills and were asserting also their claim to a language. They did not have the blas but, by God, they had the enthusiasm that too many of today's Highlanders have forgotten.

I spoke to one of the singers and asked him if he was in the Creag Dhu. He seemed surprised that his accent had given him away, but he seized the opportunity to give me a gleeful appraisal of a grievance.

'I used to be, Mac', he said, 'but no' now. They're too soft. They threw me oot. They widnae let me take ma rifle on the bus. So I'm in the New Creag Dhu now.'

The non sequiturs took a moment or two to clarify but eventually we both agreed that there was no point in remaining in a mountaineering club whose members had Lowland scruples about poaching. After all, we agreed, there is no Gaelic word for poaching. Then he returned cheerfully to his singing.

These young men and others like them have put a stamp on the hills, sometimes recklessly, but they have played their part in pushing back the frontiers of experience and skill. In the bygoing, they have found their country and themselves.

Sailing or yachting was never only a rich man's hobby here. It couldn't be with our western and northern seaboards so profusely indented with sea lochs and hedged by the Northern and Western Isles. Sailing around these coasts and from these islands was more than a sport or a hobby. It was an art and on it depended the survival of whole communities. Measured against that background, individual life was expendable. As the Hanseatic motto has it, 'To navigate is necessary, to live is not'. But with the hardihood there was always the trim craft to be matched against another and a skilly crew to challenge.

There were plenty of races and much fine sailing for those who lived by and on the sea, who had the boats and who relaxed boisterously to forget the grimmer tensions.

By the way, watch your step if you should find yourself in a small harbour where they are in the throes of the local regatta. I have been involved in rowing races and swimming races more or less immediately after arriving. It is no joke to find yourself as I did taking part in a rowing race in Tobermory Regatta in Calum Macdonald's boat. Calum was a hefty farmer and a man who used his boat summer and winter. No matter how hard I pulled, when he put his weight behind his oar, our boat tended to birl like a peerie, or, if you prefer it in English, to spin like a top.

Then nothing would satisfy the Macdonalds but that I would uphold the honour of Calve by entering for the swimming. In due course, I was lined up with half a dozen others on the deck of a trawler out in the bay. The race was to be to the 'coal hulk' and back. I looked around me and decided that two lithe young twins had the look of good crawl swimmers. I looked again and decided that, since everyone else was intending to jump from the deck, I would do a racing dive and that come hell or high water, or the crawl-stroke twins, I would get to the hulk first. I did. But I have ever since wished that I could have seen that racing dive. It seemed to be from an awful height. I didn't win. I came in second and I don't mind admitting now that I infringed my amateur status by accepting 17/6d.

What we have seen in the past twenty years or so has been an explosion in leisure sailing to match the explosion in climbing. A whole generation has been exposed. A large number of people of all ages have been introduced to sailing. They have been taught the crafts and the lore at sailing schools. They have graduated to the larger yachts, some of which are also used for training holidays. They now have a wide range of choice for charter and, of course, the boat trailer has put weekend sailing within the reach of increasing numbers of enthusiasts.

I think it fair to include canoeing along with climbing and sailing as a traditional outdoor sport. After all, the current popularity can be traced to John 'Rob Roy' MacGregor who had canoes built for him in timber and modelled on the Eskimo kayak. His canoes or kayaks had good lines but they were heavy and cumbersome to transport. Nevertheless let no one denigrate these canoes or the young men who used them in the late nineteenth century. They made some wild sea journeys in them around the

West Coast and crossed the Minch in them. They pioneered a new sport, a new craft, and a new kind of adventure for which there was quite a vogue. Robert Louis Stevenson found himself caught up in it and wrote about it in his *Inland Voyage*; 'Rob Roy' Mac-Gregor wrote several books about it and his nickname of Rob Roy was used to describe the style and design of these modern kayaks. The interest in canoeing languished until the 1920s when German manufacturers produced a folding kayak of jointed rods, laminated frames, and a rubberized envelope. They called it a faltboot and Young Germany took to the rivers in it and the interest in the kayak revived throughout Europe. At home, the prospect of trundling down rivers seemed a little on the dull side and the kayak was used for some exciting sea journeys along the coast and out to the Hebrides. That was in the thirties but as with climbing, the pre-war pioneering efforts have been rapidly overtaken and today, journeys through tricky and turbulent passages are now taken as a matter of course.

Since then, too, there has been a remarkable return to the rivers for 'white-water' canoeing. The standards of today's slalom canoeists are almost incredibly high. They take their fibre glass canoes into what look like impassable cataracts, not only to navigate through gates but to come back up against the mass of the foaming river from time to time. To see the eskimo roll being carried out by a competitor who has couped in a cataract is to begin to believe in the impossible. These slalom competitions are held regularly and one of the courses is on the River Tay at Grandtully. There is another splendid course on the Welsh Dee at Llangollen where the British champions of the Chester Canoe Club practise.

Slaloms are a spectacle that ought to be included in everyone's diary. Depending on the time of the year, there can be more than physical hardihood involved. I remember standing on the bridge at Grandtully early in the year watching the slalom. Three local men crossing the bridge stopped to see. They looked at the grey swollen spate underneath and one of them said thoughtfully, 'Aye, there's a gey lot o' snaw bree there.'

It is perhaps in the newer fields post-war that there was the most spectacular development.

Pony-trekking is now a common activity in many places but it had its beginning at Newtonmore with the late Ewen Ormiston who started it all off in 1952. Even the word was coined to name the

229

new idea. Ewen had some fine Highland ponies eating their heads off and no way of getting a return out of them. In discussions with Jock Kerr Hunter the idea of formalizing pony hire into a holiday adventure context was born.

'We must give it a name,' said Ewen.

'Call it pony-trekking,' replied Jock and a new sport with a new name came into being – and as an important by-product, there was a new use and life for the garron, as we call our hill pony.

Pony-trekking in the Highlands tends to be a more rugged experience than jogging along a bridle path. For one thing there are few such paths in the Highlands and the pony-trekker on a Highland jaunt has to be prepared to go where his garron will go, and that is just about anywhere on any hill.

The advent of winter gives rise to mixed feelings according to one's point of view. Snow can be a curse or a blessing. Bud Neill, one of our more fey cartoonists, hailed winter in a zany verse of which I am inordinately fond:

> Winter's came,
> The snow has fell.
> Wee Josie's nose is froze as well.
> Wee Josie's frozis nose is skinted.
> Winter's diabolic.
> Intit!

That verse first appeared in the *Glasgow Evening Times* and I am not alone in my addiction to its joyously nonsensical fracturing of language. Alongside the irresistible onward march of its twisted cadences, 'Summer is Icumen in. Then loudly sing cucu' can only be described as alone and palely loitering. I like Bud Neill's verse because it affirms that winter is important to us.

The great romantic development in recent years has been in the field of winter ski-ing. On Glencoe and in Glenshee there are independent and excellent facilities. Before long the Ben Wyvis snow will also be exploited. The spectacular growth has been in the Spey Valley where the corries of Cairngorm are threaded by a steadily increasing number of ski lifts and ski tows.

In the early days – and that was only a matter of a dozen years or more ago – Jock Kerr Hunter worked hard at getting a Committee to represent the hoteliers of the area, the landowners, skiers and publicists. Today, the Cairngorm Winter Sports Board has an expanding commerical asset and a full and understanding support from the Highlands and Islands Development Board. There are many encouraging by-products. A short summer tourist season has now been extended to cover at least ten months of the year. New hotels have been built in the Spey Valley. New houses have been needed and new schools. In this area, at least, a population drift to the towns has been reversed. Townies have headed for the hills, found a congenial livelihood, and have settled in that lovely healthy part of the Highlands.

The most exciting and rewarding by-product of all is that the new generation have already demonstrated international ski-ing capability. They have grown up with snow and winter sports as a major interest in their formative years and the first crop have tested their new native skills against Continental youth who have long traditions and generations of ski-ing behind them. Once again the provision of the basic facilities, opportunities and training has shown that the latent talent is there.

When David Murray founded his motor racing stable, Ecurie Ecosse, and provided the outlets for the young racing motorist, he opened the door to a new expression of national aptitude. We have had a glittering international representation in recent world events from Ron Flockhart and Ninian Sanderson to the late Jim Clark and Jackie Stewart. A significant boost to motor racing was the setting up of the Ecurie Ecosse Association in 1957 through which, since then, some six thousand people have subscribed funds annually to help finance this costly sport. It is interesting that the pattern of the Ecurie Ecosse Association is being discussed as a possible way of finding the money to assist the young skiers of the Spey Valley and elsewhere to go to the Continental snow slopes for further training and experience. When that is achieved there is the confidence that in this field also a natural talent for physical co-ordination will once again be demonstrated on a world stage.

Before 1939 when work or holidays took me north into the Highlands in the winter months I used to feel that everything changed colour and dimension at the Pass of Leny. To walk the length of Loch Lubnaig on a frost-bound road on a day of crisp clear sunshine with snow on the tops, the lower slopes in their autumnal browns, reds and purples and with the loch a silent mirror, was to be back in the days when the world was a quiet place.

There was little traffic on these roads in the pre-war winters and the lonely walker could enjoy that road up past Balquhidder and on to Loch Earn. It was a road of tranquillity with beauty in the far view and in the near.

When I arrived at Lochearnhead Hotel in those days, it was a typical comfortable small well-run Highland hotel. Today it is different. The roads are busy and Lochearnhead's Highland hotel does the equivalent of a town trade. Ewen Cameron, the hotel's Highland Games athlete proprietor, has developed a popular water ski-ing activity at Lochearnhead and the area throbs with youthful vigour, and not only the young. Loch Earn at that point is in a sheltered scenic setting and it is a convenient distance from Glasgow and Edinburgh for a short run into the Highlands by car, a view of the lively activity on the loch, and a meal in the hotel. At the east end of the loch under the colourful bulk of Ben Vorlich there is sailing and yachting for those who prefer to be a little less close to the water.

Of all our outdoor sports, none is more widely enjoyed or on a more classless democratic basis than golf, the game we developed and exported to every corner of the world. The name of St Andrews may to some convey an appreciation of an early devotion to the brother of Peter and the second disciple to be called to fish for men; our link with Andrew is one that we share with Russia and with Greece, an association which may itself prove a rewarding subject for speculation. To others, St Andrews may recall a delightful little town by the grey North Sea and site of our first university founded in 1411. Or again, St Andrews may recall turbulent passionate periods in our story when men held views so strongly that they did not shirk the awful climax of the stake and the flame. All of these are thoughts that the name of St Andrews may conjure but I am certain that to most people their first thought will be of golf and the Royal and Ancient Club building presiding over the historic courses.

Despite its venerable and awe-inspiring authority, in St Andrews golf is cheap and accessible. Indeed, throughout the country, golf courses proliferate to the happy convenience of citizen and visitor alike.

Nowadays, there is a convention that golfers are not properly equipped unless they are humping great bags stuffed with a vast assortment of expensive clubs. But, there are still boys and girls who start on their nearby links with two or maybe three old clubs and who learn early and naturally a co-ordination of hand and eye, who develop a natural and instinctive sense of timing and rhythm by just 'skelping the gutty'.

The *Glasgow Daily Record* has an office golf competition for a trophy named after a popular colleague who was one such natural golfer. Tommie Crawford's advice was often sought by aspiring golfers on the staff. It was always freely given and it never varied. His secret was not one he wanted to hide. 'It's simple,' he would say. 'Just stand up and hit the ba'.'

In *The Scotsman* head office in Edinburgh they take a character-istically wider view of how they should mark the origin of this world-wide game. Their trophy, the Frank Moran Trophy, is named for their golf correspondent, happily still with us at eighty-seven years of age, who for fifty years delighted *The Scotsman* readers with his percipient and sprightly golf reports and is still writing a fortnightly article. The trophy designed and made for *The Scotsman* by Hamilton & Inches of Edinburgh is awarded annually to the Scot, wherever he may be, who has done most for golf.

My own recollections of my childhood are of holidays spent in Carnoustie and Monifieth. I had cousins in Monifieth and as the links were almost next door they grew up on them and with worn-out old clubs in their hands. I remember one of my cousins telling me, still with the light of battle in her eye, that she had been on the links the day before and had had an encounter with two men players. They were in front of her and were dawdling so she gave them the customary courteous golfers' hint. She teed her ball and shouted 'Fore!'

'They looked round,' she said, 'and when they saw it was only a lassie, they ignored me. They thocht I couldna drive the distance.'

Only a lassie! But she had been golfing since she could toddle and she had Buchan as well as Angus blood in her veins, and red hair forby. So she belted a screamer at them, saw them duck and heard them swear.

As I say, it was the day after when she was telling me and it was a year or two back but I can still see and hear her, a young golfing suffragette.

'I gied them a richt guid fleg. They'll no' dae that again the next time a lassie's ahent them on the links.'

The moral of this anecdote is to warn you that when you are enjoying the exhilaration and freedom of our inexpensive courses

233

and you see a youngster behind you, don't underestimate him or her. Or if you do, get ready to duck. You could be in for a richt guid fleg.

During the summer in all the best places and in some un-expected byways, a kind of madness is likely to break out, a frenzy that finds an outlet in hurling large objects around the landscape. Highland Games is the name by which the symptom is known. It is not possible for a visitor to be left unaware of the imminence of any Highland Games. There is too much of a stir. Bunting sprouts on the roads and buildings. Pipers can be heard practising. Stalwart young men in farm fields and on convenient hillsides are throwing stones around and are staggering about with tree trunks trying to throw them end over end. Even the practice itself is a stark demonstration of young manhood flexing its muscles. The Games themselves, however, are a glorious pageantry of movement and music, tartan and toughness, a satisfying spectacle seen at its best in a Highland setting of green sward amid the pine-clad hills.

For the tourist, undoubtedly the most rewarding of these Highland Games spectaculars are the Aboyne Games and the Braemar Games both in incomparable Royal Deeside and both claiming Balmoral Castle and the Royal Family as neighbours.

It was at the Aboyne Games that the organizers took a stand against the practice of young girl dancers competing in male kilt outfits. The organizers decreed that girl dancers at Aboyne would be allowed to compete only if dressed in skirt and blouse and that there would be no further masquerade in the kilt. The fury that erupted in the central industrial belt was spectacular. The mothers who toured their small daughters round the games to compete for the not inconsiderable cash prizes were a fearsome prospect in their mass anger. They had invested sizeable sums in their daughters' Prince Charlie jackets, jabots and kilts. Indeed, one slander went that with the original purchase of the original pristine jacket went a purchase of the dozen or so medals sewn on the jacket for the wee lassie's first appearance. Slander it may have been although few dancers, however inexperienced, could ever be seen without medals. It was my old colleague, the late Harold Stewart, who wrote the definitive joke in the *Daily Record*:

> I think that the saddest of songs
> is the one that to Gaeldom belongs.

It tells how a dancer,
a bonny wee prancer
was battered to death by her gongs.

At one time, when the *Aberdeen Press & Journal* sent a reporter and photographer to the Aboyne Games, a luncheon basket with chicken and a bottle of wine was ordered for them from the Atheneum in Aberdeen. That was in the 'bad old days' and that custom has fallen into desuetude but I keep hoping that some day we will be able to defeat today's miserable egalitarianism and that the *Press & Journal* may once again feel free to revert to the pernicious practice of paternalism with its concomitants of chicken and good red wine.

May I here enter a careful caveat for the unwary. Not all Highland Games are for experts and professionals. (Incidentally, don't let anyone confuse with talk of Yorkshiremen competing at Highland Games and winning. One Yorkshireman may and good luck to him. Yorkshire should belong to us anyway.) Until quite recently, the tallest recruits into the British Army regiments came from the Highlands. Whether that reflects the influence of the Highland Games or whether the Highland Games are a reflex from the national physique is a moot point. But there are a lot of Highland Games held all over the country in wee places as well as the big centres. The competitors are local people and here is the warning. When the frenzy of preparation is in full swing, watch out. You may well find yourself more actively involved than you are prepared for. I know. I have had the experience.

There was one young Hebridean farmer I used to visit. He lived on a small island. When the Games were due I had a full exposure to his practice. I had hardly come down the steamer's gangway and had scarcely had time to savour the keen delight of rowing over to the little island he farmed before I was at the back of the house. There he had a six-foot bar and a 56lb weight. My poor puny town wrists were sorely tested with snatch throws before I even got a drink. On another occasion it was the caber he was at. He had a tree out of the wood and there I was with the city dust still on my shoes staggering around his fields trying to toss his muckle tree.

Caber (pronounced cabber, not cayber) means a branch from a tree. In practice, it is a tree. There is no standard of weight or size. A tree trunk is trimmed and the heavy men have a go. If it is too

235

big and bulky for all of them, a piece is sawn off and so on until one of them succeeds in throwing it end over end. The whole affair is a splendid example of sporting empiricism at its striving best.

Angling is usually synonymous with salmon fishing and high cost but this need not be so. There is good salmon and trout fishing to be had from many a small Highland hotel and at a modest cost. The Scottish Tourist Board can give you helpful advice here.

There has, however, been a remarkable and fast development in sea angling. A few years ago the energetic Jock Kerr Hunter organized the setting up of a committee to investigate the potential of sea angling. Here again there has been an explosive development and each year sees a new listing and chartering of the areas round the coasts where exciting sea angling can be enjoyed. The late Laurie Robinson, a retired schoolmaster from Whitley Bay, was organizer for ten years and, as a consequence, there are hundreds of Geordies and their families who now know the delights of fishing off Lamlash on the Island of Arran, the thrills of luring skate at Ullapool and the zest of trying for big ones of almost any kind off the Orkneys or Shetland.

The other kind of big game hunting, for the red deer, is a carefully guarded activity, and with good reason. We live in a small country, albeit picturesque, and anyone who is setting out to stalk the red deer stag with a rifle must be a good shot for preference, but, whether or not, he must put himself unreservedly in the charge and under the orders of the stalker or gillie. This is an expensive sport and is not for the man with a short pocket, a weak physique, or a tender skin. Head stalkers are the kind of men who gave the Lovat Scouts their fearsome reputation as snipers and marksmen. They are men who, in the course of their job of leading a guest up to a stag, will crawl and belly their way over miles of moor and heather and peat. At the end of that crawling and bellying, they are not the kind of men who suffer a fool with a gun gladly. And incidentally you will never taste venison properly until you are accepted by a head stalker and taken home for a meal. A beast carefully chosen by the head stalker, the best cut, and all the past venison roasting experience of the stalker's wife, will give you a feast the gods here enjoy.

Throughout this account of what is available in sport in the countryside, one name keeps cropping up. Jock Kerr Hunter, senior technical adviser to the Scottish Council of Physical Recreation, has probably done more than any other person in a notably rich field of enthusiasts to get new activities under way. Pony-trekking, water ski-ing, snow ski-ing, and sea angling in particular owe much of their present vigorous development to his imagination, his eye for potential, and his hard work in the gathering-together and the launching of the exploratory committees. Having faced his formidable enthusiasms and having worked with him on some of the original committees, I gladly take this opportunity to pay a tribute to him. Jock Kerr Hunter's contribution has not yet been fully realized but when it has been evaluated, his country and countrymen will, I hope, mark their indebtedness in some signal and suitable form.

There are four key organizations to whom reference may be made: The Scottish Tourist Board, 2 Rutland Place, Edinburgh EH1 2YU; The Highland and Islands Development Board, Bridge House, Bank Street, Inverness; The Scottish Youth Hostels Association, National Office, 7 Glebe Crescent, Stirling; The Scottish Council of Physical Recreation (The General Secretary), 4 Queensferry Street, Edinburgh EH2 4PB. Each of these organizations is staffed by knowledgeable enthusiasts who can advise you how best to enjoy the many opportunities that lie on every hand in this incomparable and lovely Land of Adventure.

Art the Hard Way

Ronald Mavor

The telephone rings and an urgent voice says 'I have got the most fantastic man here. He used to run the Corcoran Museum in Washington and now he's got this great gallery in New York and has evenings for the Black Panthers. . . . He thinks Edinburgh's the greatest city in the world.' Richard Demarco, one of the most recent flowerings of the steady Italian immigration into Scotland and, in his mid-thirties, Director of one of the liveliest art galleries in Great Britain, has just arrived back from a four weeks' tour in America. He has picked up Jim Harithas in New York and persuaded him on the spur of the moment to come and see Edinburgh, throwing in as bait the possibility of meeting Josef Beuys, the grand old *enfant terrible* of the German avant-garde who might be arriving a day later. So we had lunch and were joined by Richard England, from Malta, who was exhibiting architectural drawings at the Demarco Gallery.

One of the great pleasures of Edinburgh is that it has perhaps the most distinguished piece of residential town planning in Europe right in the centre of the city. Edinburgh decided to move out of its Old Town, perched on the hog's back of the Royal Mile between the Castle and Holyrood Palace, at a time when there were living and working in Edinburgh a handful of the finest architects alive, and the New Town, with its noble rooms, fine ceilings, and fireplaces, remains after two hundred years a place of beauty and elegance. I had the good fortune to live in a New Town house and asked Harithas and England for a drink in the evening. In the event about twenty people turned up including Beuys, three Maltese artists, the art critic of the *Frankfurter Allgemeine Zeitung*, a publisher from Brussels, and God knows who else. We have become used to this kind of thing during the Edinburgh Festival but now it is occurring all the year round.

It may be objected that this kind of lively gathering is not available to the casual visitor to Edinburgh. I am not sure that this

238

is so. The Scots have a passionate affection for informal conversation and they seize upon an interested visitor, as the Ancient Mariner held the unfortunate wedding guest, and drag him into their homes, clubs or pubs, talking not only of Michelangelo but of Bartok, Bob Dylan, Aznavour, Denis Law, Yevtushenko, God, and the Devil. I met Harithas the following evening sitting wearily on the bottom step of a flight of stairs. He and Beuys had had a wonderful day walking about the closes and terraces of Edinburgh in what most people would call a light rain, but which in Edinburgh is described as a sea mist. He said they had just been talking to people.

In many ways it is a defect of the Scottish approach to the arts that they prefer talking about them to practising them or studying them. Claret and conversation were always in great supply in old Edinburgh and, even today, the heady seductions of the literary pub keep too many Scottish writers away from their desks. There is a particularly Scottish atmosphere, however, compounded of a sometimes dismal climate, a puritanical suspicion of anything that is graceful or charming, a reliance upon strong liquors to overcome a lack of self-confidence, and a holy dread of what the neighbours may say, which, while it is not the most encouraging compost for the young artist, gives to the arts in Scotland a particular flavour which visitors rapidly come to relish.

The Edinburgh Festival, for example, is never without its scandal. City Councillors express themselves shocked and horrified. Young ladies are hastily thrust into dressing gowns. Unsuitable words are painted out. But the effect of such vigilante activity is rather to heighten the sense of enjoyment. It is like the Ball on the eve of Waterloo. The noise of battle echoes from the cliffs of the Salisbury Crags and we settle down to our string quartets and our experimental drama with a little bit more acuteness than we would in, say, Vienna or New York.

A somewhat testing environment is not, perhaps, although it is a typically Scottish Calvinist thing to say, altogether a bad thing for a young artist and those that survive may, indeed, be the better for it. Certainly there is a vigour and an assurance about many of our established artists which comes from having learned in a hard school.

The church still exerts its influence in a hundred, often subliminal, ways and for many years the sermon was the most practised art form in Scotland and the most rigorously attended and criticized. The Scottish aesthetic might even have been evolved, indeed was probably evolved, specifically for this purpose. Not only must the sermon be long and nobly delivered, but it must be sound in doctrine, shapely and, as the Germans say, *durch-komponiert*, all-of-a-piece. Ideas should be expressed with intelligence, but clarity is not a necessity. The audience must expect, and does expect, to work as hard as the performer.

So the visitor to Scotland must not expect to find string bands playing waltzes in the open air while the citizens sip their Pernod in the shade of walnut trees beside a lake. If, however, he hunts diligently in the advertisement columns of the newspapers and takes the trouble to find the unsignposted hall, which will be up three flights of stairs and originally designed as a court room or a stock exchange, he will find a large audience listening, rapt, to the complete piano sonatas of Beethoven on seven successive nights.

It was a Scotsman who remarked that he did not care who made the laws of the country as long as the right person wrote the songs. Any small country has a problem of identity, not only in the political sense, but in the cultural one. It is easy, even on the smallest Mediterranean island, to preserve a unique and character-istic nose-flute, but do you also want Shakespeare and Beethoven, Boulez and Rothko? If you only have the former you will create a heaven for middle-aged ladies with wooden beads and sandals and slim young men on the run from the University of California. On the other hand, if you want an electronics factory and a petro-chemical industry to set themselves up and boost your economy you will find they will demand a more cosmopolitan infra-structure. Scotland is no Mediterranean island and it has a noble and individual sub-culture with a language, a literature and a music of its own. For better or for worse, however, the Gaelic has retreated to the north and west, leaving little pockets of resistance in the universities and the Glasgow Police Force. To the vast majority of Scots, books are written in English and music is purveyed by the radio and performed by musicians schooled in the traditions of Europe. A remarkable number of Scottish writers of distinction have come from the Gaelic peoples and places, and continue to do so, some writing with equal skill in both languages. The music of the Gael focuses on an annual gathering, or Mod, which mixes song and sociability in a particularly

Highland brew and is notable for not only the purity of its best singers and the liveliness of its children's choirs, but for the insouciance of its administrative arrangements and for the firmly held traditional belief that hotel bedrooms are for singing in rather than for sleeping. Celtic design, weaving, carving and other crafts have been famous for several thousand years, but the recent notion that the summit of the visual arts consists of squeezing oil paints on to a bit of stretched cloth has never been accepted by the Gaelic mind. The art of painting in Scotland is exclusively a Lowland art and as the waves of fashion have flowed across from Europe, and more recently from America, Scottish painters have alternately been carried well forward in the surf and been left rather high and dry on our northern rocks.

A fair attitude would be that Scotland must have some kind of brief for her own artists but that she must not allow them to become bloated fish in a tiny pond, that barriers must never be erected along the Tweed to preserve some mythical, innocent, and delicate Scottish flower of culture from the depraved and sophisticated influences of the south, but that everything possible must be done to provide in Scotland an ambience welcoming and apt for all artists, whether Scottish or not. A good model for the Scottish artist is the salmon, which heads out for the open sea, for a wider nourishment and longer horizons, but returns in its own good time to its native river.

One of our salmon is Alexander Gibson, CBE, who became the youngest Musical Director of Sadler's Wells Opera in London but returned, still in his early thirties, to become the first ever Scottish permanent Musical Director of the Scottish National Orchestra in 1959. The Scottish National Orchestra grew out of the old Scottish Orchestra which gave winter seasons in Glasgow and Edinburgh and numbered among its conductors, Richter, George Szell and Barbirolli. Since 1950 it has been a permanent orchestra and, under Gibson, has gone from strength to strength. One of the hardest worked orchestras in the country it gives a winter season of weekly concerts on Friday nights in Edinburgh and Saturday nights in Glasgow, plays for Scottish Opera, tours quite extensively throughout Scotland and occasionally in England and abroad, gives a large number of children's concerts and an enthusiastically supported season of summer promenade concerts in the Kelvin Hall, Glasgow.

The magnificent St Andrew's Hall, in Glasgow, acoustically

241

one of the finest in Europe, was burned down in 1962, and the orchestra has not been adequately housed in Glasgow since. The present City Hall is splendid for chamber music but it seats only 1,200 and the orchestra has had to drop from its repertoire any large choral, or indeed orchestral, pieces until a new concert hall is provided for it. In Edinburgh the orchestra plays in the very large Usher Hall and while it must be interesting every week to play the same programme in two such different buildings, it is sad that an orchestra which is based in a city of over a million inhabitants should not have an adequate hall in which to perform.

The creation of Scottish Opera has perhaps been Mr Gibson's greatest contribution to the arts in Scotland and is Scotland's artistic success story of the last ten years. There are those who claim that Alexander Gibson is essentially an operatic conductor and the fact that many eminent singers will come thousands of miles to perform for him at substantially lower fees than they would accept elsewhere is a tribute both to the company and to him. I have always suspected that a major bait is Mr Gibson's idiorhythmic left arm, which sometimes seems to be operated by a quite separate dwarf repetiteur crouched somewhere on his left shoulder. Whatever the right arm, and the orchestra, may be doing, a long finger shoots out and indicates in the most precise manner who is to sing what and when. It must be a great comfort to a singer performing a new role. Also, of course, Scottish Opera has already an established international reputation as a company whose operas, musically, scenically, and dramatically, are very carefully prepared and stylishly presented.

The Company began life only in June 1962 with performances of *Pelléas et Mélisande* and *Madam Butterfly* but has already scaled the heights of Wagner's *Ring*, and Berlioz's *The Trojans* in the complete version, with Janet Baker as Dido – a production which most critics felt to be superior to that at Covent Garden. They have also taken on the English Opera Group in its own field of the smaller Britten operas and there are those who claim that it has won.

It is a lively company which brings a sense of theatrical excitement to all that it does and which has extended its season from a couple of weeks in June eight years ago to nearly twenty weeks, spread through the year. The Scottish National Orchestra plays for the big works, the BBC Scottish Symphony Orchestra for some, and its own instrumental ensemble for the chamber works. Singers of the first quality are brought from all over the world, and surprisingly often, to sing for the first time roles for which they have later become famous. It is in this way that Scottish Opera, unable to pay the enormous fees offered by the big houses of Europe and America, has established and maintained its reputation for quality.

The Scottish Opera Chorus, which has become progressively more professional, in the technical sense of the word – it was never amateur in the pejorative sense – has won the highest praise, as has the Edinburgh Festival Chorus, recruited from all over Scotland, and both are trained by Arthur Oldham who commutes between these commitments and the London Philharmonic Choir every few days. The achievements of the Scottish choruses have established him as one of the great European chorus masters of our time.

It is said that when the Administrative Director of the Edinburgh Festival was recovering from a serious operation a year or two ago his first visitor when he emerged from the anaesthetic was Arthur demanding that he arrange extra rehearsals for the Festival Chorus. He is a man of driving energy.

The major cities are reasonably rich in concert-giving throughout the year but Edinburgh can claim to have an average of three or four concerts a week throughout the winter. A notable series now, alas, terminated were the lunch-hour concerts held in the National Gallery of Scotland for thirty years by Miss Tertia Liebenthal. Miss Liebenthal was one of the great figures of Edinburgh life and lived for over 70 years in the house in which she was born in Regent Terrace. She had been a pupil and friend of Sir Donald Tovey and she ran the lunch-hour concerts single-handed and according to her own very high standards. Many young musicians went on to greater fame and many of them returned, for love not money, to give concerts for her in the National Gallery. Every concert began as the one o'clock gun resounded from the Castle Rock and Miss Liebenthal insisted that every concert, with the rare exception of certain specialized concerts as, for example, when Peter Williams played Bach's Goldberg Variations, should contain at least one contemporary work.

Peter Pears, with Joan Dickson, the Scottish cellist, gave Miss Liebenthal's 600th concert and Pears and Benjamin Britten

243

insisted upon coming to Edinburgh to give her 700th concert in April 1970, for which Britten had composed a new song cycle. It was after announcing this concert, in the middle of the previous one, that Miss Liebenthal collapsed, and died shortly afterwards. Everyone felt that it was exactly as she would have wished, to die at one of her own concerts, but only Tertia would have had the finesse to do so at her 699th. She will be much missed. Her home in Regent Terrace was both a mecca and a retreat for great artists coming to the Edinburgh Festival.

Outside the cities, the Scottish Arts Council has been active for many years in helping local music clubs and art clubs to promote concerts and performances of all kinds and there are few towns of any size in Scotland which have not profited from this service. There has been a steady increase in concert giving and many towns have long established music clubs, to which visitors are welcome, promoting, either on their own account or with the help of the Council, chamber music concerts of the highest quality.

Such is the quality of Scottish country life, however, that the hard working organizers have to fight with the various commitments of the Women's Rural Institute, the Flower Show, the Sheep Dog Ball, the Brownies and goodness knows what other rural saturnalia to find a spare evening on which to promote the claims of Mozart and Schubert. The music clubs tend to be seasonal and to operate from September to March but the visitor will sometimes be surprised to find the village hall in some remote West Highland archipelago advertising a concert or a play in the middle of summer. There are many professional, or semi-professional, artists who like to combine a holiday jaunt with the exercise of their art and, particularly from the universities, there emerge ensembles of all kinds who carry their gear north and west for their own entertainment and that of the citizens and tourists wherever they go.

The theatre, again helped by the Arts Council, has, over the past twenty years, penetrated to most corners of Scotland but it is an expensive business to put on a play and the main centres of drama are, of course, the main cities.

An exception to this is the Pitlochry Festival Theatre which started life in a terrace drawing-room in Glasgow, expanded to Pitlochry after the war, and has continued under the inspired management of Kenneth Ireland, OBE, to provide a summer feast of drama from spring to autumn. 'Stay six days and see six plays' is the theatre's banner and the visitor to Pitlochry is further invited to eat, drink and be merry in the theatre's foyer restaurant and bar, and to drink morning coffee under the umbrellas on its lawn.

The theatre prides itself on its sense of occasion, but it is not only on gala nights when a piper welcomes the glittering collection of local dukes, civic dignitaries and long-range urban sophisticates, that a visit to Pitlochry is an agreeable and rewarding experience. Like a good restaurant, the Pitlochry Theatre owes its success to the personal touch of its Director. There is a London restaurant which advertises, *'Le patron mange ici'*. Every night of the season Mr Ireland, in full Highland dress, is there half an hour before the doors open to check that the radiators are warm, the salads are crisp, the panatrope at the right number of decibels, and that the Commissionaire has cleaned his finger nails. When the doors are flung open he greets all his customers like old friends, frequently remembering their previous visits in 1962 and the fact that they come from Brownsville, Nebraska. The plays range from Shaw and Shakespeare to frothy comedy. There is something for every taste.

There is no Scottish National Theatre and any proposal that there ought to be one becomes very rapidly bogged down in discussions about the degree of Scottishness which would be expected of it. Should it perform in Gaelic? Must all the actors be fluent and expert in Lallans? Apart from Scottish plays, should the best of the world's drama be performed in Scots? With a Scots accent? Or in English?

There is a good deal of valuable experience on the Continent to suggest that a National Theatre is not necessarily superior to municipal theatres and, amid the fluctuating changes and chances of the theatre world in Scotland, the present writer is inclined to feel that a National Theatre, if it comes at all, should be allowed to evolve in its own good time. Until quite recently the Glasgow Citizens' Theatre seemed to be several noses ahead in the race and reliable critics were heard to say that it was to all intents and purposes the Scottish National Theatre.

Founded by the late James Bridie in 1943, it built up the reputation of being one of the leading repertory theatres and it added to its status by becoming, in 1965, the first British repertory theatre to have two auditoria under the same roof. The little Close Theatre, so called because it is 'up a close' and because the audience is close to the actors, is administered as a theatre club but is staffed by the Artistic Director and company of the Citizens' Theatre. It has been used for more experimental productions than can be ventured in the large theatre and has proved a success.

Unfortunately the re-development of the Gorbals area and a number of domestic difficulties considerably affected attendances in the main theatre and, although they have recently been rising, all seems now to depend upon the theatre company getting itself rehoused in a new building at the earliest moment.

While Glasgow has struck a bad patch, Edinburgh is on the crest of a wave. The Corporation purchased the Royal Lyceum Theatre and set up a Civic Theatre Trust to run it. After a difficult start and the appointment of Clive Perry as Director, the theatre has steadily built up a following and, thanks to generous subsidy from the municipality, as well as from the Scottish Arts Council, is putting on distinguished productions to large audiences and even exporting occasional productions to Aberdeen. With the Edinburgh Festival, the Lyceum Theatre Company, the recently-purchased King's Theatre, which is essential for opera at the Edinburgh Festival, and the Church Hill Theatre, which was lavishly refurnished from an old church for the benefit of the amateurs, Edinburgh Corporation is in the theatre business in a big way and when the promised new opera house is built will have taken a substantial step towards the realization of the late Sir John Falconer's dream of the city as an arts centre, not only for the three weeks of the Festival but throughout the year.

Dundee has a gallant repertory theatre company which, like the Scottish National Orchestra, has had to survive the aftermath of a disastrous fire in its home. The old theatre in Nicoll Street had recently been redecorated at lowish cost but with considerable flair thanks to the advice of Mr Richard Buckle, the ballet critic and exhibition designer. The rather severe oblong hall had come out in a rash of powder blue poppies on a red background, which made one critic fear that his frequent attendances at the theatre would make him feel like a laryngologist after a long day at the tonsil clinic. He might have been spared that anxiety as the building went up in flames a few months afterwards and the company now plays in a converted church a little bit too far out from the centre of the city. Plans are afoot, however, for a new building on the University campus, which is fine.

The oldest of the Scottish repertory theatres, and one whose escutcheon carries as many honours as scars, is the Perth Theatre. In 1936 two young actors were standing on a railway station between dates. David Steuart pointed to Perth in the centre of Scotland on the map and said, 'That is where I would like to run a theatre'. His friend, Marjorie Dence, happened to be reading *The Stage* a few days later over breakfast and explained to her startled parents that the theatre that David wanted to run was for sale. So her generous father offered to buy it, and the two of them began what was to be more than thirty years of endeavour.

It is a beautiful little theatre but Perth has only some 30,000 inhabitants, so that the battle for an audience has never been easy. Latterly Miss Dence, a commanding and rather Edwardian figure in a green chiffon evening dress on theatre nights, started a football pool to help finance the theatre. Just before the war they had a festival to which Ivor Brown, Lionel Hale, W. A. Darlington and other leading drama critics came (employing their spare time in driving golf balls across the River Tay from the North Inch into Miss Dence's garden) and at which a young Mr Guinness (later Sir Alec) played Romeo. Had it not been for the war Perth might have become a Scottish Malvern but, in fact, it was only by superhuman effort – for long periods the company lived in the theatre, did all the chores themselves and divided the takings at the end of the week – that the theatre survived at all. Following Miss Dence's death in 1967 the theatre was acquired by the Corporation and it continues to provide a season of plays for the citizens of Perth, a remarkably high proportion of whom attend the theatre, although the struggle to make ends meet is no easier now than it was.

One is struck by the very different character of the various Scottish theatres and there is none with a stronger personality than the little Byre Theatre in St Andrews. Started before the war by a group of local amateurs, the theatre has for over twenty years employed a young professional company and director, and Alex Paterson, MBE, who has guided its fortunes from the beginning, gives them their heads. The theatre used to occupy a converted cowshed or byre and could seat seventy people. Those in the front row were instructed not to put their feet on the stage, and actors could only leave the stage by jumping over the prompter and rushing out into the rain to scramble up a ship's ladder to their dressing-rooms in the loft; it was also possible with a skilful stage designer to arrange an exit from a trap door on the roof of the stage, and I am told that ladies in crinolines once used this unladylike entrance during a production of *She Stoops to Conquer*. The Byre Theatre is the theatre most rooted in its community. Young actresses working there find that they can get their hair done and their shoes repaired for nothing in the town. It is also one of the most enterprising and has recently demonstrated this by getting itself the first new theatre to be built in Scotland since Pitlochry erected a tent in a Pitlochry garden in the late 1940s. The new building was remarkably inexpensive and erected with remarkable speed. St Andrews continues to show the way down the fairway, and not only in the field of golf.

The claim of St Andrew's to be the smallest professional theatre in Scotland, however, has been undermined by two recent foundations. In 1963 a lively group of young men in Edinburgh, all of them influenced to a greater or lesser extent by the viviparous and guru-like personality of Jim Haynes, started the Traverse Theatre and, more recently, Mr and Mrs Barrie Hesketh have begun their Mull Little Theatre at Dervaig.

Jim Haynes, challenged only by Richard Demarco, who is in a sense his disciple, must be regarded as the most powerful animator of the arts in Edinburgh of recent years. A serving airman at a neighbouring American Air Force Base, he volunteered for the one job for which there was no competition, that of writing two reports, at midnight and five in the morning, which, it appears, were demanded by regulations. This gave him the day free and he spent it, because he was a man of an enquiring mind, attending, without too much diligence, lectures at Edinburgh University. This droll way of life he preferred to explain to himself in the terms that he was in fact a student at Edinburgh University who worked nights for the American Air Force to put himself through college. When he was demobilized, for all good things come to an end, he took a local release from the US Air Force and opened a paperback bookshop near the University which was decorated outside with the head of a stuffed rhinoceros and furnished inside with free coffee, guitar players, folk singers and the unfailing presence of such wits and philosophers as Edinburgh could muster.

During successive Edinburgh Festivals he promoted late-night discussions, one of which began with a performance in costume with claret and a dialogue by the Scottish philosopher, David Hume, and then spread out into the audience whose voices continued to echo from the walls of the Old Town as they argued their way home at three or four in the morning.

It is probable that Jim Haynes did not in fact start the Traverse Theatre, but it is equally probable that it could not have started without him. Anyway, about that time the mysterious Tom Mitchell acquired a rather gaunt property, for many years a celebrated brothel, in James' Court and, as is the way of all empty large spaces during the Edinburgh Festival, it was occupied by a student group appearing on, what is called, the Fringe. It seemed to work and a group was formed who converted the building and opened as a professional Theatre Club. The history of the Club has been quite as dramatic as anything that appeared on its tiny stage but on a quick conspectus one distinguishes two major periods. There was the Jim period where at any time of the day or night one would meet the *genius loci* himself in the middle of fantastic plans for a festival of Javanese dancing on the Calton Hill, a performance of *Aida* in a brewer's vault or a conference of oriental short story writers during the General Assembly of the Church of Scotland. Norman Mailer would just have left to visit friends of Jim's in Achiltibuie, and you would be introduced to Otto Klemperer and Sandie Shaw, who would be sitting on the floor in the bar eating bacon and eggs. Down in the theatre there would be a new version of *Hamlet* performed by six ten-year-old schoolchildren under the direction of Charles Marowitz, and one had only to wait until one o'clock in the morning to hear a discussion on sewage disposal between the City Planning Officer, the Medical Officer of Health, a Catholic priest and Mr Nicholas Fairbairn.

After Jim left to start an arts laboratory in London (and that is a story which would take too long in the telling although it would fascinate you) there was a period in which Max Stafford Clark, much influenced by La Mama and the off-off-Broadway theatre generally, did dozens of new plays and added to the theatre's reputation as one of the most go-ahead enterprises in the arts in Great Britain, without greatly contributing to the solution of the Club's financial and administrative problems, the relics of the first fine careless rapture of those early years.

At the time of writing the Traverse has found itself an exciting new building in the Grassmarket, is intelligently run and never fails to provide a stimulating evening. One has to be a member, but it is not too difficult to become one.

The Mull Little Theatre began when art proved too powerful an influence in the lives of two young actors, Barrie and Marianne

249

Hesketh, who had decided, sensibly enough, to escape from London and the rat race and run a boarding house at Dervaig in Mull. A cowshed beside the boarding house looked too like a theatre to be neglected and what began as an occasional performance, just to keep their hands in, soon became a full time activity, the boarding house having been transferred to the care of a manager. The Heskeths now tour widely through the Highlands and Islands, presenting their two or three-handed productions of Shaw, Strindberg and Shakespeare with great acceptance everywhere.

It is disappointing that all this activity in the theatre has proved singularly unproductive of Scottish dramatists. The history of the drama in Scotland consists of no more than four or five peaks on a rather flat landscape. In music it is different. There have perhaps been no peaks, only an occasional respectable eminence, but the generally healthy nature of Scottish musical life has produced at the present time, if not a nest of singing birds, at least a substantial and lively group of working composers. In the theatre, however, it is otherwise.

The revival of Sir Tyrone Guthrie's production of *The Three Estates* by Sir David Lyndsay of the Mount in the early days of the Edinburgh Festival astonished everyone. Here was a considerable masterpiece, virtually unperformed for 500 years, full of action and wit and written in a broad Scots language to which our indigenous actors took like ducks to water and which, more surprisingly, proved thoroughly comprehensible to the cosmopolitan audience that flocked to the Assembly Hall to see it. But between *The Three Estates* and J. M. Barrie there is nothing, except perhaps Home's *Douglas*, a revival of which, even with Dame Sybil Thorndyke in the lead, showed it to be no more than another Drury Lane tragedy in kilts.

I am not sure that we are very happy about J. M. Barrie at the moment. The picture of the Scotsman which he presented to the world is one which we find uncomfortable to inhabit. His plays now seem very sentimental, much too coy, and pervaded by a kind of spitefulness, the taste of which still penetrates through the layers of charm. He was, however, a splendid craftsman and it would be a foolish man who would deny that he may yet have a come-back.

The plays of James Bridie have also sunk almost without trace under the wave of Socialist realism, and later Beckett/Pinterism, which flowed across the English theatre in the 1950s and 1960s.

This writer, who is certainly biased, believes that the plays, which were very successful in the forties and fifties are due a re-examination and will prove to be more important and serious (although they are nearly all extremely funny) than they were adjudged to be when they were first performed. At that time the theatre-going audience demanded that a funny play should be funny. The very significant changes in British humour, which date from the magnificent Goon Show on the BBC have changed all that and we have come much nearer to Bridie's view, a view which would not have astonished a Zen master, that the joke is almost the most serious, revealing and enlightening kind of statement which one can make.

In the wake of Guthrie's revival of *The Three Estates* there came an interesting period in which the three most active playwrights in Scotland all wrote, at least for the main part, in Lallans (the speech of the lowland Scot) rather than in English. Robert McLellan, Robert Kemp and Alexander Reid provided for the Citizens' Theatre in Glasgow, and later the Gateway Theatre in Edinburgh, a succession of worthwhile and entertaining plays, a modest renaissance which, however, petered out and seems unlikely to have any successors. Currently we can claim the exiled Glasgow writer Cecil P. Taylor, the north of England man Stanley Eveling, who has a residential qualification as a lecturer at Edinburgh University, and the locals Tom Wright and Jack Ronder and Stuart Corr, all of whom are capable of writing a distinguished play but none of whom has yet quite fulfilled his promise.

These are all abstemious men but Scotland, as has already been noted, has often seemed to suffer from an excess of public bar literati and a shortage of completed works. It is the Scot's love of argument. A small flower pushes itself through the hard crust, but rather than plant it in a small corner of his attic workshop the Scottish writer too often thumps it on the counter of the nearest bar and by the time his friends have finished discussing whether it is an orchid or the common eyebright, and he has slept too long the next morning, he has lost interest in it. Perhaps it is the lack of central heating which has driven too many Scottish authors to the cosy pub and away from their typewriters. Robert Louis Stevenson said that any man of imagination who was not called to the church went instead to the pub, 'And what else,' he asked, 'could you do in this dogs' weather?'

However, there have been those who have survived. The early Makars, among them Dunbar, Henryson and Montgomerie are worth the study of anybody who has the patience to attune his inner ear to their language, and one need only mention such names as Scott, Stevenson, Carlyle, Hume, Smollet, Drummond of Hawthornden, Byron, Urquhart, the translator of Rabelais, to demonstrate that the contemporary writer has a tradition – which Neil Gunn defined as 'a place where a writer can be at home with himself' – which he can treat with affection or disdain as he feels inclined.

Neil Gunn, himself, brought the very feel of the Highlands into a succession of admirable novels. An earlier Neil, Neil Munro, had captured much of the West Highland ways of speaking and thinking but his novels have an air of Victorian romanticism about them which probably deters the modern reader, and he is likely to be best remembered for the magnificent *Para Handy* stories about the little puffer, The Vital Spark, which plied between Highland harbours with no great urgency and at the whim of its philosophical captain and characterful crew. The stories are much quoted among the yachting fraternity on the West Coast. Neil Gunn, however, remains a contemporary writer from his concentration on the very essence of life itself, a life always distanced geographically and spiritually from the fads and fashions of the urban literary scene.

His notable contemporary was, and is, Eric Linklater, a stylist and a virtuoso, a misplaced Viking, never happier than in wars (*Private Angelo*) or on forays to foreign parts (*Juan in America*) but now turned to the re-writing of history.

These were writers of a distinction which none of their successors has quite reached, although Robin Jenkins has published very nearly as many novels and one masterpiece in *The Cone Gatherers*.

The Grand Old Man of the Scottish novel, however, has been for most of his eighty-nine years Sir Compton Mackenzie, whose *Sinister Street* and *Carnival* were written long enough ago to have been a major influence on Scott Fitzgerald. Gifted with an incredibly accurate memory and a passion and talent for hard work, but becoming progressively hampered by failing eyesight, he resolved not to commence his autobiography until his 80th birthday because it was a work which he could do without too much reading. As if this were not enough, he planned the work in ten volumes and brought it to a successful conclusion. It must be one of the great literary feats of all time. He divides his time between an idyllic house near Cahors in France, to which he retreats in order to escape from his friends and get on with his work, and the most hospitable house in Edinburgh, in Drummond Place. The arrival of the most casual visitor will lead Sir Compton, who may be reclining on a four-poster bed or watching his favourite television serial, to embark upon the most fascinating flow of anecdotal conversation which is liable to continue (or was, because one must admit that he is beginning to show the slightest signs of middle age) until two or three in the morning. If the visitor attempted to go home at or about midnight his host would exclaim that he could not understand why young people nowadays tended to go home to bed in the middle of the afternoon.

It is perhaps in poetry that Scotland today has most to offer. There is a different kind of Grand Old Man in Hugh MacDiarmid, a fiery antagonist of the English in his public persona and a kindly sage in his private. *A Drunk Man Looks at the Thistle* is one of the finest lyrical and philosophical poems in any language. His early lyrics rival the best of Burns and his later, and longer, poems extend the possibilities of the language. Almost single-handed he created in the twenties and thirties a revival of writing in Lallans and a widespread interest in the language and its possibilities. His great friend Norman McCaig never followed him into that field but has achieved almost equal distinction as a poet.

Of the younger poets there are many and worthwhile. Anthologies of Scottish poetry shower from the presses and in Ian Hamilton Finlay, Scotland may claim one of the founder fathers of concrete poetry and the creator of a number of works of real beauty and originality. As in the cases of Linklater and Gunn, who came from Orkney and Caithness respectively, however, it is in the North that the two younger masters are to be found. George Mackay Brown is another Orcadian who conjures up an eternal Orkney, set in some northern dream time in fine poetry and no less notable stories. Ian Crichton Smith, who comes from Lochinver, is both an established novelist and a leading poet in Gaelic and English. If, to begin with, his works in the former language seemed to have an altogether more vivid imagery than his English poetry, he has now an established mastery of both languages and both media.

I suggested earlier that the Highland mind had not seen fit to apply itself to the field of painting as to that of literature. On the other hand the accessibility of the dramatic landscape of Scotland to even the most urban Scot has an influence on the whole national character and, more particularly, on the artist. Nowadays our paintings do not depict romantic castles and shaggy cattle looming amid the swirling mist. Indeed, there has been a great explosion of non-figurative painting in recent years. Until then, however, the pace was set largely by a remarkable group of painters based in Edinburgh. Anne Redpath, John Maxwell, Sir William Gillies and Sir William MacTaggart dominated not only the Royal Scottish Academy but the large number of talented young painters who studied or worked in Edinburgh. Characteristic of the group was an affection for thick and luxuriant pigment, simplification of landscape and still-life forms, and a light-hearted and romantic imagination. English critics would talk about the Edinburgh obsession with 'belle peinture', with the air of progressive mothers who could not persuade their children to eat wholemeal bread rather than sticky cakes, but if Edinburgh was a back water, at least the artists knew what they wanted to do and did it with great skill and to the pleasure of thousands. Their painting was also very notably the work of people who knew and loved their craft.

In this they followed a distinguished tradition. 'The Glasgow Boys' of the beginning of the century brought a new kind of fresh air into stuffy Victorian galleries and the elder McTaggart was painting wild sunlit seascapes which still look modern while the Impressionist movement was only just getting under way in France. The later group of Cadell, Hunter and Peploe, all of whom died in 1930, were equally at home in France and in Scotland and as the 'Scottish Colourists' achieved an intense lyrical view of the Scottish scene which continues to inspire painters up to the present day.

Edinburgh has not had it all its own way, of course, in recent years and perhaps the finest of our recent painters was Joan Eardley, who died at the age of forty-three, and worked in Glasgow for most of her life, moving later to the little village of Catterline on the Kincardineshire coast. In her Glasgow studio she painted the street children who wandered in and out and in Catterline she painted enormously beautiful land and seascapes which seemed to have grown out of either a creative fury or an involvement with the very earth itself. A strong but gentle character, she would paint in the open air in all weathers, often painting from the same spot, her easel held down with rope and boulders for weeks on end through the changing weathers and seasons.

A younger group of Glasgow painters, unlike their Edinburgh counterparts tending to subdued colours, have also established themselves, but the arrival of the Richard Demarco Gallery in Edinburgh and his promotion of the Edinburgh Open 100 at the Festival of 1967 brought a belated blast of non-figurative painting through the newly opened windows of Scottish art and the art of international experiment is now in full swing throughout the country.

In a survey of this kind one cannot cover every aspect of the arts without producing a long and perhaps not altogether inspiring catalogue. I have not mentioned sculpture (we have at least one distinguished figure in Benno Schotz), or architecture, where the last two recipients of the Queen's Gold Medal of the Royal Institute of British Architects have been Scots and resident in Scotland, nor ballet, where the lively Western Theatre Ballet, originally founded in Bristol, has recently established itself in Scotland, becoming Scottish Theatre Ballet in the process. Nor, perhaps, have I dealt adequately with the more specifically Scottish arts. The great music of the bagpipe, the pibroch, an art form often compared with, and little less intricate than, the fugue, has interested distinguished musicians from Heifetz to Menuhin, but it is difficult to get to hear – although worth the effort. Pipe bands march at unexpected times through Border towns and city streets, and the lucky visitor may catch a Tattoo, a kind of military musical spectacle, of a summer evening in a barracks or town square. Gaelic song and lowland poetry readings break out with total spontaneity at the unlikeliest times and places, and dancing, whether in the wild Highland or more genteel country style, is a frequent physical and aesthetic exercise among our people.

But we must keep our ears and eyes open to the world. We must hear and see what Shelley called 'the record of the best and happiest thoughts of the best and happiest men'. At all costs we must not be provincial. It is our good fortune then, to have every autumn perhaps the greatest jamboree of the arts in the world occurring in the shadow of Edinburgh's Castle Rock. Not only do we have the most superb performances of the acknowledged musical and operatic masterpieces, but we have plays, exhibitions and, from time to time, literary conferences. For three weeks, as Rudolph Bing claimed of his first Festival in 1947, Edinburgh becomes the art capital of the world and it does so, in spite of what unkind tongues have said, with a truly regal air. Yes, Edinburgh can be a gloomy and a puritanical city, but when she cares to wake up to her responsibilities she has a sense of history and a confidence which makes her the ideal hostess to such a gathering. Nor is the Festival simply a parade of the approved high art of the high bourgeoisie. Edinburgh becomes an open city and hairy students and blue-jeaned musicians flock into its courts and closes, setting up their platforms and preparing their shows like pedlars in some North African *souks* because there is an audience there, and ready to listen. This phenomenon, which arose spontaneously in the earliest year of the Festival and has flourished without deliberate cultivation, is known as the Fringe, and has perhaps done as much to stimulate creativity and water the seedbeds of living Scottish culture as the Festival itself.

It would be difficult to plead the cause of the arts in Scotland before some World Court. We have not the galleries of Italy, the opera houses of Austria, the musicians of Germany or the per-fervid ingenuity of the American avant-garde, but according to our character, our history and our climate, so have we developed our arts and so do they continue to flourish, and without them what meaning would there be in a nation?

THE DUCA   L I DON   SEA

ORCA
DES.

6   5   4   3

J. Rewnogh
J. Dunkey
Corbet
Segram
Visca
Bol
Telladar
Keill
Kell
S. Breuich
Loch Tua
Korbigh
Charlgh
I. Adam

Bernera I.
Bulwer
merqh
Kellifs
Flanna
Bragh
Isle
Ballishill
Greifett
R. and Loke
Greifetter
Dun
Pag
Challediill
Scalpa
Lewis
Tevay's
Telesta

HARRANOBLE

Stair
Liura

Viste
Shon

Kilmori
Kilnaby
Pladla
Kilmartin
Tasin

P. Comerd
Lough Broom
Assynt

Heslip
Kerwalth
Raswdall

Hoghanes
Kilchalms

Borg en Bernera
Kilchalankt

Daruing

Cnighinan

Christmas

SKYE

Bay Ayr
Hessir

Nissar

Kanad
Kanats
Kilmory
Muck
Aich
Pin of Ardna
Murchin

Kilchadro
Brysloil
Baifs I.
Brey

Soltfild
Col I.
Broockah C.

LOCHQUABER

MUL

Fitzgray
Cload C.
Rawig
Kirkbud
Howard
Lowgn
Bud

Turril I.
Eilogrin
Kandam

LOR

Barra I.
I Megeda

Keriera
Seil
Torren

DunStag
Kilmore

A Scale of Scotch Miles

A Scale of English Miles

LORNE

Kildawan
Killmore
Ardhaich
Ormsfa

Killuran
Collonsa I.

Kilmartel
Krachak

KNAPDAILE
Kilmer

ARGILE

Bincengad Port

JURA

Kilkhuban
Proig
Kilchd
Grops
Paligh

VLE

Balnay
Onsay
Ogg
Kava

ARROW

Clos
CARR

Freasons
Kilon
Kilderhigton
Kilerwan
Graphmygh
Gygharigh

The Mul
Cantyr
Yarderley
Panavwy C.
Kendo P.

GALL

THE
Fair head

IRISH

Rathlin

Green C.

Loch Bay
Glenarms

P. Moulin

Lachas
Mavs

SEA.

PART   OF   IRELAND

Lindun
Derry

5   4   3

The Mul of Gallo